From the Pages of Essays and Poems
by Ralph Waldo Emerson

In the woods, we return to reason and faith.

(from "Nature," page 12)

The Transcendentalist adopts the whole connection of spiritual doctrine. He believes in miracle, in the perpetual openness of the human mind to new influx of light and power; he believes in inspiration, and in ecstasy.   (from "The Transcendentalist," page 101)

To believe your own thought, to believe that what is true for you in your private heart, is true for all men—that is genius.

(from "Self-Reliance," page 113)

Society everywhere is in conspiracy against the manhood of every one of its members. Society is a joint stock company in which the members agree for the better securing of his bread to each shareholder, to surrender the liberty and culture of the eater. The virtue in most request is conformity. Self-reliance is its aversion. It loves not realities and creators, but names and customs. Whoso would be a man must be a nonconformist.   (from "Self-Reliance," page 116)

To be great is to be misunderstood.   (from "Self-Reliance," page 120)

A friend may well be reckoned the masterpiece of nature.

(from "Friendship," page 179)

The only reward of virtue, is virtue: the only way to have a friend, is to be one.   (from "Friendship," page 183)

There is not yet any inventory of a man's faculties, and more than a bible of his opinions.   (from "Power," page 000)

> When I heard the Earth-song,
> I was no longer brave;
> My avarice cooled
> Like lust in the chill of the grave.
>
> (from "Earth-song," page 000)

Essays and Poems by Ralph Waldo Emerson

*With an Introduction and Notes
by Peter Norberg*

*George Stade
Consulting Editorial Director*

BARNES & NOBLE CLASSICS
NEW YORK

$\mathcal{NB}$

BARNES & NOBLE CLASSICS

NEW YORK

Published by Barnes & Noble Books
122 Fifth Avenue
New York, NY 10011

www.barnesandnoble.com/classics

The present texts of Emerson's essays and poems all derive from
The Complete Works of Ralph Waldo Emerson (1903-1904),
prepared by his son, Edward Waldo Emerson.

Published in 2004 by Barnes & Noble Classics with new Introduction,
Notes, Biography, Chronology, Inspired By, Comments & Questions,
and For Further Reading.

Essays and Poems by Ralph Waldo Emerson
ISBN-13: 978-1-59308-076-1
ISBN-10: 1-59308-076-X
LC Control Number 2003112461

Produced and published in conjunction with:
Fine Creative Media, Inc.
322 Eighth Avenue
New York, NY 10001

Michael J. Fine, President and Publisher

Printed in the United States of America

QM

15 17 19 20 18 16 14

Ralph Waldo Emerson

Ralph Waldo Emerson was born in Boston on May 25, 1803, to William and Ruth Emerson. In 1811 Emerson's father died, leaving his mother limited resources for raising the family. Three of Emerson's siblings died during childhood and two before age thirty; one was mentally handicapped. His elder brother William, who became a lawyer in New York City, was the only other Emerson child to have a lengthy career. The family was so impoverished in Emerson's early years that one winter he and his brother Edward had to share a single overcoat. Ruth was aided in child-rearing by her sister-in-law Mary Moody Emerson, who instilled in her young nephew a love of learning; her influence helped Emerson enter the distinguished Boston Latin School at age nine and Harvard University at fourteen.

At Harvard Emerson was at best an average student, chosen class poet only after seven classmates had declined the offer. He studied rhetoric, won the Boylston oratory prize, and formed a club for public speaking. Upon graduation he worked first as a schoolteacher but in 1826 decided to become a minister. While preaching in New Hampshire, he met his great love, Ellen Tucker. They married and settled in Massachusetts, and Emerson secured a prominent position at the Second Church of Boston.

Ellen's death from tuberculosis in 1831 permanently altered the course of Emerson's life. His religious faith shaken to the core, he left his post as minister and toured Europe, where he saw Paris and the museums of Italy. In England he met Samuel Taylor Coleridge, William Wordsworth, and Thomas Carlyle; he subsequently began an intellectual correspondence with Carlyle that lasted thirty-eight years. Returning to America in 1833, Emerson achieved financial security through an inheritance from his late wife, and his creative period began. Freed from the obligations of the ministry, he began to lecture publicly on a variety of topics, including natural history, biography, literature, and ethics. Throughout the rest of his career, public lectures provided him with a steady source of income and gradually increased his reputation as one of America's leading intellectuals. In 1835 he married Lydia Jackson and with her had four children; in 1842 Emerson painfully watched his firstborn son, Waldo, die when the boy was only five. In the late 1830s he published *Nature* and gave two important speeches at Harvard: "The American Scholar," which Oliver Wendell Holmes called the declaration of independence of American intellectual life, and "The Divinity School Address," for which Harvard banned him for the next twenty-five years.

In the early 1840s, while serving as editor of the *Dial*, Emerson published *Essays* and *Essays: Second Series*, confirming his reputation as one of the leading spokespersons of the transcendental movement. Although his verse was never as successful as he intended and a lack of organizational sense kept him from compiling a universal philosophic scheme, Emerson produced prodigiously throughout his later years, publishing *Representative Men* (1850), *The Conduct of Life* (1860), *Society and Solitude* (1870), and two collections of poetry (1846, 1867). He made two more trips to Europe, the second after fire destroyed his longtime home in Concord.

Emerson was a leading thinker, lecturer, and writer during a period when the literary character of the United States was being formed. In his role as spokesman for the American philosophical and ethical movement known as transcendentalism, he gave voice to a belief in the spiritual potential of every man. Ralph Waldo Emerson died quietly on April 27, 1882, and was buried at Sleepy Hollow Cemetery in Concord.

Table of Contents

The World of Ralph Waldo Emerson

1803   Ralph Waldo Emerson is born on May 25 in Boston, the fourth of eight children of William and Ruth Emerson. The United States greatly increases its landholdings with the Louisiana Purchase.

1804   Nathaniel Hawthorne is born.

1807   Henry Wadsworth Longfellow is born. England bans the slave trade. William Wordsworth's ode "Intimations of Immortality from Recollections of Early Childhood" appears.

1808   The first part of Goethe's *Faust* appears.

1809   Edgar Allan Poe is born.

1811   Emerson's father dies. Ruth Emerson must raise her family on her limited income from taking in boarders. Harriet Beecher Stowe is born.

1812–   Emerson attends Boston Latin School. War with Britain lasts
1817   from 1812 to 1814. Henry David Thoreau is born in 1817.

1817–   Emerson attends Harvard College. His earliest surviving jour-
1821   nals appear during this period; he will keep them continuously until the last years of his life. In 1819 James Russell Lowell, Herman Melville, and Walt Whitman are born. In 1820 the government negotiates the Missouri Compromise, which keeps equal the number of states where slavery is legal and illegal.

1821–   A college graduate, Emerson takes a variety of teaching jobs in
1825   and around Boston. In 1822 his first published essay, "Thoughts on the Religion of the Middle Ages," appears in the *Christian Disciple and Theological Review.*

1825   Emerson enrolls in Harvard Divinity School but withdraws because of eyesight problems and early signs of tuberculosis.

1826   In October the Middlesex Association of Ministers licenses Emerson to preach, and he delivers his first sermon in Waltham, Massachusetts. A month later, again showing signs of tuberculosis, Emerson sails to Charleston, South Carolina, and St. Augustine, Florida, seeking to recover in the warm climate. James Fenimore Cooper publishes *The Last of the Mohicans.*

1827   Emerson returns to New England, where he preaches in Unitarian churches in Massachusetts and New Hampshire. He receives his master's degree from Harvard Divinity School. In December he meets Ellen Louisa Tucker while preaching in Concord, New Hampshire.

1829   In January Emerson becomes junior pastor of the Reverend Henry Ware, Jr., at the respected Second Church of Boston, where he is ordained in March; he becomes pastor in July. He marries Ellen Tucker in September.

1830   Emily Dickinson is born.

1831   Ellen Emerson dies, shaking Emerson's religious faith. Nat Turner leads an insurrection of slaves in Virginia. William Lloyd Garrison begins publishing the anti-slavery magazine the *Liberator* in Boston.

1832   In late December Emerson resigns as minister and three days later travels to Europe, where he meets writers William Wordsworth, Samuel Taylor Coleridge, John Stuart Mill, and Thomas Carlyle; the relationship with Carlyle, largely maintained via correspondence, will last many years. Louisa May Alcott is born. Goethe dies; the second part of *Faust* is published posthumously.

1833   Emerson returns to America and begins a career as a lecturer. He gives his first public lecture, "The Uses of Natural History," in Boston.

1834   Emerson meets Lydia Jackson and receives the first half of an inheritance from the estate of Ellen Emerson. Emerson's brother Edward dies of tuberculosis. Emerson moves to Concord, Massachusetts. Coleridge dies.

1835   Emerson and Lydia Jackson become engaged and marry. He begins his first lecture series, "Biography," in Boston. Mark Twain is born.

1836   *Nature*, Emerson's first book, appears, and the Transcendental Club begins. Lydia gives birth to a son, Waldo. Emerson's brother Charles dies of tuberculosis in New York City. Davy Crockett is killed at the Alamo.

1837   Emerson delivers his speech "The American Scholar" at Harvard; Oliver Wendell Holmes calls it the declaration of independence of American intellectual life. Emerson receives the second half of his inheritance from the estate of Ellen Emerson.

1838   Emerson delivers "The Divinity School Address" at Harvard, for which the school bans him for what will be twenty-five years.

1839   Lydia gives birth to the couple's first daughter, Ellen Tucker Emerson. Emerson preaches his last sermon at Concord.

1840 The first issue of the *Dial* appears, under the editorship of Margaret Fuller.

1841 Emerson's first series of *Essays* is published. Brook Farm, an experiment in communal living, is founded near Boston; Emerson declines membership. The Emersons' second daughter, Edith, is born.

1842 Waldo Emerson dies of scarlet fever. Emerson's deep grief colors his second series of essays, which he begins to write and compile. Emerson assumes editorship of the *Dial*. Charles Dickens's *American Notes* appears.

1843 Henry James is born.

1844 Emerson's *Essays: Second Series* is published. He gives the speech "Emancipation in the British West Indies" at the Concord Court House. Emerson's second son, Edward, is born. The *Dial* ceases publication because of low subscription rates.

1845 Emerson purchases land at Walden Pond. Edgar Allan Poe's *The Raven* appears.

1846 *Poems*, Emerson's first collection of verse, appears. The United States declares war on Mexico.

1847 Emerson takes his second trip to Europe; his lectures in England and Scotland are well attended.

1848 Emerson returns to the United States. Advocates of women's rights convene at Seneca Falls. Gold is discovered in California. The United States defeats Mexico, gaining control of most of the modern Southwest.

1849 Emerson republishes *Nature* in the collection *Nature, Addresses, and Lectures*, which includes "The American Scholar" and "The Divinity School Address," along with other early lectures.

1850 Emerson's *Representative Men* is published. Nathaniel Hawthorne's *The Scarlet Letter* appears. The second Fugitive Slave Law is enacted, making it illegal to assist escaped slaves. Margaret Fuller dies. When William Wordsworth dies, Alfred, Lord Tennyson succeeds him as poet laureate of England.

1851 Herman Melville publishes *Moby-Dick*, and James Fenimore Cooper dies.

1852 Harriet Beecher Stowe's *Uncle Tom's Cabin* appears.

1853 Emerson's mother dies.

1854 *Walden: or Life in the Woods*, by Henry David Thoreau, is published.

1855 Henry Wadsworth Longfellow's *The Song of Hiawatha* and the first edition of Walt Whitman's *Leaves of Grass* appear.

1856   Emerson's *English Traits* is published.

1857   Melville's *The Confidence-Man* appears, with what some believe is anti-Emersonian sentiment.

1859   Emerson's brother Robert dies. Washington Irving dies.

1860   *The Conduct of Life* is published.

1861   The American Civil War begins.

1862   U.S. President Abraham Lincoln issues the Emancipation Proclamation. Henry David Thoreau dies.

1863   Emerson's aunt, Mary Moody Emerson, dies.

1864   Nathaniel Hawthorne dies.

1865   The Confederates surrender at Appomattox Courthouse, Virginia, ending the American Civil War. Lincoln is assassinated.

1866   Emerson recites to his son his poem *Terminus*, in which he recognizes his declining creative power. Harvard honors Emerson with the Doctor of Laws degree.

1867   *May-Day and Other Pieces*, Emerson's second and final collection of poems, appears. He lectures in nine western states. Harvard University names him an Overseer of the Corporation.

1868   Louisa May Alcott publishes *Little Women*. Emerson's brother William dies in New York City.

1870   *Society and Solitude* is published. This year and the next Emerson presents at Harvard the lecture series "The Natural History of the Intellect."

1871   Emerson travels to California by railroad at the urging of his son-in-law, who works in the railroad industry.

1872–   Fire destroys Emerson's home. During its reconstruction a dev-
1873   astated Emerson and his daughter Ellen travel to Europe and Egypt. He visits Carlyle for the last time.

1874   *Parnassus*, an anthology of favorite poems Emerson compiled throughout his lifetime, appears.

1875   James Elliot Cabot, Emerson's literary executor and future biographer, compiles and publishes *Letters and Social Aims*, the last book by Emerson to be published in his lifetime.

1876–   Mark Twain's *The Adventures of Tom Sawyer* appears in 1876.
1881   Emerson stops making entries to his journal as his mental faculties slowly decline. Henry James's *The American*, *Daisy Miller*, and *Hawthorne* appear.

1882   Barely able to speak, Emerson attends the funeral of Henry Wadsworth Longfellow. Ralph Waldo Emerson dies on April 27 and is buried at Sleepy Hollow Cemetery in Concord.

Introduction

Optimist and Realist

Ralph Waldo Emerson was one of the most influential American writers of the nineteenth century. His essays, lectures, and poems significantly shaped the cultural values and intellectual traditions that remain central to our understanding of American culture. He inspired a poetic tradition that has passed down from Walt Whitman and Emily Dickinson to Robert Frost and William Carlos Williams. He anticipated a pragmatic style of thinking that has influenced American philosophers from William James to John Dewey to Richard Rorty. He was a leading figure among the transcendentalists, a group of writers, intellectuals, and social reformers whose ideas helped transform American culture during the period of rapid industrial growth and westward expansion that occurred from 1830 to 1860. Margaret Fuller, Henry David Thoreau, Theodore Parker, and Nathaniel Hawthorne are just a few of the contemporary writers who were inspired and antagonized by Emerson's words and example. His philosophy of self-reliance, his optimistic faith in the progress of American civilization, and his insistence on each individual's capacity for greatness continue to inspire new generations of writers, intellectuals, artists, and entrepreneurs. His essays, especially, offer readers an opportunity to engage in conscious acts of self-reflection modeled after his own contemplative engagement with the natural world. For Emerson, to enter into nature meant to enter an environment, free from society's conventional attitudes and opinions, where one could discover one's self, unique and apart from all other relations. "In the woods, we return to reason and faith," he wrote in *Nature*. "There I feel that nothing can befall me in life . . . which nature cannot repair" (p. 12). A similar experience may be had by those who enter into Emerson's essays. Often written in an elliptical style, and punctuated with epigrammatic statements such as "That is always best which gives me to myself" (p. 73) and "Insist on yourself; never imitate" (p. 132), Emerson's essays regularly turn readers back on themselves, reminding us that it is not in his writings, but in ourselves that we will find the purpose and motivation that defines our lives.

The appeal of Emerson's writings, however, has as much to do with their radicalism as with their affirmation of the individual. He maintained that if we would but trust ourselves, we would discover unlimited resources for the accomplishment of our will, but this belief was inseparable from his equally strong conviction that the opinions of the majority in American society lead away from self-trust and into conformity. "Society everywhere is in conspiracy against the manhood of every one of its members," he wrote famously in "Self-Reliance." "Society is a joint stock company in which the members agree for the better securing of his bread to each shareholder, to surrender the liberty and culture of the eater. The virtue in most request is conformity. . . . Whoso would be a man must be a nonconformist" (p. 116). Yet Emerson was not simply calling his readers to be iconoclastic. He knew that he lived in a time of unprecedented political change, one that gave, as he wrote in "The American Scholar," "new importance . . . to the single person" (p. 65). Democracies had begun to displace monarchies and limited monarchies throughout Europe. With the election of Andrew Jackson in 1828, it became clear that in America, too, the majority would no longer consist of established property owners aligned with the conservative Whig party but would include the immigrants, laborers, and farmers who were settling the western territories. Emerson saw that a newly emergent middle class of merchants, skilled workers, and entrepreneurs was becoming the dominant political class, and he recognized the immense opportunities that were now available to the average citizen of the United States. At the same time, as his metaphor of society as a joint stock company implies, he saw these opportunities being squandered as the ambitions and values of every citizen were determined for them by the marketplace mentality that had come to dominate American culture.

In the face of this new materialism, Emerson feared that America was losing its most valuable resource—the individual—as men and women increasingly defined themselves in terms of their professions and their possessions. "The tradesman scarcely ever gives an ideal worth to his work, but is ridden by the routine of his craft, and the soul is subject to dollars," he lamented in "The American Scholar." "The priest becomes a form; the attorney, a statute-book; the mechanic, a machine; the sailor, a rope of a ship" (p. 51). The alienation that results from conformity could be overcome only by a radical break with custom and tradition. "If you maintain a dead church, contribute to a dead Bible society, vote with a great party either for the Government or against it," he wrote in "Self-Reliance," ". . . under all these screens I have difficulty to detect the precise man you are. . . . But do your work, and I shall know you. Do your work, and you shall reinforce yourself" (p. 118). For Emerson, our ability to think and act on our own terms was ultimately the strongest corrective to conformity. "In all of my lectures," he wrote in his journal in 1840, "I have preached one doctrine, namely, the infinitude of the private man" (*Journals and Miscellaneous Notebooks*, vol. 7, p. 342; see "For Further Reading"). By keeping this a continual refrain throughout his career, he placed the individual at the center of American culture as a critical counterforce to the mentality of mass consumerism. Today, when the pressures placed on individuals to conform to the material values of American culture are perhaps stronger than ever, readers young and old will find Emerson's essays a resource for personal, intellectual, and professional renewal.

The emphasis Emerson placed on the individual was grounded in his theological beliefs. Human life, as well as nature, was a manifestation of divinity. In moments of genuine inspiration or original action, the individual did not think or act from himself but was a conduit for what Emerson variously referred to as "Supreme Mind," "Universal Being," or "the Over-soul." "We lie in the lap of immense intelligence, which makes us organs of its activity and receivers of its truth," he wrote in "Self-Reliance." "When we discern justice, when we discern truth, we do nothing of ourselves, but allow a passage to its beams" (p. 123). This fact is easy to overlook in an increasingly secular world, but it is essential for understanding the difference between Emersonian self-reliance and what Albert J. von Frank has termed the "predatory individualism" of the expansionist era.

Equally important is some knowledge of Emerson's personal experience of the transient nature of human life. From his childhood until the middle of his life, Emerson lived through the tragic loss of those closest to him. His father died less than two weeks before Emerson's eighth birthday; his three-year-old sister, Mary Caroline, when he was ten. His first wife, Ellen Tucker, suffered from tuberculosis, and Emerson probably knew she would die young when they married. Still, when she succumbed to the disease at the age of nineteen, before their second wedding anniversary, he was devastated. Tuberculosis was widespread in New England. Emerson showed symptoms of it himself. It claimed the lives of two of his brothers, Edward at the age of twenty-nine and Charles at thirty-two. They were his closest confidants. Following Charles's funeral, Emerson is reported to have said, "When one has never had but little society—and all that society is taken away—what is there worth living for?" Finally, in 1842, when Emerson was thirty-eight and happily married to his second wife, Lydia Jackson, their eldest son,

Waldo, died of scarlet fever. He was five. Emerson's optimistic affirmations of the individual take on new urgency when read in light of this litany of loss.

When he writes in *Nature* that our "relation to the world . . . is not to be learned by any addition or subtraction or other comparison of known quantities, but is arrived at by untaught sallies of the spirit, by a continual self-recovery, and by entire humility" (p. 44), the "self-recovery" he speaks of is not simply a return to one's sense of self. It is a recovery from our failures, and especially from the failure of what we thought we knew, in the face of experiences that indicate otherwise. At times in his essays, Emerson will entertain the deepest skepticism. "No picture of life can have any veracity that does not admit the odious facts" (p. 375), he wrote in "Fate." Among these facts is the awful truth that not just our knowledge, but our loves and friendships are partial and temporary. "Souls never touch their objects," he wrote in "Experience." "An unnavigable sea washes with silent waves between us and the things we aim at and converse with" (p. 236). And yet, in the face of these facts, Emerson still affirms the beauty and value of human life. Confronting the mixed bag of human experience—what he jokingly calls "the pot-luck of the day"—he insists that "if we will take the good we find, asking no questions, we shall have heaping measures" (pp. 242–243). These are not the words of an idealistic dreamer, as Emerson has sometimes been portrayed. They are an expression of his confidence in man's ability to meet and master his circumstances; they are a call for a pragmatic engagement of the world in which we find ourselves.

The world in which Emerson found himself was decidedly mixed. He was born May 25, 1803, in Boston, Massachusetts, the fourth of eight children. His father, William Emerson, was the minister of First Church, Boston, one of the leading congregations in the city. His mother, Ruth Haskins, was the daughter of a wealthy merchant family. However, his father's untimely death left his mother responsible for raising six children (Emerson's oldest sister, Phebe Ripley, died before he was born; his oldest brother, John Clarke, when he was three). She was able to do so with the help of family and friends, but she was no longer a member of Boston's social elite. The congregation of the First Church allowed her to continue living in the parsonage for the next year, and she then managed a series of boardinghouses in Boston and the vicinity. While Emerson and his brothers never suffered the deprivations of poverty, neither did they lead a life of wealth and privilege. Above all, Ruth Emerson made sure that her children were educated. Before he was three, Emerson attended a dame school (an early form of nursery school) and by the age of nine he was enrolled in Boston Latin, the preparatory school that sent many of its students on to Harvard. During the break between morning and afternoon classes, Emerson attended a second school, the South Writing School, with his close friend William Henry Furness. At Boston Latin, Emerson first began writing poetry, and in his final year, at the age of thirteen, he delivered his "Poem on Eloquence" as part of the school's annual exhibition.

The next year he attended Harvard, where his older brother William was beginning his senior year. Emerson was one of the youngest in his class, but it was common practice at that time for students to enter college at fourteen and to graduate at eighteen. Emerson worked his way through college. He was fortunate to be appointed "the President's freshman" in his first year by the college president, John Thornton Kirkland, a friend and classmate of his father, and that January, during the semester break, he began teaching at his uncle Samuel Ripley's grammar school, a job he would work at during summers as well. He also tutored his classmates and entered most of the academic prize competitions, which usually carried a cash award. He earned distinction in philosophy, oratory, and poetry, and in his senior year he was elected class poet, but only after seven other students declined the honor.

Emerson received a broad education at Harvard. He studied Latin and Greek, English rhetoric and oratory, mathematics, logic, and history both ancient and modern. He was fluent in French when he entered, and he would later learn German. By his senior year he was spending more and more time studying British empiricism and Scottish common sense philosophy, especially the work of John Locke and Dugald Stewart. Much of this reading went into his "Dissertation on the Present State of Ethical Philosophy," which placed second in the annual Bowdoin Prize competition. This course of reading was excellent preparation for the ministry, but when he graduated in 1821 he was ambivalent about a career at the pulpit. He moved in with his mother in Boston and began teaching in the school for young ladies that his brother William had established. William was planning to travel to Germany to study theology at Göttingen. For a time, Emerson entertained the idea of joining him, but he had assumed responsibility for the school (the tuition fees were helping to fund William's studies), and his interest in a career in divinity continued to fluctuate. In January 1823 he wrote to a friend, "My sole answer and apology to those who inquire about my studies is—I keep school—I study neither law, medicine, or divinity, and write neither poetry nor prose" (*The Letters of Ralph Waldo Emerson*, vol. 1, p. 127). A little over a year later, though, he declared in his journal, "I am beginning my professional studies. In a month I shall be legally a man. And I deliberately dedicate my time, my talents, & my hopes to the Church" (*Journals and Miscellaneous Notebooks*, vol. 2, p. 237). Soon thereafter, Emerson requested a reading list from William Ellery Channing, a prominent Unitarian preacher and theologian who had been one of his professors at Harvard, and began studying on his own in preparation to enter the Divinity School at Harvard. He met with Channing weekly, and by the end of the year, had closed his school and enrolled for the spring term. His independent study under Channing's direction made it possible for him to complete his training in two years (rather than the usual three), but economic considerations forced him back to teaching in the summer. He also began to experience severe health problems. He contracted an eye infection that drastically limited his ability to read and caused him constant headaches. He also experienced inflammation in one of his hips that was diagnosed as rheumatoid arthritis; Emerson believed these symptoms were related to tuberculosis, the disease that plagued his younger brothers Edward and Charles. Although he was officially approbated to preach in October 1826, Emerson suspended his studies and traveled south for the winter, first to Charleston, South Carolina, and then to St. Augustine, Florida, in the hope that a change in climate would improve his health.

It was perhaps fortunate that Emerson's poor health disrupted his studies. He had found the readings in Unitarian theology somewhat stifling, and during his illness he decided to pursue his own interests, reading the *Essais* of Michel de Montaigne for the first time, and returning to Plutarch and Marcus Aurelius, as well as Madame de Staël's *Germany* and Samuel Taylor Coleridge's *Biographia Literaria*. This return to stoic philosophy and literary romanticism was perhaps the antidote Emerson needed to the rationalist theology he was hearing from Channing and the other faculty of the Harvard Divinity School. Emerson's education coincided with Harvard's institutionalization of Unitarianism, a liberal approach to theology that challenged the Calvinistic traditions of the New England churches. Strongly influenced by the rational empiricism of Locke, New England Unitarians rejected the orthodox position on original sin, grace, and revelation. For example, Channing, one of the most eloquent and outspoken of the Boston Unitarians, insisted that "revelation is addressed to us as rational beings" and condemned those who claimed to preach from divine inspiration. In "Unitarian Christianity" he wrote, "We cannot sacrifice our reason to the reputation of zeal. We owe it to truth and religion to maintain that fanaticism, partial insanity, sudden impressions, and ungovernable transports are anything rather than piety." Grounding religion on a strict rationalism, however, had its drawbacks for students of Emerson's generation. A religion devoid of emotional enthusiasm seemed to many lifeless— "corpse-cold" in Emerson's phrase. At the same time, though, the Unitarian insistence on reason helped liberate Emerson and his peers— in ways more radical than their teachers imagined—from the hidebound strictures of doctrine. If scripture was not divine revelation, but written in the language of men, as Channing claimed, then why not write a new scripture suitable for today, instead of simply repeating the words of past generations?

Emerson found a model for such an endeavor in a book written by one of his peers, Sampson Reed's *Observations on the Growth of the Mind*, which Emerson read just before his departure for Florida. Only two years his senior, Reed received his M.A. the year Emerson graduated from Harvard, and Emerson heard him read his "Oration on Genius" as part of the commencement ceremonies that year. *Observations on the Growth of the Mind* was an expanded treatment of the same subject— namely, that the mind contains within itself "the germ of every science" and that nature exists "to draw forth and mature" these "latent energies of the soul." The emphasis Reed placed on the mind's organic capacity for growth and development challenged the mechanistic view of Lockean rationalism and gave new importance to human creativity. "Syllogistic reasoning is passing away," he proclaimed, "in the progress of moral improvement, the imagination (which is called the creative power of man) shall coincide with the actively creative power of God." Reed's *Observations* helped fill the void in Emerson's training for the ministry. What frustrated Emerson most with the Divinity School curriculum was the amount of time spent studying the history of Christian doctrine. Elated with Reed, Emerson wrote to his Aunt Mary Moody, who had long been his confidant in matters relating to his spiritual life: "It is one of the feelings of modern philosophy, that it is wrong to regard ourselves so much in a *historical* light as we do, putting time between God & us; and that it were fitter to account every moment of the existence of the Universe as a new Creation and *all* as a revelation proceeding every moment from the Divinity to the mind of the observer" (*Letters*, vol. 1, p. 174). This insight would remain central to Emerson's thinking, and would provide the foundation for his philosophy of self-reliance.

Emerson returned from Florida having recovered his health, but his ambitions for the ministry had been tempered. He settled into a routine of preaching, but unlike his classmates from the Divinity School, he did not take a permanent position in a congregation. Instead he served as substitute or replacement preacher, first in Boston and then throughout New England. Emerson was invited to join a number of congregations but declined out of concern for his health. Because he was not constrained to meet the expectations of the same congregation week in and week out, he had the freedom to experiment with rhetorical devices and develop his own interpretations of scripture and doctrine. In the weeks between his stints preaching, he pursued his interests in philosophy, literary criticism, and the natural sciences. Emerson had started keeping a journal during his sophomore year in college, a practice he maintained throughout his life, and now his journals became the forum in which he debated with himself the competing truth claims of the scientists, theologians, philosophers, and poets he encountered in his copious reading.

During this time he met his first wife, Ellen Tucker, while preaching in Concord, New Hampshire. Like Emerson, she was an aspiring poet, and as their correspondence shows, they fell deeply in love with one another. Tragically, she already had been diagnosed with tuberculosis. Her brother had died of the disease, and she knew it was likely to claim her life, too, at a young age. Nevertheless she and Emerson found great joy in their marriage, and when they returned to Boston, Emerson accepted a permanent position as a minister of Boston's Second Church. "My history has had its important days," he wrote in his journal. "Whilst I enjoy the luxury of an unmeasured affection for an object so deserving of it all & who requites it all,—I am called by an ancient & respectable church to be its pastor" (*Journals and Miscellaneous Notebooks*, vol. 3, p. 149). Over the next year and a half Emerson settled into Boston society. He was made an honorary member of Phi Beta Kappa, appointed chaplain of the Massachusetts senate, and elected to serve on the school board. All signs pointed to his becoming a respectable member of Boston's Brahmin elite, and the obligations of family probably would have assured that. After a severe attack of bleeding at the lungs, Ellen's condition steadily worsened, and on February 8, 1831, she died. Emerson tried to find solace in his conviction that her spiritual presence in his life would persist, but his bereavement was profound. He wrote to his Aunt Mary in the hours after Ellen's death, "I have never known a person in the world in whose separate existence as a soul I could so readily & fully believe." A few lines later, however, he admitted that "things & duties will look coarse & vulgar enough to me when I find the romance of her presence withdrawn from them all" (*Letters*, vol. 1, p. 318). Emerson knew himself well. Over the next six months, the daily obligations of ministering to the congregation of the Second Church began to wear on him, and by October 1831 he was exasperated with the forms and rituals of organized religion. "How little love is at the bottom of these great religious shows," he wrote in his journal; "congregations and temples and sermons,—how much sham!" (*Journals and Miscellaneous Notebooks*, vol. 3, p. 301). In early June 1832, Emerson wrote a letter to his congregation proposing to change the ritual for administering communion. Apparently Emerson believed that, in the minds of his parishioners, the formal ritual of "the Lord's Supper" was more important than following Christ's example in their daily lives. When the church committee rejected his proposal, Emerson preached a final sermon defending his position, and then tendered his resignation.

For Emerson, leaving the church was not a repudiation of his faith but a reaffirmation of it. He was increasingly convinced of the immediacy of God in human experience. There was no need for the intermediate forms of the liturgy once one realized, as Emerson had, that "my own mind is the direct revelation I have from God" (*Journals and Miscellaneous Notebooks*, vol. 3, p. 312). Having severed his ties with the Church, he had to find a new way to communicate his revelation to the world. Inspired by a number of articles published anonymously in the British periodicals *Frazer's Magazine* and the *New Monthly Magazine*, Emerson considered starting a magazine of his own. He soon discovered that the anonymous author was Thomas Carlyle. However, his newfound literary ambitions were dampened by illness. The emotional and mental strain of leaving the ministry had taken its toll, and Emerson continued to mourn Ellen's death. He planned to sail for Puerto Rico for the winter, to join his brother Edward, who was convalescing there, but he suddenly changed his mind on hearing that a ship was preparing to sail for Naples, Italy. Emerson seized the opportunity to see the "Old Europe" his brother William had described in his letters from Germany. Perhaps he would also find an opportunity to meet some of the prominent scientists, artists, and men of letters whose work he had been reading with such enthusiasm—perhaps this Carlyle, "who gives us confidence in our philosophy" and "assures the truth-lover everywhere of sympathy" (*Journals and Miscellaneous Notebooks*, vol. 4, p. 45).

Emerson spent five months in Italy touring architectural sites and museums, absorbing visual images of ancient Greek and Roman culture and the art of the Italian Renaissance, often in the company of the English poet Walter Savage Landor. He then traveled via Switzerland to Paris, where he attended lectures on chemistry and the natural sciences at the Sorbonne. He visited the Jardin des Plantes, the famous botanical gardens, and marveled at its "cabinet of natural history," which displayed specimens collected from around the world. Before embarking from Boston, Emerson had been reading books about natural history with great interest. The evolutionary views of the French naturalist Lamarck had been gaining favor over the past decade, and Charles Darwin was two years into his voyage aboard the HMS *Beagle*, collecting the data that would inform the theory of evolution outlined in *The Origin of Species*. Natural history was the field in which the most innovative science was being done, and Emerson responded powerfully to the new image of the natural world that was emerging, in which all life forms were seen to be intricately interrelated. Viewing the meticulous classification of plant and animal specimens at the Jardin des Plantes confirmed visually what he had been reading and led him in a moment of enthusiasm to declare in his journals, "I will be a naturalist" (*Journals and Miscellaneous Notebooks*, vol. 4, pp. 198–200). What Emerson was discovering, though, was scientific confirmation for the beliefs that had led him to abandon the forms of organized religion. The systematic exhibition of species displayed in the Paris museums struck him as an elaborate argument from design; even the minute, detailed patterns of a seashell or a fern leaf were indications of the order that permeates creation and gives mute testimony of a Creator.

Emerson left Paris for England on July 18, 1833, pondering how he could direct his own intellectual abilities into productive work on the scale of that of the great naturalists of the nineteenth century. Just as natural science had begun systematically to classify the various life forms of the natural world, Emerson began thinking about how to classify the various intellectual patterns in the spiritual world of human consciousness. He arranged to visit Samuel Taylor Coleridge, the romantic poet and critic, whose writings on philosophy, religion, and the human imagination had played a significant role in Emerson's education. He also visited William Wordsworth, whom he considered the greatest living poet. However, the person who influenced his intellectual ambitions most during his travels in Britain was Thomas Carlyle, the social critic and historian he had encountered years earlier. Coleridge and Wordsworth were in their sixties and nearing the end of their careers. Carlyle, at thirty-seven, was much more nearly Emerson's contemporary. Carlyle was opinionated, an advocate of progressive ideas, and a writer determined to address contemporary social and political issues even when writing as a historian or literary critic. It was Carlyle who served as the model for Emerson's ambitions as a writer and intellectual on his return to America, even if many of Emerson's more idealistic beliefs antagonized the practical Scotsman.

Emerson's travels in Europe and England planted the seeds of the idealist philosophy he would outline in his first book, *Nature*. It would take him three years to finish that work, but he began to work out its argument on the voyage home to Boston. Within a few weeks of his return he delivered a lecture on "The Uses of Natural History," which can be considered a prospectus for *Nature*. This lecture was partly an account of what he had learned in Paris and in his own reading on the subject, and partly an effort to tease out a series of moral lessons from these new scientific discoveries about the natural world. The proper "use" of natural history, Emerson believed, was not to be found in what it could teach us about the material world, but in what it demonstrated about the mind's powers of observation. Our capacity to perceive and comprehend order in nature indicates a deeper truth about the autonomy of human consciousness. The mental processes used to discover the heretofore hidden interrelation of flora and fauna provide a disciplined education in how each individual can discover his or her own relation to the world. "Our dealing with sensible objects," he would write in *Nature*, "is a constant exercise in the necessary lessons of difference, of likeness, of order, of being and seeming, of progressive arrangement. . . . and all to form the Hand of the mind;—to instruct us that 'good thoughts are no better than good dreams, unless they be executed!'" (p. 27).

At the lecture podium, Emerson was beginning to discover how to translate his spiritual convictions into the language of natural science, which was rapidly becoming the dominant language among the academic and professional classes. *Nature* was his first and most concerted effort to present a systematic account of how studying the natural world will lead individuals to discover fundamental moral, or spiritual, truths—truths that, in turn, are the ethical basis for action in the world. His argument can start to sound fairly Puritanical when he claims in the "Discipline" chapter that "every natural process is a version of a moral sentence" (p. 30), and insists on our duty to read out the ethical lesson of every event that befalls us in life. However, in the final three chapters, "Idealism," "Spirit," and "Prospects," his argument turns in a radically forward-looking direction. Because the phenomena of the natural world are ultimately symbolic of higher spiritual ideals, the natural world—as well as the human societies built up from its resources—are subject to the ideas of men and, therefore, can be reformed and improved by better ideas. "'Nature is not fixed but fluid. Spirit alters, moulds, makes it'" (p. 49). Just three generations after the Declaration of Independence, America was searching for its cultural identity. In *Nature*, Emerson provided a philosophical foundation for the production of a new set of cultural values and beliefs. The interaction between the natural world and human consciousness provided unlimited possibilities for the production of the values and beliefs that comprise a genuinely democratic culture, in which each individual must "build [his] own world" (p. 49) from experiences that are common to all.

As *Nature* slowly took shape, Emerson was actively re-engaging with life and New England society. He agreed to preach on an interim basis at several congregations but he made it clear that he had no intention of returning to the ministry full-time. Instead he sought out opportunities to lecture on topics of his own choosing, including "On the Relation of Man to the Globe," "Literary Ethics," and a series of biographical sketches modeled after Plutarch's *Lives*. An inheritance from Ellen Tucker's estate freed him from the necessity of having to seek full-time employment and made it possible for him to pour his energies into his new intellectual pursuits. He struck up a correspondence with Carlyle and was soon encouraging him to come and lecture in America. He continued to make plans for a new magazine, to be called the *Transcendentalist*. He continued to write poetry, producing, among others, "The Rhodora," "Each and All," and "The Snowstorm," which capture in poetic form the philosophy he expressed in prose in *Nature*. During this time, Emerson also met Lydia Jackson, the woman who would become his second wife. Without pretending to recapture the youthful romance he shared with Ellen, Emerson courted Lydian (as he came to call her) with an intensity born of their mutual admiration and respect. Their marriage coincided with Emerson's return to his ancestral home in Concord, where his grandfather William Emerson had served as minister of the First Church prior to his death in the Revolutionary War, and where his step-grandfather, Ezra Ripley, continued to occupy the pulpit in his place. Ripley was nearing retirement, and there may have been some speculation that Emerson would succeed him, in turn. Clearly an effort was made to welcome him into the community. He was invited to be the principal speaker at the town's celebration of its two-hundredth anniversary, and the speech he delivered on the history of Concord became his first published address. He purchased a house for himself and his new bride, and arranged to have his mother move in with them, while finding rooms in town for his Aunt Mary and his brother Charles. Even as he settled with his family into the familiar confines of Concord society however, his intellectual and literary ambitions were growing to national proportions.

Emerson was thirty-two when he and Lydian were married, and having re-established a private life for himself with his family, he was ready to embark on a public career with renewed vigor and spirit. His stint as a public lecturer had exposed him to a new audience of intellectuals, artists, and entrepreneurs, and soon after the publication of *Nature* in 1836, he organized a symposium of people interested in discussing the leading intellectual trends in American culture. This group, which came to be known as the Transcendental Club, included George Ripley, the founder of the Brook Farm commune; Orestes Brownson, soon to be editor of the *Boston Quarterly Review*; Bronson Alcott, the educational reformer whose Temple school anticipated many of the modern methods of education; Frederic Henry Hedge, a brilliant young professor of German philosophy; Theodore Parker, who became a prominent leader of the abolitionist movement in Boston; and James Freeman Clarke, who as editor of the *Western Messenger* would bring Emerson's transcendental philosophy to the Ohio River Valley. Emerson would later invite his young friend Henry David Thoreau to attend, and when the club met at Emerson's house he arranged for Margaret Fuller, Elizabeth Hoar, and Sarah Ripley to be present, and in subsequent meetings women often participated in the conversation and debate. Fuller became a frequent visitor to his home, and with her he would plan and edit the *Dial*, the literary journal that served as a publishing venue for many writers associated with the transcendental movement.

The meetings of the Transcendental Club inspired Emerson to make bold pronouncements of the idealist philosophy he had outlined in *Nature* on two prominent occasions. The first was his invitation to address Harvard's Phi Beta Kappa society on August 31, 1837, the morning after commencement. Although his chosen topic, "The American Scholar," was a traditional one, Emerson poured into it his fierce conviction that each individual possesses unique talents and ability, and that education should cultivate those talents rather than transmit the intellectual traditions of the past. "Why should we not have a literature of our own?" he had asked in *Nature*. Now he made the same rhetorical appeal to Harvard's leading graduates. "Meek young men grow up in libraries," he chided them, "believing it their duty to accept the views, which Cicero, which Locke, which Bacon, have given, forgetful that Cicero, Locke and Bacon were only young men in libraries, when they wrote these books" (p. 54). In the strongest terms he could imagine, Emerson reminded these students that education was of value only insofar as it drew out their own intellectual force. Colleges "can only highly serve us," he said, "when they aim not to drill, but to create; when they gather from far every ray of various genius . . . and, by the concentrated fires, set the hearts of their youth on flame" (p. 56). Even though the country was mired in economic recession, Emerson warned that, if education merely trained students for a career, it would lead them to despair. "The American Scholar" address was somewhat controversial (Edward Everett Hale remarked, "It was not very good, but very transcendental"), but when published as a pamphlet in an edition of 500 copies, it quickly sold out.

The following year Emerson was invited back to Harvard to speak to the graduating class of the Divinity School. The ideas he expressed on that occasion were essentially the same as those in "The American Scholar" address, but in the halls of the Divinity School they were much more controversial. He urged the newly appointed ministers to preach from their own experience: "Be to [your congregation] a divine man; be to them thought and virtue . . . let their doubts know that you have doubted, and their wonder feel that you have wondered" (p. 79). In order to do this, though, he declared, the ministers must forget the "historical Christianity" they had been taught, and unlearn the formal methods of scriptural interpretation in which they had been trained— a method Emerson claimed was responsible for "the universal decay and now almost death of faith in society" (p. 74). Although some in attendance were greatly inspired, others were outraged, especially those faculty members whose methodology was dismissed as damaging to true religious faith. Five weeks after the talk, Andrews Norton, a distinguished professor of theology at Harvard, published a newspaper article condemning Emerson's address as "an incoherent rhapsody" and "an insult to religion," the words of an atheist. Emerson's supporters rushed to his defense, but he refused to take part in the public controversy. He set about his work, and the lessons he learned by his public censure eventually found their way into "Self-Reliance," his most defiant—but also most pragmatic—account of the constraints of conformity.

The public reaction to his Divinity School address may have confirmed Emerson in his decision to give up preaching in favor of the lecture circuit, which was proving to be more lucrative. In January 1839 he delivered his final sermon and committed himself to the work of compiling an edition of essays from his numerous lectures and journal entries. However, it would take him another two years to decide on a suitable arrangement and to revise and rework the material he published in 1841 as _Essays_. During this time he continued to lecture regularly, and he assisted Margaret Fuller as co-editor of the *Dial*. He also continued to manage the publication of Carlyle's writings in America, a task he had begun in 1836 when he arranged and wrote the introduction for an American edition of *Sartor Resartus*. Emerson also edited a collection of essays and poems by Jones Very, a young man struck with such religious enthusiasm that for a time he believed himself a literal incarnation of the Holy Spirit. While he sometimes complained that these other publishing ventures were a distraction from his own writing, their success helped spur him to complete his own volume of essays.

Essays was published during a time of political intensity and social transformation. The generation Emerson had addressed in "The American Scholar" was coming of age. The belief was widespread that the fundamental structures of society could and would be changed. Abolition, women's suffrage, the rights of labor, the temperance movement, and the establishment of numerous communes committed to socialist principles of shared labor—all indicated that large portions of the population were committed to social reform. Yet even as he was being recognized as a leading voice among the transcendentalists, Emerson held himself aloof from direct involvement in many of their projects of reform. He refused to join Brook Farm, the utopian commune founded by George Ripley, and though he did speak out against slavery on several occasions, he was hesitant to associate himself with abolitionist organizations or their publications. He stated his reasons publicly in an address to the Mechanics' Apprentices Association titled "Man the Reformer," delivered on January 25, 1841, just a few weeks after he sent *Essays* to press. "The power, which is at once spring and regulator in all efforts of reform, is the conviction that there is an infinite worthiness in man which will appear at the call of worth" (p. 93). From Emerson's perspective, in order for social reform to be effective, it must necessarily be preceded by self-reform. *Essays* was Emerson's contribution to the reform movement insofar as each essay in the series was meant to liberate the reader from conventional ways of knowing and turn him back on his own inner resources. "A greater self-reliance," Emerson declared in the essay of that name, ". . . must work a revolution in all the offices and relations of men; in their religion; in their education; in their pursuits; their modes of living; their association; in their property; in their speculative views" (p. 129). Emerson imagined the self-reliant individual as engaged in an ongoing process of self-becoming. "Every man believes that he has a greater possibility" (p. 204), he wrote in "Circles"—also included in *Essays*—and the same is true for society as a whole. "The things which are dear to men at this hour, are so on account of the ideas which have emerged on their mental horizon. . . . A new degree of culture would instantly revolutionize the entire system of human pursuits" (p. 206). The key word in this sentence is "culture." Unlike many of his fellow transcendentalists, Emerson did not believe one could simply change society by changing the laws, or imposing new regulations. In order to effectively change the laws of a state, one must first change the minds of its citizens, and this could best be done through "culture," or education. Emerson made this point explicitly in "Politics," an essay he published in *Essays: Second Series* (1844). "Foolish legislation is a rope of sand, which perishes in the twisting; . . . the State must follow, and not lead the character and progress of the citizen" (p. 256).

As a public lecturer, Emerson had dedicated himself to improving the character and progress of citizens. In the essay, he found the literary form best suited to that endeavor. Over the next few years, though, his faith in individual and social progress would be severely tested, yet still he would persist in his affirmation of human potential. In January 1842, his first-born child, Waldo, would die of scarlet fever. The death of his son necessarily recalled the other tragic and untimely deaths he had endured: Following Ellen's death, his brother Edward had passed away in Puerto Rico soon after Emerson returned from England; his brother Charles had died just as Emerson was preparing *Nature* for the press. Waldo's death was both familiar and unimaginable. He was only five. In "Spiritual Laws," included in *Essays*, Emerson had written, "No man ever stated his griefs as lightly as he might. . . . For it is only the finite that has wrought and suffered; the infinite lies stretched in smiling repose" (p. 154). Now he was forced to reconsider his belief in the infinite goodness of human life. Perhaps there were some events with no redeeming characteristics. "I comprehend nothing of this fact but its bitterness," he wrote of Waldo's death. In the essay "Experience," which he published two years later in *Essays: Second Series*, Emerson grappled directly with the issue of potentially meaningless experience. "I grieve that grief can teach me nothing," he wrote (p. 236). Even in his agony, Emerson was still able to recognize that this mood would be supplanted by other moods, including future moments of insight and joy.

In his essay "The Poet," also included in *Essays: Second Series*, he made it the poet's task to liberate us from such settled moods. "Every thought is also a prison," he wrote. "Therefore we love the poet, the inventor, who in any form . . . has yielded us a new thought. He unlocks our chains, and admits us to a new scene" (p. 228). Emerson defines the office of the poet to be the work of liberation. His essay on the poet can be taken as defining a much larger social role for himself as a public intellectual, a role he had began to perform in August 1844 when he agreed to deliver an address, "Emancipation in the British West Indies," at the Concord Court House to mark the anniversary of the abolition of slavery in the British colonies. Emerson had come to realize that his philosophy of self-reliance applied to all individuals, regardless of race. He returned to the lecture circuit with a new sense of his calling to influence the nature and direction of American culture, and slavery had no place in it. His lecturing increased, and soon he was traveling as far west as Ohio and as far north as Toronto. In 1846 he published *Poems*, his first volume of poetry. It included "Threnody," an elegy for his son Waldo. Emerson had recovered from the boy's death and found new purpose in his work.

With the publication of *Essays*, *Essays: Second Series*, and *Poems*, as well as his growing reputation as a lecturer, Emerson gained prominence as one of America's leading men of letters. His reputation led Alexander Ireland to invite him in to lecture in England. Emerson agreed, and a series of lectures was planned from October 1847 to July 1848 that would take him throughout the industrial North, from Liverpool to Manchester, to Edinburgh, Scotland, and then on to London. Emerson's lecture tour occurred during a time of political unrest in England. The Chartist movement was organizing the working class into a powerful political force, and many feared a social revolution. Emerson was sympathetic toward the movement. He was distressed by the poverty he witnessed in the Midland cities of Liverpool and Manchester, but he had also seen the high standard of living that these industrial centers had brought to the Midlands. He believed the working class deserved the same opportunities, but he criticized the "gross and bloody" methods of the Chartist leaders, whose demonstrations he felt were organized more to intimidate with the threat of force than to exhibit the justice of their cause. There was even greater political turmoil in France. The February Revolution of 1848 had ousted Louis Phillipe and established an interim government under the leadership of poet and statesman Alphonse-Marie-Louis de Lamartine. While in London during the following May, Emerson decided to make a trip to Paris during a break in his lecturing itinerary. He witnessed an uprising of union workers and socialists to overthrow Lamartine's predominantly middle-class leadership and establish a more socialist democracy. Emerson was appalled by such senseless violence and he became convinced that social reform must be accomplished by other means. How could the benefits of modern technology and a marketplace economy be made available to all members of society? Emerson set about answering this question in his lectures. In *Nature* he had looked for a way to translate his spiritual convictions into the language of natural science. Now he sought to translate his political convictions into the language of business and political economy.

On his return to America, Emerson threw himself into his work with renewed commitment. He decided to republish *Nature* in a collection that would include "The American Scholar" and his address to the Divinity School, along with some of his other early lectures. This volume *Nature, Addresses, and Lectures* (1849) presented the stages in thinking that led to the philosophy of self-reliance outlined in *Essays*. The following year he published *Representative Men*, a series of biographical sketches that Emerson believed exemplified the human potential for greatness. "Great men exist," he reminded his readers, "that there may be greater men" (p. 295). Both of these volumes were designed to promote a culture of self-improvement that might help ameliorate class differences, but in America these differences were complicated by the existence of slavery, which presented the greatest barrier to progress in the United States. In 1850 Congress passed the compromise legislation that included the Fugitive Slave Law, which required northern states to cooperate fully in the arrest and return of those who had escaped enslavement and fled north to freedom. Emerson was outraged when Daniel Webster, the eloquent and much admired senator from Massachusetts, gave a speech defending the compromise as essential to the maintenance of the Union. Emerson filled pages of his journal with paragraphs condemning Webster for his political expediency and lack of moral principle. When a group of Concord citizens petitioned him to speak publicly on the matter, Emerson had plenty of material to draw on. His "Address to the Citizens of Concord" on the Fugitive Slave Law restates his philosophy of self-reliance in an explicitly political context and deserves to be ranked alongside Thoreau's "Resistance to Civil Government" as one of the most powerful justifications for civil disobedience written in the nineteenth century.

As the political crisis over slavery intensified as a result of the passage of the Fugitive Slave Law, Emerson continued to work on a series of lectures called "The Conduct of Life." The series was meant to further the project Emerson had envisioned while lecturing in England: the cultivation of the middle class into the leading wave of reform in America. Now that project became shot through with the task of overcoming slavery. In the introductory lecture of that series, "Fate," Emerson proposed a heroic overcoming of the limitations of human experience, and presented race as one of the predominant factors that must be overcome. Emerson published *The Conduct of Life* in 1860, on the eve of the Civil War. His essay "Power" unabashedly celebrates the entrepreneurial strength of the industrial north. "The alarmists in Congress, and in the newspapers . . . sectional interests urged with a fury which shuts its eyes to consequences," these are "unimportant," once we realize that "personal power, freedom, and the resources of nature strain every faculty of every citizen" (p. 394). The power of the human will comes into being precisely through its encounter with limitations, and what was true for the individual would also be true for the nation. From Emerson's perspective, the Civil War itself was necessary to overcome the limitation of slavery and create a democratic society in which all individuals are free and equal.

With the publication of *The Conduct of Life*, the major phase of Emerson's career was over. After Thoreau's death in 1862, Emerson devoted time to editing Thoreau's papers, and he continued to lecture throughout the country. In 1866, with the Civil War finally over, he compiled a second volume of poetry, *May-Day and Other Pieces*, which was published in 1867. That year is also notable because Harvard named him an Overseer of the Corporation—it seemed his address to the Divinity School was finally forgiven. However, Emerson was not generating significant new material. Most of his lectures, as well as the poems in *May-Day*, had been written earlier in his career, and the new lectures he did produce were often efforts to complete half-finished projects he dredged up from his journals and notebooks. A notable exception is the series of lectures he delivered at Harvard in 1870 and 1871, "The Natural History of the Intellect." In this series, Emerson returned to the themes of *Nature* and made a concerted effort to offer a final, synthetic exposition of his theory that the physical laws of the universe correspond to ethical laws in the mind. But the effort left him exhausted. It soon was apparent that Emerson was experiencing short-term memory loss, and over the next decade he slowly declined into senility. With the help of his daughters, Ellen and Edith, and his literary executor, James Elliot Cabot, he continued to lecture and to advise on the publication of his miscellaneous lectures and addresses, but what he had foretold two decades earlier in his poem "Terminus" had now come to pass, "It is time to be old, / To take in sail," he had written. ". . . Fancy departs: no more invent" (p. 463). He died on April 27, 1882, at the age of seventy-nine.

Emerson's philosophy of self-reliance is an indelible part of the American character. Some scholars condemn it for giving license to the worst sort of materialism—the "me first" mentality that sees wealth as equivalent to worth. They fail to see that this mentality is exactly the condition of conformity from which Emerson would liberate us. Their mistake is understandable because in our thoroughly secular society it is easy to overlook the fact that Emerson's claims for the individual are based on a theory of natural right. Fortunately, the political crisis caused by the passage of the Fugitive Slave Law makes that basis easier to comprehend. In his "Address to the Citizens of Concord," he explained in no uncertain terms that human society is grounded in a common experience of the sanctity of human life.

> I thought that all men of all conditions had been made sharers of a certain experience, that in certain rare and retired moments they had been made to see . . . what makes the essence of rational beings, namely, that whilst animals have to do with eating the fruits of the ground, men have to do with rectitude, with benefit, with truth, with something which *is*, independent of appearances: and that this tie makes the substantiality of life, this, and not their ploughing, or sailing, their trade or the breeding of families. . . . I thought it was this fair mystery, . . . which made the basis of human society, and of law; and that to pretend anything else, as that the acquisition of property was the end of living, was to confound all distinctions, to make the world a greasy hotel, and, instead of noble motives and inspirations, and a heaven of companions and angels around and before us, to leave us in a grimacing menagerie of monkeys and idiots (p. 000).

The Fugitive Slave Law attempted to elevate property rights over the individual's natural right to liberty. For Emerson, this abomination made a mockery of democracy. Yet in American culture today, the right to get and keep whatever you can hold often seems to take precedence over the rights of others to a peaceable existence. Emerson was not naive to this fact. "I know that the world I converse with, in the city and in the farms, is not the world I *think*," he wrote in "Experience" (p. 253), but he made this distinction to remind us that the world we think oftentimes is better than the world in which we find ourselves, and that such thoughts have the power to transform our lives. "We must be very suspicious of the deceptions of the element of time," he wrote. "It takes a good deal of time to eat or to sleep, or to earn a hundred dollars, and a very little time to entertain a hope and an insight which becomes the light of our life" (p. 253). To read Emerson is to make time for such insights, and in so doing, to remember the power we have as intelligent beings to change our circumstances. "Every law and usage was a man's expedient to meet a particular case; . . . we may make as good; we may make better" (p. 256).

Peter Norberg received his Ph.D. from Rice University in 1998. Since 1997 he has been Assistant Professor of English at Saint Joseph's University in Philadelphia. A specialist on the writers associated with the transcendentalist movement, he has written and lectured extensively on Emerson, Henry David Thoreau, Margaret Fuller, and the critical reaction to transcendentalism in the writings of Nathaniel Hawthorne and Edgar Allan Poe. He also has published articles on Herman Melville and the poetry of Richard Henry Stoddard. His future projects include a history of Emerson's career as a public lecturer.

A Note on the Text

This edition contains selections from five of Emerson's works—*Essays* (1841), *Essays: Second Series* (1844), *Nature, Addresses, and Lectures* (1849), *Representative Men* (1850), and *The Conduct of Life* (1860)—as well as "An Address to the Citizens of Concord" on the Fugitive Slave Law (1851), the expanded version of Emerson's eulogy for Thoreau that was published in the *Atlantic Monthly*, and a short selection of poetry. The essays collected here are meant to introduce readers to the major phases of Emerson's career; however, no essays have been included from *English Traits* (1856), a volume of essays based on Emerson's observations of British culture during his 1847–1848 lecture tour.

The text of this edition is based on *The Complete Works of Ralph Waldo Emerson*, edited by Emerson's son, Edward Waldo Emerson. With the exception of the essays "Fate," "Power," "Thoreau," and the poetry, I have corrected each essay to bring it into accordance with *The Collected Works of Ralph Waldo Emerson* (5 volumes to date, edited by Alfred R. Ferguson, Joseph Slater, and Douglas Emory Wilson, Harvard University Press, 1971–). I have done the same with "An Address to the Citizens of Concord" on the Fugitive Slave Law, correcting it against the text given in *The Later Lectures of Ralph Waldo Emerson, 1843–1871* (2 vols., edited by Ronald A. Bosco and Joel Myerson, Athens: University of Georgia Press, 2001). Readers interested in textual matters for "Fate," "Power," and "Thoreau" should consult future volumes of *The Collected Works* as they become available.

Emerson makes numerous references to historical persons and mythology. Unless otherwise annotated, names of people and mythological figures have been identified in the Glossary of Names on page 465.

Essays and Poems by Ralph Waldo Emerson

Contents

Essays

Poems

Contents

ESSAYS

Nature[1]

A subtle chain of countless rings
The next unto the farthest brings;
The eye reads omens where it goes,
And speaks all languages the rose;
And, striving to be man, the worm
Mounts through all the spires of form.[2]

Introduction

OUR AGE IS RETROSPECTIVE. It builds the sepulchres of the fathers.[3] It writes biographies, histories, and criticism. The foregoing generations beheld God and nature face to face; we, through their eyes. Why should not we also enjoy an original relation to the universe? Why should not we have a poetry and philosophy of insight and not of tradition, and a religion by revelation to us, and not the history of theirs? Embosomed for a season in nature, whose floods of life stream around and through us, and invite us by the powers they supply, to action proportioned to nature, why should we grope among the dry bones* of the past, or put the living generation into masquerade out of its faded wardrobe? The sun shines to-day also. There is more wool and flax in the fields. There are new lands, new men, new thoughts. Let us demand our own works and laws and worship.

Undoubtedly we have no questions to ask which are unanswerable. We must trust the perfection of the creation so far, as to believe that whatever curiosity the order of things has awakened in our minds, the order of things can satisfy. Every man's condition is a solution in hiero-glyphic[4] to those inquiries he would put. He acts it as life, before he ap-prehends it as truth. In like manner, nature is already, in its forms and tendencies, describing its own design. Let us interrogate the great ap-parition, that shines so peacefully around us. Let us inquire, to what end is nature?

All science has one aim, namely, to find a theory of nature. We have theories of races and of functions, but scarcely yet a remote approach to an idea of creation. We are now so far from the road to truth, that reli-gious teachers dispute and hate each other, and speculative men are es-teemed unsound and frivolous. But to a sound judgment, the most abstract truth is the most practical. Whenever a true theory appears, it will be its own evidence. Its test is, that it will explain all phenomena.

---

*Reference to the Bible, Ezekiel 37:1–14: "The hand of the Lord was upon me . . . and set me down in the midst of the valley which was full of bones . . . and, lo, they were very dry. . . . Again he said unto me, Prophesy upon these bones, and say unto them, O ye dry bones, hear the word of the Lord" (King James Version; henceforth, KJV).

Now many are thought not only unexplained but inexplicable; as language, sleep, madness, dreams, beasts, sex.

Philosophically considered, the universe is composed of Nature and the Soul. Strictly speaking, therefore, all that is separate from us, all which Philosophy distinguishes as the NOT ME,[5] that is, both nature and art, all other men and my own body, must be ranked under this name, NATURE. In enumerating the values of nature and casting up their sum, I shall use the word in both senses;—in its common and in its philosophical import. In inquiries so general as our present one, the inaccuracy is not material; no confusion of thought will occur. *Nature*, in the common sense, refers to essences unchanged by man; space, the air, the river, the leaf. *Art* is applied to the mixture of his will with the same things, as in a house, a canal, a statue, a picture. But his operations taken together are so insignificant, a little chipping, baking, patching, and washing, that in an impression so grand as that of the world on the human mind, they do not vary the result.

Chapter I

To go into solitude, a man needs to retire as much from his chamber as from society. I am not solitary whilst I read and write, though nobody is with me. But if a man would be alone, let him look at the stars. The rays that come from those heavenly worlds, will separate between him and what he touches. One might think the atmosphere was made transparent with this design, to give man, in the heavenly bodies, the perpetual presence of the sublime. Seen in the streets of cities, how great they are! If the stars should appear one night in a thousand years, how would men believe and adore; and preserve for many generations the remembrance of the city of God which had been shown! But every night come out these envoys of beauty, and light the universe with their admonishing smile.

The stars awaken a certain reverence, because though always present, they are inaccessible; but all natural objects make a kindred impression, when the mind is open to their influence. Nature never wears a mean appearance. Neither does the wisest man extort her secret, and lose his curiosity by finding out all her perfection. Nature never became a toy to a wise spirit. The flowers, the animals, the mountains, reflected the wisdom of his best hour, as much as they had delighted the simplicity of his childhood.

When we speak of nature in this manner, we have a distinct but most poetical sense in the mind. We mean the integrity of impression made by manifold natural objects. It is this which distinguishes the stick of timber of the wood-cutter, from the tree of the poet. The charming landscape which I saw this morning, is indubitably made up of some twenty or thirty farms. Miller owns this field, Locke that, and Manning the woodland beyond. But none of them owns the landscape. There is a property in the horizon which no man has but he whose eye can integrate all the parts, that is, the poet. This is the best part of these men's farms, yet to this their warranty-deeds give no title.

To speak truly, few adult persons can see nature. Most persons do not see the sun. At least they have a very superficial seeing. The sun illuminates only the eye of the man, but shines into the eye and the heart of the child. The lover of nature is he whose inward and outward senses are still truly adjusted to each other; who has retained the spirit of infancy even into the era of manhood. His intercourse with heaven and earth, becomes part of his daily food. In the presence of nature, a wild delight runs through the man, in spite of real sorrows. Nature says,—he is my creature, and maugre* all his impertinent griefs, he shall be glad with me. Not the sun or the summer alone, but every hour and season yields its tribute of delight; for every hour and change corresponds to and authorizes a different state of the mind, from breathless noon to grimmest midnight. Nature is a setting that fits equally well a comic or a mourning piece. In good health, the air is a cordial of incredible virtue. Crossing a bare common, in snow puddles, at twilight, under a clouded sky, without having in my thoughts any occurrence of special good fortune, I have enjoyed a perfect exhilaration. I am glad to the brink of fear.† In the woods too, a man casts off his years, as the snake his slough, and at what period soever of life, always is a child. In the woods, is perpetual youth. Within these plantations of God, a decorum and sanctity reign, a perennial festival is dressed, and the guest sees not how he should tire of them in a thousand years. In the woods, we return to reason and faith. There I feel that nothing can befall me in life,—no disgrace, no calamity, (leaving me my eyes,) which nature cannot repair. Standing on the bare ground,—my head bathed by the blithe air, and uplifted into infinite space,—all mean egotism vanishes. I become a transparent eyeball;[6] I am nothing; I see all; the currents of the Universal Being circulate through me; I am part or particle of God. The name of the nearest friend sounds then foreign and accidental: to be brothers, to be acquaintances,—master or servant, is then a trifle and a disturbance. I am the lover of uncontained and immortal beauty. In the wilderness, I find something more dear and connate‡ than in streets or villages. In the tranquil landscape, and especially in the distant line of the horizon, man beholds somewhat as beautiful as his own nature.

The greatest delight which the fields and woods minister, is the suggestion of an occult§ relation between man and the vegetable. I am not alone and unacknowledged. They nod to me, and I to them. The waving of the boughs in the storm, is new to me and old. It takes me by surprise, and yet is not unknown. Its effect is like that of a higher thought

---

*Archaic word that derives from French and means "in spite of."
†In the 1836 edition Emerson wrote: "Almost I fear to think how glad I am."
‡Inborn; associated in birth or origin.
§Spiritual.

or a better emotion coming over me, when I deemed I was thinking justly or doing right.

Yet it is certain that the power to produce this delight, does not reside in nature, but in man, or in a harmony of both. It is necessary to use these pleasures with great temperance. For, nature is not always tricked in holiday attire, but the same scene which yesterday breathed perfume and glittered as for the frolic of the nymphs, is overspread with melancholy to-day. Nature always wears the colors of the spirit. To a man laboring under calamity, the heat of his own fire hath sadness in it. Then, there is a kind of contempt of the landscape felt by him who has just lost by death a dear friend. The sky is less grand as it shuts down over less worth in the population.

Chapter II

Commodity

WHOEVER CONSIDERS THE FINAL cause* of the world will discern a multitude of uses that enter as parts into that result. They all admit of being thrown into one of the following classes; Commodity; Beauty; Language; and Discipline.[7]

Under the general name of Commodity, I rank all those advantages which our senses owe to nature. This, of course, is a benefit which is temporary and mediate, not ultimate, like its service to the soul. Yet although low, it is perfect in its kind, and is the only use of nature which all men apprehend. The misery of man appears like childish petulance, when we explore the steady and prodigal provision that has been made for his support and delight on this green ball which floats him through the heavens. What angels invented these splendid ornaments, these rich conveniences, this ocean of air above, this ocean of water beneath, this firmament of earth between? this zodiac of lights, this tent of dropping clouds, this striped coat of climates, this fourfold year. Beasts, fire, water, stones, and corn serve him. The field is at once his floor, his work-yard, his play-ground, his garden, and his bed.

> "More servants wait on man
> Than he'll take notice of."——[†]

Nature, in its ministry to man, is not only the material, but is also the process and the result. All the parts incessantly work into each other's hands for the profit of man. The wind sows the seed; the sun evaporates the sea; the wind blows the vapor to the field; the ice, on the other side of the planet, condenses rain on this; the rain feeds the plant; the plant feeds the animal; and thus the endless circulations of the divine charity nourish man.

---

*Purpose.
†From the poem "Man," by George Herbert (1593–1633); Emerson quotes this poem at length in chapter VIII, "Prospects."

The useful arts are reproductions or new combinations by the wit of man, of the same natural benefactors. He no longer waits for favoring gales, but by means of steam, he realizes the fable of Æolus's bag,[8] and carries the two and thirty winds in the boiler of his boat. To diminish friction, he paves the road with iron bars, and, mounting a coach with a ship-load of men, animals, and merchandise behind him, he darts through the country, from town to town, like an eagle or a swallow through the air. By the aggregate of these aids, how is the face of the world changed from the era of Noah to that of Napoleon! The private poor man hath cities, ships, canals, bridges, built for him. He goes to the post-office, and the human race run on his errands; to the book-shop, and the human race read and write of all that happens, for him; to the court-house, and nations repair his wrongs. He sets his house upon the road, and the human race go forth every morning, and shovel out the snow, and cut a path for him.

But there is no need of specifying particulars in this class of uses. The catalogue is endless, and the examples so obvious, that I shall leave them to the reader's reflection, with the general remark, that this mercenary benefit is one which has respect to a farther good. A man is fed, not that he may be fed, but that he may work.

Chapter III

Beauty

A NOBLER WANT OF man is served by nature, namely, the love of Beauty.

The ancient Greeks called the world χοσμος,* beauty. Such is the constitution of all things, or such the plastic power† of the human eye, that the primary forms, as the sky, the mountain, the tree, the animal, give us a delight *in and for themselves;* a pleasure arising from outline, color, motion, and grouping. This seems partly owing to the eye itself. The eye is the best of artists. By the mutual action of its structure and of the laws of light, perspective is produced, which integrates every mass of objects, of what character soever, into a well colored and shaded globe, so that where the particular objects are mean and unaffecting, the landscape which they compose, is round and symmetrical. And as the eye is the best composer, so light is the first of painters. There is no object so foul that intense light will not make beautiful. And the stimulus it affords to the sense, and a sort of infinitude which it hath, like space and time, make all matter gay. Even the corpse has its own beauty. But beside this general grace diffused over nature, almost all the individual forms are agreeable to the eye, as is proved by our endless imitations of some of them, as the acorn, the grape, the pine-cone, the wheat-ear, the egg, the wings and forms of most birds, the lion's claw, the serpent, the butterfly, sea-shells, flames, clouds, buds, leaves, and the forms of many trees, as the palm.

For better consideration, we may distribute the aspects of Beauty in a threefold manner.

1. First, the simple perception of natural forms is a delight. The influence of the forms and actions in nature, is so needful to man, that, in its lowest functions, it seems to lie on the confines of commodity and beauty. To the body and mind which have been cramped by noxious work or company, nature is medicinal and restores their tone. The tradesman, the attorney comes out of the din and craft of the street, and

*Cosmos, or order (Greek).
†The power to mold and shape as a sculptor would clay.

sees the sky and the woods, and is a man again. In their eternal calm, he finds himself. The health of the eye seems to demand a horizon. We are never tired, so long as we can see far enough.

But in other hours, Nature satisfies by its loveliness, and without any mixture of corporeal benefit. I see the spectacle of morning from the hill-top over against my house, from daybreak to sunrise, with emotions which an angel might share. The long slender bars of cloud float like fishes in the sea of crimson light. From the earth as a shore, I look out into that silent sea. I seem to partake its rapid transformations: the active enchantment reaches my dust, and I dilate and conspire with the morning wind. How does Nature deify us with a few and cheap elements? Give me health and a day, and I will make the pomp of emperors ridiculous. The dawn is my Assyria; the sun-set and moon-rise my Paphos, and unimaginable realms of faerie; broad noon shall be my England of the senses and the understanding; the night shall be my Germany of mystic philosophy and dreams.[9]

Not less excellent, except for our less susceptibility in the afternoon, was the charm, last evening, of a January sunset. The western clouds divided and subdivided themselves into pink flakes modulated with tints of unspeakable softness; and the air had so much life and sweetness, that it was a pain to come within doors. What was it that nature would say? Was there no meaning in the live repose of the valley behind the mill, and which Homer or Shakspeare could not re-form for me in words? The leafless trees become spires of flame in the sunset, with the blue east for their back-ground, and the stars of the dead calices* of flowers, and every withered stem and stubble rimed† with frost, contribute something to the mute music.

The inhabitants of cities suppose that the country landscape is pleasant only half the year. I please myself with the graces of the winter scenery, and believe that we are as much touched by it as by the genial influences of summer. To the attentive eye, each moment of the year has its own beauty, and in the same field, it beholds, every hour, a picture which was never seen before, and which shall never be seen again. The heavens change every moment, and reflect their glory or gloom on the plains beneath. The state of the crop in the surrounding farms alters the expression of the earth from week to week. The succession of native plants in the pastures and roadsides, which makes the silent clock by

---

*That is, calyxes: the outermost leaves, or sepals, at the base of a flower.
†Coated.

which time tells the summer hours, will make even the divisions of the day sensible to a keen observer. The tribes of birds and insects, like the plants punctual to their time, follow each other, and the year has room for all. By water courses, the variety is greater. In July, the blue ponte-deria or pickerel-weed blooms in large beds in the shallow parts of our pleasant river, and swarms with yellow butterflies in continual motion. Art cannot rival this pomp of purple and gold. Indeed the river is a per-petual gala, and boasts each month a new ornament.

But this beauty of Nature which is seen and felt as beauty, is the least part. The shows of day, the dewy morning, the rainbow, mountains, or-chards in blossom, stars, moonlight, shadows in still water, and the like, if too eagerly hunted, become shows merely, and mock us with their un-reality. Go out of the house to see the moon, and 't is mere tinsel; it will not please as when its light shines upon your necessary journey. The beauty that shimmers in the yellow afternoons of October, who ever could clutch it? Go forth to find it, and it is gone: 't is only a mirage as you look from the windows of diligence.

2. The presence of a higher, namely, of the spiritual element is essen-tial to its perfection. The high and divine beauty which can be loved without effeminacy, is that which is found in combination with the human will. Beauty is the mark God sets upon virtue. Every natural ac-tion is graceful. Every heroic act is also decent, and causes the place and the bystanders to shine. We are taught by great actions that the universe is the property of every individual in it. Every rational creature has all nature for his dowry and estate. It is his, if he will. He may divest him-self of it, he may creep into a corner, and abdicate his kingdom, as most men do, but he is entitled to the world by his constitution. In propor-tion to the energy of his thought and will, he takes up the world into himself. "All those things for which men plough, build, or sail, obey virtue;" said Sallust.* "The winds and waves," said Gibbon,† "are always on the side of the ablest navigators." So are the sun and moon and all the stars of heaven. When a noble act is done,—perchance in a scene of great natural beauty; when Leonidas and his three hundred martyrs consume one day in dying,[10] and the sun and moon come each and look at them once in the steep defile of Thermopylæ; when Arnold Winkel-ried, in the high Alps, under the shadow of the avalanche, gathers in his

---

*For the names of most people and groups of people, see "Glossary of Names" on p. 465.

†English historian Edward Gibbon; the quote is from *The History of the Decline and Fall of the Roman Empire* (1776–1788), chapter 68.

side a sheaf of Austrian spears to break the line for his comrades; are not these heroes entitled to add the beauty of the scene to the beauty of the deed? When the bark of Columbus nears the shore of America;—before it, the beach lined with savages, fleeing out of all their huts of cane; the sea behind; and the purple mountains of the Indian Archipelago around, can we separate the man from the living picture? Does not the New World clothe his form with her palm-groves and savannahs as fit drapery? Ever does natural beauty steal in like air, and envelop great actions. When Sir Harry Vane was dragged up the Tower-hill, sitting on a sled, to suffer death, as the champion of the English laws, one of the multitude cried out to him, "You never sate on so glorious a seat." Charles II., to intimidate the citizens of London, caused the patriot Lord Russel to be drawn in an open coach, through the principal streets of the city, on his way to the scaffold. "But," his biographer says, "the multitude imagined they saw liberty and virtue sitting by his side." In private places, among sordid objects, an act of truth or heroism seems at once to draw to itself the sky as its temple, the sun as its candle. Nature stretcheth out her arms to embrace man, only let his thoughts be of equal greatness. Willingly does she follow his steps with the rose and the violet, and bend her lines of grandeur and grace to the decoration of her darling child. Only let his thoughts be of equal scope, and the frame will suit the picture. A virtuous man is in unison with her works, and makes the central figure of the visible sphere. Homer, Pindar, Socrates, Phocion, associate themselves fitly in our memory with the geography and climate of Greece. The visible heavens and earth sympathize with Jesus. And in common life, whosoever has seen a person of powerful character and happy genius, will have remarked how easily he took all things along with him,—the persons, the opinions, and the day, and nature became ancillary* to a man.

3. There is still another aspect under which the beauty of the world may be viewed, namely, as it becomes an object of the intellect. Beside the relation of things to virtue, they have a relation to thought. The intellect searches out the absolute order of things as they stand in the mind of God, and without the colors of affection.† The intellectual and the active powers seem to succeed each other, and the exclusive activity of the one, generates the exclusive activity of the other. There is something unfriendly in each to the other, but they are like the alternate pe-

---

*Subordinate; assisting.

†Emotions that may bias the objectivity of "the intellect."

riods of feeding and working in animals; each prepares and will be followed by the other. Therefore does beauty, which, in relation to actions, as we have seen, comes unsought, and comes because it is unsought, remain for the apprehension and pursuit of the intellect; and then again, in its turn, of the active power. Nothing divine dies. All good is eternally reproductive. The beauty of nature re-forms itself in the mind, and not for barren contemplation, but for new creation.

All men are in some degree impressed by the face of the world; some men even to delight. This love of beauty is Taste. Others have the same love in such excess, that, not content with admiring, they seek to embody it in new forms. The creation of beauty is Art.

The production of a work of art throws a light upon the mystery of humanity. A work of art is an abstract or epitome of the world. It is the result or expression of nature, in miniature. For, although the works of nature are innumerable and all different, the result or the expression of them all is similar and single. Nature is a sea of forms radically alike and even unique. A leaf, a sun-beam, a landscape, the ocean, make an analogous impression on the mind. What is common to them all,—that perfectness and harmony, is beauty. The standard of beauty is the entire circuit of natural forms,—the totality of nature; which the Italians expressed by defining beauty "il piu nell' uno."* Nothing is quite beautiful alone: nothing but is beautiful in the whole. A single object is only so far beautiful as it suggests this universal grace. The poet, the painter, the sculptor, the musician, the architect, seek each to concentrate this radiance of the world on one point, and each in his several work to satisfy the love of beauty which stimulates him to produce. Thus is Art, a nature passed through the alembic† of man. Thus in art, does nature work through the will of a man filled with the beauty of her first works.

The world thus exists to the soul to satisfy the desire of beauty. This element I call an ultimate end. No reason can be asked or given why the soul seeks beauty. Beauty, in its largest and profoundest sense, is one expression for the universe. God is the all-fair. Truth, and goodness, and beauty, are but different faces of the same All. But beauty in nature is not ultimate. It is the herald of inward and eternal beauty, and is not alone a solid and satisfactory good. It must stand as a part, and not as yet the last or highest expression of the final cause of Nature.

---

*The many in one (Italian).

†Device used for distilling; anything that transforms, purifies, or refines.

Chapter IV

Language

LANGUAGE IS A THIRD use which Nature subserves to man. Nature is the vehicle of thought, and in a simple, double, and threefold degree.

1. Words are signs of natural facts.
2. Particular natural facts are symbols of particular spiritual facts.
3. Nature is the symbol of spirit.

1. Words are signs of natural facts. The use of natural history is to give us aid in supernatural history: the use of the outer creation, to give us language for the beings and changes of the inward creation. Every word which is used to express a moral or intellectual fact, if traced to its root, is found to be borrowed from some material appearance. *Right* means *straight, wrong* means *twisted. Spirit* primarily means *wind; transgression,* the crossing of a *line; supercilious,* the *raising of the eyebrow.* We say the *heart* to express emotion, the *head* to denote thought; and *thought* and *emotion* are words borrowed from sensible things, and now appropriated to spiritual nature. Most of the process by which this transformation is made, is hidden from us in the remote time when language was framed; but the same tendency may be daily observed in children. Children and savages use only nouns or names of things, which they convert into verbs, and apply to analogous mental acts.

2. But this origin of all words that convey a spiritual import,—so conspicuous a fact in the history of language,—is our least debt to nature. It is not words only that are emblematic; it is things which are emblematic. Every natural fact is a symbol of some spiritual fact.[11] Every appearance in nature corresponds to some state of the mind, and that state of the mind can only be described by presenting that natural appearance as its picture. An enraged man is a lion, a cunning man is a fox, a firm man is a rock, a learned man is a torch. A lamb is innocence; a snake is subtle spite; flowers express to us the delicate affections. Light and darkness are our familiar expression for knowledge and ignorance; and heat for love. Visible distance behind and before us, is respectively our image of memory and hope.

Who looks upon a river in a meditative hour, and is not reminded of the flux of all things? Throw a stone into the stream, and the circles that propagate themselves are the beautiful type of all influence. Man is conscious of a universal soul within or behind his individual life, wherein, as in a firmament, the natures of Justice, Truth, Love, Freedom, arise and shine. This universal soul, he calls Reason: it is not mine, or thine, or his, but we are its; we are its property and men. And the blue sky in which the private earth is buried, the sky with its eternal calm, and full of everlasting orbs, is the type of Reason. That which, intellectually considered, we call Reason, considered in relation to nature, we call Spirit. Spirit is the Creator. Spirit hath life in itself. And man in all ages and countries, embodies it in his language, as the FATHER.

It is easily seen that there is nothing lucky or capricious in these analogies, but that they are constant, and pervade nature. These are not the dreams of a few poets, here and there, but man is an analogist, and studies relations in all objects. He is placed in the centre of beings, and a ray of relation passes from every other being to him. And neither can man be understood without these objects, nor these objects without man. All the facts in natural history taken by themselves, have no value, but are barren, like a single sex. But marry it to human history, and it is full of life. Whole Floras, all Linnæus's and Buffon's volumes, are dry catalogues of facts; but the most trivial of these facts, the habit of a plant, the organs, or work, or noise of an insect, applied to the illustration of a fact in intellectual philosophy, or in any way associated to human nature, affects us in the most lively and agreeable manner. The seed of a plant,—to what affecting analogies in the nature of man, is that little fruit made use of, in all discourse, up to the voice of Paul, who calls the human corpse a seed,—"It is sown a natural body; it is raised a spiritual body."* The motion of the earth round its axis, and round the sun makes the day, and the year. These are certain amounts of brute light and heat. But is there no intent of an analogy between man's life and the seasons? And do the seasons gain no grandeur or pathos from that analogy? The instincts of the ant are very unimportant, considered as the ant's; but the moment a ray of relation is seen to extend from it to man, and the little drudge is seen to be a monitor, a little body with a mighty heart, then all its habits, even that said to be recently observed, that it never sleeps, become sublime.

---

*Quotation from the Bible, I Corinthians 15:44 (KJV).

Because of this radical* correspondence between visible things and human thoughts, savages, who have only what is necessary, converse in figures. As we go back in history, language becomes more picturesque, until its infancy, when it is all poetry; or all spiritual facts are represented by natural symbols. The same symbols are found to make the original elements of all languages.[12] It has moreover been observed, that the idioms of all languages approach each other in passages of the greatest eloquence and power. And as this is the first language, so is it the last. This immediate dependence of language upon nature, this conversion of an outward phenomenon into a type of somewhat in human life, never loses its power to affect us. It is this which gives that piquancy to the conversation of a strong-natured farmer or back-woodsman, which all men relish.

A man's power to connect his thought with its proper symbol, and so to utter it, depends on the simplicity of his character, that is, upon his love of truth, and his desire to communicate it without loss. The corruption of man is followed by the corruption of language. When simplicity of character and the sovereignty of ideas is broken up by the prevalence of secondary desires, the desire of riches, of pleasure, of power, and of praise,—and duplicity and falsehood take place of simplicity and truth, the power over nature as an interpreter of the will, is in a degree lost; new imagery ceases to be created, and old words are perverted to stand for things which are not; a paper currency is employed, when there is no bullion in the vaults. In due time, the fraud is manifest, and words lose all power to stimulate the understanding or the affections. Hundreds of writers may be found in every long-civilized nation, who for a short time believe, and make others believe, that they see and utter truths, who do not of themselves clothe one thought in its natural garment, but who feed unconsciously on the language created by the primary writers of the country, those, namely, who hold primarily on nature.

But wise men pierce this rotten diction and fasten words again to visible things; so that picturesque language is at once a commanding certificate that he who employs it, is a man in alliance with truth and God. The moment our discourse rises above the ground line of familiar facts, and is inflamed with passion or exalted by thought, it clothes itself in images. A man conversing in earnest, if he watch his intellectual processes, will find that a material image, more or less luminous, arises in his mind, contemporaneous with every thought, which furnishes the vestment of the thought. Hence, good writing and brilliant discourse are perpetual

---

*Fundamental; literally, "from the root."

allegories. This imagery is spontaneous. It is the blending of experience with the present action of the mind. It is proper creation. It is the working of the Original Cause through the instruments he has already made.

These facts may suggest the advantage which the country-life possesses for a powerful mind, over the artificial and curtailed life of cities. We know more from nature than we can at will communicate. Its light flows into the mind evermore, and we forget its presence. The poet, the orator, bred in the woods, whose senses have been nourished by their fair and appeasing changes, year after year, without design and without heed,—shall not lose their lesson altogether, in the roar of cities or the broil of politics. Long hereafter, amidst agitation and terror in national councils,—in the hour of revolution,—these solemn images shall reappear in their morning lustre, as fit symbols and words of the thoughts which the passing events shall awaken. At the call of a noble sentiment, again the woods wave, the pines murmur, the river rolls and shines, and the cattle low upon the mountains, as he saw and heard them in his infancy. And with these forms, the spells of persuasion, the keys of power are put into his hands.

3. We are thus assisted by natural objects in the expression of particular meanings. But how great a language to convey such pepper-corn informations! Did it need such noble races of creatures, this profusion of forms, this host of orbs in heaven, to furnish man with the dictionary and grammar of his municipal speech? Whilst we use this grand cipher to expedite the affairs of our pot and kettle, we feel that we have not yet put it to its use, neither are able. We are like travellers using the cinders of a volcano to roast their eggs. Whilst we see that it always stands ready to clothe what we would say, we cannot avoid the question, whether the characters are not significant of themselves. Have mountains, and waves, and skies, no significance but what we consciously give them, when we employ them as emblems of our thoughts? The world is emblematic. Parts of speech are metaphors, because the whole of nature is a metaphor, of the human mind. The laws of moral nature answer to those of matter as face to face in a glass. "The visible world and the relation of its parts, is the dial plate of the invisible."* The axioms of physics translate the laws of ethics.† Thus, "the whole is greater than its part;" "reaction is equal to action;" "the smallest weight may be made to

---

*The words were written by Emanuel Swedenborg in the *New Jerusalem Magazine* (July 1832).

†Adapted from Madame de Staël's *De l'Allemagne* (1810; translated to English as *Germany* in 1813): "Not a mathematical axiom but is a moral rule."

lift the greatest, the difference of weight being compensated by time;" and many the like propositions, which have an ethical as well as physical sense. These propositions have a much more extensive and universal sense when applied to human life, than when confined to technical use.

In like manner, the memorable words of history, and the proverbs of nations, consist usually of a natural fact, selected as a picture or parable of a moral truth. Thus; a rolling stone gathers no moss; A bird in the hand is worth two in the bush; A cripple in the right way, will beat a racer in the wrong; Make hay while the sun shines; 'T is hard to carry a full cup even; Vinegar is the son of wine; The last ounce broke the camel's back; Long-lived trees make roots first;—and the like. In their primary sense these are trivial facts, but we repeat them for the value of their analogical import. What is true of proverbs, is true of all fables, parables, and allegories.

This relation between the mind and matter is not fancied by some poet, but stands in the will of God, and so is free to be known by all men. It appears to men, or it does not appear. When in fortunate hours we ponder this miracle, the wise man doubts, if, at all other times, he is not blind and deaf;

> ——"Can these things be,
> And overcome us like a summer's cloud
> Without our special wonder?"*

for the universe becomes transparent, and the light of higher laws than its own, shines through it. It is the standing problem which has exercised the wonder and the study of every fine genius since the world began; from the era of the Egyptians and the Brahmins, to that of Pythagoras, of Plato, of Bacon, of Leibnitz, of Swedenborg.[13] There sits the Sphinx at the roadside, and from age to age, as each prophet comes by, he tries his fortune at reading her riddle.[14] There seems to be a necessity in spirit to manifest itself in material forms; and day and night, river and storm, beast and bird, acid and alkali, preëxist in necessary Ideas in the mind of God, and are what they are by virtue of preceding affections, in the world of spirit. A Fact is the end or last issue of spirit. The visible creation is the terminus or the circumference of the invisible world. "Material objects," said a French philosopher, "are necessarily kinds of *scoriæ* of the substantial thoughts of the Creator, which must

---

*From Shakespeare's *Macbeth* (act 3, scene 4).

always preserve an exact relation to their first origin; in other words, visible nature must have a spiritual and moral side."*

This doctrine is abstruse, and though the images of "garment," "scoriæ," " mirror," &c., may stimulate the fancy, we must summon the aid of subtler and more vital expositors to make it plain. "Every scripture is to be interpreted by the same spirit which gave it forth,"†—is the fundamental law of criticism. A life in harmony with nature, the love of truth and of virtue, will purge the eyes to understand her text. By degrees we may come to know the primitive sense of the permanent objects of nature, so that the world shall be to us an open book, and every form significant of its hidden life and final cause.

A new interest surprises us, whilst, under the view now suggested, we contemplate the fearful extent and multitude of objects; since "every object rightly seen, unlocks a new faculty of the soul."‡ That which was unconscious truth, becomes, when interpreted and defined in an object, a part of the domain of knowledge,—a new weapon in the magazine of power.

---

*The words were written by Guillaume Oegger in *The True Messiah* (1829). Scoria is the slag or refuse left after metal has been smelted from ore.
†Written by the English Quaker George Fox.
‡From Samuel Taylor Coleridge's *Aids to Reflection* (1825).

Chapter V
Discipline [15]

IN VIEW OF THE significance of nature, we arrive at once at a new fact, that nature is a discipline. This use of the world includes the preceding uses, as parts of itself.

Space, time, society, labor, climate, food, locomotion, the animals, the mechanical forces, give us sincerest lessons, day by day, whose meaning is unlimited. They educate both the Understanding and the Reason. Every property of matter is a school for the understanding,— its solidity or resistance, its inertia, its extension, its figure, its divisibility. The understanding adds, divides, combines, measures, and finds nutriment and room for its activity in this worthy scene. Meantime Reason transfers all these lessons into its own world of thought, by perceiving the analogy that marries Matter and Mind.

1. Nature is a discipline of the understanding in intellectual truths. Our dealing with sensible objects is a constant exercise in the necessary lessons of difference, of likeness, of order, of being and seeming, of progressive arrangement; of ascent from particular to general; of combination to one end of manifold forces. Proportioned to the importance of the organ to be formed, is the extreme care with which its tuition is provided,—a care pretermitted* in no single case. What tedious training, day after day, year after year, never ending, to form the common sense; what continual reproduction of annoyances, inconveniences, dilemmas; what rejoicing over us of little men; what disputing of prices, what reckonings of interest,—and all to form the Hand of the mind;—to instruct us that "good thoughts are no better than good dreams, unless they be executed!"†

The same good office is performed by Property and its filial systems of debt and credit. Debt, grinding debt, whose iron face the widow, the orphan, and the sons of genius fear and hate;—debt, which consumes

---

*Tuition: protection necessary for growth and development. *Pretermitted:* neglected or omitted.

†Adapted from the essay "Of Great Place," by Francis Bacon.

so much time, which so cripples and disheartens a great spirit with cares that seem so base, is a preceptor whose lessons cannot be foregone, and is needed most by those who suffer from it most. Moreover, property, which has been well compared to snow,—"if it fall level to-day, it will be blown into drifts to-morrow,"—is the surface action of internal ma-chinery, like the index on the face of a clock. Whilst now it is the gym-nastics of the understanding, it is hiving in the foresight of the spirit, experience in profounder laws.

The whole character and fortune of the individual are affected by the least inequalities in the culture of the understanding; for example, in the perception of differences. Therefore is Space, and therefore Time, that man may know that things are not huddled and lumped, but sun-dered and individual. A bell and a plough have each their use, and nei-ther can do the office of the other. Water is good to drink, coal to burn, wool to wear; but wool cannot be drunk, nor water spun, nor coal eaten. The wise man shows his wisdom in separation, in gradation, and his scale of creatures and of merits is as wide as nature. The foolish have no range in their scale, but suppose every man is as every other man. What is not good they call the worst, and what is not hateful they call the best.

In like manner, what good heed, nature forms in us! She pardons no mistakes. Her yea is yea, and her nay, nay.

The first steps in Agriculture, Astronomy, Zoology, (those first steps which the farmer, the hunter, and the sailor take,) teach that nature's dice are always loaded; that in her heaps and rubbish are concealed sure and useful results.

How calmly and genially the mind apprehends one after another the laws of physics! What noble emotions dilate the mortal as he enters into the counsels of the creation, and feels by knowledge the privilege to BE! His insight refines him. The beauty of nature shines in his own breast. Man is greater that he can see this, and the universe less, because Time and Space relations vanish as laws are known.

Here again we are impressed and even daunted by the immense Uni-verse to be explored. "What we know, is a point to what we do not know." Open any recent journal of science, and weigh the problems suggested concerning Light, Heat, Electricity, Magnetism, Physiology, Geology, and judge whether the interest of natural science is likely to be soon exhausted.

Passing by many particulars of the discipline of nature, we must not omit to specify two.

The exercise of the Will or the lesson of power is taught in every event. From the child's successive possession of his several senses up to the hour when he saith, "Thy will be done!"* he is learning the secret, that he can reduce under his will, not only particular events, but great classes, nay the whole series of events, and so conform all facts to his character. Nature is thoroughly mediate. It is made to serve. It receives the dominion of man as meekly as the ass on which the Saviour rode!† It offers all its kingdoms to man as the raw material which he may mould into what is useful. Man is never weary of working it up. He forges the subtle and delicate air into wise and melodious words, and gives them wing as angels of persuasion and command. One after another, his victorious thought comes up with and reduces all things, until the world becomes, at last, only a realized will,—the double of the man.

2. Sensible objects conform to the premonitions of Reason and reflect the conscience. All things are moral; and in their boundless changes have an unceasing reference to spiritual nature. Therefore is nature glorious with form, color, and motion, that every globe in the remotest heaven; every chemical change from the rudest crystal up to the laws of life; every change of vegetation from the first principle of growth in the eye of a leaf, to the tropical forest and antediluvian‡ coalmine; every animal function from the sponge up to Hercules, shall hint or thunder to man the laws of right and wrong, and echo the Ten Commandments. Therefore is nature ever the ally of Religion: lends all her pomp and riches to the religious sentiment. Prophet and priest, David, Isaiah, Jesus, have drawn deeply from this source. This ethical character so penetrates the bone and marrow of nature, as to seem the end for which it was made. Whatever private purpose is answered by any member or part, this is its public and universal function, and is never omitted. Nothing in nature is exhausted in its first use. When a thing has served an end to the uttermost, it is wholly new for an ulterior service. In God, every end is converted into a new means. Thus the use of commodity, regarded by itself, is mean and squalid. But it is to the mind an education in the doctrine of Use, namely, that a thing is good only so far as it serves; that a conspiring of parts and efforts to the production of an end, is essential to any being. The first and gross manifestation of this truth, is our inevitable and hated training in values and wants, in corn and meat.

---

*Reference to the Bible, Matthew 6:10 and 26:42.
†Reference to the Bible, Matthew 21:5.
‡Before the Flood; see the Bible, Genesis 6–9.

It has already been illustrated, that every natural process is a version of a moral sentence. The moral law lies at the centre of nature and radiates to the circumference. It is the pith and marrow of every substance, every relation, and every process. All things with which we deal, preach to us. What is a farm but a mute gospel? The chaff and the wheat, weeds and plants, blight, rain, insects, sun,—it is a sacred emblem from the first furrow of spring to the last stack which the snow of winter overtakes in the fields. But the sailor, the shepherd, the miner, the merchant, in their several resorts, have each an experience precisely parallel, and leading to the same conclusion: because all organizations are radically alike. Nor can it be doubted that this moral sentiment which thus scents the air, grows in the grain, and impregnates the waters of the world, is caught by man and sinks into his soul. The moral influence of nature upon every individual is that amount of truth which it illustrates to him. Who can estimate this? Who can guess how much firmness the sea-beaten rock has taught the fisherman? how much tranquillity has been reflected to man from the azure sky, over whose unspotted deeps the winds forevermore drive flocks of stormy clouds, and leave no wrinkle or stain? how much industry and providence and affection we have caught from the pantomime of brutes? What a searching preacher of self-command is the varying phenomenon of Health!

Herein is especially apprehended the unity of Nature,—the unity in variety,—which meets us everywhere. All the endless variety of things make an identical impression. Xenophanes complained in his old age, that, look where he would, all things hastened back to Unity. He was weary of seeing the same entity in the tedious variety of forms. The fable of Proteus has a cordial truth.[16] A leaf, a drop, a crystal, a moment of time is related to the whole, and partakes of the perfection of the whole. Each particle is a microcosm, and faithfully renders the likeness of the world.

Not only resemblances exist in things whose analogy is obvious, as when we detect the type of the human hand in the flipper of the fossil saurus, but also in objects wherein there is great superficial unlikeness. Thus architecture is called "frozen music," by De Staël and Goethe.* Vitruvius thought an architect should be a musician. "A Gothic church," said Coleridge, "is a petrified religion."† Michael Angelo maintained,

---

*Madame de Staël, in *Corinne* (1807), book 4, chapter 3. Goethe, in Johann Eckermann's *Conversations with Goethe in the Last Years of His Life* (1839), translated by Margaret Fuller.

†In his "Lecture on the General Character of the Gothic Mind on the Middle Ages" (1836).

that, to an architect, a knowledge of anatomy is essential.* In Haydn's oratorios, the notes present to the imagination not only motions, as of the snake, the stag, and the elephant, but colors also; as the green grass. The law of harmonic sounds reappears in the harmonic colors. The granite is differenced in its laws only by the more or less of heat, from the river that wears it away. The river, as it flows, resembles the air that flows over it; the air resembles the light which traverses it with more subtle currents; the light resembles the heat which rides with it through Space. Each creature is only a modification of the other; the likeness in them is more than the difference, and their radical law is one and the same. A rule of one art, or a law of one organization, holds true throughout nature. So intimate is this Unity, that, it is easily seen, it lies under the undermost garment of nature, and betrays its source in Universal Spirit. For, it pervades Thought also. Every universal truth which we express in words, implies or supposes every other truth. *Omne verum vero consonat.*† It is like a great circle on a sphere, comprising all possible circles; which, however, may be drawn, and comprise it, in like manner. Every such truth is the absolute Ens‡ seen from one side. But it has innumerable sides.

The central Unity is still more conspicuous in actions. Words are finite organs of the infinite mind. They cannot cover the dimensions of what is in truth. They break, chop, and impoverish it. An action is the perfection and publication of thought. A right action seems to fill the eye, and to be related to all nature. "The wise man, in doing one thing, does all; or, in the one thing he does rightly, he sees the likeness of all which is done rightly."§

Words and actions are not the attributes of brute nature. They introduce us to the human form, of which all other organizations appear to be degradations. When this appears among so many that surround it, the spirit prefers it to all others. It says, 'From such as this, have I drawn joy and knowledge; in such as this, have I found and beheld myself; I will speak to it; it can speak again; it can yield me thought already formed and alive.' In fact, the eye,—the mind,—is always accompanied by these forms, male and female; and these are incomparably the rich-

---

*From the sketch of Michelangelo in *Lives of Eminent Persons* (1833), published by the Society for the Diffusion of Useful Knowledge (Great Britain).

†Every truth agrees with every other truth (Latin).

‡Absolute existence.

§Paraphrase of a quotation from Goethe's *The Apprenticeship of Wilhelm Meister* (1795–1796) from the translation by Thomas Carlyle.

est informations of the power and order that lie at the heart of things. Unfortunately, every one of them bears the marks as of some injury; is marred and superficially defective. Nevertheless, far different from the deaf and dumb nature around them, those all rest like fountain-pipes on the unfathomed sea of thought and virtue whereto they alone, of all organizations, are the entrances.

It were a pleasant inquiry to follow into detail their ministry to our education, but where would it stop? We are associated in adolescent and adult life with some friends, who, like skies and waters, are coextensive with our idea; who, answering each to a certain affection of the soul, satisfy our desire on that side; whom we lack power to put at such focal distance from us, that we can mend or even analyze them. We cannot choose but love them. When much intercourse with a friend has supplied us with a standard of excellence, and has increased our respect for the resources of God who thus sends a real person to outgo our ideal; when he has, moreover, become an object of thought, and, whilst his character retains all its unconscious effect, is converted in the mind into solid and sweet wisdom,—it is a sign to us that his office is closing, and he is commonly withdrawn from our sight in a short time.

Chapter VI

Idealism

THUS IS THE UNSPEAKABLE but intelligible and practicable meaning of the world conveyed to man, the immortal pupil, in every object of sense. To this one end of Discipline, all parts of nature conspire.

A noble doubt perpetually suggests itself, whether this end be not the Final Cause of the Universe; and whether nature outwardly exists. It is a sufficient account of that Appearance we call the World, that God will teach a human mind, and so makes it the receiver of a certain number of congruent sensations, which we call sun and moon, man and woman, house and trade. In my utter impotence to test the authenticity of the report of my senses, to know whether the impressions they make on me correspond with outlying objects, what difference does it make, whether Orion is up there in heaven, or some god paints the image in the firmament of the soul? The relations of parts and the end of the whole remaining the same, what is the difference, whether land and sea interact, and worlds revolve and intermingle without number or end,— deep yawning under deep, and galaxy balancing galaxy, throughout absolute space,—or, whether, without relations of time and space, the same appearances are inscribed in the constant faith of man? Whether nature enjoy a substantial existence without, or is only in the apocalypse of the mind, it is alike useful and alike venerable to me. Be it what it may, it is ideal to me, so long as I cannot try the accuracy of my senses.

The frivolous make themselves merry with the Ideal theory,[17] as if its consequences were burlesque; as if it affected the stability of nature. It surely does not. God never jests with us, and will not compromise the end of nature, by permitting any inconsequence in its procession. Any distrust of the permanence of laws, would paralyze the faculties of man. Their permanence is sacredly respected, and his faith therein is perfect. The wheels and springs of man are all set to the hypothesis of the permanence of nature. We are not built like a ship to be tossed, but like a house to stand, it is a natural consequence of the structure, that, so long as the active powers predominate over the reflective, we resist with indignation any hint that nature is more short-lived or mutable than spirit. The broker, the wheelwright, the carpenter, the tollman, are much displeased at the intimation.

But whilst we acquiese entirely in the permanence of natural laws, the question of the absolute existence of nature still remains open. It is the uniform effect of culture on the human mind, not to shake our faith in the stability of particular phenomena, as of heat, water, azote;* but to lead us to regard nature as a phenomenon, not a substance; to attribute necessary existence to spirit; to esteem nature as an accident and an effect.

To the senses and the unrenewed understanding, belongs a sort of instinctive belief in the absolute existence of nature. In their view, man and nature are indissolubly joined. Things are ultimates, and they never look beyond their sphere. The presence of Reason mars this faith. The first effort of thought tends to relax this despotism of the senses, which binds us to nature as if we were a part of it, and shows us nature aloof, and, as it were, afloat. Until this higher agency intervened, the animal eye sees, with wonderful accuracy, sharp outlines and colored surfaces. When the eye of Reason opens, to outline and surface are at once added, grace and expression. These proceed from imagination and affection, and abate somewhat of the angular distinctness of objects. If the Reason be stimulated to more earnest vision, outlines and surface become transparent, and are no longer seen; causes and spirits are seen through them. The best moments of life are these delicious awakenings of the higher powers, and the reverential withdrawing of nature before its God.

Let us proceed to indicate the effects of culture. 1. Our first institution† in the Ideal philosophy is a hint from nature herself.

Nature is made to conspire with spirit to emancipate us. Certain mechanical changes, a small alteration in our local position apprises us of a dualism. We are strangely affected by seeing the shore from a moving ship, from a balloon, or through the tints of an unusual sky. The least change in our point of view, gives the whole world a pictorial air. A man who seldom rides, needs only to get into a coach and traverse his own town, to turn the street into a puppet show. The men, the women,—talking, running, bartering, fighting,—the earnest mechanic, the lounger, the beggar, the boys, the dogs, are unrealized at once, or, at least, wholly detached from all relation to the observer, and seen as ap-

---

*Nitrogen.

†Instruction by example; initiation into. Emerson is using the ecclesiastical meaning of "institution," which refers to the origination of the sacrament of the Eucharist in its enactment by Christ at the Last Supper.

parent, not substantial beings. What new thoughts are suggested by seeing a face of country quite familiar, in the rapid movement of the railroad car! Nay, the most wonted objects, (make a very slight change in the point of vision,) please us most. In a camera obscura,* the butcher's cart, and the figure of one of our own family amuse us. So a portrait of a well-known face gratifies us. Turn the eyes upside down, by looking at the landscape through your legs, and how agreeable is the picture, though you have seen it any time these twenty years!

In these cases, by mechanical means, is suggested the difference between the observer and the spectacle,—between man and nature. Hence arises a pleasure mixed with awe; I may say, a low degree of the sublime is felt from the fact, probably, that man is hereby apprised, that, whilst the world is a spectacle, something in himself is stable.

2. In a higher manner, the poet communicates the same pleasure. By a few strokes, he delineates, as on air, the mountain, the camp, the city, the hero, the maiden, not different from what we know them, but only lifted from the ground and afloat before the eye. He unfixes the land and the sea, makes them revolve around the axis of his primary thought, and disposes them anew. Possessed himself by a heroic passion, he uses matter as symbols of it. The sensual man conforms thoughts to things; the poet conforms things to his thoughts. The one esteems nature as rooted and fast; the other, as fluid, and impresses his being thereon. To him, the refractory world is ductile and flexible; he invests dust and stones with humanity, and makes them the words of the Reason. The Imagination may be defined to be, the use which the Reason makes of the material world. Shakspeare possesses the power of subordinating nature for the purposes of expression, beyond all poets. His imperial muse tosses the creation like a bauble from hand to hand, and uses it to embody any caprice of thought that is uppermost in his mind. The remotest spaces of nature are visited, and the farthest sundered things are brought together, by a subtle spiritual connection. We are made aware that magnitude of material things is relative, and all objects shrink and expand to serve the passion of the poet. Thus, in his sonnets, the lays of birds, the scents and dyes of flowers, he finds to be the *shadow* of his beloved; time, which keeps her from him, is his *chest*; the suspicion she has awakened, is her *ornament*;†

---

*Device used for sketching or exhibiting pictures.
†Compare Shakespeare's Sonnet 98.

> The ornament of beauty in Suspect,
> A crow which flies in heaven's sweetest air.*

His passion is not the fruit of chance; it swells, as he speaks, to a city, or a state.

> No, it was builded far from accident;
> It suffers not in smiling pomp, nor falls
> Under the brow of thralling discontent;
> It fears not policy, that heretic,
> That works on leases of short numbered hours,
> But all alone stands hugely politic.†

In the strength of his constancy, the Pyramids‡ seem to him recent and transitory. The freshness of youth and love dazzles him with its resemblance to morning.

> Take those lips away
> Which so sweetly were forsworn;
> And those eyes,—the break of day,
> Lights that do mislead the morn.§

The wild beauty of this hyperbole, I may say, in passing, it would not be easy to match in literature.

This transfiguration which all material objects undergo through the passion of the poet,—this power which he exerts to dwarf the great, to magnify the small,—might be illustrated by a thousand examples from his Plays. I have before me the Tempest, and will cite only these few lines.

> PROSPERO: The strong based promontory
> Have I made shake, and by the spurs plucked up
> The pine and cedar.‖

---

*Near quotation from Shakespeare's Sonnet 70.
†Near quotation from Shakespeare's Sonnet 124.
‡See Shakespeare's Sonnet 123.
§From Shakespeare's *Measure for Measure* (act 4, scene 1).
‖From Shakespeare's *The Tempest* (act 5, scene 1); the quotations that follow are from the same scene of *The Tempest*.

Prospero calls for music to soothe the frantic Alonzo, and his compan-
ions;

> A solemn air, and the best comforter
> To an unsettled fancy, cure thy brains
> Now useless, boiled within thy skull.

Again;

> The charm dissolves apace,
> And, as the morning steals upon the night,
> Melting the darkness, so their rising senses
> Begin to chase the ignorant fumes that mantle
> Their clearer reason.
> Their understanding
> Begins to swell: and the approaching tide
> Will shortly fill the reasonable shores
> That now lie foul and muddy.

The perception of real affinities between events, (that is to say, of
ideal affinities, for those only are real,) enables the poet thus to make
free with the most imposing forms and phenomena of the world, and
to assert the predominance of the soul.

3. Whilst thus the poet animates nature with his own thoughts, he
differs from the philosopher only herein, that the one proposes Beauty
as his main end; the other Truth. But the philosopher, not less than the
poet, postpones the apparent order and relations of things to the em-
pire of thought. "The problem of philosophy," according to Plato, "is,
for all that exists conditionally, to find a ground unconditioned and ab-
solute." It proceeds on the faith that a law determines all phenomena,
which being known, the phenomena can be predicted. That law, when
in the mind, is an idea. Its beauty is infinite. The true philosopher and
the true poet are one, and a beauty, which is truth, and a truth, which is
beauty, is the aim of both. Is not the charm of one of Plato's or Aristo-
tle's definitions, strictly like that of the Antigone of Sophocles? It is, in
both cases, that a spiritual life has been imparted to nature; that the
solid seeming block of matter has been pervaded and dissolved by a
thought; that this feeble human being has penetrated the vast masses of
nature with an informing soul, and recognized itself in their harmony,
that is, seized their law. In physics, when this is attained, the memory

disburthens itself of its cumbrous catalogues of particulars and carries centuries of observation in a single formula.

Thus even in physics, the material is degraded before the spiritual. The astronomer, the geometer, rely on their irrefragable analysis, and disdain the results of observation. The sublime remark of Euler on his law of arches, "This will be found contrary to all experience, yet is true;" had already transferred nature into the mind, and left matter like an outcast corpse.

4. Intellectual science has been observed to beget invariably a doubt of the existence of matter. Turgot said, "He that has never doubted the existence of matter, may be assured he has no aptitude for metaphysical inquiries." It fastens the attention upon immortal necessary uncreated natures, that is, upon Ideas; and in their presence, we feel that the outward circumstance is a dream and a shade. Whilst we wait in this Olympus of gods,* we think of nature as an appendix to the soul. We ascend into their region, and know that these are the thoughts of the Supreme Being. "These are they who were set up from everlasting, from the beginning, or ever the earth was. When he prepared the heavens, they were there; when he established the clouds above, when he strengthened the fountains of the deep, then they were by him, as one brought up with him. Of them took he counsel."†

Their influence is proportionate. As objects of science, they are accessible to few men. Yet all men are capable of being raised by piety or by passion, into their region. And no man touches these divine natures, without becoming, in some degree, himself divine. Like a new soul, they renew the body. We become physically nimble and lightsome; we tread on air; life is no longer irksome, and we think it will never be so. No man fears age or misfortune or death, in their serene company, for he is transported out of the district of change. Whilst we behold unveiled the nature of Justice and Truth, we learn the difference between the absolute and the conditional or relative. We apprehend the absolute. As it were, for the first time, *we exist*. We become immortal, for we learn that time and space are relations of matter; that, with a perception of truth, or a virtuous will, they have no affinity.

5. Finally, religion and ethics, which may be fitly called,—the practice of ideas, or the introduction of ideas into life,—have an analogous effect with all lower culture, in degrading nature and suggesting its de-

---

*In Greek mythology, the home of the gods.
†Compare the Bible, Proverbs 8:23–30.

pendence on spirit. Ethics and religion differ herein; that the one is the system of human duties commencing from man; the other, from God. Religion includes the personality of God; Ethics does not. They are one to our present design. They both put nature under foot. The first and last lesson of religion is, "The things that are seen, are temporal; the things that are unseen, are eternal."* It puts an affront upon nature. It does that for the unschooled, which philosophy does for Berkeley and Viasa. The uniform language that may be heard in the churches of the most ignorant sects, is,—"Contemn the unsubstantial shows of the world; they are vanities, dreams, shadows, unrealities; seek the realities of religion." The devotee flouts nature. Some theosophists have arrived at a certain hostility and indignation towards matter, as the Manichean and Plotinus. They distrusted in themselves any looking back to these flesh-pots of Egypt.† Plotinus was ashamed of his body. In short, they might all say of matter, what Michael Angelo said of external beauty, "it is the frail and weary weed, in which God dresses the soul, which he has called into time."‡

It appears that motion, poetry, physical and intellectual science, and religion, all tend to affect our convictions of the reality of the external world. But I own there is something ungrateful in expanding too curiously the particulars of the general proposition, that all culture tends to imbue us with idealism. I have no hostility to nature, but a child's love to it. I expand and live in the warm day like corn and melons. Let us speak her fair. I do not wish to fling stones at my beautiful mother, nor soil my gentle nest. I only wish to indicate the true position of nature in regard to man, wherein to establish man, all right education tends; as the ground which to attain is the object of human life, that is, of man's connection with nature. Culture inverts the vulgar views of nature, and brings the mind to call that apparent, which it uses to call real, and that real, which it uses to call visionary. Children, it is true, believe in the external world. The belief that it appears only, is an afterthought, but with culture, this faith will as surely arise on the mind as did the first.

The advantage of the ideal theory over the popular faith, is this, that it presents the world in precisely that view which is most desirable to

---

*Paraphrase of the Bible, 2 Corinthians 4:18.

†Reference to the Bible, Exodus 16:3: "And the children of Israel said unto them, Would to God we had died by the hand of the Lord in the land of Egypt, when we sat by the flesh pots, and when we did eat bread to the full; for ye have brought us forth into this wilderness, to kill this whole assembly with hunger" (KJV).

‡From Michelangelo's Sonnet 51.

the mind. It is, in fact, the view which Reason, both speculative and practical, that is, philosophy and virtue, take. For, seen in the light of thought, the world always is phenomenal;* and virtue subordinates it to the mind. Idealism sees the world in God. It beholds the whole circle of persons and things, of actions and events, of country and religion, not as painfully accumulated, atom after atom, act after act, in an aged creeping Past, but as one vast picture, which God paints on the instant eternity, for the contemplation of the soul. Therefore the soul holds itself off from a too trivial and microscopic study of the universal tablet. It respects the end too much, to immerse itself in the means. It sees something more important in Christianity, than the scandals of ecclesiastical history, or the niceties of criticism; and, very incurious concerning persons or miracles, and not at all disturbed by chasms of historical evidence, it accepts from God the phenomenon, as it finds it, as the pure and awful form of religion in the world. It is not hot and passionate at the appearance of what it calls its own good or bad fortune, at the union or opposition of other persons. No man is its enemy. It accepts whatsoever befalls, as part of its lesson. It is a watcher more than a doer, and it is a doer, only that it may the better watch.

---

*Consisting of our experience of it.

Chapter VII

Spirit

IT IS ESSENTIAL TO a true theory of nature and of man, that it should contain somewhat progressive. Uses that are exhausted or that may be, and facts that end in the statement, cannot be all that is true of this brave lodging wherein man is harbored, and wherein all his faculties find appropriate and endless exercise. And all the uses of nature admit of being summed in one, which yields the activity of man an infinite scope. Through all its kingdoms, to the suburbs and outskirts of things, it is faithful to the cause whence it had its origin. It always speaks of Spirit. It suggests the absolute. It is a perpetual effect. It is a great shadow pointing always to the sun behind us.

The aspect of nature is devout. Like the figure of Jesus, she stands with bended head, and hands folded upon the breast. The happiest man is he who learns from nature the lesson of worship.

Of that ineffable essence which we call Spirit, he that thinks most, will say least. We can foresee God in the coarse, and, as it were, distant phenomena of matter; but when we try to define and describe himself, both language and thought desert us, and we are as helpless as fools and savages. That essence refuses to be recorded in propositions, but when man has worshipped him intellectually, the noblest ministry of nature is to stand as the apparition of God. It is the organ through which the universal spirit speaks to the individual, and strives to lead back the individual to it.

When we consider Spirit, we see that the views already presented do not include the whole circumference of man. We must add some related thoughts.

Three problems are put by nature to the mind; What is matter? Whence is it? and Whereto? The first of these questions only, the ideal theory answers. Idealism saith: matter is a phenomenon, not a substance. Idealism acquaints us with the total disparity between the evidence of our own being, and the evidence of the world's being. The one is perfect; the other, incapable of any assurance; the mind is a part of the nature of things; the world is a divine dream, from which we may presently awake to the glories and certainties of day. Idealism is a hypothesis to account for nature by other principles than those of carpentry and chemistry. Yet, if it only deny the existence of matter, it does not satisfy the demands of the spirit. It leaves God out of me. It leaves me in the splendid labyrinth of my perceptions, to wander without end. Then the heart resists it, because it balks the affections in denying substantive being to men and women. Nature is so pervaded with human life, that there is something of humanity in all, and in every particular. But this theory makes nature foreign to me, and does not account for that consanguinity* which we acknowledge to it.

Let it stand, then, in the present state of our knowledge, merely as a useful introductory hypothesis, serving to apprise us of the eternal distinction between the soul and the world.

But when following the invisible steps of thought, we come to inquire, Whence is matter? and Whereto? many truths arise to us out of the recesses of consciousness. We learn that the highest is present to the soul of man, that the dread universal essence, which is not wisdom, or love, or power, but all in one, and each entirely, is that for which all things exist, and that by which they are; that spirit creates; that behind nature, throughout nature, spirit is present; one and not compound, it does not act upon us from without, that is, in space and time, but spiritually, or through ourselves: therefore, that spirit, that is, the Supreme Being, does not build up nature around us, but puts it forth through us, as the life of the tree puts forth new branches and leaves through the pores of the old. As a plant upon the earth, so a man rests upon the bosom of God; he is nourished by unfailing fountains, and draws, at his need, inexhaustible power. Who can set bounds to the possibilities of man? Once inhale the upper air, being admitted to behold the absolute natures of justice and truth, and we learn that man has access to the entire mind of the Creator, is himself the creator in the finite.[18] This view, which admonishes me where the sources of wisdom and power lie, and points to virtue as to

> "The golden key
> Which opes the palace of eternity,"†

and carries upon its face the highest certificate of truth, because it animates me to create my own world through the purification of my soul.

---

*Kinship.

†From John Milton's *Comus* (1634), lines 13–14.

The world proceeds from the same spirit as the body of man. It is a remoter and inferior incarnation of God, a projection of God in the unconscious. But it differs from the body in one important respect. It is not, like that, now subjected to the human will. Its serene order is inviolable by us. It is, therefore, to us, the present expositor of the divine mind. It is a fixed point whereby we may measure our departure. As we degenerate, the contrast between us and our house is more evident. We are as much strangers in nature, as we are aliens from God. We do not understand the notes of birds. The fox and the deer run away from us; the bear and tiger rend us. We do not know the uses of more than a few plants, as corn and the apple, the potato and the vine. Is not the landscape, every glimpse of which hath a grandeur, a face of him? Yet this may show us what discord is between man and nature, for you cannot freely admire a noble landscape, if laborers are digging in the field hard by. The poet finds something ridiculous in his delight, until he is out of the sight of men.

Chapter VIII

Prospects

IN INQUIRIES RESPECTING THE laws of the world and the frame of things, the highest reason is always the truest. That which seems faintly possible—it is so refined, is often faint and dim because it is deepest seated in the mind among the eternal verities.* Empirical science is apt to cloud the sight, and, by the very knowledge of functions and processes, to bereave the student of the manly contemplation of the whole. The savant† becomes unpoetic. But the best read naturalist who lends an entire and devout attention to truth, will see that there remains much to learn of his relation to the world, and that it is not to be learned by any addition or subtraction or other comparison of known quantities, but is arrived at by untaught sallies of the spirit, by a continual self-recovery, and by entire humility. He will perceive that there are far more excellent qualities in the student than preciseness and infallibility; that a guess is often more fruitful than an indisputable affirmation, and that a dream may let us deeper into the secret of nature than a hundred concerted experiments.

For, the problems to be solved are precisely those which the physiologist and the naturalist omit to state. It is not so pertinent to man to know all the individuals of the animal kingdom, as it is to know whence and whereto is this tyrannizing unity in his constitution, which evermore separates and classifies things, endeavoring to reduce the most diverse to one form. When I behold a rich landscape, it is less to my purpose to recite correctly the order and superposition of the strata, than to know why all thought of multitude is lost in a tranquil sense of unity. I cannot greatly honor minuteness in details, so long as there is no hint to explain the relation between things and thoughts; no ray upon the *metaphysics* of conchology, of botany, of the arts, to show the relation of the forms of flowers, shells, animals, architecture, to the mind, and build science upon ideas. In a cabinet of natural history, we

---

*Truths.
†Learned person.

become sensible of a certain occult recognition and sympathy in regard to the most unwieldy and eccentric forms of beast, fish, and insect. The American who has been confined, in his own country, to the sight of buildings designed after foreign models, is surprised on entering York Minster or St. Peter's at Rome, by the feeling that these structures are imitations also,—faint copies of an invisible archetype. Nor has science sufficient humanity, so long as the naturalist overlooks that wonderful congruity which subsists between man and the world; of which he is lord, not because he is the most subtile inhabitant, but because he is its head and heart, and finds something of himself in every great and small thing, in every mountain stratum, in every new law of color, fact of astronomy, or atmospheric influence which observation or analysis lay open. A perception of this mystery inspires the muse of George Herbert, the beautiful psalmist of the seventeenth century. The following lines are part of his little poem on Man.

> "Man is all symmetry,
> Full of proportions, one limb to another,
> And to all the world besides.
> Each part may call the farthest, brother;
> For head with foot hath private amity,
> And both with moons and tides.
>
> "Nothing hath got so far
> But man hath caught and kept it as his prey;
> His eyes dismount the highest star;
> He is in little all the sphere.
> Herbs gladly cure our flesh, because that they
> Find their acquaintance there.
>
> "For us, the winds do blow,
> The earth doth rest, heaven move, and fountains flow;
> Nothing we see, but means our good,
> As our delight, or as our treasure;
> The whole is either our cupboard of food,
> Or cabinet of pleasure.
>
> "The stars have us to bed:
> Night draws the curtain; which the sun withdraws.
> Music and light attend our head.
> All things unto our flesh are kind,

In their descent and being; to our mind,
   In their ascent and cause.

"More servants wait on man
Than he'll take notice of. In every path,
   He treads down that which doth befriend him
   When sickness makes him pale and wan.
Oh mighty love! Man is one world, and hath
   Another to attend him."

The perception of this class of truths makes the attraction which draws men to science, but the end is lost sight of in attention to the means. In view of this half-sight of science, we accept the sentence of Plato, that, "poetry comes nearer to vital truth than history."* Every surmise and vaticination† of the mind is entitled to a certain respect, and we learn to prefer imperfect theories, and sentences, which contain glimpses of truth, to digested systems which have no one valuable suggestion.[19] A wise writer will feel that the ends of study and composition are best answered by announcing undiscovered regions of thought, and so communicating, through hope, new activity to the torpid spirit.

I shall therefore conclude this essay with some traditions of man and nature, which a certain poet sang to me; and which, as they have always been in the world, and perhaps reappear to every bard, may be both history and prophecy.

"The foundations of man are not in matter, but in spirit. But the element of spirit is eternity. To it, therefore, the longest series of events, the oldest chronologies are young and recent. In the cycle of the universal man, from whom the known individuals proceed, centuries are points, and all history is but the epoch of one degradation.

"We distrust and deny inwardly our sympathy with nature. We own and disown our relation to it, by turns. We are, like Nebuchadnezzar, dethroned, bereft of reason, and eating grass like an ox.‡ But who can set limits to the remedial force of spirit?

"A man is a god in ruins. When men are innocent, life shall be longer, and shall pass into the immortal, as gently as we awake from dreams.

---

*From Aristotle's *Poetics*, section 9.

†Prophesy.

‡Compare the Bible, Daniel 4:31–33: "Nebuchadnezzar . . . was driven from men, and did eat grass as oxen, and his body was wet with the dew of heaven, till his hairs were grown like eagles' feathers, and his nails like birds' claws" (KJV).

Now, the world would be insane and rabid, if these disorganizations should last for hundreds of years. It is kept in check by death and infancy. Infancy is the perpetual Messiah, which comes into the arms of fallen men, and pleads with them to return to paradise.

"Man is the dwarf of himself. Once he was permeated and dissolved by spirit. He filled nature with his overflowing currents. Out from him sprang the sun and moon; from man, the sun; from woman, the moon. The laws of his mind, the periods of his actions externized themselves into day and night, into the year and the seasons. But, having made for himself this huge shell, his waters retired; he no longer fills the veins and veinlets; he is shrunk to a drop. He sees, that the structure still fits him, but fits him colossally. Say, rather, once it fitted him, now it corresponds to him from far and on high. He adores timidly his own work. Now is man the follower of the sun, and woman the follower of the moon. Yet sometimes he starts in his slumber, and wonders at himself and his house and muses strangely at the resemblance betwixt him and it. He perceives that if his law is still paramount, if still he have elemental power, if his word is sterling yet in nature, it is not conscious power, it is not inferior but superior to his will. It is Instinct." Thus my Orphic poet sang.[20]

At present, man applies to nature but half his force. He works on the world with his understanding alone. He lives in it, and masters it by a penny-wisdom; and he that works most in it, is but a half-man, and whilst his arms are strong and his digestion good, his mind is imbruted, and he is a selfish savage. His relation to nature, his power over it, is through the understanding; as by manure; the economic use of fire, wind, water, and the mariner's needle; steam, coal, chemical agriculture; the repairs of the human body by the dentist and the surgeon. This is such a resumption of power, as if a banished king should buy his territories inch by inch, instead of vaulting at once into his throne. Meantime, in the thick darkness, there are not wanting gleams of a better light,—occasional examples of the action of man upon nature with his entire force,—with reason as well as understanding. Such examples are; the traditions of miracles in the earliest antiquity of all nations; the history of Jesus Christ; the achievements of a principle, as in religious and political revolutions, and in the abolition of the Slave-trade; the miracles of enthusiasm, as those reported of Swedenborg, Hohenlohe, and the Shakers; many obscure and yet contested facts, now arranged under the name of Animal Magnetism;* prayer; eloquence; self-healing; and the wisdom of children. These are ex-

---

*Early term for hypnotism.

amples of Reason's momentary grasp of the sceptre; the exertions of a power which exists not in time or space, but an instantaneous in-streaming causing power. The difference between the actual and the ideal force of man is happily figured by the schoolmen, in saying, that the knowledge of man is an evening knowledge, *vespertina cognitio*, but that of God is a morning knowledge, *matutina cognitio.**

The problem of restoring to the world original and eternal beauty, is solved by the redemption of the soul. The ruin or the blank, that we see when we look at nature, is in our own eye. The axis of vision is not coincident with the axis of things, and so they appear not transparent but opaque. The reason why the world lacks unity, and lies broken and in heaps, is, because man is disunited with himself. He cannot be a naturalist, until he satisfies all the demands of the spirit. Love is as much its demand, as perception. Indeed, neither can be perfect without the other. In the uttermost meaning of the words, thought is devout, and devotion is thought. Deep calls unto deep.† But in actual life, the marriage is not celebrated. There are innocent men who worship God after the tradition of their fathers, but their sense of duty has not yet extended to the use of all their faculties. And there are patient naturalists, but they freeze their subject under the wintry light of the understanding. Is not prayer also a study of truth,—a sally of the soul into the unfound infinite? No man ever prayed heartily, without learning something. But when a faithful thinker, resolute to detach every object from personal relations, and see it in the light of thought, shall, at the same time, kindle science with the fire of the holiest affections, then will God go forth anew into the creation.

It will not need, when the mind is prepared for study, to search for objects. The invariable mark of wisdom is to see the miraculous in the common. What is a day? What is a year? What is summer? What is woman? What is a child? What is sleep? To our blindness, these things seem unaffected. We make fables to hide the baldness of the fact and conform it, as we say, to the higher law of the mind. But when the fact is seen under the light of an idea, the gaudy fable fades and shrivels. We behold the real higher law. To the wise, therefore, a fact is true poetry, and the most beautiful of fables. These wonders are brought to our own door. You also are a man. Man and woman, and their social life, poverty, labor, sleep, fear, fortune, are known to you. Learn that none of these

---

*The two Latin phrases here are terms from medieval scholastic philosophy.
†Reference to the Bible, Psalm 42:7: "Deep calleth unto deep at the noise of thy waterspouts: all thy waves and thy billows are gone over me" (KJV).

things is superficial, but that each phenomenon has its roots in the faculties and affections of the mind. Whilst the abstract question occupies your intellect, nature brings it in the concrete to be solved by your hands. It were a wise inquiry for the closet,* to compare, point by point, especially at remarkable crises in life, our daily history, with the rise and progress of ideas in the mind.

So shall we come to look at the world with new eyes. It shall answer the endless inquiry of the intellect,—What is truth? and of the affections,—What is good? by yielding itself passive to the educated Will. Then shall come to pass what my poet said; "Nature is not fixed but fluid. Spirit alters, moulds, makes it. The immobility or bruteness of nature, is the absence of spirit; to pure spirit, it is fluid, it is volatile, it is obedient. Every spirit builds itself a house; and beyond its house a world; and beyond its world a heaven. Know then, that the world exists for you. For you is the phenomenon perfect. What we are, that only can we see. All that Adam had, all that Cæsar could, you have and can do. Adam called his house, heaven and earth; Cæsar called his house, Rome; you perhaps call yours, a cobbler's trade; a hundred acres of ploughed land; or a scholar's garret. Yet line for line and point for point, your dominion is as great as theirs, though without fine names. Build, therefore, your own world. As fast as you conform your life to the pure idea in your mind, that will unfold its great proportions. A correspondent revolution in things will attend the influx of the spirit. So fast will disagreeable appearances, swine, spiders, snakes, pets, madhouses, prisons, enemies, vanish; they are temporary and shall be no more seen. The sordor and filths of nature, the sun shall dry up, and the wind exhale. As when the summer comes from the south; the snow-banks melt, and the face of the earth becomes green before it, so shall the advancing spirit create its ornaments along its path, and carry with it the beauty it visits, and the song which enchants it; it shall draw beautiful faces, warm hearts, wise discourse, and heroic acts, around its way, until evil is no more seen. The kingdom of man over nature, which cometh not with observation,†—a dominion such as now is beyond his dream of God,— he shall enter without more wonder than the blind man feels who is gradually restored to perfect sight."

---

*Scholar's study.

†Reference to the Bible, Luke 17:20: "And when he was demanded of the Pharisees, when the kingdom of God should come, he answered them and said, The kingdom of God cometh not with observation" (KJV).

The American Scholar[1]

An Oration Delivered before the Phi Beta Kappa Society, at Cambridge, August 31, 1837.

MR. PRESIDENT AND GENTLEMEN,

I greet you on the re-commencement of our literary year. Our anniversary is one of hope, and, perhaps, not enough of labor. We do not meet for games of strength or skill, for the recitation of histories, tragedies, and odes, like the ancient Greeks; for parliaments of love and poesy, like the Troubadours; nor for the advancement of science, like our contemporaries in the British and European capitals. Thus far, our holiday has been simply a friendly sign of the survival of the love of letters amongst a people too busy to give to letters any more. As such, it is precious as the sign of an indestructible instinct. Perhaps the time is already come, when it ought to be, and will be something else; when the sluggard intellect of this continent will look from under its iron lids, and fill the postponed expectation of the world with something better than the exertions of mechanical skill. Our day of dependence, our long apprenticeship to the learning of other lands, draws to a close. The millions, that around us are rushing into life, cannot always be fed on the sere* remains of foreign harvests. Events, actions arise, that must be sung, that will sing themselves. Who can doubt, that poetry will revive and lead in a new age, as the star in the constellation Harp, which now flames in our zenith, astronomers announce, shall one day be the pole-star for a thousand years?

In this hope, I accept the topic which not only usage, but the nature of our association, seem to prescribe to this day,—the AMERICAN SCHOLAR. Year by year, we come up hither to read one more chapter of his biography. Let us inquire what light new days and events have thrown on his character, and his hopes.

It is one of those fables, which, out of an unknown antiquity, convey an unlooked-for wisdom, that the gods, in the beginning, divided Man into men, that he might be more helpful to himself;† just as the hand was divided into fingers, the better to answer its end.

---

*Dry; withered.

†A version of this fable is given in Plato's *Symposium*.

The old fable covers a doctrine ever new and sublime; that there is One Man,—present to all particular men only partially, or through one faculty; and that you must take the whole society to find the whole man. Man is not a farmer, or professor, or an enginer, but he is all. Man is priest, and scholar, and statesman, and producer, and soldier. In the *divided* or social state these functions are parcelled out to individuals, each of whom aims to do his stint of the joint work, whilst each other performs his. The fable implies, that the individual, to possess himself, must sometimes return from his own labor to embrace all the other laborers. But unfortunately, this original unit, this fountain of power, has been so distributed to multitudes, has been so minutely subdivided and peddled out, that it is spilled into drops, and cannot be gathered. The state of society is one in which the members have suffered amputation from the trunk, and strut about so many walking monsters,—a good finger, a neck, a stomach, an elbow, but never a man.

Man is thus metamorphosed into a thing, into many things. The planter, who is Man sent out into the field to gather food, is seldom cheered by any idea of the true dignity of his ministry. He sees his bushel and his cart, and nothing beyond, and sinks into the farmer, instead of Man on the farm. The tradesman scarcely ever gives an ideal worth to his work, but is ridden by the routine of his craft, and the soul is subject to dollars. The priest becomes a form; the attorney, a statute-book; the mechanic, a machine; the sailor, a rope of a ship.

In this distribution of functions, the scholar is the delegated intellect. In the right state, he is *Man Thinking*. In the degenerate state, when the victim of society, he tends to become a mere thinker, or, still worse, the parrot of other men's thinking.

In this view of him, as Man Thinking, the theory of his office is contained. Him nature solicits with all her placid, all her monitory* pictures; him the past instructs; him the future invites. Is not, indeed, every man a student, and do not all things exist for the student's behoof? And, finally, is not the true scholar the only true master? But the old oracle said, 'All things have two handles: beware of the wrong one.' In life, too often, the scholar errs with mankind and forfeits his privilege. Let us see him in his school, and consider him in reference to the main influences he receives.

I. The first in time and first in importance of the influences upon the mind is that of nature. Every day, the sun; and, after sunset, night and

---

*Serving to admonish or warn.

her stars. Ever the winds blow; ever the grass grows. Every day, men and women, conversing, beholding and beholden. The scholar is he of all men whom this spectacle most engages. He must settle its value in his mind. What is nature to him? There is never a beginning, there is never an end, to the inexplicable continuity of this web of God, but always circular power returning into itself. Therein it resembles his own spirit, whose beginning, whose ending, he never can find,—so entire, so boundless. Far, too, as her splendors shine, system on system shooting like rays, upward, downward, without centre, without circumference,— in the mass and in the particle, nature hastens to render account of herself to the mind. Classification begins. To the young mind, every thing in individuals, stands by itself. By and by, it finds how to join two things, and see in them one nature; then three, then three thousand; and so, tyrannized over by its own unifying instinct, it goes on tying things together, diminishing anomalies, discovering roots running under ground, whereby contrary and remote things cohere, and flower out from one stem. It presently learns, that, since the dawn of history, there has been a constant accumulation and classifying of facts. But what is classification but the perceiving that these objects are not chaotic, and are not foreign, but have a law which is also a law of the human mind? The astronomer discovers that geometry, a pure abstraction of the human mind, is the measure of planetary motion. The chemist finds proportions and intelligible method throughout matter; and science is nothing but the finding of analogy, identity, in the most remote parts. The ambitious soul sits down before each refractory fact; one after another, reduces all strange constitutions, all new powers, to their class and their law, and goes on for ever to animate the last fibre of organization, the outskirts of nature, by insight.

Thus to him, to this school-boy under the bending dome of day, is suggested, that he and it proceed from one root; one is leaf and one is flower; relation, sympathy, stirring in every vein. And what is that Root? Is not that the soul of his soul?—A thought too bold,—a dream too wild. Yet when this spiritual light shall have revealed the law of more earthly natures,—when he has learned to worship the soul, and to see that the natural philosophy that now is, is only the first gropings of its gigantic hand, he shall look forward to an ever expanding knowledge as to a becoming creator. He shall see, that nature is the opposite of the soul, answering to it part for part. One is seal, and one is print. Its beauty is the beauty of his own mind. Its laws are the laws of his own mind. Nature then becomes to him the measure of his attainments. So much of nature as he is ignorant of, so much of his own mind does he not yet possess. And, in fine, the ancient precept, "Know thyself," and the modern precept, "Study nature," become at last the one maxim.

II. The next great influence into the spirit of the scholar, is, the mind of the Past,—in whatever form, whether of literature, of art, of institutions, that mind is inscribed. Books are the best type of the influence of the past, and perhaps we shall get at the truth,—learn the amount of this influence more conveniently,—by considering their value alone.

The theory of books is noble. The scholar of the first age received into him the world around; brooded thereon; gave it the new arrangement of his own mind, and uttered it again. It came into him, life; it went out from him, truth. It came to him, short-lived actions; it went out from him, immortal thoughts. It came to him, business; it went from him, poetry. It was dead fact; now, it is quick* thought. It can stand, and it can go. It now endures, it now flies, it now inspires. Precisely in proportion to the depth of mind from which it issued, so high does it soar, so long does it sing.

Or, I might say, it depends on how far the process had gone, of transmuting life into truth. In proportion to the completeness of the distillation, so will the purity and imperishableness of the product be. But none is quite perfect. As no air-pump can by any means make a perfect vacuum, so neither can any artist entirely exclude the conventional, the local, the perishable from his book, or write a book of pure thought, that shall be as efficient, in all respects, to a remote posterity, as to contemporaries, or rather to the second age. Each age, it is found, must write its own books; or rather, each generation for the next succeeding. The books of an older period will not fit this.

Yet hence arises a grave mischief. The sacredness which attaches to the act of creation,—the act of thought,—is transferred to the record. The poet chanting, was felt to be a divine man: henceforth the chant is divine also. The writer was a just and wise spirit: henceforward it is settled, the book is perfect; as love of the hero corrupts into worship of his statue. Instantly, the book becomes noxious: the guide is a tyrant. The sluggish and perverted mind of the multitude, slow to open to the incursions of Reason, having once so opened, having once received this book, stands upon it, and makes an outcry, if it is disparaged. Colleges are built on it. Books are written on it by thinkers, not by Man Thinking; by men of talent, that is, who start wrong, who set out from ac-

---

*Living.

cepted dogmas, not from their own sight of principles. Meek young men grow up in libraries, believing it their duty to accept the views, which Cicero, which Locke, which Bacon, have given, forgetful that Cicero, Locke and Bacon were only young men in libraries, when they wrote these books.

Hence, instead of Man Thinking, we have the bookworm. Hence, the book-learned class, who value books, as such; not as related to nature and the human constitution, but as making a sort of Third Estate* with the world and the soul. Hence, the restorers of readings, the emendators, the bibliomaniacs of all degrees.

Books are the best of things, well used; abused, among the worst. What is the right use? What is the one end, which all means go to effect? They are for nothing but to inspire. I had better never see a book, than to be warped by its attraction clean out of my own orbit, and made a satellite instead of a system. The one thing in the world, of value, is the active soul. This every man is entitled to; this every man contains within him, although, in almost all men, obstructed, and as yet unborn. The soul active sees absolute truth; and utters truth, or creates. In this action, it is genius; not the privilege of here and there a favorite, but the sound estate of every man. In its essence, it is progressive. The book, the college, the school of art, the institution of any kind, stop with some past utterance of genius. This is good, say they,—let us hold by this. They pin me down. They look backward and not forward. But genius looks forward: the eyes of man are set in his forehead: not in his hindhead: man hopes: genius creates. Whatever talents may be, if the man create not, the pure efflux† of the Deity is not his;—cinders and smoke there may be, but not yet flame. There are creative manners, there are creative actions, and creative words; manners, actions, words, that is, indicative of no custom or authority, but springing spontaneous from the mind's own sense of good and fair.

On the other part, instead of being its own seer, let it receive from another mind its truth, though it were in torrents of light, without periods of solitude, inquest, and self-recovery, and a fatal disservice is done. Genius is always sufficiently the enemy of genius by over influence. The literature of every nation bear me witness. The English dramatic poets have Shakspearized now for two hundred years.

---

*In political science, the third estate refers to the common people; the second estate, the nobility; and the first estate, the clergy.
†Outflowing.

Undoubtedly there is a right way of reading, so it be sternly subordi-nated. Man Thinking must not be subdued by his instruments. Books are for the scholar's idle times. When he can read God directly, the hour is too precious to be wasted in other men's transcripts of their readings. But when the intervals of darkness come, as come they must, when the sun is hid, and the stars withdraw their shining,—we repair to the lamps which were kindled by their ray, to guide our steps to the East again, where the dawn is. We hear, that we may speak. The Arabian proverb says, "A fig tree, looking on a fig tree, becometh fruitful."

It is remarkable, the character of the pleasure we derive from the best books. They impress us with the conviction, that one nature wrote and the same reads. We read the verses of one of the great English poets, of Chaucer, of Marvell, of Dryden, with the most modern joy,—with a pleasure, I mean, which is in great part caused by the abstraction of all *time* from their verses. There is some awe mixed with the joy of our sur-prise, when this poet, who lived in some past world, two or three hun-dred years ago, says that which lies close to my own soul, that which I also had wellnigh thought and said. But for the evidence thence af-forded to the philosophical doctrine of the identity of all minds, we should suppose some preëstablished harmony, some foresight of souls that were to be, and some preparation of stores for their future wants, like the fact observed in insects, who lay up food before death for the young grub they shall never see.

I would not be hurried by any love of system, by any exaggeration of instincts, to underrate the Book. We all know, that as the human body can be nourished on any food, though it were boiled grass and the broth of shoes, so the human mind can be fed by any knowledge. And great and heroic men have existed, who had almost no other information than by the printed page. I only would say, that it needs a strong head to bear that diet. One must be an inventor to read well. As the proverb says, "He that would bring home the wealth of the Indies, must carry out the wealth of the Indies." There is then creative reading as well as creative writing.[2] When the mind is braced by labor and invention, the page of whatever book we read becomes luminous with manifold allu-sion. Every sentence is doubly significant, and the sense of our author is as broad as the world. We then see, what is always true, that, as the seer's hour of vision is short and rare among heavy days and months, so is its record, perchance, the least part of his volume. The discerning will read, in his Plato or Shakspeare, only that least part,—only the authentic ut-terances of the oracle;—all the rest he rejects, were it never so many times Plato's and Shakspeare's.

Of course, there is a portion of reading quite indispensable to a wise man. History and exact science he must learn by laborious reading. Colleges, in like manner, have their indispensable office,—to teach elements. But they can only highly serve us, when they aim not to drill, but to create; when they gather from far every ray of various genius to their hospitable halls, and, by the concentrated fires, set the hearts of their youth on flame. Thought and knowledge are natures in which apparatus and pretension avail nothing. Gowns, and pecuniary* foundations, though of towns of gold, can never countervail the least sentence or syllable of wit. Forget this, and our American colleges will recede in their public importance, whilst they grow rich every year.

III. There goes in the world a notion, that the scholar should be a recluse, a valetudinarian,†—as unfit for any handiwork or public labor, as a penknife for an axe. The so-called 'practical men' sneer at speculative men, as if, because they speculate or *see*, they could do nothing. I have heard it said that the clergy,—who are always, more universally than any other class, the scholars of their day,—are addressed as women; that the rough, spontaneous conversation of men they do not hear, but only a mincing and diluted speech. They are often virtually disfranchised;‡ and, indeed, there are advocates for their celibacy. As far as this is true of the studious classes, it is not just and wise. Action is with the scholar subordinate, but it is essential. Without it, he is not yet man. Without it, thought can never ripen into truth. Whilst the world hangs before the eye as a cloud of beauty, we cannot even see its beauty. Inaction is cowardice, but there can be no scholar without the heroic mind. The preamble of thought, the transition through which it passes from the unconscious to the conscious, is action.[3] Only so much do I know, as I have lived. Instantly we know whose words are loaded with life, and whose not.

The world,—this shadow of the soul, or *other me*, lies wide around. Its attractions are the keys which unlock my thoughts and make me acquainted with myself. I run eagerly into this resounding tumult. I grasp the hands of those next me, and take my place in the ring to suffer and to work, taught by an instinct, that so shall the dumb abyss be vocal with speech. I pierce its order; I dissipate its fear; I dispose of it within

---

*Pertaining to money.
†An invalid.
‡Without the rights of citizenship, especially the right to vote.

the circuit of my expanding life. So much only of life as I know by experience, so much of the wilderness have I vanquished and planted, or so far have I extended my being, my dominion. I do not see how any man can afford, for the sake of his nerves and his nap, to spare any action in which he can partake. It is pearls and rubies to his discourse. Drudgery, calamity, exasperation, want, are instructors in eloquence and wisdom. The true scholar grudges every opportunity of action past by, as a loss of power.

It is the raw material out of which the intellect moulds her splendid products. A strange process too, this, by which experience is converted into thought, as a mulberry leaf is converted into satin.* The manufacture goes forward at all hours.

The actions and events of our childhood and youth, are now matters of calmest observation. They lie like fair pictures in the air. Not so with our recent actions,—with the business which we now have in hand. On this we are quite unable to speculate. Our affections as yet circulate through it. We no more feel or know it, than we feel the feet, or the hand, or the brain of our body. The new deed is yet a part of life,—remains for a time immersed in our unconscious life. In some contemplative hour, it detaches itself from the life like a ripe fruit, to become a thought of the mind. Instantly, it is raised, transfigured; the corruptible has put on incorruption.† Henceforth it is an object of beauty, however base its origin and neighborhood. Observe, too, the impossibility of antedating this act. In its grub state, it cannot fly, it cannot shine, it is a dull grub. But suddenly, without observation, the selfsame thing unfurls beautiful wings, and is an angel of wisdom. So is there no fact, no event in our private history, which shall not, sooner or later, lose its adhesive, inert form, and astonish us by soaring from our body into the empyrean.‡ Cradle and infancy, school and playground, the fear of boys, and dogs, and ferules,§ the love of little maids and berries, and many another fact that once filled the whole sky, are gone already; friend and relative, profession and party, town and country, nation and world, must also soar and sing.

Of course, he who has put forth his total strength in fit actions, has

---

*An allusion to silkworms, which feed on mulberry leaves.
†Reference to the Bible, I Corinthians 15:53: "For this corruptible must put on incorruption" (KJV).
‡In ancient cosmology, the highest heaven.
§Rods used for punishing children.

the richest return of wisdom. I will not shut myself out of this globe of action, and transplant an oak into a flower-pot, there to hunger and pine; nor trust the revenue of some single faculty, and exhaust one vein of thought, much like those Savoyards,* who, getting their livelihood by carving shepherds, shepherdesses, and smoking Dutchmen, for all Europe, went out one day to the mountain to find stock, and discovered that they had whittled up the last of their pine-trees. Authors we have, in numbers, who have written out their vein, and who, moved by a commendable prudence, sail for Greece or Palestine, follow the trapper into the prairie, or ramble round Algiers, to replenish their merchantable stock.[4]

If it were only for a vocabulary, the scholar would be covetous of action. Life is our dictionary. Years are well spent in country labors; in town,—in the insight into trades and manufactures; in frank intercourse with many men and women; in science; in art; to the one end of mastering in all their facts a language by which to illustrate and embody our perceptions. I learn immediately from any speaker how much he has already lived, through the poverty or the splendor of his speech. Life lies behind us as the quarry from whence we get tiles and cope-stones for the masonry of to-day. This is the way to learn grammar. Colleges and books only copy the language which the field and the work-yard made.

But the final value of action, like that of books, and better than books, is, that it is a resource. That great principle of Undulation in nature, that shows itself in the inspiring and expiring of the breath; in desire and satiety; in the ebb and flow of the sea; in day and night; in heat and cold; and as yet more deeply ingrained in every atom and every fluid, is known to us under the name of Polarity,—these "fits of easy transmission and reflection,"† as Newton called them, are the law of nature because they are the law of spirit.

The mind now thinks; now acts; and each fit reproduces the other. When the artist has exhausted his materials, when the fancy no longer paints, when thoughts are no longer apprehended, and books are a weariness,—he has always the resource *to live.* Character is higher than intellect. Thinking is the function. Living is the functionary. The stream retreats to its source. A great soul will be strong to live, as well as strong to think. Does he lack organ or medium to impart his truths? He can

---

*Savoy is a region in the western Alps.
†From the *Optics* (1704) of Sir Isaac Newton.

still fall back on this elemental force of living them. This is a total act. Thinking is a partial act. Let the grandeur of justice shine in his affairs. Let the beauty of affection cheer his lowly roof. Those "far from fame,"* who dwell and act with him, will feel the force of his constitution in the doings and passages of the day better than it can be measured by any public and designed display. Time shall teach him, that the scholar loses no hour which the man lives. Herein he unfolds the sacred germ of his instinct, screened from influence. What is lost in seemliness is gained in strength. Not out of those, on whom systems of education have exhausted their culture, comes the helpful giant to destroy the old or to build the new, but out of unhandselled† savage nature, out of terrible Druids and berserkirs, come at last Alfred and Shakspeare.

I hear therefore with joy whatever is beginning to be said of the dignity and necessity of labor to every citizen.[5] There is virtue yet in the hoe and the spade, for learned as well as for unlearned hands. And labor is everywhere welcome; always we are invited to work; only be this limitation observed, that a man shall not for the sake of wider activity sacrifice any opinion to the popular judgments and modes of action.

I have now spoken of the education of the scholar by nature, by books, and by action. It remains to say somewhat of his duties.

They are such as become Man Thinking. They may all be comprised in self-trust. The office of the scholar is to cheer, to raise, and to guide men by showing them facts amidst appearances. He plies the slow, unhonored, and unpaid task of observation. Flamsteed and Herschel, in their glazed‡ observatories, may catalogue the stars with the praise of all men, and, the results being splendid and useful, honor is sure. But he, in his private observatory, cataloguing obscure and nebulous stars of the human mind, which as yet no man has thought of as such,—watching days and months, sometimes, for a few facts; correcting still his old records;—must relinquish display and immediate fame. In the long period of his preparation, he must betray often an ignorance and shiftlessness in popular arts, incurring the disdain of the able who shoulder

---

*Possibly an allusion to William Wordsworth's poem "June 1820": "Fame tells of groves—from England far away."

†A "handsel" is an initial experience of something—a foretaste, or token, of what is to come. Emerson is referring to how truly original thinkers come unannounced and are beyond, or outside, our prior experience.

‡Glass-roofed.

him aside. Long he must stammer in his speech; often forego the living for the dead. Worse yet, he must accept,—how often! poverty and solitude. For the ease and pleasure of treading the old road, accepting the fashions, the education, the religion of society, he takes the cross of making his own, and of course, the self-accusation, the faint heart, the frequent uncertainty and loss of time, which are the nettles and tangling vines in the way of the self-relying and self-directed; and the state of virtual hostility in which he seems to stand to society, and especially to educated society. For all this loss and scorn, what offset? He is to find consolation in exercising the highest functions of human nature. He is one, who raises himself from private considerations, and breathes and lives on public and illustrious thoughts. He is the world's eye. He is the world's heart. He is to resist the vulgar prosperity that retrogrades ever to barbarism, by preserving and communicating heroic sentiments, noble biographies, melodious verse, and the conclusions of history. Whatsoever oracles the human heart, in all emergencies, in all solemn hours, has uttered as its commentary on the world of actions,—these he shall receive and impart. And whatsoever new verdict Reason from her inviolable seat pronounces on the passing men and events of to-day—this he shall hear and promulgate.

These being his functions, it becomes him to feel all confidence in himself, and to defer never to the popular cry. He and he only knows the world. The world of any moment is the merest appearance. Some great decorum, some fetish of a government, some ephemeral trade, or war, or man, is cried up by half mankind and cried down by the other half, as if all depended on this particular up or down. The odds are that the whole question is not worth the poorest thought which the scholar has lost in listening to the controversy. Let him not quit his belief that a popgun is a popgun, though the ancient and honorable of the earth affirm it to be the crack of doom. In silence, in steadiness, in severe abstraction, let him hold by himself; add observation to observation, patient of neglect, patient of reproach; and bide his own time,—happy enough, if he can satisfy himself alone, that this day he has seen something truly. Success treads on every right step. For the instinct is sure, that prompts him to tell his brother what he thinks. He then learns, that in going down into the secrets of his own mind, he has descended into the secrets of all minds. He learns that he who has mastered any law in his private thoughts, is master to that extent of all men whose language he speaks, and of all into whose language his own can be translated. The poet, in utter solitude remembering his spontaneous thoughts and recording them, is found to have recorded that, which men in crowded cities find true for them also. The orator distrusts at first the fitness of his frank confessions,—his want of knowledge of the persons he addresses,—until he finds that he is the complement of his hearers;—that they drink his words because he fulfils for them their own nature; the deeper he dives into his privatest, secretest presentiment, to his wonder he finds, this is the most acceptable, most public, and universally true. The people delight in it; the better part of every man feels, This is my music; this is myself.

In self-trust, all the virtues are comprehended. Free should the scholar be,—free and brave. Free even to the definition of freedom, "without any hindrance that does not arise out of his own constitution." Brave; for fear is a thing, which a scholar by his very function puts behind him. Fear always springs from ignorance. It is a shame to him if his tranquillity, amid dangerous times, arise from the presumption, that, like children and women, his is a protected class; or if he seek a temporary peace by the diversion of his thoughts from politics or vexed questions, hiding his head like an ostrich in the flowering bushes, peeping into microscopes, and turning rhymes, as a boy whistles to keep his courage up. So is the danger a danger still; so is the fear worse. Manlike let him turn and face it. Let him look into its eye and search its nature, inspect its origin,—see the whelping of this lion, which lies no great way back; he will then find in himself a perfect comprehension of its nature and extent; he will have made his hands meet on the other side, and can henceforth defy it, and pass on superior. The world is his, who can see through its pretension. What deafness, what stone-blind custom, what overgrown error you behold, is there only by sufferance,—by your sufferance. See it to be a lie, and you have already dealt it its mortal blow.

Yes, we are the cowed,—we the trustless. It is a mischievous notion that we are come late into nature; that the world was finished a long time ago. As the world was plastic and fluid in the hands of God, so it is ever to so much of his attributes as we bring to it. To ignorance and sin, it is flint. They adapt themselves to it as they may; but in proportion as a man has any thing in him divine, the firmament flows before him and takes his signet* and form. Not he is great who can alter matter, but he who can alter my state of mind. They are the kings of the world who give the color of their present thought to all nature and all art, and persuade men by the cheerful serenity of their carrying the matter, that this thing which they do, is the apple which the ages have desired to pluck,

---

*Impression, or signature, made by a signet ring.

now at last ripe, and inviting nations to the harvest. The great man makes the great thing. Wherever Macdonald sits, there is the head of the table.* Linnæus makes botany the most alluring of studies, and wins it from the farmer and the herd-woman; Davy, chemistry; and Cuvier, fossils. The day is always his, who works in it with serenity and great aims. The unstable estimates of men crowd to him whose mind is filled with a truth, as the heaped waves of the Atlantic follow the moon.

For this self-trust, the reason is deeper than can be fathomed,— darker than can be enlightened. I might not carry with me the feeling of my audience in stating my own belief. But I have already shown the ground of my hope, in adverting† to the doctrine that man is one. I believe man has been wronged; he has wronged himself. He has almost lost the light, that can lead him back to his prerogatives. Men are become of no account. Men in history, men in the world of to-day are bugs, are spawn, and are called "the mass" and "the herd." In a century, in a millennium, one or two men; that is to say,—one or two approximations to the right state of every man. All the rest behold in the hero or the poet their own green and crude being,—ripened, yes, and are content to be less, so *that* may attain to its full stature. What a testimony,—full of grandeur, full of pity, is borne to the demands of his own nature, by the poor clansman, the poor partisan, who rejoices in the glory of his chief. The poor and the low find some amends to their immense moral capacity, for their acquiescence in a political and social inferiority. They are content to be brushed like flies from the path of a great person, so that justice shall be done by him to that common nature which it is the dearest desire of all to see enlarged and glorified. They sun themselves in the great man's light, and feel it to be their own element. They cast the dignity of man from their downtrod selves upon the shoulders of a hero, and will perish to add one drop of blood to make that great heart beat, those giant sinews combat and conquer. He lives for us, and we live in him.

Men such as they are, very naturally seek money or power; and power because it is as good as money,—the "spoils," so called, "of office." And why not? for they aspire to the highest, and this, in their sleep-walking, they dream is highest. Wake them, and they shall quit the false good, and leap to the true, and leave governments to clerks and desks.

---

*Variation on the Scottish proverb "Where Macgregor sits, there is the head of the table."
†Referring.

This revolution is to be wrought by the gradual domestication of the idea of Culture. The main enterprise of the world for splendor, for extent, is the upbuilding of a man. Here are the materials strown along the ground. The private life of one man shall be a more illustrious monarchy,—more formidable to its enemy, more sweet and serene in its influence to its friend, than any kingdom in history. For a man, rightly viewed, comprehendeth the particular natures, of all men. Each philosopher, each bard, each actor, has only done for me, as by a delegate, what one day I can do for myself. The books which once we valued more than the apple of the eye, we have quite exhausted. What is that but saying, that we have come up with the point of view which the universal mind took through the eyes of one scribe; we have been that man, and have passed on. First, one; then, another; we drain all cisterns, and waxing greater by all these supplies, we crave a better and more abundant food. The man has never lived that can feed us ever. The human mind cannot be enshrined in a person, who shall set a barrier on any one side to this unbounded, unboundable empire. It is one central fire, which, flaming now out of the lips of Etna, lightens the capes of Sicily; and, now out of the throat of Vesuvius, illuminates the towers and vineyards of Naples.* It is one light which beams out of a thousand stars. It is one soul which animates all men.

But I have dwelt perhaps tediously upon this abstraction of the Scholar. I ought not to delay longer to add what I have to say, of nearer reference to the time and to this country.

Historically, there is thought to be a difference in the ideas which predominate over successive epochs, and there are data for marking the genius of the Classic, of the Romantic, and now of the Reflective or Philosophical age. With the views I have intimated of the oneness or the identity of the mind through all individuals, I do not much dwell on these differences. In fact, I believe each individual passes through all three. The boy is a Greek; the youth, romantic; the adult, reflective. I deny not, however, that a revolution in the leading idea may be distinctly enough traced.

Our age is bewailed as the age of Introversion. Must that needs be evil? We, it seems, are critical; we are embarrassed with second thoughts; we cannot enjoy anything for hankering to know whereof the

---

*Etna and Vesuvius are volcanoes in Sicily and Italy.

pleasure consists; we are lined with eyes; we see with our feet; the time is infected with Hamlet's unhappiness,—

"Sicklied o'er with the pale cast of thought."*

Is it so bad then? Sight is the last thing to be pitied. Would we be blind? Do we fear lest we should outsee nature and God, and drink truth dry? I look upon the discontent of the literary class, as a mere announcement of the fact, that they find themselves not in the state of mind of their fathers, and regret the coming state as untried; as a boy dreads the water before he has learned that he can swim. If there is any period one would desire to be born in,—is it not the age of Revolution; when the old and the new stand side by side, and admit of being compared; when the energies of all men are searched by fear and by hope; when the historic glories of the old can be compensated by the rich possibilities of the new era? This time, like all times, is a very good one, if we but know what to do with it.

I read with joy some of the auspicious signs of the coming days, as they glimmer already through poetry and art, through philosophy and science, through church and state.

One of these signs is the fact, that the same movement which effected the elevation of what was called the lowest class in the state, assumed in literature a very marked and as benign an aspect. Instead of the sublime and beautiful; the near, the low, the common, was explored and poetized. That, which had been negligently trodden under foot by those who were harnessing and provisioning themselves for long journeys into far countries, is suddenly found to be richer than all foreign parts. The literature of the poor, the feelings of the child, the philosophy of the street, the meaning of household life, are the topics of the time. It is a great stride. It is a sign—is it not? of new vigor, when the extremities are made active, when currents of warm life run into the hands and the feet. I ask not for the great, the remote, the romantic; what is doing in Italy or Arabia; what is Greek art, or Provençal minstrelsy; I embrace the common, I explore and sit at the feet of the familiar, the low. Give me insight into to-day, and you may have the antique and future worlds. What would we really know the meaning of? The meal in the firkin; the milk in the pan; the ballad in the street; the news of the boat; the glance of the eye; the form and the gait of the body;—show me the ultimate reason of these matters; show me the

---

*From Shakespeare's *Hamlet* (act 3, scene 1).

sublime presence of the highest spiritual cause lurking, as always it does lurk, in these suburbs and extremities of nature; let me see every trifle bristling with the polarity that ranges it instantly on an eternal law; and the shop, the plough, and the ledger, referred to the like cause by which light undulates and poets sing;—and the world lies no longer a dull miscellany and lumber-room, but has form and order; there is no trifle; there is no puzzle; but one design unites and animates the farthest pinnacle and the lowest trench.

This idea has inspired the genius of Goldsmith, Burns, Cowper, and, in a newer time, of Goethe, Wordsworth, and Carlyle. This idea they have differently followed and with various success. In contrast with their writing, the style of Pope, of Johnson, of Gibbon, looks cold and pedantic.[6] This writing is blood-warm. Man is surprised to find that things near are not less beautiful and wondrous than things remote. The near explains the far. The drop is a small ocean. A man is related to all nature. This perception of the worth of the vulgar is fruitful in discoveries. Goethe, in this very thing the most modern of the moderns, has shown us, as none ever did, the genius of the ancients.

There is one man of genius, who has done much for this philosophy of life, whose literary value has never yet been rightly estimated;—I mean Emanuel Swedenborg. The most imaginative of men, yet writing with the precision of a mathematician, he endeavored to engraft a purely philosophical Ethics on the popular Christianity of his time. Such an attempt, of course, must have difficulty, which no genius could surmount. But he saw and showed the connection between nature and the affections of the soul. He pierced the emblematic or spiritual character of the visible, audible, tangible world. Especially did his shade-loving muse hover over and interpret the lower parts of nature; he showed the mysterious bond that allies moral evil to the foul material forms, and has given in epical parables a theory of insanity, of beasts, of unclean and fearful things.

Another sign of our times, also marked by an analogous political movement, is, the new importance given to the single person. Everything that tends to insulate the individual,—to surround him with barriers of natural respect, so that each man shall feel the world is his, and man shall treat with man as a sovereign state with a sovereign state,—tends to true union as well as greatness. "I learned," said the melancholy Pestalozzi, "that no man in God's wide earth is either willing or able to help any other man." Help must come from the bosom alone. The scholar is that man who must take up into himself all the ability of the time, all the contributions of the past, all the hopes of the future. He must be an university of knowledges. If there be one lesson more than another, which should pierce his ear, it is, The world is nothing, the man is all; in yourself is the law of all nature, and you know not yet how a globule of sap ascends; in yourself slumbers the whole of Reason; it is for you to know all, it is for you to dare all. Mr. President and Gentlemen, this confidence in the unsearched might of man belongs, by all motives, by all prophecy, by all preparation, to the American Scholar. We have listened too long to the courtly muses of Europe. The spirit of the American freeman is already suspected to be timid, imitative, tame. Public and private avarice* make the air we breathe thick and fat. The scholar is decent, indolent, complaisant. See already the tragic consequence. The mind of this country, taught to aim at low objects, eats upon itself. There is no work for any but the decorous and the complaisant. Young men of the fairest promise, who begin life upon our shores, inflated by the mountain winds, shined upon by all the stars of God, find the earth below not in unison with these,—but are hindered from action by the disgust which the principles on which business is managed inspire, and turn drudges, or die of disgust,—some of them suicides. What is the remedy? They did not yet see, and thousands of young men as hopeful now crowding to the barriers for the career, do not yet see, that, if the single man plant himself indomitably on his instincts, and there abide, the huge world will come round to him. Patience,—patience;—with the shades† of all the good and great for company; and for solace, the perspective of your own infinite life; and for work, the study and the communication of principles, the making those instincts prevalent, the conversion of the world. Is it not the chief disgrace in the world, not to be an unit;—not to be reckoned one character;—not to yield that peculiar fruit which each man was created to bear, but to be reckoned in the gross, in the hundred, or the thousand, of the party, the section, to which we belong; and our opinion predicted geographically, as the north, or the south? Not so, brothers, and friends,—please God, ours shall not be so. We will walk on our own feet; we will work with our own hands; we will speak our own minds. The study of letters shall be no longer a name for pity, for doubt, and for sensual indulgence. The dread of man and the love of man shall be a wall of defence and a wreath of joy around all. A nation of men will for the first time exist, because each believes himself inspired by the Divine Soul which also inspires all men.

---

*Greed.
†Spirits.

An Address[1]

Delivered before the Senior Class
in Divinity College, Cambridge,
Sunday Evening, July 15, 1838.

IN THIS REFULGENT* SUMMER, it has been a luxury to draw the breath of life. The grass grows, the buds burst, the meadow is spotted with fire and gold in the tint of flowers. The air is full of birds, and sweet with the breath of the pine, the balm-of-Gilead,† and the new hay. Night brings no gloom to the heart with its welcome shade. Through the transparent darkness the stars pour their almost spiritual rays. Man under them seems a young child, and his huge globe a toy. The cool night bathes the world as with a river, and prepares his eyes again for the crimson dawn. The mystery of nature was never displayed more happily. The corn and the wine have been freely dealt to all creatures, and the never-broken silence with which the old bounty goes forward, has not yielded yet one word of explanation. One is constrained to respect the perfection of this world, in which our senses converse. How wide; how rich; what invitation from every property it gives to every faculty of man! In its fruitful soils; in its navigable sea; in its mountains of metal and stone; in its forests of all woods; in its animals; in its chemical ingredients; in the powers and path of light, heat, attraction, and life, it is well worth the pith and heart of great men to subdue and enjoy it. The planters, the mechanics, the inventors, the astronomers, the builders of cities, and the captains, history delights to honor.

But when the mind opens, and reveals the laws which traverse the universe, and make things what they are, then shrinks the great world at once into a mere illustration and fable of this mind. What am I? and What is? asks the human spirit with a curiosity new-kindled, but never to be quenched. Behold these out-running laws, which our imperfect apprehension can see tend this way and that, but not come full circle. Behold these infinite relations, so like, so unlike; many, yet one. I would study, I would know, I would admire forever. These works of thought have been the entertainments of the human spirit in all ages.

---

*Radiant.

†A flowering poplar tree, so called for the curative resin associated with Gilead in the Bible, Jeremiah 8:22.

A more secret, sweet, and overpowering beauty appears to man when his heart and mind open to the sentiment of virtue. Then he is instructed in what is above him. He learns that his being is without bound; that, to the good, to the perfect, he is born, low as he now lies in evil and weakness. That which he venerates is still his own, though he has not realized it yet. *He ought.* He knows the sense of that grand word, though his analysis fails entirely to render account of it. When in innocency, or when by intellectual perception, he attains to say,—"I love the Right; Truth is beautiful within and without, forevermore. Virtue, I am thine: save me: use me: thee will I serve, day and night, in great, in small, that I may be not virtuous, but virtue;"—then is the end of the creation answered, and God is well pleased.

The sentiment of virtue is a reverence and delight in the presence of certain divine laws. It perceives that this homely game of life we play, covers, under what seem foolish details, principles that astonish. The child amidst his baubles, is learning the action of light, motion, gravity, muscular force; and in the game of human life, love, fear, justice, appetite, man, and God, interact. These laws refuse to be adequately stated. They will not be written out on paper, or spoken by the tongue. They elude our persevering thought; yet we read them hourly in each other's faces, in each other's actions, in our own remorse. The moral traits which are all globed into every virtuous act and thought,—in speech, we must sever, and describe or suggest by painful enumeration of many particulars. Yet, as this sentiment is the essence of all religion, let me guide your eye to the precise objects of the sentiment, by an enumeration of some of those classes of facts in which this element is conspicuous.

The intuition of the moral sentiment is an insight of the perfection of the laws of the soul. These laws execute themselves. They are out of time, out of space, and not subject to circumstance. Thus; in the soul of man there is a justice whose retributions are instant and entire. He who does a good deed, is instantly ennobled. He who does a mean deed, is by the action itself contracted. He who puts off impurity, thereby puts on purity. If a man is at heart just, then in so far is he God; the safety of God, the immortality of God, the majesty of God do enter into that man with justice. If a man dissemble, deceive, he deceives himself, and goes out of acquaintance with his own being. A man in the view of absolute goodness, adores, with total humility. Every step so downward, is a step upward. The man who renounces himself, comes to himself.

See how this rapid intrinsic energy worketh everywhere, righting wrongs, correcting appearances, and bringing up facts to a harmony with thoughts. Its operation in life, though slow to the senses, is, at last, as sure as in the soul. By it, a man is made the Providence to himself, dispensing good to his goodness, and evil to his sin. Character is always known. Thefts never enrich; alms never impoverish; murder will speak out of stone walls. The least admixture of a lie,—for example, the taint of vanity, the least attempt to make a good impression, a favorable appearance,—will instantly vitiate* the effect. But speak the truth, and all nature and all spirits help you with unexpected furtherance. Speak the truth, and all things alive or brute are vouchers, and the very roots of the grass underground there, do seem to stir and move to bear you witness. See again the perfection of the Law as it applies itself to the affections, and becomes the law of society. As we are, so we associate. The good, by affinity, seek the good; the vile, by affinity, the vile. Thus of their own volition, souls proceed into heaven, into hell.

These facts have always suggested to man the sublime creed, that the world is not the product of manifold power, but of one will, of one mind; and that one mind is everywhere active, in each ray of the star, in each wavelet of the pool; and whatever opposes that will, is everywhere balked and baffled, because things are made so, and not otherwise. Good is positive. Evil is merely privative, not absolute: it is like cold, which is the privation of heat. All evil is so much death or nonentity. Benevolence is absolute and real. So much benevolence as a man hath, so much life hath he. For all things proceed out of this same spirit which is differently named love, justice, temperance, in its different applications, just as the ocean receives different names on the several shores which it washes. All things proceed out of the same spirit, and all things conspire with it. Whilst a man seeks good ends, he is strong by the whole strength of nature. In so far as he roves from these ends, he bereaves himself of power, of auxiliaries; his being shrinks out of all remote channels, he becomes less, and less, a mote, a point, until absolute badness is absolute death.

The perception of this law of laws awakens in the mind a sentiment which we call the religious sentiment, and which makes our highest happiness. Wonderful is its power to charm and to command. It is a mountain air. It is the embalmer of the world. It is myrrh and storax, and chlorine and rosemary.† It makes the sky and the hills sublime, and

---

*To spoil; corrupt.

†*Myrrh:* an aromatic resin used in perfume and incense—it was one of the gifts given to the infant Jesus by the three wise men. *Storax:* an aromatic resin. *Chlorine:* a greenish-yellow gas used for purifying. *Rosemary:* an aromatic evergreen herb used in cooking and in perfume.

the silent song of the stars is it. By it, is the universe made safe and habitable, not by science or power. Thought may work cold and intransitive in things, and find no end or unity; but the dawn of the sentiment of virtue on the heart, gives and is the assurance that Law is sovereign over all natures; and the worlds, time, space, eternity, do seem to break out into joy.

This sentiment is divine and deifying. It is the beatitude of man. It makes him illimitable. Through it, the soul first knows itself. It corrects the capital mistake of the infant man, who seeks to be great by following the great, and hopes to derive advantages *from another*,—by showing the fountain of all good to be in himself, and that he, equally with every man, is an inlet into the deeps of Reason. When he says, "I ought"; when love warms him; when he chooses, warned from on high, the good and great deed; then, deep melodies wander through his soul from Supreme Wisdom. Then he can worship, and be enlarged by his worship; for he can never go behind this sentiment. In the sublimest flights of the soul, rectitude is never surmounted, love is never outgrown.

This sentiment lies at the foundation of society; and successively creates all forms of worship. The principle of veneration never dies out. Man fallen into superstition, into sensuality, is never quite without the visions of the moral sentiment. In like manner, all the expressions of this sentiment are sacred and permanent in proportion to their purity. The expressions of this sentiment affect us more than all other compositions. The sentences of the oldest time, which ejaculate this piety, are still fresh and fragrant. This thought dwelled always deepest in the minds of men in the devout and contemplative East; not alone in Palestine, where it reached its purest expression, but in Egypt, in Persia, in India, in China. Europe has always owed to oriental genius, its divine impulses. What these holy bards said, all sane men found agreeable and true. And the unique impression of Jesus upon mankind, whose name is not so much written as ploughed into the history of this world, is proof of the subtle virtue of this infusion.

Meantime, whilst the doors of the temple stand open, night and day before every man, and the oracles of this truth cease never, it is guarded by one stern condition; this, namely; it is an intuition. It cannot be received at second hand. Truly speaking, it is not instruction, but provocation, that I can receive from another soul. What he announces, I must find true in me, or wholly reject; and on his word, or as his second, be he who he may, I can accept nothing. On the contrary, the absence of this primary faith is the presence of degradation. As is the flood, so is the ebb. Let this faith depart, and the very words it spake, and the things it made, become false and hurtful. Then falls the church, the state, art, letters, life. The doctrine of the divine nature being forgotten, a sickness infects and dwarfs the constitution. Once man was all; now he is an appendage, a nuisance. And because the indwelling Supreme Spirit cannot wholly be got rid of, the doctrine of it suffers this perversion, that the divine nature is attributed to one or two persons, and denied to all the rest, and denied with fury. The doctrine of inspiration is lost; the base doctrine of the majority of voices, usurps the place of the doctrine of the soul. Miracles, prophecy, poetry; the ideal life, the holy life, exist as ancient history merely; they are not in the belief, nor in the aspiration of society; but, when suggested, seem ridiculous. Life is comic or pitiful, as soon as the high ends of being fade out of sight and man becomes near-sighted, and can only attend to what addresses the senses.

These general views, which, whilst they are general, none will contest, find abundant illustration in the history of religion, and especially in the history of the Christian church. In that, all of us have had our birth and nurture. The truth contained in that, you, my young friends, are now setting forth to teach. As the Cultus, or established worship of the civilized world, it has great historical interest for us. Of its blessed words, which have been the consolation of humanity, you need not that I should speak. I shall endeavor to discharge my duty to you, on this occasion, by pointing out two errors in its administration, which daily appear more gross from the point of view we have just now taken.

Jesus Christ belonged to the true race of prophets. He saw with open eye the mystery of the soul. Drawn by its severe harmony, ravished with its beauty, he lived in it, and had his being there. Alone in all history, he estimated the greatness of man. One man was true to what is in you and me. He saw that God incarnates himself in man, and evermore goes forth anew to take possession of his world. He said, in this jubilee of sublime emotion, "I am divine. Through me, God acts; through me, speaks. Would you see God, see me; or, see thee, when thou also thinkest as I now think." But what a distortion did his doctrine and memory suffer in the same, in the next, and the following ages! There is no doctrine of the Reason which will bear to be taught by the Understanding. The understanding caught this high chant from the poet's lips, and said, in the next age, "This was Jehovah come down out of heaven. I will kill you, if you say he was a man." The idioms of his language, and the figures of his rhetoric, have usurped the place of his truth; and churches are not built on his principles, but on his tropes. Christianity became a Mythus,* as the poetic teaching of Greece and of Egypt, before. He spoke of miracles; for he felt that man's life was a miracle, and all that man doth, and he knew that this daily miracle shines, as the character ascends. But the word Miracle, as pronounced by Christian churches, gives a false impression; it is Monster. It is not one with the blowing clover and the falling rain.

He felt respect for Moses and the prophets; but no unfit tenderness at postponing their initial revelations, to the hour and the man that now is; to the eternal revelation in the heart. Thus was he a true man. Having seen that the law in us is commanding, he would not suffer it to be commanded. Boldly, with hand, and heart, and life, he declared it was God. Thus is he, as I think, the only soul in history who has appreciated the worth of a man.

1. In this point of view we become very sensible of the first defect of historical Christianity.[2] Historical Christianity has fallen into the error that corrupts all attempts to communicate religion. As it appears to us, and as it has appeared for ages, it is not the doctrine of the soul, but an exaggeration of the personal, the positive, the ritual. It has dwelt, it dwells, with noxious exaggeration about the *person* of Jesus. The soul knows no persons. It invites every man to expand to the full circle of the universe, and will have no preferences but those of spontaneous love. But by this eastern monarchy of a Christianity, which indolence and fear have built, the friend of man is made the injurer of man. The manner in which his name is surrounded with expressions, which were once sallies of admiration and love, but are now petrified into official titles, kills all generous sympathy and liking. All who hear me, feel, that the language that describes Christ to Europe and America, is not the style of friendship and enthusiasm to a good and noble heart, but is appropriated and formal,—paints a demigod, as the Orientals or the Greeks would describe Osiris or Apollo.[3] Accept the injurious impositions of our early catechetical instruction, and even honesty and self-denial were but splendid sins, if they did not wear the Christian name. One would rather be

"A pagan, suckled in a creed outworn,"†

---

*A literature to be studied, a story to be told rather than a religion to be lived out in one's daily life.

†From William Wordsworth's sonnet "The World Is Too Much with Us" (1807).

than to be defrauded of his manly right in coming into nature, and finding not names and places, not land and professions, but even virtue and truth foreclosed and monopolized. You shall not be a man even. You shall not own the world; you shall not dare, and live after the infinite Law that is in you, and in company with the infinite Beauty which heaven and earth reflect to you in all lovely forms; but you must subordinate your nature to Christ's nature; you must accept our interpretations; and take his portrait as the vulgar draw it.

That is always best which gives me to myself. The sublime is excited in me by the great stoical doctrine, Obey thyself. That which shows God in me, fortifies me. That which shows God out of me, makes me a wart and a wen. There is no longer a necessary reason for my being. Already the long shadows of untimely oblivion creep over me, and I shall decease forever.

The divine bards are the friends of my virtue, of my intellect, of my strength. They admonish me, that the gleams which flash across my mind, are not mine, but God's; that they had the like, and were not disobedient to the heavenly vision. So I love them. Noble provocations go out from them, inviting me to resist evil; to subdue the world; and to Be. And thus by his holy thoughts, Jesus serves us, and thus only. To aim to convert a man by miracles, is a profanation of the soul. A true conversion, a true Christ, is now, as always, to be made, by the reception of beautiful sentiments. It is true that a great and rich soul, like his, falling among the simple, does so preponderate, that, as his did, it names the world. The world seems to them to exist for him, and they have not yet drunk so deeply of his sense, as to see that only by coming again to themselves, or to God in themselves, can they grow, forevermore. It is a low benefit to give me something; it is a high benefit to enable me to do somewhat of myself. The time is coming when all men will see, that the gift of God to the soul is not a vaunting, overpowering, excluding sanctity, but a sweet, natural goodness, a goodness like thine and mine, and that so invites thine and mine to be and to grow.

The injustice of the vulgar tone of preaching is not less flagrant to Jesus, than to the souls which it profanes. The preachers do not see that they make his gospel not glad, and shear him of the locks of beauty and the attributes of heaven. When I see a majestic Epaminondas, or Washington; when I see among my contemporaries, a true orator, an upright judge, a dear friend; when I vibrate to the melody and fancy of a poem; I see beauty that is to be desired. And so lovely, and with yet more entire consent of my human being, sounds in my ear the severe music of the bards that have sung of the true God in all ages. Now do not degrade the life and dialogues of Christ out of the circle of this charm, by insulation and peculiarity. Let them lie as they befel, alive and warm, part of human life, and of the landscape, and of the cheerful day.

2. The second defect of the traditionary and limited way of using the mind of Christ is a consequence of the first; this, namely; that the Moral Nature, that Law of laws, whose revelations introduce greatness,—yea, God himself, into the open soul, is not explored as the fountain of the established teaching in society. Men have come to speak of the revelation as somewhat long ago given and done, as if God were dead. The injury to faith throttles the preacher; and the goodliest of institutions becomes an uncertain and inarticulate voice.

It is very certain that it is the effect of conversation with the beauty of the soul, to beget a desire and need to impart to others the same knowledge and love. If utterance is denied, the thought lies like a burden on the man. Always the seer is a sayer. Somehow his dream is told; somehow he publishes it with solemn joy: sometimes with pencil on canvas; sometimes with chisel on stone; sometimes in towers and aisles of granite, his soul's worship is builded; sometimes in anthems of indefinite music; but clearest and most permanent, in words.

The man enamored of this excellency, becomes its priest or poet. The office is coeval* with the world. But observe the condition, the spiritual limitation of the office. The spirit only can teach. Not any profane man, not any sensual, not any liar, not any slave can teach but only he can give, who has; he only can create, who is. The man on whom the soul descends, through whom the soul speaks, alone can teach. Courage, piety, love, wisdom, can teach; and every man can open his door to these angels, and they shall bring him the gift of tongues. But the man who aims to speak as books enable, as synods use, as the fashion guides, and as interest commands, babbles. Let him hush.

To this holy office, you propose to devote yourselves. I wish you may feel your call in throbs of desire and hope. The office is the first in the world. It is of that reality, that it cannot suffer the deduction of any falsehood. And it is my duty to say to you, that the need was never greater of new revelation than now. From the views I have already expressed, you will infer the sad conviction, which I share, I believe, with numbers, of the universal decay and now almost death of faith in society. The soul is not preached. The Church seems to totter to its fall, almost all life extinct. On this occasion, any complaisance would be

---

*Of contemporaneous origin.

criminal, which told you, whose hope and commission it is to preach the faith of Christ, that the faith of Christ is preached.

It is time that this ill-suppressed murmur of all thoughtful men against the famine of our churches; this moaning of the heart because it is bereaved of the consolation, the hope, the grandeur, that come alone out of that culture of the moral nature, should be heard through the sleep of indolence, and over the din of routine. This great and perpetual office of the preacher is not discharged. Preaching is the expression of the moral sentiment in application to the duties of life. In how many churches, by how many prophets, tell me, is man made sensible that he is an infinite soul; that the earth and heavens are passing into his mind; that he is drinking forever the soul of God? Where now sounds the persuasion, that by its very melody imparadises my heart, and so affirms its own origin in heaven? Where shall I hear words such as in elder ages drew men to leave all and follow,—father and mother, house and land, wife and child?* Where shall I hear these august laws of moral being so pronounced, as to fill my ear, and I feel ennobled by the offer of my uttermost action and passion? The test of the true faith, certainly, should be its power to charm and command the soul, as the laws of nature control the activity of the hands,—so commanding that we find pleasure and honor in obeying. The faith should blend with the light of rising and of setting suns, with the flying cloud, the singing bird, and the breath of flowers. But now the priest's Sabbath has lost the splendor of nature; it is unlovely; we are glad when it is done; we can make, we do make, even sitting in our pews, a far better, holier, sweeter, for ourselves.

Whenever the pulpit is usurped by a formalist, then is the worshipper defrauded and disconsolate. We shrink as soon as the prayers begin, which do not uplift, but smite and offend us. We are fain to wrap our cloaks about us, and secure, as best we can, a solitude that hears not. I once heard a preacher who sorely tempted me to say, I would go to church no more. Men go, thought I, where they are wont to go, else had no soul entered the temple in the afternoon. A snow storm was falling around us. The snow storm was real; the preacher merely spectral; and the eye felt the sad contrast in looking at him, and then out of the window behind him, into the beautiful meteor of the snow. He had lived in

---

*Compare the Bible, Matthew 19:28–29: ". . . And every one that hath forsaken houses, or brethren, or sisters, or father, or mother, or wife, or children, or lands, for my name's sake, shall receive an hundredfold, and shall inherit everlasting life" (KJV).

vain. He had no one word intimating that he had laughed or wept, was married or in love, had been commended, or cheated, or chagrined. If he had ever lived and acted, we were none the wiser for it. The capital secret of his profession, namely, to convert life into truth, he had not learned. Not one fact in all his experience, had he yet imported into his doctrine. This man had ploughed, and planted, and talked, and bought, and sold; he had read books; he had eaten and drunken; his head aches; his heart throbs; he smiles and suffers; yet was there not a surmise, a hint, in all the discourse, that he had ever lived at all. Not a line did he draw out of real history. The true preacher can be known by this, that he deals out to the people his life,—life passed through the fire of thought. But of the bad preacher, it could not be told from his sermon, what age of the world he fell in; whether he had a father or a child; whether he was a freeholder or a pauper; whether he was a citizen or a countryman; or any other fact of his biography. It seemed strange that the people should come to church. It seemed as if their houses were very unentertaining, that they should prefer this thoughtless clamor. It shows that there is a commanding attraction in the moral sentiment, that can lend a faint tint of light to dulness and ignorance, coming in its name and place. The good hearer is sure he has been touched some-times; is sure there is somewhat to be reached, and some word that can reach it. When he listens to these vain words, he comforts himself by their relation to his remembrance of better hours, and so they clatter and echo unchallenged.

I am not ignorant that when we preach unworthily, it is not always quite in vain. There is a good ear, in some men, that draws supplies to virtue out of very indifferent nutriment. There is poetic truth concealed in all the common-places of prayer and of sermons, and though fool-ishly spoken, they may be wisely heard; for, each is some select expres-sion that broke out in a moment of piety from some stricken or jubilant soul, and its excellency made it remembered. The prayers and even the dogmas of our church, are like the zodiac of Denderah, and the astro-nomical monuments of the Hindoos,* wholly insulated from anything now extant in the life and business of the people. They mark the height to which the waters once rose. But this docility is a check upon the mis-chief from the good and devout. In a large portion of the community, the religious service gives rise to quite other thoughts and emotions. We need not chide the negligent servant. We are struck with pity, rather, at

---

*Archaeological remnants of the religions central to Egyptian and Indian culture.

the swift retribution of his sloth. Alas for the unhappy man that is called to stand in the pulpit, and *not* give bread of life. Everything that befalls, accuses him. Would he ask contributions for the missions, foreign or domestic? Instantly his face is suffused with shame, to propose to his parish, that they should send money a hundred or a thousand miles, to furnish such poor fare as they have at home, and would do well to go the hundred or the thousand miles to escape. Would he urge people to a godly way of living;—and can he ask a fellow-creature to come to Sabbath meetings, when he and they all know what is the poor uttermost they can hope for therein? Will he invite them privately to the Lord's Supper? He dares not. If no heart warm this rite, the hollow, dry, creaking formality is too plain, than that he can face a man of wit and energy, and put the invitation without terror. In the street, what has he to say to the bold village blasphemer? The village blasphemer sees fear in the face, form and gait of the minister.

Let me not taint the sincerity of this plea by any oversight of the claims of good men. I know and honor the purity and strict conscience of numbers of the clergy. What life the public worship retains, it owns to the scattered company of pious men, who minister here and there in the churches, and who, sometimes accepting with too great tenderness the tenet of the elders, have not accepted from others, but from their own heart, the genuine impulses of virtue, and so still command our love and awe, to the sanctity of character. Moreover, the exceptions are not so much to be found in a few eminent preachers, as in the better hours, the truer inspirations of all,—nay, in the sincere moments of every man. But with whatever exception, it is still true that tradition characterizes the preaching of this country; that it comes out of the memory, and not out of the soul; that it aims at what is usual, and not at what is necessary and eternal; that thus, historical Christianity destroys the power of preaching, by withdrawing it from the exploration of the moral nature of man, where the sublime is, where are the resources of astonishment and power. What a cruel injustice it is to that Law, the joy of the whole earth, which alone can make thought dear and rich; that Law whose fatal sureness the astronomical orbits poorly emulate, that it is travestied and depreciated, that it is behooted and behowled, and not a trait, not a word of it articulated. The pulpit in losing sight of this Law, loses its reason, and gropes after it knows not what. And for want of this culture, the soul of the community is sick and faithless. It wants nothing so much as a stern, high, stoical, Christian discipline, to make it know itself and the divinity that speaks through it. Now man is ashamed of himself; he skulks and sneaks through the world, to be tolerated, to be pitied, and scarcely in a thousand years does any man dare to be wise and good, and so draw after him the tears and blessings of his kind.

Certainly there have been periods when, from the inactivity of the intellect on certain truths, a greater faith was possible in names and persons. The Puritans in England and America, found in the Christ of the Catholic Church, and in the dogmas inherited from Rome, scope for their austere piety, and their longings for civil freedom. But their creed is passing away, and none arises in its room. I think no man can go with his thoughts about him into one of our churches, without feeling, that what hold the public worship had on men is gone, or going. It has lost its grasp on the affection of the good, and the fear of the bad. In the country, neighborhoods, half parishes are *signing off,*—to use the local term. It is already beginning to indicate character and religion to withdraw from the religious meetings. I have heard a devout person, who prized the Sabbath, say in bitterness of heart, "On Sundays, it seems wicked to go to church." And the motive, that holds the best there, is now only a hope and a waiting. What was once a mere circumstance, that the best and the worst men in the parish, the poor and the rich, the learned and the ignorant, young and old, should meet one day as fellows in one house, in sign of an equal right in the soul,—has come to be a paramount motive for going thither.

My friends, in these two errors, I think, I find the causes of a decaying church and a wasting unbelief. And what greater calamity can fall upon a nation, than the loss of worship? Then all things go to decay. Genius leaves the temple, to haunt the senate, or the market. Literature becomes frivolous. Science is cold. The eye of youth is not lighted by the hope of other worlds, and age is without honor. Society lives to trifles, and when men die, we do not mention them.

And now, my brothers, you will ask, What in these desponding days can be done by us? The remedy is already declared in the ground of our complaint of the Church. We have contrasted the Church with the soul. In the soul, then, let the redemption be sought. Wherever a man comes, there comes revolution. The old is for slaves. When a man comes, all books are legible, all things transparent, all religions are forms. He is religious. Man is the wonderworker. He is seen amid miracles. All men bless and curse. He saith yea and nay, only. The stationariness of religion; the assumption that the age of inspiration is past, that the Bible is closed; the fear of degrading the character of Jesus by representing him as a man; indicate with sufficient clearness the falsehood of our theology. It is the office of a true teacher to show us that God is, not was; that He speaketh, not spake. The true Christianity,—a faith like Christ's in the infinitude of man,—is lost. None believeth in the soul of man, but only in some man or person old and departed. Ah me! no man goeth alone. All men go in flocks to this saint or that poet, avoiding the God who seeth in secret. They cannot see in secret; they love to be blind in public. They think society wiser than their soul, and know not that one soul, and their soul, is wiser than the whole world. See how nations and races flit by on the sea of time, and leave no ripple to tell where they floated or sunk, and one good soul shall make the name of Moses, or of Zeno, or of Zoroaster, reverend forever. None essayeth the stern ambition to be the Self of the nation, and of nature, but each would be an easy secondary to some Christian scheme, or sectarian connection, or some eminent man. Once leave your own knowledge of God, your own sentiment, and take secondary knowledge, as St. Paul's, or George Fox's, or Swedenborg's, and you get wide from God with every year this secondary form lasts, and if, as now, for centuries,—the chasm yawns to that breadth, that man can scarcely be convinced there is in them anything divine.

Let me admonish you, first of all, to go alone; to refuse the good models, even those which are sacred in the imagination of men, and dare to love God without mediator or veil. Friends enough you shall find who will hold up to your emulation Wesleys and Oberlins, Saints and Prophets. Thank God for these good men, but say, "I also am a man." Imitation cannot go above its model. The imitator dooms himself to hopeless mediocrity.[4] The inventor did it, because it was natural to him, and so in him it has a charm. In the imitator, something else is natural, and he bereaves himself of his own beauty, to come short of another man's.

Yourself a newborn bard of the Holy Ghost,—cast behind you all conformity, and acquaint men at first hand with Deity. Look to it first and only, that fashion, custom, authority, pleasure, and money, are nothing to you,—are not bandages over your eyes, that you cannot see,—but live with the privilege of the immeasurable mind. Not too anxious to visit periodically all families and each family in your parish connection,—when you meet one of these men or women, be to them a divine man; be to them thought and virtue; let their timid aspirations find in you a friend; let their trampled instincts be genially tempted out in your atmosphere; let their doubts know that you have doubted, and their wonder feel that you have wondered. By trusting your own heart, you shall gain more confidence in other men. For all our penny-wisdom, for all our soul-destroying slavery to habit, it is not to be doubted, that all men have sublime thoughts; that all men value the few real hours of life; they love to be heard; they love to be caught up into the vision of principles. We mark with light in the memory the few interviews we have had, in the dreary years of routine and of sin, with souls that made our souls wiser; that spoke what we thought; that told us what we knew; that gave us leave to be what we inly were. Discharge to men the priestly office, and, present or absent, you shall be followed with their love as by an angel.

And, to this end, let us not aim at common degrees of merit. Can we not leave, to such as love it, the virtue that glitters for the commendation of society, and ourselves pierce the deep solitudes of absolute ability and worth? We easily come up to the standard of goodness in society. Society's praise can be cheaply secured, and almost all men are content with those easy merits; but the instant effect of conversing with God, will be, to put them away. There are persons who are not actors, not speakers, but influences; persons too great for fame, for display; who disdain eloquence; to whom all we call art and artist, seems too nearly allied to show and by-ends, to the exaggeration of the finite and selfish, and loss of the universal. The orators, the poets, the commanders encroach on us only as fair women do, by our allowance and homage. Slight them by preoccupation of mind, slight them, as you can well afford to do, by high and universal aims, and they instantly feel that you have right, and that it is in lower places that they must shine. They also feel your right; for they with you are open to the influx of the all-knowing Spirit, which annihilates before its broad noon the little shades and gradations of intelligence in the composition we call wiser and wisest.

In such high communion, let us study the grand strokes of rectitude: a bold benevolence, an independence of friends, so that not the unjust wishes of those who love us, shall impair our freedom, but we shall resist for truth's sake the freest flow of kindness, and appeal to sympathies far in advance; and,—what is the highest form in which we know this beautiful element,—a certain solidity of merit, that has nothing to do with opinion, and which is so essentially and manifestly virtue, that it is taken for granted, that the right, the brave, the generous step will be taken by it, and nobody thinks of commending it. You would compliment a coxcomb* doing a good act, but you would not praise an angel. The silence that accepts merit as the most natural thing in the world, is the highest applause. Such souls, when they appear, are the Imperial Guard of Virtue, the perpetual reserve, the dictators of fortune. One

---

*A fool.

needs not praise their courage,—they are the heart and soul of nature. O my friends, there are resources in us on which we have not drawn. There are men who rise refreshed on hearing a threat; men to whom a crisis which intimidates and paralyzes the majority,—demanding not the faculties of prudence and thrift, but comprehension, immovableness, the readiness of sacrifice,—comes graceful and beloved as a bride. Napoleon said of Massena, that he was not himself until the battle began to go against him; then, when the dead began to fall in ranks around him, awoke his powers of combination, and he put on terror and victory as a robe. So it is in rugged crises, in unweariable endurance, and in aims which put sympathy out of question, that the angel is shown. But these are heights that we can scarce remember and look up to, without contrition and shame. Let us thank God that such things exist.

And now let us do what we can to rekindle the smouldering, nigh quenched fire on the altar. The evils of the church that now is are manifest. The question returns, What shall we do? I confess, all attempts to project and establish a Cultus with new rites and forms seem to me vain. Faith makes us, and not we it, and faith makes its own forms. All attempts to contrive a system are as cold as the new worship introduced by the French to the goddess of Reason,—to-day, pasteboard and filigree, and ending to-morrow in madness and murder.[5] Rather let the breath of new life be breathed by you through the forms already existing. For, if once you are alive, you shall find they shall become plastic* and new. The remedy to their deformity is, first, soul, and second, soul, and evermore, soul. A whole popedom† of forms, one pulsation of virtue can uplift and vivify. Two inestimable advantages Christianity has given us; first; the Sabbath, the jubilee of the whole world; whose light dawns welcome alike into the closet of the philosopher, into the garret of toil, and into prison cells, and everywhere suggests, even to the vile, the dignity of spiritual being. Let it stand forevermore, a temple, which new love, new faith, new sight shall restore to more than its first splendor to mankind. And secondly, the institution of preaching,—the speech of man to men,—essentially the most flexible of all organs, of all forms. What hinders that now, everywhere, in pulpits, in lecture-rooms, in houses, in fields, wherever the invitation of men or your own occasions lead you, you speak the very truth, as your life and conscience

---

*Malleable.

†That is, a rigid hierarchy, as in the Roman Catholic Church.

teach it, and cheer the waiting, fainting hearts of men with new hope and new revelation?

I look for the hour when that supreme Beauty, which ravished the souls of those eastern men, and chiefly of those Hebrews, and through their lips spoke oracles to all time, shall speak in the West also. The Hebrew and Greek Scriptures contain immortal sentences, that have been bread of life to millions. But they have no epical integrity; are fragmentary; are not shown in their order to the intellect. I look for the new Teacher, that shall follow so far those shining laws that he shall see them come full circle; shall see their rounding complete grace; shall see the world to be the mirror of the soul, shall see the identity of the law of gravitation with purity of heart; and shall show that the Ought, that Duty, is one thing with Science, with Beauty, and with Joy.

Man the Reformer[1]

A Lecture Read before the Mechanics' Apprentices' Library Association, Boston, January 25, 1841.

MR. PRESIDENT, AND GENTLEMEN,

I wish to offer to your consideration some thoughts on the particular and general relations of man as a reformer. I shall assume that the aim of each young man in this association is the very highest that belongs to a rational mind. Let it be granted, that our life, as we lead it, is common and mean; that some of those offices and functions for which we were mainly created are grown so rare in society, that the memory of them is only kept alive in old books and in dim traditions; that prophets and poets, that beautiful and perfect men, we are not now, no, nor have even seen such; that some sources of human instruction are almost unnamed and unknown among us; that the community in which we live will hardly bear to be told that every man should be open to ecstasy or a divine illumination, and his daily walk elevated by intercourse with the spiritual world. Grant all this, as we must, yet I suppose none of my auditors will deny that we ought to seek to establish ourselves in such disciplines and courses as will deserve that guidance and clearer communication with the spiritual nature. And further, I will not dissemble my hope, that each person whom I address has felt his own call to cast aside all evil customs, timidities, and limitations, and to be in his place a free and helpful man, a reformer, a benefactor, not content to slip along through the world like a footman or a spy, escaping by his nimbleness and apologies as many knocks as he can, but a brave and upright man, who must find or cut a straight road to everything excellent in the earth, and not only go honorably himself, but make it easier for all who follow him, to go in honor and with benefit.

In the history of the world the doctrine of Reform had never such scope as at the present hour. Lutherans, Hernhutters, Jesuits, Monks, Quakers, Knox, Wesley, Swedenborg, Bentham, in their accusations of society, all respected something,—church or state, literature or history, domestic usages, the market town, the dinner table, coined money. But now all these and all things else hear the trumpet, and must rush to judgment,—Christianity, the laws, commerce, schools, the farm, the laboratory; and not a kingdom, town, statute, rite, calling, man, or woman, but is threatened by the new spirit.

What if some of the objections whereby our institutions are assailed are extreme and speculative, and the reformers tend to idealism; that only shows the extravagance of the abuses which have driven the mind into the opposite extreme. It is when your facts and persons grow unreal and fantastic by too much falsehood, that the scholar flies for refuge to the world of ideas, and aims to recruit and replenish nature from that source. Let ideas establish their legitimate sway again in society, let life be fair and poetic, and the scholars will gladly be lovers, citizens, and philanthropists.

It will afford no security from the new ideas, that the old nations, the laws of centuries, the property and institutions of a hundred cities, are built on other foundations. The demon of reform has a secret door into the heart of every lawmaker, of every inhabitant of every city. The fact, that a new thought and hope have dawned in your breast, should apprise you that in the same hour a new light broke in upon a thousand private hearts. That secret which you would fain keep,—as soon as you go abroad, lo! there is one standing on the doorstep, to tell you the same. There is not the most bronzed and sharpened money-catcher, who does not, to your consternation, almost, quail and shake the moment he hears a question prompted by the new ideas. We thought he had some semblance of ground to stand upon, that such as he at least would die hard; but he trembles and flees. Then the scholar says, "Cities and coaches shall never impose on me again; for, behold, every solitary dream of mine is rushing to fulfilment. That fancy I had, and hesitated to utter because you would laugh,—the broker, the attorney, the market-man are saying the same thing. Had I waited a day longer to speak, I had been too late. Behold, State Street* thinks, and Wall Street doubts, and begins to prophecy!"

It cannot be wondered at, that this general inquest into abuses should arise in the bosom of society, when one considers the practical impediments that stand in the way of virtuous young men. The young man, on entering life, finds the way to lucrative employments blocked with abuses. The ways of trade are grown selfish to the borders of theft, and supple to the borders (if not beyond the borders) of fraud. The employments of commerce are not intrinsically unfit for a man, or less

---

*The symbol of mercantile interests in Boston, as Wall Street is the symbol of financial interests in New York.

genial to his faculties, but these are now in their general course so viti-
ated by derelictions and abuses at which all connive, that it requires
more vigor and resources than can be expected of every young man, to
right himself in them; he is lost in them; he cannot move hand or foot
in them. Has he genius and virtue? the less does he find them fit for him
to grow in, and if he would thrive in them, he must sacrifice all the bril-
liant dreams of boyhood and youth as dreams; he must forget the
prayers of his childhood; and must take on him the harness of routine
and obsequiousness. If not so minded, nothing is left him but to begin
the world anew, as he does who puts the spade into the ground for food.
We are all implicated, of course, in this charge; it is only necessary to ask
a few questions as to the progress of the articles of commerce from the
fields where they grew, to our houses, to become aware that we eat and
drink and wear perjury and fraud in a hundred commodities. How
many articles of daily consumption are furnished us from the West In-
dies; yet it is said, that, in the Spanish islands, the venality of the officers
of the government has passed into usage, and that no article passes into
our ships which has not been fraudulently cheapened. In the Spanish is-
lands, every agent or factor of the Americans, unless he be a consul, has
taken oath that he is a Catholic, or has caused a priest to make that dec-
laration for him. The abolitionist has shown us our dreadful debt to the
Southern negro. In the island of Cuba, in addition to the ordinary
abominations of slavery, it appears, only men are bought for the plan-
tations, and one dies in ten every year, of these miserable bachelors, to
yield us sugar. I leave for those who have the knowledge the part of sift-
ing the oaths of our custom-houses; I will not inquire into the oppres-
sion of the sailors; I will not pry into the usages of our retail trade. I
content myself with the fact, that the general system of our trade, (apart
from the blacker traits which, I hope, are exceptions denounced and un-
shared by all reputable men,) is a system of selfishness; is not dictated
by the high sentiments of human nature; is not measured by the exact
law of reciprocity; much less by the sentiments of love and heroism, but
is a system of distrust, of concealment, of superior keenness, not of giv-
ing but of taking advantage. It is not that which a man delights to un-
lock to a noble friend; which he meditates on with joy and self-approval
in his hour of love and aspiration; but rather what he then puts out of
sight, only showing the brilliant result, and atoning for the manner of
acquiring, by the manner of expending it. I do not charge the merchant
or the manufacturer. The sins of our trade belong to no class, to no in-
dividual. One plucks, one distributes, one eats. Every body partakes,
every body confesses,—with cap and knee volunteers his confession, yet

none feels himself accountable. He did not create the abuse; he cannot alter it. What is he? an obscure private person who must get his bread. That is the vice,—that no one feels himself called to act for man, but only as a fraction of man. It happens therefore that all such ingenuous souls as feel within themselves the irrepressible strivings of a noble aim, who by the law of their nature must act simply, find these ways of trade unfit for them, and they come forth from it. Such cases are becoming more numerous every year.

But by coming out of trade you have not cleared yourself. The trail of the serpent reaches into all the lucrative professions and practices of man. Each has its own wrongs. Each finds a tender and very intelligent conscience a disqualification for success. Each requires of the practitioner a certain shutting of the eyes, a certain dapperness and compliance, an acceptance of customs, a sequestration from the sentiments of generosity and love, a compromise of private opinion and lofty integrity. Nay, the evil custom reaches into the whole institution of property, until our laws which establish and protect it, seem not to be the issue of love and reason, but of selfishness. Suppose a man is so unhappy as to be born a saint, with keen perceptions, but with the conscience and love of an angel, and he is to get his living in the world; he finds himself excluded from all lucrative works; he has no farm, and he cannot get one; for, to earn money enough to buy one, requires a sort of concentration toward money, which is the selling himself for a number of years, and to him the present hour is as sacred and inviolable as any future hour. Of course, whilst another man has no land, my title to mine, your title to yours, is at once vitiated. Inextricable seem to be the twinings and tendrils of this evil, and we all involve ourselves in it the deeper by forming connections, by wives and children, by benefits and debts.

Considerations of this kind have turned the attention of many philanthropic and intelligent persons to the claims of manual labor, as a part of the education of every young man. If the accumulated wealth of the past generation is thus tainted,—no matter how much of it is offered to us,—we must begin to consider if it were not the nobler part to renounce it, and to put ourselves into primary relations with the soil and nature, and abstaining from whatever is dishonest and unclean, to take each of us bravely his part, with his own hands, in the manual labor of the world.

But it is said, "What! will you give up the immense advantages reaped from the division of labor, and set every man to make his own shoes, bureau, knife, wagon, sails, and needle? This would be to put men back into barbarism by their own act." I see no instant prospect of a virtuous revolution; yet I confess, I should not be pained at a change which threatened a loss of some of the luxuries or conveniences of society, if it proceeded from a preference of the agricultural life out of the belief, that our primary duties as men could be better discharged in that calling. Who could regret to see a high conscience and a purer taste exercising a sensible effect on young men in their choice of occupation, and thinning the ranks of competition in the labors of commerce, of law, and of state? It is easy to see that the inconvenience would last but a short time. This would be great action, which always opens the eyes of men. When many persons shall have done this, when the majority shall admit the necessity of reform in all these institutions, their abuses will be redressed, and the way will be open again to the advantages which arise from the division of labor, and a man may select the fittest employment for his peculiar talent again, without compromise.

But quite apart from the emphasis which the times give to the doctrine, that the manual labor of society ought to be shared among all the members, there are reasons proper to every individual, why he should not be deprived of it. The use of manual labor is one which never grows obsolete, and which is inapplicable to no person. A man should have a farm or a mechanical craft for his culture. We must have a basis for our higher accomplishments, our delicate entertainments of poetry and philosophy, in the work of our hands. We must have an antagonism in the tough world for all the variety of our spiritual faculties, or they will not be born. Manual labor is the study of the external world. The advantage of riches remains with him who procured them, not with the heir. When I go into my garden with a spade, and dig a bed, I feel such an exhilaration and health, that I discover that I have been defrauding myself all this time in letting others do for me what I should have done with my own hands. But not only health, but education is in the work. Is it possible that I who get indefinite quantities of sugar, hominy,* cotton, buckets, crockery ware, and letter paper, by simply signing my name once in three months to a cheque in favor of John Smith and Co., traders, get the fair share of exercise to my faculties by that act, which nature intended for me in making all these far-fetched matters important to my comfort? It is Smith himself, and his carriers, and dealers, and manufacturers, it is the sailor, the hidedrogher,† the butcher, the

---

*Whole or ground hulled corn from which the bran and germ have been removed, used to make grits.

†Coastal vessel trading in hides; the master of such a vessel.

negro, the hunter, and the planter, who have intercepted the sugar of the sugar, and the cotton of the cotton. They have got the education, I only the commodity. This were all very well if I were necessarily absent, being detained by work of my own, like theirs, work of the same faculties; then should I be sure of my hands and feet, but now I feel some shame before my wood-chopper, my ploughman, and my cook, for they have some sort of self-sufficiency, they can contrive without my aid to bring the day and year round, but I depend on them, and have not earned by use a right to my arms and feet.

Consider further the difference between the first and second owner of property. Every species of property is preyed on by its own enemies, as iron by rust; timber by rot; cloth by moths; provisions by mould, putridity, or vermin; money by thieves; an orchard by insects; a planted field by weeds and the inroad of cattle; a stock of cattle by hunger; a road by rain and frost; a bridge by freshets. And whoever takes any of these things into his possession, takes the charge of defending them from this troop of enemies, or of keeping them in repair. A man who supplies his own want, who builds a raft or a boat to go a fishing, finds it easy to caulk it, or put in a thole-pin, or mend the rudder. What he gets only as fast as he wants for his own ends, does not embarrass him, or take away his sleep with looking after. But when he comes to give all the goods he has year after year collected, in one estate to his son, house, orchard, ploughed land, cattle, bridges, hardware, wooden-ware, carpets, cloths, provisions, books, money, and cannot give him the skill and experience which made or collected these, and the method and place they have in his own life, the son finds his hands full,—not to use these things,—but to look after them and defend them from their natural enemies. To him they are not means, but masters. Their enemies will not remit; rust, mould, vermin, rain, sun, freshet, fire, all seize their own, fill him with vexation, and he is converted from the owner into a watchman or a watch-dog to this magazine* of old and new chattels. What a change! Instead of the masterly good humor, and sense of power, and fertility of resource in himself; instead of those strong and learned hands, those piercing and learned eyes, that supple body, and that mighty and prevailing heart, which the father had, whom nature loved and feared, whom snow and rain, water and land, beast and fish seemed all to know and to serve, we have now a puny, protected person, guarded by walls and curtains, stoves and down beds, coaches, and men-servants

---

*Place for keeping military stores, weapons, ammunition, provisions, etc.

and women-servants from the earth and the sky, and who, bred to depend on all these, is made anxious by all that endangers those possessions, and is forced to spend so much time in guarding them, that he has quite lost sight of their original use, namely, to help him to his ends,—to the prosecution of his love; to the helping of his friend, to the worship of his God, to the enlargement of his knowledge, to the serving of his country, to the indulgence of his sentiment, and he is now what is called a rich man,—the menial and runner of his riches.

Hence it happens that the whole interest of history lies in the fortunes of the poor. Knowledge, Virtue, Power are the victories of man over his necessities, his march to the dominion of the world. Every man ought to have this opportunity to conquer the world for himself. Only such persons interest us, Spartans, Romans, Saracens, English, Americans, who have stood in the jaws of need, and have by their own wit and might extricated themselves, and made man victorious.

I do not wish to overstate this doctrine of labor, or insist that every man should be a farmer, any more than that every man should be a lexicographer.* In general, one may say, that the husbandman's† is the oldest, and most universal profession, and that where a man does not yet discover in himself any fitness for one work more than another, this may be preferred. But the doctrine of the Farm is merely this, that every man ought to stand in primary relations with the work of the world, ought to do it himself, and not to suffer the accident of his having a purse in his pocket, or his having been bred to some dishonorable and injurious craft, to sever him from those duties; and for this reason, that labor is God's education; that he only is a sincere learner, he only can become a master, who learns the secrets of labor, and who by real cunning extorts from nature its sceptre.

Neither would I shut my ears to the plea of the learned professions, of the poet, the priest, the lawgiver, and men of study generally; namely, that in the experience of all men of that class, the amount of manual labor which is necessary to the maintenance of a family, indisposes and disqualifies for intellectual exertion. I know, it often, perhaps usually, happens, that where there is a fine organization apt for poetry and philosophy, that individual finds himself compelled to wait on his thoughts, to waste several days that he may enhance and glorify one; and is better taught by a moderate and dainty exercise, such as rambling

---

*Writer of dictionaries.
†Farmer.

in the fields, rowing, skating, hunting, than by the downright drudgery of the farmer and the smith. I would not quite forget the venerable counsel of the Egyptian mysteries, which declared that "there were two pairs of eyes in man, and it is requisite that the pair which are beneath should be closed, when the pair that are above them perceive, and that when the pair above are closed, those which are beneath should be opened." Yet I will suggest that no separation from labor can be without some loss of power and of truth to the seer himself; that, I doubt not, the faults and vices of our literature and philosophy, their too great fineness, effeminacy, and melancholy, are attributable to the enervated and sickly habits of the literary class. Better that the book should not be quite so good, and the bookmaker abler and better, and not himself often a ludicrous contrast to all that he has written.

But granting that for ends so sacred and dear, some relaxation must be had, I think, that if a man find in himself any strong bias to poetry, to art, to the contemplative life, drawing him to these things with a devotion incompatible with good husbandry, that man ought to reckon early with himself, and, respecting the compensations of the Universe, ought to ransom himself from the duties of economy, by a certain rigor and privation in his habits. For privileges so rare and grand, let him not stint to pay a great tax. Let him be a cænobite,* a pauper, and if need be, celibate also. Let him learn to eat his meals standing, and to relish the taste of fair water and black bread. He may leave to others the costly conveniences of housekeeping, and large hospitality, and the possession of works of art. Let him feel that genius is a hospitality, and that he who can create works of art needs not collect them. He must live in a chamber, and postpone his self-indulgence, forewarned and forearmed against that frequent misfortune of men of genius,—the taste for luxury. This is the tragedy of genius,—attempting to drive along the ecliptic† with one horse of the heavens and one horse of the earth, there is only discord and ruin and downfall to chariot and charioteer.

The duty that every man should assume his own vows, should call the institutions of society to account, and examine their fitness to him, gains in emphasis, if we look at our modes of living. Is our housekeeping sacred and honorable? Does it raise and inspire us, or does it cripple us instead? I ought to be armed by every part and function of my

---

*Member of a religious order living in community, as in a convent or monastery.
†The great circle formed by the intersection of the plane of Earth's orbit with the celestial sphere; the apparent annual path of the sun in the heavens.

household, by all my social function, by my economy, by my feastings, by my voting, by my traffic. Yet I am almost no party to any of these things. Custom does it for me, gives me no power therefrom, and runs me in debt to boot. We spend our incomes for paint and paper, for a hundred trifles, I know not what, and not for the things of a man. Our expense is almost all for conformity. It is for cake that we run in debt; 't is not the intellect, not the heart, not beauty, not worship, that costs so much. Why needs any man be rich? Why must he have horses, fine garments, handsome apartments, access to public houses, and places of amusement? Only for want of thought. Give his mind a new image, and he flees into a solitary garden or garret to enjoy it, and is richer with that dream, than the fee of a county could make him. But we are first thoughtless, and then find that we are moneyless. We are first sensual, and then must be rich. We dare not trust our wit for making our house pleasant to our friend, and so we buy ice-creams. He is accustomed to carpets, and we have not sufficient character to put floor-cloths out of his mind whilst he stays in the house, and so we pile the floor with carpets. Let the house rather be a temple of the Furies of Lacedæmon,* formidable and holy to all, which none but a Spartan may enter or so much as behold. As soon as there is faith, as soon as there is society, comfits†️ and cushions will be left to slaves. Expense will be inventive and heroic. We shall eat hard and lie hard, we shall dwell like the ancient Romans in narrow tenements, whilst our public edifices, like theirs, will be worthy for their proportion of the landscape in which we set them, for conversation, for art, for music, for worship. We shall be rich to great purposes; poor only for selfish ones.

Now what help for these evils? How can the man who has learned but one art, procure all the conveniences of life honestly? Shall we say all we think?—Perhaps with his own hands. Suppose he collects or makes them ill;—yet he has learned their lesson. If he cannot do that.— Then perhaps he can go without. Immense wisdom and riches are in that. It is better to go without, than to have them at too great a cost. Let us learn the meaning of economy. Economy is a high, humane office, a sacrament, when its aim is grand; when it is the prudence of simple tastes, when it is practised for freedom, or love, or devotion. Much of the economy which we see in houses, is of a base origin, and is best kept out of sight. Parched corn eaten to-day that I may have roast fowl to my

---

*Lacedaemon was another name for the Greek city-state Sparta.
†Candy containing a nut or pieces of fruit, often offered to guests.

dinner on Sunday, is a baseness; but parched corn and a house with one apartment, that I may be free of all perturbations, that I may be serene and docile to what the mind shall speak, and girt and road-ready for the lowest mission of knowledge or goodwill, is frugality for gods and heroes.

Can we not learn the lesson of self-help? Society is full of infirm people, who incessantly summon others to serve them. They contrive everywhere to exhaust for their single comfort the entire means and appliances of that luxury to which our invention has yet attained. Sofas, ottomans, stoves, wine, game-fowl, spices, perfumes, rides, the theatre, entertainments,—all these they want, they need, and whatever can be suggested more than these, they crave also, as if it was the bread which should keep them from starving; and if they miss any one, they represent themselves as the most wronged and most wretched persons on earth. One must have been born and bred with them to know how to prepare a meal for their learned stomach. Meantime, they never bestir themselves to serve another person; not they! they have a great deal more to do for themselves than they can possibly perform, nor do they once perceive the cruel joke of their lives, but the more odious they grow, the sharper is the tone of their complaining and craving. Can anything be so elegant as to have few wants and to serve them one's self, so as to have somewhat left to give, instead of being always prompt to grab? It is more elegant to answer one's own needs, than to be richly served; inelegant perhaps it may look to-day, and to a few, but it is an elegance forever and to all.

I do not wish to be absurd and pedantic in reform. I do not wish to push my criticism on the state of things around me to that extravagant mark, that shall compel me to suicide, or to an absolute isolation from the advantages of civil society. If we suddenly plant our foot, and say,— I will neither eat nor drink nor wear nor touch any food or fabric which I do not know to be innocent, or deal with any person whose whole manner of life is not clear and rational, we shall stand still. Whose is so? Not mine; not thine; not his. But I think we must clear ourselves each one by the interrogation, whether we have earned our bread to-day by the hearty contribution of our energies to the common benefit? and we must not cease to *tend* to the correction of these flagrant wrongs, by laying one stone aright every day.

But the idea which now begins to agitate society has a wider scope than our daily employments, our households, and the institutions of property. We are to revise the whole of our social structure, the state, the school, religion, marriage, trade, science, and explore their foundations

in our own nature; we are to see that the world not only fitted the for-
mer men, but fits us, and to clear ourselves of every usage which has not
its roots in our own mind. What is a man born for but to be a Reformer,
a Re-maker of what man has made; a renouncer of lies; a restorer of
truth and good, imitating that great Nature which embosoms us all, and
which sleeps no moment on an old past, but every hour repairs herself,
yielding us every morning a new day, and with every pulsation a new
life? Let him renounce everything which is not true to him, and put all
his practices back on their first thoughts, and do nothing for which he
has not the whole world for his reason. If there are inconveniences, and
what is called ruin in the way, because we have so enervated and
maimed ourselves, yet it would be like dying of perfumes to sink in the
effort to reattach the deeds of every day to the holy and mysterious re-
cesses of life.

The power, which is at once spring and regulator in all efforts of re-
form, is the conviction that there is an infinite worthiness in man which
will appear at the call of worth, and that all particular reforms are the
removing of some impediment. Is it not the highest duty that man
should be honored in us? I ought not to allow any man, because he has
broad lands, to feel that he is rich in my presence. I ought to make him
feel that I can do without his riches, that I cannot be bought,—neither
by comfort, neither by pride,—and though I be utterly penniless, and
receiving bread from him, that he is the poor man beside me. And if, at
the same time, a woman or a child discovers a sentiment of piety, or a
juster way of thinking than mine, I ought to confess it by my respect and
obedience, though it go to alter my whole way of life.

The Americans have many virtues, but they have not Faith and
Hope. I know no two words whose meaning is more lost sight of. We
use these words as if they were as obsolete as Selah and Amen.* And yet
they have the broadest meaning, and the most cogent application to
Boston in 1841. The Americans have no faith. They rely on the power of
a dollar; they are deaf to a sentiment. They think you may talk the north
wind down as easily as raise society; and no class more faithless than the
scholars or intellectual men. Now if I talk with a sincere wise man, and
my friend, with a poet, with a conscientious youth who is still under the
dominion of his own wild thoughts, and not yet harnessed in the team

---

Selah: term that appears regularly in the biblical book of Psalms, thought to indi-
cate a change in intonation, or a pause. *Amen:* Hebrew term meaning "it is so; so
be it."

of society to drag with us all in the ruts of custom, I see at once how paltry is all this generation of unbelievers, and what a house of cards their institutions are, and I see what one brave man, what one great thought executed might effect. I see that the reason of the distrust of the practical man in all theory, is his inability to perceive the means whereby we work. Look, he says, at the tools with which this world of yours is to be built. As we cannot make a planet, with atmosphere, rivers, and forests, by means of the best carpenters' or engineers' tools, with chemist's laboratory and smith's forge to boot,—so neither can we ever construct that heavenly society you prate of, out of foolish, sick, selfish men and women, such as we know them to be. But the believer not only beholds his heaven to be possible, but already to begin to exist,—not by the men or materials the statesman uses, but by men transfigured and raised above themselves by the power of principles. To principles something else is possible that transcends all the power of expedients.

Every great and commanding moment in the annals of the world is the triumph of some enthusiasm. The victories of the Arabs after Mahomet, who, in a few years, from a small and mean beginning, established a larger empire than that of Rome, is an example. They did they knew not what. The naked Derar,* horsed on an idea, was found an overmatch for a troop of Roman cavalry. The women fought like men, and conquered the Roman men. They were miserably equipped, miserably fed. They were Temperance troops. There was neither brandy nor flesh needed to feed them. They conquered Asia, and Africa, and Spain, on barley. The Caliph Omar's walking stick struck more terror into those who saw it, than another man's sword. His diet was barley bread: his sauce was salt; and oftentimes by way of abstinence he ate his bread without salt. His drink was water. His palace was built of mud; and when he left Medina to go to the conquest of Jerusalem, he rode on a red camel, with a wooden platter hanging at his saddle, with a bottle of water and two sacks, one holding barley, and the other dried fruits.

But there will dawn ere long on our politics, on our modes of living, a nobler morning than that Arabian faith, in the sentiment of love. This is the one remedy for all ills, the panacea of nature. We must be lovers, and at once the impossible becomes possible. Our age and history, for these thousand years, has not been the history of kindness, but of self-

---

*Reference to Derar Ebn Alazar, which Emerson took from Simon Ockley, *The History of the Saracens*, third edition (1757). The description below of the Caliph Omar is also taken from Ockley.

ishness. Our distrust is very expensive. The money we spend for courts and prisons is very ill laid out. We make, by distrust, the thief, and burglar, and incendiary, and by our court and jail we keep him so. An acceptance of the sentiment of love throughout Christendom for a season, would bring the felon and the outcast to our side in tears, with the devotion of his faculties to our service. See this wide society of laboring men and women. We allow ourselves to be served by them, we live apart from them, and meet them without a salute in the streets. We do not greet their talents, nor rejoice in their good fortune, nor foster their hopes, nor in the assembly of the people vote for what is dear to them. Thus we enact the part of the selfish noble and king from the foundation of the world. See, this tree always bears one fruit. In every household, the peace of a pair is poisoned by the malice, slyness, indolence, and alienation of domestics. Let any two matrons meet, and observe how soon their conversation turns on the troubles from their "*help*," as our phrase is. In every knot of laborers, the rich man does not feel himself among his friends,—and at the polls he finds them arrayed in a mass in distinct opposition to him. We complain that the politics of masses of the people are controlled by designing men, and led in opposition to manifest justice and the common weal, and to their own interest. But the people do not wish to be represented or ruled by the ignorant and base. They only vote for these, because they were asked with the voice and semblance of kindness. They will not vote for them long. They inevitably prefer wit and probity. To use an Egyptian metaphor, it is not their will for any long time "to raise the nails of wild beasts, and to depress the heads of the sacred birds."* Let our affection flow out to our fellows; it would operate in a day the greatest of all revolutions. It is better to work on institutions by the sun than by the wind. The state must consider the poor man, and all voices must speak for him. Every child that is born must have a just chance for his bread. Let the amelioration in our laws of property proceed from the concession of the rich, not from the grasping of the poor. Let us begin by habitual imparting. Let us understand that the equitable rule is, that no one should take more than his share, let him be ever so rich. Let me feel that I am to be a lover. I am to see to it that the world is the better for me, and to find my reward in the act. Love would put a new face on this weary old world in which we dwell as pagans and enemies too long, and

---

*From *Treatise of Synesius on Providence*, translated by Thomas Taylor and printed with his *Select Works of Plotinus* (1817).

it would warm the heart to see how fast the vain diplomacy of statesmen, the impotence of armies, and navies, and lines of defence, would be superseded by this unarmed child. Love will creep where it cannot go, will accomplish that by imperceptible methods,—being its own lever, fulcrum, and power,—which force could never achieve. Have you not seen in the woods, in a late autumn morning, a poor fungus or mushroom,—a plant without any solidity, nay, that seemed nothing but a soft mush or jelly,—by its constant, total, and inconceivably gentle pushing, manage to break its way up through the frosty ground, and actually to lift a hard crust on its head? It is the symbol of the power of kindness. The virtue of this principle in human society in application to great interests is obsolete and forgotten. Once or twice in history it has been tried in illustrious instances, with signal success. This great, overgrown, dead Christendom of ours still keeps alive at least the name of a lover of mankind. But one day all men will be lovers; and every calamity will be dissolved in the universal sunshine.

Will you suffer me to add one trait more to this portrait of man the reformer? The mediator between the spiritual and the actual world should have a great prospective prudence. An Arabian poet describes his hero by saying,

> "Sunshine was he
> In the winter day;
> And in the midsummer
> Coolness and shade."*

He who would help himself and others, should not be a subject of irregular and interrupted impulses of virtue, but a continent, persisting, immovable person,—such as we have seen a few scattered up and down in time for the blessing of the world, men who have in the gravity of their nature a quality which answers to the fly-wheel in a mill, which distributes the motion equally over all the wheels, and hinders it from falling unequally and suddenly in destructive shocks. It is better that joy should be spread over all the day in the form of strength, than that it should be concentrated into ecstasies, full of danger and followed by reactions. There is a sublime prudence, which is the very highest that we know of man, which, believing in a vast future,—sure of more to come

---

*Emerson notes in his journals that the translation from the Arabic was by Goethe; the English version is apparently Emerson's translation from the German.

than is yet seen,—postpones always the present hour to the whole life; postpones talent to genius, and special results to character. As the merchant gladly takes money from his income to add to his capital, so is the great man very willing to lose particular powers and talents, so that he gain in the elevation of his life. The opening of the spiritual senses disposes men ever to greater sacrifices, to leave their signal talents, their best means and skill of procuring a present success, their power and their fame,—to cast all things behind, in the insatiable thirst for divine communications. A purer fame, a greater power rewards the sacrifice. It is the conversion of our harvest into seed. As the farmer casts into the ground the finest ears of his grain, the time will come when we too shall hold nothing back, but shall eagerly convert more than we now possess into means and powers,[2] when we shall be willing to sow the sun and the moon for seeds.

The Transcendentalist[1]

A Lecture Read at the Masonic Temple, Boston, January, 1842.

THE FIRST THING WE have to say respecting what are called *new views* here in New England, at the present time, is, that they are not new, but the very oldest of thoughts cast into the mould of these new times. The light is always identical in its composition, but it falls on a great variety of objects, and by so falling is first revealed to us, not in its own form, for it is formless, but in theirs; in like manner, thought only appears in the objects it classifies. What is popularly called Transcendentalism among us, is Idealism; Idealism as it appears in 1842. As thinkers, mankind have ever divided into two sects, Materialists and Idealists; the first class founding on experience, the second on consciousness; the first class beginning to think from the data of the senses, the second class perceive that the senses are not final, and say, the senses give us representations of things, but what are the things themselves, they cannot tell. The materialist insists on facts, on history, on the force of circumstances, and the animal wants of man; the idealist on the power of Thought and of Will, on inspiration, on miracle, on individual culture. These two modes of thinking are both natural, but the idealist contends that his way of thinking is in higher nature. He concedes all that the other affirms, admits the impressions of sense, admits their coherency, their use and beauty, and then asks the materialist for his grounds of assurance, that things are as his senses represent them. But I, he says, affirm facts not affected by the illusions of sense, facts which are of the same nature as the faculty which reports them, and not liable to doubt; facts which in their first appearance to us assume a native superiority to material facts, degrading these into a language by which the first are to be spoken; facts which it only needs a retirement from the senses to discern. Every materialist will be an idealist; but an idealist can never go backward to be a materialist.

The idealist, in speaking of events, sees them as spirits. He does not deny the sensuous fact: by no means; but he will not see that alone. He does not deny the presence of this table, this chair, and the walls of this room, but he looks at these things as the reverse side of the tapestry, as the *other end*, each being a sequel of completion of a spiritual fact which nearly concerns him. This manner of looking at things, transfers every object in nature from an independent and anomalous position without there, into the consciousness. Even the materialist Condillac, perhaps the most logical expounder of materialism, was constrained to say, "Though we should soar into the heavens, though we should sink into the abyss, we never go out of ourselves; it is always our own thought that we perceive." What more could an idealist say?

The materialist, secure in the certainty of sensation, mocks at fine-spun theories, at star-gazers and dreamers, and believes that his life is solid, that he at least takes nothing for granted, but knows where he stands, and what he does. Yet how easy it is to show him, that he also is a phantom walking and working amid phantoms, and that he need only ask a question or two beyond his daily questions, to find his solid universe growing dim and impalpable before his sense. The sturdy capitalist, no matter how deep and square on blocks of Quincy granite* he lays the foundations of his banking-house or Exchange, must set it, at last, not on a cube corresponding to the angles of his structure, but on a mass of unknown materials and solidity, red-hot or white-hot, perhaps at the core, which rounds off to an almost perfect sphericity, and lies floating in soft air, and goes spinning away, dragging bank and banker with it at a rate of thousands of miles the hour, he knows not whither,— a bit of bullet, now glimmering, now darkling through a small cubic space on the edge of an unimaginable pit of emptiness. And this wild balloon, in which his whole venture is embarked, is a just symbol of his whole state and faculty. One thing, at least, he says is certain, and does not give me the headache, that figures do not lie; the multiplication table has been hitherto found unimpeachable truth; and moreover, if I put a gold eagle† in my safe, I find it again to-morrow;—but for these thoughts, I know not whence they are. They change and pass away. But ask him why he believes that an uniform experience will continue uniform, or on what grounds he founds his faith in his figures, and he will perceive that his mental fabric is built up on just as strange and quaking foundations as his proud edifice of stone.

In the order of thought, the materialist takes his departure from the external world, and esteems a man as one product of that. The idealist takes his departure from his consciousness, and reckons the world an appearance. The materialist respects sensible masses, Society, Govern-

---

*From the quarry in Quincy, Massachusetts, south of Boston.
†Gold coin of the United States valued at $10.

ment, social art, and luxury, every establishment, every mass, whether majority of numbers, or extent of space, or amount of objects, every social action. The idealist has another measure, which is metaphysical, namely, the *rank* which things themselves take in his consciousness; not at all, the size or appearance. Mind is the only reality, of which man and all other natures are better or worse reflectors. Nature, literature, history, are only subjective phenomena. Although in his action overpowered by the laws of action, and so, warmly coöperating with men, even preferring them to himself, yet when he speaks scientifically, or after the order of thought, he is constrained to degrade persons into representatives of truths. He does not respect labor, or the products of labor, namely, property, otherwise than as a manifold symbol, illustrating with wonderful fidelity of details the laws of being; he does not respect government, except as far as it reiterates the law of his mind; nor the church; nor charities; nor arts, for themselves; but hears, as at a vast distance, what they say, as if his consciousness would speak to him through a pantomimic scene. His thought,—that is the Universe. His experience inclines him to behold the procession of facts you call the world, as flowing perpetually outward from an invisible, unsounded centre in himself, centre alike of him and of them, and necessitating him to regard all things as having a subjective or relative existence, relative to that aforesaid Unknown Centre of him.

From this transfer of the world into the consciousness, this beholding of all things in the mind, follow easily his whole ethics. It is simpler to be self-dependent. The height, the deity of man is, to be self-sustained, to need no gift, no foreign force. Society is good when it does not violate me; but best when it is likest to solitude. Everything real is self-existent. Everything divine shares the self-existence of Deity. All that you call the world is the shadow of that substance which you are, the perpetual creation of the powers of thought, of those that are dependent and of those that are independent of your will. Do not cumber yourself with fruitless pains to mend and remedy remote effects; let the soul be erect, and all things will go well. You think me the child of my circumstances; I make my circumstance. Let any thought or motive of mine be different from that they are, the difference will transform my condition and economy. I—this thought which is called I,—is the mould into which the world is poured like melted wax. The mould is invisible, but the world betrays the shape of the mould. You call it the power of circumstance, but it is the power of me. Am I in harmony with myself? my position will seem to you just and commanding. Am I vicious and insane? my fortunes will seem to you obscure and descending. As I am, so shall I associate, and so shall I act; Cæsar's history will paint out Cæsar. Jesus acted so, because he thought so. I do not wish to overlook or to gainsay any reality; I say, I make my circumstance: but if you ask me, Whence am I? I feel like other men my relation to that Fact which cannot be spoken, or defined, nor even thought, but which exists, and will exist.

The Transcendentalist adopts the whole connection of spiritual doctrine. He believes in miracle, in the perpetual openness of the human mind to new influx of light and power; he believes in inspiration, and in ecstasy. He wishes that the spiritual principle should be suffered to demonstrate itself to the end, in all possible applications to the state of man, without the admission of anything unspiritual; that is, anything positive, dogmatic, personal. Thus, the spiritual measure of inspiration is the depth of the thought, and never, who said it? And so he resists all attempts to palm other rules and measures on the spirit than its own.

In action, he easily incurs the charge of antinomianism* by his avowal that he, who has the Lawgiver, may with safety not only neglect, but even contravene every written commandment. In the play of Othello, the expiring Desdemona absolves her husband of the murder, to her attendant Emilia. Afterwards, when Emilia charges him with the crime, Othello exclaims,

> "You heard her say herself it was not I."

Emilia replies,

> "The more angel she, and thou the blacker devil."†

Of this fine incident, Jacobi, the Transcendental moralist, makes use, with other parallel instances, in his reply to Fichte. Jacobi, refusing all measure of right and wrong except the determinations of the private spirit, remarks that there is no crime but has sometimes been a virtue. "I," he says, "am that atheist, that godless person who, in opposition to an imaginary doctrine of calculation, would lie as the dying Desdemona lied; would lie and deceive, as Pylades when he personated Orestes;

---

*Belief that one is exempt from the laws of church or state because one has received grace and therefore obeys the higher laws of God.

†Emerson quotes, somewhat inaccurately, from Shakespeare's *Othello* (act 5, scene 2). Emilia's words follow Othello's admission of guilt.

would assassinate like Timoleon; would perjure myself like Epaminondas, and John de Witt; I would resolve on suicide like Cato; I would commit sacrilege with David;* yea, and pluck ears of corn on the Sabbath,† for no other reason than that I was fainting for lack of food. For, I have assurance in myself, that, in pardoning these faults according to the letter, man exerts the sovereign right which the majesty of his being confers on him; he sets the seal of his divine nature to the grace he accords."‡

In like manner, if there is anything grand and daring in human thought or virtue, any reliance on the vast, the unknown; any presentiment; any extravagance of faith, the spiritualist adopts it as most in nature. The oriental mind has always tended to this largeness. Buddhism is an expression of it. The Buddhist who thanks no man, who says, "do not flatter your benefactors,"§ but who, in his conviction that every good deed can by no possibility escape its reward, will not deceive the benefactor by pretending that he has done more than he should, is a Transcendentalist.

You will see by this sketch that there is no such thing as a Transcendental *party;* that there is no pure Transcendentalist; that we know of none but prophets and heralds of such a philosophy; that all who by strong bias of nature have leaned to the spiritual side in doctrine, have stopped short of their goal. We have had many harbingers and forerunners; but of a purely spiritual life, history has afforded no example. I mean, we have yet no man who has leaned entirely on his character, and eaten angels' food, who, trusting to his sentiments, found life made of miracles; who, working for universal aims, found himself fed, he knew not how: clothed, sheltered, and weaponed, he knew not how, and yet it was done by his own hands. Only in the instinct of the lower animals, we find the suggestion of the methods of it, and something higher than our understanding. The squirrel hoards nuts, and the bee gathers honey, without knowing what they do, and they are thus provided for without selfishness or disgrace.

Shall we say, then, that Transcendentalism is the Saturnalia‖ or excess of Faith; the presentiment of a faith proper to man in his integrity, ex-

---

*Reference to the Bible, 1 Samuel 21.
†Reference to the Bible, Matthew 12:1.
‡Coleridge's translation (author's note).
§This unattributed quotation occurs frequently in Emerson's letters and journals.
‖Unrestrained celebration.

cessive only when his imperfect obedience hinders the satisfaction of his wish. Nature is transcendental, exists primarily, necessarily, ever works and advances, yet takes no thought for the morrow. Man owns the dignity of the life which throbs around him in chemistry, and tree, and animal, and in the involuntary functions of his own body; yet he is balked when he tries to fling himself into this enchanted circle, where all is done without degradation. Yet genius and virtue predict in man the same absence of private ends, and of condescension to circumstances, united with every trait and talent of beauty and power.

This way of thinking, falling on Roman times, made Stoic philosophers; falling on despotic times, made patriot Catos and Brutuses; falling on superstitious times, made prophets and apostles; on popish times, made protestants and ascetic monks, preachers of Faith against the preachers of Works; on prelatical times, made Puritans and Quakers; and falling on Unitarian and commercial times, makes the peculiar shades of Idealism which we know.

It is well known to most of my audience, that the Idealism of the present day acquired the name of Transcendental, from the use of that term by Immanuel Kant,[2] of Konigsberg, who replied to the skeptical philosophy of Locke, which insisted that there was nothing in the intellect which was not previously in the experience of the senses, by showing that there was a very important class of ideas, or imperative forms, which did not come by experience, but through which experience was acquired; that these were intuitions of the mind itself; and he denominated them *Transcendental* forms. The extraordinary profoundness and precision of that man's thinking have given vogue to his nomenclature, in Europe and America, to that extent, that whatever belongs to the class of intuitive thought, is popularly called at the present day *Transcendental*.

Although, as we have said, there is no pure Transcendentalist, yet the tendency to respect the intuitions, and to give them, at least in our creed, all authority over our experience, has deeply colored the conversation and poetry of the present day; and the history of genius and of religion in these times, though impure, and as yet not incarnated in any powerful individual, will be the history of this tendency.

It is a sign of our times, conspicuous to the coarsest observer, that many intelligent and religious persons withdraw themselves from the common labors and competitions of the market and the caucus, and betake themselves to a certain solitary and critical way of living, from which no solid fruit has yet appeared to justify their separation. They hold themselves aloof: they feel the disproportion between their faculties and the work offered them, and they prefer to ramble in the country and perish of ennui, to the degradation of such charities and such ambitions as the city can propose to them. They are striking work, and crying out for somewhat worthy to do! What they do, is done only because they are overpowered by the humanities that speak on all sides; and they consent to such labor as is open to them, though to their lofty dream the writing of Iliads or Hamlets, or the building of cities or empires seems drudgery.

Now every one must do after his kind, be he asp or angel, and these must. The question, which a wise man and a student of modern history will ask, is, what that kind is? And truly, as in ecclesiastical history we take so much pains to know what the Gnostics, what the Essenes, what the Manichees, and what the Reformers believed, it would not misbecome us to inquire nearer home, what these companions and contemporaries of ours think and do, at least so far as those thoughts and actions appear to be not accidental and personal, but common to many, and the inevitable flower of the Tree of Time. Our American literature and spiritual history are, we confess, in the optative mood; but whoso knows these seething brains, these admirable radicals, these unsocial worshippers, these talkers who talk the sun and moon away, will believe that this heresy cannot pass away without leaving its mark.

They are lonely; the spirit of their writing and conversation is lonely; they repel influences; they shun general society; they incline to shut themselves in their chamber in the house, to live in the country rather than in the town, and to find their tasks and amusements in solitude. Society, to be sure, does not like this very well; it saith, Whoso goes to walk alone, accuses the whole world; he declareth all to be unfit to be his companions; it is very uncivil, nay, insulting; Society will retaliate. Meantime, this retirement does not proceed from any whim on the part of these separators; but if any one will take pains to talk with them, he will find that this part is chosen both from temperament and from principle; with some unwillingness, too, and as a choice of the less of two evils; for these persons are not by nature melancholy, sour, and unsocial,—they are not stockish or brute,—but joyous, susceptible, affectionate; they have even more than others a great wish to be loved. Like the young Mozart, they are rather ready to cry ten times a day, "But are you sure you love me?" Nay, if they tell you their whole thought, they will own that love seems to them the last and highest gift of nature; that there are persons whom in their hearts they daily thank for existing,— persons whose faces are perhaps unknown to them, but whose fame and spirit have penetrated their solitude,—and for whose sake they wish to exist. To behold the beauty of another character, which inspires a new interest in our own; to behold the beauty lodged in a human being, with such vivacity of apprehension that I am instantly forced home to inquire if I am not deformity itself: to behold in another the expression of a love so high that it assures itself,—assures itself also to me against every possible casualty except my unworthiness;—these are degrees on the scale of human happiness, to which they have ascended; and it is a fidelity to this sentiment which has made common association distasteful to them. They wish a just and even fellowship, or none. They cannot gossip with you, and they do not wish, as they are sincere and religious, to gratify any mere curiosity which you may entertain. Like fairies, they do not wish to be spoken of. Love me, they say, but do not ask who is my cousin and my uncle. If you do not need to hear my thought, because you can read it in my face and behavior, then I will tell it you from sunrise to sunset. If you cannot divine it, you would not understand what I say. I will not molest myself for you. I do not wish to be profaned.

And yet, it seems as if this loneliness, and not this love, would prevail in their circumstances, because of the extravagant demand they make on human nature. That, indeed, constitutes a new feature in their portrait, that they are the most exacting and extortionate critics. Their quarrel with every man they meet, is not with his kind, but with his degree. There is not enough of him,—that is the only fault. They prolong their privilege of childhood in this wise, of doing nothing,—but making immense demands on all the gladiators in the lists of action and fame. They make us feel the strange disappointment which overcasts every human youth. So many promising youths, and never a finished man! The profound nature will have a savage rudeness; the delicate one will be shallow, or the victim of sensibility; the richly accomplished will have some capital absurdity; and so every piece has a crack. 'Tis strange, but this masterpiece is a result of such an extreme delicacy, that the most unobserved flaw in the boy will neutralize the most aspiring genius, and spoil the work. Talk with a seaman of the hazards to life in his profession, and he will ask you, "Where are the old sailors? do you not see that all are young men?" And we, on this sea of human thought, in like manner inquire, Where are the old idealists? where are they who represented to the last generation that extravagant hope, which a few happy aspirants suggest to ours? In looking at the class of counsel, and power, and wealth, and at the matronage of the land, amidst all the prudence and all the triviality, one asks, Where are they who represented genius, virtue, the invisible and heavenly world, to these? Are they dead,—taken in early ripeness to the gods,—as ancient wisdom foretold their fate? Or did the high idea die out of them, and leave their unper-fumed body as its tomb and tablet, announcing to all that the celestial inhabitant, who once gave them beauty, had departed? Will it be better with the new generation? We easily predict a fair future to each new candidate who enters the lists, but we are frivolous and volatile, and by low aims and ill example do what we can to defeat this hope. Then these youths bring us a rough but effectual aid. By their unconcealed dissat-isfaction, they expose our poverty, and the insignificance of man to man. A man is a poor limitary benefactor. He ought to be a shower of benefits—a great influence, which should never let his brother go, but should refresh old merits continually with new ones; so that, though ab-sent, he should never be out of my mind, his name never far from my lips; but if the earth should open at my side, or my last hour were come, his name should be the prayer I should utter to the Universe. But in our experience, man is cheap, and friendship wants its deep sense. We affect to dwell with our friends in their absence, but we do not; when deed, word, or letter comes not, they let us go. These exacting children adver-tise us of our wants. There is no compliment, no smooth speech with them; they pay you only this one compliment, of insatiable expectation; they aspire, they severely exact, and if they only stand fast in this watch-tower, and persist in demanding unto the end, and without end, then are they terrible* friends, whereof poet and priest cannot choose but stand in awe; and what if they eat clouds, and drink wind, they have not been without service to the race of man.

With this passion for what is great and extraordinary, it cannot be wondered at, that they are repelled by vulgarity and frivolity in people. They say to themselves, It is better to be alone than in bad company. And it is really a wish to be met,—the wish to find society for their hope and religion,—which prompts them to shun what is called society. They feel that they are never so fit for friendship, as when they have quitted mankind, and taken themselves to friend. A picture, a book, a favorite spot in the hills or the woods, which they can people with the fair and worthy creation of the fancy, can give them often forms so vivid, that these for the time shall seem real, and society the illusion.

But their solitary and fastidious manners not only withdraw them from the conversation, but from the labors of the world; they are not good citizens, not good members of society; unwillingly they bear their

---

*In the sense of terrific, awe-inspiring.

part of the public and private burdens; they do not willingly share in the public charities, in the public religious rites, in the enterprises of education, of missions foreign or domestic, in the abolition of the slave-trade, or in the temperance society. They do not even like to vote. The philanthropists inquire whether Transcendentalism does not mean sloth: they had as lief hear that their friend is dead, as that he is a Transcendentalist; for then is he paralyzed, and can never do anything for humanity. What right, cries the good world, has the man of genius to retreat from work, and indulge himself? The popular literary creed seems to be, "I am a sublime genius; I ought not therefore to labor." But genius is the power to labor better and more availably. Deserve thy genius: exalt it. The good, the illuminated, sit apart from the rest, censuring their dulness and vices, as if they thought that, by sitting very grand in their chairs, the very brokers, attorneys, and congressmen would see the error of their ways, and flock to them. But the good and wise must learn to act, and carry salvation to the combatants and demagogues in the dusty arena below.

On the part of these children, it is replied, that life and their faculty seem to them gifts too rich to be squandered on such trifles as you propose to them. What you call your fundamental institutions, your great and holy causes, seem to them great abuses, and, when nearly seen, paltry matters. Each "Cause," as it is called,—say Abolition, Temperance, say Calvinism, or Unitarianism,—becomes speedily a little shop, where the article, let it have been at first never so subtle and ethereal, is now made up into portable and convenient cakes, and retailed in small quantities to suit purchasers. You make very free use of these words, "great" and "holy" but few things appear to them such. Few persons have any magnificence of nature to inspire enthusiasm, and the philanthropies and charities have a certain air of quackery.* As to the general course of living, and the daily employments of men, they cannot see much virtue in these, since they are parts of this vicious circle; and as no great ends are answered by the men, there is nothing noble in the arts by which they are maintained. Nay, they have made the experiment, and found that, from the liberal professions to the coarsest manual labor, and from the courtesies of the academy and the college to the conventions of the cotillon-room† and the morning call, there is

---

*The selling of fake or ineffective medicines.
†Ballroom for formal dances.

a spirit of cowardly compromise and seeming, which intimates a frightful skepticism, a life without love, and an activity without an aim.

Unless the action is necessary, unless it is adequate, I do not wish to perform it. I do not wish to do one thing but once. I do not love routine. Once possessed of the principle, it is equally easy to make four or forty thousand applications of it. A great man will be content to have indicated in any the slightest manner his perception of the reigning Idea of his time, and will leave to those who like it the multiplication of examples. When he has hit the white, the rest may shatter the target. Every thing admonishes us how needlessly long life is. Every moment of a hero so raises and cheers us, that a twelvemonth is an age. All that the brave Xanthus brings home from his wars, is the recollection that, at the storming of Samos, "in the heat of the battle, Pericles smiled on me, and passed on to another detachment."* It is the quality of the moment, not the number of days, of events, or of actors, that imports.

New, we confess, and by no means happy, is our condition: if you want the aid of our labor, we ourselves stand in greater want of the labor. We are miserable with inaction. We perish of rest and rust: but we do not like your work.

"Then," says the world, "show me your own.

"We have none."

"What will you do, then?" cries the world.

"We will wait."

"How long?"

"Until the Universe rises up and calls us to work."

"But whilst you wait, you grow old and useless."

"Be it so: I can sit in a corner and *perish*, (as you call it,) but I will not move until I have the highest command. If no call should come for years, for centuries, then I know that the want of the Universe is the attestation of faith by my abstinence. Your virtuous projects, so called, do not cheer me. I know that which shall come will cheer me. If I cannot work, at least I need not lie. All that is clearly due to-day is not to lie. In other places, other men have encountered sharp trials, and have behaved themselves well. The martyrs were sawn asunder, or hung alive on meat-hooks. Cannot we screw our courage to patience and truth, and without complaint, or even with good-humor, await our turn of action in the Infinite Counsels?"

But, to come a little closer to the secret of these persons, we must say,

---

*From *Pericles and Aspasia* (1836), by Walter Savage Landor.

that to them it seems a very easy matter to answer the objections of the man of the world, but not so easy to dispose of the doubts and objections that occur to themselves. They are exercised in their own spirit with queries, which acquaint them with all adversity, and with the trials of the bravest heroes. When I asked them concerning their private experience, they answered somewhat in this wise: It is not to be denied that there must be some wide difference between my faith and other faith; and mine is a certain brief experience, which surprised me in the highway or in the market, in some place, at some time,—whether in the body or out of the body, God knoweth,*—and made me aware that I had played the fool with fools all this time, but that law existed for me and for all; that to me belong trust, a child's trust and obedience, and the worship of ideas, and I should never be fool more. Well, in the space of an hour, probably, I was let down from this height; I was at my old tricks, the selfish member of a selfish society. My life is superficial, takes no root in the deep world; I ask, When shall I die, and be relieved of the responsibility of seeing an Universe which I do not use? I wish to exchange this flash-of-lightning faith for continuous daylight, this fever-glow for a benign climate.

These two states of thought diverge every moment, and stand in wild contrast. To him who looks at his life from these moments of illumination, it will seem that he skulks and plays a mean, shiftless, and subaltern† part in the world. That is to be done which he has not skill to do, or to be said which others can say better, and he lies by, or occupies his hands with some plaything, until his hour comes again.‡ Much of our reading, much of our labor, seems mere waiting: it was not that we were born for.§ Any other could do it as well, or better. So little skill enters into these works, so little do they mix with the divine life, that it really signifies little what we do, whether we turn a grindstone, or ride, or run, or make fortunes, or govern the state. The worst feature of this double consciousness is, that the two lives, of the understanding and of the

---

*Reference to the Bible, 2 Corinthians 12:2: "I knew a man in Christ above fourteen years ago, (whether in the body, I cannot tell; or whether out of the body, I cannot tell: God knoweth;) such an one caught up to the third heaven" (KJV).

†Subordinate.

‡"Until his hour comes again" is a phrase used frequently by Saint John in his gospel and epistles.

§Reference to the Bible, John 18:37: "Pilate therefore said unto him, Art thou a king then? Jesus answered, Thou sayest that I am a king. To this end was I born, and for this cause came I into the world, that I should bear witness unto the truth" (KJV).

soul, which we lead, really show very little relation to each other, never meet and measure each other: one prevails now, all buzz and din, and the other prevails then, all infinitude and paradise; and, with the progress of life, the two discover no greater disposition to reconcile themselves.[3] Yet, what is my faith? What am I? What but a thought of serenity and independence, an abode in the deep blue sky? Presently the clouds shut down again; yet we retain the belief that this petty web we weave will at last be overshot and reticulated with veins of the blue, and that the moments will characterize the days. Patience, then, is for us, is it not? Patience, and still patience.[4] When we pass, as presently we shall, into some new infinitude, out of this Iceland of negations, it will please us to reflect that, though we had few virtues or consolations, we bore with our indigence, nor once strove to repair it with hypocrisy or false heat of any kind.

But this class are not sufficiently characterized, if we omit to add that they are lovers and worshippers of Beauty. In the eternal trinity of Truth, Goodness, and Beauty,[5] each in its perfection including the three, they prefer to make Beauty the sign and head. Something of the same taste is observable in all the moral movements of the time, in the religious and benevolent enterprises. They have a liberal, even an æsthetic spirit. A reference to Beauty in action sounds, to be sure, a little hollow and ridiculous in the ears of the old church. In politics, it has often sufficed, when they treated of justice, if they kept the bounds of selfish calculation. If they granted restitution, it was prudence which granted it. But the justice which is now claimed for the black, and the pauper, and the drunkard is for Beauty,—is for a necessity to the soul of the agent, not of the beneficiary. I say, this is the tendency, not yet the realization. Our virtue totters and trips, does not yet walk firmly. Its representatives are austere; they preach and denounce; their rectitude is not yet a grace. They are still liable to that slight taint of burlesque which, in our strange world, attaches to the zealot. A saint should be as dear as the apple of the eye. Yet we are tempted to smile, and we flee from the working to the speculative reformer, to escape that same slight ridicule. Alas for these days of derision and criticism! We call the Beautiful the highest, because it appears to us the golden mean, escaping the dowdiness of the good, and the heartlessness of the true.—They are lovers of nature also, and find an indemnity in the inviolable order of the world for the violated order and grace of man.

There is, no doubt, a great deal of well-founded objection to be spoken or felt against the sayings and doings of this class, some of whose traits we have selected; no doubt, they will lay themselves open to criticism and to lampoons, and as ridiculous stories will be to be told of them as of any. There will be cant and pretension; there will be subtilty and moonshine. These persons are of unequal strength, and do not all prosper. They complain that everything around them must be denied; and if feeble, it takes all their strength to deny, before they can begin to lead their own life. Grave seniors insist on their respect to this institution, and that usage; to an obsolete history; to some vocation, or college, or etiquette, or beneficiary, or charity, or morning or evening call, which they resist, as what does not concern them. But it costs such sleepless nights, alienations and misgivings,—they have so many moods about it;—these old guardians never change *their* minds; they have but one mood on their subject, namely, that Antony[6] is very perverse,—that it is quite as much as Antony can do, to assert his rights, abstain from what he thinks foolish, and keep his temper. He cannot help the reaction of this injustice in his own mind. He is braced-up and stilted; all freedom and flowing genius, all sallies of wit and frolic nature are quite out of the question; it is well if he can keep from lying, injustice, and suicide. This is no time for gayety and grace. His strength and spirits are wasted in rejection. But the strong spirits overpower those around them without effort. Their thought and emotion comes in like a flood, quite withdraws them from all notice of these carping critics; they surrender themselves with glad heart to the heavenly guide, and only by implication reject the clamorous nonsense of the hour. Grave serious talk to the deaf,—church and old book mumble and ritualize to an unheeding, preoccupied and advancing mind, and thus they by happiness of greater momentum lose no time, but take the right road at first.

But all these of whom I speak are not proficients; they are novices; they only show the road in which man should travel, when the soul has greater health and prowess. Yet let them feel the dignity of their charge, and deserve a larger power. Their heart is the ark* in which the fire is concealed, which shall burn in a broader and universal flame. Let them obey the Genius then most when his impulse is wildest; then most when he seems to lead to uninhabitable deserts of thought and life; for the path which the hero travels alone is the highway of health and benefit to mankind. What is the privilege and nobility of our nature, but its persistency, through its power to attach itself to what is permanent?

Society also has its duties in reference to this class, and must behold

---

*Allusion to the Ark of the Covenant, the sacred wooden chest of the Hebrews representative of God's bond with his chosen people; see the Bible, Exodus 25:10–22.

them with what charity it can. Possibly some benefit may yet accrue from them to the state. In our Mechanics' Fair, there must be not only bridges, ploughs, carpenter's planes, and baking troughs, but also some few finer instruments,—raingauges, thermometers, and telescopes; and in society, besides farmers, sailors, and weavers, there must be a few persons of purer fire kept specially as gauges and meters of character; persons of a fine, detecting instinct, who betray the smallest accumulations of wit and feeling in the bystander. Perhaps too there might be room for the exciters and monitors;* collectors of the heavenly spark with power to convey the electricity to others. Or, as the storm-tossed vessel at sea speaks the frigate or "line packet"† to learn its longitude, so it may not be without its advantage that we should now and then encounter rare and gifted men, to compare the points of our spiritual compass, and verify our bearings from superior chronometers.

Amidst the downward tendency and proneness of things, when every voice is raised for a new road or another statute, or a subscription of stock, for an improvement in dress, or in dentistry, for a new house or a larger business, for a political party, or the division of an estate,—will you not tolerate one or two solitary voices in the land, speaking for thoughts and principles not marketable or perishable? Soon these improvements and mechanical inventions will be superseded; these modes of living lost out of memory; these cities rotted, ruined by war, by new inventions, by new seats of trade, or the geologic changes:—all gone, like the shells which sprinkle the sea-beach with a white colony to-day, forever renewed to be forever destroyed. But the thoughts which these few hermits strove to proclaim by silence, as well as by speech, not only by what they did, but by what they forbore to do, shall abide in beauty and strength, to reorganize themselves in nature, to invest themselves anew in other, perhaps higher endowed and happier mixed clay than ours, in fuller union with the surrounding system.

---

*Instruments used in early scientific experiments with electricity.
†Vessel that carries mail and passengers on a regular route.

Self-Reliance[1]

Ne te quæsiveris extra.*

"Man is his own star, and the soul that can
Render an honest and a perfect man,
Command all light, all influence, all fate,
Nothing to him falls early or too late.
Our acts our angels are, or good or ill,
Our fatal shadows that walk by us still."
    —*Epilogue to Beaumont and Fletcher's*
        Honest Man's Fortune.

Cast the bantling[†] on the rocks,
Suckle him with the she-wolf's teat:
Wintered with the hawk and fox,
Power and speed be hands and feet.

I READ THE OTHER day some verses written by an eminent painter which were original and not conventional. Always the soul hears an admonition in such lines, let the subject be what it may. The sentiment they instill is of more value than any thought they may contain. To believe your own thought, to believe that what is true for you in your private heart, is true for all men—that is genius. Speak your latent conviction and it shall be the universal sense; for always the inmost becomes the outmost, and our first thought is rendered back to us by the trumpets of the Last Judgment. Familiar as the voice of the mind is to each, the highest merit we ascribe to Moses, Plato, and Milton, is that they set at naught books and traditions, and spoke not what men, but what they, thought. A man should learn to detect and watch that gleam of light which flashes across his mind from

---

*Do not search outside yourself (Latin), from Persius's *Satire* 1.7.
†Infant; "bantling" often refers to orphaned or abandoned children. These verses are Emerson's own.

within, more than the luster of the firmament of bards and sages. Yet he dismisses without notice his thought, because it is his. In every work of genius we recognize our own rejected thoughts: they come back to us with a certain alienated majesty. Great works of art have no more affecting lesson for us than this. They teach us to abide by our spontaneous impression with good-humored inflexibility then most when the whole cry of voices is on the other side. Else, to-morrow a stranger will say with masterly good sense precisely what we have thought and felt all the time, and we shall be forced to take with shame our own opinion from another.

There is a time in every man's education when he arrives at the conviction that envy is ignorance; that imitation is suicide; that he must take himself for better, for worse, as his portion; that though the wide universe is full of good, no kernel of nourishing corn can come to him but through his toil bestowed on that lot of ground which is given to him to till. The power which resides in him is new in nature, and none but he knows what that is which he can do, nor does he know until he has tried. Not for nothing one face, one character, one fact makes much impression on him, and another none. It is not without pre-established harmony, this sculpture in the memory. The eye was placed where one ray should fall, that it might testify of that particular ray. Bravely let him speak the utmost syllable of his confession. We but half express ourselves, and are ashamed of that divine idea which each of us represents. It may be safely trusted as proportionate and of good issues, so it be faithfully imparted, but God will not have his work made manifest by cowards. It needs a divine man to exhibit anything divine. A man is relieved and gay when he has put his heart into his work and done his best; but what he has said or done otherwise, shall give him no peace. It is a deliverance which does not deliver. In the attempt his genius deserts him; no muse befriends; no invention, no hope.

Trust thyself: every heart vibrates to that iron string. Accept the place the divine Providence has found for you; the society of your contemporaries, the connection of events. Great men have always done so and confided themselves childlike to the genius of their age, betraying their perception that the Eternal was stirring at their heart, working through their hands, predominating in all their being. And we are now men, and must accept in the highest mind the same transcendent destiny; and not pinched in a corner, not cowards fleeing before a revolution, but redeemers and benefactors, pious aspirants to be noble clay plastic* under the Almighty effort, let us advance and advance on Chaos and the Dark.

---

*Capable of being molded into new forms.

What pretty oracles nature yields us on this text in the face and behavior of children, babes and even brutes. That divided and rebel mind, that distrust of a sentiment because our arithmetic has computed the strength and means opposed to our purpose, these have not. Their mind being whole, their eye is as yet unconquered, and when we look in their faces, we are disconcerted. Infancy conforms to nobody: all conform to it, so that one babe commonly makes four or five out of the adults who prattle and play to it. So God has armed youth and puberty and manhood no less with its own piquancy and charm, and made it enviable and gracious and its claims not to be put by, if it will stand by itself. Do not think the youth has no force because he cannot speak to you and me. Hark! in the next room, who spoke so clear and emphatic? Good Heaven! it is he! it is that very lump of bashfulness and phlegm which for weeks has done nothing but eat when you were by, that now rolls out these words like bell-strokes. It seems he knows how to speak to his contemporaries. Bashful or bold, then, he will know how to make us seniors very unnecessary.

The nonchalance of boys who are sure of a dinner, and would disdain as much as a lord to do or say aught to conciliate one, is the healthy attitude of human nature. How is a boy the master of society!—independent, irresponsible, looking out from his corner on such people and facts as pass by, he tries and sentences them on their merits, in the swift summary ways of boys, as good, bad, interesting, silly, eloquent, troublesome. He cumbers himself never about consequences, about interests: he gives an independent, genuine verdict. You must court him: he does not court you. But the man is, as it were, clapped into jail by his consciousness. As soon as he has once acted or spoken with eclat, he is a committed person, watched by the sympathy or the hatred of hundreds whose affections must now enter into his account. There is no Lethe* for this. Ah, that he could pass again into his neutral, god-like independence! Who can thus lose all pledge, and having observed, observe again from the same unaffected, unbiased, unbribable, unaffrighted innocence, must always be formidable, must always engage the poet's and the man's regards. Of such an immortal youth the force would be felt. He would utter opinions on all passing affairs, which being seen to be not private but necessary, would sink like darts into the ear of men, and put them in fear.

---

*Waters of forgetfulness. In Greek mythology, Lethe is a river in the underworld; all who die drink its water, which makes them forget their actions while alive.

These are the voices which we hear in solitude, but they grow faint and inaudible as we enter into the world. Society everywhere is in conspiracy against the manhood of every one of its members. Society is a joint stock company* in which the members agree for the better securing of his bread to each shareholder, to surrender the liberty and culture of the eater. The virtue in most request is conformity. Self-reliance is its aversion. It† loves not realities and creators, but names and customs.

Whoso would be a man must be a nonconformist. He who would gather immortal palms must not be hindered by the name of goodness, but must explore if it be goodness. Nothing is at last sacred but the integrity of our own mind. Absolve you to yourself, and you shall have the suffrage of the world. I remember an answer which when quite young I was prompted to make to a valued adviser who was wont to importune me with the dear old doctrines of the church. On my saying, What have I to do with the sacredness of traditions, if I live wholly from within? my friend suggested—"But these impulses may be from below, not from above." I replied, "They do not seem to me to be such; but if I am the devil's child, I will live then from the devil." No law can be sacred to me but that of my nature. Good and bad are but names very readily transferable to that or this; the only right is what is after my constitution, the only wrong what is against it. A man is to carry himself in the presence of all opposition as if everything were titular and ephemeral but he. I am ashamed to think how easily we capitulate to badges and names, to large societies and dead institutions. Every decent and well-spoken individual affects and sways me more than is right. I ought to go upright and vital, and speak the rude truth in all ways. If malice and vanity wear the coat of philanthropy, shall that pass? If an angry bigot assumes this bountiful cause of Abolition, and comes to me with his last news from Barbadoes,‡ why should I not say to him, "Go love thy infant; love thy wood-chopper; be good-natured and modest; have that grace; and never varnish your hard, uncharitable ambition with this incredible tenderness for black folk a thousand miles off. Thy love afar is spite at home." Rough and graceless would be such greeting, but truth is handsomer than the affectation of love. Your goodness must have some edge to it—else it is none. The doctrine of hatred must be preached as the counteraction of the doctrine of love when that pules and whines. I

---

*Business in which capital is held by the owners in transferable shares.
†That is, conformity.
‡Island in the Caribbean where slavery was abolished in 1834.

shun father and mother and wife and brother, when my genius calls me.* I would write on the lintels of the door-post, *Whim*.[2] I hope it is somewhat better than whim at last, but we cannot spend the day in explanation. Expect me not to show cause why I seek or why I exclude company. Then, again, do not tell me, as a good man did to-day, of my obligation to put all poor men in good situations. Are they *my* poor? I tell thee, thou foolish philanthropist, that I grudge the dollar, the dime, the cent I give to such men as do not belong to me and to whom I do not belong. There is a class of persons to whom by all spiritual affinity I am bought and sold; for them I will go to prison, if need be; but your miscellaneous popular charities; the education at college of fools; the building of meeting-houses to the vain end to which many now stand; alms to sots; and the thousandfold relief societies; though I confess with shame I sometimes succumb and give the dollar, it is a wicked dollar which by-and-by I shall have the manhood to withold.

Virtues are in the popular estimate rather the exception than the rule. There is the man *and* his virtues. Men do what is called a good action, as some piece of courage or charity, much as they would pay a fine in expiation of daily non-appearance on parade. Their works are done as an apology or extenuation of their living in the world, as invalids and the insane pay a high board. Their virtues are penances. I do not wish to expiate, but to live. My life is not an apology, but a life. It is for itself and not for a spectacle. I much prefer that it should be of a lower strain, so it be genuine and equal, than that it should be glittering and unsteady. I wish it to be sound and sweet, and not to need diet and bleeding.† My life should be unique; it should be an alms, a battle, a conquest, a medicine. I ask primary evidence that you are a man, and refuse this appeal from the man to his actions. I know that for myself it makes no difference whether I do or forebear those actions which are reckoned excellent. I cannot consent to pay for a privilege where I have intrinsic right. Few and mean as my gifts may be, I actually am, and do not need for my own assurance, or the assurance of my fellows, any secondary testimony.

What I must do, is all that concerns me, not what the people think. This rule, equally arduous in actual and in intellectual life, may serve for the whole distinction between greatness and meanness. It is the harder

---

*See the Bible, Matthew 19:28–29, 10:35. Compare with "The Divinity School Address": "Where shall I hear words such as in elder ages drew men to leave all and follow,—father and mother, house and land, wife and child?" (p. 75).

†The outdated medical practice of bloodletting.

because you will always find those who think they know what is your duty better than you know it. It is easy in the world to live after the world's opinion; it is easy in solitude to live after our own; but the great man is he who in the midst of the crowd keeps with perfect sweetness the independence of solitude.

The objection to conforming to usages that have become dead to you, is that it scatters your force. It loses your time and blurs the impression of your character. If you maintain a dead church, contribute to a dead Bible society, vote with a great party either for the Government or against it, spread your table like base housekeepers—under all these screens I have difficulty to detect the precise man you are. And, of course, so much force is withdrawn from your proper life. But do your work, and I shall know you. Do your work, and you shall reinforce yourself. A man must consider what a blind-man's-buff* is this game of conformity. If I know your sect, I anticipate your argument. I hear a preacher announce for his text and topic the expediency of one of the institutions of his church. Do I not know beforehand that not possibly can he say a new and spontaneous word? Do I not know that with all the ostentation of examining the grounds of the institution, he will do no such thing? Do I not know that he is pledged to himself not to look but at one side; the permitted side, not as a man, but as a parish minister? He is a retained attorney, and these airs of the bench are the emptiest affectation. Well, most men have bound their eyes with one or another handkerchief, and attached themselves to some one of these communities of opinion. This conformity makes them not false in a few particulars, authors of a few lies, but false in all particulars. Their every truth is not quite true. Their two is not the real two, their four not the real four; so that every word they say chagrins us, and we know not where to begin to set them right. Meantime nature is not slow to equip us in the prison uniform of the party to which we adhere. We come to wear one cut of face and figure, and acquire by degrees the gentlest asinine expression. There is a mortifying experience in particular which does not fail to wreck itself also in the general history: I mean, "the foolish face of praise,"† the forced smile which we put on in company where we do not feel at ease in answer to conversation which does not interest us. The muscles, not spontaneously moved, but moved by a low usurping wilfulness, grow tight about the outline of the face, and make the

---

*Parlor game in which a blindfolded player tries to catch and identify other players.
†Alexander Pope's "Epistle to Doctor Arbuthnot" (1735), line 212.

most disagreeable sensation, a sensation of rebuke and warning which no brave young man will suffer twice.

For non-conformity the world whips you with its displeasure. And therefore a man must know how to estimate a sour face. The bystanders look askance on him in the public street or in the friend's parlor. If this aversation had its origin in contempt and resistance like his own, he might well go home with a sad countenance; but the sour faces of the multitude, like their sweet faces, have no deep cause—disguise no god, but are put on and off as the wind blows, and a newspaper directs. Yet is the discontent of the multitude more formidable than that of the senate and the college. It is easy enough for a firm man who knows the world to brook the rage of the cultivated classes. Their rage is decorous and prudent, for they are timid as being very vulnerable themselves. But when to their feminine rage the indignation of the people is added, when the ignorant and the poor are aroused, when the unintelligent brute force that lies at the bottom of society is made to growl and mow, it needs the habit of magnanimity and religion to treat it godlike as a trifle of no concernment.

The other terror that scares us from self-trust is our consistency; a reverence for our past act or word, because the eyes of others have no other data for computing our orbit than our past acts, and we are loath to disappoint them.

But why should you keep your head over your shoulder? Why drag about this monstrous corpse of your memory, lest you contradict somewhat you have stated in this or that public place? Suppose you should contradict yourself; what then? It seems to be a rule of wisdom never to rely on your memory alone, scarcely even in acts of pure memory, but bring the past for judgment into the thousand-eyed present, and live ever in a new day. Trust your emotion. In your metaphysics you have denied personality to the Deity; yet when the devout motions of the soul come, yield to them heart and life, though they should clothe God with shape and color. Leave your theory as Joseph his coat in the hand of the harlot, and flee.*

A foolish consistency is the hobgoblin of little minds, adored by little statesmen and philosophers and divines. With consistency a great soul has simply nothing to do. He may as well concern himself with his shadow on the wall. Out upon your guarded lips! Sew them up with pack-thread, do. Else, if you would be a man, speak what you think to-

---

*Compare the Bible, Genesis 39.

day in words as hard as cannon-balls, and to-morrow speak what to-morrow thinks in hard words again, though it contradict everything you said to-day. Ah, then, exclaimed the aged ladies, you shall be sure to be misunderstood. Misunderstood! It is a right fool's word. Is it so bad then to be misunderstood? Pythagoras was misunderstood, and Socrates, and Jesus, and Luther, and Copernicus, and Galileo, and Newton,[3] and every pure and wise spirit that ever took flesh. To be great is to be misunderstood.

I suppose no man can violate his nature. All the sallies of his will are rounded in by the law of his being as the inequalities of the Andes and Himalaya* are insignificant in the curve of the sphere. Nor does it matter how you gauge and try him. A character is like an acrostic† or Alexandrian stanza—read it forward, backward, or across, it still spells the same thing. In this pleasing contrite wood-life which God allows me, let me record day by day my honest thought without prospect or retrospect, and, I cannot doubt, it will be found symmetrical, though I mean it not, and see it not. My book should smell of pines and resound with the hum of insects. The swallow over my window should interweave that thread or straw he carries in his bill into my web also. We pass for what we are. Character teaches above our wills. Men imagine that they communicate their virtue or vice only by overt actions and do not see that virtue or vice emit a breath every moment.

Fear never but you shall be consistent in whatever variety of actions, so they be each honest and natural in their hour. For of one will, the actions will be harmonious, however unlike they seem. These varieties are lost sight of when seen at a little distance, at a little height of thought. One tendency unites them all. The voyage of the best ship is a zigzag line of a hundred tacks. This is only microscopic criticism. See the line from a sufficient distance, and it straightens itself to the average tendency. Your genuine action will explain your other genuine actions. Your conformity explains nothing. Act singly, and what you have already done singly, will justify you now. Greatness always appears to the future. If I can be great enough now to do right and scorn eyes, I must have done so much right before, as to defend me now. Be it how it will, do right now. Always scorn appearances, and you always may. The force of char-

---

*Mountain ranges in South America and Asia, respectively.
†Series of lines or verse in which the first, last, or other particular letters when taken in order spell out a word or phrase.

acter is cumulative. All the foregone days of virtue work their health into this. What makes the majesty of the heroes of the senate and the field, which so fills the imagination? The consciousness of a train of great days and victories behind. There they all stand and shed an united light on the advancing actor. He is attended as by a visible escort of angels to every man's eye. That is it which throws thunder into Chatham's voice, and dignity into Washington's port, and America into Adam's eye. Honor is venerable to us because it is no ephemeris. It is always ancient virtue. We worship it to-day, because it is not of to-day. We love it and pay it homage, because it is not a trap for our love and homage, but is self-dependent, self-derived, and therefore of an old immaculate pedigree, even if shown in a young person.

I hope in these days we have heard the last of conformity and consistency. Let the words be gazetted* and ridiculous henceforward. Instead of the gong for dinner, let us hear a whistle from the Spartan fife. Let us bow and apologize never more. A great man is coming to eat at my house. I do not wish to please him: I wish that he should wish to please me. I will stand here for humanity, and though I would make it kind, I would make it true. Let us affront and reprimand the smooth mediocrity and squalid contentment of the times, and hurl in the face of custom, and trade, and office, the fact which is the upshot of all history, that there is a great responsible Thinker and Actor moving wherever moves a man; that a true man belongs to no other time or place, but is the center of things. Where he is, there is nature. He measures you, and all men, and all events. You are constrained to accept his standard. Ordinarily every body in society reminds us of somewhat else or of some other person. Character, reality, reminds you of nothing else. It takes place of the whole creation. The man must be so much that he must make all circumstances indifferent—put all means into the shade. This all great men are and do. Every true man is a cause, a country, and an age; requires infinite spaces and numbers and time fully to accomplish his thought—and posterity seem to follow his steps as a procession. A man Cæsar is born, and for ages after, we have a Roman Empire. Christ is born, and millions of minds so grow and cleave to his genius, that he is confounded with virtue and the possible of man. An institution is the lengthened shadow of one man; as, the Reformation, of

---

*Gazettes printed public announcements, including lists of businesses that had gone bankrupt and of officers who had resigned or been dismissed from their posts. Compare with Emerson's use of the word in "Power," p. 401.

Luther; Quakerism, of Fox; Methodism, of Wesley; Abolition, of Clarkson. Scipio, Milton called "the height of Rome;" and all history resolves itself very easily into the biography of a few stout and earnest persons.

Let a man then know his worth, and keep things under his feet. Let him not peep or steal, or skulk up and down with the air of a charity-boy, a bastard, or an interloper, in the world which exists for him. But the man in the street finding no worth in himself which corresponds to the force which built a tower or sculptured a marble god, feels poor when he looks on these. To him a palace, a statue, or a costly book have an alien and forbidding air, much like a gay equipage, and seem to say like that, "Who are you, sir?" Yet they all are his, suitors for his notice, petitioners to his faculties that they will come out and take possession. The picture waits for my verdict; it is not to command me, but I am to settle its claims to praise. That popular fable of the sot who was picked up dead drunk in the street, carried to the duke's house, washed and dressed and laid in the duke's bed, and, on his waking, treated with all obsequious ceremony like the duke, and assured that he had been insane, owes its popularity to the fact, that it symbolizes so well the state of man, who is in the world a sort of sot, but now and then wakes up, exercises his reason, and finds himself a true prince.

Our reading is mendicant and sycophantic. In history, our imagination makes fools of us, plays us false. Kingdom and lordship, power and estate are a gaudier vocabulary than private John and Edward in a small house and common day's work; but the things of life are the same to both; the sum total of both is the same. Why all this deference to Alfred, and Scanderbeg, and Gustavus? Suppose they were virtuous; did they wear out virtue? As great a stake depends on your private act to-day, as followed their public and renowned steps. When private men shall act with vast views, the luster will be transferred from the actions of kings to those of gentlemen.

The world has indeed been instructed by its kings who have so magnetized the eyes of nations. It has been taught by this colossal symbol the mutual reverence that is due from man to man. The joyful loyalty with which men have everywhere suffered the king, the noble, or the great proprietor to walk among them by a law of his own, make his own scale of men and things, and reverse theirs, pay for benefits, not with money but with honor, and represent the Law in his person, was the hieroglyphic by which they obscurely signified their consciousness of their own right and comeliness, the right of every man.

The magnetism which all original action exerts is explained when we inquire the reason of self-trust. Who is the Trustee? What is the aboriginal* Self on which a universal reliance may be grounded? What is the nature and power of that science-baffling star, without parallax,[†] without calculable elements, which shoots a ray of beauty even into trivial and impure actions, if the least mark of independence appear? The inquiry leads us to that source, at once the essence of genius, the essence of virtue, and the essence of life, which we call Spontaneity or Instinct. We denote this primary wisdom as Intuition, while all lateral teachings are tuitions.[‡] In that deep force, the last fact behind which analysis cannot go, all things find their common origin. For the sense of being which in calm hours rises, we know not how, in the soul, is not diverse from things, from space, from light, from time, from man, but one with them, and proceedeth obviously from the same source whence their life and being also proceedeth. We first share the life by which things exist, and afterward see them as appearances in nature, and forget that we have shared their cause. Here is the fountain of action and the fountain of thought. Here are the lungs of that inspiration which giveth man wisdom, of that inspiration of man which cannot be denied without impiety and atheism. We lie in the lap of immense intelligence, which makes us organs of its activity and receivers of its truth. When we discern justice, when we discern truth, we do nothing of ourselves, but allow a passage to its beams. If we ask whence this comes, if we seek to pry into the soul that causes—all metaphysics, all philosophy is at fault. Its presence or its absence is all we can affirm. Every man discerns between the voluntary acts of his mind, and his involuntary perceptions. And to his involuntary perceptions, he knows a perfect respect is due. He may err in the expression of them, but he knows that these things are so, like day and night, not to be disputed. All my wilful actions and acquisitions are but roving—the most trivial reverie, the faintest native emotion, are domestic and divine. Thoughtless people contradict as readily the statement of perceptions as of opinions, or rather much more readily; for, they do not distinguish between perception and notion. They fancy that I choose to see this or that thing. But perception is not whimsical, but fatal. If I see a trait, my children will see it after me, and in course of time, all mankind—although it may chance that no one has seen it before me. For my perception of it is as much a fact as the sun.

The relations of the soul to the divine spirit are so pure that it is pro-

---

*Native.

†Apparent displacement of an object due to a change in the position of the observer; Emerson seems to mean "without a position from which it can be observed."

‡In this sense, knowledge that is paid for.

fane to seek to interpose helps. It must be that when God speaketh, he should communicate not one thing, but all things; should fill the world with his voice; should scatter forth light, nature, time, souls, from the center of the present thought; and new date and new create the whole. Whenever a mind is simple, and receives a divine wisdom, then old things pass away—means, teachers, texts, temples fall; it lives now and absorbs past and future into the present hour. All things are made sacred by relation to it—one thing as much as another. All things are dissolved to their center by their cause, and in the universal miracle petty and particular miracles disappear. This is and must be. If, therefore, a man claims to know and speak of God, and carries you backward to the phraseology of some old moldered nation in another country, in another world, believe him not. Is the acorn better than the oak which is its fulness and completion? Is the parent better than the child into whom he has cast his ripened being? Whence then this worship of the past? The centuries are conspirators against the sanity and majesty of the soul. Time and space are but physiological colors which the eye maketh, but the soul is light; where it is, is day; where it was, is night; and history is an impertinence and an injury, if it be anything more than a cheerful apologue or parable of my being and becoming.

Man is timid and apologetic. He is no longer upright. He dares not say "I think," "I am," but quotes some saint or sage. He is ashamed before the blade of grass or the blowing rose. These roses under my window make no reference to former roses or to better ones; they are for what they are; they exist with God to-day. There is no time to them. There is simply the rose; it is perfect in every moment of its existence. Before a leaf-bud has burst, its whole life acts; in the full-blown flower, there is no more; in the leafless root, there is no less. Its nature is satisfied, and it satisfies nature, in all moments alike. There is no time to it. But man postpones or remembers; he does not live in the present, but with reverted eye laments the past, or, heedless of the riches that surround him, stands on tiptoe to foresee the future. He cannot be happy and strong until he too lives with nature in the present, above time.

This should be plain enough. Yet see what strong intellects dare not yet hear God himself, unless he speak the phraseology of I know not what David, or Jeremiah, or Paul. We shall not always set so great a price on a few texts, on a few lives. We are like children who repeat by rote the sentences of grandames and tutors, and, as they grow older, of the men of talents and character they chance to see—painfully recollecting the exact words they spoke; afterward, when they come into the point of view which those had who uttered these sayings, they understand them, and are willing to let the words go; for, at any time, they can use words as good, when occasion comes. So was it with us, so will it be, if we proceed. If we live truly, we shall see truly. It is as easy for the strong man to be strong, as it is for the weak to be weak. When we have new perception, we shall gladly disburden the memory of its hoarded treasures as old rubbish. When a man lives with God, his voice shall be as sweet as the murmur of the brook and the rustle of the corn.

And now at last the highest truth on this subject remains unsaid; probably, cannot be said; for all that we say is the far off remembering of the intuition. That thought, by what I can now nearest approach to say it, is this. When good is near you, when you have life in yourself—it is not by any known or appointed way; you shall not discern the footprints of any other; you shall not see the face of man; you shall not hear any name—the way, the thought, the good shall be wholly strange and new. It shall exclude all other being. You take the way from man not to man. All persons that ever existed are its fugitive ministers. There shall be no fear in it. Fear and hope are alike beneath it. It asks nothing. There is somewhat low even in hope. We are then in vision. There is nothing that can be called gratitude nor properly joy. The soul is raised over passion. It seeth identity and eternal causation. It is a perceiving that Truth and Right are. Hence it becomes a Tranquillity out of the knowing that all things go well. Vast spaces of nature; the Atlantic Ocean, the South Sea; vast intervals of time, years, centuries, are of no account. This which I think and feel, underlay that former state of life and circumstances, as it does underlie my present, and will always all circumstance, and what is called life, and what is called death.

Life only avails, not the having lived. Power ceases in the instant of repose; it resides in the moment of transition from a past to a new state; in the shooting of the gulf; in the darting to an aim. This one fact the world hates, that the soul *becomes;* for, that forever degrades the past; turns all riches to poverty; all reputation to a shame; confounds the saint with the rogue; shoves Jesus and Judas equally aside. Why then do we prate of self-reliance? In as much as the soul is present, there will be power not confident but agent. To talk of reliance, is a poor external way of speaking. Speak rather of that which relies, because it works and is. Who has more soul than I masters me, though he should not raise his finger. Round him I must revolve by the gravitation of spirits; who has less, I rule with like facility. We fancy it rhetoric when we speak of eminent virtue. We do not yet see that virtue is Height, and that a man or a company of men plastic and permeable to principles, by the law of nature must overpower and ride all cities, nations, kings, rich men, poets, who are not.

This is the ultimate fact which we so quickly reach on this as on every topic, the resolution of all into the ever blessed ONE. Virtue is the governor, the creator, the reality. All things real are so by so much of virtue as they contain. Hardship, husbandry, hunting, whaling, war, eloquence, personal weight, are somewhat, and engage my respect as examples of the soul's presence and impure action. I see the same law working in nature for conservation and growth. The poise of a planet, the bended tree recovering itself from the strong wind, the vital resources of every vegetable and animal, are also demonstrations of the self-sufficing, and therefore self-relying soul. All history from its highest to its trivial passages is the various record of this power.

Thus all concentrates; let us not rove; let us sit at home with the cause. Let us stun and astonish the intruding rabble of men and books and institutions by a simple declaration of the divine fact. Bid them take the shoes from off their feet,* for God is here within. Let our simplicity judge them, and our docility to our own law demonstrate the poverty of nature and fortune beside our native riches.

But now we are a mob. Man does not stand in awe of man, nor is the soul admonished to stay at home, to put itself in communication with the internal ocean, but it goes abroad to beg a cup of water of the urns of men. We must go alone. Isolation must precede true society. I like the silent church before the service begins, better than any preaching. How far off, how cool, how chaste the persons look, begirt each one with a precinct or sanctuary. So let us always sit. Why should we assume the faults of our friend, or wife, or father, or child, because they sit around our hearth, or are said to have the same blood? All men have my blood, and I have all men's. Not for that will I adopt their petulance or folly, even to the extent of being ashamed of it. But your isolation must not be mechanical, but spiritual, that is, must be elevation. At times the whole world seems to be in conspiracy to importune you with emphatic trifles. Friend, client, child, sickness, fear, want, charity, all knock at once at thy closet door and say: "Come out unto us." Do not spill thy soul; do not all descend; keep thy state; stay at home in thine own heaven; come not for a moment into their facts, into their hubbub of conflicting appearances, but let in the light of thy law on their confusion. The power

---

*The Bible, Exodus 3:5: "Put off thy shoes from off thy feet, for the place whereon thou standest is holy ground" (KJV).

men possess to annoy me I give them by a weak curiosity. No man can come near me but through my act. "What we love that we have, but by desire we bereave ourselves of the love."

If we cannot at once rise to the sanctities of obedience and faith, let us at least resist our temptations, let us enter into the state of war, and wake Thor and Woden, courage and constancy in our Saxon breasts. This is to be done in our smooth times by speaking the truth. Check this lying hospitality and lying affection. Live no longer to the expectation of these deceived and deceiving people with whom we converse. Say to them, O father, O mother, O wife, O brother, O friend, I have lived with you after appearances hitherto. Henceforward I am the truth's. Be it known unto you that henceforward I obey no law less than the eternal law. I will have no covenants but proximities. I shall endeavor to nourish my parents, to support my family, to be the chaste husband of one wife—but these relations I must fill after a new and unprecedented way. I appeal from your customs, I must be myself. I cannot break myself any longer for you, or you. If you can love me for what I am, we shall be happier. If you cannot, I will still seek to deserve that you should. I must be myself. I will not hide my tastes or aversions. I will so trust that what is deep is holy, that I will do strongly before the sun and moon whatever inly rejoices me, and the heart appoints. If you are noble, I will love you; if you are not, I will not hurt you and myself by hypocritical attentions. If you are true, but not in the same truth with me, cleave to your companions; I will seek my own. I do this not selfishly, but humbly and truly. It is alike your interest and mine and all men's, however long we have dwelt in lies, to live in truth. Does this sound harsh to-day? You will soon love what is dictated by your nature as well as mine, and if we follow the truth, it will bring us out safe at last. But so you may give these friends pain. Yes, but I cannot sell my liberty and my power, to save their sensibility. Besides, all persons have their moments of reason when they look out into the region of absolute truth; then will they justify me and do the same thing.

The populace think that your rejection of popular standards is a rejection of all standard, and mere antinomianism; and the bold sensualist will use the name of philosophy to gild his crimes. But the law of consciousness abides. There are two confessionals, in one or the other of which we must be shriven. You may fulfil your round of duties by clearing yourself in the *direct*, or, in the *reflex* way. Consider whether you have satisfied your relations to father, mother, cousin, neighbor, town, cat and dog; whether any of these can upbraid you. But I may also neglect this reflex standard, and absolve me to myself. I have my own stern claims and perfect circle. It denies the name of duty to many offices that are called duties. But if I can discharge its debts, it enables me to dispense with the popular code. If any one imagines that this law is lax, let him keep its commandment one day.

And truly it demands something godlike in him who has cast off the common motives of humanity, and has ventured to trust himself for a task-master. High be his heart, faithful his will, clear his sight, that he may in good earnest be doctrine, society, law to himself, that a simple purpose may be to him as strong as iron necessity is to others.

If any man consider the present aspects of what is called by distinction *society*, he will see the need of these ethics. The sinew and heart of man seem to be drawn out, and we are become timorous, desponding whimperers. We are afraid of truth, afraid of fortune, afraid of death, and afraid of each other. Our age yields no great and perfect persons. We want men and women who shall renovate life and our social state, but we see that most natures are insolvent; cannot satisfy their own wants, have an ambition out of all proportion to their practical force, and so do lean and beg day and night continually. Our housekeeping is mendicant, our arts, our occupations, our marriages, our religion we have not chosen, but society has chosen for us. We are parlor soldiers. The rugged battle of fate, where strength is born, we shun.

If our young men miscarry in their first enterprises, they lose all heart. If the young merchant fails, men say he is *ruined*. If the finest genius studies at one of our colleges, and is not installed in an office within one year afterward in the cities or suburbs of Boston or New York, it seems to his friends and to himself that he is right in being disheartened and in complaining the rest of his life. A sturdy lad from New Hampshire or Vermont, who in turn tries all the professions, who *teams it, farms it, peddles*, keeps a school, preaches, edits a newspaper, goes to Congress, buys a township, and so forth, in successive years, and always, like a cat, falls on his feet, is worth a hundred of these city dolls. He walks abreast with his days, and feels no shame in not "studying a profession," for he does not postpone his life, but lives already. He has not one chance, but a hundred chances. Let a stoic arise who shall reveal the resources of man, and tell men they are not leaning willows, but can and must detach themselves; that with the exercise of self-trust, new powers shall appear; that a man is the word made flesh, born to shed healing to the nations, that we should be ashamed of our compassion, and that the moment he acts from himself, tossing the laws, the books, idolatries, and customs out of the window, we pity him no more but thank and revere him, and that teacher shall restore the life of man to splendor, and make his name dear to all History.

It is easy to see that a greater self-reliance, a new respect for the divinity in man, must work a revolution in all the offices and relations of men; in their religion; in their education; in their pursuits; their modes of living; their association; in their property; in their speculative views.

1. In what prayers do men allow themselves! That which they call a holy office, is not so much as brave and manly. Prayer looks abroad and asks for some foreign addition to come through some foreign virtue, and loses itself in endless mazes of natural and supernatural, and mediatorial and miraculous. Prayer that craves a particular commodity— any thing less than all good, is vicious. Prayer is the contemplation of the facts of life from the highest point of view. It is the soliloquy of a beholding and jubilant soul. It is the spirit of God pronouncing his works good. But prayer as a means to effect a private end, is theft and meanness. It supposes dualism and not unity in nature and consciousness. As soon as the man is at one with God, he will not beg. He will then see prayer in all action. The prayer of the farmer kneeling in his field to weed it, the prayer of the rower kneeling with the stroke of his oar, are true prayers heard throughout nature, though for cheap ends. Caratach, in Fletcher's Bonduca, when admonished to inquire the mind of the god Audate, replies:

> "His hidden meaning lies in our endeavors,
> Our valors are our best gods."*

Another sort of false prayers are our regrets. Discontent is the want of self-reliance: it is infirmity of will. Regret calamities, if you can thereby help the sufferer; if not, attend your own work, and already the evil begins to be repaired. Our sympathy is just as base. We come to them who weep foolishly, and sit down and cry for company, instead of imparting to them truth and health in rough electric shocks, putting them once more in communication with the soul. The secret of fortune is joy in our hands. Welcome evermore to gods and men is the self-helping man. For him all doors are flung wide. Him all tongues greet, all honors crown, all eyes follow with desire. Our love goes out to him and embraces him, because he did not need it. We solicitously and apologetically caress and celebrate him, because he held on his way

---

*Near quotation from John Fletcher's *Bonduca* (1614; act 3, scene 1).

and scorned our disapprobation. The gods love him because men hated him. "To the persevering mortal" said Zoroaster, "the blessed Immortals are swift."*

As men's prayers are a disease of the will, so are their creeds a disease of the intellect. They say with those foolish Israelites, "Let not God speak to us, lest we die. Speak thou, speak any man with us, and we will obey."† Everywhere I am bereaved of meeting God in my brother, because he has shut his own temple doors, and recites fables merely of his brother's, or his brother's brother's God. Every new mind is a new classification. If it prove a mind of uncommon activity and power, a Locke, a Lavoisier, a Hutton, a Bentham, a Spurzheim, it imposes its classification on other men, and lo! a new system. In proportion always to the depth of the thought, and so to the number of the objects it touches and brings within reach of the pupil, in his complacency. But chiefly is this apparent in creeds and churches, which are also classifications of some powerful mind acting on the great elemental thought of Duty, and man's relation to the Highest. Such is Calvinism, Quakerism, Swedenborgianism. The pupil takes the same delight in subordinating everything to the new terminology that a girl does who has just learned botany, in seeing a new earth and new seasons thereby. It will happen for a time, that the pupil will feel a real debt to the teacher—will find his intellectual power has grown by the study of his writings. This will continue until he has exhausted his master's mind. But in all unbalanced minds the classification is idolized, passes for the end, and not for a speedily exhaustible means, so that the walls of the system blend to their eye in the remote horizon with the walls of the universe; the luminaries of heaven seem to them hung on the arch their master built. They cannot imagine how you aliens have any right to see—how you can see. "It must be somehow that you stole the light from us." They do not yet perceive that light, unsystematic, indomitable, will break into any cabin, even into theirs. Let them chirp a while and call it their own. If they are honest and do well, presently their neat new pinfold‡ will be too straight and low, will crack, will lean, will rot and vanish, and the immortal light, all young and joyful, million-orbed, million-colored, will beam over the universe as on the first morning.

2. It is for want of self-culture that the idol of Traveling, the idol of

---

*From *The Chaldean Oracles*.
†Paraphrase of the Bible, Exodus 20:19.
‡Enclosure for sheep or cattle.

Italy, of England, of Egypt, remains for all educated Americans. They who made England, Italy or Greece venerable in the imagination, did so not by rambling round creation as a moth round a lamp, but by sticking fast where they were, like an axis of the earth. In manly hours, we feel that duty is our place, and that the merry men of circumstance should follow as they may. The soul is no traveler: the wise man stays at home with the soul, and when his necessities, his duties, on any occasion call him from his house, or into foreign lands, he is at home still, and is not gadding abroad from himself, and shall make men sensible by the expression of his countenance, that he goes the missionary of wisdom and virtue, and visits cities and men like a sovereign, and not like an interloper or a valet.

I have no churlish objection to the circumnavigation of the globe, for the purposes of art, of study and benevolence, so that the man is first domesticated, or does not go abroad with the hope of finding somewhat greater than he knows. He who travels to be amused, or to get somewhat which he does not carry, travels away from himself, and grows old even in youth among old things. In Thebes, in Palmyra,* his will and mind have become old and dilapidated as they. He carries ruins to ruins.

Traveling is a fool's paradise. We owe to our first journeys the discovery that place is nothing. At home I dream that at Naples, at Rome, I can be intoxicated with beauty, and lose my sadness. I pack my trunk, embrace my friends, embark on the sea, and at last wake up in Naples, and there beside me is the stern Fact, the sad self, unrelenting, identical, that I fled from. I seek the Vatican, and the palaces. I affect to be intoxicated with sights and suggestions, but I am not intoxicated. My giant goes with me wherever I go.

3. But the rage of traveling is itself only a symptom of a deeper unsoundness affecting the whole intellectual action. The intellect is vagabond, and the universal system of education fosters restlessness. Our minds travel when our bodies are forced to stay at home. We imitate; and what is imitation but the traveling of the mind? Our houses are built with foreign taste; our shelves are garnished with foreign ornaments; our opinions, our tastes, our whole minds lean, and follow the Past and Distant, as the eyes of a maid follow her mistress. The soul created the arts wherever they have flourished. It was in his own mind that

---

Thebes: ancient city in Upper Egypt, on the Nile. *Palmyra:* ancient city in central Syria.

the artist sought his model. It was an application of his own thought to the thing to be done and the conditions to be observed. And why need we copy the Doric or the Gothic model?* Beauty, convenience, grandeur of thought, and quaint expression are as near to us as to any, and if the American artist will study with hope and love the precise thing to be done by him, considering the climate, the soil, the length of the day, the wants of the people, the habit and form of the government, he will create a house in which all these will find themselves fitted, and taste and sentiment will be satisfied also.

Insist on yourself; never imitate. Your own gift you can present every moment with the cumulative force of a whole life's cultivation; but of the adopted talent of another you have only an extemporaneous, half possession. That which each can do best, none but his Maker can teach him. No man yet knows what it is, nor can, till that person has exhibited it. Where is the master who could have taught Shakespeare? Where is the master who could have instructed Franklin, or Washington or Bacon, or Newton? Every great man is an unique. The Scipionism of Scipio is precisely that part he could not borrow. If anybody will tell me whom the great man imitates in the original crisis when he performs a great act, I will tell him who else than himself can teach him. Shakespeare will never be made by the study of Shakespeare. Do that which is assigned thee, and thou canst not hope too much or dare too much. There is at this moment, there is for me an utterance bare and grand as that of the colossal chisel of Phidias, or trowel of the Egyptians,† or the pen of Moses, or Dante, but different from all these. Not possibly will the soul all rich, all eloquent, with thousand-cloven tongue, deign to repeat itself; but if I can hear what these patriarchs say, surely I can reply to them in the same pitch of voice: for the ear and the tongue are two organs of one nature. Dwell up there in the simple and noble regions of thy life, obey thy heart, and thou shalt reproduce the Foreworld again.

4. As our Religion, our Education, our Art look abroad, so does our spirit of society. All men plume themselves on the improvement of society, and no man improves.

Society never advances. It recedes as fast on one side as it gains on the other. Its progress is only apparent, like the workers of a tread-mill. It undergoes continual changes; it is barbarous, it is civilized, it is chris-

---

*Doric and Gothic are architectural styles based on ancient Greek and medieval European structures, respectively.
†That is, the building of the pyramids of Giza.

tianized, it is rich, it is scientific; but this change is not amelioration. For every thing that is given, something is taken. Society acquires new arts and loses old instincts. What a contrast between the well-clad, reading, writing, thinking American, with a watch, a pencil, and a bill of exchange in his pocket, and the naked New Zealander, whose property is a club, a spear, a mat, and an undivided twentieth of a shed to sleep under. But compare the health of the two men, and you shall see that his aboriginal strength the white man has lost. If the traveler tell us truly, strike the savage with a broad-ax, and in a day or two the flesh shall unite and heal as if you struck the blow into soft pitch, and the same blow shall send the white to his grave.

The civilized man has built a coach, but has lost the use of his feet. He is supported on crutches, but loses so much support of muscle. He has got a fine Geneva watch, but he has lost the skill to tell the hour by the sun. A Greenwich nautical almanac he has, as so being sure of the information when he wants it, the man in the street does not know a star in the sky. The solstice he does not observe; the equinox he knows as little; and the whole bright calendar of the year is without a dial in his mind. His note-books impair his memory; his libraries overload his wit; the insurance office increases the number of accidents; and it may be a question whether machinery does not incumber; whether we have not lost by refinement some energy, by a christianity intrenched in establishments and forms, some vigor of wild virtue. For every stoic was a stoic; but in Christendom where is the Christian?

There is no more deviation in the moral standard than in the standard of height or bulk. No greater men are now than ever were. A singular equality may be observed between the great men of the first and of the last ages; nor can all the science, art, religion and philosophy of the nineteenth century avail to educate greater men than Plutarch's heroes, three or four and twenty centuries ago. Not in time is the race progressive. Phocion, Socrates, Anaxagoras, Diogenes, are great men, but they leave no class. He who is really of their class will not be called by their name, but be wholly his own man, and in his turn the founder of a sect. The arts and inventions of each period are only its costume, and do not invigorate men. The harm of the improved machinery may compensate its good. Hudson and Behring accomplished so much in their fishing-boats as to astonish Parry and Franklin, whose equipment exhausted the resources of science and art.[4] Galileo, with an opera-glass, discovered a more splendid series of facts than any one since. Columbus found the New World in an undecked boat. It is curious to see the periodical disuse and perishing of means and machinery which were introduced with loud laudation, a few years or centuries before. The great genius returns to essential man. We reckoned the improvements of the art of war among the triumphs of science, and yet Napoleon conquered Europe by the Bivouac, which consisted of falling back on naked valor, and disencumbering it of all aids. "The Emperor held it impossible to make a perfect army," says Las Casas, "without abolishing our arms, magazines, commissaries, and carriages, until in imitation of the Roman custom, the soldier should receive his supply of corn, grind it in his hand-mill, and bake his bread himself."*

Society is a wave. The wave moves onward, but the water of which it is composed, does not. The same particle does not rise from the valley to the ridge. Its unity is only phenomenal. The persons who make up a nation to-day, next year die, and their experience with them.

And so the reliance on Property, including the reliance on governments which protect it, is the want of self-reliance. Men have looked away from themselves and at things so long, that they have come to esteem what they call the soul's progress, namely, the religious, learned, and civil institutions, as guards of property, and they deprecate assaults on these, because they feel them to be assaults on property. They measure their esteem of each other, by what each has, and not by what each is. But a cultivated man becomes ashamed of his property, ashamed of what he has, out of new respect for his being. Especially he hates what he has, if he sees that it is accidental—came to him by inheritance, or gift, or crime; then he feels that it is not having; it does not belong to him, has no root in him, and merely lies there, because no revolution or no robber takes it away. But that which a man is, does always by necessity acquire, and what the man acquires is permanent and living property, which does not wait the beck of rulers, or mobs, or revolutions, or fire, or storm, or bankruptcies, but perpetually renews itself wherever the man is put. "Thy lot or portion of life," said the Caliph Ali, "is seeking after thee; therefore be at rest from seeking after it."† Our dependence on these foreign goods leads us to our slavish respect for numbers. The political parties meet in numerous conventions; the greater the concourse, and with each new uproar of announcement, The delegation from Essex! The Democrats from New Hampshire! The Whigs of

---

*From *Mémorial de Sainte Hélène: Journal of the Private Life and Conversations of the Emperor Napoleon at Saint Helena* (1823), which records Las Cases's conversations with Napoleon during his exile at Saint Helena.
†From Simon Ockley's *The History of the Saracens* (1718).

Maine! the young patriot feels himself stronger than before by a new thousand of eyes and arms. In like manner the reformers summon conventions, and vote and resolve in multitude. But not so, O friends! will the God deign to enter and inhabit you, but by a method precisely the reverse. It is only as a man puts off from himself all external support, and stands alone, that I see him to be strong and to prevail. He is weaker by every recruit to his banner. Is not a man better than a town? Ask nothing of men, and in the endless mutation, thou only firm column must presently appear the upholder of all that surrounds thee. He who knows that power is in the soul, that he is weak only because he has looked for good out of him and elsewhere, and so perceiving, throws himself unhesitatingly on his thought, instantly rights himself, stands in the erect position, commands his limbs, works miracles; just as a man who stands on his feet is stronger than a man who stands on his head.

So use all that is called Fortune. Most men gamble with her, and gain all, and lose all, as her wheel rolls. But do thou leave as unlawful these winnings, and deal with Cause and Effect, the chancellors of God. In the Will work and acquire, and thou hast chained the wheel of Chance, and shalt always drag her after thee. A political victory, a rise of rents, the recovery of your sick, or the return of your absent friend, or some other quite external event, raises your spirits, and you think good days are preparing for you. Do not believe it. It can never be so. Nothing can bring you peace but yourself. Nothing can bring you peace but the triumph of principles.

Compensation[1]

The wings of Time are black and white,
Pied with morning and with night.
Mountain tall and ocean deep
Trembling balance duly keep.
In changing moon, in tidal wave,
Glows the feud of Want and Have.
Gauge of more and less through space
Electric star and pencil plays.
The lonely Earth amid the balls
That hurry through the eternal halls,
A makeweight flying to the void,
Supplemental asteroid,
Or compensatory spark,
Shoots across the neutral Dark.

Man's the elm, and Wealth the vine,
Stanch and strong the tendrils twine:
Though the frail ringlets thee deceive,
None from its stock that vine can reave.
Fear not, then, thou child infirm,
There's no god dare wrong a worm.
Laurel crowns cleave to deserts
And power to him who power exerts;
Hast not thy share? On winged feet,
Lo! it rushes thee to meet;
And all that Nature made thy own,
Floating in air or pent in stone,
Will rive the hills and swim the sea
And, like thy shadow, follow thee.

EVER SINCE I WAS a boy I have wished to write a discourse on Compensation; for it seemed to me when very young that on this subject life was ahead of theology and the people knew more than the preachers taught.

The documents too from which the doctrine is to be drawn, charmed my fancy by their endless variety, and lay always before me, even in sleep; for they are the tools in our hands, the bread in our basket, the transactions of the street, the farm and the dwelling-house; greetings, relations, debts and credits, the influence of character, the nature and endowment of all men. It seemed to me also that in it might be shown men a ray of divinity, the present action of the soul of this world, clean from all vestige of tradition; and so the heart of man might be bathed by an inundation of eternal love, conversing with that which he knows was always and always must be, because it really is now. It appeared moreover that if this doctrine could be stated in terms with any resemblance to those bright intuitions in which this truth is sometimes revealed to us, it would be a star in many dark hours and crooked passages in our journey, that would not suffer us to lose our way.

I was lately confirmed in these desires by hearing a sermon at church. The preacher, a man esteemed for his orthodoxy, unfolded in the ordinary manner the doctrine of the Last Judgment. He assumed that judgment is not executed in this world; that the wicked are successful; that the good are miserable; and then urged from reason and from Scripture a compensation to be made to both parties in the next life. No offence appeared to be taken by the congregation at this doctrine. As far as I could observe when the meeting broke up they separated without remark on the sermon.

Yet what was the import of this teaching? What did the preacher mean by saying that the good are miserable in the present life? Was it that houses and lands, offices, wine, horses, dress, luxury, are had by unprincipled men, whilst the saints are poor and despised; and that a compensation is to be made to these last hereafter, by giving them the like gratifications another day,—bank-stock and doubloons, venison and champagne? This must be the compensation intended; for what else? Is it that they are to have leave to pray and praise? to love and serve men? Why, that they can do now. The legitimate inference the disciple would draw was,—'We are to have *such* a good time as the sinners have now';—or, to push it to its extreme import,—'You sin now, we shall sin by and by; we would sin now, if we could; not being successful we expect our revenge to-morrow.'

The fallacy lay in the immense concession that the bad are successful; that justice is not done now. The blindness of the preacher consisted in deferring to the base estimate of the market of what constitutes a manly success, instead of confronting and convicting the world from the truth; announcing the presence of the soul; the omnipotence of the will; and so establishing the standard of good and ill, of success and falsehood.

I find a similar base tone in the popular religious works of the day and the same doctrines assumed by the literary men when occasionally they treat the related topics. I think that our popular theology has gained in decorum, and not in principle, over the superstitions it has displaced. But men are better than their theology. Their daily life gives it the lie. Every ingenuous and aspiring soul leaves the doctrine behind him in his own experience, and all men feel sometimes the falsehood which they cannot demonstrate. For men are wiser than they know. That which they hear in schools and pulpits without afterthought, if said in conversation would probably be questioned in silence. If a man dogmatize in a mixed company on Providence and the divine laws, he is answered by a silence which conveys well enough to an observer the dissatisfaction of the hearer, but his incapacity to make his own statement.

I shall attempt in this and the following chapter* to record some facts that indicate the path of the law of Compensation; happy beyond my expectation if I shall truly draw the smallest arc of this circle.

Polarity, or action and reaction, we meet in every part of nature; in darkness and light; in heat and cold; in the ebb and flow of waters; in male and female; in the inspiration and expiration of plants and animals; in the equation of quantity and quality in the fluids of the animal body; in the systole and diastole of the heart; in the undulations of fluids and of sound; in the centrifugal and centripetal gravity; in electricity, galvanism, and chemical affinity. Superinduce magnetism at one end of a needle, the opposite magnetism takes place at the other end. If the south attracts, the north repels. To empty here, you must condense there. An inevitable dualism bisects nature, so that each thing is a half, and suggests another thing to make it whole; as, spirit, matter; man, woman; odd, even; subjective, objective; in, out; upper, under; motion, rest; yea, nay.

Whilst the world is thus dual, so is every one of its parts. The entire system of things gets represented in every particle. There is somewhat that resembles the ebb and flow of the sea, day and night, man and woman, in a single needle of the pine, in a kernel of corn, in each indi-

---

*In *Essays: First Series*, the following chapter is "Spiritual Laws," which is included in this edition.

vidual of every animal tribe. The reaction, so grand in the elements, is repeated within these small boundaries. For example, in the animal kingdom the physiologist has observed that no creatures are favorites, but a certain compensation balances every gift and every defect. A surplusage given to one part is paid out of a reduction from another part of the same creature. If the head and neck are enlarged, the trunk and extremities are cut short.

The theory of the mechanic forces is another example. What we gain in power is lost in time, and the converse. The periodic or compensating errors of the planets is another instance. The influences of climate and soil in political history are another. The cold climate invigorates. The barren soil does not breed fevers, crocodiles, tigers or scorpions.

The same dualism underlies the nature and condition of man. Every excess causes a defect; every defect an excess. Every sweet hath its sour; every evil its good. Every faculty which is a receiver of pleasure has an equal penalty put on its abuse. It is to answer for its moderation with its life. For every grain of wit there is a grain of folly. For every thing you have missed, you have gained something else; and for every thing you gain, you lose something. If riches increase, they are increased that use them. If the gatherer gathers too much, Nature takes out of the man what she puts into his chest; swells the estate, but kills the owner. Nature hates monopolies and exceptions. The waves of the sea do not more speedily seek a level from their loftiest tossing than the varieties of condition tend to equalize themselves. There is always some levelling circumstance that puts down the overbearing, the strong, the rich, the fortunate, substantially on the same ground with all others. Is a man too strong and fierce for society and by temper and position a bad citizen,—a morose ruffian, with a dash of the pirate in him?—Nature sends him a troop of pretty sons and daughters who are getting along in the dame's classes at the village school, and love and fear for them smooths his grim scowl to courtesy. Thus she contrives to intenerate* the granite and felspar, takes the boar out and puts the lamb in and keeps her balance true.

The farmer imagines power and place are fine things. But the President has paid dear for his White House. It has commonly cost him all his peace, and the best of his manly attributes. To preserve for a short time so conspicuous an appearance before the world, he is content to eat dust before the real masters who stand erect behind the throne. Or

---

*Soften.

do men desire the more substantial and permanent grandeur of genius? Neither has this an immunity. He who by force of will or of thought is great and overlooks thousands, has the charges of that eminence. With every influx of light comes new danger. Has he light? he must bear witness to the light, and always outrun that sympathy which gives him such keen satisfaction, by his fidelity to new revelations of the incessant soul. He must hate father and mother, wife and child. Has he all that the world loves and admires and covets?—he must cast behind him their admiration and afflict them by faithfulness to his truth and become a byword and a hissing.

This law writes the laws of cities and nations. It is in vain to build or plot or combine against it. Things refuse to be mismanaged long. *Res nolunt diu male administrari.** Though no checks to a new evil appear, the checks exist, and will appear. If the government is cruel, the governor's life is not safe. If you tax too high, the revenue will yield nothing. If you make the criminal code sanguinary, juries will not convict. If the law is too mild, private vengeance comes in. If the government is a terrific democracy, the pressure is resisted by an over-charge of energy in the citizen, and life glows with a fiercer flame. The true life and satisfactions of man seem to elude the utmost rigors or felicities of condition and to establish themselves with great indifferency under all varieties of circumstances. Under all governments the influence of character remains the same,—in Turkey and in New England about alike. Under the primeval despots of Egypt, history honestly confesses that man must have been as free as culture could make him.

These appearances indicate the fact that the universe is represented in every one of its particles. Every thing in nature contains all the powers of nature. Every thing is made of one hidden stuff; as the naturalist sees one type under every metamorphosis, and regards a horse as a running man, a fish as a swimming man, a bird as a flying man, a tree as a rooted man. Each new form repeats not only the main character of the type, but part for part all the details, all the aims, furtherances, hindrances, energies and whole system of every other. Every occupation, trade, art, transaction, is a compend† of the world and a correlative of

---

*Emerson's source for this well-known Latin saying (translated in the preceding sentence) is *The Poetical Writings of Alexander Pope*, 9 vols. (London, 1760). It occurs in a letter from Jonathan Swift to Lord Bolingbroke, dated April 5, 1729. See the discussion in *The Collected Works.*
†Comprehensive summary.

every other. Each one is an entire emblem of human life; of its good and ill, its trials, its enemies, its course and its end. And each one must somehow accommodate the whole man and recite all his destiny.

The world globes itself in a drop of dew. The microscope cannot find the animalcule which is less perfect for being little. Eyes, ears, taste, smell, motion, resistance, appetite, and organs of reproduction that take hold on eternity,—all find room to consist in the small creature. So do we put our life into every act. The true doctrine of omnipresence is that God reappears with all his parts in every moss and cobweb. The value of the universe contrives to throw itself into every point. If the good is there, so is the evil; if the affinity, so the repulsion; if the force, so the limitation.

Thus is the universe alive. All things are moral. That soul which within us is a sentiment, outside of us is a law. We feel its inspiration; out there in history we can see its fatal strength. "It is in the world, and the world was made by it."* Justice is not postponed. A perfect equity adjusts its balance in all parts of life. *Οἱ κύβοι Διὸς ἀεὶ εὐπίπτουσι,*—The dice of God are always loaded.† The world looks like a multiplication-table, or a mathematical equation, which, turn it how you will, balances itself. Take what figure you will, its exact value, nor more nor less, still returns to you. Every secret is told, every crime is punished, every virtue rewarded, every wrong redressed, in silence and certainty. What we call retribution is the universal necessity by which the whole appears wherever a part appears. If you see smoke, there must be fire. If you see a hand or a limb, you know that the trunk to which it belongs is there behind.

Every act rewards itself, or in other words integrates itself, in a twofold manner; first in the thing, or in real nature; and secondly in the circumstance, or in apparent nature. Men call the circumstance the retribution. The causal retribution is in the thing and is seen by the soul. The retribution in the circumstance is seen by the understanding; it is inseparable from the thing, but is often spread over a long time and so does not become distinct until after many years. The specific stripes may follow late after the offence, but they follow because they accompany it. Crime and punishment grow out of one stem. Punishment is a fruit that unsuspected ripens within the flower of the pleasure which

---

*Paraphrase from the Bible, John 1:10: "He was in the world, and the world was made by him, and the world knew him not" (KJV).

†Well-known fragment of Sophocles. According to the editors of *The Collected Works*, Emerson's translation is colloquial, and possibly his own.

concealed it. Cause and effect, means and ends, seed and fruit, cannot be severed; for the effect already blooms in the cause, the end preëxists in the means, the fruit in the seed.

Whilst thus the world will be whole and refuses to be disparted, we seek to act partially, to sunder, to appropriate; for example,—to gratify the senses we sever the pleasure of the senses from the needs of the character. The ingenuity of man has always been dedicated to the solution of one problem,—how to detach the sensual sweet, the sensual strong, the sensual bright, etc., from the moral sweet, the moral deep, the moral fair; that is, again to contrive to cut clean off this upper surface so thin as to leave it bottomless; to get a *one end*, without an *other end*. The soul says, "Eat;" the body would feast. The soul says, "The man and woman shall be one flesh and one soul;" the body would join the flesh only. The soul says, "Have dominion over all things to the ends of virtue;" the body would have the power over things to its own ends.

The soul strives amain to live and work through all things. It would be the only fact. All things shall be added unto it,—power, pleasure, knowledge, beauty. The particular man aims to be somebody; to set up for himself; to truck and higgle for a private good; and, in particulars, to ride that he may ride; to dress that he may be dressed; to eat that he may eat; and to govern, that he may be seen. Men seek to be great; they would have offices, wealth, power and fame. They think that to be great is to possess one side of nature,—the sweet, without the other side, the bitter.

This dividing and detaching is steadily counteracted. Up to this day it must be owned no projector has had the smallest success. The parted water reunites behind our hand. Pleasure is taken out of pleasant things, profit out of profitable things, power out of strong things, as soon as we seek to separate them from the whole. We can no more halve things and get the sensual good, by itself, than we can get an inside that shall have no outside, or a light without a shadow. "Drive out Nature with a fork, she comes running back."*

Life invests itself with inevitable conditions, which the unwise seek to dodge, which one and another brags that he does not know, that they do not touch him;—but the brag is on his lips, the conditions are in his soul. If he escapes them in one part they attack him in another more vital part. If he has escaped them in form and in the appearance, it is because he has resisted his life and fled from himself, and the retribution

---

*Compare Horace's *Epistles*, I, x, 24.

is so much death. So signal is the failure of all attempts to make this separation of the good from the tax, that the experiment would not be tried,—since to try it is to be mad,—but for the circumstance that when the disease began in the will, of rebellion and separation, the intellect is at once infected, so that the man ceases to see God whole in each object, but is able to see the sensual allurement of an object and not see the sensual hurt, he sees the mermaid's head but not the dragon's tail, and thinks he can cut off that which he would have from that which he would not have. "How secret art thou who dwellest in the highest heavens in silence, O thou only great God, sprinkling with an unwearied providence certain penal blindnesses upon such as have unbridled desires!"*

The human soul is true to these facts in the painting of fable, of history, of law, of proverbs, of conversation. It finds a tongue in literature unawares. Thus the Greeks called Jupiter, Supreme Mind; but having traditionally ascribed to him many base actions, they involuntarily made amends to reason by tying up the hands of so bad a god. He is made as helpless as a king of England. Prometheus knows one secret which Jove must bargain for; Minerva, another. He cannot get his own thunders; Minerva keeps the key of them:—

> "Of all the gods, I only know the keys
> That ope the solid doors within whose vaults
> His thunders sleep."†

A plain confession of the in-working of the All and of its moral aim. The Indian mythology ends in the same ethics; and it would seem impossible for any fable to be invented and get any currency which was not moral. Aurora forgot to ask youth for her lover, and though Tithonus is immortal, he is old. Achilles is not quite invulnerable; the sacred waters did not wash the heel by which Thetis held him. Siegfried, in the Nibelungen, is not quite immortal, for a leaf fell on his back whilst he was bathing in the dragon's blood, and that spot which it covered is mortal. And so it must be. There is a crack in every thing God has made. It would seem there is always this vindictive circumstance stealing in at unawares even into the wild poesy in which the human fancy attempted to make bold holiday and to shake itself free of the old laws,—this back-

---

*Saint Augustine, *Confessions*, B. [book] 1 (author's note).
†From Aeschylus's *Eumenides*.

stroke, this kick of the gun, certifying that the law is fatal; that in nature nothing can be given, all things are sold.

This is that ancient doctrine of Nemesis, who keeps watch in the universe and lets no offence go unchastised. The Furies they said are attendants on justice, and if the sun in heaven should transgress his path they would punish him.* The poets related that stone walls and iron swords and leathern thongs had an occult sympathy with the wrongs of their owners; that the belt which Ajax gave Hector dragged the Trojan hero over the field at the wheels of the car of Achilles, and the sword which Hector gave Ajax was that on whose point Ajax fell.† They recorded that when the Thasians erected a statue to Theagenes, a victor in the games, one of his rivals went to it by night and endeavored to throw it down by repeated blows, until at last he moved it from its pedestal and was crushed to death beneath its fall.‡

This voice of fable has in it somewhat divine. It came from thought above the will of the writer. That is the best part of each writer which has nothing private in it; that which he does not know; that which flowed out of his constitution and not from his too active invention; that which in the study of a single artist you might not easily find, but in the study of many you would abstract as the spirit of them all. Phidias it is not, but the work of man in that early Hellenic world that I would know. The name and circumstance of Phidias, however convenient for history, embarrass when we come to the highest criticism. We are to see that which man was tending to do in a given period, and was hindered, or, if you will, modified in doing, by the interfering volitions of Phidias, of Dante, of Shakspeare, the organ whereby man at the moment wrought.

Still more striking is the expression of this fact in the proverbs of all nations, which are always the literature of reason, or the statements of an absolute truth without qualification. Proverbs, like the sacred books of each nation, are the sanctuary of the intuitions. That which the droning world, chained to appearances, will not allow the realist to say in his own words, it will suffer him to say in proverbs without contradiction. And this law of laws, which the pulpit, the senate and the college deny,

---

*Compare Plutarch's *Moralia*, "On Exile," 11; see also p. 91.
†Compare Sophocles' *Ajax*, lines 1029–1034.
‡Emerson's source for this anecdote is Thomas Brown's *Lectures on the Philosophy of the Human Mind*, 4 vols. (Edinburgh, 1820).

is hourly preached in all markets and work-shops by flights of proverbs, whose teaching is as true and as omnipresent as that of birds and flies.

All things are double, one against another.—Tit for tat; an eye for an eye; a tooth for a tooth; blood for blood; measure for measure; love for love.—Give, and it shall be given you.—He that watereth shall be watered himself.—What will you have? quoth God; pay for it and take it.—Nothing venture, nothing have.—Thou shalt be paid exactly for what thou hast done, no more, no less.—Who doth not work shall not eat.—Harm watch, harm catch.—Curses always recoil on the head of him who imprecates them.—If you put a chain around the neck of a slave, the other end fastens itself around your own.—Bad counsel confounds the adviser.—The Devil is an ass.

It is thus written, because it is thus in life. Our action is overmastered and characterized above our will by the law of nature. We aim at a petty end quite aside from the public good, but our act arranges itself by irresistible magnetism in a line with the poles of the world.

A man cannot speak but he judges himself. With his will or against his will he draws his portrait to the eye of his companions by every word. Every opinion reacts on him who utters it. It is a thread-ball thrown at a mark, but the other end remains in the thrower's bag. Or rather it is a harpoon hurled at the whale, unwinding, as it flies, a coil of cord in the boat, and, if the harpoon is not good, or not well thrown, it will go nigh to cut the steersman in twain or to sink the boat.

You cannot do wrong without suffering wrong. "No man had ever a point of pride that was not injurious to him," said Burke.* The exclusive in fashionable life does not see that he excludes himself from enjoyment, in the attempt to appropriate it. The exclusionist in religion does not see that he shuts the door of heaven on himself, in striving to shut out others. Treat men as pawns and ninepins and you shall suffer as well as they. If you leave out their heart, you shall lose your own. The senses would make things of all persons; of women, of children, of the poor. The vulgar proverb, "I will get it from his purse or get it from his skin," is sound philosophy.

All infractions of love and equity in our social relations are speedily punished. They are punished by fear. Whilst I stand in simple relations to my fellow-man, I have no displeasure in meeting him. We meet as water meets water, or as two currents of air mix, with perfect diffusion

---

*Emerson's source for this quotation is James Prior's *Memoir of the Life and Character of the Right Hon. Edmund Burke* (London, 1824).

and interpenetration of nature. But as soon as there is any departure from simplicity and attempt at halfness, or good for me that is not good for him, my neighbor feels the wrong; he shrinks from me as far as I have shrunk from him; his eyes no longer seek mine; there is war between us; there is hate in him and fear in me.

All the old abuses in society, universal and particular, all unjust accumulations of property and power, are avenged in the same manner. Fear is an instructor of great sagacity and the herald of all revolutions. One thing he teaches, that there is rottenness where he appears. He is a carrion crow, and though you see not well what he hovers for, there is death somewhere. Our property is timid, our laws are timid, our cultivated classes are timid. Fear for ages has boded and mowed and gibbered over government and property. That obscene bird is not there for nothing. He indicates great wrongs which must be revised.

Of the like nature is that expectation of change which instantly follows the suspension of our voluntary activity. The terror of cloudless noon, the emerald of Polycrates,[2] the awe of prosperity, the instinct which leads every generous soul to impose on itself tasks of a noble asceticism and vicarious virtue, are the tremblings of the balance of justice through the heart and mind of man.

Experienced men of the world know very well that it is best to pay scot and lot as they go along, and that a man often pays dear for a small frugality. The borrower runs in his own debt. Has a man gained any thing who has received a hundred favors and rendered none? Has he gained by borrowing, through indolence or cunning, his neighbor's wares, or horses, or money? There arises on the deed the instant acknowledgment of benefit on the one part and of debt on the other; that is, of superiority and inferiority. The transaction remains in the memory of himself and his neighbor; and every new transaction alters according to its nature their relation to each other. He may soon come to see that he had better have broken his own bones than to have ridden in his neighbor's coach, and that "the highest price he can pay for a thing is to ask for it."*

A wise man will extend this lesson to all parts of life, and know that it is the part of prudence to face every claimant and pay every just demand on your time, your talents, or your heart. Always pay; for first or last you must pay your entire debt. Persons and events may stand for a time between you and justice, but it is only a postponement. You must

---

*From "Eschines and Phocion," by Walter Savage Landor.

pay at last your own debt. If you are wise you will dread a prosperity which only loads you with more. Benefit is the end of nature. But for every benefit which you receive, a tax is levied. He is great who confers the most benefits. He is base,—and that is the one base thing in the universe,—to receive favors and render none. In the order of nature we cannot render benefits to those from whom we receive them, or only seldom. But the benefit we receive must be rendered again, line for line, deed for deed, cent for cent, to somebody. Beware of too much good staying in your hand. It will fast corrupt and worm worms. Pay it away quickly in some sort.

Labor is watched over by the same pitiless laws. Cheapest, say the prudent, is the dearest labor. What we buy in a broom, a mat, a wagon, a knife, is some application of good sense to a common want. It is best to pay in your land a skilful gardener, or to buy good sense applied to gardening; in your sailor, good sense applied to navigation; in the house, good sense applied to cooking, sewing, serving; in your agent, good sense applied to accounts and affairs. So do you multiply your presence, or spread yourself throughout your estate. But because of the dual constitution of things, in labor as in life there can be no cheating. The thief steals from himself. The swindler swindles himself. For the real price of labor is knowledge and virtue, whereof wealth and credit are signs. These signs, like paper money, may be counterfeited or stolen, but that which they represent, namely, knowledge and virtue, cannot be counterfeited or stolen. These ends of labor cannot be answered but by real exertions of the mind, and in obedience to pure motives. The cheat, the defaulter, the gambler, cannot extort the knowledge of material and moral nature which his honest care and pains yield to the operative. The law of nature is, Do the thing, and you shall have the power; but they who do not the thing have not the power.

Human labor, through all its forms, from the sharpening of a stake to the construction of a city or an epic, is one immense illustration of the perfect compensation of the universe. The absolute balance of Give and Take, the doctrine that every thing has its price,—and if that price is not paid, not that thing but something else is obtained, and that it is impossible to get any thing without its price,—is not less sublime in the columns of a leger than in the budgets of states, in the laws of light and darkness, in all the action and reaction of nature. I cannot doubt that the high laws which each man sees implicated in those processes with which he is conversant, the stern ethics which sparkle on his chisel-edge, which are measured out by his plumb and foot-rule, which stand as manifest in the footing of the shop-bill as in the history of a state,—

do recommend to him his trade, and though seldom named, exalt his business to his imagination.

The league between virtue and nature engages all things to assume a hostile front to vice. The beautiful laws and substances of the world persecute and whip the traitor. He finds that things are arranged for truth and benefit, but there is no den in the wide world to hide a rogue. Commit a crime, and the earth is made of glass. Commit a crime, and it seems as if a coat of snow fell on the ground, such as reveals in the woods the track of every partridge and fox and squirrel and mole. You cannot recall the spoken word, you cannot wipe out the foot-track, you cannot draw up the ladder, so as to leave no inlet or clew. Some damning circumstance always transpires. The laws and substances of nature,—water, snow, wind, gravitation,—become penalties to the thief.

On the other hand the law holds with equal sureness for all right action. Love, and you shall be loved. All love is mathematically just, as much as the two sides of an algebraic equation. The good man has absolute good, which like fire turns every thing to its own nature, so that you cannot do him any harm; but as the royal armies sent against Napoleon, when he approached cast down their colors and from enemies became friends, so disasters of all kinds, as sickness, offence, poverty, prove benefactors:—

> "Winds blow and waters roll
> Strength to the brave and power and deity,
> Yet in themselves are nothing."*

The good are befriended even by weakness and defect. As no man had ever a point of pride that was not injurious to him, so no man had ever a defect that was not somewhere made useful to him. The stag in the fable† admired his horns and blamed his feet, but when the hunter came, his feet saved him, and afterwards, caught in the thicket, his horns destroyed him. Every man in his lifetime needs to thank his faults. As no man thoroughly understands a truth until he has contended against it, so no man has a thorough acquaintance with the hindrances or talents of men until he has suffered from the one and seen the triumph of the other over his own want of the same. Has he a defect of temper that unfits him to live in society? Thereby he is driven to entertain himself

---

*William Wordsworth's sonnet "September 1802. Near Dover," lines 10–12.
†Emerson is referring to Aesop's fable "The Stag at the Pool."

alone and acquire habits of self-help; and thus, like the wounded oyster, he mends his shell with pearl.

Our strength grows out of our weakness. The indignation which arms itself with secret forces does not awaken until we are pricked and stung and sorely assailed. A great man is always willing to be little. Whilst he sits on the cushion of advantages, he goes to sleep. When he is pushed, tormented, defeated, he has a chance to learn something; he has been put on his wits, on his manhood; he has gained facts; learns his ignorance; is cured of the insanity of conceit; has got moderation and real skill. The wise man throws himself on the side of his assailants. It is more his interest than it is theirs to find his weak point. The wound cicatrizes* and falls off from him like a dead skin and when they would triumph, lo! he has passed on invulnerable. Blame is safer than praise. I hate to be defended in a newspaper. As long as all that is said is said against me, I feel a certain assurance of success. But as soon as honeyed words of praise are spoken for me I feel as one that lies unprotected before his enemies. In general, every evil to which we do not succumb is a benefactor. As the Sandwich Islander† believes that the strength and valor of the enemy he kills passes into himself, so we gain the strength of the temptation we resist.

The same guards which protect us from disaster, defect and enmity, defend us, if we will, from selfishness and fraud. Bolts and bars are not the best of our institutions, nor is shrewdness in trade a mark of wisdom. Men suffer all their life long under the foolish superstition that they can be cheated. But it is as impossible for a man to be cheated by any one but himself, as for a thing to be and not to be at the same time. There is a third silent party to all our bargains. The nature and soul of things takes on itself the guaranty of the fulfilment of every contract, so that honest service cannot come to loss. If you serve an ungrateful master, serve him the more. Put God in your debt. Every stroke shall be repaid. The longer the payment is withholden, the better for you; for compound interest on compound interest is the rate and usage of this exchequer.

The history of persecution is a history of endeavors to cheat nature, to make water run up hill, to twist a rope of sand. It makes no difference whether the actors be many or one, a tyrant or a mob. A mob is a society of bodies voluntarily bereaving themselves of reason and traversing

---

*Scars over.
†The islands of Hawaii were formerly called the Sandwich Islands.

its work. The mob is man voluntarily descending to the nature of the beast. Its fit hour of activity is night. Its actions are insane, like its whole constitution. It persecutes a principle; it would whip a right; it would tar and feather justice, by inflicting fire and outrage upon the houses and persons of those who have these. It resembles the prank of boys, who run with fire-engines to put out the ruddy aurora streaming to the stars. The inviolate spirit turns their spite against the wrongdoers. The martyr cannot be dishonored. Every lash inflicted is a tongue of fame; every prison a more illustrious abode; every burned book or house enlightens the world; every suppressed or expunged word reverberates through the earth from side to side. Hours of sanity and consideration are always arriving to communities, as to individuals, when the truth is seen and the martyrs are justified.

Thus do all things preach the indifferency of circumstances. The man is all. Every thing has two sides, a good and an evil. Every advantage has its tax. I learn to be content. But the doctrine of compensation is not the doctrine of indifferency. The thoughtless say, on hearing these representations,—What boots it to do well? there is one event to good and evil; if I gain any good I must pay for it; if I lose any good I gain some other; all actions are indifferent.

There is a deeper fact in the soul than compensation, to wit, its own nature. The soul is not a compensation, but a life. The soul *is.* Under all this running sea of circumstance, whose waters ebb and flow with perfect balance, lies the aboriginal abyss of real Being. Essence, or God, is not a relation or a part, but the whole. Being is the vast affirmative, excluding negation, self-balanced, and swallowing up all relations, parts and times within itself. Nature, truth, virtue, are the influx from thence. Vice is the absence or departure of the same. Nothing, Falsehood, may indeed stand as the great Night or shade on which as a background the living universe paints itself forth, but no fact is begotten by it; it cannot work, for it is not. It cannot work any good; it cannot work any harm. It is harm inasmuch as it is worse not to be than to be.

We feel defrauded of the retribution due to evil acts, because the criminal adheres to his vice and contumacy and does not come to a crisis or judgment anywhere in visible nature. There is no stunning confutation of his nonsense before men and angels. Has he therefore outwitted the law? Inasmuch as he carries the malignity and the lie with him he so far deceases from nature. In some manner there will be a demonstration of the wrong to the understanding also; but, should we not see it, this deadly deduction makes square the eternal account.

Neither can it be said, on the other hand, that the gain of rectitude must be bought by any loss. There is no penalty to virtue; no penalty to wisdom; they are proper additions of being. In a virtuous action I properly *am;* in a virtuous act I add to the world; I plant into deserts conquered from Chaos and Nothing and see the darkness receding on the limits of the horizon. There can be no excess to love, none to knowledge, none to beauty, when these attributes are considered in the purest sense. The soul refuses limits, and always affirms an Optimism, never a Pessimism.

His life is a progress, and not a station. His instinct is trust. Our instinct uses "more" and "less" in application to man, of the *presence of the soul,* and not of its absence; the brave man is greater than the coward; the true, the benevolent, the wise, is more a man and not less, than the fool and knave. There is no tax on the good of virtue, for that is the incoming of God himself, or absolute existence, without any comparative. Material good has its tax, and if it came without desert or sweat, has no root in me, and the next wind will blow it away. But all the good of nature is the soul's, and may be had if paid for in nature's lawful coin, that is, by labor which the heart and the head allow. I no longer wish to meet a good I do not earn, for example to find a pot of buried gold, knowing that it brings with it new burdens. I do not wish more external goods,— neither possessions, nor honors, nor powers, nor persons. The gain is apparent; the tax is certain. But there is no tax on the knowledge that the compensation exists and that it is not desirable to dig up treasure. Herein I rejoice with a serene eternal peace. I contract the boundaries of possible mischief. I learn the wisdom of St. Bernard,—"Nothing can work me damage except myself; the harm that I sustain I carry about with me, and never am a real sufferer but by my own fault."*

In the nature of the soul is the compensation for the inequalities of condition. The radical tragedy of nature seems to be the distinction of More and Less. How can Less not feel the pain; how not feel indignation or malevolence towards More? Look at those who have less faculty, and one feels sad and knows not well what to make of it. He almost shuns their eye; he fears they will upbraid God. What should they do? It seems a great injustice. But see the facts nearly and these mountainous inequalities vanish. Love reduces them as the sun melts the iceberg in the sea. The heart and soul of all men being one, this bitterness of *His* and *Mine* ceases. His is mine. I am my brother and my brother is me. If I feel

---

*Compare *The Meditations of St. Augustine . . . with Select Contemplations from St. Anselm and St. Bernard,* translated by George Stanhope (London, 1818).

overshadowed and outdone by great neighbors, I can yet love; I can still receive; and he that loveth maketh his own the grandeur he loves. Thereby I make the discovery that my brother is my guardian, acting for me with the friendliest designs, and the estate I so admired and envied is my own. It is the nature of the soul to appropriate all things. Jesus and Shakspeare are fragments of the soul, and by love I conquer and incorporate them in my own conscious domain. His virtue,—is not that mine? His wit,—if it cannot be made mine, it is not wit.

Such also is the natural history of calamity. The changes which break up at short intervals the prosperity of men are advertisements of a nature whose law is growth. Every soul is by this intrinsic necessity quitting its whole system of things, its friends and home and laws and faith, as the shellfish crawls out of its beautiful but stony case, because it no longer admits of its growth, and slowly forms a new house. In proportion to the vigor of the individual these revolutions are frequent, until in some happier mind they are incessant and all worldly relations hang very loosely about him, becoming as it were a transparent fluid membrane through which the living form is seen, and not, as in most men, an indurated* heterogeneous fabric of many dates and of no settled character, in which the man is imprisoned. Then there can be enlargement, and the man of to-day scarcely recognizes the man of yesterday. And such should be the outward biography of man in time, a putting off of dead circumstances day by day, as he renews his raiment day by day. But to us, in our lapsed estate, resting, not advancing, resisting, not coöperating with the divine expansion, this growth comes by shocks.

We cannot part with our friends. We cannot let our angels go. We do not see that they only go out that archangels may come in. We are idolators of the old. We do not believe in the riches of the soul, in its proper eternity and omnipresence. We do not believe there is any force in to-day to rival or recreate that beautiful yesterday. We linger in the ruins of the old tent where once we had bread and shelter and organs, nor believe that the spirit can feed, cover, and nerve us again. We cannot again find aught so dear, so sweet, so graceful. But we sit and weep in vain. The voice of the Almighty saith, 'Up and onward for evermore!'[3] We cannot stay amid the ruins. Neither will we rely on the new; and so we walk ever with reverted eyes, like those monsters who look backwards.

And yet the compensations of calamity are made apparent to the understanding also, after long intervals of time. A fever, a mutilation, a

---

*Hardened.

cruel disappointment, a loss of wealth, a loss of friends, seems at the moment unpaid loss, and unpayable. But the sure years reveal the deep remedial force that underlies all facts. The death of a dear friend, wife, brother, lover, which seemed nothing but privation, somewhat later assumes the aspect of a guide or genius; for it commonly operates revolutions in our way of life, terminates an epoch of infancy or of youth which was waiting to be closed, breaks up a wonted occupation, or a household, or style of living, and allows the formation of new ones more friendly to the growth of character. It permits or constrains the formation of new acquaintances and the reception of new influences that prove of the first importance to the next years; and the man or woman who would have remained a sunny garden-flower, with no room for its roots and too much sunshine for its head, by the falling of the walls and the neglect of the gardener is made the banian* of the forest, yielding shade and fruit to wide neighborhoods of men.

---

*That is, the banyan, a large, spreading tree.

Spiritual Laws[1]

The living Heaven thy prayers respect,
House at once and architect,
Quarrying man's rejected hours,
Builds therewith eternal towers;
Sole and self-commanded works,
Fear not undermining days,
Grows by decays,
And, by the famous might that lurks
In reaction and recoil,
Makes flame to freeze, and ice to boil;
Forging, through swart arms of Offence,
The silver seat of Innocence.

WHEN THE ACT OF reflection takes place in the mind, when we look at ourselves in the light of thought, we discover that our life is embosomed in beauty. Behind us, as we go, all things assume pleasing forms, as clouds do far off. Not only things familiar and stale, but even the tragic and terrible are comely, as they take their place in the pictures of memory. The river-bank, the weed at the water-side, the old house, the foolish person—however neglected in the passing—have a grace in the past. Even the corpse that has lain in the chambers has added a solemn ornament to the house. The soul will not know either deformity or pain. If in the hour of clear reason we should speak the severest truth, we should say, that we had never made a sacrifice. In these hours the mind seems so great that nothing can be taken from us that seems much.[2] All loss, all pain is particular: the universe remains to the heart unhurt. Distress never, trifles never abate our trust. No man ever stated his griefs as lightly as he might. Allow for exaggeration in the most patient and sorely ridden hack that ever was driven. For it is only the finite that has wrought and suffered; the infinite lies stretched in smiling repose.

The intellectual life may be kept clean and healthful, if man will live the life of nature, and not import into his mind difficulties which are none of his. No man need be perplexed in his speculations. Let him do and say what strictly belongs to him, and though very ignorant of books, his nature shall not yield him any intellectual obstructions and doubts. Our young people are diseased with the theological problems of original sin, origin of evil, predestination, and the like. These never presented a practical difficulty to any man—never darkened across any man's road, who did not go out of his way to seek them. These are the soul's mumps and measles, and whooping-coughs, and those who have not caught them, cannot describe their health or prescribe the cure. A simple mind will not know these enemies. It is quite another thing that he should be able to give account of his faith, and expound to another the theory of his self-union and freedom. This requires rare gifts. Yet without this self-knowledge, there may be a sylvan strength and integrity in that which he is. "A few strong instincts and a few plain rules" suffice us.*

My will never gave the images in my mind the rank they now take. The regular course of studies, the years of academical and professional education have yielded me better facts than some idle books under the bench at the Latin school. What we do not call education is more precious than that which we call so.[3] We form no guess at the time of receiving a thought, of its comparative value. And education often wastes its effort in attempts to thwart and balk this natural magnetism which with sure discrimination selects its own.

In like manner, our moral nature is vitiated by any interference of our will. People represent virtue as a struggle, and take to themselves great airs upon their attainments, and the question is everywhere vexed, when a noble nature is commended, Whether the man is not better who strives with temptation? But there is no merit in the matter. Either God is there, or he is not there. We love characters in proportion as they are impulsive and spontaneous. The less a man thinks or knows about his virtues, the better we like him. Timoleon's victories are the best victories; which ran and flowed like Homer's verses, Plutarch said.† When we see a soul whose acts are all regal, graceful and pleasant as roses, we must thank God that such things can be and are, and not turn sourly on

---

*From William Wordsworth's poem "Alas! What Boots the Long Laborius Quest" (1809): "And may not we with sorrow say— / A few strong instincts and a few plain rules, / Among the herdsmen of the Alps, have wrought / More for mankind at this unhappy day / Then all the pride of intellect and thought?"

†Emerson takes the comparison of Timoleon's victories with Homer's verses from Plutarch's *Lives*.

the angel, and say, "Crump is a better man with his grunting resistance to all his native devils."*

Not less conspicuous is the preponderance of nature over will in all practical life. There is less intention in history than we ascribe to it. We impute deep-laid, far-sighted plans to Cæsar and Napoleon; but the best of their power was in nature, not in them. Men of an extraordinary success, in their honest moments, have always sung, "Not unto us, not unto us."† According to the faith of their times, they have built altars to Fortune or to Destiny, or to St. Julian. Their success lay in their parallelism to the course of thought, which found in them an unobstructed channel; and the wonders of which they were the visible conductors, seemed to the eye their deed. Did the wires generate the galvanism?‡ It is even true that there was less in them on which they could reflect, than in another; as the virtue of a pipe is to be smooth and hollow. That which externally seemed will and immovableness was willingness and self-annihilation. Could Shakespeare give a theory of Shakespeare? Could ever a man of prodigious mathematical genius convey to others any insight into his methods? If he could communicate that secret, instantly it would lose all its exaggerated value, blending with the daylight and the vital energy, the power to stand and to go.

The lesson is forcibly taught by these observations that our life might be much easier and simpler than we make it, that the world might be a happier place than it is, that there is no need of struggles, convulsions, and despairs, of the wringing of the hands and the gnashing of the teeth; that we miscreate our own evils. We interfere with the optimism of nature; for, whenever we get this vantage-ground of the past, or of a wiser mind in the present, we are able to discern that we are begirt with spiritual laws which execute themselves.

The face of external nature teaches the same lesson with calm superiority. Nature will not have us fret and fume.

She does not like our benevolence or our learning, much better than she likes our frauds and wars. When we come out of the caucus, or the bank, or the Abolition convention, or the temperance meeting or the Transcendental club,⁴ into the fields and woods, she says to us, "So hot? my little sir."

We are full of mechanical actions. We must needs intermeddle, and

---

*"Crump" was a common name for a member of the middle class.
†Reference to the Bible, Psalms 115:1: "Not unto us, O Lord, not unto us, but unto thy name give glory, for thy mercy, and for thy truth's sake" (KJV).
‡Direct electrical current.

have things in our own way, until the sacrifices and virtues of society are odious. Love should make joy; but our benevolence is unhappy. Our Sunday-schools and churches and pauper societies are yokes to the neck. We pain ourselves to please nobody. There are natural ways of arriving at the same ends at which these aim, but do not arrive. Why should all virtue work in one and the same way? Why should all give dollars? It is very inconvenient to us country folk, and we do not think any good will come of it. We have not dollars. Merchants have. Let them give them. Farmers will give corn. Poets will sing. Women will sew. Laborers will lend a hand. The children will bring flowers. And why drag this dead weight of a Sunday-school over the whole Christendom? It is natural and beautiful that childhood should inquire, and maturity should teach; but it is time enough to answer questions when they are asked. Do not shut up the young people against their will in a pew, and force the children to ask them questions for an hour against their will.

If we look wider, things are all alike; laws and letters, and creeds and modes of living, seem a travesty of truth. Our society is encumbered by ponderous machinery which resembles the endless aqueducts which the Romans built over hill and dale, and which are superseded by the discovery of the law that water rises to the level of its source. It is a Chinese wall which any nimble Tartar can leap over. It is a standing army not so good as a peace. It is a graduated, titled, richly appointed Empire, quite superfluous when town-meetings are found to answer just as well.

Let us draw a lesson from nature, which always works by short ways. When the fruit is ripe, it falls. When the fruit is despatched, the leaf falls. The circuit of the waters is mere falling. The walking of man and all animals is a falling forward. All our manual labor and works of strength, as prying, splitting, digging, rowing and so forth, are done by dint of continual falling, and the globe, earth, moon, comet, sun, star, fall forever and ever.

The simplicity of the universe is very different from the simplicity of a machine. He who sees moral nature out and out and thoroughly knows how knowledge is acquired and character formed, is a pedant. The simplicity of nature is not that which may easily be read, but is inexhaustible. The last analysis can nowise be made. We judge of a man's wisdom by his hope, knowing that the perception of the inexhaustibleness of nature is an immortal youth. The wild fertility of nature is felt in comparing our rigid names and reputations with our fluid consciousness. We pass in the world for sects and schools, for erudition and piety, and we are all the time jejune* babes. One sees very well how Pyrrhonism† grew up. Every man sees that he is that middle point whereof everything may be affirmed and denied with equal reason. He is old, he is young, he is very wise, he is altogether ignorant. He hears and feels what you say of the seraphim, and of the tin-peddler. There is no permanent wise man, except in the figment of the stoics. We side with the hero, as we read or paint, against the coward and the robber; but we have been ourselves that coward and robber, and shall be again, not in the low circumstance, but in comparison with the grandeurs possible to the soul.

A little consideration of what takes place around us every day, would show us that a higher law than that of our will, regulates events; that our painful labors are very unnecessary, and altogether fruitless; that only in our easy, simple, spontaneous action we are strong, and by contenting ourselves with obedience we become divine. Belief and love—a believing love will relieve us of a vast load of care. O my brothers, God exists. There is a soul at the center of nature, and over the will of every man, so that none of us can wrong the universe. It has so infused its strong enchantment into nature, that we prosper when we accept its advice, and when we struggle to wound its creatures, our hands are glued to our sides, or they beat our own breasts. The whole course of things goes to teach us faith. We need only obey. There is guidance for each of us, and by lowly listening we shall hear the right word. Why need you choose so painfully your place, and occupation, and associates, and modes of action, and of entertainment? Certainly there is a possible right for you that precludes the need of balance and wilful election. For you there is a reality, a fit place and congenial duties. Place yourself in the middle of the stream of power and wisdom which flows into you as life, place yourself in the full center of that flood, then you are without effort impelled to truth, to right, and a perfect contentment. Then you put all gainsayers in the wrong. Then you are the world, the measure of right, of truth, of beauty. If we will not be marplots‡ with our miserable interferences, the work, the society, letters, arts, science, religion of men, would go on far better than now, and the Heaven predicted from the be-

---

*Inexperienced.
†Philosophy of skepticism, named after the Greek philosopher Pyrrho (c.360–270 B.C.), who maintained that nothing could be known with certainty.
‡A marplot frustrates or ruins a plan.

ginning of the world, and still predicted from the bottom of the heart, would organize itself, as do now the rose, and the air, and the sun.

I say, *do not choose;* but that is a figure of speech by which I would distinguish what is commonly called *choice* among men, and which is a partial act, the choice of the hands, of the eyes, of the appetites, and not a whole act of the man. But that which I call right or goodness, is the choice of my constitution; and that which I call heaven, and inwardly aspire after, is the state or circumstance desirable to my constitution; and the action which I in all my years tend to do, is the work for my faculties. We must hold a man amendable to reason for the choice of his daily craft or profession. It is not an excuse any longer for his deeds that they are the custom of his trade. What business has he with an evil trade? Has he not a *calling* in his character?

Each man has his own vocation. The talent is the call. There is one direction in which all space is open to him. He has faculties silently inviting him thither to endless exertion. He is like a ship in a river; he runs against obstructions on every side but one; on that side, all obstruction is taken away, and he sweeps serenely over God's depths into an infinite sea. This talent and this call depend on his organization, or the mode in which the general soul incarnates itself in him. He inclines to do something which is easy to him, and good when it is done, but which no other man can do. He has no rival. For the more truly he consults his own powers, the more difference will his work exhibit from the work of any other. When he is true and faithful, his ambition is exactly proportioned to his powers. The height of the pinnacle is determined by the breadth of the base. Every man has this call of the power to do somewhat unique, and no man has any other call. The pretense that he has another call, a summons by name and personal election and outward "signs that mark him extraordinary, and not in the roll of common men," is fanaticism, and betrays obtuseness to perceive that there is one mind in all the individuals, and no respect of persons therein.

By doing his work, he makes the need felt which he can supply. He creates the taste by which he is enjoyed. He provokes the wants to which he can minister. By doing his own work, he unfolds himself. It is the vice of our public speaking, that it has not abandonment. Somewhere, not only every orator but every man should let out all the length of all the reins; should find or make a frank and hearty expression of what force and meaning is in him. The common experience is, that the man fits himself as well as he can to the customary details of that work or trade he falls into, and tends it as a dog turns a spit. Then is he a part of the machine he moves; the man is lost. Until he can manage to communicate himself to others in his full stature and proportion as a wise and good man, he does not yet find his vocation. He must find in that an outlet for his character, so that he may justify himself to their eyes for doing what he does. If the labor is trivial, let him by his thinking and character make it liberal. Whatever he knows and thinks, whatever in his apprehension is worth doing, that let him communicate, or men will never know and honor him aright. Foolish, whenever you take the meanness and formality of that thing you do, instead of converting it into the obedient spiracle* of your character and aims.

We like only such actions as have already long had the praise of men, and do not perceive that anything man can do may be divinely done. We think greatness entailed or organized in some places or duties, in certain offices or occasions, and do not see that Paganini can extract rapture from a catgut, and Eulenstein from a jews-harp, and a nimble-fingered lad out of shreds of paper with his scissors; and Landseer out of swine, and the hero out of the pitiful habitation and company in which he was hidden. What we call obscure condition or vulgar society, is that condition and society whose poetry is not yet written, but which you shall presently make as enviable and renowned as any. Accept your genius, and say what you think. In our estimates, let us take a lesson from kings. The parts of hospitality, the connection of families, the impressiveness of death, and a thousand other things royalty makes its own estimate of, and a royal mind will. To make habitually a new estimate—that is elevation.

What a man does, that he has. What has he to do with hope or fear? In himself is his might. Let him regard no good as solid, but that which is in his nature, and which must grow out of him as long as he exists. The goods of fortune may come and go like summer leaves; let him play with them, and scatter them on every wind as the momentary signs of his infinite productiveness.[5]

He may have his own. A man's genius, the quality that differences him from every other, the susceptibility to one class of influences, the selection of what is fit for him, the rejection of what is unfit, determines for him the character of the universe. As a man thinketh, so is he, and as a man chooseth, so is he and so is nature. A man is a method, a progressive arrangement; a selecting principle, gathering his like to him, wherever he goes. He takes only his own out of the multiplicity that sweeps and circles round him. He is like one of those booms which are

---

*Breath, spirit; an aperture for breathing.

set out from the shore on rivers to catch drift-wood, or like the load-stone* among splinters of steel.

Those facts, words, persons which dwell in his memory without his being able to say why, remain, because they have a relation to him not less real for being as yet unapprehended. They are symbols of value to him, as they can interpret parts of his consciousness which he would vainly seek words for in the conventional images of books and other minds. What attracts my attention shall have it, as I will go to the man who knocks at my door, while a thousand persons, as worthy, go by it, to whom I give no regard. It is enough that these particulars speak to me. A few anecdotes, a few traits of character, manners, face, a few incidents have an emphasis in your memory out of all proportion to their apparent significance, if you measure them by the ordinary standards. They relate to your gift. Let them have their weight, and do not reject them and cast about for illustration and facts more usual in literature. Respect them, for they have their origin in deepest nature. What your heart thinks great, is great. The soul's emphasis is always right.

Over all things that are agreeable to his nature and genius, the man has the highest right. Everywhere he may take what belongs to his spiritual estate, nor can he take anything else, though all doors were open, nor can all the force of men hinder him from taking so much. It is vain to attempt to keep a secret from one who has a right to know it. It will tell itself. That mood into which a friend can bring us, is his dominion over us. To the thoughts of that state of mind, he has a right. All the secrets of that state of mind, he can compel. This is a law which statesmen use in practice. All the terrors of the French Republic, which held Austria in awe, were unable to command her diplomacy. But Napoleon sent to Vienna M. de Narbonne, one of the old noblesse, with the morals, manners and name of that interest, saying, that it was indispensable to send to the old aristocracy of Europe, men of the same connection, which, in fact, constitutes a sort of free masonry.† M. Narbonne, in less than a fortnight, penetrated all the secrets of the Imperial Cabinet.‡

A mutual understanding is ever the firmest chain. Nothing seems so easy as to speak and to be understood. Yet a man may come to find *that* the strongest of defenses and of ties—that he has been understood; and

---

*Magnet.
†Secret society or brotherhood.
‡From *Mémorial de Sainte Hélène* (1823), by Comte Emmanuel de Las Cases; see note on p. 134.

he who has received an opinion, may come to find it the most inconvenient of bonds.

If a teacher have any opinion which he wishes to conceal, his pupils will become as fully indoctrinated into that as into any which he publishes. If you pour water into a vessel twisted into coils and angles, it is vain to say, I will pour it only into this or that—it will find its own level in all. Men feel and act the consequences of your doctrine, without being able to show how they follow. Show us an arc of the curve, and a good mathematician will find out the whole figure. We are always reasoning from the seen to the unseen. Hence the perfect intelligence that subsists between wise men of remote ages. A man cannot bury his meanings so deep in his book, but time and like-minded men will find them. Plato had a secret doctrine, had he? What secret can he conceal from the eyes of Bacon? of Montaigne? of Kant? Therefore, *Aristotle* said of his works, "They are published and not published."*

No man can learn what he has not preparation for learning, however near to his eyes is the object. A chemist may tell his most precious secrets to a carpenter, and he shall be never the wiser—the secrets he would not utter to a chemist for an estate. God screens us evermore from premature ideas. Our eyes are *holden* that we cannot see things that stare us in the face,† until the hour arrives when the mind is ripened, then we behold them, and the time when we saw them not, is like a dream.

Not in nature but in man is all the beauty and worth he sees. The world is very empty, and is indebted to this gilding, exalting soul for all its pride. "Earth fills her lap with splendors" *not her own.*‡ The vale of Tempe, Tivoli§ and Rome are earth and water, rocks and sky. There are as good earth and water in a thousand places, yet how unaffecting!

People are not the better for the sun and the moon, the horizon and the trees; as it is not observed that the keepers of Roman galleries, or the valets of painters have any elevation of thought, or that librarians are wiser men than others. There are graces in the demeanor of a polished and noble person, which are lost upon the eye of a churl.‖ These are like the stars whose light has not yet reached us.

---

*Emerson takes this quotation from Plutarch's "Life of Alexander."

†Reference to the Bible, Luke 24:16: "But their eyes were holden that they should not know him" (KJV).

‡Reference to William Wordsworth's poem "Ode: Intimations of Immortality" (1807; line 77): "Earth fills her lap with pleasures of her own."

§*Tempe:* beautiful valley in ancient Thessaly; *Tivoli:* pleasure resort near Rome.

‖Peasant; ill-mannered person.

He may see what he maketh. Our dreams are the sequel of our waking knowledge. The visions of the night always bear some proportion to the visions of the day. Hideous dreams are only exaggerations of the sins of the day. We see our own evil affections embodied in bad physiognomies. On the Alps, the traveler sometimes sees his own shadow magnified to a giant, so that every gesture of his hand is terrific. "My children," said an old man to his boys scared by a figure in the dark entry, "my children, you will never see anything worse than yourselves."[6] As in dreams, so in the scarcely less fluid events of the world, every man sees himself in colossal, without knowing that it is himself that he sees. The good which he sees, compared to the evil which he sees, is as his own good to his own evil. Every quality of his mind is magnified in some one acquaintance, and every emotion of his heart in some one. He is like a quincunx of trees, which counts five, east, west, north, or south;* or, an initial, medial, and terminal acrostic.† And why not? He cleaves to one person, and avoids another, according to their likeness or unlikeness to himself, truly seeking himself in his associates, and moreover in his trade, and habits, and gestures, and meats, and drinks; and comes at last to be faithfully represented by every view you take of his circumstances.

He may read what he writeth. What can we see or acquire, but what we are? You have seen a skilful man reading Virgil. Well, that author is a thousand books to a thousand persons. Take the book into your two hands, and read your eyes out; you will never find what I find. If any ingenious reader would have a monopoly of the wisdom or delight he gets, he is as secure now the book is Englished, as if it were imprisoned in the Pelews tongue.‡ It is with a good book as it is with good company. Introduce a base person among gentlemen: it is all to no purpose; he is not their fellow. Every society protects itself. The company is perfectly safe, and he is not one of them, though his body is in the room.

What avails it to fight with the eternal laws of mind, which adjust the relation of all persons to each other, by the mathematical measure of their havings and beings? Gertrude is enamored of Guy; how high, how aristocratic, how Roman his mien and manners! to live with him were life indeed: and no purchase is too great; and heaven and earth are

---

*Pattern in which four trees are planted in a square with a fifth tree in the middle of the square.

†Arrangement of letters that reads the same way forward and backward, up and down, and along the diagonal.

‡Polynesian language spoken in the Caroline islands of the western Pacific.

moved to that end. Well, Gertrude has Guy: but what now avails how high, how aristocratic, how Roman his mien and manners, if his heart and aims are in the senate, in the theater and in the billiard-room, and she has no aims, no conversation that can enchant her graceful lord?

He shall have his own society. We can love nothing but nature. The most wonderful talents, the most meritorious exertions really avail very little with us; but nearness or likeness of nature, how beautiful is the case of its victory! Persons approach us famous for their beauty, for their accomplishments, worthy of all wonder for their charms and gifts: they dedicate their whole skill to the hour and the company, with very imperfect result. To be sure, it would be very ungrateful in us not to praise them very loudly. Then, when all is done, a person of related mind, a brother or sister by nature, comes to us so softly and easily, so nearly and intimately, as if it were the blood in our proper veins, that we feel as if some one was gone, instead of another having come: we are utterly relieved and refreshed: it is a sort of joyful solitude. We foolishly think, in our days of sin, that we must court friends by compliance to the customs of society, to its dress, its breeding and its estimates. But later, if we are so happy, we learn that only that soul can be my friend, which I encounter on the line of my own march, that soul to which I do not decline, and which does not decline to me, but, native of the same celestial latitude, repeats in its own all my experience. The scholar and the prophet forget themselves, and ape the customs and costumes of the man of the world, to deserve the smile of beauty. He is a fool and follows some giddy girl, and not with religious, ennobling passion, a woman with all that is serene, oracular and beautiful in her soul. Let him be great, and love shall follow him. Nothing is more deeply punished than the neglect of the affinities by which alone society should be formed, and the insane levity of choosing associates by others' eyes.

He may set his own rate. It is an universal maxim, worthy of all acceptation, that a man may have that allowance he takes. Take the place and attitude to which you see your unquestionable right, and all men acquiesce. The world must be just. It always leaves every man with profound unconcern to set his own rate. Hero or driveler, it meddles not in the matter. It will certainly accept your own measure of your doing and being, whether you sneak about and deny your own name, or, whether you see your work produced to the concave sphere of the heavens, one with the revolution of the stars.

The same reality pervades all teaching. The man may teach by doing, and not otherwise. If he can communicate himself, he can teach, but not by words. He teaches who gives, and he learns who receives. There

is no teaching until the pupil is brought into the same state or principle
in which you are; a transfusion takes place: he is you, and you are he;
then is a teaching, and by no unfriendly chance or bad company can he
ever quite lose the benefit. But your propositions run out of one ear as
they run in at the other. We see it advertised that Mr. Grand will deliver
an oration on the Fourth of July, and Mr. Hand before the Mechanics'
Association, and we do not go thither, because we know that these gen-
tlemen will not communicate their own character and being to the au-
dience. If we had reason to expect such a communication, we should go
through all inconvenience and opposition. The sick would be carried in
litters. But a public oration is an escapade, a non-committal, an apol-
ogy, a gag, and not a communication, not a speech, not a man.

A like Nemesis presides over all intellectual works. We have yet to
learn, that the thing uttered in words is not therefore affirmed. It must
affirm itself, or no forms of grammar and no plausibility can give it ev-
idence, and no array of arguments. The sentence must also contain its
own apology for being spoken.

The effect of any writing on the public mind is mathematically
measurable by its depth of thought. How much water does it draw? If it
awaken you to think; if it lift you from your feet with the great voice of
eloquence; then the effect is to be wide, slow, permanent, over the
minds of men; if the pages instruct you not, they will die like flies in the
hour. The way to speak and write what shall not go out of fashion, is to
speak and write sincerely. The argument which has not power to reach
my own practice, I may well doubt, will fail to reach yours. But take
Sidney's maxim: "Look in thy heart, and write."* He that writes to him-
self, writes to an eternal public. That statement only is fit to be made
public which you have come at in attempting to satisfy your own cu-
riosity. The writer who takes his subject from his ear and not from his
heart, should know that he has lost as much as he seems to have gained,
and when the empty book has gathered all its praise, and half the peo-
ple say—"what poetry! what genius!" it still needs fuel to make fire.
That only profits which is profitable. Life alone can impart life; and
though we should burst, we can only be valued as we make ourselves
valuable. There is no luck in literary reputation. They who make up the
final verdict upon every book, are not the partial and noisy readers of
the hour when it appears; but a court as of angels, a public not to be
bribed, not to be entreated, and not to be overawed, decides upon every

---

*From Sir Philip Sidney's *Astrophel and Stella* (1591), sonnet 1, line 14.

man's title to fame. Only those books come down which deserve to last. All the gilt edges and vellum and morocco, all the presentation-copies to all the libraries will not preserve a book in circulation beyond its intrinsic date. It must go with all Walpole's Noble and Royal Authors to its fate.* Blackmore, Kotzebue, or Pollok may endure for a night, but Moses and Homer stand forever. There are not in the world at any one time more than a dozen persons who read and understand Plato—never enough to pay for an edition of his works; yet to every generation these come duly down, for the sake of those few persons, as if God brought them in his hand. "No book," said Bentley, "was ever written down by any one but itself."† The permanence of all books is fixed by no effort friendly or hostile, but by their own specific gravity, or the intrinsic importance of their contents to the constant mind of man. "Do not trouble yourself too much about the light on your statue," said Michael Angelo to the young sculptor; "the light of the public square will test its value."‡

In like manner the effect of every action is measured by the depth of the sentiments from which it proceeds. The great man knew not that he was great. It took a century or two, for that fact to appear. What he did, he did because he must: he used no election: it was the most natural thing in the world, and grew out of the circumstances of the moment. But now everything he did, even to the lifting of his finger, or the eating of bread, looks large, all-related, and is called an institution.

These are the demonstrations in a few particulars of the genius of nature: they show the direction of the stream. But the stream is blood: every drop is alive. Truth has not single victories: all things are its organs, not only dust and stones, but errors and lies. The laws of disease, physicians say, are as beautiful as the laws of health. Our philosophy is affirmative, and readily accepts the testimony of negative facts, as every shadow points to the sun.[7] By a divine necessity, every fact in nature is constrained to offer its testimony.

Human character does evermore publish itself. It will not be concealed. It hates darkness—it rushes into light. The most fugitive deed and word, the mere air of doing a thing, the intimated purpose, expresses character. If you act, you show character; if you sit still, you show it; if you sleep, you show it. You think because you have spoken nothing,

---

*Horace Walpole's *A Catalogue of the Royal and Noble Authors of England* (1758) lists numerous books that are now unheard of.

†From James Henry Monk's *The Life of Richard Bentley* (1833), vol. 1, p. 116.

‡From Thomas Roscoe, "The Life of Michael Angelo Buonaroti," in *Lives of Eminent Persons* (London, 1833), p. 72.

when others spoke, and have given no opinion on the times, on the church, on slavery, on the college, on parties and persons, that your verdict is still expected with curiosity as a reserved wisdom. Far otherwise; your silence answers very loud. You have no oracle to utter, and your fellow-men have learned that you cannot help them; for, oracles speak. Doth not wisdom cry, and understanding put forth her voice?*

Dreadful limits are set in nature to the powers of dissimulation. Truth tyrannizes over the unwilling members of the body. Faces never lie, it is said. No man need be deceived, who will study the changes of expression. When a man speaks the truth in the spirit of truth, his eye is as clear as the heavens. When he has base ends, and speaks falsely, the eye is muddy and sometimes asquint.

I have heard an experienced counselor say, that he feared never the effect upon a jury, of a lawyer who does not believe in his heart that his client ought to have a verdict. If he does not believe it, his unbelief will appear to the jury, despite all his protestations, and will become their unbelief. This is that law whereby a work of art, of whatever kind, sets us in the same state of mind wherein the artist was, when he made it. That which we do not believe, we cannot adequately say, though we may repeat the words never so often. It was this conviction which Swedenborg expressed, when he described a group of persons in the spiritual world endeavoring in vain to articulate a proposition which they did not believe; but they could not, though they twisted and folded their lips even to indignation.†

A man passes for that he is worth. Very idle is all curiosity concerning other people's estimate of us, and idle is all fear of remaining unknown. If a man know that he can do anything—that he can do it better than any one else—he has a pledge of the acknowledgment of that fact by all persons. The world is full of judgment days, and into every assembly that a man enters, in every action that he attempts, he is gauged and stamped. In every troop of boys that whoop and run in each yard and square, a newcomer is as well and accurately weighed in the balance, in the course of a few days, and stamped with his right number, as if he had undergone a formal trial of his strength, speed and temper. A stranger comes from a distant school, with better dress, with trinkets in his pockets, with airs and pretension; an old boy sniffs thereat, and says to himself, "It's of no use: we shall find him out to-morrow." "What hath he done?" is the divine question which searches men, and transpierces

---

*This passage is from the Bible, Proverbs 8:1.
†The anecdote is taken from *The Apocalypse Revealed* (Boston, 1836).

every false reputation. A fop may sit in any chair of the world, nor be distinguished for his hour from Homer and Washington; but there can never be any doubt concerning the respective ability of human beings, when we seek the truth. Pretension may sit still, but cannot act. Pretension never feigned an act of real greatness. Pretension never wrote an *Iliad*, nor drove back Xerxes, nor christianized the world, nor abolished slavery.

Always as much virtue as there is, so much appears; as much goodness as there is, so much reverence it commands. All the devils respect virtue. The high, the generous, the self-devoted sect will always instruct and command mankind. Never a sincere word was utterly lost. Never a magnanimity fell to the ground. Always the heart of man greets and accepts it unexpectedly. A man passes for that he is worth. What he is, engraves itself on his face, on his form, on his fortunes, in letters of light which all men may read but himself. Concealment avails him nothing, boasting nothing. There is confession in the glances of our eyes, in our smiles, in salutations, and the grasp of hands. His sin bedaubs him, mars all his good impression. Men know not why they do not trust him; but they do not trust him. His vice glasses his eye, demeans his cheek, pinches the nose, sets the mark of the beast on the back of the head, and writes O fool! fool! on the forehead of a king.

If you would not be known to do anything, never do it. A man may play the fool in the drifts of a desert, but every grain of sand shall seem to see. He may be a solitary eater, but he cannot keep his foolish counsel. A broken complexion, a swinish look, ungenerous acts, and the want of due knowledge—all blab. Can a cook, a Chiffinch, an Iachimo be mistaken for Zeno or Paul? Confucius exclaimed, "How can a man be concealed! How can a man be concealed!"*

On the other hand, the hero fears not, that if he withhold the avowal of a just and brave act, it will go unwitnessed and unloved. One knows it—himself—and is pledged by it to sweetness of peace, and to nobleness of aim, which will prove in the end a better proclamation of it than the relating of the incident. Virtue is the adherence in action to the nature of things, and the nature of things makes it prevalent. It consists in a perpetual substitution of being for seeming, and with sublime propriety God is described as saying, I AM.†

---

*From *Analects*, II, x, 4.

†Reference to the Bible, Exodus 3:14: "And God said unto Moses, I AM THAT I AM: and he said, Thus shalt thou say unto the children of Israel, I AM hath sent me unto you" (KJV).

The lesson which all these observations convey is, Be and not seem. Let us acquiesce. Let us take our bloated nothingness out of the path of the divine circuits. Let us unlearn our wisdom of the world. Let us lie low in the Lord's power, and learn that truth alone makes rich and great.

If you visit your friend, why need you apologize for not having visited him, and waste his time and deface your own act? Visit him now. Let him feel that the highest love has come to see him, in thee its lowest organ. Or why need you torment yourself and friend by secret self-reproaches that you have not assisted him or complimented him with gifts and salutations heretofore? Be a gift and a benediction. Shine with real light, and not with the borrowed reflection of gifts. Common men are apologies for men; they bow the head, they excuse themselves with prolix reasons, they accumulate appearances, because the substance is not.

We are full of these superstitions of sense, the worship of magnitude. God loveth not size: whale and minnow are of like dimension. But we call the poet inactive, because he is not a president, a merchant, or a porter. We adore an institution, and do not see that it is founded on a thought which we have. But real action is in silent moments. The epochs of our life are not in the visible facts of our choice of a calling, our marriage, our acquisition of an office, and the like, but in a silent thought by the wayside as we walk; in a thought which revises our entire manner of life, and says, "Thus hast thou done, but it were better thus." And all our after years, like menials, do serve and wait on this, and, according to their ability, do execute its will. This revisal or correction is a constant force, which, as a tendency, reaches through our lifetime. The object of the man, the aim of these moments is to make daylight shine through him, to suffer the law to traverse his whole being without obstruction, so that, on what point soever of his doing your eye falls, it shall report truly of his character, whether it be his diet, his house, his religious forms, his society, his mirth, his vote, his opposition. Now he is not homogeneous, but heterogeneous, and the ray does not traverse; there are no thorough lights: but the eye of the beholder is puzzled, detecting many unlike tendencies, and a life not yet at one.

Why should we make it a point with our false modesty to disparage that man we are, and that form of being assigned to us? A good man is contented. I love and honor Epaminondas, but I do not wish to be Epaminondas. I hold it more just to love the world of this hour, than the world of his hour. Nor can you, if I am true, excite me to the least uneasiness by saying, "he acted, and thou sittest still." I see action to be good, when the need is, and sitting still to be also good. Epaminondas, if he was the man I take him for, would have sat still with joy and peace, if his lot had been mine. Heaven is large, and affords space for all modes of love and fortitude. Why should we be busy-bodies and superserviceable? Action and inaction are alike to the true. One piece of the tree is cut for a weathercock, and one for the sleeper of a bridge; the virtue of the wood is apparent in both.

I desire not to disgrace the soul. The fact that I am here, certainly shows me that the soul had need of an organ here. Shall I not assume the post? Shall I skulk and dodge and duck with my unseasonable apologies and vain modesty, and imagine my being here impertinent? Less pertinent than Epaminondas or Homer being there? and that the soul did not know its own needs? Besides, without any reasoning on the matter, I have no discontent. The good soul nourishes me always, unlocks new magazines of power and enjoyment to me every day. I will not merely decline the immensity of good, because I have heard that it has come to others in another shape.

Besides, why should we not be cowed by the name of Action? 'Tis a trick of the senses—no more. We know that the ancestor of every action is a thought. The poor mind does not seem to itself to be anything, unless it have an outside badge—some Gentoo diet, or Quaker coat, or Calvinistic prayer-meeting, or philanthropic society, or a great donation, or a high office, or, anyhow, some wild contrasting action to testify that it is somewhat. The rich mind lies in the sun and sleeps, and is Nature. To think is to act.

Let us, if we must have great actions, make our own so. All action is of an infinite elasticity, and the least admits of being inflated with the celestial air until it eclipses the sun and moon. Let us seek *one* peace by fidelity. Let me do my duties. Why should I go gadding into the scenes and philosophy of Greek and Italian history, before I have washed my own face, or justified myself to my own benefactors? How dare I read Washington's campaigns, when I have not answered the letters of my own correspondents? Is not that a just objection to much of our reading? It is a pusillanimous desertion of our work to gaze after our neighbors. It is peeping. Byron says of Jack Bunting:

"He knew not what to say, and so, he swore."*

---

*Compare Byron's poem *The Island*, canto 3, stanza 5; Emerson mistakenly conflates two characters, Jack Skyscrape and Ben Bunting.

I may say it of our preposterous use of books: He knew not what to do, and so, *he read.* I can think of nothing to fill my time with, and so, without any constraint, I find the Life of Brant. It is a very extravagant compliment to pay to Brant, or to General Schuyler, or to General Washington. My time should be as good as their time; my world, my facts, all my net of relations as good as theirs, or either of theirs. Rather let me do my work so well that other idlers, if they choose, may compare my texture with the texture of these and find it identical with the best.

This over-estimate of the possibilities of Paul and Pericles, this under-estimate of our own, comes from a neglect of the fact of an identical nature. Bonaparte knew but one Merit, and rewarded in one and the same way the good soldier, the good astronomer, the good poet, the good player. Thus he signified his sense of a great fact. The poet uses the name of Cæsar, of Tamerlane, of Bonduca, of Belisarius;[8] the painter uses the conventional story of the Virgin Mary, of Paul, of Peter. He does not, therefore, defer to the nature of these accidental men, of these stock heroes. If the poet write a true drama, then he is Cæsar, and not the player of Cæsar; then the self-same strain of thought, emotion as pure, wit as subtle, motions as swift, mounting, extravagant, and a heart as great, self-sufficing, dauntless, which on the waves of its love and hope can uplift all that is reckoned solid and precious in the world, palaces, gardens, money, navies, kingdoms—marking its own incomparable worth by the slight it casts on these gauds of men—these all are his and by the power of these he rouses the nations. But the great names cannot stead him, if he have not life himself. Let a man believe in God, and not in names and places and persons. Let the great soul incarnated in some woman's form, poor and sad and single, in some Dolly or Joan, go out to service, and sweep chambers and scour floors, and its effulgent day-beams cannot be muffled or hid, but to sweep and scour will instantly appear supreme and beautiful actions, the top and radiance of human life, and all people will get mops and brooms; until, lo, suddenly the great soul has enshrined itself in some other form, and done some other deed, and that is now the flower and head of all living nature.

We are the photometers, we the irritable gold-leaf and tin-foil* that measure the accumulations of the subtle element. We know the authentic effects of the true fire through every one of its million disguises.

---

*Instruments used to measure the intensity of light.

Friendship[1]

A ruddy drop of manly blood
The surging sea outweighs,
The world uncertain comes and goes,
The lover rooted stays.
I fancied he was fled,
And, after many a year,
Glowed unexhausted kindliness
Like daily sunrise there.
My careful heart was free again,—
O friend, my bosom said,
Through thee alone the sky is arched,
Through thee the rose is red,
All things through thee take nobler form,
And look beyond the earth,
And is the mill-round of our fate
A sun-path in thy worth.
Me too thy nobleness has taught
To master my despair;
The fountains of my hidden life
Are through thy friendship fair.

WE HAVE A GREAT deal more kindness than is ever spoken. Barring all the selfishness that chills like east winds the world, the whole human family is bathed with an element of love like a fine ether. How many persons we meet in houses, whom we scarcely speak to, whom yet we honor, and who honor us! How many we see in the street, or sit with in church, whom, though silently, we warmly rejoice to be with! Read the language of these wandering eye-beams. The heart knoweth.*

The effect of the indulgence of this human affection is a certain cor-

*Reference to the Bible, Proverbs 14:10: "The heart knoweth his own bitterness" (KJV).

172

dial exhilaration. In poetry, and in common speech, the emotions of benevolence and complacency which are felt toward others, are likened to the material effects of fire; so swift, or much more swift, more active, more cheering are these fine inward irradiations. From the highest degree of passionate love, to the lowest degree of good will, they make the sweetness of life.

Our intellectual and active powers increase with our affection. The scholar sits down to write, and all his years of meditation do not furnish him with one good thought or happy expression; but it is necessary to write a letter to a friend, and, forthwith, troops of gentle thoughts invest themselves, on every hand, with chosen words. See in any house where virtue and self-respect abide, the palpitation which the approach of a stranger causes. A commended stranger is expected and announced, and an uneasiness between pleasure and pain invades all the hearts of a household. His arrival almost brings fear to the good hearts that would welcome him. The house is dusted, all things fly into their places, the old coat is exchanged for the new, and they must get up a dinner if they can. Of a commended stranger, only the good report is told by others, only the good and new is heard by us. He stands to us for humanity. He is, what we wish. Having imagined and invested him, we ask how we should stand related in conversation and action with such a man, and are uneasy with fear. The same idea exalts conversation with him. We talk better than we are wont. We have the nimblest fancy, a richer memory, and our dumb devil has taken leave for the time. For long hours we can continue a series of sincere, graceful, rich communications, drawn from the oldest, secretest experience, so that they who sit by, of our own kinsfolk and acquaintance, shall feel a lively surprise at our unusual powers. But as soon as the stranger begins to intrude his partialities, his definitions, his defects, into the conversation, it is all over. He has heard the first, the last and best, he will ever hear from us. He is no stranger now. Vulgarity, ignorance, misapprehension, are old acquaintances. Now, when he comes, he may get the order, the dress, and the dinner, but the throbbing of the heart, and the communications of the soul, no more.

Pleasant are these jets of affection which relume a young world for me again. Delicious is a just and firm encounter of two, in a thought, in a feeling. How beautiful, on their approach to this beating heart, the steps and forms of the gifted and the true! The moment we indulge our affections, the earth is metamorphosed: there is no winter, and no night: all tragedies, all ennuis vanish; all duties even; nothing fills the proceeding eternity but the forms all radiant of beloved persons. Let the soul be assured that somewhere in the universe it should rejoin its friend, and it would be content and cheerful alone for a thousand years.

I awoke this morning with devout thanksgiving for my friends, the old and the new. Shall I not call God, the Beautiful, who daily showeth himself so to me in his gifts? I chide society, I embrace solitude, and yet I am not so ungrateful as not to see the wise, the lovely, and the noble-minded, as from time to time they pass my gate. Who hears me, who understands me, becomes mine—a possession for all time. Nor is nature so poor, but she gives me this joy several times, and thus we weave social threads of our own, a new web of relations; and, as many thoughts in succession substantiate themselves, we shall by-and-by stand in a new world of our own creation, and no longer strangers and pilgrims in a traditionary globe. My friends have come to me unsought. The great God gave them to me. By oldest right, by the divine affinity of virtue with itself, I find them, or rather, not I, but the Deity in me and in them, both deride and cancel the thick walls of individual character, relation, age, sex and circumstance, at which he usually connives, and now makes many one. High thanks I owe you, excellent lovers, who carry out the world for me to new and noble depths, and enlarge the meaning of all my thoughts. These are not stark and stiffened persons, but the newborn poetry of God—poetry without stop—hymn, ode and epic, poetry still flowing, and not yet caked in dead books with annotation and grammar, but Apollo and the Muses chanting still. Will these two separate themselves from me again, or some of them? I know not, but I fear it not; for my relation to them is so pure, that we hold by simple affinity, and the Genius of my life being thus social, the same affinity will exert its energy on whomsoever is as noble as these men and women, wherever I may be.

I confess to an extreme tenderness of nature on this point. It is almost dangerous to me to "crush the sweet poison of misused wine"* of the affections. A new person is to me always a great event, and hinders me from sleep. I have had such fine fancies lately about two or three persons, as have given me delicious hours; but the joy ends in the day: it yields no fruit. Thought is not born of it; my action is very little modified. I must feel pride in my friend's accomplishments as if they were mine—wild, delicate, throbbing property in his virtues. I feel as warmly when he is praised, as the lover when he hears applause of his engaged maiden. We overestimate the conscience of our friend. His goodness

---

*From John Milton's *Comus* (1634; line 47).

seems better than our goodness, his nature finer, his temptations less. Everything that is his, his name, his form, his dress, books and instruments, fancy enhances. Our own thought sounds new and larger from his mouth.

Yet the systole and diastole of the heart are not without their analogy in the ebb and flow of love. Friendship, like the immortality of the soul, is too good to be believed. The lover, beholding his maiden, half knows that she is not verily that which he worships; and in the golden hour of friendship, we are surprised with shades of suspicion and unbelief. We doubt that we bestow on our hero the virtues in which he shines, and afterward worship the form to which we have ascribed this divine inhabitation. In strictness, the soul does not respect men as it respects itself. In strict science, all persons underlie the same condition of an infinite remoteness. Shall we fear to cool our love by facing the fact, by mining for the metaphysical foundation of this Elysian temple?* Shall I not be as real as the things I see? If I am, I shall not fear to know them for what they are. Their essence is not less beautiful than their appearance, though it needs finer organs for its apprehension. The root of the plant is not unsightly to science, though for chaplets and festoons we cut the stem short. And I must hazard the production of the bald fact amid these pleasing reveries, though it should prove an Egyptian skull at our banquet.[2] A man who stands united with his thought, conceives magnificently to himself. He is conscious of a universal success, even though bought by uniform particular failures. No advantages, no powers, no gold or force can be any match for him. I cannot choose but rely on my own property, more than on your wealth. I cannot make your consciousness tantamount to mine. Only the star dazzles; the planet has a faint, moon-like ray. I hear what you say of the admirable parts and tried temper of the party you praise, but I see well that for all his purple cloaks I shall not like him, unless he is at last a poor Greek like me. I cannot deny it, O friend, that the vast shadow of the phenomenal includes thee, also, in its pied and painted immensity—thee, also, compared with whom all else is shadow. Thou art not Being, as Truth is, as Justice is—thou art not my soul, but a picture and effigy of that. Thou hast come to me lately, and already thou art seizing thy hat and cloak. Is it not that the soul puts forth friends, as the tree puts forth leaves, and presently, by the germination of new buds, extrudes the old leaf? The

---

*In ancient Greek and Roman culture, Elysium was the name given to the dwelling place of happy souls in the afterlife.

law of nature is alternation forevermore. Each electrical state superinduces the opposite. The soul environs itself with friends, that it may enter into a grander self-acquaintance or solitude; and it goes alone, for a season, that it may exalt its conversation or society. This method betrays itself along the whole history of our personal relations. Ever the instinct of affection revives the hope of union with our mates, and ever the returning sense of insulation recalls us from the chase. Thus every man passes his life in the search after friendship, and if he should record his true sentiment, he might write a letter like this, to each new candidate for his love:

DEAR FRIEND:

If I was sure of thee, sure of thy capacity, sure to match my mood with thine, I should never think again of trifles, in relation to thy comings and goings. I am not very wise: my moods are quite attainable: and I respect thy genius: it is to me as yet unfathomed; yet dare I not presume in thee a perfect intelligence of me, and so thou art to me a delicious torment. Thine ever, or never.

Yet these uneasy pleasures and fine pains are for curiosity, and not for life. They are not to be indulged. This is to weave cobweb, and not cloth. Our friendships hurry to short and poor conclusions, because we have made them a texture of wine and dreams, instead of the tough fiber of the human heart. The laws of friendship are great, austere, and eternal, of one web with the laws of nature and of morals. But we have aimed at a swift and petty benefit, to suck a sudden sweetness. We snatch at the slowest fruit in the whole garden of God, which many summers and many winters must ripen. We seek our friend not sacredly but with an adulterate passion which would appropriate him to ourselves. In vain. We are armed all over with subtle antagonisms, which, as soon as we meet, begin to play, and translate all poetry into stale prose. Almost all people descend to meet. All association must be a compromise, and, what is worst, the very flower and aroma of the flower of each of the beautiful natures disappears as they approach each other. What a perpetual disappointment is actual society, even of the virtuous and gifted! After interviews have been compassed with long foresight, we must be tormented presently by baffled blows, by sudden, unseasonable apathies, by epilepsies of wit and of animal spirits, in the heyday of friendship and thought. Our faculties do not play us true, and both parties are relieved by solitude.

I ought to be equal to every relation. It makes no difference how many friends I have, and what content I can find in conversing with each, if there be one to whom I am not equal. If I have shrunk unequal from one contest instantly the joy I find in all the rest becomes mean and cowardly. I should hate myself, if then I made my other friends my asylum.

> "The valiant warrior famoused for fight,
>   After a hundred victories, once foiled,
> Is from the book of honor razed quite,
>   And all the rest forgot for which he toiled."*

Our impatience is thus sharply rebuked. Bashfulness and apathy are a tough husk in which a delicate organization is protected from premature ripening. It would be lost if it knew itself before any of the best souls were yet ripe enough to know and own it. Respect the naturlangsamkeit† which hardens the ruby in a million years, and works in duration, in which Alps and Andes come and go as rainbows. The good spirit of our life has no heaven which is the price of rashness. Love, which is the essence of God, is not for levity, but for the total worth of man. Let us not have this childish luxury in our regards; but the austerest worth; let us approach our friend with an audacious trust in the truth of his heart, in the breadth, impossible to be overturned, of his foundations.

The attractions of this subject are not to be resisted, and I leave, for the time, all account of subordinate social benefit, to speak of that select and sacred relation which is a kind of absolute, and which even leaves the language of love suspicious and common, so much is this purer, and nothing is so much divine.

I do not wish to treat friendships daintily, but with roughest courage. When they are real, they are not glass threads or frost-work, but the solidest thing we know. For now, after so many ages of experience, what do we know of nature, or of ourselves? Not one step has man taken toward the solution of the problem of his destiny. In one condemnation of folly stand the whole universe of men. But the sweet sincerity of joy and peace, which I draw from this alliance with my brother's soul, is the nut itself whereof all nature and all thought is but the husk and shell.

---

*Near quotation from Shakespeare's sonnet 25, lines 9–12; Emerson substitutes "valiant" for "painful."

†Emerson borrows from Goethe this German term that refers to the long, slow processes of evolution.

Happy is the house that shelters a friend! It might well be built, like a festal bower or arch, to entertain him a single day. Happier, if he know the solemnity of that relation, and honor its law! It is no idle band, no holiday engagement. He who offers himself a candidate for that covenant comes up, like an Olympian, to the great games, where the first-born of the world are the competitors. He proposes himself for contests where Time, Want, Danger are in the lists, and he alone is victor who has truth enough in his constitution to preserve the delicacy of his beauty from the wear and tear of all these. The gifts of fortune may be present or absent, but all the hap in that contest depends on intrinsic nobleness, and the contempt of trifles. There are two elements that go to the composition of friendship, each so sovereign, that I can detect no superiority in either, no reason why either should be first named. One is Truth. A friend is a person with whom I may be sincere. Before him, I may think aloud. I am arrived at last in the presence of a man so real and equal that I may drop even those undermost garments of dissimulation, courtesy, and second thought, which men never put off, and may deal with him with the simplicity and wholeness, with which one chemical atom meets another. Sincerity is the luxury allowed, like diadems and authority, only to the highest rank, *that* being permitted to speak truth, as having none above it to court or conform unto. Every man alone is sincere. At the entrance of a second person, hypocrisy begins.[3] We parry and fend the approach of our fellow man by compliments, by gossip, by amusements, by affairs. We cover up our thought from him under a hundred folds. I knew a man who, under a certain religious frenzy, cast off his drapery and omitting all compliments and commonplace, spoke to the conscience of every person he encountered, and that with great insight and beauty.[*] At first he was resisted, and all men agreed he was mad. But persisting, as indeed he could not help doing, for some time in this course, he attained to the advantage of bringing every man of his acquaintance into true relations with him. No man would think of speaking falsely with him, or of putting him off with any chat of markets or reading-rooms. But every man was constrained by so much sincerity to face him, and what love of nature, what poetry, what symbol of truth he had, he did certainly show him. But to most of us society shows not its face and eye, but its side and its back. To stand in true relations with men in a false age, is worth a fit of in-

---

[*]Probably the poet Jones Very (1813–1880); Emerson edited Very's *Essays and Poems* (1839).

sanity, is it not? We can seldom go erect. Almost every man we meet re-
quires some civility, requires to be humored—he has some fame, some
talent, some whim of religion or philanthropy in his head that is not to
be questioned, and so spoils all conversation with him. But a friend is a
sane man who exercises not my ingenuity but me. My friend gives me
entertainment without requiring me to stoop, or to lisp, or to mask my-
self. A friend, therefore, is a sort of paradox in nature. I who alone am,
I who see nothing in nature whose existence I can affirm with equal ev-
idence to my own, behold now the semblance of my being in all its
height, variety and curiosity, reiterated in a foreign form; so that a
friend may well be reckoned the masterpiece of nature.

The other element of friendship is Tenderness. We are holden to men
by every sort of tie, by blood, by pride, by fear, by hope, by lucre, by lust,
by hate, by admiration, by every circumstance and badge and trifle, but
we can scarce believe that so much character can subsist in another as
to draw us by love. Can another be so blessed, and we so pure, that we
can offer him tenderness? When a man becomes dear to me, I have
touched the goal of fortune. I find very little written directly to the heart
of this matter in books. And yet I have one text which I cannot choose
but remember. My author* says, "I offer myself faintly and bluntly to
those whose I effectually am, and tender myself least to him to whom I
am the most devoted." I wish that friendship should have feet, as well as
eyes and eloquence. It must plant itself on the ground, before it walks
over the moon. I wish it to be a little of a citizen, before it is quite a
cherub. We chide the citizen because he makes love a commodity. It is
an exchange of gifts, of useful loans; it is good neighborhood; it watches
with the sick; it holds the pall at the funeral; and quite loses sight of the
delicacies and nobility of the relation. But though we cannot find the
god under this disguise of a sutler,† yet, on the other hand, we cannot
forgive the poet if he spins his thread too fine, and does not substanti-
ate his romance by the municipal virtues of justice, punctuality, fidelity
and pity. I hate the prostitution of the name of friendship to signify
modish and worldly alliances. I much prefer the company of plow-boys
and tin-peddlers, to the silken and perfumed amity which only cele-
brates its days of encounter by a frivolous display, by rides in a curricle,‡

---

*Michel de Montaigne, from his essay "A Consideration upon Cicero": Montaigne's
essay "On Friendship" is also worth comparing.
†Person who does sloppy work.
‡Two-wheeled chaise drawn by horses.

and dinners at the best taverns. The end of friendship is a commerce the most strict and homely that can be joined; more strict than any of which we have experience. It is for aid and comfort through all the relations and passages of life and death. It is fit for serene days, and graceful gifts, and country rambles, but also for rough roads and hard fare, shipwreck, poverty, and persecution. It keeps company with the sallies of the wit and the trances of religion. We are to dignify to each other the daily needs and offices of man's life, and embellish it by courage, wisdom and unity. It should never fall into something usual and settled, but should be alert and inventive, and add rhyme and reason to what was drudgery.

For perfect friendship it may be said to require natures so rare and costly, so well tempered each, and so happily adapted, and withal so circumstanced (for even in that particular, a poet says, love demands that the parties be altogether paired), that very seldom can its satisfaction be realized. It cannot subsist in its perfection, say some of those who are learned in this warm lore of the heart, betwixt more than two. I am not quite so strict in my terms, perhaps because I have never known so high a fellowship as others. I please my imagination more with a circle of godlike men and women variously related to each other, and between whom subsists a lofty intelligence. But I find, this law of *one to one*, peremptory for conversation, which is the practice and consummation of friendship. Do not mix waters too much. The best mix as ill as good and bad. You shall have very useful and cheering discourse at several times with two several men, but let all three of you come together, and you shall not have one new and hearty word. Two may talk and one may hear, but three cannot take part in a conversation of the most sincere and searching sort. In good company there is never such discourse between two, across the table, as takes place when you leave them alone. In good company, the individuals at once merge their egotism into a social soul exactly co-extensive with the several consciousnesses there present. No partialities of friend to friend, no fondnesses of brother to sister, of wife to husband, are there pertinent, but quite otherwise. Only he may then speak who can sail on the common thought of the party, and not poorly limited to his own. Now this convention, which good sense demands, destroys the high freedom of great conversation, which requires an absolute running of two souls into one.

No two men but being left alone with each other, enter into simpler relations. Yet it is affinity that determines *which* two shall converse. Unrelated men give little joy to each other; will never suspect the latent powers of each. We talk sometimes of a great talent for conversation, as if it were a permanent property in some individuals. Conversation is an evanescent relation—no more. A man is reputed to have thought and eloquence; he cannot, for all that, say a word to his cousin or his uncle. They accuse his silence with as much reason as they would blame the insignificance of a dial in the shade. In the sun it will mark the hour. Among those who enjoy his thought, he will regain his tongue.

Friendship requires that rare mean betwixt likeness and unlikeness, that piques each with the presence of power and of consent in the other party. Let me be alone to the end of the world, rather than that my friend should overstep by a word or a look his real sympathy. I am equally balked by antagonism and by compliance. Let him not cease an instant to be himself. The only joy I have in his being mine, is that the *not mine* is *mine*. It turns the stomach, it blots the daylight; where I looked for a manly furtherance, or at least a manly resistance, to find a mush of concession. Better be a nettle in the side of your friend, than his echo. The condition which high friendship demands is ability to do without it. To be capable of that high office requires great and sublime parts. There must be very two before there can be very one. Let it be an alliance of two large formidable natures, mutually beheld, mutually feared, before yet they recognize the deep identity which beneath these disparities unites them.

He only is fit for this society who is magnanimous. He must be so, to know its law. He must be one who is sure that greatness and goodness are always economy. He must be one who is not swift to intermeddle with his fortunes. Let him not dare to intermeddle with this. Leave to the diamond its ages to grow, nor expect to accelerate the births of the eternal. Friendship demands a religious treatment. We must not be wilful, we must not provide. We talk of choosing our friends, but friends are self-elected. Reverence is a great part of it. Treat your friend as a spectacle. Of course, if he be a man, he has merits that are not yours, and that you cannot honor, if you must needs hold him close to your person. Stand aside. Give those merits room. Let them mount and expand. Be not so much his friend that you can never know his peculiar energies, like fond mammas who shut up their boy in the house until he is almost grown a girl. Are you the friend of your friend's buttons, or of his thought? To a great heart he will still be a stranger in a thousand particulars, that he may come near in the holiest ground. Leave it to girls and boys to regard a friend as property, and to suck a short and all-confounding pleasure instead of the pure nectar of God.

Let us buy our entrance to this guild by a long probation. Why should we desecrate noble and beautiful souls by intruding on them?

Why insist on rash personal relations with your friend? Why go to his house, or know his mother and brother and sisters? Why be visited by him at your own? Are these things material to our covenant? Leave this touching and clawing. Let him be to me a spirit. A message, a thought, a sincerity, a glance from him I want, but not news, nor pottage. I can get politics, and chat, and neighborly conveniences, from cheaper companions. Should not the society of my friend be to me poetic, pure, universal, and great as nature itself? Ought I to feel that our tie is profane in comparison with yonder bar of cloud that sleeps on the horizon, or that clump of waving grass that divides the brook? Let us not vilify but raise it to that standard. That great defying eye, that scornful beauty of his mien and action, do not pique yourself on reducing, but rather fortify and enhance. Worship his superiorities. Wish him not less by a thought, but hoard and tell them all. Guard him as thy great counterpart; have a princedom to thy friend. Let him be to thee forever a sort of beautiful enemy, untamable, devoutly revered, and not a trivial conveniency to be soon outgrown and cast aside. The hues of the opal, the light of the diamond, are not to be seen, if the eye is too near. To my friend I write a letter, and from him I receive a letter. That seems to you a little. Me it suffices. It is a spiritual gift worthy of him to give and of me to receive. It profanes nobody. In these warm lines the heart will trust itself, as it will not to the tongue, and pour out the prophesy of a godlier existence than all the annals of heroism have yet made good.

Respect so far the holy laws of this fellowship as not to prejudice its perfect flower by your impatience for its opening. We must be our own before we can be another's. There is at least this satisfaction in crime, according to the Latin proverb: you can speak to your accomplice on even terms. *Crimen quos inquinat, æquat.** To those whom we admire and love, at first we cannot. Yet the least defect of self-possession vitiates, in my judgment, the entire relation. There can never be deep peace between two spirits, never mutual respect until, in their dialogue, each stands for the whole world.

What is so great as friendship, let us carry with what grandeur of spirit we can. Let us be silent—so we may hear the whisper of the gods. Let us not interfere. Who set you to cast about what you should say to the select souls, or to say anything to such? No matter how in genius, no matter how graceful and bland. There are innumerable degrees of folly

---

*Compare the following line from *Pharsalia*, by Lucan: *Facinus, quos inquinat, aequat* (Crime levels those whom it pollutes).

and wisdom, and for you to say aught is to be frivolous. Wait, and thy soul shall speak. Wait until the necessary and everlasting overpowers you, until day and night avail themselves of your lips. The only money of God is God. He pays never with anything less or anything else. The only reward of virtue, is virtue: the only way to have a friend, is to be one. Vain to hope to come nearer a man by getting into his house. If unlike, his soul only flees the faster from you, and you shall catch never a true glance of his eye. We see the noble afar off, and they repel us; why should we intrude? Late—very late—we perceive that no arrangements, no introductions, no consuetudes,* or habits of society, would be of any avail to establish us in such relations with them as we desire—but solely the uprise of nature in us to the same degree it is in them: then shall we meet as water with water: and if we should not meet them then, we shall not want them, for we are already they. In the last analysis, love is only the reflection of a man's own worthiness from other men. Men have sometimes exchanged names with their friends, as if they would signify that in their friend each loved his own soul.

The higher the style we demand of friendship, of course the less easy to establish it with flesh and blood. We walk alone in the world. Friends, such as we desire, are dreams and fables. But a sublime hope cheers ever the faithful heart, that elsewhere, in other regions of the universal power, souls are now acting, enduring and daring, which can love us, and which we can love. We may congratulate ourselves that the period of nonage, of follies, of blunders, and of shame, is passed in solitude, and when we are finished men, we shall grasp heroic hands in heroic hands. Only be admonished by what you already see, not to strike leagues of friendship with cheap persons, where no friendship can be. Our impatience betrays us into rash and foolish alliances which no God attends. By persisting in your path, though you forfeit the little, you gain the great. You become pronounced. You demonstrate yourself, so as to put yourself out of the reach of false relations, and you draw to you the first-born of the world, those rare pilgrims whereof only one or two wander in nature at once, and before whom the vulgar great show as specters and shadows merely.

It is foolish to be afraid of making our ties too spiritual, as if so we could lose any genuine love. Whatever correction of our popular views we make from insight, nature will be sure to bear us out in, and though it seem to rob us of some joy, will repay us with a greater. Let us feel, if

---

*Social customs.

we will, the absolute insulation of man. We are sure that we have all in us. We go to Europe, or we pursue persons, or we read books, in the instinctive faith that these will call it out and reveal us to ourselves. Beggars all. The persons are such as we; the Europe, an old faded garment of dead persons; the books, their ghosts. Let us drop this idolatry. Let us give over this mendicancy. Let us even bid our dearest friends farewell, and defy them, saying, "Who are you? Unhand me. I will be dependent no more." Ah! seest thou not, O brother, that thus we part only to meet again on a higher platform, and only be more each other's, because we are more our own? A friend is Janus-faced:* he looks to the past and the future. He is the child of all my foregoing hours, the prophet of those to come. He is the harbinger of a greater friend. It is the property of the divine to be reproductive.

I do then with my friends as I do with my books. I would have them where I can find them, but I seldom use them. We must have society on our own terms, and admit or exclude it on the slightest cause. I cannot afford to speak much with my friend. If he is great, he makes me so great that I cannot descend to converse. In the great days, presentiments hover before me, far before me in the firmament. I ought then to dedicate myself to them. I go in that I may seize them; I go out that I may seize them. I fear only that I may lose them receding into the sky in which now they are only a patch of brighter light. Then, though I prize my friends, I cannot afford to talk with them and study their visions, lest I lose my own. It would indeed give me a certain household joy to quit this lofty seeking, this spiritual astronomy, or search of stars, and come down to warm sympathies with you; but then I know well I shall mourn always the vanishing of my mighty gods. It is true, next week I shall have languid times, when I can well afford to occupy myself with foreign objects; then I shall regret the lost literature of your mind, and wish you were by my side again. But if you come, perhaps you will fill my mind only with new visions, not with yourself but with your lusters, and I shall not be able any more than now to converse with you. So I will owe to my friends this evanescent intercourse. I will receive from them not what they have, but what they are. They shall give me that which properly they cannot give me, but which radiates from them. But they shall not hold me by any relations less subtle and pure. We will meet as though we met not, and part as though we parted not.

---

*After the Roman god Janus, god of beginnings, who was often represented as having two faces because he looked to both the future and the past.

It has seemed to me lately more possible than I knew, to carry a friendship greatly, on one side, without due correspondence on the other. Why shall I cumber myself with the poor fact that the receiver is not capacious? It never troubles the sun that some of his rays fall wide and vain into ungrateful space, and only a small part on the reflecting planet. Let your greatness educate the crude and cold companion. If he is unequal, he will presently pass away, but thou art enlarged by thy own shining; and, no longer a mate for frogs and worms, dost soar and burn with the gods of the empyrean. It is thought a disgrace to love unrequited. But the great will see that true love cannot be unrequited. True love transcends instantly the unworthy object, and dwells and broods on the eternal, and when the poor, interposed mask crumbles, it is not sad, but feels rid of so much earth, and feels its independency the surer. Yet these things may hardly be said without a sort of treachery to the relation. The essence of friendship is entireness, a total magnanimity and trust. It must not surmise or provide for infirmity. It treats its object as a god, that it may deify both.

The Over-Soul[1]

"But souls that of his own good life partake,
    He loves as his own self; dear as his eye
    They are to Him: He'll never them forsake:
    When they shall die, then God himself shall die:
    They live, they live in blest eternity."
                                    —*Henry More**

        Space is ample, east and west,
        But two cannot go abreast,
        Cannot travel in it two:
        Yonder masterful cuckoo
        Crowds every egg out of the nest,
        Quick or dead, except it's own;
        A spell is laid on sod and stone,
        Night and Day 've been tampered with,
        Every quality and pith
        Surcharged and sultry with a power
        That works its will on age and hour.

THERE IS A DIFFERENCE between one and another hour of life, in their authority and subsequent effect. Our faith comes in moments; our vice is habitual. Yet is there a depth in those brief moments, which constrains us to ascribe more reality to them than to all other experiences. For this reason, the argument, which is always forthcoming to silence those who conceive extraordinary hopes of man, namely, the appeal to experience, is forever invalid and vain. A mightier hope abolishes despair. We give up the past to the objector, and yet we hope. He must explain this hope. We grant that human life is mean; but how did we find out that it was mean? What is the ground of this uneasiness of ours; of this old dis-

---

*"Psychozia, or the Life of the Soul," in *Philosophical Poems* (1647), canto II, stanza 19.

content? What is the universal sense of want and ignorance, but the fine inuendo by which the great soul makes its enormous claim? Why do men feel that the natural history of man has never been written, but always he is leaving behind what you have said of him, and it becomes old, and books of metaphysics worthless? The philosophy of six thousand years has not searched the chambers and magazines of the soul. In its experiments there has always remained, in the last analysis, a residuum it could not resolve. Man is a stream whose source is hidden. Always our being is descended into us from we know not whence. The most exact calculator has no prescience that somewhat incalculable may not balk the very next moment. I am constrained every moment to acknowledge a higher origin for events than the will I call mine.

As with events, so is it with thoughts. When I watch that flowing river, which, out of regions I see not, pours for a season its streams into me—I see that I am a pensioner—not a cause, but a surprised spectator of this ethereal water; that I desire and look up, and put myself in the attitude of reception, but from some alien energy the visions come.

The Supreme Critic on all the errors of the past and the present, and the only prophet of that which must be, is that great nature in which we rest, as the earth lies in the soft arms of the atmosphere; that Unity, that Over-Soul, within which every man's particular being is contained and made one with all other; that common heart, of which all sincere conversation is the worship, to which all right action is submission; that overpowering reality which confutes our tricks and talents, and constrains every one to pass for what he is, and to speak from his character and not from his tongue; and which evermore tends and aims to pass into our thought and hand, and become wisdom, and virtue, and power, and beauty. We live in succession, in division, in parts, in particles. Meantime within man is the soul of the whole; the wise silence; the universal beauty, to which every part and particle is equally related; the eternal ONE. And this deep power in which we exist, and whose beatitude is all accessible to us, is not only self-sufficing and perfect in every hour, but the act of seeing, and the thing seen, the seer and the spectacle, the subject and the object, are one. We see the world piece by piece, as the sun, the moon, the animal, the tree; but the whole, of which these are the shining parts, is the soul. It is only by the vision of that Wisdom, that the horoscope of the ages can be read, and it is only by falling back on our better thoughts, by yielding to the spirit of prophesy which is innate in every man, that we can know what it saith. Every man's words, who speaks from that life, must sound vain to those who do not dwell in the same thought on their own part. I dare not speak for it. My words do not carry its august sense; they fall short and cold. Only itself can aspire whom it will, and behold, their speech shall be lyrical, and sweet, and universal as the rising of the wind. Yet I desire, even by profane words, if sacred I may not use, to indicate the heaven of this deity, and to report what hints I have collected of the transcendent simplicity and energy of the Highest Law.

If we consider what happens in conversation, in reveries, in remorse, in times of passion, in surprises, in the instructions of dreams wherein often we see ourselves in masquerade—the droll disguises only magnifying and enhancing a real element, and forcing it on our distinct notice—we shall catch many hints that will broaden and lighten into knowledge of the secret of nature. All goes to show that the soul in man is not an organ, but animates and exercises all the organs; is not a function, like the power of memory, of calculation, of comparison, but uses these as hands and feet; is not a faculty, but a light; is not the intellect or the will, but the master of the intellect and the will; is the vast background of our being, in which they lie, an immensity not possessed and that cannot be possessed. From within or from behind, a light shines through us upon things, and makes us aware that we are nothing, but the light is all. A man is the façade of a temple wherein all wisdom and all good abide. What we commonly call man, the eating, drinking, planting, counting man, does not, as we know him represent himself, but misrepresents himself. Him we do not respect, but the soul, whose organ he is, would he let it appear through his action, would make our knees bend. When it breathes through his intellect, it is genius; when it breathes through his will, it is virtue; when it flows through his affection, it is love. And the blindness of the intellect begins, when it would be something of itself. The weakness of the will begins when the individual would be something of himself. All reform aims, in some one particular, to let the great soul have its way through us; in other words, to engage us to obey.

Of this pure nature every man is at some time sensible. Language cannot paint it with his colors. It is too subtle. It is undefinable, unmeasurable, but we know that it pervades and contains us. We know that all spiritual being is in man. A wise old proverb says, "God comes to see us without bell:" that is, as there is no screen or ceiling between our heads and the infinite heavens, so is there no bar or wall in the soul where man, the effect, ceases, and God, the cause, begins. The walls are taken away. We lie open on one side to the deeps of spiritual nature, to all the attributes of God. Justice we see and know, Love, Freedom, Power. These natures no man ever got above, but always they tower over us, and most in the moment when our interests tempt us to wound them.

The sovereignty of this nature whereof we speak, is made known by its independency of those limitations which circumscribe us on every hand. The soul circumscribeth all things. As I have said, it contradicts all experience. In like manner it abolishes time and space. The influence of the senses has, in most men, overpowered the mind to that degree, that the walls of time and space have come to look solid, real and insurmountable; and to speak with levity of these limits is, in the world, the sign of insanity. Yet time and space are but inverse measures of the force of the soul. A man is capable of abolishing them both. The spirit sports with time—

> "Can crowd eternity into an hour,
> Or stretch an hour to eternity."*

We are often made to feel that there is another youth and age than that which is measured from the year of our natural birth. Some thoughts always find us young and keep us so. Such a thought is the love of the universal and eternal beauty. Every man parts from that contemplation with the feeling that it rather belongs to ages than to mortal life. The least activity of the intellectual powers redeems us in a degree from the influences of time. In sickness, in languor, give us a strain of poetry or a profound sentence, and we are refreshed; or produce a volume of Plato, or Shakespeare, or remind us of their names, and instantly we come into a feeling of longevity. See how the deep, divine thought demolishes centuries, and millenniums, and makes itself present through all ages. Is the teaching of Christ less effective now than it was when first his mouth was opened? The emphasis of facts and persons to my soul has nothing to do with time. And so, always, the soul's scale is one; the scale of the senses and the understanding is another. Before the great revelations of the soul, Time, Space find Nature shrink away. In common speech, we refer all things to time, as we habitually refer the immensely sundered stars to one concave sphere. And so we say that the Judgment is distant or near, that the Millennium approaches, that a day of certain political, moral, social reforms is at hand, and the like, when we mean, that in the nature of things, one of the facts that we contemplate is external and fugitive, and the other is permanent and connate

---

*From *Cain* (act 1, scene 1, lines 536–537), by George Gordon, Lord Byron.

with the soul. The things we now esteem fixed, shall, one by one, detach themselves, like ripe fruit, from our experience, and fall. The wind shall blow them none knows whither. The landscapes, the figures, Boston, London, are facts as fugitive as any institution past, or any whiff of mist or smoke, and so is society, and so is the world. The soul looketh steadily forward, creating a world always before her, and leaving worlds always behind her. She has no dates, nor rites, nor persons, nor specialties, nor men. The soul knows only the soul. All else is idle weeds* for her wearing.

After its own law and not by arithmetic is the rate of its progress to be computed. The soul's advances are not made by gradation, such as can be represented by motion in a straight line; but rather by ascension of state, such as can be represented by metamorphosis—from the egg to the worm, from the worm to the fly. The growths of genius are of a certain *total* character, that does not advance the elect individual first over John, then Adam, then Richard, and give to each the pain of discovered inferiority, but by every throe of growth, the man expands there where he works, passing, at each pulsation, classes, populations of men. With each divine impulse the mind rends the thin rinds of the visible and finite, and comes out into eternity, and inspires and expires its air. It converses with truths that have always been spoken in the world, and becomes conscious of a closer sympathy with Zeno and Arrian, than with persons in the house.

This is the law of moral and of mental gain. The simple rise as by specific levity, not into a particular virtue, but into the region of all the virtues. They are in the spirit which contains them all. The soul is superior to all the particulars of merit. The soul requires purity, but purity is not it; requires justice, but justice is not that; requires beneficence, but is somewhat better: so that there is a kind of descent and accommodation felt when we leave speaking of moral nature to urge a virtue which it enjoins. For, to the soul in her pure action, all the virtues are natural, and not painfully acquired. Speak to his heart, and the man becomes suddenly virtuous.

Within the same sentiment is the germ of intellectual growth, which obeys the same law. Those who are capable of humility, of justice, of love, of aspiration, are already on a platform that commands the sciences and arts, speech and poetry, action and grace. For whoso dwells in this moral beatitude, does already anticipate those special powers which men prize

---

*Religious dress of a person on pilgrimage; veil or other garments worn to signify mourning.

so highly; just as love does justice to all the gifts of the object beloved. The lover has no talent, no skill, which passes for quite nothing with his enamored maiden, however little she may possess of related faculty. And the heart, which abandons itself to the Supreme Mind, finds itself related to all its works and will travel a royal road to particular knowledges and powers. For, in ascending to this primary and aboriginal sentiment, we have come from our remote station on the circumference instantaneously to the center of the world, where, as in the closet of God, we see causes, and anticipate the universe, which is but a slow effect.

One mode of the divine teaching is the incarnation of the spirit in a form—in forms, like my own. I live in society; with persons who answer to thoughts in my own mind, or outwardly express to me a certain obedience to the great instincts to which I live. I see its presence to them. I am certified of a common nature; and so these other souls, these separated selves, draw me as nothing else can. They stir in me the new emotions we call passion; of love, hatred, fear, admiration, pity; thence comes conversation, competition, persuasion, cities, and war. Persons are supplementary to the primary teaching of the soul. In youth we are mad for persons. Childhood and youth see all the world in them. But the larger experience of man discovers the identical nature appearing through them all. Persons themselves acquaint us with the impersonal. In all conversation between two persons, tacit reference is made as to a third party, to a common nature. That third party or common nature is not social; it is impersonal; is God.[2] And so in groups where debate is earnest, and especially on great questions of thought, the company become aware of their unity; aware that the thought rises to an equal height in all bosoms, that all have a spiritual property in what was said, as well as the sayer. They all wax wiser than they were. It arches over them like a temple, this unity of thought, in which every heart beats with nobler sense of power and duty, and thinks and acts with unusual solemnity. All are conscious of attaining to a higher self-possession. It shines for all. There is a certain wisdom of humanity which is common to the greatest men with the lowest, and which our ordinary education often labors to silence and obstruct. The mind is one, and the best minds who love truth for its own sake think much less of property in truth. Thankfully they accept it everywhere, and do not label or stamp it with any man's name, for it is theirs long beforehand. It is theirs from eternity. The learned and the studious of thought have no monopoly of wisdom. Their violence of direction in some degree disqualifies them to think truly. We owe many valuable observations to people who are not very acute or profound, and who say the thing without effort, which we .

want and have long been hunting in vain. The action of the soul is of-
tener in that which is felt and left unsaid than in that which is said in
any conversation. It broods over every society, and they unconsciously
seek for it in each other. We know better than we do. We do not yet pos-
sess ourselves, and we know at the same time that we are much more. I
feel the same truth how often in my trivial conversation with my neigh-
bors, that somewhat higher in each of us overlooks this by-play, and
Jove nods to Jove from behind each of us.

Men descend to meet. In their habitual and mean service to the
world, for which they forsake their native nobleness, they resemble
those Arabian Sheiks, who dwell in mean houses and affect an external
poverty, to escape the rapacity of the Pasha,* and reserve all their dis-
play of wealth for their interior and guarded retirements.

As it is present in all persons, so it is in every period of life. It is adult
already in the infant man. In my dealing with my child, my Latin and
Greek, my accomplishments and my money stead me nothing. They are
all lost on him: but as much soul as I have, avails. If I am merely wilful,
he gives me a Roland for an Oliver,† sets his will against mine, one for
one, and leaves me, if I please, the degradation of beating him by my su-
periority of strength. But if I renounce my will, and act for the soul, set-
ting that up as umpire between us two, out of his young eyes looks the
same soul; he reveres and loves with me.

The soul is the perceiver and revealer of truth. We know truth when
we see it, let skeptic and scoffer say what they choose. Foolish people ask
you, when you have spoken what they do not wish to hear, "How do you
know it is truth, and not an error of your own?" We know truth when
we see it, from opinion, as we know when we are awake that we are
awake. It was a grand sentence of Emanuel Swedenborg, which would
alone indicate the greatness of that man's perception—"It is no proof of
a man's understanding to be able to affirm whatever he pleases, but to
be able to discern that what is true is true, and that what is false is false;
this is the mark and character of intelligence."‡ In the book I read, the
good thought returns to me, as every truth will, the image of the whole

---

*Turkish term for a leader placed in charge of conquered territory.

†Roland is the hero of the French epic poem *Chanson de Roland* (eleventh or twelfth
century); Oliver was Roland's friend and brother in arms. Their characters stood in
contrast: Roland acted on impulse; Oliver was prudent.

‡The editors of *The Collected Works* identify this quotation as a paraphrase by Caleb
Reed that appeared in "The Nature and Character of True Wisdom and Intelligence,"
New Jerusalem Magazine 3 (January 1830).

soul. To the bad thought which I find in it, the same soul becomes a discerning, separating sword that lops it away. We are wiser than we know. If we will not interfere with our thought, but will act entirely, or see how the thing stands in God, we know the particular thing, and everything, and every man. For, the Maker of all things and all persons stands behind us, and casts his dread omniscience through us over things.

But beyond this recognition of its own in particular passages of the individual's experience, it also reveals truth. And here we should seek to reinforce ourselves by its very presence, and to speak with a worthier, loftier strain of that advent. For the soul's communication of truth is the highest event in nature, for it then does not give somewhat from itself, but it gives itself, or passes into and becomes that man whom it enlightens; or in proportion to that truth he receives, it takes him to itself.

We distinguish the announcements of the soul, its manifestations of its own nature, by the term *Revelation*. These are always attended by the emotion of the sublime. For this communication is an influx of the Divine mind into our mind. It is an ebb of the individual rivulet before the flowing surges of the sea of life. Every distinct apprehension of this central commandment agitates men with awe and delight. A thrill passes through all men at the reception of new truths, or at the performance of a great action, which comes out of the heart of nature. In these communications, the power to see, is not separated from the will to do, but the insight proceeds from obedience, and the obedience proceeds from a joyful perception. Every moment when the individual feels himself invaded by it, is memorable. Always, I believe, by the necessity of our constitution, a certain enthusiasm attends the individual's consciousness of that divine presence. The character and duration of this enthusiasm varies with the state of the individual, from an ecstasy and trance and prophetic inspiration—which is its rarer appearance—to the faintest glow of virtuous emotion, in which form it warms, like our household fires, all the families and associations of men, and makes society possible. A certain tendency to insanity has always attended the opening of the religious sense in men, as if "blasted with excess of light."* The trances of Socrates; the "union" of Plotinus; the vision of Porphyry; the conversion of Paul; the aurora of Behmen; the convulsions of George Fox and his Quakers; the illumination of Swedenborg; are of this kind.[3] What was in the case of these remarkable persons a ravishment, has in innumerable instances in common life, been exhibited in less striking

*From Thomas Gray's "Progress of Poesy" (1757; line 101).

manner. Everywhere the history of religion betrays a tendency to enthusiasm. The rapture of the Moravian and Quietist; the opening of the internal sense of the Word, in the language of the New Jerusalem Church;* the revival of the Calvinistic Churches; the experiences of the Methodists, are varying forms of that shudder of awe and delight with which the individual soul always mingles with the universal soul.

The nature of these revelations is always the same: they are perceptions of the absolute law. They are solutions of the soul's own questions. They do not answer the questions which the understanding asks. The soul answers never by words, but by the thing itself that is inquired after.

Revelation is the disclosure of the soul. The popular notion of a revelation is, that it is a telling of fortunes. In past oracles of the soul, the understanding seeks to find answers to sensual questions, and undertakes to tell from God how long men shall exist, what their hands shall do, and who shall be their company, adding even names, and dates, and places. But we must pick no locks. We must check this low curiosity. An answer in words is delusive; it is really no answer to the questions you ask. Do not ask a description of the countries toward which you sail. The description does not describe them to you, and to-morrow you arrive there, and know them by inhabiting them. Men ask of the immortality of the soul, and the employments of heaven, and the state of the sinner, and so forth. They even dream that Jesus has left replies to precisely these interrogatories. Never a moment did that sublime spirit speak in their patois.† To truth, justice, love, the attributes of the soul, the idea of immutableness is essentially associated. Jesus, living in these moral sentiments, heedless of sensual fortunes, heeding only the manifestations of these, never made the separation of the idea of duration from the essence of these attributes; never uttered a syllable concerning the duration of the soul. It was left to his disciples to sever duration from the moral elements and to teach the immortality of the soul as a doctrine and maintain it by evidences. The moment the doctrine of the immortality is separately taught, man is already fallen. In the flowing of love, in the adoration of humility, there is no question of continuance. No inspired man ever asks this question, or condescends to these evidences. For the soul is true to itself, and the man in whom it is shed

---

*Church founded on the teachings of Emanuel Swedenborg.
†Dialect.

abroad cannot wander from the present, which is infinite, to a future which would be finite.

These questions which we lust to ask about the future, are a confession of sin. God has no answer for them. No answer in words can reply to a question of things. It is not in an arbitrary "decree of God," but in the nature of man that a veil shuts down on the facts of to-morrow; for the soul will not have us read any other cipher but that of cause and effect. By this veil, which curtains events, it instructs the children of men to live in to-day. The only mode of obtaining an answer to these questions of the senses is to forego all low curiosity, and accepting the tide of being which floats us into the secret of nature, work and live, work and live, and all unawares, the advancing soul has built and forged for itself a new condition, and the question and the answer are one.

Thus is the soul the perceiver and revealer of truth. By the same fire, serene, impersonal, perfect, which burns until it shall dissolve all things into the waves and surges of an ocean of light, we see and know each other, and what spirit each is of. Who can tell the grounds of his knowledge of the character of the several individuals in his circle of friends? No man. Yet their acts and words do not disappoint him. In that man, though he knew no ill of him, he put no trust. In that other, though they had seldom met, authentic signs had yet passed, to signify that he might be trusted as one who had an interest in his own character. We know each other very well—which of us has been just to himself, and whether that which we teach or behold is only an aspiration, or is our honest effort also.

We are all discerners of spirits. That diagnosis lies aloft in our life or unconscious power, not in the understanding. The whole intercourse of society, its trade, its religion, its friendships, its quarrels—is one wide, judicial investigation of character. In full court, or in small committee, or confronted face to face, accuser and accused, men offer themselves to be judged. Against their will they exhibit those decisive trifles by which character is read. But who judges? and what? Not our understanding. We do not read them by learning or craft. No; the wisdom of the wise man consists herein, that he does not judge them; he lets them judge themselves, and merely reads and records their own verdict.

By virtue of this inevitable nature, private will is overpowered, and, mauger* our efforts, or our imperfections, your genius will speak from you, and mine from me. That which we are, we shall teach, not volun-

---

*In spite of.

tarily, but involuntarily. Thoughts come into our minds by avenues which we never left open, and thoughts go out of our minds through avenues which we never voluntarily open. Character teaches over our head. The infallible index of true progress is found in the tone the man takes. Neither his age, nor his breeding, nor company, nor books, nor actions, nor talents, nor all together, can hinder him from being deferential to a higher spirit than his own. If he have not found his home in God, his manners, his forms of speech, the turn of his sentences, the build, shall I say, of all his opinions will involuntarily confess it, let him brave it out how he will. If he have found his center, the Deity will shine through him, through all the disguises of ignorance, of ungenial temperament, of unfavorable circumstance. The tone of seeking is one, and the tone of having is another.

The great distinction between teachers, sacred or literary; between poets like Herbert, and poets like Pope; between philosophers like Spinoza, Kant and Coleridge, and philosophers like Locke, Paley, Mackintosh and Stewart;[4] between men of the world who are reckoned accomplished talkers, and here and there a fervent mystic, prophesying, half-insane under the infinitude of his thought, is, that one class speak from within, or from experience, as parties and possessors of the fact; and the other class, from without, as spectators merely, or perhaps as acquainted with the fact, on the evidence of third persons. It is of no use to preach to me from without. I can do that too easily myself. Jesus speaks always from within, and in a degree that transcends all others. In that is the miracle. That includes the miracle. My soul believes beforehand that it ought so to be. All men stand continually in the expectation of the appearance of such a teacher.[5] But if a man do not speak from within the veil, where the word is one with that it tells of, let him lowly confess it.

The same Omniscience flows into the intellect and makes what we call genius. Much of the wisdom of the world is not wisdom, and the most illuminated class of men are no doubt superior to literary fame, and are not writers. Among the multitude of scholars and authors we feel no hallowing presence; we are sensible of a knack and skill rather than of inspiration; they have a light, and know not whence it comes, and call it their own; their talent is some exaggerated faculty, some overgrown member, so that their strength is a disease. In these instances, the intellectual gifts do not make the impression of virtue, but almost of vice; and we feel that a man's talents stand in his way of his advancement in truth. But genius is religion. It is a larger imbibing of the common heart. It is not anomalous, but more like, and not less like, other men. There is in all great poets a wisdom of humanity which is superior to any talents they exercise. The author, the wit, the partisan, the fine gentleman, does not take place of the man. Humanity shines in Homer, in Chaucer, in Spenser, in Shakespeare, in Milton. They are content with truth. They use the positive degree. They seem frigid and phlegmatic to those who have been spiced with the frantic passion and violent coloring of inferior, but popular writers. For, they are poets by the free course which they allow to the informing soul, though their eyes beholdeth again and blesseth the things which it hath made.

The soul is superior to its knowledge; wiser than any of its works. The great poet makes us feel our own wealth, and then we think less of his compositions. His greatest communication to our mind is to teach us to despise all he has done. Shakespeare carries us to such a lofty strain of intelligent activity as to suggest a wealth which beggars his own; and we then feel that the splendid works which he has created, and which in other hours we extol as a sort of self-existent poetry, take no stronger hold of real nature than the shadow of a passing traveler on the rock. The inspiration which uttered itself in Hamlet and Lear, could utter things as good from day to day, forever. Why then should I make account of Hamlet and Lear, as if we had not the soul from which they fell as syllables from the tongue?

This energy does not descend into individual life, on any other condition than entire possession. It comes to the lowly and simple; it comes to whomsoever will put off what is foreign and proud; it comes as insight; it comes as serenity and grandeur. When we see those whom it inhabits, we are apprised of new degrees of greatness. From that inspiration the man comes back with a changed tone. He does not talk with men, with an eye to their opinion. He tries them. It requires of us to be plain and true. The vain traveler attempts to embellish his life by quoting my Lord, and the Prince, and the Countess, who thus said or did to *him*. The ambitious vulgar show you their spoons, and brooches, and rings, and preserve their cards and compliments. The more cultivated, in their account of their own experience, cull out the pleasing poetic circumstance; the visit to Rome; the man of genius they saw; the brilliant friend they know; still further on, perhaps, the gorgeous landscape, the mountain lights, the mountain thoughts, they enjoyed yesterday—and so seek to throw a romantic color over their life. But the soul that ascendeth to worship the great God, is plain and true; has no rose color; no fine friends; no chivalry; no adventures; does not want admiration; dwells in the hour that now is, in the earnest experience of

the common day[6]—by reason of the present moment, and the mere tri-
fle having become porous to thought, and bibulous* of the sea of light.

Converse with a mind that is grandly simple, and literature looks like
word-catching. The simplest utterances are worthiest to be written, yet
are they so cheap, and so things of course, that in the infinite riches of
the soul, it is like gathering a few pebbles off the ground, or bottling a
little air in a vial, when the whole earth, and the whole atmosphere are
ours. The mere author, in such society, is like a pickpocket among gen-
tlemen, who has come in to steal a gold button or a pin. Nothing can
pass there, or make you one of the circle, but the casting aside your
trappings, and dealing man to man in naked truth, plain confession and
omniscient affirmation.

Souls, such as these, treat you as gods would; walk as gods in the
earth, accepting without any admiration, your wit, your bounty, your
virtue, even, say rather your act of duty, for your virtue they own as
their proper blood, royal as themselves, and over-royal, and the father
of the gods. But what rebuke their plain fraternal bearing casts on the
mutual flattery with which authors solace each other, and wound them-
selves! These flatter not. I do not wonder that these men go to see
Cromwell, and Christina, and Charles II, and James I, and the Grand
Turk.[†] For they are in their own elevation, the fellows of kings, and must
feel the servile tone of conversation in the world. They must always be
a godsend to princes, for they confront them, a king to a king, without
ducking or concession, and give a high nature the refreshment and sat-
isfaction of resistance, of plain humanity, of even companionship, and
of new ideas. They leave them wiser and superior men. Souls like these
make us feel that sincerity is more excellent than flattery. Deal so plainly
with man and woman, as to constrain the utmost sincerity, and destroy
all hope of trifling with you. It is the highest compliment you can pay.
Their "highest praising," said Milton, "is not flattery, and their plainest
advice is a kind of praising."[‡]

Ineffable is the union of man and God in every act of the soul. The
simplest person, who in his integrity worships God, becomes God; yet
for ever and ever the influx of this better and universal self is new and
unsearchable. Ever it inspires awe and astonishment. How dear, how
soothing to man, arises the idea of God, peopling the lonely place, ef-

---

*Absorbent.

†Each of these rulers was considered a patron of the arts.

‡From *Aeropagitica* (1644; paragraph 4).

facing the scars of our mistakes and disappointments! When we have broken our god of tradition, and ceased from our god of rhetoric, then may God fire the heart with his presence. It is the doubling of the heart itself, nay, the infinite enlargement of the heart with a power of growth to a new infinity on every side. It inspires in man an infallible trust. He has not the conviction, but the sight that the best is the true, and may in that thought easily dismiss all particular uncertainties and fears, and adjourn to the sure revelation of time, the solution of his private riddles. He is sure that his welfare is dear to the heart of being. In the presence of law to his mind, he is overflowed with a reliance so universal, that it sweeps away all cherished hopes and the most stable projects of the mortal condition in its flood. He believes that he cannot escape from his good. The things that are really for thee, gravitate to thee. You are running to seek your friend. Let your feet run, but your mind need not. If you do not find him, will you not acquiesce that it is best that you should not find him? For there is a power, which, as it is in you, is in him also, and could therefore very well bring you together, if it were for the best. You are preparing with eagerness to go and render a service to which your talent and your tastes invite you, the love of men, and the hope of fame. Has it not occurred to you that you have no right to go, unless you are equally willing to be prevented from going? O believe, as thou livest, that every sound that is spoken over the round world, which thou oughtest to hear, will vibrate on thine ear. Every proverb, every book, every by-word that belongs to thee for aid or comfort shall surely come home through open or winding passages. Every friend whom not thy fantastic will, but the great and tender heart in thee craveth, shall lock thee in his embrace. And this, because the heart in thee is the heart of all; not a valve, not a wall, not an intersection is there anywhere in nature, but one blood rolls uninterruptedly, an endless circulation through all men, as the water of the globe is all one sea, and, truly seen, its tide is one.

Let man then learn the revelation of all nature, and all thought to his heart; this, namely: that the Highest dwells with him; that the sources of nature are in his own mind, if the sentiment of duty is there. But if he would know that the great God speaketh, he must "go into his closet and shut the door," as Jesus said.* God will not make himself manifest

---

*Reference to the Bible, Matthew 6:6: "When thou prayest, enter into thy closet, and when thou hast shut thy door, pray to thy Father which is in secret; and thy Father which seeth in secret shall reward thee openly" (KJV).

to cowards. He must greatly listen to himself, withdrawing himself from all the accents of other men's devotion. Their prayers even are hurtful to him, until he have made his own. The soul makes no appeal from itself. Our religion vulgarly stands on numbers of believers. Whenever the appeal is made—no matter how indirectly—to numbers, proclamation is then and there made that religion is not. He that finds God a sweet, enveloping thought to him never counts his company. When I sit in that presence, who shall dare to come in? When I rest in perfect humility, when I burn with pure love, what can Calvin or Swedenborg say?

It makes no difference whether the appeal is to numbers or to one. The faith that stands on authority is not faith. The reliance on authority, measures the decline of religion, the withdrawal of the soul. The position men have given to Jesus, now for many centuries of history, is a position of authority. It characterizes themselves. It cannot alter the eternal facts. Great is the soul, and plain. It is no flatterer, it is no follower; it never appeals from itself. It always believes in itself. Before the immense possibilities of man, all mere experiences, all past biography, however spotless and sainted, shrinks away. Before that holy heaven which our presentiments foreshow us, we cannot easily praise any form of life we have seen or read of. We not only affirm that we have few great men, but, absolutely speaking, that we have none; that we have no history, no record of any character or mode of living that entirely contents us. The saints and demigods whom history worships we are constrained to accept with a grain of allowance. Though in our lonely hours we draw a new strength out of their memory, yet pressed on our attention, as they are by the thoughtless and customary, they fatigue and invade. The soul gives itself alone, original and pure, to the Lonely, Original, and Pure, who, on that condition, gladly inhabits, leads, and speaks through it. Then is it glad, young and nimble. It is not wise, but it sees through all things. It is not called religious, but it is innocent. It calls the light its own, and feels that the grass grows, and the stone falls by a law inferior to, and dependent on its nature. Behold, it saith, I am born into the great, the universal mind. I the imperfect, adore my own Perfect. I am somehow receptive of the great soul, and thereby I do overlook the sun and the stars, and feel them to be but the fair accidents and effects which change and pass. More and more the surges of everlasting nature enter into me, and I become public and human in my regards and actions. So come I to live in thoughts, and act with energies which are immortal. Thus revering the soul, and learning, as the ancient said, that "its beauty is immense,"* man will come to see that the world is the perennial miracle which the soul worketh, and be less astonished at particular wonders; he will learn that there is no profane history; that all history is sacred; that the universe is represented in an atom, in a moment of time. He will weave no longer a spotted life of shreds and patches, but he will live with a divine unity. He will cease from what is base and frivolous in his own life, and be content with all places and any service he can render. He will calmly front the morrow in the negligency of that trust which carries God with it, and so hath already the whole future in the bottom of the heart.

---

*Possibly a line from Plotinus's "On Beauty."

Circles[1]

Nature centres into balls,
And her proud ephemerals,
Fast to surface and outside,
Scan the profile of the sphere;
Knew they what that signified,
A new genesis were here.

THE EYE IN THE first circle; the horizon which it forms is the second; and throughout nature this primary figure is repeated without end. It is the highest emblem in the cipher of the world. St. Augustine described the nature of God as a circle whose center was everwhere, and its circumference nowhere.[2] We are all our lifetime reading the copious sense of this first of forms. One moral we have already deduced in considering the circular or compensatory character of every human action. Another analogy we shall now trace; that every action admits of being outdone. Our life is an apprenticeship to the truth, that around every circle another can be drawn; that there is no end in nature, but every end is a beginning; that there is always another dawn risen on mid-noon, and under every deep a lower deep opens.

This fact, as far as it symbolizes the moral facts of the Unattainable, the flying Perfect, around which the hands of man can never meet, at once the inspirer and the condemner of every success, may conveniently serve us to connect many illustrations of human power in every department.

There are no fixtures in nature. The universe is fluid and volatile: Permanence is but a word of degrees. Our globe seen by God, is a transparent law, not a mass of facts. The law dissolves the fact and holds it fluid. Our culture is the predominance of an idea which draws after it all this train of cities and institutions. Let us rise into another idea: they will disappear. The Greek sculpture is all melted away, as if it had been statues of ice: here and there a solitary figure or fragment remaining, as we see flecks and scraps of snow left in cold dells and mountain clefts in June and July. For, the genius that created it creates now somewhat else.

202

The Greek letters last a little longer, but are already passing under the same sentence, and tumbling into the inevitable pit which the creation of new thought opens for all that is old. The new continents are built out of the ruins of an old planet: the new races fed out of the decomposition of the foregoing. New arts destroy the old. See the investment of capital in aqueducts, made useless by hydraulics; fortifications, by gunpowder; roads and canals, by railways; sails, by steam; steam by electricity.

You admire his tower of granite, weathering the hurts of so many ages. Yet a little waving hand built this huge wall, and that which builds, is better than that which is built. The hand that built, can tear it down much faster. Better than the hand, and nimbler, was the invisible thought which wrought through it, and thus ever behind the coarse effect, is a fine cause, which being narrowly seen, is itself the effect of a finer cause.[3] Everything looks permanent until its secret is known. A rich estate appears to women and children, a firm and lasting fact; to a merchant, one easily created out of any materials, and easily lost. An orchard, good tillage, good grounds, seem a fixture, like a gold mine, or a river, to a citizen, but to a large farmer, not much more fixed than the state of the crop. Nature looks provokingly stable and secular, but it has a cause like all the rest; and when once I comprehend that, Will these fields stretch so immovably wide, these leaves hang so individually considerable? Permanence is a word of degrees. Everything is medial. Moons are no more bounds to spiritual power than bat-balls.

The key to every man is his thought. Sturdy and defying though he look, he has a helm which he obeys, which is the idea after which all his facts are classified. He can only be reformed by showing him a new idea which commands his own. The life of man is a self-evolving circle, which, from a ring imperceptibly small, rushes on all sides outward to new and larger circles, and that without end. The extent to which this generation of circles, wheel without wheel, will go, depends on the force or truth of the individual soul. For, it is the inert effort of each thought having formed itself into a circular wave of circumstance, as, for instance, an empire, rules of an art, a local usage, a religious rite, to heap itself on that ridge, and to solidify, and hem in the life. But if the soul is quick and strong it bursts over that boundary on all sides, and expands another orbit on the great deep, which also runs up into a high wave, with attempt again to stop and to bind. But the heart refuses to be imprisoned; in its first and narrowest pulses, it already tends outward with a vast force, and to immense and innumerable expansions.

Every ultimate fact is only the first of a new series. Every general law only a particular fact of some more general law presently to disclose itself. There is no outside, no inclosing wall, no circumference to us. The man finishes his story—how good! how final! how it puts a new face on all things! He fills the sky. Lo, on the other side, rises also a man, and draws a circle around the circle we had just pronounced the outline of the sphere. Then already is our first speaker, not man, but only a first speaker. His only redress is forthwith to draw a circle outside of his antagonist. And so men do by themselves. The result of to-day which haunts the mind and cannot be escaped will presently be abridged into a word, and the principle that seemed to explain nature will itself be included as one example of a bolder generalization. In the thought of to-morrow there is a power to upheave all thy creed, all the creeds, all the literatures of the nations, and marshal thee to a heaven which no epic dream has yet depicted. Every man is not so much a workman in the world, as he is a suggestion of that he should be. Men walk as prophecies of the next age.

Step by step we scale this mysterious ladder: the steps are actions; the new prospect is power. Every several result is threatened and judged by that which follows. Every one seems to be contradicted by the new; it is only limited by the new. The new statement is always hated by the old, and, to those dwelling in the old, comes like an abyss of skepticism. But the eye soon gets wonted to it, for the eye and it are effects of one cause; then its innocency and benefit appear, and, presently, all its energy spent, it pales and dwindles before the revelation of the new hour.

Fear not the new generalization. Does the fact look crass and material, threatening to degrade thy theory of spirit? Resist it not; it goes to refine and raise thy theory of matter just as much.[4]

There are no fixtures to men, if we appeal to consciousness. Every man supposes himself not to be fully understood; and if there is any truth in him, if he rests at last on the divine soul, I see not how it can be otherwise. The last chamber, the last closet, he must feel, was never opened; there is always a residuum unknown, unanalyzable. That is, every man believes that he has a greater possibility.

Our moods do not believe in each other. To-day, I am full of thoughts, and can write what I please. I see no reason why I should not have the same thought, the same power of expression to-morrow. What I write, while I write it, seems the most natural thing in the world; but, yesterday, I saw a dreary vacuity in this direction in which now I see so much; and a month hence, I doubt not, I shall wonder who he was that wrote so many continuous pages. Alas for this infirm faith, this will not strenuous, this vast ebb of a vast flow! I am God in nature; I am a weed by the wall.

The continual effort to raise himself above himself, to work a pitch above his last height, betrays itself in a man's relations. We thirst for approbation, yet cannot forgive the approver. The sweet of nature is love; yet if I have a friend, I am tormented by my imperfection. The love of me accuses the other party. If he were high enough to slight me, then could I love him, and rise by my affection to new heights. A man's growth is seen in the successive choirs of his friends. For every friend whom he loses for truth, he gains a better. I thought, as I walked in the woods and mused on my friends, why should I play with them this game of idolatry? I know and see too well, when not voluntarily blind, the speedy limits of persons called high and worthy. Rich, noble, and great they are by the liberality of our speech, but truth is sad. O blessed Spirit, whom I forsake for these, they are not thee! Every personal consideration that we allow, costs us heavenly state. We sell the thrones of angels for a short and turbulent pleasure.

How often must we learn this lesson? Men cease to interest us when we find their limitations. The only sin is limitation. As soon as you once come up with a man's limitations, it is all over with him. Has he talents? has he enterprises? has he knowledge? it boots not. Infinitely alluring and attractive was he to you yesterday, a great hope, a sea to swim in; now, you have found his shores, found it a pond, and you care not if you never see it again.

Each new step we take in thought reconciles twenty seemingly discordant facts, as expressions of one law. Aristotle and Plato are reckoned the respective heads of two schools. A wise man will see that Aristotle Platonizes. By going one step further back in thought, discordant opinions are reconciled, by being seen to be two extremes of one principle, and we can never go so far back as to preclude a still higher vision.

Beware when the great God lets loose a thinker on this planet. Then all things are at risk. It is as when a conflagration has broken out in a great city, and no man knows what is safe, or where it will end. There is not a piece of science, but its flank may be turned to-morrow; there is not any literary reputation, not the so-called eternal names of fame, that may not be reviled and condemned. The very hopes of man, the thoughts of his heart, the religion of nations, the manners and morals of mankind, are all at the mercy of a new generalization. Generalization is always a new influx of the divinity into the mind. Hence the thrill that attends it.

Valor consists in the power of self-recovery, so that a man cannot have his flank turned, cannot be outgeneraled, but put him where you will, he stands. This can only be by his preferring truth to his past apprehension of truth; and his alert acceptance of it from whatever quarter; the intrepid conviction that his laws, his relations to society, his christianity, his world, may at any time be superseded and decease.

There are degrees in idealism. We learn first to play with it academically, as the magnet was once a toy. Then we see in the heyday of youth and poetry that it may be true, that it is true in gleams and fragments. Then, its countenance waxes stern and grand, and we see that it must be true. It now shows itself ethical and practical. We learn that God *is;* that he is in me; and that all things are shadows of him. The idealism of Berkeley is only a crude statement of the idealism of Jesus, and that, again, is a crude statement of the fact that all nature is the rapid efflux of goodness executing and organizing itself. Much more obviously is history and the state of the world at any one time, directly dependent on the intellectual classification then existing in the minds of men. The things which are dear to men at this hour, are so on account of the ideas which have emerged on their mental horizon, and which cause the present order of things as a tree bears its apples. A new degree of culture would instantly revolutionize the entire system of human pursuits.

Conversation is a game of circles. In conversation we pluck up the *termini* which bound the common of silence on every side. The parties are not to be judged by the spirit they partake and even express under this Pentecost.* To-morrow they will have receded from this high-water mark. To-morrow you shall find them stooping under the old pack-saddles. Yet let us enjoy the cloven flame while it glows on our walls. When each new speaker strikes a new light, emancipates us from the oppression of the last speaker, to oppress us with the greatness and exclusiveness of his own thought, then yields us to another redeemer, we seem to recover our rights, to become men. O what truths profound and executable only in ages and orbs, are supposed in the announcement of every truth! In common hours, society sits cold and statuesque. We all stand waiting, empty—knowing, possibly, that we can be full, surrounded by mighty symbols which are not symbols to us, but prose and trivial toys. Then cometh the god, and converts the statues into fiery men, and by a flash of his eye burns up the veil which shrouded all

---

*Term given to the descent of the Holy Spirit upon the Apostles, in the Bible, Acts 2.

things, and the meaning of the very furniture, of cup and saucer, of chair and clock and tester,* is manifest. The facts which loomed so large in the fogs of yesterday—property, climate, breeding, personal beauty, and the like, have strangely changed their proportions. All that we reckoned settled, shakes now and rattles; and literatures, cities, climates, religions, leave their foundations, and dance before our eyes. And yet here again see the swift circumscription. Good as is discourse, silence is better, and shames it. The length of the discourse indicates the distance of thought betwixt the speaker and the hearer. If they were at a perfect understanding in any part, no words would be necessary thereon. If at one in all parts, no words would be suffered.

Literature is a point outside of our hodiernal† circle, through which a new one may be described. The use of literature is to afford us a platform whence we may command a view of our present life, a purchase by which we may move it. We fill ourselves with ancient learning; install ourselves the best we can in Greek, in Punic, in Roman houses, only that we may wiselier see French, English, and American houses and modes of living.‡ In like manner we see literature best from the midst of wild nature, or from the din of affairs, or from a high religion. The field cannot be well seen from within the field. The astronomer must have his diameter of the earth's orbit, as a base to find the parallax of any star.

Therefore, we value the poet. All the argument, and all the wisdom, is not in the encyclopedia, or the treatise on metaphysics, or the Body of Divinity, but in the sonnet or the play. In my daily work I incline to repeat my old steps, and do not believe in remedial force, in the power of change and reform. But some Petrarch or Ariosto, filled with the new wine of his imagination, writes me an ode, or a brisk romance, full of daring thought and action. He smites and arouses me with his shrill tones, breaks up my whole chain of habits, and I open my eye on my own possibilities. He claps wings to the sides of all the solid old lumber of the world, and I am capable once more of choosing a straight path in theory and practice.

We have the same need to command a view of the religion of the world. We can never see Christianity from the catechism—from the pastures, from a boat in the pond, from amid the songs of wood-birds,

---

*Canopy, as over a bed.

†Of or belonging to the present day.

‡That is, we study ancient culture and history (Greek, Punic, Roman) in order to better understand our own via the contrast.

we possibly may. Cleansed by the elemental light and wind, steeped in the sea of beautiful forms which the field offers us, we may chance to cast a right glance back upon biography. Christianity is rightly dear to the best of mankind; yet was there never a young philosopher whose breeding had fallen into the Christian Church, by whom that brave text of Paul's was not specially prized, "Then shall also the Son be subject unto him who put all things under him, that God may be all in all."* Let the claims and virtues of persons be never so great and welcome, the instinct of man presses eagerly onward to the impersonal and illimitable, and gladly arms itself against the dogmatism of bigots with this generous word out of the book itself.

The natural world may be conceived of as a system of concentric circles, and we now and then detect in nature slight dislocations, which apprize us that this surface on which we now stand is not fixed, but sliding. These manifold tenacious qualities, this chemistry and vegetation, these metals and animals, which seem to stand there for their own sake, are means and methods only, are words of God, and as fugitive as other words. Has the naturalist or chemist learned his craft, who has explored the gravity of atoms and the elective affinities, who has not yet discerned the deeper law whereof this is only a partial or approximate statement, namely, that like draws to like; and that the goods which belong to you, gravitate to you, and need not be pursued with pains and cost? Yet is that statement approximate also, and not final. Omnipresence is a higher fact. Not through subtle, subterranean channels need friend and fact be drawn to their counterpart, but, rightly considered, these things proceed from the eternal generation of the soul. Cause and effect are two sides of one fact.

The same law of eternal procession ranges all that we call the virtues, and extinguishes each in the light of a better. The great man will not be prudent in the popular sense; all his prudence will be so much deduction from his grandeur. But it behooves each to see when he sacrifices prudence, to what god he devotes it; if to ease and pleasure, he had better be prudent still: if to a great trust, he can well spare his mule and panniers, who has a winged chariot instead. Geoffrey draws on his boots to go through the wood, that his feet may be safer from the bite of snakes; Aaron never thinks of such a peril. In many years, neither is harmed by such an accident. Yet it seems to me that with every precaution you take against such an evil, you put yourself into the power of the

---

*Near quotation from the Bible, I Corinthians 15:28.

evil. I suppose that the highest prudence is the lowest prudence. Is this too sudden a rushing from the center to the verge of our orbit? Think how many times we shall fall back into pitiful calculations before we take up our rest in the great sentiment, or make the verge of to-day the new center. Besides, your bravest sentiment is familiar to the humblest men. The poor and the low have their way of expressing the last facts of philosophy as well as you. "Blessed be nothing," and "the worse things are, the better they are," are the proverbs which express the transcendentalism of common life.

One man's justice is another's injustice; one man's beauty, another's ugliness; one man's wisdom, another's folly, as one beholds the same objects from a higher point of view. One man thinks justice consists in paying debts, and has no measure in his abhorrence of another who is very remiss in this duty, and makes the creditor wait tediously. But that second man has his own way of looking at things; asks himself, which debt must I pay first, the debt to the rich, or the debt to the poor? the debt of money, or the debt of thought to mankind, of genius to nature? For you, O broker, there is no other principle but arithmetic. For me, commerce is of trivial import; love, faith, truth of character, the aspiration of man, these are sacred; nor can I detach one duty, like you, from all other duties, and concentrate my forces mechanically on the payment of moneys. Let me live onward; you shall find that, though slower, the progress of my character will liquidate all these debts without injustice to higher claims. If a man should dedicate himself to the payment of notes, would not this be injustice? Owes he no debt but money? And are all claims on him to be postponed to a landlord's or a banker's?

There is no virtue which is final; all are initial. The virtues of society are vices of the saint. The terror of reform is the discovery that we must cast away our virtues, or what we have always esteemed such, into the same pit that has consumed our grosser vices.

> "Forgive his crimes, forgive his virtues too,
> Those smaller faults, half converts to the right."*

It is the highest power of divine moments that they abolish our contritions also. I accuse myself of sloth and unprofitableness, day by day; but when these waves of God flow into me, I no longer reckon lost time.

---

*From Edward Young's *Night Thoughts*, ix, lines 2316–2317. The first line should read "His crimes forgive, forgive his virtues too."

I no longer poorly compute my possible achievement by what remains to me of the month or the year; for these moments confer a sort of omnipresence and omnipotence, which asks nothing of duration, but sees that the energy of the mind is commensurate with the work to be done, without time.

And thus, O circular philosopher, I hear some reader exclaim, you have arrived at a fine pyrrhonism,* at an equivalence and indifferency of all actions, and would fain teach us that *if we are true*, forsooth, our crimes may be lively stones out of which we shall construct the temple of the true God.†

I am not careful to justify myself. I own I am gladdened by seeing the predominance of the saccharine principle throughout vegetable nature, and not less by beholding in morals that unrestrained inundation of the principle of good into every chink and hole that selfishness has left open, yea, into selfishness and sin itself; so that no evil is pure; nor hell itself without its extreme satisfactions. But lest I should mislead any when I have my own head, and obey my whims, let me remind the reader that I am only an experimenter. Do not set the least value on what I do, or the least discredit on what I do not, as if I pretended to settle anything as true or false. I unsettle all things. No facts are to me sacred; none are profane; I simply experiment, an endless seeker, with no Past at my back.[5]

Yet this incessant movement and progression, which all things partake, could never become sensible to us, but by contrast to some principle of fixture or stability in the soul. While the eternal generation of circles proceeds, the eternal generator abides. That central life is somewhat superior to creation, superior to knowledge and thought, and contains all its circles. Forever it labors to create a life and thought as large and excellent as itself; but in vain; for that which is made instructs how to make a better.

Thus there is no sleep, no pause, no preservation, but all things renew, germinate, and spring. Why should we import rags and relics into the new hour? Nature abhors the old, and old age seems the only disease; all others run into this one. We call it by many names, fever, intemperance, insanity, stupidity, and crime: they are all forms of old age; they are rest, conservatism, appropriation, inertia, not newness, not the

---

*Philosophy of skepticism, named after the Greek philosopher Pyrrho (c.360–270 B.C.), who maintained that nothing could be known with certainty.

†Quotation from the Bible, I Peter 2:5: "Ye also, as lively stones, are built up a spiritual house" (KJV).

way onward. We grizzle every day. I see no need of it. While we converse with what is above us, we do not grow old, but grow young. Infancy, youth, receptive, aspiring, with religious eye looking upward, counts itself nothing, and abandons itself to the instruction flowing from all sides. But the man and woman of seventy assume to know all; throw up their hope; renounce aspiration; accept the actual for the necessary; and talk down to the young. Let them then become organs of the Holy Ghost; let them be lovers; let them behold truth; and their eyes are uplifted, their wrinkles smoothed, they are perfumed again with hope and power. This old age ought not to creep on a human mind. In nature, every moment is new; the past is always swallowed and forgotten; the coming only is sacred. Nothing is secure but life, transition, the energizing spirit. No love can be bound by oath or covenant to secure it against a higher love. No truth so sublime but it may be trivial tomorrow in the light of new thoughts. People wish to be settled; only as far as they are unsettled is there any hope for them.

Life is a series of surprises. We do not guess to-day the mood, the pleasure, the power of to-morrow, when we are building up our being. Of lower states, of acts of routine and sense, we can tell somewhat, but the masterpieces of God, the total growths, and universal movements of the soul, he hideth; they are incalculable. I can know that truth is divine and helpful, but how it shall help me, I can have no guess, for, *so to be* is the sole inlet of *so to know*. The new position of the advancing man has all the powers of the old, yet has them all new. It carries in its bosom all the energies of the past, yet is itself an exhalation of the morning. I cast away in this new moment all my once hoarded knowledge, as vacant and vain. Now, for the first time, seem I to know anything rightly. The simplest words, we do not know what they mean, except when we love and aspire.

The difference between talents and character is adroitness to keep the old and trodden round, and power and courage to make a new road to new and better goals. Character makes an overpowering present, a cheerful, determined hour, which fortifies all the company, by making them see that much is possible and excellent that was not thought of. Character dulls the impression of particular events. When we see the conqueror, we do not think much of any one battle or success. We see that we had exaggerated the difficulty. It was easy to him. The great man is not convulsible or tormentable. He is so much that events pass over him without much impression. People say sometimes, "See what I have overcome; see how cheerful I am; see how completely I have triumphed over these black events." Not if they still remind me of the black event—

they have not yet conquered. Is it conquest to be a gay and decorated sepulcher, or a half-crazed widow hysterically laughing? True conquest is the causing the black event to fade and disappear as an early cloud of insignificant result in a history so large and advancing.

The one thing which we seek with insatiable desire, is to forget ourselves, to be surprised out of our propriety, to lose our sempiternal* memory, and to do something without knowing how or why; in short, to draw a new circle. Nothing great was ever achieved without enthusiasm.† The way of life is wonderful. It is by abandonment. The great moments of history are the facilities of performance through the strength of ideas, as the works of genius and religion. "A man," said Oliver Cromwell, "never rises so high as when he knows not whither he is going." Dreams and drunkenness, the use of opium and alcohol are the semblance and counterfeit of this oracular genius, and hence their dangerous attraction for men. For the like reason, they ask the aid of wild passions, as in gaming and war, to ape in some manner these flames and generosities of the heart.

---

*Everlasting; eternal.
†From Coleridge's *The Statesman's Manual* (1816; paragraph 18).

The Poet[1]

A moody child and wildly wise
Pursued the game with joyful eyes,
Which chose, like meteors, their way,
And rived the dark with private ray;
They overleapt the horizon's edge.
Searched with Apollo's privilege;
Through man, and woman, and sea, and star,
Saw the dance of nature forward far;
Through worlds, and races, and terms, and times,
Saw musical order, and pairing rhymes.

Olympian bards who sung
Divine ideas below,
Which always find us young,
And always keep us so.*

THOSE WHO ARE ESTEEMED umpires of taste,† are often persons who have acquired some knowledge of admired pictures or sculptures, and have an inclination for whatever is elegant; but if you inquire whether they are beautiful souls, and whether their own acts are like fair pictures, you learn that they are selfish and sensual. Their cultivation is local, as if you should rub a log of dry wood in one spot to produce fire, all the rest remaining cold. Their knowledge of fine arts is some study of rules and particulars, or some limited judgment of color or form, which is exercised for amusement or for show. It is a proof of the shallowness of the doctrine of beauty, as it lies in the minds of our amateurs, that men seem to have lost their perception of the instant dependence of form upon soul. There is no doctrine of forms in our philosophy. We were put into our bodies, as fire is put into the pan, to be carried about; but

---

*This second passage of verse is taken from Emerson's poem "Ode to Beauty."
†That is, critics.

there is no accurate adjustment between the spirit and the organ, much less is the latter the germination of the former. So in regard to other forms, the intellectual men do not believe in any essential dependence of the material world on thought and volition. Theologians think it a pretty air-castle to talk of the spiritual meaning of a ship or a cloud, of a city or a contract, but they prefer to come again to the solid ground of historical evidence; and even the poets are contented with a civil and conformed manner of living, and to write poems from the fancy, at a safe distance from their own experience. But the highest minds of the world have never ceased to explore the double meaning, or, shall I say, the quadruple, or the centuple, or much more manifold meaning, of every sensuous fact: Orpheus, Empedocles, Heraclitus, Plato, Plutarch, Dante, Swedenborg, and the masters of sculpture, picture and poetry. For we are not pans and barrows, nor even porters of the fire, and torch-bearers, but children of the fire, made of it, and only the same divinity transmuted, and at two or three removes, when we know least about it. And this hidden truth, that the fountains whence all this river of Time, and its creatures, floweth, are intrinsically ideal and beautiful, draws us to the consideration of the nature and functions of the Poet, or the man of Beauty, to the means and materials he uses, and to the general aspect of the art of the present time.

The breadth of the problem is great, for the poet is representative. He stands among partial men for complete man, and apprises us not of his wealth, but of the commonwealth. The young man reveres men of genius, because, to speak truly, they are more himself than he is. They receive of the soul as he also receives, but they more. Nature enhances her beauty, to the eye of loving men, from their belief that the poet is beholding her shows at the same time. He is isolated among his contemporaries, by truth and by his art, but with this consolation in his pursuits, that they will draw all men sooner or later. For all men live by truth, and stand in need of expression. In love, in art, in avarice, in politics, in labor, in games, we study to utter our painful secret. The man is only half himself, the other half is his expression.

Notwithstanding this necessity to be published, adequate expression is rare. I know not how it is that we need an interpreter; but the great majority of men seem to be minors, who have not yet come into possession of their own, or mutes, who cannot report the conversation they have had with nature. There is no man who does not anticipate a supersensual utility in the sun, and stars, earth, and water. These stand and wait to render him a peculiar service. But there is some obstruction, or some excess of phlegm* in our constitution, which does not suffer them to yield the due effect. Too feeble fall the impressions of nature on us to make us artists. Every touch should thrill. Every man should be so much an artist, that he could report in conversation what had befallen him. Yet, in our experience, the rays or appulses† have sufficient force to arrive at the senses, but not enough to reach the quick, and compel the reproduction of themselves in speech. The poet is the person in whom these powers are in balance, the man without inpediment, who sees and handles that which others dream of, traverses the whole scale of experience, and is representative of man in virtue of being the largest power to receive and to impart.

For the Universe has three children, born at one time, which reappear, under different names, in every system of thought, whether they be called cause, operation or effect; or, more poetically, Jove, Pluto, Neptune; or, theologically, the Father, the Spirit, and the Son; but which we will call here, the Knower, the Doer, and the Sayer.[2] These stand respectively for the love of truth, for the love of good, and for the love of beauty. These three are equal. Each is that which he is essentially, so that he cannot be surmounted or analyzed, and each of these three has the power of the others latent in him, and his own patent.

The poet is the sayer, the namer, and represents beauty. He is a sovereign, and stands on the center. For the world is not painted, or adorned, but is from the beginning beautiful; and God has not made some beautiful things, but Beauty is the creator of the universe. Therefore the poet is not any permissive potentate, but is emperor in his own right. Criticism is infested with a cant of materialism, which assumes that manual skill and activity is the first merit of all men, and disparages such as say and do not, overlooking the fact that some men, namely, poets, are natural sayers, sent into the world to the end of expression, and confounds them with those whose province is action, but who quit it to imitate the sayers. But Homer's words are as costly and admirable to Homer, as Agamemnon's victories are to Agamemnon. The poet does not wait for the hero or the sage, but, as they act and think primarily, so he writes primarily what will and must be spoken, reckoning the others, though primaries also, yet, in respect to him, sec-

---

*In medieval physiology, the bodily humor thought to cause sluggishness, indifference, or apathy.

†Energy directed to a point.

ondaries and servants; as sitters or models in the studio of a painter, or as assistants who bring building materials to an architect.

For poetry was all written before time was, and whenever we are so finely organized that we can penetrate into that region where the air is music, we hear those primal warblings, and attempt to write them down, but we lose ever and anon a word, or a verse, and substitute something of our own, and thus miswrite the poem. The men of more delicate ear write down these cadences more faithfully, and these transcripts, though imperfect, become the songs of the nations. For nature is as truly beautiful as it is good, or as it is reasonable, and must as much appear, as it must be done, or be known. Words and deeds are quite indifferent modes of the divine energy. Words are also actions, and actions are a kind of words.

The sign and credentials of the poet are, that he announces that which no man foretold. He is the true and only doctor;* he knows and tells; he is the only teller of news, for he was present and privy to the appearance which he describes. He is a beholder of ideas, and an utterer of the necessary and casual.† For we do not speak now of men of political talents, or of industry and skill in meter, but of the true poet. I took part in a conversation the other day concerning a recent writer of lyrics, a man of subtle mind, whose head appeared to be a music-box of delicate tunes and rhythms, and whose skill, and command of language, we could not sufficiently praise. But when the question arose, whether he was not only a lyrist, but a poet, we were obliged to confess that he is plainly a contemporary, not an eternal man. He does not stand out of our low limitation, like a Chimborazo‡ under the line, running up from the torrid base through all the climates of the globe, with belts of the herbage of every latitude on its high and mottled sides; but this genius is the landscape-garden of a modern house, adorned with fountains and statues, with well-bred men and women standing and sitting in the walks and terraces. We hear, through all the varied music, the ground-tone of conventional life. Our poets are men of talents who sing, and not the children of music. The argument is secondary, the finish of the verses is primary.

---

*In the older sense of teacher.

†In the sense of casuist, a person who studies and resolves cases of conscience or difficult questions regarding duty or moral obligation.

‡Inactive volcano in central Ecuador; the phrase "under the line" refers to its location on the equator.

For it is not meters, but a meter-making argument, that makes a poem—a thought so passionate and alive that, like the spirit of a plant or an animal, it has an architecture of its own, and adorns nature with a new thing. The thought and the form are equal in the order of time, but in the order of genesis the thought is prior to the form. The poet has a new thought; he has a whole new experience to unfold; he will tell us how it was with him, and all men will be the richer in his fortune. For the experience of each new age requires a new confession, and the world seems always waiting for its poet. I remember, when I was young, how much I was moved one morning by tidings that genius had appeared in a youth who sat near me at table. He had left his work, and gone rambling none knew whither, and had written hundreds of lines, but could not tell whether that which was in him was therein told; he could tell nothing but that all was changed—man, beast, heaven, earth and sea. How gladly we listened! how credulous! Society seemed to be compromised. We sat in the aurora of a sunrise which was to put out all the stars. Boston seemed to be at twice the distance it had the night before, or was much further than that. Rome—what was Rome? Plutarch and Shakespeare were in the yellow leaf,* and Homer no more should be heard of. It is much to know that poetry has been written this very day, under this very roof, by your side. What! that wonderful spirit has not expired! These stony moments are still sparkling and animated! I had fancied that the oracles were all silent, and nature had spent her fires, and behold! all night, from every pore, these fine auroras have been streaming. Every one has some interest in the advent of the poet, and no one knows how much it may concern him. We know that the secret of the world is profound, but who or what shall be our interpreter, we know not. A mountain ramble, a new style of face, a new person, may put the key into our hands. Of course, the value of genius to us is in the veracity of its report. Talent may frolic and juggle; genius realizes and adds. Mankind, in good earnest, have availed so far in understanding themselves and their work that the foremost watchman on the peak announces his news. It is the truest word ever spoken, and the phrase will be the fittest, most musical, and the unerring voice of the world for that time.

All that we call sacred history attests that the birth of a poet is the principal event in chronology. Man, never so often deceived, still

---

*In decay.

watches for the arrival of a brother who can hold him steady to a truth, until he has made it his own. With what joy I begin to read a poem, which I confide in as an inspiration! And now my chains are to be broken; and I shall mount above these clouds and opaque airs in which I live—opaque, though they seem transparent—and from the heaven of truth I shall see and comprehend my relations. That will reconcile me to life, and renovate nature, to see trifles animated by a tendency, and to know what I am doing. Life will no more be a noise; now I shall see men and women, and know the signs by which they may be discerned from fools and satans. This day shall be better than my birthday; then I became an animal; now I am invited into the science of the real. Such is the hope, but the fruition is postponed. Oftener it falls, that this winged man, who will carry me into the heaven, whirls me into the clouds, then leaps and frisks about with me from cloud to cloud, still affirming that he is bound heavenward; and I, being myself a novice, am slow in perceiving that he does not know the way into the heavens, and is merely bent that I should admire his skill to rise, like a fowl or a flying-fish, a little way from the ground or the water; but the all-piercing, all-feeding, and ocular air of heaven, that man shall never inhabit. I tumble down again soon into my old nooks, and lead the life of exaggerations as before, and have lost my faith in the possibility of any guide who can lead me thither where I would be.

But leaving these victims of vanity, let us, with new hope, observe how nature, by worthier impulses, has insured the poet's fidelity to his office of announcement and affirming, namely, by the beauty of things, which becomes a new and higher beauty when expressed. Nature offers all her creatures to him as a picture-language. Being used as a type, a second wonderful value appears in the object, far better than its old value, as the carpenter's stretched cord, if you hold your ear close enough, is musical in the breeze. "Things more excellent than every image," says Jamblichus, "are expressed through images." Things admit of being used as symbols, because nature is a symbol, in the whole, and in every part. Every line we can draw in the sand has expression; and there is nobody without its spirit or genius. All form is an effect of character; all condition, of the quality of the life; all harmony, of health; and, for this reason, a perception of beauty should be sympathetic, or proper only to the good. The beautiful rests on the foundations of the necessary. The soul makes the body, as the wise Spenser teaches:

> "So every spirit, as it is most pure,
>> And hath in it the more of heavenly light,
>> So it the fairer body doth procure
>> To habit in, and it more fairly dight,
>> With cheerful grace and amible sight.
>> For, of the soul, the body form doth take,
>> For soul is form, and doth the body make."*

Here we find ourselves, suddenly, not in a critical speculation, but in a holy place, and should go very warily and reverently. We stand before the secret of the world, there where Being passes into Appearance, and Unity into Variety.

The Universe is the externization of the soul. Wherever the life is, that bursts into appearance around it. Our science is sensual,† and therefore superficial. The earth and the heavenly bodies, physics and chemistry we sensually treat, as if they were self-existent; but these are the retinue of that Being we have. "The mighty heaven," said Proclus, "exhibits, in its transfigurations, clear images of the splendor of intellectual perceptions; being moved in conjunction with the unapparent periods of intellectual natures."‡ Therefore, science always goes abreast with the just elevation of the man, keeping step with religion and metaphysics; or, the state of science is an index of our self-knowledge. Since everything in nature answers to a moral power, if any phenomenon remains brute and dark, it is that the corresponding faculty in the observer is not yet active.

No wonder, then, if these waters be so deep, that we hover over them with a religious regard. The beauty of the fable proves the importance of the sense; to the poet, and to all others; or, if you please, every man is so far a poet as to be susceptible of these enchantments of nature: for all men have the thoughts whereof the universe is the celebration. I find that the fascination resides in the symbol. Who loves nature? Who does not? Is it only poets and men of leisure and cultivation who live with her? No; but also hunters, farmers, grooms and butchers, though they express their affection in their choice of life, and not in their choice of words. The writer wonders what the coachman or the hunter values in

---

*"An Hymne in Honour of Beautie" (1594; stanza 19).

†Based on knowledge gathered via the five senses; the opposite of spiritual.

‡From *The Commentaries of Proclus on the Timaeus of Plato*, translated by Thomas Taylor, 2 vols. (London, 1820).

riding, in horses and dogs. It is not superficial qualities. When you talk with him, he holds these at as slight a rate as you. His worship is sympathetic; he has no definitions, but he is commanded in nature by the living power which he feels to be there present. No imitation, or playing of these things would content him; he loves the earnest of the north wind, of rain, of stone, and wood and iron. A beauty not explicable is dearer than a beauty which we can see the end of. It is nature the symbol, nature certifying the supernatural, body overflowed by life, which he worships with coarse but sincere rites.

The inwardness, and mystery, of this attachment, drives men of every class to the use of emblems. The schools of poets, and philosophers, are not more intoxicated with their symbols, than the populace with theirs. In our political parties, compute the power of badges and emblems. See the great ball which they roll from Baltimore to Bunker Hill! In the political processions, Lowell goes in a loom, and Lynn in a shoe, and Salem in a ship. Witness the cider-barrel, the log-cabin, the hickory-stick, the palmetto, and all the cognizances of party. See the power of national emblems. Some stars, lilies, leopards, a crescent, a lion, an eagle, or other figure, which came into credit God knows how, on an old rag of bunting, blowing in the wind, on a fort, at the ends of the earth, shall make the blood tingle under the rudest, or the most conventional exterior. The people fancy they hate poetry, and they are all poets and mystics.[3]

Beyond this universality of the symbolic language, we are apprised of the divineness of this superior use of things, whereby the world is a temple, whose walls are covered with emblems, pictures, and commandments of the Deity, in this, that there is no fact in nature which does not carry the whole sense of nature; and the distinctions which we make in events, and in affairs, of low and high, honest and base, disappear when nature is used as a symbol. Thought makes everything fit for use. The vocabulary of an omniscient man would embrace words and images excluded from polite conversation. What would be base, or even obscene, to the obscene, becomes illustrious, spoken in a new connection of thought. The piety of the Hebrew prophets purges their grossness. The circumcision is an example of the power of poetry to raise the low and offensive. Small and mean things serve as well as great symbols. The meaner the type by which a law is expressed, the more pungent it is, and the more lasting in the memories of men: just as we choose the smallest box, or case, in which any needful utensil can be carried. Bare lists of words are found suggestive, to an imaginative and excited mind; as it is related of Lord Chatham, that he was accustomed to read in Bailey's Dictionary, when he was preparing to speak in Parliament.* The poorest experience is rich enough for all the purposes of expressing thought. Why covet a knowledge of new facts? Day and night, house and garden, a few books, a few actions, serve us as well as would all trades and all spectacles. We are far from having exhausted the significance of the few symbols we use. We can come to use them yet with a terrible simplicity. It does not need that a poem should be long. Every word was once a poem. Every new relation is a new word. Also, we use defects and deformities to a sacred purpose, so expressing our sense that the evils of the world are such only to the evil eye. In the old mythology, mythologists observe, defects are ascribed to divine natures, as lameness to Vulcan, blindness to Cupid, and the like, to signify exuberances.

For, as it is dislocation and detachment from the life of God that makes things ugly, the poet, who re-attaches things to nature and the Whole—re-attaching even artificial things, and violations of nature, to nature, by a deeper insight—disposes very easily of the most disagreeable facts. Readers of poetry see the factory-village and the railway, and fancy that the poetry of the landscape is broken up by these; for these works of art are not yet consecrated in their reading; but the poet sees them fall within the great Order not less than the bee-hive, or the spider's geometrical web. Nature adopts them very fast into her vital circles, and the gliding train of cars she loves like her own. Besides, in a centered mind, it signifies nothing how many mechanical inventions you exhibit. Though you add millions, and never so surprising, the fact of mechanics has not gained a grain's weight. The spiritual fact remains unalterable, by many or by few particulars; as no mountain is of any appreciable height to break the curve of the sphere. A shrewd country boy goes to the city for the first time, and the complacent citizen is not satisfied with his little wonder. It is not that he does not see all the fine houses, and know that he never saw such before, but he disposes of them as easily as the poet finds place for the railway. The chief value of the new fact is to enhance the great and constant fact of Life, which can dwarf any and every circumstance, and to which the belt of wampum† and the commerce of America are alike.

The world being thus put under the mind for verb and noun, the poet is he who can articulate it. For, though life is great, and fascinates,

---

*William Pitt, 1st earl of Chatham, was said to have read Nathaniel Bailey's *Universal Etymological English Dictionary* (1721) from cover to cover.
†String of beads or shells used by some Native American tribes as currency.

and absorbs—and though all men are intelligent of the symbols through which it is named—yet they cannot originally use them. We are symbols, and inhabit symbols; workman, work and tools, words and things, birth and death, all are emblems; but we sympathize with the symbols, and, being infatuated with the economical uses of things, we do not know that they are thoughts. The poet, by an ulterior intellectual perception, gives them a power which makes their old use forgotten, and puts eyes, and a tongue, into every dumb and inanimate object. He perceives the independence of the thought on the symbol, the stability of the thought, the accidency and fugacity* of the symbol. As the eyes of Lyncæus were said to see through the earth, so the poet turns the world to glass, and shows us all things in their right series and procession. For, through that better perception, he stands one step nearer to things, and sees the flowing or metamorphosis; perceives that thought is multiform; that within the form of every creature is a force impelling it to ascend into a higher form; and, following with his eyes the life, uses the forms which express that life, and so his speech flows with the flowing of nature. All the facts of the animal economy, sex, nutriment, gestation, birth, growth, are symbols of the passage of the world into the soul of man, to suffer there a change, and reappear a new and higher fact. He uses forms according to the life, and not according to the form. This is true science. The poet alone knows astronomy, chemistry, vegetation, and animation, for he does not stop at these facts, but employs them as signs. He knows why the plain, or meadow of space, was strewn with these flowers we call suns, and moons, and stars; why the great deep is adorned with animals, with men, and gods; for in every word he speaks he rides on them as the horses of thought.

By virtue of this science the poet is the Namer, or Language-maker, naming things sometimes after their appearance, sometimes after their essence, and giving to every one its own name and not another's, thereby rejoicing the intellect, which delights in detachment or boundary. The poets made all the words, and therefore language is the archives of history, and, if we must say it, a sort of tomb of the muses. For, though the origin of most of our words is forgotten, each word was at first a stroke of genius, and obtained currency, because for the moment it symbolized the world to the first speaker and to the hearer. The etymologist finds the deadest word to have been once a brilliant picture. Language is fossil poetry. As the limestone of the continent consists of

---

*Quality of being fleeting or transitory.

infinite masses of the shells of animalcules, so language is made up of images, or tropes, which now, in their secondary use, have long ceased to remind us of their poetic origin. But the poet names the thing because he sees it, or comes one step nearer to it than any other. This expression, or naming, is not art, but a second nature, grown out of the first, as a leaf out of a tree. What we call nature is a certain self-regulated motion, or change; and nature does all things by her own hands, and does not leave another to baptize her, but baptizes herself; and this through the metamorphosis again. I remember that a certain poet described it to me thus:[4]

"Genius is the activity which repairs the decays of things, whether wholly or partly of a material and finite kind. Nature, through all her kingdoms, insures herself. Nobody cares for planting the poor fungus, so she shakes down from the gills of one agarac* countless spores, any one of which, being preserved, transmits new billions of spores tomorrow or next day. The new agaric of this hour has a chance which the old one had not. This atom of seed is thrown into a new place, not subject to the accidents which destroyed its parent two rods off. She makes a man, and having brought him to ripe age, she will no longer run the risk of losing this wonder at a blow, but she detaches from him a new self, that the kind may be safe from accidents to which the individual is exposed. So when the soul of the poet has come to ripeness of thought, she detaches and sends away from it its poems or songs—a fearless, sleepless, deathless progeny, which is not exposed to the accidents of the weary kingdom of time: a fearless, vivacious offspring, clad with wings (such was the virtue of the soul out of which they came), which carry them fast and far, and infix them irrecoverably into the hearts of men. These wings are the beauty of the poet's soul. The songs, thus flying immortal from their mortal parent, are pursued by clamorous flights of censures, which swarm in far greater numbers, and threaten to devour them; but these last are not winged. At the end of a very short leap they fall plump down, and rot, having received from the souls out of which they came no beautiful wings. But the melodies of the poet ascend, and leap, and pierce into the deeps of infinite time."

So far the bard taught me, using his freer speech. But nature has a higher end, in the production of new individuals, than security, namely, *ascension*, or the passage of the soul into higher forms. I knew, in my younger days, the sculptor who made the statue of the youth which

---

*Family of fungus that includes mushrooms.

stands in the public garden. He was, as I remember, unable to tell, directly, what made him happy or unhappy, but by wonderful indirections he could tell. He rose one day, according to his habit, before the dawn, and saw the morning break, grand as the eternity out of which it came, and, for many days after, he strove to express this tranquillity, and lo! his chisel had fashioned out of marble the form of a beautiful youth, Phosphorus, whose aspect is such that it is said all persons who look on it become silent. The poet also resigns himself to his mood, and that thought which agitated him is expressed, but *alter idem,** in a manner totally new. The expression is organic, or the new type which things themselves take when liberated. As in the sun objects paint their images on the retina of the eye, so they, sharing the aspiration of the whole universe, tend to paint a far more delicate copy of their essence in his mind. Like the metamorphosis of things into higher organic forms, is their change into melodies. Over everything stands its demon, or soul, and, as the form of the thing is reflected by the eye, so the soul of the thing is reflected by a melody. The sea, the mountain-ridge, Niagara, and every flower-bed, pre-exist, or super-exist, in pre-cantations, which sail like odors in the air, and when any man goes by with an ear sufficiently fine, he overhears them, and endeavors to write down the notes, without diluting or depraving them. And herein is the legitimation of criticism, in the mind's faith, that the poems are a corrupt version of some text in nature, with which they ought to be made to tally. A rhyme in one of our sonnets should not be less pleasing than the iterated nodes of a sea-shell, or the resembling difference of a group of flowers. The pairing of the birds is an idyl, not tedious as our idyls are; a tempest is a rough ode without falsehood or rant; a summer, with its harvest sown, reaped, and stored, is an epic song, subordinating how many admirably executed parts. Why should not the symmetry and truth that modulate these glide into our spirits, and we participate the invention of nature?

This insight, which expresses itself by what is called Imagination, is a very high sort of seeing, which does not come by study, but by the intellect being where and what it sees, by sharing the path, or circuit of things through form, and so making them translucid to others. The path of things is silent. Will they suffer a speaker to go with them? A spy they will not suffer; a lover, a poet, is the transcendency of their own nature—him they will suffer. The condition of true naming on the poet's

---

*Another, but the same (Latin).

part, is his resigning himself to the divine *aura* which breathes through forms, and accompanying that.

It is a secret which every intellectual man quickly learns, that beyond the energy of his possessed and conscious intellect he is capable of a new energy (as of an intellect doubled on itself), by abandonment to the nature of things; that, besides his privacy of power as an individual man, there is a great public power on which he can draw, by unlocking, at all risks, his human doors, and suffering the ethereal tides to roll and circulate through him: then he is caught up into the life of the Universe, his speech is thunder, his thought is law, and his words are universally intelligible as the plants and animals. The poet knows that he speaks adequately, then, only when he speaks somewhat wildly, or "with the flower of the mind;"* not with the intellect used as an organ, but with the intellect released from all service, and suffered to take its direction from its celestial life; or, as the ancients were wont to express themselves, not with intellect alone, but with the intellect inebriated by nectar. As the traveler who has lost his way throws his reins on his horse's neck, and trusts to the instincts of the animal to find his road, so must we do with the divine animal who carries us through this world. For if in any manner we can stimulate this instinct, new passages are opened for us into nature, the mind flows into and through things hardest and highest, and the metamorphosis is possible.

This is the reason why bards love wine, mead, narcotics, coffee, tea, opium, the fumes of sandal-wood and tobacco, or whatever other species of animal exhilaration. All men avail themselves of such means as they can, to add this extraordinary power to their normal powers; and to this end they prize conversation, music, pictures, sculpture, dancing, theaters, traveling, war, mobs, fires, gaming, politics, or love, or science, or animal intoxication, which are several coarser or finer *quasi*-mechanical substitutes for the true nectar, which is the ravishment of the intellect by coming nearer to the fact. These are auxiliaries to the centrifugal tendency of a man, to his passage out into free space, and they help him to escape the custody of that body in which he is pent up, and of that jail-yard of individual relations in which he is inclosed. Hence a great number of such as were professionally expressors of Beauty, as painters, poets, musicians, and actors, have been more than others wont to lead a life of pleasure and indulgence; all but the few who received the true nectar; and, as it was a spurious mode of at-

---

*From *The Chaldean Oracles*, attributed to Zoroaster.

taining freedom, as it was an emancipation not into the heavens, but into the freedom of baser places, they were punished for that advantage they won by a dissipation and deterioration. But never can any advantage be taken of nature by a trick. The spirit of the world, the great calm presence of the Creator, comes not forth to the sorceries of opium or of wine. The sublime vision comes to the pure and simple soul in a clean and chaste body. That is not an inspiration which we owe to narcotics, but some counterfeit excitement and fury. Milton says that the lyric poet may drink wine and live generously, but the epic poet, he who shall sing of the gods, and their descent unto men, must drink water out of a wooden bowl.* For poetry is not "Devil's wine," but God's wine. It is with this as it is with toys. We fill the hands and nurseries of our children with all manner of dolls, drums, and horses, withdrawing their eyes from the plain face and suffing objects of nature, the sun, the moon, the animals, the water, and stones, which should be their toys. So the poet's habit of living should be set on a key so low and plain that the common influences should delight him. His cheerfulness should be the gift of the sunlight; the air should suffice for his inspiration, and he should be tipsy with water. The spirit which suffices quiet hearts, which seems to come forth to such from every dry knoll of sere grass, from every pine-stump, and half imbedded stone, on which the dull March sun shines, comes forth to the poor and hungry, and such as are of simple taste. If thou fill thy brain with Boston and New York, with fashion and covetousness, and wilt stimulate thy jaded senses with wine and French coffee, thou shalt find no radiance of wisdom in the lonely waste of the pine-woods.

If the imagination intoxicates the poet, it is not inactive in other men. The metamorphosis excites in the beholder an emotion of joy. The use of symbols has a certain power of emancipation and exhilaration of all men. We seem to be touched by a wand, which makes us dance and run about happily, like children. We are like persons who come out of a cave or cellar into the open air. This is the effect on us of tropes, fables, oracles, and all poetic forms. Poets are thus liberating gods. Men have really got a new sense, and found within their world another world or nest of worlds; for, the metamorphosis once seen, we divine that it does not stop. I will now consider how much this makes the charm of algebra and the mathematics, which also have their tropes, but it is felt in every definition; as, when Aristotle defines *space* to be an immovable

---

*Compare Milton's sixth *Latin Elegy*.

vessel, in which things are contained; or, when Plato defines a *line* to be a flowing point; or, *figure* to be a bound of solid; and many the like. What a joyful sense of freedom we have, when Vitruvius announces the old opinion of artists that no architect can build any house well who does not know something of anatomy. When Socrates, in Charmides, tells us that the soul is cured of its maladies by certain incantations and that these incantations are beautiful reasons, from which temperance is generated in souls; when Plato calls the world an animal; and Timæus affirms that the plants also are animals;* or affirms a man to be a heavenly tree, growing with his root, which is his head, upward; and, as George Chapman, following him, writes:

> "So in our tree of man, whose nervie root
> Springs in his top;"†

when Orpheus speaks of hoariness as "that white flower which marks extreme old age;" when Proclus calls the universe the statue of the intellect;‡ when Chaucer, in his praise of "Gentilesse," compares good blood in mean condition to fire, which, though carried to the darkest house between this and the mount of Caucasus, will yet hold its natural office, and burn as bright as if twenty thousand men it did behold;§ when John saw, in the apocalypse, the ruin of the world through evil, and the stars fall from heaven, as time fig-tree castest her untimely fruit;‖ when Æsop reports the whole catalogue of common daily relations through the masquerade of birds and beasts; we take the cheerful hint of the immortality of our essence, and its versatile habit and escapes, as when the gypsies say, "It is in vain to hang them, they cannot die."

The poets are thus liberating gods. The ancient British bards had for the title of their order, "Those who are free throughout the world." They are free, and they make free. An imaginative book renders us much more service at first, by stimulating us through its tropes, than

---

*Compare Plato's *Charmides*, section 157, and *Timaeus* 31 and 77.

†See the "Epistle Dedicatory" of Chapman's translation of the *Iliad*, lines 132–133.

‡Emerson's source for this and the previous quotation attributed to Orpheus is Thomas Taylor's translation of *The Six Books of Proclus* (1816).

§In "The Wife of Bath's Tale," lines 1132–1145.

‖Reference to the Bible, Revelations 6:13: "And the stars of heaven fell unto the earth, even as a fig tree casteth her untimely figs, when she is shaken of a mighty wind" (KJV).

afterward, when we arrive at the precise sense of the author. I think nothing is of any value in books excepting the transcendental and extraordinary.[5] If a man is inflamed and carried away by his thought to that degree that he forgets the authors and the public, and heeds only this one dream, which holds him like an insanity, let me read his paper, and you may have all the arguments and histories and criticism. All the value which attaches to Pythagoras, Paracelsus, Cornelius Agrippa, Cardan, Kepler, Swedenborg, Schelling, Oken or any other who introduces questionable facts into his cosmogony, as angels, devils, magic, astrology, palmistry, mesmerism, and so on, is the certificate we have of departure from routine, and that here is a new witness. That also is the best success in conversation, the magic of liberty, which puts the world, like a ball, in our hands. How cheap even the liberty then seems; how mean to study, when an emotion communicates to the intellect the power to sap and upheave nature; how great the perspective! nations, times, systems, enter and disappear, like threads in tapestry of large figure and many colors; dream delivers us to dream, and while the drunkenness lasts we will sell our bed, our philosophy, our religion, in our opulence.

There is good reason why we should prize this liberation. The fate of the poor shepherd who, blinded and lost in the snow-storm, perishes in a drift within a few feet of his cottage-door, is an emblem of the state of man. On the brink of the waters of life and truth, we are miserably dying. The inaccessibleness of every thought but that we are in is wonderful. What if you come near to it, you are as remote when you are nearest, as when you are farthest. Every thought is also a prison; every heaven is also a prison. Therefore we love the poet, the inventor, who in any form, whether in an ode, or in an action, or in looks and behavior, has yielded us a new thought. He unlocks our chains, and admits us to a new scene.

This emancipation is dear to all men, and the power to impart it, as it must come from greater depth and scope of thought, is a measure of intellect. Therefore all books of the imagination endure, all which ascend to that truth, that the writer sees nature beneath him, and uses it as his exponent. Every verse or sentence, possessing this virtue, will take care of its own immortality. The religions of the world are ejaculations of a few imaginative men.

But the quality of the imagination is to flow, and not to freeze. The poet did not stop at the color, or the form, but read their meaning; neither may he rest in this meaning, but he makes the same objects exponents of his new thought. Here is the difference between the poet and the mystic, that the last nails a symbol to one sense, which was a true sense for a moment, but soon becomes old and false. For all symbols are fluctional; all language is vehicular and transitive, and is good, as ferries and horses are, for conveyance, not as farms and houses are, for homestead. Mysticism consists in the mistake of an accidental and individual symbol for an universal one. The morning redness happens to be the favorite meteor to the eyes of Jacob Behmen, and comes to stand to him for truth and faith; and he believes should stand for the same realities to every reader. But the first reader prefers as naturally the symbol of a mother and child, or a gardener and his bulb, or a jeweler polishing a gem. Either of these, or of a myriad more, are equally good to the person to whom they are significant. Only they must be held lightly, and be very willingly translated into the equivalent terms which others use. And the mystic must be steadily told, All that you say is just as true without the tedious use of that symbol as with it. Let us have a little algebra, instead of this trite rhetoric; universal signs instead of these village symbols, and we shall both be gainers. The history of hierarchies seems to show that all religious error consisted in making the symbol too stark and solid, and, at last, nothing but an excess of the organ of language.

Swedenborg, of all men in the recent ages, stands eminently for the translator of nature into thought. I do not know the man in history to whom things stood so uniformly for words. Before him the metamorphosis continually plays. Everything on which his eye rests obeys the impulses of moral nature. The figs become grapes while he eats them. When some of his angels affirmed a truth, the laurel twig which they held blossomed in their hands. The noise which, at a distance, appeared like gnashing and thumping, on coming nearer was found to be the voice of disputants. The men, in one of his visions,* seen in heavenly light, appeared like dragons, and seemed in darkness; but to each other they appeared as men, and when the light from heaven shone into their cabin they complained of the darkness, and were compelled to shut the window that they might see.

There was this perception in him, which makes the poet or seer an object of awe and terror, namely, that the same man, or society of men, may wear one aspect to themselves and their companions, and a different aspect to higher intelligences. Certain priests, whom he describes as

---

*The "vision" is reported in Swedenborg's book *The Apocalypse Revealed* (Boston, 1836).

conversing very learnedly together, appeared to the children, who were at some distance, like dead horses; and many the like misappearances. And instantly the mind inquires, whether these fishes under the bridge, yonder oxen in the pasture, those dogs in the yard, are immutably fishes, oxen and dogs, or only so appear to me, and perchance to themselves appear upright men; and whether I appear as a man to all eyes. The Bramins and Pythagoras propounded the same question, and if any poet has witnessed the transformation, he doubtless found it in harmony with various experiences. We have all seen changes as considerable in wheat and caterpillars. He is the poet, and shall draw us with love and terror, who sees, through the flowing vest, the firm nature, and can declare it.

I look in vain for the poet whom I describe. We do not, with sufficient plainness, or sufficient profoundness, address ourselves to life, nor dare we chant our own times and social circumstance. If we filled the day with bravery, we should not shrink from celebrating it. Time and nature yield us many gifts, but not yet the timely man, the new religion, the reconciler, whom all things await. Dante's praise is, that he dared to write his autobiography in colossal cipher, or into universality. We have yet had no genius in America, with tyrannous eye, which knew the value of our incomparable materials, and saw, in the barbarism and materialism of the times, another carnival of the same gods whose picture he so much admires in Homer; then in the middle age; then in Calvinism. Banks and tariffs, the newspaper and caucus, Methodism and Unitarianism, are flat and dull to dull people, but rest on the same foundations of wonder as the town of Troy and the temple of Delphos,* and are as swiftly passing away. Our log-rolling, our stumps and their politics, our fisheries, our negroes and Indians, our boats and our repudiations, the wrath of rogues and the pusillanimity of honest men, the northern trade, the southern planting, the western clearing, Oregon and Texas, are yet unsung.† Yet America is a poem in our eyes; its ample geography dazzles the imagination, and it will not wait long for meters. If I have not found that excellent combination of gifts in my countrymen which I seek, neither could I aid myself to fix the idea of the poet by reading now and then in Chalmers' collection of five centuries of English poets. These are wits more than poets, though there have been poets among

---

Troy: city in Asia Minor besieged by the Greeks in the Trojan War; *temple of Delphos:* home of the oracle, or prophetess, of Delphi.
†List of important political issues during the 1840s.

them. But when we adhere to the ideal of the poet, we have our diffi-
culties even with Milton and Homer. Milton is too literary, and Homer
too literal and historical.

But I am not wise enough for a national criticism, and must use the
old largeness a little longer to discharge my errand from the muse to the
poet concerning his art.

Art is the path of the creator to his work. The paths or methods are
ideal and eternal, though few men ever see them, not the artist himself
for years, or for a lifetime, unless he come into the conditions. The
painter, the sculptor, the composer, the epic rhapsodist, the orator, all
partake one desire, namely, to express themselves symmetrically and
abundantly, not dwarfishly and fragmentarily. They found or put them-
selves in certain conditions, as the painter and sculptor before some im-
pressive human figures; the orator, into the assembly of the people; and
the others, in such scenes as each has found exciting to his intellect; and
each presently feels the new desire. He hears a voice, he sees a beckon-
ing. Then he is apprised, with wonder, what herds of demons hem him
in. He can no more rest, he says, with the old painter, "By God, it is in
me, and must go forth of me." He pursues a beauty, half seen, which flies
before him. The poet pours out verses in every solitude. Most of the
things he says are conventional, no doubt; but by-and-by he says some-
thing which is original and beautiful. That charms him. He would say
nothing else but such things. In our way of talking, we say: "That is
yours, this is mine;" but the poet knows well that it is not his; that it is
as strange and beautiful to him as to you; he would fain hear the like
eloquence at length. Once having tasted this immortal ichor,* he can-
not have enough of it, and, as an admirable creative power exists in
these intellections, it is of the last importance that these things get spo-
ken. What a little of all we know is said! What drops of all the sea of our
science are baled up!† And by what accident it is that these are exposed,
when so many secrets sleep in nature! Hence the necessity of speech and
song; hence these throbs and heart-beatings in the orator, at the door of
the assembly, to the end, namely, that thought may be ejaculated as
Logos, or Word.

Doubt not, O poet, but persist. Say, "It is in me, and shall out."
Stand there, balked and dumb, stuttering and stammering, hissed
and hooted, stand and strive, until at last rage draw out of thee that

---

*Ethereal fluid flowing in the veins of gods.
†Scooped up, as with a bucket.

dream-power which every night shows thee is thine own; a power transcending all limit and privacy, and by virtue of which a man is the conductor of the whole river of electricity. Nothing walks, or creeps, or grows, or exists, which must not in turn arise and walk before him as exponent of his meaning. Comes he to that power, his genius is no longer exhaustible. All the creatures, by pairs and by tribes, pour into his mind as into Noah's ark, to come forth again to people a new world. This is like the stock of air for our respiration, or for the combustion of our fireplace, not a measure of gallons, but the entire atmosphere if wanted. And therefore the rich poets, as Homer, Chaucer, Shakespeare, and Raphael, have obviously no limits to their works, except the limits of their lifetime, and resemble a mirror carried through the street, ready to render an image of every created thing.

O poet! a new nobility is conferred in groves and pastures, and not in castles, or by the sword-blade, any longer. The conditions are hard but equal. Thou shalt leave the world, and know the muse only. Thou shalt not know any longer the times, customs, graces, politics, or opinions of men, but shalt take all from the muse. For the time of towns is tolled from the world by funereal chimes, but in nature the universal hours are counted by succeeding tribes of animals and plants, and by a growth of joy on joy. God wills also that thou abdicate a manifold and duplex life, and that thou be content that others speak for thee. Others shall be thy gentlemen, and shall represent all courtesy and worldly life for thee; others shall do the great and resounding actions also. Thou shalt lie close hid with nature, and canst not be afforded to the Capitol or the Exchange. The world is full of renunciations and apprenticeships, and this is thine: thou must pass for a fool and a churl for a long season. This is the screen and sheath in which Pan has protected his well-beloved flower, and thou shalt be known only to thine own, and they shall console thee with tenderest love. And thou shalt not be able to rehearse the names of thy friends in thy verse, for an old shame before the holy ideal. And this is the reward: that the ideal shall be real to thee, and the impressions of the actual world shall fall like summer rain, copious, but not troublesome, to thy invulnerable essence. Thou shalt have the whole land for thy park and manor, the sea for thy bath and navigation, without tax and without envy; the woods and the rivers thou shalt own; and thou shalt possess that wherein others are oniy tenants and boarders. Thou true landlord! sealord! airlord! Wherever snow falls, or water flows, or birds fly, wherever day and night meet in twilight, wherever the blue heaven is hung by clouds, or sown with stars, wherever are forms with transparent boundaries, wherever are outlets into celestial space, wherever is danger, and awe, and love, there is Beauty, plenteous as rain, shed for thee, and though thou shouldest walk the world over thou shalt not be able to find a condition inopportune or ignoble.

Experience[1]

The lords of life, the lords of life—
I saw them pass,
In their own guise,
Like and unlike,
Portly and grim,
Use and Surprise,
Surface and Dream,
Succession swift, and Spectral Wrong,
Temperament without a tongue,
And the inventor of the game
Omnipresent without name;
Some to see, some to be guessed,
They marched from east to west:
Little man, least of all,
Among the legs of his guardians tall,
Walked about with puzzled look:
Him by the hand dear nature took;
Dearest nature strong and kind,
Whispered, "Darling, never mind!
To-morrow they will wear another face,
The founder thou! these are thy race!"

WHERE DO WE FIND ourselves? In a series of which we do not know the extremes, and believe that it has none. We wake and find ourselves on a stair; there are stairs below us, which we seem to have ascended; there are stairs above us, many a one, which go upward and out of sight. But the Genius which, according to the old belief, stands at the door by which we enter, and gives us the lethe* to drink, that we may tell no

---

*Waters of forgetfulness. In Greek mythology, Lethe is a river in the underworld; all who die drink its water, which makes them forget their actions while alive. See the parable of Er at the conclusion of Plato's *Republic*.

tales, mixed the cup too strongly, and we cannot shake off the lethargy now at noonday. Sleep lingers all our lifetime about our eyes, as night hovers all day in the boughs of the fir-tree. All things swim and glitter. Our life is not so much threatened as our perception. Ghost-like we glide through nature, and should not know our place again. Did our birth fall in some fit of indigence and frugality in nature, that she was so sparing of her fire and so liberal of her earth, that it appears to us that we lack the affirmative principle, and though we have health and reason, yet we have no superfluity of spirit for new creation? We have enough to live and bring the year about, but not an ounce to impart or to invest. Ah that our Genius were a little more of a genius! We are like millers on the lower levels of a stream, when the factories above them have exhausted the water. We too fancy that the upper people must have raised their dams.

If any of us knew what we were doing, or where we are going, then when we think we best know! We do not know to-day whether we are busy or idle. In times when we thought ourselves indolent, we have afterward discovered that much was accomplished, and much was begun in us. All our days are so unprofitable while they pass that 'tis wonderful where or when we ever got anything of this which we call wisdom, poetry, virtue. We never got it on any dated calendar day. Some heavenly days must have been intercalated somewhere, like those that Hermes won with dice of the Moon, that Osiris might be born.[2] It is said all martyrdoms looked mean when they were suffered. Every ship is a romantic object, except that we sail in. Embark, and the romance quits our vessel, and hangs on every other sail in the horizon. Our life looks trivial, and we shun to record it. Men seem to have learned of the horizon the art of perpetual retreating and reference. "Yonder uplands are rich pasturage, and my neighbor has fertile meadow, but my field," says the querulous farmer, "only holds the world together." I quote another man's saying; unluckily that other withdraws himself in the same way, and quotes me. "'Tis the trick of nature thus to degrade to-day; a good deal of buzz, and somewhere a result slipped magically in." Every roof is agreeable to the eye, until it is lifted; then we find tragedy and moaning women, and hard-eyed husbands, and deluges of lethe, and the men ask, "What's the news?" as if the old were so bad. How many individuals can we count in society? how many actions? how many opinions? So much of our time is preparation, so much is routine, and so much retrospect, that the pith of each man's genius contracts itself to a very few hours. The history of literature—take the net result of Tiraboschi, Warton, or Schlegel—is a sum of very few ideas, and of very few original tales—all the rest being variation of these. So in this great society wide lying around us, a critical analysis would find very few spontaneous actions. It is almost all custom and gross sense. There are even few opinions, and these seem organic in the speakers, and do not disturb the universal necessity.

What opium is instilled into all disaster! It shows formidable as we approach it, but there is at last no rough rasping friction, but the most slippery sliding surfaces. We fall soft on a thought. *Ate Dea* is gentle,

> "Over men's heads walking aloft,
>   With tender feet treading so soft."*

People grieve and bemoan themselves, but it is not half so bad with them as they say. There are moods in which we court suffering, in the hope that here at least we shall find reality, sharp peaks and edges of truth. But it turns out to be scene-painting and counterfeit. The only thing grief has taught me, is to know how shallow it is. That, like all the rest, plays about the surface, and never introduces me into the reality, for contact with which, we would even pay the costly price of sons and lovers. Was it Boscovich who found out that bodies never come in contact? Well, souls, never touch their objects. An unnavigable sea washes with silent waves between us and the things we aim at and converse with. Grief too will make us idealists. In the death of my son, now more than two years ago, I seem to have lost a beautiful estate—no more. I cannot get it nearer to me. If to-morrow I should be informed of the bankruptcy of my principal debtors, the loss of my property would be a great inconvenience to me, perhaps, for many years; but it would leave me as it found me—neither better nor worse. So is it with this calamity: it does not touch me: something which I fancied was a part of me, which could not be torn away without tearing me, nor enlarged without enriching me, falls off from me, and leaves no scar. It was caducous.† I grieve that grief can teach me nothing, nor carry me one step into real nature. The Indian who was laid under a curse, that the wind should not blow on him, nor water flow to him, nor fire burn him, is a type of us all.‡ The dearest events are summer-rain, and we

---

*From Lucian's comedy *Podagra*, but Emerson takes it from Robert Burton's *Anatomy of Melancholy* (I, 2, iii, 10).

†Dropping off early, as leaves; transitory.

‡Emerson takes this story from Robert Southey's *The Curse of Kehama* (1810), part 2, section 14.

the Para coats* that shed every drop. Nothing is left us now but death. We look to that with a grim satisfaction, saying, there at least is reality that will not dodge us.

I take this evanescence and lubricity of all objects, which lets them slip through our fingers then when we clutch hardest, to be the most unhandsome part of our condition. Nature does not like to be observed, and likes that we should be her fools and playmates. We may have the sphere for our cricketball, but not a berry for our philosophy. Direct strokes she never gave us power to make; all our blows glance, all our hits are accidents. Our relations to each other are oblique and casual.

Dream delivers us to dream, and there is no end to illusion. Life is a train of moods like a string of beads, and as we pass through them, they prove to be many-colored lenses which paint the world their own hue, and each shows only what lies in its focus. From the mountain you see the mountain. We animate what we can, and we see only what we animate. Nature and books belong to the eyes that see them. It depends on the mood of the man whether he shall see sunset or the fine poem. There are always sunsets, and there is always genius; but only a few hours so serene that we can relish nature or criticism. The more or less depends on structure or temperament. Temperament is the iron wire on which the beads are strung. Of what use is fortune or talent to a cold and defective nature? Who cares what sensibility or discrimination a man has at some time shown, if he falls asleep in his chair? or if he laugh and giggle? or if he apologize? or is affected with egotism? or thinks of his dollar? or cannot go by food? or has gotten a child in his boyhood? Of what use is genius, if the organ is too convex or too concave, and cannot find a focal distance within the actual horizon of human life? Of what use, if the brain is too cold or too hot, and the man does not care enough for results to stimulate him to experiment, and hold him up in it? or if the web is too finely woven, too irritable by pleasure and pain, so that life stagnates from too much reception, without due outlet? Of what use to make heroic vows of amendment, if the same old lawbreaker is to keep them? What cheer can the religious sentiment yield, when that is suspected to be secretly dependent on the seasons of the year, and the state of the blood? I knew a witty physician who found theology in the biliary duct, and used to affirm that if there was disease in the liver, the man became a Calvinist, and if that organ was sound, he

---

*Early type of raincoat.

became a Unitarian. Very mortifying is the reluctant experience that some unfriendly excess or imbecility neutralizes the promise of genius. We see young men who owe us a new world, so readily and lavishly they promise, but they never acquit the debt; they die young and dodge the account: or if they live, they lose themselves in the crowd.

Temperament also enters fully into the system of illusions, and shuts us in a prison of glass which we cannot see. There is an optical illusion about every person we meet. In truth, they are all creatures of given temperament, which will appear in a given character, whose boundaries they will never pass: but we look at them, they seem alive and we presume there is impulse in them. In the moment it seems impulse; in the year, in the lifetime, it turns out to be a certain uniform tune which the revolving barrel of the music-box must play. Men resist the conclusion in the morning, but adopt it as the evening wears on, that temper prevails over everything of time, place, and condition, and is inconsumable in the flames of religion. Some modifications the moral sentiment avails to impose, but the individual texture holds its dominion, if not to bias the moral judgments, yet to fix the measure of activity and of enjoyment.

I thus express the law as it is read from the platform of ordinary life, but must not leave it without noticing the capital exception. For temperament is a power which no man willingly hears any one praise but himself. On the platform of physics we cannot resist the contracting influences of so-called science. Temperament puts all divinity to rout. I know the mental proclivity of physicians. I hear the chuckle of the phrenologists. Theoretic kidnappers and slave-drivers, they esteem each man the victim of another, who winds him round his finger by knowing the law of his being, and by such cheap sign-boards as the color of his beard, or the slope of his occiput, reads the inventory of his fortunes and character. The grossest ignorance does not disgust like this impudent knowingness. The physicians say, they are not materialists; but they are: Spirit is matter reduced to an extreme thinness: O *so* thin! But the definition of *spiritual* should be, *that which is its own evidence.* What notions do they attach to love! what to religion! One would not willingly pronounce these words in their hearing, and give them the occasion to profane them. I saw a gracious gentleman who adapts his conversation to the form of the head of the man he talks with. I had fancied that the value of life lay in its inscrutable possibilities; in the fact that I never know, in addressing myself to a new individual, what may befall me. I carry the keys of my castle in my hand, ready to throw them at the feet of my lord, whenever and in what disguise soever he shall appear. I know he is in the neighborhood hidden among vagabonds. Shall I preclude my future by taking a high seat, and kindly adapting my conversation to the shape of heads? When I come to that the doctors shall buy me for a cent. "But, sir, medical history; the report to the Institute; the proven facts!" I distrust the facts and the inferences. Temperament is the veto or limitation-power in the constitution, very justly applied to restrain an opposite excess in the constitution, but absurdly offered as a bar to original equity. When virtue is in presence, all subordinate powers sleep. On its own level, or in view of nature, temperament is final. I see not, if one be once caught in this trap of so-called sciences, any escape for the man from the links of the chain of physical necessity. Given such an embryo, such a history must follow. On this platform, one lives in a sty of sensualism, and would soon come to suicide. But it is impossible that the creative power should exclude itself. Into every intelligence there is a door which is never closed, through which the creator passes. The intellect, seeker of absolute truth, or the heart, lover of absolute good, intervenes for our succor, and at one whisper of these high powers, we awake from ineffectual struggles with this nightmare. We hurl it into its own hell, and cannot again contract ourselves to so base a state.

The secret of the illusoriness is in the necessity of a succession of moods or objects. Gladly would we anchor, but the anchorage is quicksand. This onward trick of nature is too strong for us: *Pero si muove.*[3] When, at night, I look at the moon and stars, I seem stationary and they to hurry. Our love of the real draws us to permanence, but health of body consists in circulation, and sanity of mind in variety or facility of association. We need change of objects. Dedication to one thought is quickly odious. We house with the insane and must humor them; then conversation dies out. Once I took such delight in Montaigne that I thought I should not need any other book; before that, in Shakspeare; then in Plutarch; then in Plotinus; at one time in Bacon; afterward in Goethe; even in Bettine; but now I turn the pages of either of them languidly, while I still cherish their genius. So with pictures; each will bear an emphasis of attention once, which it cannot retain, though we fain would continue to be pleased in that manner. How strongly I have felt of pictures, that when you have seen one well, you must take your leave of it; you shall never see it again. I have had good lessons from pictures, which I have since seen without emotion or remark. A deduction must be made from the opinion, which even the wise express of a new book or occurrence. Their opinion gives me tidings of their mood, and some vague guess at the new fact, but is nowise to be trusted as the lasting relation between that intellect and that thing. The child asks, "Mamma, why don't I like the story as well as when you told it me yesterday?" Alas, child, it is even so with the oldest cherubim of knowledge. But will it answer thy question to say, Because thou wert born to a whole, and this story is a particular? The reason of the pain this discovery causes us (and we make it late in respect to works of art and intellect), is the plaint of tragedy which murmurs from it in regard to persons, to friendship and love.

That immobility and absence of elasticity which we find in the arts, we find with more pain in the artist. There is no power of expansion in men. Our friends early appear to us as representatives of certain ideas, which they never pass or exceed. They stand on the brink of the ocean of thought and power, but they never take the single step that would bring them there. A man is like a bit of Labrador spar,* which has no luster as you turn it in your hand, until you come to a particular angle; then it shows deep and beautiful colors. There is no adaptation or universal applicability in men, but each has his special talent, and the mastery of successful men consists in adroitly keeping themselves where and when that turn should be oftenest to be practiced. We do what we must, and call it by the best names we can, and would fain have the praise of having intended the result which ensues. I cannot recall any form of man who is not superfluous sometimes. But is not this pitiful? Life is not worth taking, to do tricks in.

Of course, it needs the whole society, to give the symmetry we seek. The parti-colored wheel must revolve very fast to appear white. Something is learned too by conversing with so much folly and defect, In fine, whoever loses, we are always of the gaining party. Divinity is behind our failures and follies also. The plays of children are nonsense, but very educative nonsense. So it is with the largest and solemnest things, with commerce, government, church, marriage, and so with the history of every man's bread, and the ways by which he is to come by it. Like a bird which alights nowhere, but hops perpetually from bough to bough, is the Power which abides in no man and in no woman, but for a moment speaks from this one, and for another moment from that one.

But what help from these fineries or pedantries? What help from thought? Life is not dialectics. We, I think, in these times, have had les-

---

*Crystalline rock found in the Labrador region of Canada.

sons enough of the futility of criticism. Our young people have thought and written much on labor and reform, and for all that they have written, neither the world nor themselves have got on a step. Intellectual tasting of life will not supersede muscular activity. If a man should consider the nicety of the passage of a piece of bread down his throat, he would starve. At Education-Farm,* the noblest theory of life sat on the noblest figures of young men and maidens, quite powerless and melancholy. It would not rake or pitch a ton of hay; it would not rub down a horse; and the men and maidens it left pale and hungry. A political orator wittily compared our party promises to western roads, which opened stately enough, with planted trees on either side, to tempt the traveler, but soon became narrow and narrower, and ended in a squirrel-track, and ran up a tree. So does culture with us; it ends in headache. Unspeakably sad and barren does life look to those, who a few months ago were dazzled with the splendor of the promise of the times. "There is now no longer any right course of action, nor any self-devotion left among the Iranis."† Objections and criticisms we have had our fill of. There are objections to every course of life and action, and the practical wisdom infers an indifferency from the omnipresence of objection. The whole frame of things preaches indifference. Do not craze yourself with thinking, but go about your business anywhere. Life is not intellectual or critical, but sturdy. Its chief good is for well-mixed people who can enjoy what they find without question. Nature hates peeping, and our mothers speak her very sense when they say, "Children, eat your victuals, and say no more of it." To fill the hour—that is happiness; to fill the hour, and leave no crevice for a repentance or an approval. We live amid surfaces and the true art of life is to skate well on them. Under the oldest, moldiest conventions, a man of native force prospers just as well as in the newest world, and that by skill of handling and treatment. He can take hold anywhere. Life itself is a mixture of power and form, and will not bear the least excess of either. To finish the moment, to find the journey's end in every step of the road, to live the greatest number of good hours, is wisdom. It is not the part of men, but of fanatics, or of mathematicians, if you will, to say that, the shortness of life considered, it is not worth caring whether for so short a duration

---

*Brook Farm, the commune in West Roxbury, Massachusetts, founded by George Ripley and other transcendentalists.

†From the *Desatir* (1818), ancient scriptures attributed to Zoroaster.

we were sprawling in want, or sitting high. Since our office is with moments, let us husband them. Five minutes of to-day are worth as much to me as five minutes in the next millennium. Let us be poised, and wise, and our own, to-day. Let us treat the men and women well: treat them as if they were real: perhaps they are. Men live in their fancy, like drunkards whose hands are too soft and tremulous for successful labor. It is a tempest of fancies, and the only ballast I know is a respect to the present hour. Without any shadow of doubt, amid this vertigo of shows and politics, I settle myself ever the firmer in the creed, that we should not postpone and refer and wish, but do broad justice where we are, by whomsoever we deal with, accepting our actual companions and circumstances, however humble or odious, as the mystic officials to whom the universe has delegated its whole pleasure for us. If these are mean and malignant, their contentment, which is the last victory of justice, is a more satisfying echo to the heart, than the voice of poets and the casual sympathy of admirable persons. I think that however a thoughtful man may suffer from the defects and absurdities of his company, he cannot without affectation deny to any set of men and women a sensibility to extraordinary merit. The coarse and frivolous have an instinct of superiority, if they have not a sympathy, and honor it in their blind capricious way with sincere homage.

The fine young people despise life, but in me, and in such as with me are free from dyspepsia,* and to whom a day is a sound and solid good, it is a great excess of politeness to look scornful and to cry for company. I am grown by sympathy a little eager and sentimental, but leave me alone, and I should relish every hour and what it brought me—the potluck of the day, as heartily as the oldest gossip in the barroom. I am thankful for small mercies. I compared notes with one of my friends who expects everything of the universe, and is disappointed when anything is less than the best, and I found that I begin at the other extreme, expecting nothing, and am always full of thanks for moderate goods. I accept the clangor and jangle of contrary tendencies. I find my account in sots and bores also. They give a reality to the circumjacent† picture, which such a vanishing meteorous appearance can ill spare. In the morning I awake, and find the old world, wife, babes, and mother, Concord and Boston, the dear old spiritual world, and even the dear old devil not far off. If we will take the good we find, asking no

---

*Indigestion; irritability.
†Surrounding.

questions, we shall have heaping measures. The great gifts are not got by analysis. Everything good is on the highway. The middle region of our being is the temperate zone. We may climb into the thin and cold realm of pure geometry and lifeless science, or sink into that of sensation. Between these extremes in the equator of life, of thought, of spirit, of poetry—a narrow belt. Moreover, in popular experience, everything good is on the highway. A collector peeps into all the picture-shops of Europe, for a landscape of Poussin, a crayon-sketch of Salvator; but the Transfiguration, the Last Judgment, the Communion of St. Jerome, and what are as transcendent as these, are on the walls of the Vatican, the Uffizii, or the Louvre,[4] where every footman may see them; to say nothing of nature's pictures in every street, of sunsets and sunrises every day, and the sculpture of the human body never absent. A collector recently bought at public auction, in London, for one hundred and fifty-seven guineas, an autograph of Shakespeare: but for nothing a schoolboy can read Hamlet, and can detect secrets of highest concernment yet unpublished therein. I think I will never read any but the commonest books—the Bible, Homer, Dante, Shakespeare, and Milton. Then we are impatient of so public a life and planet, and run hither and thither for nooks and secrets. The imagination delights in the woodcraft of Indians, trappers, and bee-hunters. We fancy that we are strangers, and not so intimately domesticated in the planet as the wild man and the wild beast and bird. But the exclusion reaches them also; reaches the climbing, flying, gliding, feathered and four-footed man. Fox and woodchuck, hawk and snipe, and bittern, when nearly seen, have no more root in the deep world than man, and are just such superficial tenants of the globe. Then the new molecular philosophy shows astronomical interspaces betwixt atom and atom, shows that the world is all outside—it has no inside.

The mid-world is best. Nature, as we know her, is no saint. The lights of the church, the ascetics, Gentoos and Grahamites, she does not distinguish by any favor. She comes eating and drinking and sinning. Her darlings, the great, the strong, the beautiful, are not children of our law, do not come out of the Sunday-school, nor weigh their food, nor punctually keep the commandments. If we will be strong with her strength, we must not harbor such disconsolate consciences, borrowed, too, from the consciences of other nations. We must set up the strong present tense against all the rumors of wrath, past or to come. So many things are unsettled which it is of the first importance to settle—and, pending their settlement, we will do as we do. While the debate goes forward on the equity of commerce, and will not be closed for a century or two,

New and Old England may keep shop. Law of copyright and international copyright is to be discussed, and in the interim we will sell our books for the most we can. Expediency of literature, reason of literature, lawfulness of writing down a thought, is questioned; much is to say on both sides, and, while the fight waxes hot, thou, dearest scholar, stick to thy foolish task, add a line every hour, and between whiles add a line. Right to hold land; right of property, is disputed, and the conventions convene, and before the vote is taken, dig away in your garden, and spend your earnings as a waif or godsend to all serene and beautiful purposes. Life itself is a bubble and a skepticism, and a sleep within a sleep.* Grant it, and as much more as they will—but thou, God's darling! heed thy private dream; thou wilt not be missed in the scorning and skepticism; there are enough of them; stay there in thy closet, and toil, until the rest are agreed what to do about it. Thy sickness, they say, and thy puny habit, require that thou do this or avoid that, but know that thy life is a flitting state, a tent for a night, and do thou, sick or well, finish that stint. Thou art sick, but shall not be worse, and the universe, which holds thee dear, shall be the better.

Human life is made up of the two elements, power and form, and the proportion must be invariably kept, if we would have it sweet and sound. Each of these elements in excess makes a mischief as hurtful as its defect. Everything runs to excess; every good quality is noxious, if unmixed, and, to carry the danger to the edge of ruin, nature causes each man's peculiarity to superabound. Here, among the farms, we adduce the scholars as examples of this treachery. They are nature's victims of expression. You who see the artist, the orator, the poet, too near, and find their life no more excellent than that of mechanics or farmers, and themselves victims of partiality, very hollow and haggard, and pronounce them failures—not heroes, but quacks—conclude very reasonably, that these arts are not for man, but are disease. Yet nature will not bear you out. Irresistible nature made men such, and makes legions more of such, every day. You love the boy reading in a book, gazing at a drawing, or a cast; yet what are these millions who read and behold, but incipient writers and sculptors? Add a little more of that quality which now reads and sees, and they will seize the pen and chisel. And if one remembers how innocently he began to be an artist, he perceives that nature joined with his enemy. A man is a golden impossibility. The line he

---

*Compare Shakespeare's *The Tempest* (act 4, scene 1): "We are such stuff / As dreams are made on, and our little life / Is rounded with a sleep."

must walk is a hair's breadth. The wise through excess of wisdom is made a fool.

How easily, if fate would suffer it, we might keep forever these beautiful limits, and adjust ourselves, once for all, to the perfect calculation of the kingdom of known cause and effect. In the street and in the newspapers, life appears so plain a business, that manly resolution and adherence to the multiplication-table through all weathers, will insure success. But ah! presently comes a day, or is it only a half-hour, with its angel-whispering—which discomfits the conclusions of nations and of years! To-morrow again, everything looks real and angular, the habitual standards are reinstated, common sense is as rare as genius—is the basis of genius, and experience is hands and feet to every enterprise—and yet, he who should do his business on this understanding, would be quickly bankrupt. Power keeps quite another road than the turnpikes of choice and will, namely, the subterranean and invisible tunnels and channels of life. It is ridiculous that we are diplomatists, and doctors, and considerate people: there are no dupes like these. Life is a series of surprises, and would not be worth taking or keeping if it were not. God delights to isolate us every day, and hide from us the past and the future. We would look about us, but with grand politeness he draws down before us an impenetrable screen of purest sky, and another behind us of purest sky. "You will not remember," he seems to say, "and you will not expect." All good conversation, manners, and action, come from a spontaneity which forgets usages, and makes the moment great. Nature hates calculators; her methods are saltatory and impulsive. Man lives by pulses; our organic movements are such; and the chemical and ethereal agents are undulatory and alternate; and the mind goes antagonizing on, and never prospers but by fits. We thrive by casualties. Our chief experiences have been casual. The most attractive class of people are those who are powerful obliquely, and not by the direct stroke; men of genius, but not yet accredited: one gets the cheer of their light, without paying too great a tax. Theirs is the beauty of the bird, or the morning light, and not of art. In the thought of genius there is always a surprise; and the moral sentiment is well called "the newness," for it is never other; as new to the oldest intelligence as to the young child—"the kingdom that cometh without observation."* In like

---

*Reference to the Bible, Luke 17:20: "And when he was demanded of the Pharisees, when the kingdom of God should come, he answered them and said, The Kingdom of God cometh not with observation" (KJV).

manner, for practical success, there must not be too much design. A man will not be observed in doing that which he can do best. There is a certain magic about his properest action which stupefies your powers of observation, so that though it is done before you, you wist not of it. The art of life has a pudency, and will not be exposed. Every man is an impossibility until he is born, everything impossible until we see a success. The ardors of piety agree at last with the coldest skepticism—that nothing is of us or our works—that all is of God. Nature will not spare us the smallest leaf of laurel. All writing comes by the grace of God, and all doing and having. I would gladly be moral, and keep due metes and bounds, which I dearly love, and allow the most to the will of man, but I have set my heart on honesty in this chapter, and I can see nothing at last, in success or failure, than more or less of vital force supplied from the Eternal. The results of life are uncalculated and uncalculable. The years teach much which the days never know. The persons who compose our company, converse, and come and go, and design and execute many things, and somewhat comes of it all, but unlooked for result. The individual is always mistaken. He designed many things, and drew in other persons as coadjutors, quarreled with some or all, blundered much, and something is done; all are a little advanced, but the individual is always mistaken. It turns out somewhat new, and very unlike what he promised himself.

The ancients, struck with this irreducibleness of the elements of human life to calculation, exalted Chance into a divinity, but that is to stay too long at the spark—which glitters truly at one point—but the universe is warm with the latency of the same fire. The miracle of life which will not be expounded, but will remain a miracle, introduces a new element. In the growth of the embryo, Sir Everard Home, I think, noticed that the evolution was not from one central point, but co-active from three or more points. Life has no memory. That which proceeds in succession might be remembered, but that which is co-existent, or ejaculated from a deeper cause, as yet far from being conscious, knows not its own tendency. So is it with us, now skeptical, or without unity, because immersed in forms and effects all seeming to be of equal yet hostile value, and now religious while in the reception of spiritual law. Bear with these distractions, with this co-etaneous* growth of the parts; they will one day be *members* and obey one will. On that one will, on that secret cause, they nail our attention and hope. Life is hereby melted into

---

*Of the same age or duration.

an expectation or a religion. Underneath the inharmonious and trivial particulars is a musical perfection, the Ideal journeying always with as, the heaven without rent or seam. Do but observe the mode of our illumination. When I converse with a profound mind, or if at any time being alone I have good thoughts, I do not at once arrive at satisfactions, as when, being thirsty, I drink water, or go to the fire, being cold; no! but I am at first apprised of my vicinity to a new and excellent region of life. By persisting to read or to think, this region gives further sign of itself, as it were, in flashes of light, in sudden discoveries of its profound beauty and repose, as if the clouds that covered it parted at intervals, and showed the approaching traveler the inland mountains, with the tranquil eternal meadows spread at their base, whereon flocks graze and shepherds pipe and dance. But every insight from this realm of thought is felt as initial, and promises a sequel. I do not make it; I arrive there, and behold what was there already. I make! O no! I clap my hands in infantine joy and amazement, before the first opening to me of this august magnificence, old with the love and homage of innumerable ages, young with the life of life, the sunbright Mecca of the desert. And what a future it opens! I feel a new heart beating with the love of the new beauty. I am ready to die out of nature, and be born again into this new yet unapproachable America I have found in the West.

> "Since neither now nor yesterday began
> These thoughts, which have been ever, nor yet can
> A man be found who their first entrance knew."*

If I have described life as a flux of moods, I must now add, that there is that in us which changes not, and which ranks all sensations and states of mind. The consciousness in each man is a sliding scale, which identifies him now with the First Cause, and now with the flesh of his body; life above life, in infinite degrees. The sentiment from which it sprung determines the dignity of any deed, and the question ever is, not what you have done or forborne, but at whose command you have done or forborne it.

Fortune, Minerva, Muse, Holy Ghost, these are quaint names, too narrow to cover this unbounded substance. The baffled intellect must still kneel before this cause, which refuses to be named, ineffable cause,

---

*Translation by seventeenth-century physician Samuel White of lines 455–457 of the ancient Greek tragedy *Antigone* by Sophocles.

which every fine genius has essayed to represent by some emphatic symbol, as, Thales by water, Anaximenes by air, Anaxagoras by (Νους) thought, Zoroater by fire, Jesus and the moderns by love: and the metaphor of each has become a national religion. The Chinese Mencius has not been the least successful in his generalization. "I fully understand language," he said, "and nourish well my vast-flowing vigor." "I beg to ask what you call vast-flowing vigor?" said his companion. "The explanation," replied Mencius, "is difficult. This vigor is supremely great, and in the highest degree unbending. Nourish it correctly, and do it no injury, and it will fill up the vacancy between heaven and earth. This vigor accords with and assists justice and reason, and leaves no hunger." In our more correct writing, we give to this generalization the name of Being, and thereby confess that we have arrived as far as we can go. Suffice it for the joy of the universe, that we have not arrived at a wall, but at interminable oceans. Our life seems not present, so much as prospective; not for the affairs on which it is wasted, but as a hint of this vast-flowing vigor. Most of life seems to be mere advertisement of faculty: information is given us not to sell ourselves cheap; that we are very great. So, in particulars, our greatness is always in a tendency or direction, not in an action. It is for us to believe in the rule, not in the exception. The noble are thus known from the ignoble. So in accepting the leading of the sentiments, it is not what we believe concerning the immortality of the soul, or the like, but *the universal impulse to believe*, that is the material circumstance, and is the principal fact in the history of the globe. Shall we describe this cause as that which works directly? The spirit is not helpless or needful of mediate organs. It has plentiful powers and direct effects. I am explained without explaining, I am felt without acting, and where I am not. Therefore all just persons are satisfied with their own praise. They refuse to explain themselves, and are content that new actions should do them that office. They believe that we communicate without speech, and above speech, and that no right action of ours is quite unaffecting to our friends, at whatever distance; for the influence of action is not to be measured by miles. Why should I fret myself because a circumstance has occurred which hinders my presence where I was expected? If I am not at the meeting, my presence where I am should be as useful to the commonwealth of friendship and wisdom as would be my presence in that place. I exert the same quality of power in all places. Thus journeys the mighty Ideal before us; it never was known to fall into the rear. No man ever came to an experience which was satiating, but his good is tidings of a better. Onward and onward. In liberated moments we know that a new picture of life and duty is already possible; the elements already exist in many minds around you of a doctrine of life which shall transcend any written record we have. The new statement will comprise the skepticisms as well as the faiths of a society, and out of unbeliefs a creed shall be formed. For skepticisms are not gratuitous or lawless, but are limitations of the affirmative statement, and the new philosophy must take them in and make affirmations outside of them, just as much as it must include the oldest beliefs.

It is very unhappy, but too late to be helped, the discovery we have made, that we exist. That discovery is called the Fall of Man. Ever afterward we suspect our instruments. We have learned that we do not see directly, but mediately, and that we have no means of correcting these colored and distorting lenses which we are, or of computing the amount of their errors. Perhaps these subject-lenses have a creative power; perhaps there are no objects. Once we lived in what we saw; now, the rapaciousness of this new power, which threatens to absorb all things, engages us. Nature, art, persons, letters, religions—objects, successively tumble in, and God is but one of its ideas. Nature and literature are subjective phenomena; every evil and every good thing is a shadow which we cast. The street is full of humiliations to the proud. As the fop contrived to dress his bailiffs in his livery, and make them wait on his guests at table, so the chagrins which the bad heart gives off as bubbles at once take form as ladies and gentlemen in the street, shopmen or barkeepers in hotels, and threaten or insult whatever is threatenable and insultable in us. 'Tis the same with our idolatries. People forget that it is the eye which makes the horizon, and the rounding mind's-eye which makes this or that man a type or representative of humanity with the name of hero or saint. Jesus, the "providential man," is a good man on whom many people are agreed that these optical laws shall take effect. By love on one part, and by forbearance to press objection on the other part, it is for a time settled that we will look at him in the center of the horizon, and ascribe to him the properties that will attach to any man so seen. But the longest love or aversion has a speedy term. The great and crescive* self, rooted in absolute nature, supplants all relative existence, and ruins the kingdom of mortal friendship and love. Marriage (in what is called the spiritual world) is impossible, because of the inequality between every subject and every object. The subject is the receiver of Godhead, and at every comparison must feel his

---

*That is, growing.

being enhanced by that cryptic might. Though not in energy, yet by presence, this magazine of substance cannot be otherwise than felt: nor can any force of intellect attribute to the object the proper deity which sleeps or wakes forever in every subject. Never can love make consciousness and ascription equal in force. There will be the same gulf between every me and thee, as between the original and the picture. The universe is the bride of the soul. All private sympathy is partial. Two human beings are like globes, which can touch only in a point, and, while they remain in contact, all other points of each of the spheres are inert; their turn must alone come, and the longer a particular union lasts, the more energy of appetency the parts not in union acquire.

Life will be imaged, but cannot be divided nor doubled. Any invasion of its unity would be chaos. The soul is not twin-born, but the only begotten, and though revealing itself as child in time, child in appearance, is of a fatal and universal power, admitting no co-life. Every day, every act betrays the ill-concealed deity. We believe in ourselves, as we do not believe in others. We permit all things to ourselves, and that which we call sin in others is experiment for us. It is an instance of our faith in ourselves that men never speak of crime as lightly as they think: or, every man thinks a latitude safe for himself which is nowise to be indulged to another. The act looks very differently on the inside, and on the outside; in its quality, and in its consequences. Murder in the murderer is no such ruinous thought as poets and romancers will have it; it does not unsettle him, or fright him from his ordinary notice of trifles: it is an act quite easy to be contemplated, but in its sequel it turns out to be a horrible jangle and confounding of all relations. Especially the crimes that spring from love seem right and fair from the actor's point of view, but when acted are found destructive of society. No man at last believes that he can be lost, nor that the crime in him is as black as in the felon. Because the intellect qualifies in our own case the moral judgments. For there is no crime to the intellect. That is antinomian or hypernomian, and judges law as well as fact. "It is worse than a crime, it is a blunder," said Napoleon,* speaking the language of the intellect. To it the world is a problem in mathematics or the science of quality, and it leaves out praise and blame, and all weak emotions. All stealing is comparative. If you come to absolutes, pray who does not steal? Saints are sad, because they behold sin (even when they speculate), from the point of view of the conscience, and not of the intellect; a confusion of

---

*Possibly taken from Sir Walter Scott's *The Life of Napoleon Buonoparte* (1827).

thought. Sin seen from the thought is a diminution or *less:* seen from the conscience or will it is pravity or *bad*. The intellect names it shade, absence of light, and no essence. The conscience must feel it as essence, essential evil. This it is not: it has an objective existence, but no subjective.

Thus inevitably does the universe wear our color, and every object fall successively into the subject itself. The subject exists, the subject enlarges; all things sooner or later fall into place. As I am, so I see; use what language we will, we can never say anything but what we are; Hermes, Cadmus, Columbus, Newton, Bonaparte, are the mind's ministers. Instead of feeling a poverty when we encounter a great man, let us treat the newcomer like a traveling geologist who passes through our estate and shows us good slate, or limestone, or anthracite, in our brush pasture. The partial action of each strong mind in one direction is a telescope for the objects on which it is pointed. But every other part of knowledge is to be pushed to the same extravagance ere the soul attains her due sphericity. Do you see that kitten chasing so prettily her own tail? If you could look with her eyes, you might see her surrounded with hundreds of figures performing complex dramas, with tragic and comic issues, long conversations, many characters, many ups and downs of fate—and meantime it is only puss and her tail. How long before our masquerade will end its noise of tambourines, laughter, and shouting, and we shall find it was a solitary performance? A subject and an object—it takes so much to make the galvanic circuit complete, but magnitude adds nothing. What imports it whether it is Kepler and the sphere;* Columbus and America; a reader and his book; or puss with her tail?

It is true that all the muses and love and religion hate these developments, and will find a way to punish the chemist, who publishes in the parlor the secrets of the laboratory. And we cannot say too little of our constitutional necessity of seeing things under private aspects, or saturated with our humors. And yet is the God the nature of these bleak rocks. That need makes in morals the capital virtue of self-trust. We must hold hard to this poverty, however scandalous, and by more vigorous self-recoveries, after the sallies of action, possess our axis more firmly. The life of truth is cold, and so far mournful; but it is not the slave of tears, contritions, and perturbations. It does not attempt another's work, nor adopt another's facts. It is a main lesson of wisdom to

---

*Kepler discovered that Mars is in an elliptical orbit around the sun.

know your own from another's. I have learned that I cannot dispose of other people's facts; but I possess such a key to my own as persuades me against all their denials, that they also have a key to theirs. A sympathetic person is placed in the dilemma of a swimmer among drowning men, who all catch at him, and if he give so much as a leg or a finger, they will drown him. They wish to be saved from the mischiefs of their vices, but not from their vices. Charity would be wasted on this poor waiting on the symptoms. A wise and hardy physician will say, *Come out of that,* as the first condition of advice.

In this our talking America we are ruined by our good nature and listening on all sides. This compliance takes away the power of being greatly useful. A man should not be able to look other than directly and forthright. A preoccupied attention is the only answer to the importunate frivolity of other people: an attention, and to an aim which makes their wants frivolous. This is a divine answer, and leaves no appeal, and no hard thoughts. In Flaxman's drawing of the Eumenides of Æschylus, Orestes supplicates Apollo, while the Furies sleep on the threshold.[5] The face of the god expresses a shade of regret and compassion, but calm with the conviction of the irreconcilableness of the two spheres. He is born into other politics, into the eternal and beautiful. The man at his feet asks for his interest in turmoils of the earth, into which his nature cannot enter. And the Eumenides there lying express pictorially this disparity. The god is surcharged with his divine destiny.

Illusion, Temperament, Succession, Surface, Surprise, Reality, Subjectiveness—these are threads on the loom of time, these are the lords of life. I dare not assume to give their order, but I name them as I find them in my way. I know better than to claim any completeness for my picture. I am a fragment, and this is a fragment of me. I can very confidently announce one or another law, which throws itself into relief and form, but I am too young yet by some ages to compile a code. I gossip for my hour concerning the eternal politics. I have seen many fair pictures not in vain. A wonderful time I have lived in. I am not the novice I was fourteen, nor yet seven years ago. Let who will ask, where is the fruit? I find a private fruit sufficient. This is a fruit—that I should not ask for a rash effect from meditations, counsels and the hiving of truths. I should feel it pitiful to demand a result on this town and county, an overt effect on the instant month and year. The effect is deep and secular as the cause. It works on periods in which mortal lifetime is lost. All I know is reception; I am and I have; but I do not

get, and when I have fancied I had gotten anything, I found I did not.
I worship with wonder the great Fortune. My reception has been so
large that I am not annoyed by receiving this or that superabundantly.
I say to the Genius, if he will pardon the proverb, *In for a mill, in for a
million.* When I receive a new gift, I do not macerate my body to make
the account square, for if I should die I could not make the account
square. The benefit overran the merit the first day, and has overran the
merit ever since. The merit itself, so-called, I reckon part of the re-
ceiving.

Also that hankering after an overt or practical effect seems to me an
apostasy. In good earnest, I am willing to spare this most unnecessary
deal of doing. Life wears to me a visionary face. Hardest, roughest ac-
tion is visionary also. It is but a choice between soft and turbulent
dreams. People disparage knowing and the intellectual life, and urge
doing. I am very content with knowing, if only I could know. That is an
august entertainment, and would suffice me a great while. To know a
little would be worth the expense of this world. I hear always the law of
Adrastia, "that every soul which had acquired any truth should be safe
from harm until another period."*

I know that the world I converse with, in the city and in the farms,
is not the world I *think*. I observe that difference, and shall observe it.
One day I shall know the value and law of this discrepance. But I have
not found that much was gained by manipular attempts to realize the
world to thought. Many eager persons successively make an experi-
ment in this way and make themselves ridiculous. They acquire demo-
cratic manners, they foam at the mouth, they hate and deny. Worse, I
observe that, in the history of mankind, there is never a solitary exam-
ple of success—taking their own test of success. I say this polemically,
or in reply to the inquiry, why not realize your world. But far be from
me the despair which prejudges the law by a paltry empiricism—since
there never was a right endeavor, but it succeeded. Patience and pa-
tience, we shall win at the last. We must be very suspicious of the de-
ceptions of the element of time. It takes a good deal of time to eat or
to sleep, or to earn a hundred dollars, and a very little time to entertain
a hope and an insight which becomes the light of our life. We dress our
garden, eat our dinners, discuss the household with our wives, and
these things make no impression, are forgotten next week; but in the
solitude to which every man is always returning, he has a sanity and

*Compare Plato's *Phaedrus*; Adrastia is the goddess of justice or retribution.

revelations, which in his passage into new worlds he will carry with him. Never mind the ridicule, never mind the defeat; up again, old heart! it seems to say, there is victory yet for all justice; and the true romance which the world exists to realize will be the transformation of genius into practical power.

Politics[1]

Gold and iron are good
To buy iron and gold;
All earth's fleece and food
For their like are sold.
Boded Merlin wise,
Proved Napoleon great—
Nor kind nor coinage buys
Aught above its rate.
Fear, Craft, and Avarice
Cannot rear a State.
Out of dust to build
What is more than dust—
Walls Amphion piled
Phœbus stablish must.[2]
When the Muses nine
With the Virtues meet,
Find to their design
An Atlantic seat,
By green orchard boughs
Fended from the heat,
Where the statesman ploughs
Furrow for the wheat;
When the Church is social worth,
When the state-house is the hearth,
Then the perfect State is come,
The republican at home.

IN DEALING WITH THE State, we ought to remember that its institutions are not aboriginal,* though they existed before we were born: that they are not superior to the citizen: that every one of them was once the act

---

*Natural.

of a single man: every law and usage was a man's expedient to meet a particular case: that they all are imitable, all alterable; we may make as good; we may make better. Society is an illusion to the young citizen. It lies before him in rigid repose, with certain names, men, and institutions, rooted like oak-trees to the center, round which all arrange themselves the best they can. But the old statesman knows that society is fluid; there are no such roots and centers; but any particle may suddenly become the center of the movement, and compel the system to gyrate round it, as every man of strong will, like Pisistratus, or Cromwell, does for a time, and every man of truth, like Plato, or Paul, does forever. But politics rest on necessary foundations, and cannot be treated with levity. Republics abound in young civilians, who believe that the laws make the city, that grave modifications of the policy and modes of living, and employments of the population, that commerce, education, and religion, may be voted in or out; and that any measure, though it were absurd, may be imposed on a people, if only you can get sufficient voices to make it a law. But the wise know that foolish legislation is a rope of sand, which perishes in the twisting; that the State must follow, and not lead the character and progress of the citizen; the strongest usurper is quickly got rid of; and they only who build on Ideas, build for eternity; and that the form of government which prevails is the expression of what cultivation exists in the population which permits it. The law is only a memorandum. We are superstitious, and esteem the statute somewhat: so much life as it has in the character of living men, is its force. The statute stands there to say, yesterday we agreed so and so, but how feel ye this article to-day? Our statute is a currency which we stamp with our own portrait: it soon becomes unrecognizable, and in process of time will return to the mint. Nature is not democratic, nor limited-monarchical, but despotic, and will not be fooled or abated of any jot of her authority, by the pertest* of her sons: and as fast as the public mind is opened to more intelligence, the code is seen to be brute and stammering. It speaks not articulately, and must be made to. Meantime the education of the general mind never stops. The reveries of the true and simple are prophetic. What the tender poetic youth dreams, and prays, and paints to-day, but shuns the ridicule of saying aloud, shall presently be the resolutions of public bodies, then shall be carried as grievance and bill of rights through conflict and war, and then shall be tri-

---

*Possibly an error for "protest" or an obscure form of "partake"—taking part in; participation.

umphant law and establishment for a hundred years, until it gives place, in turn, to new prayers and pictures. The history of the State sketches in coarse outline the progress of thought, and follows at a distance the delicacy of culture and of aspiration.

The theory of politics, which has possessed the mind of men, and which they have expressed the best they could in their laws and in their revolutions, considers persons and property as the two objects for whose protection government exists. Of persons, all have equal rights in virtue of being identical in nature. This interest, of course, with its whole power demands a democracy. While the rights of all as persons are equal in virtue of their access to reason, their rights in property are very unequal. One man owns his clothes and another owns a county. This accident, depending primarily on the skill and virtue of the parties of which there is every degree, and, secondarily, on patrimony, falls unequally, and its rights, of course, are unequal. Personal rights, universally the same, demand a government framed on the ratio of the census; property demands a government framed on the ratio of owners and of owning. Laban, who has flocks and herds, wishes them looked after by an officer on the frontiers, lest the Midianites shall drive them off, and pays a tax to that end.* Jacob has no flocks or herds, and no fear of the Midianites, and pays no tax to the officer. It seemed fit that Laban and Jacob should have equal rights to elect the officer who is to defend their persons, but that Laban and not Jacob should elect the officer who is to guard the sheep and cattle. And if question arise whether additional officers or watch-towers should be provided, must not Laban and Isaac, and those who must sell part of their herds to buy protection for the rest, judge better of this and with more right than Jacob, who, because he is a youth and a traveler, eats their bread and not his own.

In the earliest society the proprietors made their own wealth, and so long as it comes to the owners in the direct way, no other opinion would arise in any equitable community than that property should make the law for property, and persons the law for persons.

But property passes through donation or inheritance to those who do not create it. Gift, in one case, makes it as really the new owner's, as labor made it the first owner's; in the other case, of patrimony, the law makes an ownership which will be valid in each man's view according to the estimate which he sets on the public tranquillity.

It was not, however, found easy to embody the readily admitted prin-

---

*Compare the Bible, Genesis 28–31.

ciple that property should make law for property and persons for persons, since persons and property mixed themselves in every transaction. At last it seemed settled that the rightful distinction was that the proprietors should have more elective franchise than non-proprietors, on the Spartan principle of "calling that which is just, equal; not that which is equal, just."*

That principle no longer looks so self-evident as it appeared in former times, partly because doubts have arisen whether too much weight had not been allowed in the laws to property, and such a structure given to our usages as allowed the rich to encroach on the poor, and to keep them poor; but mainly because there is an instinctive sense, however obscure and yet inarticulate, that the whole constitution of property, on its present tenures, is injurious, and its influence on persons deteriorating and degrading; that truly the only interest for the consideration of the State is persons; that property will always follow persons; that the highest end of government is the culture of men; and if men can be educated the institutions will share their improvement, and the moral sentiment will write the law of the land.

If it be not easy to settle the equity of this question, the peril is less when we take note of our natural defenses. We are kept by better guards than the vigilance of such magistrates as we commonly elect. Society always consists, in greatest part, of young and foolish persons. The old, who have seen through the hypocrisy of courts and statesmen, die, and leave no wisdom to their sons. They believe their own newspaper, as their fathers did at their age. With such an ignorant and deceivable majority, States would soon run to ruin, but that there are limitations beyond which the folly and ambition of governors cannot go. Things have their laws, as well as men; and things refuse to be trifled with. Property will be protected. Corn will not grow unless it is planted and manured; but the farmer will not plant or hoe it unless the chances are a hundred to one that he will cut and harvest it. Under any forms, persons and property must and will have their just sway. They exert their power as steadily as matter its attraction. Cover up a pound of earth never so cunningly, divide and subdivide it, melt it to liquid, convert it to gas; it will always weigh a pound: it will always attract and resist other matter by the full virtue of one pound weight; and the attributes of a person, his wit and his moral energy, will exercise, under any law or extinguishing tyranny, their proper force—if not overtly, then covertly, if not for

*From Plutarch's "Symposiacs," in *Morals*, book 8.

the law, then against it; with right, or by might. The boundaries of personal influence it is impossible to fix, as persons are organs of moral or supernatural force. Under the dominion of an idea, which posesses the minds of multitudes, as civil freedom, or the religious sentiment, the powers of persons are no longer subjects of calculation. A nation of men unanimously bent on freedom, or conquest, can easily confound the arithmetic of statists, and achieve extravagant actions, out of all proportion to their means; as the Greeks, the Saracens, the Swiss, the Americans and the French have done.

In like manner to every particle of property belongs its own attractions. A cent is the representative of a certain quantity of corn or other commodity. Its value is in the necessities of the animal man. It is so much warmth, so much bread, so much water, so much land. The law may do what it will with the owner of property, its just power will still attach to the cent. The law may in a mad freak say that all shall have power except the owners of property: they shall have no vote. Nevertheless, by a higher law, the property will, year after year, write every statute that respects property. The non-proprietor will be the scribe of the proprietor. What the owners wish to do, the whole power of property will do, either through the law, or else in defiance of it. Of course, I speak of all the property, not merely of the great estates. When the rich are outvoted, as frequently happens, it is the joint treasury of the poor which exceeds their accumulations. Every man owns something, if it is only a cow, or a wheelbarrow, or his arms, and so has that property to dispose of.

The same necessity which secures the rights of person and property against the malignity or folly of the magistrate, determines the form methods of governing which are proper to each nation, and to its habits of thought, and nowise transferable to other states of society. In this country we are very vain of our political institutions, which are singular in this, that they sprung, within the memory of living men, from the character and condition of the people, which they still express with sufficient fidelity, and we ostentatiously prefer them to any other in history. They are not better, but only fitter for us. We may be wise in asserting the advantage in modern times of the democratic form, but to other states of society, in which religion consecrated the monarchical, that and not this was expedient. Democracy is better for us because the religious sentiment of the present time accords better with it. Born democrats, we are nowise qualified to judge of monarchy, which, to our fathers living in the monarchical idea, was also relatively right. But our institutions, though in coincidence with the spirit of the age, have not any exemption from the practical defects which have discredited other forms. Every actual State is corrupt. Good men must not obey the laws too well. What satire on government can equal the severity of censure conveyed in the word *politic*, which now for ages has signified *cunning*, intimating that the State is a trick?

The same benign necessity and the same practical abuse appear in the parties into which each State divides itself, of opponents and defenders of the administration of the government. Parties are also founded on instincts and have better guides to their own humble aims than the sagacity of their leaders. They have nothing perverse in their origin, but rudely mark some real and lasting relation. We might as wisely reprove the east wind, or the frost, as a political party whose members, for the most part, could give no account of their position, but stand for the defense of those interests in which they find themselves. Our quarrel with them begins when they quit this deep natural ground at the bidding of some leader, and obeying personal considerations throw themselves into the maintenance and defense of points nowise belonging to their system. A party is perpetually corrupted by personality. While we absolve the association from dishonesty we cannot extend the same charity to their leaders. They reap the rewards of the docility and zeal of the masses which they direct. Ordinarily our parties are parties of circumstance and not of principle; as the planting interest in conflict with the commercial; the party of capitalists, and that of operatives; parties which are identical in their moral character, and which can easily change ground with each other in the support of many of their measures. Parties of principle, as religious sects, or the party of free-trade, or universal suffrage, of abolition of slavery, of abolition of capital punishment, degenerate into personalities, or would inspire enthusiasm. The vice of our leading parties in this country (which may be cited as a fair specimen of these societies of opinion), is that they do not plant themselves on the deep and necessary grounds to which they are respectively entitled, but lash themselves to fury in the carrying of some local and momentary measure nowise useful to the commonwealth. Of the two great parties which, at this hour, almost share the nation between them, I should say that one has the best cause, and the other contains the best men. The philosopher, the poet, or the religious man will, of course, wish to cast his vote with the democrat, for free-trade, for wide suffrage, for the abolition of legal cruelties in the penal code, and for facilitating in every manner the access of the young and the poor to the sources of wealth and power. But he can rarely accept the persons whom the so-called popular party proposes to him as representatives of these liberalities. They have not at heart the ends which give to the name of democracy what hope and virtue are in it. The spirit of our American radicalism is destructive and aimless; it is not loving; it has no ulterior and divine ends; but is destructive only out of hatred and selfishness. On the other side, the conservative party, composed of the most moderate, able and cultivated part of the population, is timid, and merely defensive of property. It vindicates no right, it aspires to no real good, it brands no crime, it proposes no generous policy, it does not build, nor write, nor cherish the arts, nor foster religion, nor establish schools, nor encourage science, nor emancipate the slave, nor befriend the poor, or the Indian, or the immigrant. From neither party, when in power, has the world any benefit to expect in science, art or humanity at all commensurate with the resources of the nation.

I do not for these defects despair of our republic. We are not at the mercy of any waves of chance. In the strife of ferocious parties, human nature always finds itself cherished, as the children of the convicts at Botany Bay* are found to have as healthy a moral sentiment as other children. Citizens of feudal states are alarmed at our democratic institutions lapsing into anarchy; and the older and more cautious among ourselves are learning from Europeans to look with some terror at our turbulent freedom. It is said that in our license of construing the Constitution, and in the despotism of public opinion, we have no anchor; and one foreign observer† thinks he has found the safeguard in the sanctity of Marriage among us; and another thinks he has found it in our Calvinism. Fisher Ames expressed the popular security more wisely, when he compared a monarchy and a republic, saying, "That a monarchy is a merchantman, which sails well, but will sometimes strike on a rock and go to the bottom; while a republic is a raft, which would never sink, but then your feet are always in water." No forms can have any dangerous importance while we are befriended by the laws of things. It makes no difference how many tons weight of atmosphere presses on our heads so long as the same pressure resists it within the lungs. Augment the mass a thousand-fold, it cannot begin to crush us as long as reaction is equal to action. The fact of two poles of two forces, centripetal and centrifugal, is universal, and each force by its own activity

---

*Penal colony in New South Wales, Australia.

†Probably Alexis de Tocqueville, whose *Democracy in America* (1835–1840) Emerson had read as early as 1841.

develops the other. Wild liberty develops iron conscience. Want of liberty, by strengthening law and decorum, stupefies conscience. "Lynch-law" prevails only where there is greater hardihood and self-subsistency in the leaders. A mob cannot be a permanency; everybody's interest requires that it should not exist, and only justice satisfies all.

We must trust infinitely to the beneficent necessity which shines through all laws.[3] Human nature expresses itself in them as characteristically as in statues, or songs, or railroads, and an abstract of the codes of nations would be a transcript of the common conscience. Governments have their origin in the moral identity of men. Reason for one is seen to be reason for another and for every other. There is a middle measure which satisfies all parties, be they never so many, or so resolute for their own. Every man finds a sanction for his simplest claims and deeds in decisions of his own mind, which he calls Truth and Holiness. In these decisions all the citizens find a perfect agreement, and only in these; not in what is good to eat, good to wear, good use of time, or what amount of land, or of public aid, each is entitled to claim. This truth and justice men presently endeavor to make application of, to the measuring of land, the apportionment of service, the protection of life and property. Their first endeavors, no doubt, are very awkward. Yet absolute right is the first governor; or, every government is an impure theocracy. The idea, after which each community is aiming to make and mend its law, is the will of the wise man. The wise man it cannot find in nature, and it makes awkward but earnest efforts to secure his government by contrivance; as, by causing the entire people to give their voices on every measure; or, by a double choice to get the representation of the whole; or, by a selection of the best citizens; or, to secure the advantages of efficiency and internal peace, by confiding the government to one, who may himself select his agents. All forms of government symbolize an immortal government, common to all dynasties and independent of numbers, perfect where two men exist, perfect where there is only one man.

Every man's nature is a sufficient advertisement to him of the character of his fellows. My right and my wrong is their right and their wrong. While I do what is fit for me, and abstain from what is unfit, my neighbor and I shall often agree in our means, and work together for a time to one end. But whenever I find my dominion over myself not sufficient for me, and undertake the direction of him also, I overstep the truth, and come into false relations to him. I may have so much more skill or strength than he that he cannot express adequately his sense of wrong, but it is a lie, and hurts like a lie both him and me. Love and nature cannot maintain the assumption: it must be executed by a practical lie, namely, by force. This undertaking for another, is the blunder which stands in colossal ugliness in the governments of the world. It is the same thing in numbers as in a pair, only not quite so intelligible. I can see well enough a great difference between my setting myself down to a self-control, and my going to make somebody else act after my views: but when a quarter of the human race assume to tell me what I must do, I may be too much disturbed by the circumstances to see so clearly the absurdity of their command. Therefore, all public ends look vague and quixotic beside private ones. For any laws but those which men make for themselves are laughable. If I put myself in the place of my child, and we stand in one thought, and see that things are thus or thus, that perception is law for him and me. We are both there, both act. But if, without carrying him into the thought, I look over into his plot, and, guessing bow it is with him, ordain this or that, he will never obey me. This is the history of governments—one man does something which is to bind another. A man who cannot be acquainted with me, taxes me; looking from afar at me, ordains that a part of my labor shall go to this or that whimsical end, not as I, but as he happens to fancy. Behold the consequence. Of all debts, men are least willing to pay the taxes. What a satire is this on government! Everywhere they think they get their money's worth, except for these.

Hence, the less government we have the better—the fewer laws, and the less confided power. The antidote to this abuse of formal Government is the influence of private character, the growth of the Individual; the appearance of the principal to supersede the proxy; the appearance of the wise man, of whom the existing government is, it must be owned, but a shabby imitation. That which all things tend to educe, which freedom, cultivation, intercourse, revolutions, go to form and deliver, is character; that is the end of nature, to reach unto this coronation of her king. To educate the wise man the State exists; and with the appearance of the wise man the State expires. The appearance of character makes the State unnecessary. The wise man is the State. He needs no army, fort, or navy—he loves men too well; no bribe, or feast, or palace, to draw friends to him; no vantage ground, no favorable circumstance. He needs no library, for he has not done thinking; no church, for he is a prophet; no statute book, for he has the law-giver; no money, for he is value; no road, for he is at home where he is; no experience, for the life of the creator shoots through him, and looks from his eyes. He has no personal friends, for he who has the spell to draw the prayer and piety of all men unto him needs not husband* and educate a few, to share with him a select and poetic life. His relation to men is angelic; his memory is myrrh to them; his presence, frankincense† and flowers.

We think our civilization near its meridian, but we are yet only at the cock-crowing and the morning star. In our barbarous society the influence of character is in its infancy. As a political power, as the rightful lord who is to tumble all rulers from their chairs, its presence is hardly yet suspected. Malthus and Ricardo quite omit it; the Annual Register is silent; in the Conversations' Lexicon,‡ it is not set down; the President's Message, the Queen's Speech, have not mentioned it; and yet it is never nothing. Every thought which genius and piety throw into the world alters the world. The gladiators in the list of power feel, through all their frocks of force and simulation, the presence of worth. I think the very strife of trade and ambition are confession of this divinity; and successes in those fields are the poor amends, the fig-leaf with which the shamed soul attempts to hide its nakedness. I find the like unwilling homage in all quarters. It is because we know how much is due from us, that we are impatient to show some petty talent as a substitute for worth. We are haunted by a conscience of this right to grandeur of character, and are false to it. But each of us has some talent, can do somewhat useful, or graceful, or formidable, or amusing, or lucrative. That we do, as an apology to others and to ourselves, for not reaching the mark of a good and equal life. But it does not satisfy *us*, while we thrust it on the notice of our companions. It may throw dust in their eyes, but does not smooth our own brow, or give us the tranquillity of the strong when we walk abroad. We do penance as we go. Our talent is a sort of expiation, and we are constrained to reflect on our splendid moment, with a certain humiliation, as somewhat too fine, and not as one act of many acts, a fair expression of our permanent energy. Most persons of ability meet in society with a kind of tacit appeal. Each seems to say, "I am not all here." Senators and presidents have climbed so high with pain enough, not because they think the place specially agreeable, but as an apology for real worth, and to vindicate their manhood in our eyes. This conspicuous chair is their compensation to themselves for being of a poor, cold, hard nature. They must do what they can. Like one class of

---

*Cultivate.

†Myrrh and frankincense are resinous oils used in perfumes and incense; gold, frankincense, and myrrh were the three gifts the Magi brought to the infant Jesus.

‡The Annual Register and the Conversations' Lexicon were contemporary encyclopedias.

forest animals, they have nothing but a prehensile tail: climb they must, or crawl. If a man found himself so rich-natured that he could enter into strict relations with the best persons, and make life serene around him by the dignity and sweetness of his behavior, could he afford to circumvent the favor of the caucus and the press, and covet relations so hollow and pompous as those of a politician? Surely nobody would be a charlatan who could afford to be sincere.

The tendencies of the times favor the idea of self-government, and leave the individual, for all code, to the rewards and penalties of his own constitution, which work with more energy than we believe, while we depend on artificial restraints. The movement in this direction has been very marked in modern history. Much has been blind and discreditable, but the nature of the revolution is not affected by the vices of the revolters; for this is a purely moral force. It was never adopted by any party in history, neither can be. It separates the individual from all party, and unites him, at the same time, to the race. It promises a recognition of higher rights than those of personal freedom, or the security of property. A man has a right to be employed, to be trusted, to be loved, to be revered. The power of love, as the basis, of a State, has never been tried. We must not imagine that all things are lapsing into confusion, if every tender protestant be not compelled to bear his part in certain social conventions: nor doubt that roads can be built, letters carried and the fruit of labor secured, when the government of force is at an end. Are our methods now so excellent that all competition is hopeless? Could not a nation or friends even devise better ways? On the other hand, let not the most conservative and timid fear anything from a premature surrender of the bayonet, and the system of force. For according to the order of nature, which is quite superior to our will, it stands thus: there will always be a government of force where men are selfish; and when they are pure enough to abjure the code of force, they will be wise enough to see how these public ends of the post-office, of the highway, of commerce, and the exchange of property, of museums and libraries, of institutions of art and science, can be answered.

We live in a very low state of the world, and pay unwilling tribute to governments founded on force. There is not, among the most religious and instructed men of the most religious and civil nations, a reliance on the moral sentiment, and a sufficient belief in the unity of things, to persuade them that society can be maintained without artificial restraints, as well as the solar system; or that the private citizen might be reasonable, and a good neighbor, without the hint of a jail or a confiscation. What is strange, too, there never was in any man sufficient faith

in the power of rectitude to inspire him with the broad design of reno-
vating the State on the principle of right and love. All those who have
pretended this design have been partial reformers, and have admitted in
some manner the supremacy of the bad State. I do not call to mind a
single human being who has steadily denied the authority of the laws,
on the simple ground of his own moral nature. Such designs, full of ge-
nius and full of fate as they are, are not entertained except avowedly as
air-pictures. If the individual who exhibits them dares to think them
practicable, he disgusts scholars and churchmen; and men of talent, and
women of superior sentiment, cannot hide their contempt. Not the less
does nature continue to fill the heart of youth with suggestions of this
enthusiasm, and there are now men—if indeed I can speak in the plu-
ral number—more exactly, I will say, I have just been conversing with
one man,* to whom no weight of adverse experience will make it for a
moment appear impossible that thousands of human beings might ex-
ercise toward each other the grandest and simplest sentiments, as well
as a knot of friends, or a pair of lovers.

---

*Possibly Bronson Alcott or George Ripley, who formed utopian communities at
Fruitlands and Brook Farm, respectively.

Nominalist and Realist[1]

In countless upward-striving waves
The moon-drawn tide-wave strives;
In thousand far-transplanted grafts
The parent fruit survives;
So, in the new-born millions,
The perfect Adam lives.
Not less are summer-mornings dear
To every child they wake,
And each with novel life his sphere
Fills for his proper sake.

I CANNOT OFTEN ENOUGH say that a man is only a relative and represen-
tative nature. Each is a hint of the truth, but far enough from being that
truth, which yet he quite newly and inevitably suggests to us. If I seek it
in him, I shall not find it. Could any man conduct into me the pure
stream of that which he pretends to be! Long afterward I find that qual-
ity elsewhere which he promised me. The genius of the Platonists is in-
toxicating to the student, yet how few particulars of it can I detach from
all their books. The man momentarily stands for the thought, but will
not bear examination; and a society of men will cursorily represent well
enough a certain quality and culture, for example, chivalry or beauty of
manners, but separate them, and there is no gentleman and no lady in
the group. The least hint sets us on the pursuit of a character which no
man realizes. We have such exorbitant eyes that on seeing the smallest
arc, we complete the curve, and when the curtain is lifted from the dia-
gram which it seemed to veil, we are vexed to find that no more was
drawn than just that fragment of an arc which we first beheld. We are
greatly too liberal in our construction of each other's faculty and prom-
ise. Exactly what the parties have already done they shall do again; but
that which we inferred from their nature and inception they will not do.
That is in nature, but not in them. That happens in the world which we
often witness in a public debate. Each of the speakers expresses himself
imperfectly; no one of them hears much that another says, such is the

preoccupation of mind of each; and the audience, who have only to hear and not to speak, judge very wisely and superiorly how wrong-headed and unskilful is each of the debaters to his own affair. Great men or men of great gifts you shall easily find, but symmetrical men never. When I meet a pure intellectual force, or a generosity of affection, I believe, here then is man; and am presently mortified by the discovery that this individual is no more available to his own or to the general ends than his companions, because the power which drew my respect is not supported by the total symphony of his talents. All persons exist to society by some shining trait of beauty or utility which they have. We borrow the proportions of the man from that one fine feature, and finish the portrait symmetrically; which is false; for the rest of his body is small or deformed. I observe a person who makes a good public appearance, and conclude thence the perfection of his private character, on which this is based; but he has no private character. He is a graceful cloak or lay-figure for holidays. All our poets, heroes and saints fail utterly in some one or in many parts to satisfy our idea, fail to draw our spontaneous interest, and so leave us without any hope of realization but in our own future. Our exaggeration of all fine characters arises from the fact that we identify each in turn with the soul. But there are no such men as we fable; no Jesus, nor Pericles, nor Cæsar, nor Angelo, nor Washington, such as we have made. We consecrate a great deal of nonsense, because it was allowed by great men. There is none without his foible. I verily believe if an angel should come to chant the chorus of the moral law, he would eat too much gingerbread, or take liberties with private letters, or do some precious atrocity. It is bad enough that our geniuses cannot do anything useful, but it is worse that no man is fit for society who has fine traits. He is admired at a distance; but he cannot come near without appearing a cripple. The men of fine parts protect themselves by solitude, or by courtesy, or by satire, or by an acid worldly manner, each concealing, as he best can, his incapacity for useful association, but they want either love or self-reliance.

Our native love of reality joins with this experience to teach us a little reserve, and to dissuade a too sudden surrender to the brilliant qualities of persons. Young people admire talents or particular excellences; as we grow older we value total powers and effects, as the impression, the quality, the spirit of men and things. The genius is all. The man—it is his system: we do not try a solitary word or act, but his habit. The acts which you praise, I praise not, since they are departures from his faith, and are mere compliances. The magnetism which arranges tribes and races in one polarity, is alone to be respected; the men are steel-filings.

Yet we unjustly select a particle and say, "O steel-filing number one! what heart-drawings I feel to thee! what prodigious virtues are these of thine! how constitutional to thee, and incommunicable." While we speak the loadstone is withdrawn; down falls our filing in a heap with the rest, and we continue our mummery to the wretched shaving. Let us go for universals; for the magnetism, not for the needles. Human life and its persons are poor empirical pretensions. A personal influence is an *ignis fatuus*.* If they say it is great, it is great; if they say it is small, it is small; you see it, and you see it not, by turns; it borrows all its size from the momentary estimation of the speakers; the Will-of-the-wisp vanishes if you go too near, vanishes if you go too far, and only blazes at one angle. Who can tell if Washington be a great man or no? Who can tell if Franklin be? Yes, or any but the twelve, or six, or three great gods of fame? And they, too, loom and fade before the eternal.

We are amphibious creatures, weaponed for two elements, having two sets of faculties, the particular and the catholic.† We adjust our instrument for general observation and sweep the heavens as easily as we pick out a single figure in the terrestrial landscape. We are practically skilful in detecting elements, for which we have no place in our theory, and no name. Thus we are very sensible of an atmospheric influence in men and in bodies of men, not accounted for in an arithmetical addition of all their measurable properties. There is a genius of a nation, which is not to be found in the numerical citizens, but which characterizes the society. England, strong, punctual, practical, well-spoken England, I should not find, if I should go to the island to see it. In the Parliament, in the play-house, at dinner-tables, I might see a great number of rich, ignorant, book-read, conventional, proud men—many old women—and not anywhere the Englishmen who made the good speeches, combined the accurate engines, and did the bold and nervous deeds.‡ It is even worse in America, where, from the intellectual quickness of the race, the genius of the country is more splendid in its promise, and more slight in its performance. Webster cannot do the work of Webster.[2] We conceive distinctly enough the French, the Spanish, the German genius, and it is not the less real that perhaps we should not meet in either of those nations a single individual who corresponded

---

*Phosphorescent light seen hovering or flitting over marshy ground; another name for "will-of-the-wisp."

†Universal.

‡That is, deeds that took "nerve"; strong and courageous deeds.

with the type. We infer the spirit of the nation in great measure from the language, which is a sort of monument to which each forcible individual in a course of many hundred years has contributed a stone. And, universally, a good example of this social force is the veracity of language, which cannot be debauched. In any controversy concerning morals an appeal may be made with safety to the sentiments, which the language of the people expresses. Proverbs, words and grammar inflections convey the public sense with more purity and precision than the wisest individual.

In the famous dispute with the Nominalists the Realists had a good deal of reason. General ideas are essences. They are our gods: they round and ennoble the most partial and sordid way of living. Our proclivity to details cannot quite degrade our life, and divest it of poetry. The day-laborer is reckoned as standing at the foot of the social scale, yet he is saturated with the laws of the world. His measures are the hours; morning and night, solstice and equinox, geometry, astronomy and all the lovely accidents of nature play through his mind. Money, which represents the prose of life, and which is hardly spoken of in parlors without an apology, is, in its effects and laws, as beautiful as roses. Property keeps the accounts of the world and is always moral. The property will be found where the labor, the wisdom, and the virtue have been in nations, in classes, and (the whole lifetime considered, with the compensations) in the individual also. How wise the world appears, when the laws and usages of nations are largely detailed, and the completeness of the municipal system is considered. Nothing is left out. If you go into the markets, and the custom-houses, the insurers' and notaries' offices, the offices of sealers of weights and measures, of inspection of provisions—it will appear as if one man had made it all. Wherever you go a wit like your own has been before you, and has realized its thought. The Eleusinian mysteries,* the Egyptian architecture, the Indian astronomy, the Greek sculpture, show that there always were seeing and knowing men in the planet. The world is full of masonic ties, of guilds, of secret and public legions of honor; that of scholars, for example; and that of gentlemen fraternizing with the upper class of every country and every culture.

I am very much struck in literature by the appearance that one person wrote all the books; as if the editor of a journal planted his body

---

*Ancient Greek religious ceremonies associated with the gods Demeter and Dionysius.

of reporters in different parts of the field of action, and relieved some by others from time to time; but there is such equality and identity, both of judgment and point of view, in the narrative, that it is plainly the work of one all-seeing, all-hearing gentleman. I looked into Pope's Odyssey yesterday: it is as correct and elegant after our canon of to-day as if it were newly written. The modernness of all good books seems to give me an existence as wide as man. What is well done, I feel as if I did; what is ill-done, I reck not of. Shakespeare's passages of pas-sion (for example, in Lear and Hamlet) are in the very dialect of the year. I am faithful again to the whole over the members in my use of books. I find the most pleasure in reading a book in a manner least flattering to the author. I read Proclus, and sometimes Plato, as I might read a dictionary, for a mechanical help to the fancy and the imagination. I read for the lusters, as if one should use a fine picture in a chromatic experiment for its rich colors. 'Tis not Proclus, but a piece of nature and fate that I explore. It is a greater joy to see the au-thor's author than himself. A higher pleasure of the same kind I found lately at a concert, where I went to hear Handel's Messiah.* As the master overpowered the littleness and incapableness of the perform-ers, and made them conductors of his electricity, so it was easy to ob-serve what efforts nature was making through so many horses, wooden and imperfect persons, to produce beautiful voices, fluid and soul-guided men and women. The genius of nature was paramount at the oratorio.

This preference of the genius to the parts is the secret of that deifi-cation of art which is found in all superior minds. Art in the artist, is proportion, or a habitual respect to the whole, by an eye loving beauty in details. And the wonder and charm of it is the sanity in insanity which it denotes. Proportion is almost impossible to human beings. There is no one who does not exaggerate. In conversation, men are en-cumbered with personality and talk too much. In modern sculpture, picture, and poetry, the beauty is miscellaneous; the artist works here and there, and at all points, adding and adding, instead of unfolding the unit of his thought. Beautiful details we must have, or no artist: but they must be means and never other. The eye must not lose sight for a mo-ment of the purpose. Lively boys write to their ear and eye, and the cool reader finds nothing but sweet jingles in it. When they grow older, they respect the argument.[3]

---

*Emerson heard this oratorio performed in Boston on Christmas Day, 1843.

We obey the same intellectual integrity when we study in exceptions the law of the world. Anomalous facts, as the never quite obsolete rumors of magic and demonology, and the new allegations of phrenologists and neurologists, are of ideal use. They are good indications. Homœopathy is insignificant as an art of healing, but of great value as criticism on the hygeia or medical practice of the time. So with Mesmerism, Swedenborgism, Fourierism, and the Millennial Church; they are poor pretensions enough, but good criticism on the science, philosophy and preaching of the day. For these abnormal insights of the adepts ought to be normal, and things of course.

All things show us that on every side we are very near to the best. It seems not worth while to execute with too much pains some one intellectual, or æsthetical, or civil feat, when presently the dream will scatter, and we shall burst into universal power. The reason of idleness and of crime is the deferring of our hopes. While we are waiting we beguile the time with jokes, with sleep, with eating, and with crimes.

Thus we settle it in our cool libraries that all the agents with which we deal are subalterns* which we can well afford to let pass, and life will be simpler when we live at the center and flout the surfaces. I wish to speak with all respect of persons, but sometimes I must pinch myself to keep awake and preserve the due decorum. They melt so fast into each other that they are like grass and trees, and it needs an effort to treat them as individuals. Though the uninspired man certainly finds persons a conveniency in household matters, the divine man does not respect them: he sees them as a rack of clouds, or a fleet of ripples which the wind drives over the surface of the water. But this is flat rebellion. Nature will not be Buddhist; she resents generalizing, and insults the philosopher in every moment with a million of fresh particulars. It is all idle talking: as much as a man is a whole, so is he also a part; and it were partial not to see it. What you say in your pompous distribution only distributes you into your class and section. You have not got rid of parts by denying them, but are the more partial. You are one thing, but nature is *one thing and the other thing* in the same moment. She will not remain orbed in a thought, but rushes into persons; and when each person, inflamed to a fury of personality, would conquer all things to his poor crotchet, she raises up against him another person, and by many persons incarnates again a sort of whole.

---

*Subordinates; lesser authorities.

She will have all. Nick Bottom cannot play all the parts,* work it how he may; there will be somebody else, and the world will be round. Everything must have its flower or effort at the beautiful, coarser or finer according to its stuff. They relieve and recommend each other, and the sanity of society is a balance of a thousand insanities. She punishes abstractionists, and will only forgive an induction which is rare and casual.† We like to come to a height of land and see the landscape, just as we value a general remark in conversation. But it is not the intention of nature that we should live by general views. We fetch fire and water, run about all day among the shops and markets, and get our clothes and shoes made and mended, and are the victims of these details, and once in a fortnight we arrive perhaps at a rational moment. If we were not thus infatuated, if we saw the real from hour to hour, we should not be here to write and to read, but should have been burned or frozen long ago. She would never get anything done if she suffered admirable Crichtons and universal geniuses. She loves better a wheelwright who dreams all night of wheels, and a groom who is part of his horse; for she is full of work, and these are her hands. As the frugal farmer takes care that his cattle shall eat down the rowan,‡ and swine shall eat the waste of his house, and poultry shall pick the crumbs, so our economical mother dispatches a new genius and habit of mind into every district and condition of existence, plants an eye wherever a new ray of light can fall, and gathering up into some man every property in the universe, establishes thousandfold occult mutual attractions among her offspring, that all this wash and waste of power may be imparted and exchanged.

Great dangers undoubtedly accrue from this incarnation and distribution of the godhead, and hence nature has her maligners, as if she were Circe; and Alphonso of Castille fancied he could have given useful advice.⁴ But she does not go unprovided; she has hellebore§ at the bottom of the cup. Solitude would ripen a plentiful crop of despots. The recluse thinks of men as having his manner, or as not having his manner; and as having degrees of it, more and less. But when he comes into a public assembly, he sees that men have very

---

*See Shakespeare's *Midsummer Night's Dream* (act 1, scene 2).

†That resolves matters; see p. 216 for a similar use of this word.

‡Stubble left in a field after harvest.

§Both poisonous and medicinal substances are derived from plants of the genus *Helleborus.*

different manners from his own, and in their way admirable. In his childhood and youth he has had many checks and censures, and thinks modestly enough of his own endowment. When afterward he comes to unfold it in propitious circumstance, it seems the only talent: he is delighted with his success, and accounts himself already the fellow of the great. But he goes into a mob, into a banking-house, into a mechanic's shop, into a mill, into a laboratory, into a ship, into a camp, and in each new place he is no better than an idiot: other talents take place and rule the hour. The rotation which whirls every leaf and pebble to the meridian reaches to every gift of man, and we all take turns at the top.

For nature, who abhors mannerism, has set her heart on breaking up all styles and tricks, and it is so much easier to do what one has done before than to do a new thing that there is a perpetual tendency to a set mode. In every conversation, even the highest, there is a certain trick which may be soon learned by an acute person, and then that particular style continued indefinitely. Each man, too, is a tyrant in tendency, because he would impose his idea on others; and their trick is their natural defense. Jesus would absorb the race; but Tom Paine* or the coarsest blasphemer helps humanity by resisting this exuberance of power. Hence the immense benefit of party in politics, as it reveals faults of character in a chief, which the intellectual force of the persons, with ordinary opportunity, and not hurled into aphelion† by hatred, could not have seen. Since we are all so stupid, what benefit that there should be two stupidities! It is like that brute advantage so essential to astronomy, of having the diameter of the earth's orbit for a base of its triangles. Democracy is morose, and runs to anarchy, but in the state, and in the schools, it is indispensable to resist the consolidation of all men into a few men. If John was perfect, why are you and I alive? As long as any man exists there is some need of him; let him fight for his own. A new poet has appeared; a new character approached us; why should we refuse to eat bread until we have found his regiment and section in our old army-files? Why not a new man? Here is a new enterprise of Brook Farm, of Skeneateles, of Northampton: why so impatient to baptize them Essenes, or Port-Royalists, or Shakers, or by any known and effete name? Let it be a new way of liv-

---

*Paine's *Age of Reason* (in 2 parts, 1794 and 1795) dismissed the Bible as mythology and promoted a deistic, rational view of the universe as the basis for civil society.
†Point in the orbit of a planet when it is farthest from the sun.

ing. Why have only two or three ways of life, and not thousands? Every man is wanted, and no man is wanted much. We came this time for condiments, not for corn. We want the great genius only for joy; for one star more in our constellation, for one tree more in our grove. But he thinks we wish to belong to him, as he wishes to occupy us. He greatly mistakes us. I think I have done well if I have acquired a new word from a good author; and my business with him is to find my own, though it were only to melt him down into an epithet or an image for daily use.

"Into paint I will grind thee, my bride!"*

To embroil the confusion, and make it impossible to arrive at any general statement, when we have insisted on the imperfection of individuals, our affections and our experience urge that every individual is entitled to honor, and a very generous treatment is sure to be repaid. A recluse sees only two or three persons, and allows them all their room; they spread themselves at large. The man of state looks at many, and compares the few habitually with others, and these look less. Yet are they not entitled to this generosity of reception? And is not munificence the means of insight? For though gamesters say that the cards beat all the players, though they were never so skilful, yet in the contest we are now considering the players are also the game, and share the power of the cards. If you criticise a fine genius, the odds are that you are out of your reckoning, and, instead of the poet, are censuring your own caricature for him. For there is somewhat spheral and infinite in every man, especially in every genius, which, if you can come very near him, sports with all your limitations. For, rightly, every man is a channel through which heaven floweth, and, while I fancied I was criticising him, I was censuring or rather terminating my own soul. After taxing Goethe as a courtier, artificial, unbelieving, worldly, I took up this book of Helena,† and found him an Indian of the wilderness, a piece of pure nature like an apple or an oak, large as morning or night, and virtuous as a briar-rose.

But care is taken that the whole tune shall be played. If we were not

---

*From the poem "The Paint King," by Washington Allston.
†The editors of *The Collected Works* point out that in his *Journals* Emerson regularly referred to *Faust, Part II*, as "Helena," the title Goethe used when he published the Helen of Troy episode separately in 1827.

kept among surfaces, every thing would be large and universal; now the excluded attributes burst in on us with the more brightness that they have been excluded. "Your turn now, my turn next," is the rule of the game. The universality being hindered in its primary form, comes in the secondary form of *all sides;* the points come in succession to the meridian and by the speed of rotation a new whole is formed. Nature keeps herself whole and her representation complete in the experience of each mind. She suffers no seat to be vacant in her college. It is the secret of the world that all things subsist and do not die, but only retire a little from sight, and afterward return again. Whatever does not concern us is concealed from us. As soon as a person is no longer related to our present well-being he is concealed, or *dies*, as we say. Really all things and persons are related to us, but according to our nature they act on us not at once, but in succession, and we are made aware of their presence one at a time. All persons, all things which we have known, are here present, and many more than we see; the world is full. As the ancient said, the world is a *plenum* or solid; and if we saw all things that really surround us we should be imprisoned and unable to move. For though nothing is impassable to the soul, but all things are pervious to it, and like highways, yet this is only while the soul does not see them. As soon as the soul sees any object it stops before that object. Therefore, the divine Providence, which keeps the universe open in every direction to the soul, conceals all the furniture and all the persons that do not concern a particular soul, from the senses of that individual. Through solidest eternal things the man finds his road, as if they did not subsist, and does not once suspect their being. As soon as he needs a new object, suddenly he beholds it and no longer attempts to pass through it, but takes another way. When he has exhausted for the time the nourishment to be drawn from any one person or thing, that object is withdrawn from his observation, and though still in his immediate neighborhood he does not suspect its presence.

Nothing is dead: men feign themselves dead, and endure mock funerals and mournful obituaries, and there they stand looking out of the window, sound and well, in some new and strange disguise. Jesus is not dead; he is very well alive; nor John, nor Paul, nor Mahomet, nor Aristotle; at times we believe we have seen them all, and could easily tell the names under which they go.

If we cannot make voluntary and conscious steps in the admirable science of universals, let us see the parts wisely, and infer the genius of nature from the best particulars with a becoming charity. What is best in each kind is an index of what should be the average of that thing. Love shows me the opulence of nature by disclosing to me in my friend a hidden wealth, and I infer an equal depth of good in every other direction. It is commonly said by farmers that a good pear or apple costs no more time or pains to rear than a poor one; so I would have no work of art no speech, or action, or thought, or friend, but the best.

The end and the means, the gamester and the game—life is made up of the intermixture and reaction of these two amicable powers, whose marriage appears beforehand monstrous, as each denies and tends to abolish the other. We must reconcile the contradictions as we can, but their discord and their concord introduce wild absurdities into our thinking and speech. No sentence will hold the whole truth, and the only way in which we can be just is by giving ourselves the lie. Speech is better than silence; silence is better than speech. All things are in contact; every atom has a sphere of repulsion. Things are, and are not, at the same time—and the like. All the universe over, there is but one thing, this old Two-Face, creator-creature, mind-matter, right-wrong, of which any proposition may be affirmed or denied. Very fitly, there-fore, I assert, that every man is a partialist, that nature secures him as an instrument by self-conceit, preventing the tendencies to religion and science; and now further assert, that, each man's genius being nearly and affectionately explored, he is justified in his individuality, as his nature is found to be immense; and now I add, that every man is a universalist also, and, as our earth, while it spins on its own axis, spins all the time around the sun through the celestial spaces, so the least of its rational children, the most dedicated to his private affair, works out, though as it were under a disguise, the universal problem. We fancy men are individuals; so are the pumpkins; but every pumpkin in the field goes through every point of pumpkin history. The rabid demo-crat, as soon as he is senator and rich man, has ripened beyond possi-bility of sincere radicalism, and unless he can resist the sun, he must be conservative the remainder of his days. Lord Eldon said in his old age, "That if he were to begin life again, he would be damned but he would begin as agitator."

We hide this universality, if we can, but it appears at all points. We are as ungrateful as children. There is nothing we cherish and strive to draw to us, but in some hour we turn and rend it. We keep a running fire of sarcasm at ignorance and the life of the senses; then goes by, per-chance, a fair girl, a piece of life, gay and happy, and making the com-monest offices beautiful, by the energy and heart with which she does them, and seeing this, we admire and love her and them, and say, "Lo! a genuine creature of the fair earth, not dissipated or too early ripened by books, philosophy, religion, society or care!" insinuating a treachery and contempt for all we had so long loved and wrought in ourselves and others.

If we could have any security against moods![5] If the profoundest prophet could be holden to his words, and the hearer who is ready to sell all* and join the crusades could have any certificate that to-morrow his prophet shall not unsay his testimony! But the Truth sits veiled there on the Bench and never interposes an adamantine syllable; and the most sincere and revolutionary doctrine, put as if the ark of God[†] were carried forward some furlongs and planted there for the succor of the world, shall in a few weeks be coldly set aside by the same speaker, as morbid; "I thought I was right, but I was not"—and the same immeasurable credulity demanded for new audacities. If we were not of all opinions! if we did not in any moment shift the platform on which we stand, and look and speak from another! if there could be any regulation, any "one-hour-rule,"[‡] that a man should never leave his point of view without sound of trumpet. I am always insincere, as always knowing there are other moods.

How sincere and confidential we can be, saying all that lies in the mind, and yet go away feeling that all is yet unsaid, from the incapacity of the parties to know each other, although they use the same words! My companion assumes to know my mood and habit of thought, and we go on from explanation to explanation, until all is said which words can, and we leave matters just as they were at first, because of that vicious assumption. It is that every man believes every other to be an incurable partialist, and himself an universalist? I talked yesterday with a pair of philosophers:[§] I endeavored to show my good men that I love everything by turns, and nothing long; that I loved the center, but doated on the superficies; that I loved man, if men seemed to me mice

---

*Compare the Bible, Luke 18:22–28: ". . . sell all that thou hast, and distribute unto the poor, and thou shalt have treasure in heaven: and come, follow me. . . . Then Peter said, Lo, we have left all, and followed thee" (KJV).

†The Ark of the Covenant, the sacred wooden chest of the Hebrews representative of God's bond with his chosen people; see the Bible, Exodus 25:10–22.

‡Time limit placed on speeches in debate.

§Some scholars suppose that these two philosophers are Charles Lane and Bronson Alcott, who repeatedly tried to persuade Emerson to join them in their efforts to establish a utopian community.

and rats; that I revered saints, but woke up glad that the old pagan world stood its ground and died hard; that I was glad of men of every gift and nobility, but would not live in their arms. Could they but once understand that I loved to know that they existed, and heartily wished them Godspeed, yet, out of my poverty of life and thought, had no word or welcome for them when they came to see me, and could well consent to their living in Oregon; for any claim I felt on them, it would be a great satisfaction.

Uses of Great Men[1]

It is natural to believe in great men. If the companions of our childhood should turn out to be heroes, and their condition regal, it would not surprise us. All mythology opens with demigods, and the circumstance is high and poetic; that is, their genius is paramount. In the legends of the Gautama, the first men ate the earth and found it deliciously sweet.

Nature seems to exist for the excellent. The world is upheld by the veracity of good men: they make the earth wholesome. They who lived with them found life glad and nutritious. Life is sweet and tolerable only in our belief in such society; and, actually or ideally, we manage to live with superiors. We call our children and our lands by their names. Their names are wrought into the verbs of language, their works and effigies are in our houses, and every circumstance of the day recalls an anecdote of them.

The search after the great man is the dream of youth and the most serious occupation of manhood. We travel into foreign parts to find his works,—if possible, to get a glimpse of him. But we are put off with fortune instead. You say, the English are practical; the Germans are hospitable; in Valencia the climate is delicious; and in the hills of the Sacramento* there is gold for the gathering. Yes, but I do not travel to find comfortable, rich and hospitable people, or clear sky, or ingots that cost too much. But if there were any magnet that would point to the countries and houses where are the persons who are intrinsically rich and powerful, I would sell all and buy it, and put myself on the road today.

The race goes with us on their credit. The knowledge that in the city is a man who invented the railroad, raises the credit of all the citizens. But enormous populations, if they be beggars, are disgusting, like moving cheese, like hills of ants or of fleas,—the more, the worse.

Our religion is the love and cherishing of these patrons. The gods of fable are the shining moments of great men. We run all our vessels into

---

*Valencia is a fertile region in Spain; the Sacramento River in California was one of the main sites where gold was mined during the gold rush of 1849.

one mould. Our colossal theologies of Judaism, Christism, Buddhism, Mahometism,* are the necessary and structural action of the human mind. The student of history is like a man going into a warehouse to buy cloths or carpets. He fancies he has a new article. If he go to the factory, he shall find that his new stuff still repeats the scrolls and rosettes which are found on the interior walls of the pyramids of Thebes.† Our theism is the purification of the human mind. Man can paint, or make, or think, nothing but man. He believes that the great material elements had their origin from his thought. And our philosophy finds one essence collected or distributed.

If now we proceed to inquire into the kinds of service we derive from others, let us be warned of the danger of modern studies, and begin low enough. We must not contend against love, or deny the substantial existence of other people. I know not what would happen to us. We have social strengths. Our affection towards others creates a sort of vantage or purchase which nothing will supply. I can do that by another which I cannot do alone. I can say to you what I cannot first say to myself. Other men are lenses through which we read our own minds. Each man seeks those of different quality from his own, and such as are good of their kind; that is, he seeks other men, and the *otherest*. The stronger the nature, the more it is reactive. Let us have the quality pure. A little genius let us leave alone. A main difference betwixt men is, whether they attend their own affair or not. Man is that noble endogenous plant which grows, like the palm, from within outward. His own affair, though impossible to others, he can open with celerity and in sport. It is easy to sugar to be sweet and to nitre to be salt. We take a great deal of pains to waylay and entrap that which of itself will fall into our hands. I count him a great man who inhabits a higher sphere of thought, into which other men rise with labor and difficulty; he has but to open his eyes to see things in a true light and in large relations, whilst they must make painful corrections and keep a vigilant eye on many sources of error. His service to us is of like sort. It costs a beautiful person no exertion to paint her image on our eyes; yet how splendid is that benefit! It costs no more for a wise soul to convey his quality to other men. And every one can do his best thing easiest. "*Peu de moyens, beau-*

---

*Another name for the religion of Islam.
†Ancient city in Upper Egypt, on the Nile.

coup d'effét."* He is great who is what he is from nature, and who never reminds us of others.

But he must be related to us, and our life receive from him some promise of explanation. I cannot tell what I would know; but I have observed there are persons who, in their character and actions, answer questions which I have not skill to put. One man answers some question which none of his contemporaries put, and is isolated. The past and passing religions and philosophies answer some other question. Certain men affect us as rich possibilities, but helpless to themselves and to their times,—the sport perhaps of some instinct that rules in the air;—they do not speak to our want. But the great are near; we know them at sight. They satisfy expectation and fall into place. What is good is effective, generative; makes for itself room, food and allies. A sound apple produces seed,—a hybrid does not. Is a man in his place, he is constructive, fertile, magnetic, inundating armies with his purpose, which is thus executed. The river makes its own shores, and each legitimate idea makes its own channels and welcome,—harvests for food, institutions for expression, weapons to fight with and disciples to explain it. The true artist has the planet for his pedestal; the adventurer, after years of strife, has nothing broader than his own shoes.

Our common discourse respects two kinds of use or service from superior men. Direct giving is agreeable to the early belief of men; direct giving of material or metaphysical aid, as of health, eternal youth, fine senses, arts of healing, magical power and prophecy. The boy believes there is a teacher who can sell him wisdom. Churches believe in imputed merit. But, in strictness, we are not much cognizant of direct serving. Man is endogenous, and education is his unfolding. The aid we have from others is mechanical compared with the discoveries of nature in us. What is thus learned is delightful in the doing, and the effect remains. Right ethics are central and go from the soul outward. Gift is contrary to the law of the universe. Serving others is serving us. I must absolve me to myself. 'Mind thy affair,' says the spirit:—'coxcomb,† would you meddle with the skies, or with other people?' Indirect service is left. Men have a pictorial or representative quality, and serve us in the intellect. Behmen and Swedenborg saw that things were representative. Men are also representative; first, of things, and secondly, of ideas.

---

*From small means, great effect (French); from George Sand's novel *Le Compagnon du Tour de France* (1843).
†Conceited or pretentious person.

As plants convert the minerals into food for animals, so each man converts some raw material in nature to human use. The inventors of fire, electricity, magnetism, iron, lead, glass, linen, silk, cotton; the makers of tools; the inventor of decimal notation; the geometer; the engineer; the musician,—severally make an easy way for all, through unknown and impossible confusions. Each man is by secret liking connected with some district of nature, whose agent and interpreter he is; as Linnæus, of plants; Huber, of bees; Fries, of lichens; Van Mons, of pears; Dalton, of atomic forms; Euclid, of lines; Newton, of fluxions.

A man is a centre for nature, running out threads of relation through every thing, fluid and solid, material and elemental. The earth rolls; every clod and stone comes to the meridian: so every organ, function, acid, crystal, grain of dust, has its relation to the brain. It waits long, but its turn comes. Each plant has its parasite, and each created thing its lover and poet. Justice has already been done to steam, to iron, to wood, to coal, to loadstone, to iodine, to corn and cotton; but how few materials are yet used by our arts! The mass of creatures and of qualities are still hid and expectant. It would seem as if each waited, like the enchanted princess in fairy tales, for a destined human deliverer. Each must be disenchanted and walk forth to the day in human shape. In the history of discovery, the ripe and latent truth seems to have fashioned a brain for itself. A magnet must be made man in some Gilbert, or Swedenborg, or Oersted, before the general mind can come to entertain its powers.

If we limit ourselves to the first advantages, a sober grace adheres to the mineral and botanic kingdoms, which, in the highest moments, comes up as the charm of nature,—the glitter of the spar, the sureness of affinity, the veracity of angles. Light and darkness, heat and cold, hunger and food, sweet and sour, solid, liquid and gas, circle us round in a wreath of pleasures, and, by their agreeable quarrel, beguile the day of life. The eye repeats every day the first eulogy on things,—"He saw that they were good."* We know where to find them; and these performers are relished all the more, after a little experience of the pretending races. We are entitled also to higher advantages. Something is wanting to science until it has been humanized. The table of logarithms is one thing, and its vital play in botany, music, optics and architecture, another. There are advancements to numbers, anatomy, architecture, astronomy, little suspected at first, when, by union with intellect and

---

*Reference to God's comment on his creation; see the Bible, Genesis 1.

will, they ascend into the life and reappear in conversation, character and politics.

But this comes later. We speak now only of our acquaintance with them in their own sphere and the way in which they seem to fascinate and draw to them some genius who occupies himself with one thing, all his life long. The possibility of interpretation lies in the identity of the observer with the observed. Each material thing has its celestial side; has its translation, through humanity, into the spiritual and necessary sphere where it plays a part as indestructible as any other. And to these, their ends, all things continually ascend. The gases gather to the solid firmament: the chemic lump arrives at the plant, and grows; arrives at the quadruped, and walks; arrives at the man, and thinks. But also the constituency determines the vote of the representative. He is not only representative, but participant. Like can only be known by like. The reason why he knows about them is that he is of them; he has just come out of nature, or from being a part of that thing. Animated chlorine knows of chlorine, and incarnate zinc, of zinc. Their quality makes his career; and he can variously publish their virtues, because they compose him. Man, made of the dust of the world, does not forget his origin; and all that is yet inanimate will one day speak and reason. Unpublished nature will have its whole secret told. Shall we say that quartz mountains will pulverize into innumerable Werners, Von Buchs and Beaumonts, and the laboratory of the atmosphere holds in solution I know not what Berzeliuses and Davys?

Thus we sit by the fire and take hold on the poles of the earth. This *quasi* omnipresence supplies the imbecility of our condition. In one of those celestial days when heaven and earth meet and adorn each other, it seems a poverty that we can only spend it once: we wish for a thousand heads, a thousand bodies, that we might celebrate its immense beauty in many ways and places. Is this fancy? Well, in good faith, we are multiplied by our proxies. How easily we adopt their labors! Every ship that comes to America got its chart from Columbus. Every novel is a debtor to Homer. Every carpenter who shaves with a foreplane borrows the genius of a forgotten inventor. Life is girt all round with a zodiac of sciences, the contributions of men who have perished to add their point of light to our sky. Engineer, broker, jurist, physician, moralist, theologian, and every man, inasmuch as he has any science,—is a definer and map-maker of the latitudes and longitudes of our condition. These road-makers on every hand enrich us. We must extend the area of life and multiply our relations. We are as much gainers by finding a new property in the old earth as by acquiring a new planet.

We are too passive in the reception of these material or semi-material aids. We must not be sacks and stomachs. To ascend one step,—we are better served through our sympathy. Activity is contagious. Looking where others look, and conversing with the same things, we catch the charm which lured them. Napoleon said, "You must not fight too often with one enemy, or you will teach him all your art of war."* Talk much with any man of vigorous mind, and we acquire very fast the habit of looking at things in the same light, and on each occurrence we anticipate his thought.

Men are helpful through the intellect and the affections. Other help I find a false appearance. If you affect to give me bread and fire, I perceive that I pay for it the full price, and at last it leaves me as it found me, neither better nor worse: but all mental and moral force is a positive good. It goes out from you, whether you will or not, and profits me whom you never thought of. I cannot even hear of personal vigor of any kind, great power of performance, without fresh resolution. We are emulous of all that man can do. Cecil's saying of Sir Walter Raleigh, "I know that he can toil terribly," is an electric touch. So are Clarendon's portraits,† of Hampden, "who was of an industry and vigilance not to be tired out or wearied by the most laborious, and of parts not to be imposed on by the most subtle and sharp, and of a personal courage equal to his best parts;"—of Falkland, "who was so severe an adorer of truth, that he could as easily have given himself leave to steal, as to dissemble." We cannot read Plutarch without a tingling of the blood; and I accept the saying of the Chinese Mencius: "A sage is the instructor of a hundred ages. When the manners of Loo are heard of, the stupid become intelligent, and the wavering, determined."‡

This is the moral of biography; yet it is hard for departed men to touch the quick like our own companions, whose names may not last as long. What is he whom I never think of? Whilst in every solitude are those who succor our genius and stimulate us in wonderful manners. There is a power in love to divine another's destiny better than that

---

*The source for this quotation has not been identified.
†In his *History of the Rebellion and Civil Wars in England* (1702–1704).
‡From "The Works of Mencius," in *The Chinese Classical Work Commonly Called the Four Books* (1828).

other can, and, by heroic encouragements, hold him to his task. What has friendship so signal as its sublime attraction to whatever virtue is in us? We will never more think cheaply of ourselves, or of life. We are piqued to some purpose, and the industry of the diggers on the railroad will not again shame us.

Under this head too falls that homage, very pure as I think, which all ranks pay to the hero of the day, from Coriolanus and Gracchus down to Pitt, Lafayette, Wellington, Webster, Lamartine. Hear the shouts in the street! The people cannot see him enough. They delight in a man. Here is a head and a trunk! What a front! what eyes! Atlantean shoulders, and the whole carriage heroic, with equal inward force to guide the great machine! This pleasure of full expression to that which, in their private experience is usually cramped and obstructed, runs also much higher, and is the secret of the reader's joy in literary genius. Nothing is kept back. There is fire enough to fuse the mountain of ore. Shakspeare's principal merit may be conveyed in saying that he of all men best understands the English language, and can say what he will. Yet these unchoked channels and floodgates of expression are only health or fortunate constitution. Shakspeare's name suggests other and purely intellectual benefits.

Senates and sovereigns have no compliment, with their medals, swords and armorial coats, like the addressing to a human being thoughts out of a certain height, and presupposing his intelligence. This honor, which is possible in personal intercourse scarcely twice in a lifetime, genius perpetually pays; contented if now and then in a century the proffer is accepted. The indicators of the values of matter are degraded to a sort of cooks and confectioners, on the appearance of the indicators of ideas. Genius is the naturalist or geographer of the supersensible regions, and draws their map; and, by acquainting us with new fields of activity, cools our affection for the old. These are at once accepted as the reality, of which the world we have conversed with is the show.

We go to the gymnasium and the swimming school to see the power and beauty of the body; there is the like pleasure and a higher benefit from witnessing intellectual feats of all kinds; as feats of memory, of mathematical combination, great power of abstraction, the transmutings of the imagination, even versatility and concentration,—as these acts expose the invisible organs and members of the mind, which respond, member for member, to the parts of the body. For we thus enter a new gymnasium, and learn to choose men by their truest marks, taught, with Plato, "to choose those who can, without aid from the eyes or any other sense, proceed to truth and to being."* Foremost among these activities are the summersaults, spells and resurrections wrought by the imagination. When this wakes, a man seems to multiply ten times or a thousand times his force. It opens the delicious sense of indeterminate size and inspires an audacious mental habit. We are as elastic as the gas of gunpowder, and a sentence in a book, or a word dropped in conversation, sets free our fancy, and instantly our heads are bathed with galaxies, and our feet tread the floor of the Pit. And this benefit is real because we are entitled to these enlargements, and once having passed the bounds shall never again be quite the miserable pedants we were.

The high functions of the intellect are so allied that some imaginative power usually appears in all eminent minds, even in arithmeticians of the first class, but especially in meditative men of an intuitive habit of thought. This class serve us, so that they have the perception of identity and the perception of reaction. The eyes of Plato, Shakspeare, Swedenborg, Goethe, never shut on either of these laws. The perception of these laws is a kind of metre of the mind. Little minds are little through failure to see them.

Even these feasts have their surfeit. Our delight in reason degenerates into idolatry of the herald. Especially when a mind of powerful method has instructed men, we find the examples of oppression. The dominion of Aristotle, the Ptolemaic astronomy, the credit of Luther, of Bacon, of Locke;[2] in religion the history of hierarchies, of saints, and the sects which have taken the name of each founder, are in point. Alas! every man is such a victim. The imbecility of men is always inviting the impudence of power. It is the delight of vulgar talent to dazzle and to blind the beholder. But true genius seeks to defend us from itself. True genius will not impoverish, but will liberate, and add new senses. If a wise man should appear in our village he would create, in those who conversed with him, a new consciousness of wealth, by opening their eyes to unobserved advantages; he would establish a sense of immovable equality, calm us with assurances that we could not be cheated; as every one would discern the checks and guaranties of condition. The rich would see their mistakes and poverty, the poor their escapes and their resources.

But nature brings all this about in due time. Rotation is her remedy. The soul is impatient of masters and eager for change. Housekeepers say of a domestic who has been valuable, "She had lived with me long

---

*Plato's *Republic*, book 7, chapter 16.

enough." We are tendencies, or rather, symptoms, and none of us complete. We touch and go, and sip the foam of many lives. Rotation is the law of nature. When nature removes a great man, people explore the horizon for a successor; but none comes, and none will. His class is extinguished with him. In some other and quite different field the next man will appear; not Jefferson, not Franklin, but now a great salesman, then a road-contractor, then a student of fishes, then a buffalo-hunting explorer, or a semi-savage Western general. Thus we make a stand against our rougher masters; but against the best there is a finer remedy. The power which they communicate is not theirs. When we are exalted by ideas, we do not owe this to Plato, but to the idea, to which also Plato was debtor.

I must not forget that we have a special debt to a single class. Life is a scale of degrees. Between rank and rank of our great men are wide intervals. Mankind have in all ages attached themselves to a few persons who either by the quality of that idea they embodied or by the largeness of their reception were entitled to the position of leaders and law-givers. These teach us the qualities of primary nature,—admit us to the constitution of things. We swim, day by day, on a river of delusions and are effectually amused with houses and towns in the air, of which the men about us are dupes. But life is a sincerity. In lucid intervals we say, 'Let there be an entrance opened for me into realities; I have worn the fool's cap too long.' We will know the meaning of our economies and politics. Give us the cipher, and if persons and things are scores of a celestial music, let us read off the strains. We have been cheated of our reason; yet there have been sane men, who enjoyed a rich and related existence. What they know, they know for us. With each new mind, a new secret of nature transpires; nor can the Bible be closed until the last great man is born. These men correct the delirium of the animal spirits, make us considerate and engage us to new aims and powers. The veneration of mankind selects these for the highest place. Witness the multitude of statues, pictures and memorials which recall their genius in every city, village, house and ship:—

> "Ever their phantoms arise before us,
>   Our loftier brothers, but one in blood;
>   At bed and table they lord it o'er us
>   With looks of beauty and words of good."*

---

*From the poem "Dædalus," by John Sterling.

How to illustrate the distinctive benefit of ideas, the service rendered by those who introduce moral truths into the general mind?—I am plagued, in all my living, with a perpetual tariff of prices. If I work in my garden and prune an apple-tree, I am well enough entertained, and could continue indefinitely in the like occupation. But it comes to mind that a day is gone, and I have got this precious nothing done. I go to Boston or New York and run up and down on my affairs: they are sped, but so is the day. I am vexed by the recollection of this price I have paid for a trifling advantage. I remember the *peau d'âne* on which whoso sat should have his desire, but a piece of the skin was gone for every wish.*
I go to a convention of philanthropists. Do what I can, I cannot keep my eyes off the clock. But if there should appear in the company some gentle soul who knows little of persons or parties, of Carolina or Cuba, but who announces a law that disposes these particulars, and so certifies me of the equity which checkmates every false player, bankrupts every self-seeker, and apprises me of my independence on any conditions of country, or time, or human body,—that man liberates me; I forget the clock. I pass out of the sore relation to persons. I am healed of my hurts. I am made immortal by apprehending my possession of incorruptible goods. Here is great competition of rich and poor. We live in a market, where is only so much wheat, or wool, or land; and if I have so much more, every other must have so much less. I seem to have no good without breach of good manners. Nobody is glad in the gladness of another, and our system is one of war, of an injurious superiority. Every child of the Saxon race is educated to wish to be first. It is our system; and a man comes to measure his greatness by the regrets, envies and hatreds of his competitors. But in these new fields there is room: here are no self-esteems, no exclusions.

I admire great men of all classes, those who stand for facts, and for thoughts; I like rough and smooth, "Scourges of God," and "Darlings of the human race." I like the first Cæsar; and Charles V., of Spain; and Charles XII., of Sweden; Richard Plantagenet; and Bonaparte, in France.† I applaud a sufficient man, an officer equal to his office; captains, ministers, senators. I like a master standing firm on legs of iron, well-born, rich, handsome, eloquent, loaded with advantages, drawing

---

*Reference to Honoré Balzac's novel *La Peau de Chagrin* (1831). The plot involves a magic blanket made of animal hide that shrinks each time a wish is granted; when it disappears completely its owner dies.

†List of powerful military leaders who engaged in the conquest of neighboring nation-states.

all men by fascination into tributaries and supporters of his power. Sword and staff, or talents sword-like or staff-like, carry on the work of the world. But I find him greater when he can abolish himself and all heroes, by letting in this element of reason, irrespective of persons, this subtilizer and irresistible upward force, into our thought, destroying individualism; the power so great that the potentate is nothing. Then he is a monarch who gives a constitution to his people; a pontiff who preaches the equality of souls and releases his servants from their barbarous homages; an emperor who can spare his empire.

But I intended to specify, with a little minuteness, two or three points of service. Nature never spares the opium or nepenthe,* but wherever she mars her creature with some deformity or defect, lays her poppies plentifully on the bruise, and the sufferer goes joyfully through life, ignorant of the ruin and incapable of seeing it, though all the world point their finger at it every day. The worthless and offensive members of society, whose existence is a social pest, invariably think themselves the most ill-used people alive, and never get over their astonishment at the ingratitude and selfishness of their contemporaries. Our globe discovers its hidden virtues, not only in heroes and archangels, but in gossips and nurses. Is it not a rare contrivance that lodged the due inertia in every creature, the conserving, resisting energy, the anger at being waked or changed? Altogether independent of the intellectual force in each is the pride of opinion, the security that we are right. Not the feeblest grandame, not a mowing idiot, but uses what spark of perception and faculty is left, to chuckle and. triumph in his or her opinion over the absurdities of all the rest. Difference from me is the measure of absurdity. Not one has a misgiving of being wrong. Was it not a bright thought that made things cohere with this bitumen, fastest of cements? But, in the midst of this chuckle of self-gratulation, some figure goes by which Thersites too can love and admire. This is he that should marshall us the way we were going. There is no end to his aid. Without Plato we should almost lose our faith in the possibility of a reasonable book. We seem to want but one, but we want one. We love to associate with heroic persons, since our receptivity is unlimited; and, with the great, our thoughts and manners easily become great. We are all wise in capacity, though so few in energy. There needs but one wise man in a company and all are wise, so rapid is the contagion.

---

*Drug that induces forgetfulness.

Great men are thus a collyrium* to clear our eyes from egotism and enable us to see other people and their works. But there are vices and follies incident to whole populations and ages. Men resemble their contemporaries even more than their progenitors. It is observed in old couples, or in persons who have been housemates for a course of years, that they grow like, and if they should live long enough we should not be able to know them apart. Nature abhors these complaisances which threaten to melt the world into a lump, and hastens to break up such maudlin agglutinations. The like assimilation goes on between men of one town, of one sect, of one political party; and the ideas of the time are in the air, and infect all who breathe it. Viewed from any high point, this city of New York, yonder city of London, the Western civilization, would seem a bundle of insanities. We keep each other in countenance and exasperate by emulation the frenzy of the time. The shield against the stingings of conscience is the universal practice, or our contemporaries. Again, it is very easy to be as wise and good as your companions. We learn of our contemporaries what they know, without effort, and almost through the pores of the skin. We catch it by sympathy, or as a wife arrives at the intellectual and moral elevations of her husband. But we stop where they stop. Very hardly can we take another step. The great, or such as hold of nature, and transcend fashions, by their fidelity to universal ideas, are saviors from these federal errors, and defend us from our contemporaries. They are the exceptions which we want, where all grows like. A foreign greatness is the antidote for cabalism.

Thus we feed on genius, and refresh ourselves from too much conversation with our mates, and exult in the depth of nature in that direction in which he leads us. What indemnification is one great man for populations of pigmies! Every mother wishes one son a genius, though all the rest should be mediocre. But a new danger appears in the excess of influence of the great man. His attractions warp us from our place. We have become underlings and intellectual suicides. Ah! yonder in the horizon is our help;—other great men, new qualities, counterweights and checks on each other. We cloy of the honey of each peculiar greatness. Every hero becomes a bore at last. Perhaps Voltaire was not bad-hearted, yet he said of the good Jesus, even, "I pray you, let me never hear that man's name again." They cry up the virtues of George Washington,—"Damn George Washington!" is the poor Jacobin's whole speech and confutation. But it is human nature's indispensable defence.

---

*An eyewash.

The centripetence augments the centrifugence. We balance one man with his opposite, and the health of the state depends on the see-saw.

There is however a speedy limit to the use of heroes. Every genius is defended from approach by quantities of unavailableness. They are very attractive, and seem at a distance our own: but we are hindered on all sides from approach. The more we are drawn, the more we are repelled. There is something not solid in the good that is done for us. The best discovery the discoverer makes for himself. It has something unreal for his companion until he too has substantiated it. It seems as if the Deity dressed each soul which he sends into nature in certain virtues and powers not communicable to other men, and sending it to perform one more turn through the circle of beings, wrote "*Not transferable*" and "*Good for this trip only*," on these garments of the soul. There is somewhat deceptive about the intercourse of minds. The boundaries are invisible, but they are never crossed. There is such good will to impart, and such good will to receive, that each threatens to become the other; but the law of individuality collects its secret strength: you are you, and I am I, and so we remain.

For nature wishes every thing to remain itself; and whilst every individual strives to grow and exclude and to exclude and grow, to the extremities of the universe, and to impose the law of its being on every other creature, Nature steadily aims to protect each against every other. Each is self-defended. Nothing is more marked than the power by which individuals are guarded from individuals, in a world where every benefactor becomes so easily a malefactor only by continuation of his activity into places where it is not due; where children seem so much at the mercy of their foolish parents, and where almost all men are too social and interfering. We rightly speak of the guardian angels of children. How superior in their security from infusions of evil persons, from vulgarity and second thought! They shed their own abundant beauty on the objects they behold. Therefore they are not at the mercy of such poor educators as we adults. If we huff and chide them they soon come not to mind it and get a self-reliance; and if we indulge them to folly, they learn the limitation elsewhere.

We need not fear excessive influence. A more generous trust is permitted. Serve the great. Stick at no humiliation. Grudge no office thou canst render. Be the limb of their body, the breath of their mouth. Compromise thy egotism. Who cares for that, so thou gain aught wider and nobler? Never mind the taunt of Boswellism: the devotion may easily be greater than the wretched pride which is guarding its own skirts. Be another: not thyself, but a Platonist; not a soul, but a Christian; not a naturalist, but a Cartesian; not a poet, but a Shaksperian. In vain, the wheels of tendency will not stop, nor will all the forces of inertia, fear, or of love itself hold thee there. On, and forever onward! The microscope observes a monad or wheel-insect among the infusories circulating in water. Presently a dot appears on the animal, which enlarges to a slit, and it becomes two perfect animals.* The ever-proceeding detachment appears not less in all thought and in society. Children think they cannot live without their parents. But, long before they are aware of it, the black dot has appeared and the detachment taken place. Any accident will now reveal to them their independence.

But *great men:*——the word is injurious. Is there caste? is there fate? What becomes of the promise to virtue? The thoughtful youth laments the superfœtation of nature. 'Generous and handsome,' he says, 'is your hero; but look at yonder poor Paddy,[†] whose country is his wheelbarrow; look at his whole nation of Paddies.' Why are the masses, from the dawn of history down, food for knives and powder? The idea dignifies a few leaders, who have sentiment, opinion, love, self-devotion; and they make war and death sacred;——but what for the wretches whom they hire and kill? The cheapness of man is every day's tragedy. It is as real a loss that others should be low as that we should be low; for we must have society.

Is it a reply to these suggestions to say, Society is a Pestalozzian school: all are teachers and pupils in turn? We are equally served by receiving and by imparting. Men who know the same things are not long the best company for each other. But bring to each an intelligent person of another experience, and it is as if you let off water from a lake by cutting a lower basin. It seems a mechanical advantage, and great benefit it is to each speaker, as he can now paint out his thought to himself. We pass very fast, in our personal moods, from dignity to dependence. And if any appear never to assume the chair, but always to stand and serve, it is because we do not see the company in a sufficiently long period for the whole rotation of parts to come about. As to what we call the masses, and common men,——there are no common men. All men are at last of a size; and true art is only possible on the conviction that every talent has its apotheosis somewhere. Fair play and an open field and freshest laurels to all who have won them! But heaven reserves an equal

---

*Reference to microscopic organisms that reproduce through division.
†Derogatory term for those of Irish descent.

scope for every creature. Each is uneasy until he has produced his private ray unto the concave sphere and beheld his talent also in its last nobility and exaltation.

The heroes of the hour are relatively great; of a faster growth; or they are such in whom, at the moment of success, a quality is ripe which is then in request. Other days will demand other qualities. Some rays escape the common observer, and want a finely adapted eye. Ask the great man if there be none greater. His companions are; and not the less great but the more that society cannot see them. Nature never sends a great man into the planet without confiding the secret to another soul.

One gracious fact emerges from these studies,—that there is true ascension in our love. The reputations of the nineteenth century will one day be quoted to prove its barbarism. The genius of humanity is the real subject whose biography is written in our annals. We must infer much, and supply many chasms in the record. The history of the universe is symptomatic, and life is mnemonical. No man, in all the procession of famous men, is reason or illumination or that essence we were looking for; but is an exhibition, in some quarter, of new possibilities. Could we one day complete the immense figure which these flagrant points compose! The study of many individuals leads us to an elemental region wherein the individual is lost, or wherein all touch by their summits. Thought and feeling that break out there cannot be impounded by any fence of personality. This is the key to the power of the greatest men,— their spirit diffuses itself. A new quality of mind travels by night and by day, in concentric circles from its origin, and publishes itself by unknown methods: the union of all minds appears intimate; what gets admission to one, cannot be kept out of any other; the smallest acquisition of truth or of energy, in any quarter, is so much good to the commonwealth of souls. If the disparities of talent and position vanish when the individuals are seen in the duration which is necessary to complete the career of each, even more swiftly the seeming injustice disappears when we ascend to the central identity of all the individuals, and know that they are made of the substance which ordaineth and doeth.

The genius of humanity is the right point of view of history. The qualities abide; the men who exhibit them have now more, now less, and pass away; the qualities remain on another brow. No experience is more familiar. Once you saw phœnixes:* they are gone; the world is not

---

*Legendary birds that burst into flames when they die and are reborn from their
own ashes.

therefore disenchanted. The vessels on which you read sacred emblems turn out to be common pottery; but the sense of the pictures is sacred, and you may still read them transferred to the walls of the world. For a time our teachers serve us personally, as metres or milestones of progress. Once they were angels of knowledge and their figures touched the sky. Then we drew near, saw their means, culture and limits; and they yielded their place to other geniuses. Happy, if a few names remain so high that we have not been able to read them nearer, and age and comparison have not robbed them of a ray. But at last we shall cease to look in men for completeness, and shall content ourselves with their social and delegated quality. All that respects the individual is temporary and prospective, like the individual himself, who is ascending out of his limits into a catholic existence. We have never come at the true and best benefit of any genius so long as we believe him an original force. In the moment when he ceases to help us as a cause, he begins to help us more as an effect. Then he appears as an exponent of a vaster mind and will. The opaque self becomes transparent with the light of the First Cause.

Yet, within the limits of human education and agency, we may say great men exist that there may be greater men. The destiny of organized nature is amelioration,* and who can tell its limits? It is for man to tame the chaos; on every side, whilst he lives, to scatter the seeds of science and of song, that climate, corn, animals, men, may be milder, and the germs of love and benefit may be multiplied.

---

*Successive improvement.

Plato; or, The Philosopher

AMONG SECULAR BOOKS, PLATO only is entitled to Omar's fanatical compliment to the Koran, when he said, "Burn the libraries; for their value is in this book."* These sentences contain the culture of nations; these are the corner-stone of schools; these are the fountain-head of literatures. A discipline it is in logic, arithmetic, taste, symmetry, poetry, language, rhetoric, ontology, morals or practical wisdom. There was never such range of speculation. Out of Plato come all things that are still written and debated among men of thought. Great havoc makes he among our originalities. We have reached the mountain from which all these drift boulders were detached. The Bible of the learned for twenty-two hundred years, every brisk young man who says in succession fine things to each reluctant generation,—Boethius, Rabelais, Erasmus, Bruno, Locke, Rousseau, Alfieri, Coleridge,—is some reader of Plato, translating into the vernacular, wittily, his good things. Even the men of grander proportion suffer some deduction from the misfortune (shall I say?) of coming after this exhausting generalizer. St. Augustine, Copernicus, Newton, Behmen, Swedenborg, Goethe, are likewise his debtors and must say after him. For it is fair to credit the broadest generalizer with all the particulars deducible from his thesis.

Plato is philosophy, and philosophy, Plato,—at once the glory and the shame of mankind, since neither Saxon nor Roman have availed to add any idea to his categories. No wife, no children had he, and the thinkers of all civilized nations are his posterity and are tinged with his mind. How many great men Nature is incessantly sending up out of night, to be *his men*,—Platonists! the Alexandrians, a constellation of genius; the Elizabethans, not less; Sir Thomas More, Henry More, John Hales, John Smith, Lord Bacon, Jeremy Taylor, Ralph Cudworth, Sydenham, Thomas Taylor; Marcilius Ficinus and Picus Mirandola.[1] Calvinism is in his Phædo: Christianity is in it. Mahometanism draws all its philosophy, in its hand-book of morals, the Akhlak-y-Jalaly, from him. Mysticism finds in Plato all its texts. This citizen of a town in Greece is

---

*Omar supposedly made this comment when he gave the order to burn the libraries at Alexandria.

no villager nor patriot. An Englishman reads and says, 'how English!' a German,—'how Teutonic!' an Italian,—'how Roman and how Greek!' As they say that Helen of Argos had that universal beauty that every body felt related to her, so Plato seems to a reader in New England an American genius. His broad humanity transcends all sectional lines.

This range of Plato instructs us what to think of the vexed question concerning his reputed works,—what are genuine, what spurious. It is singular that wherever we find a man higher by a whole head than any of his contemporaries, it is sure to come into doubt what are his real works. Thus Homer, Plato, Raffaelle, Shakspeare. For these men magnetise their contemporaries, so that their companions can do for them what they can never do for themselves; and the great man does thus live in several bodies, and write, or paint or act, by many hands; and after some time it is not easy to say what is the authentic work of the master and what is only of his school.

Plato, too, like every great man, consumed his own times. What is a great man but one of great affinities, who takes up into himself all arts, sciences, all knowables, as his food? He can spare nothing; he can dispose of every thing. What is not good for virtue, is good for knowledge. Hence his contemporaries tax him with plagiarism. But the inventor only knows how to borrow; and society is glad to forget the innumerable laborers who ministered to this architect, and reserves all its gratitude for him. When we are praising Plato, it seems we are praising quotations from Solon and Sophron and Philolaus.* Be it so. Every book is a quotation; and every house is a quotation out of all forests and mines and stone quarries; and every man is a quotation from all his ancestors. And this grasping inventor puts all nations under contribution.

Plato absorbed the learning of his times,—Philolaus, Timæus, Heraclitus, Parmenides, and what else; then his master, Socrates; and finding himself still capable of a larger synthesis,—beyond all example then or since,—he travelled into Italy, to gain what Pythagoras had for him; then into Egypt, and perhaps still farther East, to import the other element, which Europe wanted, into the European mind. This breadth entitles him to stand as the representative of philosophy. He says, in the Republic, "Such a genius as philosophers must of necessity have, is wont but seldom in all its parts to meet in one man, but its different parts generally spring up in different persons."† Every man who would do

---

*Legend suggests that Plato's *Timaeus* was plagiarized from Philolaus.
†*Republic*, 503B (book VI, chapter 15).

anything well, must come to it from a higher ground. A philosopher must be more than a philosopher. Plato is clothed with the powers of a poet, stands upon the highest place of the poet, and (though I doubt he wanted the decisive gift of lyric expression), mainly is not a poet because he chose to use the poetic gift to an ulterior purpose.

Great geniuses have the shortest biographies. Their cousins can tell you nothing about them. They lived in their writings, and so their house and street life was trivial and commonplace. If you would know their tastes and complexions, the most admiring of their readers most resembles them. Plato especially has no external biography. If he had lover, wife, or children, we hear nothing of them. He ground them all into paint. As a good chimney burns its smoke, so a philosopher converts the value of all his fortunes into his intellectual performances.

He was born 427 A.C., about the time of the death of Pericles; was of patrician connection in his times and city, and is said to have had an early inclination for war, but, in his twentieth year, meeting with Socrates, was easily dissuaded from this pursuit and remained for ten years his scholar, until the death of Socrates. He then went to Megara, accepted the invitations of Dion and of Dionysius to the court of Sicily, and went thither three times, though very capriciously treated. He travelled into Italy; then into Egypt, where he stayed a long time; some say three,—some say thirteen years. It is said he went farther, into Babylonia: this is uncertain. Returning to Athens, he gave lessons in the Academy to those whom his fame drew thither; and died, as we have received it, in the act of writing, at eighty-one years.[2]

But the biography of Plato is interior. We are to account for the supreme elevation of this man in the intellectual history of our race,— how it happens that in proportion to the culture of men they become his scholars; that, as our Jewish Bible has implanted itself in the table-talk and household life of every man and woman in the European and American nations, so the writings of Plato have preoccupied every school of learning, every lover of thought, every church, every poet,— making it impossible to think, on certain levels, except through him. He stands between the truth and every man's mind, and has almost impressed language and the primary forms of thought with his name and seal. I am struck, in reading him, with the extreme modernness of his style and spirit. Here is the germ of that Europe we know so well, in its long history of arts and arms; here are all its traits, already discernible in the mind of Plato,—and in none before him. It has spread itself since into a hundred histories, but has added no new element. This perpetual modernness is the measure of merit in every work of art; since the author of it was not misled by any thing short-lived or local, but abode by real and abiding traits. How Plato came thus to be Europe, and philosophy, and almost literature, is the problem for us to solve.

This could not have happened without a sound, sincere and catholic man, able to honor, at the same time, the ideal, or laws of the mind, and fate, or the order of nature. The first period of a nation, as of an individual, is the period of unconscious strength. Children cry, scream and stamp with fury, unable to express their desires. As soon as they can speak and tell their want and the reason of it, they become gentle. In adult life, whilst the perceptions are obtuse, men and women talk vehemently and superlatively, blunder and quarrel: their manners are full of desperation; their speech is full of oaths. As soon as, with culture, things have cleared up a little, and they see them no longer in lumps and masses but accurately distributed, they desist from that weak vehemence and explain their meaning in detail. If the tongue had not been framed for articulation, man would still be a beast in the forest. The same weakness and want, on a higher plane, occurs daily in the education of ardent young men and women. 'Ah! you don't understand me; I have never met with any one who comprehends me:' and they sigh and weep, write verses and walk alone,—fault of power to express their precise meaning. In a month or two, through the favor of their good genius, they meet some one so related as to assist their volcanic estate, and, good communication being once established, they are thenceforward good citizens. It is ever thus. The progress is to accuracy, to skill, to truth, from blind force.

There is a moment in the history of every nation, when, proceeding out of this brute youth, the perceptive powers reach their ripeness and have not yet become microscopic: so that man, at that instant, extends across the entire scale, and, with his feet still planted on the immense forces of night, converses by his eyes and brain with solar and stellar creation. That is the moment of adult health, the culmination of power.

Such is the history of Europe, in all points; and such in philosophy. Its early records, almost perished, are of the immigrations from Asia, bringing with them the dreams of barbarians; a confusion of crude notions of morals and of natural philosophy, gradually subsiding through the partial insight of single teachers.

Before Pericles came the Seven Wise Masters, and we have the beginnings of geometry, metaphysics and ethics: then the partialists,—deducing the origin of things from flux or water, or from air, or from fire, or from mind.[3] All mix with these causes mythologic pictures. At last comes Plato, the distributor, who needs no barbaric paint, or tattoo, or whooping; for he can define. He leaves with Asia the vast and superlative; he is the arrival of accuracy and intelligence. "He shall be as a god to me, who can rightly divide and define."*

This defining is philosophy. Philosophy is the account which the human mind gives to itself of the constitution of the world. Two cardinal facts lie forever at the base; the one, and the two.—1. Unity, or Identity; and, 2. Variety. We unite all things by perceiving the law which pervades them; by perceiving the superficial differences and the profound resemblances. But every mental act,—this very perception of identity or oneness, recognizes the difference of things. Oneness and otherness. It is impossible to speak or to think without embracing both.

The mind is urged to ask for one cause of many effects; then for the cause of that; and again the cause, diving still into the profound: self-assured that it shall arrive at an absolute and sufficient one,—a one that shall be all. "In the midst of the sun is the light, in the midst of the light is truth, and in the midst of truth is the imperishable being," say the Vedas.[4] All philosophy, of East and West, has the same centripetence. Urged by an opposite necessity, the mind returns from the one to that which is not one, but other or many; from cause to effect; and affirms the necessary existence of variety, the self-existence of both, as each is involved in the other. These strictly-blended elements it is the problem of thought to separate and to reconcile. Their existence is mutually contradictory and exclusive; and each so fast slides into the other that we can never say what is one, and what it is not. The Proteus is as nimble in the highest as in the lowest grounds; when we contemplate the one, the true, the good,—as in the surfaces and extremities of matter.

In all nations there are minds which incline to dwell in the conception of the fundamental Unity. The raptures of prayer and ecstasy of devotion lose all being in one Being. This tendency finds its highest expression in the religious writings of the East, and chiefly in the Indian Scriptures, in the Vedas, the Bhagavat Geeta, and the Vishnu Purana.†️ Those writings contain little else than this idea, and they rise to pure and sublime strains in celebrating it.

The Same, the Same: friend and foe are of one stuff; the ploughman, the plough and the furrow are of one stuff; and the stuff is such and so much that the variations of form are unimportant. "You are fit" (says

---

*See *Phaedo*, 266 B.

†The Vedas, the Bhagavat Geeta, and the Vishnu Purana are sacred texts of Hinduism.

the supreme Krishna to a sage) "to apprehend that you are not distinct from me. That which I am, thou art, and that also is this world, with its gods and heroes and mankind. Men contemplate distinctions, because they are stupefied with ignorance." "The words *I* and *mine* constitute ignorance. What is the great end of all, you shall now learn from me. It is soul,—one in all bodies, pervading, uniform, perfect, preeminent over nature, exempt from birth, growth and decay, omnipresent, made up of true knowledge, independent, unconnected with unrealities, with name, species and the rest, in time past, present and to come. The knowledge that this spirit, which is essentially one, is in one's own and in all other bodies, is the wisdom of one who knows the unity of things. As one diffusive air, passing through the perforations of a flute, is distinguished as the notes of a scale, so the nature of the Great Spirit is single, though its forms be manifold, arising from the consequences of acts. When the difference of the investing form, as that of god or the rest, is destroyed, there is no distinction." "The whole world is but a manifestation of Vishnu, who is identical with all things, and is to be regarded by the wise as not differing from, but as the same as themselves. I neither am going nor coming; nor is my dwelling in any one place; nor art thou, thou; nor are others, others; nor am I, I."* As if he had said, 'All is for the soul, and the soul is Vishnu; and animals and stars are transient paintings; and light is whitewash; and durations are deceptive; and form is imprisonment; and heaven itself a decoy.' That which the soul seeks is resolution into being above form, out of Tartarus† and out of heaven,—liberation from nature.

If speculation tends thus to a terrific unity, in which all things are absorbed, action tends directly backwards to diversity. The first is the course or gravitation of mind; the second is the power of nature. Nature is the manifold. The unity absorbs, and melts or reduces. Nature opens and creates. These two principles reappear and interpenetrate all things, all thought; the one, the many. One is being; the other, intellect: one is necessity; the other, freedom: one, rest; the other, motion: one, power; the other, distribution: one, strength; the other, pleasure: one, consciousness; the other, definition: one, genius; the other, talent: one, earnestness; the other, knowledge: one, possession; the other, trade: one, caste; the other, culture: one, king; the other, democracy: and, if we dare

---

*The preceeding quotations are a conflation of a number of passages taken from the Vishnu Purana.

†In Greek mythology, the place below Hades, where Zeus imprisoned the Titans.

carry these generalizations a step higher, and name the last tendency of both, we might say, that the end of the one is escape from organization,—pure science; and the end of the other is the highest instrumentality, or use of means, or executive deity.

Each student adheres, by temperament and by habit, to the first or to the second of these gods of the mind. By religion, he tends to unity; by intellect, or by the senses, to the many. A too rapid unification, and an excessive appliance to parts and particulars, are the twin dangers of speculation.

To this partiality the history of nations corresponded. The country of unity, of immovable institutions, the seat of a philosophy delighting in abstractions, of men faithful in doctrine and in practice to the idea of a deaf, unimplorable, immense fate, is Asia; and it realizes this faith in the social institution of caste. On the other side, the genius of Europe is active and creative: it resists caste by culture; its philosophy was a discipline; it is a land of arts, inventions, trade, freedom. If the East loved infinity, the West delighted in boundaries.

European civility is the triumph of talent, the extension of system, the sharpened understanding, adaptive skill, delight in forms, delight in manifestation, in comprehensible results. Pericles, Athens, Greece, had been working in this element with the joy of genius not yet chilled by any foresight of the detriment of an excess. They saw before them no sinister political economy; no ominous Malthus; no Paris or London; no pitiless subdivision of classes,—the doom of the pin-makers, the doom of the weavers, of dressers, of stockingers, of carders, of spinners, of colliers; no Ireland; no Indian caste, superinduced by the efforts of Europe to throw it off. The understanding was in its health and prime. Art was in its splendid novelty. They cut the Pentelican marble as if it were snow, and their perfect works in architecture and sculpture seemed things of course, not more difficult than the completion of a new ship at the Medford yards, or new mills at Lowell. These things are in course, and may be taken for granted. The Roman legion, Byzantine legislation, English trade, the saloons of Versailles, the cafés of Paris, the steam-mill, steamboat, steam-coach, may all be seen in perspective; the town-meeting, the ballot-box, the newspaper and cheap press.

Meantime, Plato, in Egypt and in Eastern pilgrimages, imbibed the idea of one Deity, in which all things are absorbed. The unity of Asia and the detail of Europe; the infinitude of the Asiatic soul and the defining, result-loving, machine-making, surface-seeking, opera-going Europe,—Plato came to join, and, by contact, to enhance the energy of each. The excellence of Europe and Asia are in his brain. Metaphysics and natural phiosophy expressed the genius of Europe; he substructs the religion of Asia, as the base.

In short, *a* balanced soul was born, perceptive of the two elements. It is as easy to be great as to be small. The reason why we do not at once believe in admirable souls is because they are not in our experience. In actual life, they are so rare as to be incredible; but primarily there is not only no presumption against them, but the strongest presumption in favor of their appearance. But whether voices were heard in the sky, or not; whether his mother or his father dreamed that the infant man-child was the son of Apollo; whether a swarm of bees settled on his lips, or not;[5] a man who could see two sides of a thing was born. The wonderful synthesis so familiar in nature; the upper and the under side of the medal of Jove the union of impossibilities, which reappears in every object; its real and its ideal power,—was now also transferred entire to the consciousness of a man.

The balanced soul came. If he loved abstract truth, he saved himself by propounding the most popular of all principles, the absolute good, which rules rulers, and judges the judge. If he made transcendental distinctions, he fortified himself by drawing all his illustrations from sources disdained by orators and polite conversers; from mares and puppies; from pitchers and soup-ladles; from cooks and criers; the shops of potters, horse-doctors, butchers and fishmongers. He cannot forgive in himself a partiality, but is resolved that the two poles of thought shall appear in his statement. His argument and his sentence are self-poised and spherical. The two poles appear; yes, and become two hands, to grasp and appropriate their own.

Every great artist has been such by synthesis. Our strength is transitional, alternating; or, shall I say, a thread of two strands. The sea-shore, sea seen from shore, shore seen from sea; the taste of two metals in contact; and our enlarged powers at the approach and at the departure of a friend; the experience of poetic creativeness, which is not found in staying at home, nor yet in travelling, but in transitions from one to the other, which must therefore be adroitly managed to present as much transitional surface as possible; this command of two elements must explain the power and the charm of Plato. Art expresses the one or the same by the different. Thought seeks to know unity in unity; poetry to show it by variety; that is, always by an object or symbol. Plato keeps the two vases, one of æther and one of pigment, at his side, and invariably uses both. Things added to things, as statistics, civil history, are inventories. Things used as language are inexhaustibly attractive. Plato turns incessantly the obverse and the reverse of the medal of Jove.

To take an example:—The physical philosophers had sketched each his theory of the world; the theory of atoms, of fire, of flux, of spirit; theories mechanical and chemical in their genius. Plato, a master of mathematics, studious of all natural laws and causes, feels these, as second causes, to be no theories of the world but bare inventories and lists. To the study of nature he therefore prefixes the dogma,—"Let us declare the cause which led the Supreme Ordainer to produce and compose the universe. He was good; and he who is good has no kind of envy. Exempt from envy, he wished that all things should be as much as possible like himself. Whosoever, taught by wise men, shall admit this as the prime cause of the origin and foundation of the world, will be in the truth."* "All things are for the sake of the good, and it is the cause of every thing beautiful."† This dogma animates and impersonates‡ his philosophy.

The synthesis which makes the character of his mind appears in all his talents. Where there is great compass of wit, we usually find excellencies that combine easily in the living man, but in description appear incompatible. The mind of Plato is not to be exhibited by a Chinese catalogue, but is to be apprehended by an original mind in the exercise of its original power. In him the freest abandonment is united with the precision of a geometer. His daring imagination gives him the more solid grasp of facts; as the birds of highest flight have the strongest alar bones.§ His patrician polish, his intrinsic elegance, edged by an irony so subtle that it stings and paralyzes, adorn the soundest health and strength of frame. According to the old sentence, "If Jove should descend to the earth, he would speak in the style of Plato."‖

With this palatial air there is, for the direct aim of several of his works and running through the tenor of them all, a certain earnestness, which mounts, in the Republic and in the Phædo, to piety. He has been charged with feigning sickness at the time of the death of Socrates. But the anecdotes that have come down from the times attest his manly interference before the people in his master's behalf, since even the savage cry of the assembly to Plato is preserved; and the indignation towards popular government, in many of his pieces, expresses a personal exasperation. He has a probity, a native reverence for justice and honor, and

---

*From *Timaeus*, 29 E-30, A.
†From Thomas Taylor's *The Six Books of Proclus* (1816).
‡Gives character to.
§Bones in the wings of birds.
‖From Thomas Taylor's "General Introduction" to *The Works of Plato* (1804).

a humanity which makes him tender for the superstitions of the people. Add to this, he believes that poetry, prophecy and the high insight are from a wisdom of which man is not master; that the gods never philosophize, but by a celestial mania these miracles are accomplished. Horsed on these winged steeds, he sweeps the dim regions, visits worlds which flesh cannot enter; he saw the souls in pain, he hears the doom of the judge, he beholds the penal metempsychosis, the Fates, with the rock and shears, and hears the intoxicating hum of their spindle.*

But his circumspection never forsook him. One would say he had read the inscription on the gates of Busyrane,—"Be bold;" and on the second gate,—"Be bold, be bold, and evermore be bold;" and then again had paused well at the third gate,—"Be not too bold."† His strength is like the momentum of a falling planet, and his discretion the return of its due and perfect curve,—so excellent is his Greek love of boundary and his skill in definition. In reading logarithms one is not more secure than in following Plato in his flights. Nothing can be colder than his head, when the lightnings of his imagination are playing in the sky. He has finished his thinking before he brings it to the reader, and he abounds in the surprises of a literary master. He has that opulence which furnishes, at every turn, the precise weapon he needs. As the rich man wears no more garments, drives no more horses, sits in no more chambers than the poor,—but has that one dress, or equipage, or instrument, which is fit for the hour and the need; so Plato, in his plenty, is never restricted, but has the fit word. There is indeed no weapon in all the armory of wit which he did not possess and use,—epic, analysis, mania, intuition, music, satire and irony, down to the customary and polite. His illustrations are poetry and his jests illustrations. Socrates' profession of obstetric art is good philosophy; and his finding that word "cookery," and "adulatory art," for rhetoric, in the Gorgias, does us a substantial service still.‡ No orator can measure in effect with him who can give good nicknames.

What moderation and understatement and checking his thunder in mid volley! He has good-naturedly furnished the courtier and citizen with all that can be said against the schools. "For philosophy is an elegant thing, if any one modestly meddles with it; but if he is conversant

---

*Compare the fable of Er at the conclusion of the *Republic*.

†Compare Edmund Spenser, *The Fairie Queene*, book 3, canto 11, stanzas 50–54.

‡Compare *Theaetetus*, 148E–151E, and *Gorgias*, 464B–466A.

with it more than is becoming, it corrupts the man."* He could well afford to be generous,—he, who from the sunlike centrality and reach of his vision, had a faith without cloud. Such as his perception, was his speech: he plays with the doubt and makes the most of it: he paints and quibbles; and by and by comes a sentence that moves the sea and land. The admirable earnest comes not only at intervals, in the perfect yes and no of the dialogue, but in bursts of light. "I, therefore, Callicles, am persuaded by these accounts, and consider how I may exhibit my soul before the judge in a healthy condition. Wherefore, disregarding the honors that most men value, and looking to the truth, I shall endeavor in reality to live as virtuously as I can; and when I die, to die so. And I invite all other men, to the utmost of my power; and you too I in turn invite to this contest, which, I affirm, surpasses all contests here."†

He is a great average man; one who, to the best thinking, adds a proportion and equality in his faculties, so that men see in him their own dreams and glimpses made available and made to pass for what they are. A great common-sense is his warrant and qualification to be the world's interpreter. He has reason, as all the philosophic and poetic class have: but he has also what they have not,—this strong solving sense to reconcile his poetry with the appearances of the world, and build a bridge from the streets of cities to the Atlantis.‡ He omits never this graduation, but slopes his thought, however picturesque the precipice on one side, to an access from the plain. He never writes in ecstacy, or catches us up into poetic raptures.

Plato apprehended the cardinal facts. He could prostrate himself on the earth and cover his eyes whilst he adored that which cannot be numbered, or gauged, or known, or named: that of which every thing can be affirmed and denied: that "which is entity and nonentity." He called it super-essential. He even stood ready, as in the Parmenides, to demonstrate that it was so,—that this Being exceeded the limits of intellect. No man ever more fully acknowledged the Ineffable. Having paid his homage, as for the human race, to the Illimitable, he then stood erect, and for the human race affirmed, 'And yet things are knowable!'—that is, the Asia in his mind was first heartily honored,—the ocean of love and power, before form, before will, before knowledge, the

Same, the Good, the One; and now, refreshed and empowered by this worship, the instinct of Europe, namely, culture, returns; and he cries, 'Yet things are knowable!' They are knowable, because being from one, things correspond. There is a scale; and the correspondence of heaven to earth, of matter to mind, of the part to the whole, is our guide. As there is a science of stars, called astronomy; a science of quantities, called mathematics; a science of qualities, called chemistry; so there is a science of sciences,—I call it Dialectic,—which is the Intellect discriminating the false and the true. It rests on the observation of identity and diversity; for to judge is to unite to an object the notion which belongs to it. The sciences, even the best,—mathematics and astronomy,—are like sportsmen, who seize whatever prey offers, even without being able to make any use of it. Dialectic must teach the use of them. "This is of that rank that no intellectual man will enter on any study for its own sake, but only with a view to advance himself in that one sole science which embraces all."

"The essence or peculiarity of man is to comprehend a whole; or that which in the diversity of sensations can be comprised under a rational unity." "The soul which has never perceived the truth, cannot pass into the human form."* I announce to men the Intellect. I announce the good of being interpenetrated by the mind that made nature: this benefit, namely, that it can understand nature, which it made and maketh. Nature is good, but intellect is better: as the law-giver is before the law-receiver. I give you joy, O sons of men! that truth is altogether wholesome; that we have hope to search out what might be the very self of everything. The misery of man is to be baulked of the sight of essence and to be stuffed with conjectures; but the supreme good is reality; the supreme beauty is reality; and all virtue and all felicity depend on this science of the real: for courage is nothing else than knowledge; the fairest fortune that can befall man is to be guided by his dæmon to that which is truly his own. This also is the essence of justice,—to attend every one his own: nay, the notion of virtue is not to be arrived at except through direct contemplation of the divine essence. Courage then! for "the persuasion that we must search that which we do not know, will render us, beyond comparison, better, braver and more industrious than if we thought it impossible to discover what we do not know, and useless to search for it." He secures a position not to be commanded, by

---

*See *Phaedrus*, 249 B–C.

his passion for reality; valuing philosophy only as it is the pleasure of conversing with real being.

Thus, full of the genius of Europe, he said, *Culture*. He saw the institutions of Sparta and recognized, more genially one would say than any since, the hope of education. He delighted in every accomplishment, in every graceful and useful and truthful performance; above all in the splendors of genius and intellectual achievement. "The whole of life, O Socrates," said Glauco, "is, with the wise, the measure of hearing such discourses as these."* What a price he sets on the feats of talent, on the powers of Pericles, of Isocrates, of Parmenides! What price above price on the talents themselves! He called the several faculties, gods, in his beautiful personation. What value he gives to the art of gymnastic in education; what to geometry; what to music; what to astronomy, whose appeasing and medicinal power he celebrates! In the Timæus he indicates the highest employment of the eyes. "By us it is asserted that God invented and bestowed sight on us for this purpose,—that on surveying the circles of intelligence in the heavens, we might properly employ those of our own minds, which, though disturbed when compared with the others that are uniform, are still allied to their circulations; and that having thus learned, and being naturally possessed of a correct reasoning faculty, we might, by imitating the uniform revolutions of divinity, set right our own wanderings and blunders."† And in the Republic,— "By each of these disciplines a certain organ of the soul is both purified and reanimated which is blinded and buried by studies of another kind; an organ better worth saving than ten thousand eyes, since truth is perceived by this alone."‡

He said, Culture; but he first admitted its basis, and gave immeasurably the first place to advantages of nature. His patrician tastes laid stress on the distinctions of birth. In the doctrine of the organic character and disposition is the origin of caste. "Such as were fit to govern, into their composition the informing Deity mingled gold; into the military, silver; iron and brass for husbandmen and artificers." The East confirms itself, in all ages, in this faith. The Koran is explicit on this point of caste.§ "Men have their metal, as of gold and silver. Those of

---

Republic, 450 B (book 5, chapter 2).

† *Timaeus*, 47 B–C.

‡*Republic*, 527 D–E.

§Emerson takes the quotation from the Koran, as well as the discussion of caste and the comparison with Plato, from *Practical Philosophy of the Muhammadan People . . . the Akhlak-i-Jalay*.

you who were the worthy ones in the state of ignorance, will be the worthy ones in the state of faith, as soon as you embrace it." Plato was not less firm. "Of the five orders of things, only four can be taught to the generality of men." In the Republic he insists on the temperaments of the youth, as first of the first.*

A happier example of the stress laid on nature is in the dialogue with the young Theages, who wishes to receive lessons from Socrates. Socrates declares that if some have grown wise by associating with him, no thanks are due to him; but, simply, whilst they were with him they grew wise, not because of him; he pretends not to know the way of it. "It is adverse to many, nor can those be benefited by associating with me whom the Dæmon opposes; so that it is not possible for me to live with these. With many however he does not prevent me from conversing, who yet are not at all benefited by associating with me. Such, O Theages, is the association with me; for, if it pleases the God, you will make great and rapid proficiency: you will not, if he does not please. Judge whether it is not safer to be instructed by some one of those who have power over the benefit which they impart to men, than by me, who benefit or not, just as it may happen."† As if he had said, 'I have no system. I cannot be answerable for you. You will be what you must. If there is love between us, inconceivably delicious and profitable will our intercourse be; if not, your time is lost and you will only annoy me. I shall seem to you stupid, and the reputation I have, false. Quite above us, beyond the will of you or me, is this secret affinity or repulsion laid. All my good is magnetic, and I educate, not by lessons, but by going about my business.'

He said, Culture; he said, Nature; and he failed not to add, 'There is also the divine.' There is no thought in any mind but it quickly tends to convert itself into a power and organizes a huge instrumentality of means. Plato, lover of limits, loved the illimitable, saw the enlargement and nobility which come from truth itself and good itself, and attempted as if on the part of the human intellect, once for all to do it adequate homage,—homage fit for the immense soul to receive, and yet homage becoming the intellect to render. He said then, 'Our faculties run out into infinity, and return to us thence. We can define but a little way; but here is a fact which will not be skipped, and which to shut our eyes upon is suicide. All things are in a scale; and, begin where we will,

---

*Compare *Republic*, book 4, chapters 15 and 16.
† *Theages*, 129E–130E.

ascend and ascend. All things are symbolical; and what we call results are beginnings.'

A key to the method and completeness of Plato is his twice bisected line. After he has illustrated the relation between the absolute good and true and the forms of the intelligible world, he says:—"Let there be a line cut in two unequal parts. Cut again each of these two main parts,— one representing the visible, the other the intelligible world,—and let these two new sections represent the bright part and the dark part of each of these worlds. You will have, for one of the sections of the visible world, images, that is, both shadows and reflections;—for the other section, the objects of these images, that is, plants, animals, and the works of art and nature. Then divide the intelligible world in like manner; the one section will be of opinions and hypotheses, and the other section of truths."* To these four sections, the four operations of the soul correspond,—conjecture, faith, understanding, reason. As every pool reflects the image of the sun, so every thought and thing restores us an image and creature of the supreme Good. The universe is perforated by a million channels for his activity. All things mount and mount.

All his thought has this ascension; in Phædrus, teaching that beauty is the most lovely of all things, exciting hilarity and shedding desire and confidence through the universe wherever it enters, and it enters in some degree into all things:—but that there is another, which is as much more beautiful than beauty as beauty is than chaos; namely, wisdom, which our wonderful organ of sight cannot reach unto, but which, could it be seen, would ravish us with its perfect reality. He has the same regard to it as the source of excellence in works of art. When an artificer, he says, in the fabrication of any work, looks to that which always subsists according to the same; and, employing a model of this kind, expresses its idea and power in his work,—it must follow that his production should be beautiful. But when he beholds that which is born and dies, it will be far from beautiful.†

Thus ever: the Banquet‡ is a teaching in the same spirit, familiar now to all the poetry and to all the sermons of the world, that the love of the sexes is initial, and symbolizes at a distance the passion of the soul for that immense lake of beauty it exists to seek. This faith in the Divinity is never out of mind, and constitutes the ground of all his dogmas. Body

---

*Compare *Republic* (book 6, chapters 20 and 21).

† *Timaeus* 28 A–B.

‡Alternate title for Plato's *Symposium*.

cannot teach wisdom;—God only.* In the same mind he constantly af-
firms that virtue cannot be taught; that it is not a science, but an inspi-
ration; that the greatest goods are produced to us through mania and
are assigned to us by a divine gift.

This leads me to that central figure which he has established in his
Academy as the organ through which every considered opinion shall be
announced, and whose biography he has likewise so labored that the
historic facts are lost in the light of Plato's mind. Socrates and Plato are
the double star which the most powerful instruments will not entirely
separate. Socrates again, in his traits and genius, is the best example of
that synthesis which constitutes Plato's extraordinary power. Socrates, a
man of humble stem, but honest enough; of the commonest history; of
a personal homeliness so remarkable as to be a cause of wit in others:—
the rather that his broad good nature and exquisite taste for a joke in-
vited the sally, which was sure to be paid. The players personated him
on the stage; the potters copied his ugly face on their stone jugs. He was
a cool fellow, adding to his humor a perfect temper and a knowledge of
his man, be he who he might whom he talked with, which laid the com-
panion open to certain defeat in any debate,—and in debate he im-
moderately delighted. The young men are prodigiously fond of him and
invite him to their feasts, whither he goes for conversation. He can
drink, too; has the strongest head in Athens; and after leaving the whole
party under the table, goes away as if nothing had happened, to begin
new dialogues with somebody that is sober. In short, he was what our
country-people call *an old one.*[6]

He affected a good many citizen-like tastes, was monstrously fond of
Athens, hated trees, never willingly went beyond the walls, knew the old
characters, valued the bores and philistines, thought every thing in
Athens a little better than anything in any other place. He was plain as
a Quaker in habit and speech, affected low phrases, and illustrations
from cocks and quails, soup-pans and sycamore-spoons, grooms and
farriers, and unnameable offices,—especially if he talked with any su-
perfine person. He had a Franklin-like wisdom. Thus he showed one
who was afraid to go on foot to Olympia, that it was no more than his
daily walk within doors, if continuously extended, would easily reach.

Plain old uncle as he was, with his great ears, an immense talker,—
the rumor ran that on one or two occasions, in the war with Bœotia, he
had shown a determination which had covered the retreat of a troop;

---

* *Phaedo* 65A–67C.

and there was some story that under cover of folly, he had, in the city government, when one day he chanced to hold a seat there, evinced a courage in opposing singly the popular voice, which had well-nigh ruined him. He is very poor; but then he is hardy as a soldier, and can live on a few olives; usually, in the strictest sense, on bread and water, except when entertained by his friends. His necessary expenses were exceedingly small, and no one could live as he did. He wore no under garment; his upper garment was the same for summer and winter, and he went barefooted; and it is said that to procure the pleasure, which he loves, of talking at his ease all day with the most elegant and cultivated young men, he will now and then return to his shop and carve statues, good or bad, for sale. However that be, it is certain that he had grown to delight in nothing else than this conversation; and that, under his hypocritical pretence of knowing nothing, he attacks and brings down all the fine speakers, all the fine philosophers of Athens, whether natives or strangers from Asia Minor and the islands. Nobody can refuse to talk with him, he is so honest and really curious to know; a man who was willingly confuted if he did not speak the truth, and who willingly confuted others asserting what was false; and not less pleased when confuted than when confuting; for he thought not any evil happened to men of such a magnitude as false opinion respecting the just and unjust. A pitiless disputant, who knows nothing, but the bounds of whose conquering intelligence no man had ever reached; whose temper was imperturbable; whose dreadful logic was always leisurely and sportive; so careless and ignorant as to disarm the wariest and draw them, in the pleasantest manner, into horrible doubts and confusion. But he always knew the way out; knew it, yet would not tell it. No escape; he drives them to terrible choices by his dilemmas, and tosses the Hippiases and Gorgiases with their grand reputations, as a boy tosses his balls. The tyrannous realist!—Meno has discoursed a thousand times, at length, on virtue, before many companies, and very well, as it appeared to him; but at this moment he cannot even tell what it is,—this cramp-fish* of a Socrates has so bewitched him.

This hard-headed humorist, whose strange conceits, drollery and *bonhommie*† diverted the young patricians, whilst the rumor of his sayings and quibbles gets abroad every day,—turns out, in the sequel, to have a probity as invincible as his logic, and to be either insane, or

---

*Another name for the electric eel.
†Good humor (French).

at least, under cover of this play, enthusiastic in his religion. When accused before the judges of subverting the popular creed, he affirms the immortality of the soul, the future reward and punishment; and refusing to recant, in a caprice of the popular government was condemned to die, and sent to the prison. Socrates entered the prison and took away all ignominy from the place, which could not be a prison whilst he was there. Crito bribed the jailer; but Socrates would not go out by treachery. "Whatever inconvenience ensue, nothing is to be preferred before justice. These things I hear like pipes and drums, whose sound makes me deaf to every thing you say."* The fame of this prison, the fame of the discourses there and the drinking of the hemlock are one of the most precious passages in the history of the world.

The rare coincidence, in one ugly body, of the droll and the martyr, the keen street and market debater with the sweetest saint known to any history at that time, had forcibly struck the mind of Plato, so capacious of these contrasts; and the figure of Socrates by a necessity placed itself in the foreground of the scene, as the fittest dispenser of the intellectual treasures he had to communicate. It was a rare fortune that this Æsop of the mob and this robed scholar should meet, to make each other immortal in their mutual faculty. The strange synthesis in the character of Socrates capped the synthesis in the mind of Plato. Moreover by this means he was able, in the direct way and without envy to avail himself of the wit and weight of Socrates, to which unquestionably his own debt was great; and these derived again their principal advantage from the perfect art of Plato.

It remains to say that the defect of Plato in power is only that which results inevitably from his quality. He is intellectual in his aim; and therefore, in expression, literary. Mounting into heaven, diving into the pit, expounding the laws of the state, the passion of love, the remorse of crime, the hope of the parting soul,—he is literary, and never otherwise. It is almost the sole deduction from the merit of Plato that his writings have not,—what is no doubt incident to this regnancy of intellect in his work,—the vital authority which the screams of prophets and the sermons of unlettered Arabs and Jews possess. There is an interval; and to cohesion, contact is necessary.

I know not what can be said in reply to this criticism but that we

*Compare *Crito* 54 D.

have come to a fact in the nature of things: an oak is not an orange. The qualities of sugar remain with sugar, and those of salt with salt.

In the second place, he has not a system. The dearest defenders and disciples are at fault. He attempted a theory of the universe, and his theory is not complete or self-evident. One man thinks he means this, and another that; he has said one thing in one place, and the reverse of it in another place. He is charged with having failed to make the transition from ideas to matter. Here is the world, sound as a nut, perfect, not the smallest piece of chaos left, never a stitch nor an end, not a mark of haste, or botching, or second thought; but the theory of the world is a thing of shreds and patches.

The longest wave is quickly lost in the sea. Plato would willingly have a Platonism, a known and accurate expression for the world, and it should be accurate. It shall be the world passed through the mind of Plato,—nothing less. Every atom shall have the Platonic tinge; every atom, every relation or quality you knew before, you shall know again and find here, but now ordered; not nature, but art. And you shall feel that Alexander indeed overran, with men and horses, some countries of the planet; but countries, and things of which countries are made, elements, planet itself, laws of planet and of men, have passed through this man as bread into his body, and become no longer bread, but body: so all this mammoth morsel has become Plato. He has clapped copyright on the world. This is the ambition of individualism. But the mouthful proves too large. Boa constrictor has good will to eat it, but he is foiled. He falls abroad in the attempt; and biting, gets strangled: the bitten world holds the biter fast by his own teeth. There he perishes: unconquered nature lives on and forgets him. So it fares with all: so must it fare with Plato. In view of eternal nature, Plato turns out to be philosophical exercitations. He argues on this side and on that. The acutest German, the lovingest disciple, could never tell what Platonism was; indeed, admirable texts can be quoted on both sides of every great question from him.

These things we are forced to say if we must consider the effort of Plato or of any philosopher to dispose of nature,—which will not be disposed of. No power of genius has ever yet had the smallest success in explaining existence. The perfect enigma remains. But there is an injustice in assuming this ambition for Plato. Let us not seem to treat with flippancy his venerable name. Men, in proportion to their intellect, have admitted his transcendent claims. The way to know him is to compare him, not with nature, but with other men. How many ages have gone by, and he remains unapproached! A chief structure of human wit, like

Karnac, or the mediæval cathedrals, or the Etrurian remains,* it requires all the breadth of human faculty to know it. I think it is trueliest seen when seen with the most respect. His sense deepens, his merits multiply, with study. When we say, here is a fine collection of fables; or when we praise the style, or the common sense, or arithmetic, we speak as boys, and much of our impatient criticism of the dialectic, I suspect, is no better. The criticism is like our impatience of miles, when we are in a hurry; but it is still best that a mile should have seventeen hundred and sixty yards. The great-eyed Plato proportioned the lights and shades after the genius of our life.

Karnac: an Egyptian village along the central Nile, site of the ancient city of Thebes. *Etruria:* an ancient civilization located in the Tuscany region of Italy.

Shakspeare; or, the Poet

GREAT MEN ARE MORE distinguished by range and extent than by originality. If we require the originality which consists in weaving, like a spider, their web from their own bowels; in finding clay and making bricks and building the house; no great men are original. Nor does valuable originality consist in unlikeness to other men. The hero is in the press of knights and the thick of events; and seeing what men want and sharing their desire, he adds the needful length of sight and of arm, to come at the desired point. The greatest genius is the most indebted man. A poet is no rattle-brain, saying what comes uppermost, and, because he says every thing, saying at last something good; but a heart in unison with his time and country. There is nothing whimsical and fantastic in his production, but sweet and sad earnest, freighted with the weightiest convictions and pointed with the most determined aim which any man or class knows of in his times.

The Genius of our life is jealous of individuals, and will not have any individual great, except through the general. There is no choice to genius. A great man does not wake up on some fine morning and say, 'I am full of life, I will go to sea and find an Antarctic continent: to-day I will square the circle:* I will ransack botany and find a new food for man: I have a new architecture in my mind: I foresee a new mechanic power:' no, but he finds himself in the river of the thoughts and events, forced onward by the ideas and necessities of his contemporaries. He stands where all the eyes of men look one way, and their hands all point in the direction in which he should go. The Church has reared him amidst rites and pomps, and he carries out the advice which her music gave him, and builds a cathedral needed by her chants and processions. He finds a war raging: it educates him, by trumpet, in barracks, and he betters the instruction. He finds two counties groping to bring coal, or flour, or fish, from the place of production to the place of consumption, and he hits on a railroad. Every master has found his materials collected, and his power lay in his sympathy with his people and in his love

---

*Common expression for an impossible task.

316

of the materials he wrought in. What an economy of power! and what a compensation for the shortness of life! All is done to his hand. The world has brought him thus far on his way. The human race has gone out before him, sunk the hills, filled the hollows and bridged the rivers. Men, nations, poets, artisans, women, all have worked for him, and he enters into their labors. Choose any other thing, out of the line of tendency, out of the national feeling and history, and he would have all to do for himself: his powers would be expended in the first preparations. Great genial power, one would almost say, consists in not being original at all; in being altogether receptive; in letting the world do all, and suffering the spirit of the hour to pass unobstructed through the mind.

Shakspeare's youth fell in a time when the English people were importunate for dramatic entertainments. The court took offence easily at political allusions and attempted to suppress them. The Puritans, a growing and energetic party, and the religious among the Anglican church, would suppress them. But the people wanted them. Inn-yards, houses without roofs, and extemporaneous enclosures at country fairs were the ready theatres of strolling players. The people had tasted this new joy; and, as we could not hope to suppress newspapers now,—no, not by the strongest party,—neither then could king, prelate, or puritan, alone or united, suppress an organ which was ballad, epic, newspaper, caucus, lecture, *Punch** and library, at the same time. Probably king, prelate and puritan, all found their own account in it. It had become, by all causes, a national interest,—by no means conspicuous, so that some great scholar would have thought of treating it in an English history,—but not a whit less considerable because it was cheap and of no account, like a baker's-shop. The best proof of its vitality is the crowd of writers which suddenly broke into this field; Kyd, Marlow, Greene, Jonson, Chapman, Dekker, Webster, Heywood, Middleton, Peele, Ford, Massinger, Beaumont and Fletcher.

The secure possession, by the stage, of the public mind, is of the first importance to the poet who works for it. He loses no time in idle experiments. Here is audience and expectation prepared. In the case of Shakspeare there is much more. At the time when he left Stratford and went up to London, a great body of stage-plays of all dates and writers existed in manuscript and were in turn produced on the boards. Here is the Tale of Troy, which the audience will bear hearing some part of, every week; the Death of Julius Cæsar, and other stories out of Plutarch,

---

*English magazine known for its satirical cartoons.

which they never tire of; a shelf full of English history, from the chronicles of Brut and Arthur, down to the royal Henries, which men hear eagerly; and a string of doleful tragedies, merry Italian tales and Spanish voyages, which all the London 'prentices know.[1] All the mass has been treated, with more or less skill, by every playwright, and the prompter has the soiled and tattered manuscripts. It is now no longer possible to say who wrote them first. They have been the property of the Theatre so long, and so many rising geniuses have enlarged or altered them, inserting a speech or a whole scene, or adding a song, that no man can any longer claim copyright in this work of numbers. Happily, no man wishes to. They are not yet desired in that way. We have few readers, many spectators and hearers. They had best lie where they are.

Shakspeare, in common with his comrades, esteemed the mass of old plays waste stock, in which any experiment could be freely tried. Had the prestige which hedges about a modern tragedy existed, nothing could have been done. The rude warm blood of the living England circulated in the play, as in street-ballads, and gave body which he wanted to his airy and majestic fancy. The poet needs a ground in popular tradition on which he may work, and which, again, may restrain his art within the due temperance. It holds him to the people, supplies a foundation for his edifice, and in furnishing so much work done to his hand, leaves him at leisure and in full strength for the audacities of his imagination In short, the poet owes to his legend what sculpture owed to the temple. Sculpture in Egypt and in Greece grew up in subordination to architecture. It was the ornament of the temple wall: at first a rude relief carved on pediments, then the relief became bolder and a head or arm was projected from the wall; the groups being still arranged with reference to the building, which serves also as a frame to hold the figures; and when at last the greatest freedom of style and treatment was reached, the prevailing genius of architecture still enforced a certain calmness and continence in the statue. As soon as the statue was begun for itself, and with no reference to the temple or palace, the art began to decline: freak, extravagance and exhibition took the place of the old temperance. This balance-wheel, which the sculptor found in architecture, the perilous irritability of poetic talent found in the accumulated dramatic materials to which the people were already wonted, and which had a certain excellence which no single genius, however extraordinary, could hope to create.

In point of fact it appears that Shakspeare did owe debts in all directions, and was able to use whatever he found; and the amount of indebtedness may be inferred from Malone's laborious computations in regard to the First, Second and Third parts of Henry VI., in which, "out of 6,043 lines, 1,771 were written by some author preceding Shakspeare, 2,373 by him, on the foundation laid by his predecessors, and 1,899 were entirely his own." And the proceeding investigation hardly leaves a single drama of his absolute invention. Malone's sentence is an important piece of external history. In Henry VIII. I think I see plainly the cropping out of the original rock on which his own finer stratum was laid. The first play was written by a superior, thoughtful man, with a vicious ear.[2] I can mark his lines, and know well their cadence. See Wolsey's soliloquy, and the following scene with Cromwell, where instead of the metre of Shakspeare, whose secret is that the thought constructs the tune, so that reading for the sense will best bring out the rhythm,—here the lines are constructed on a given tune, and the verse has even a trace of pulpit eloquence. But the play contains through all its length unmistakable traits of Shakspeare's hand, and some passages, as the account of the coronation, are like autographs. What is odd, the compliment to Queen Elizabeth is in the bad rhythm.

Shakspeare knew that tradition supplies a better fable than any invention can.* If he lost any credit of design, he augmented his resources; and, at that day, our petulant demand for originality was not so much pressed. There was no literature for the million. The universal reading, the cheap press, were unknown. A great poet who appears in illiterate times, absorbs into his sphere all the light which is any where radiating. Every intellectual jewel, every flower of sentiment it is his fine office to bring to his people; and he comes to value his memory equally with his invention. He is therefore little solicitous whence his thoughts have been derived; whether through translation, whether through tradition, whether by travel in distant countries, whether by inspiration; from whatever source, they are equally welcome to his uncritical audience. Nay, he borrows very near home. Other men say wise things as well as he; only they say a good many foolish things, and do not know when they have spoken wisely. He knows the sparkle of the true stone, and puts it in high place, wherever he finds it. Such is the happy position of Homer perhaps; of Chaucer, of Saadi. They felt that all wit was their wit. And they are librarians and historiographers, as well as poets.

---

*This idea is expressed in Madame de Staël's *Influence of Literature upon Society* (published as part of *De la littérature considérée dans ses rapports avec les institutions sociales* (1800); Emerson would probably have read the translation published in Boston in 1813.

Each romancer was heir and dispenser of all the hundred tales of the world,—

> "Presenting Thebes' and Pelops' line
> And the tale of Troy divine."*

The influence of Chaucer is conspicuous in all our early literature; and more recently not only Pope and Dryden have been beholden to him, but, in the whole society of English writers, a large unacknowledged debt is easily traced. One is charmed with the opulence which feeds so many pensioners. But Chaucer is a huge borrower.3 Chaucer, it seems, drew continually, through Lydgate and Caxton, from Guido di Colonna, whose Latin romance of the Trojan war was in turn a compilation from Dares Phrygius, Ovid and Statius. Then Petrarch, Boccaccio and the Provençal poets are his benefactors: the *Romaunt of the Rose* is only judicious translation from William of Lorris and John of Meung: Troilus and Creseide, from Lollius of Urbino: *The Cock and the Fox,* from the Lais of Marie: *The House of Fame,* from the French or Italian: and poor Gower he uses as if he were only a brick-kiln or stone-quarry out of which to build his house. He steals by this apology,—that what he takes has no worth where he finds it and the greatest where he leaves it. It has come to be practically a sort of rule in literature, that a man having once shown himself capable of original writing, is entitled thenceforth to steal from the writings of others at discretion. Thought is the property of him who can entertain it and of him who can adequately place it. A certain awkwardness marks the use of borrowed thoughts; but as soon as we have learned what to do with them they become our own.

Thus all originality is relative. Every thinker is retrospective. The learned member of the legislature, at Westminster or at Washington, speaks and votes for thousands. Show us the constituency, and the now invisible channels by which the senator is made aware of their wishes; the crowd of practical and knowing men, who, by correspondence or conversation, are feeding him with evidence, anecdotes and estimates, and it will bereave his fine attitude and resistance of something of their impressiveness. As Sir Robert Peel and Mr. Webster vote, so Locke and Rousseau think, for thousands; and so there were fountains all around Homer, Menu, Saadi, or Milton, from which they drew; friends, lovers,

---

*From John Milton's "Il Penseroso" (c.1632), lines 99–100.

books, traditions, proverbs,—all perished—which, if seen, would go to reduce the wonder. Did the bard speak with authority? Did he feel himself overmatched by any companion? The appeal is to the consciousness of the writer. Is there at last in his breast a Delphi* whereof to ask concerning any thought or thing, whether it be verily so, yea or nay? and to have answer, and to rely on that? All the debts which such a man could contract to other wit would never disturb his consciousness of originality; for the ministrations of books and of other minds are a whiff of smoke to that most private reality with which he has conversed.

It is easy to see that what is best written or done by genius in the world, was no man's work, but came by wide social labor, when a thousand wrought like one, sharing the same impulse. Our English Bible is a wonderful specimen of the strength and music of the English language. But it was not made by one man, or at one time; but centuries and churches brought it to perfection. There never was a time when there was not some translation existing. The Liturgy, admired for its energy and pathos, is an anthology of the piety of ages and nations, a translation of the prayers and forms of the Catholic church,—these collected, too, in long periods, from the prayers and meditations of every saint and sacred writer all over the world. Grotius makes the like remark in respect to the Lord's Prayer, that the single clauses of which it is composed were already in use in the time of Christ, in the Rabbinical forms. He picked out the grains of gold. The nervous language of the Common Law, the impressive forms of our courts and the precision and substantial truth of the legal distinctions, are the contribution of all the sharp-sighted, strong-minded men who have lived in the countries where these laws govern. The translation of Plutarch† gets its excellence by being translation on translation. There never was a time when there was none. All the truly idiomatic and national phrases are kept, and all others successively picked out and thrown away. Something like the same process had gone on, long before, with the originals of these books. The world takes liberties with world-books. Vedas, Æsop's Fables, Pilpay, Arabian Nights, Cid, Iliad, Robin Hood, Scottish Minstrelsy, are not the work of single men.[4] In the composition of such works the time thinks, the market thinks, the mason, the carpenter, the merchant, the farmer, the fop, all think for us. Every book supplies its time with one good

---

*Fortune-teller, after the oracle at Delphi.

†Shakespeare is known to have used Sir Thomas North's translation of Plutarch's *Lives*, which was itself a translation from the French of Jacques Amyot.

word; every municipal law, every trade, every folly of the day; and the generic catholic genius who is not afraid or ashamed to owe his originality to the originality of all, stands with the next age as the recorder and embodiment of his own.

We have to thank the researches of antiquaries, and the Shakspeare Society, for ascertaining the steps of the English drama, from the Mysteries celebrated in churches and by churchmen, and the final detachment from the church, and the completion of secular plays, from *Ferrex and Porrex,* and *Gammer Gurton's Needle,*[5] down to the possession of the stage by the very pieces which Shakspeare altered, remodelled and finally made his own. Elated with success and piqued by the growing interest of the problem, they have left no book-stall unsearched, no chest in a garret unopened, no file of old yellow accounts to decompose in damp and worms, so keen was the hope to discover whether the boy Shakspeare poached or not, whether he held horses at the theatre door, whether he kept school, and why he left in his will only his second-best bed to Ann Hathaway, his wife.

There is somewhat touching in the madness with which the passing age mischooses the object on which all candles shine and all eyes are turned; the care with which it registers every trifle touching Queen Elizabeth and King James, and the Essexes, Leicesters, Burleighs and Buckinghams; and lets pass without a single valuable note the founder of another dynasty, which alone will cause the Tudor dynasty to be remembered,—the man who carries the Saxon race in him by the inspiration which feeds him, and on whose thoughts the foremost people of the world are now for some ages to be nourished, and minds to receive this and not another bias. A popular player;—nobody suspected he was the poet of the human race; and the secret was kept as faithfully from poets and intellectual men as from courtiers and frivolous people. Bacon, who took the inventory of the human understanding for his times, never mentioned his name. Ben Jonson, though we have strained his few words of regard and panegyric, had no suspicion of the elastic fame whose first vibrations he was attempting.* He no doubt thought the praise he has conceded to him generous, and esteemed himself, out of all question, the better poet of the two.

If it need wit to know wit, according to the proverb, Shakspeare's time should be capable of recognizing it. Sir Henry Wotton was born

---

*See Jonson's poems "To the Reader" and "To the Memory of My Beloved, the Author Mr. William Shakespeare: and What He Hath Left Us."

four years after Shakspeare, and died twenty-three years after him; and I find, among his correspondents and acquaintances, the following persons: Theodore Beza, Isaac Casaubon, Sir Philip Sidney, the Earl of Essex, Lord Bacon, Sir Walter Raleigh, John Milton, Sir Henry Vane, Isaac Walton, Dr. Donne, Abraham Cowley, Bellarmine, Charles Cotton, John Pym, John Hales, Kepler, Vieta, Albericus Gentilis, Paul Sarpi, Arminius; with all of whom exists some token of his having communicated, without enumerating many others whom doubtless he saw,— Shakspeare, Spenser, Jonson, Beaumont, Massinger, the two Herberts, Marlow, Chapman and the rest. Since the constellation of great men who appeared in Greece in the time of Pericles, there was never any such society;—yet their genius failed them to find out the best head in the universe. Our poet's mask was impenetrable. You cannot see the mountain near. It took a century to make it suspected; and not until two centuries had passed, after his death, did any criticism which we think adequate begin to appear. It was not possible to write the history of Shakspeare till now; for he is the father of German literature: it was with the introduction of Shakspeare into German, by Lessing, and the translation of his works by Wieland and Schlegel,[6] that the rapid burst of German literature was most intimately connected. It was not until the nineteenth century, whose speculative genius is a sort of living Hamlet, that the tragedy of Hamlet could find such wondering readers. Now, literature, philosophy and thought, are Shakspearized. His mind is the horizon beyond which, at present, we do not see. Our ears are educated to music by his rhythm. Coleridge and Goethe are the only critics who have expressed our convictions with any adequate fidelity: but there is in all cultivated minds a silent appreciation of his superlative power and beauty, which, like Christianity, qualifies the period.

The Shakspeare Society have inquired in all directions, advertised the missing facts, offered money for any information that will lead to proof,—and with what result? Beside some important illustration of the history of the English stage, to which I have adverted, they have gleaned a few facts touching the property, and dealings in regard to property, of the poet. It appears that from year to year he owned a larger share in the Blackfriars' Theatre: its wardrobe and other appurtenances were his: that he bought an estate in his native village with his earnings as writer and shareholder; that he lived in the best house in Stratford; was intrusted by his neighbors with their commissions in London, as of borrowing money, and the like; that he was a veritable farmer. About the time when he was writing Macbeth, he sues Philip Rogers, in the borough-court of Stratford, for thirty-five shillings, ten pence, for corn delivered to him at different times; and in all respects appears as a good husband, with no reputation for eccentricity or excess. He was a good-natured sort of man, an actor and shareholder in the theatre, not in any striking manner distinguished from other actors and managers. I admit the importance of this information. It was well worth the pains that have been taken to procure it.

But whatever scraps of information concerning his condition these researches may have rescued, they can shed no light upon that infinite invention which is the concealed magnet of his attraction for us. We are very clumsy writers of history. We tell the chronicle of parentage, birth, birth-place, schooling, school-mates, earning of money, marriage, publication of books, celebrity, death; and when we have come to an end of this gossip, no ray of relation appears between it and the goddess-born; and it seems as if, had we dipped at random into the "Modern Plutarch," and read any other life there, it would have fitted the poems as well. It is the essence of poetry to spring, like the rainbow daughter of Wonder, from the invisible, to abolish the past and refuse all history. Malone, Warburton, Dyce and Collier, have wasted their oil. The famed theatres, Covent Garden, Drury Lane, the Park and Tremont have vainly assisted. *Betterton, Garrick, Kemble, Kean and Macready* dedicate their lives to this genius; him they crown, elucidate, obey and express. The genius knows them not. The recitation begins; one golden word leaps out immortal from all this painted pedantry and sweetly torments us with invitations to its own inaccessible homes. I remember I went once to see the Hamlet of a famed performer, the pride of the English stage; and all I then heard and all I now remember of the tragedian was that in which the tragedian had no part; simply Hamlet's question to the ghost:—

> "What may this mean,
> That thou, dead corse, again in complete steel
> Revisit'st thus the glimpses of the moon?"*

That imagination which dilates the closet he writes in to the world's dimension, crowds it with agents in rank and order, as quickly reduces the big reality to be the glimpses of the moon. These tricks of his magic spoil for us the illusions of the green-room. Can any biography shed light on the localities into which the Midsummer Night's Dream admits me? Did Shakspeare confide to any notary or parish recorder, sacristan,

---

*From Shakespeare's *Hamlet* (act 1, scene 4).

or surrogate in Stratford, the genesis of that delicate creation? The forest of Arden, the nimble air of Scone Castle, the moonlight of Portia's villa, "the antres vast and desarts idle"* of Othello's captivity,—where is the third cousin, or grand-nephew, the chancellor's file of accounts, or private letter, that has kept one word of those transcendent secrets? In fine, in this drama, as in all great works of art,—in the Cyclopæan architecture of Egypt and India, in the Phidian sculpture, the Gothic minsters, the Italian painting, the Ballads of Spain and Scotland,—the Genius draws up the ladder after him, when the creative age goes up to heaven, and gives way to a new age, which sees the works and asks in vain for a history.

Shakspeare is the only biographer of Shakspeare; and even he can tell nothing, except to the Shakspeare in us, that is, to our most apprehensive and sympathetic hour. He cannot step from off his tripod and give us anecdotes of his inspirations. Read the antique documents extricated, analyzed and compared by the assiduous Dyce and Collier, and now read one of these skiey sentences,—aerolites,†—which seem to have fallen out of heaven, and which not your experience but the man within the breast has accepted as words of fate, and tell me if they match; if the former account in any manner for the latter; or which gives the most historical insight into the man.

Hence, though our external history is so meagre, yet, with Shakspeare for biographer, instead of Aubrey and Rowe, we have really the information which is material; that which describes character and fortune, that which, if we were about to meet the man and deal with him, would most import us to know. We have his recorded convictions on those questions which knock for answer at every heart,—on life and death, on love, on wealth and poverty, on the prizes of life and the ways whereby we come at them; on the characters of men, and the influences, occult and open, which affect their fortunes; and on those mysterious and demoniacal powers which defy our science and which yet interweave their malice and their gift in our brightest hours. Who ever read the volume of the Sonnets without finding that the poet had there revealed, under masks that are no masks to the intelligent, the lore of friendship and of love; the confusion of sentiments in the most susceptible, and, at the same time, the most intellectual of men? What trait of his private mind has he hidden in his dramas? One can discern, in his

---

*From Shakespeare's *Othello* (act 1, scene 3).
†Meteorites.

ample pictures of the gentleman and the king, what forms and humanities pleased him; his delight in troops of friends, in large hospitality, in cheerful giving. Let Timon, let Warwick, let Antonio the merchant answer for his great heart. So far from Shakspeare's being the least known, he is the one person, in all modern history, known to us. What point of morals, of manners, of economy, of philosophy, of religion, of taste, of the conduct of life, has he not settled? What mystery has he not signified his knowledge of? What office, or function, or district of man's work, has he not remembered? What king has he not taught state, as Talma taught Napoleon? What maiden has not found him finer than her delicacy? What lover has he not outloved? What sage has he not outseen? What gentleman has he not instructed in the rudeness of his behavior?

Some able and appreciating critics think no criticism on Shakspeare valuable that does not rest purely on the dramatic merit; that he is falsely judged as poet and philosopher. I think as highly as these critics of his dramatic merit, but still think it secondary. He was a full man, who liked to talk; a brain exhaling thoughts and images, which, seeking vent, found the drama next at hand. Had he been less, we should have had to consider how well he filled his place, how good a dramatist he was,—and he is the best in the world. But it turns out that what he has to say is of that weight as to withdraw some attention from the vehicle; and he is like some saint whose history is to be rendered into all languages, into verse and prose, into songs and pictures, and cut up into proverbs; so that the occasion which gave the saint's meaning the form of a conversation, or of a prayer, or of a code of laws, is immaterial compared with the universality of its application. So it fares with the wise Shakspeare and his book of life. He wrote the airs for all our modern music: he wrote the text of modern life; the text of manners: he drew the man of England and Europe; the father of the man in America; he drew the man, and described the day, and what is done in it: he read the hearts of men and women, their probity, and their second thought and wiles; the wiles of innocence, and the transitions by which virtues and vices slide into their contraries: he could divide the mother's part from the father's part in the face of the child, or draw the fine demarcations of freedom and of fate: he knew the laws of repression which make the police of nature: and all the sweets and all the terrors of human lot lay in his mind as truly but as softly as the landscape lies on the eye. And the importance of this wisdom of life sinks the form, as of Drama or Epic, out of notice. 'Tis like making a question concerning the paper on which a king's message is written.

Shakspeare is as much out of the category of eminent authors, as he is out of the crowd. He is inconceivably wise; the others, conceivably. A good reader can, in a sort, nestle into Plato's brain and think from thence; but not into Shakspeare's. We are still out of doors. For executive faculty, for creation, Shakspeare is unique. No man can imagine it better. He was the farthest reach of subtlety compatible with an individual self,—the subtilest of authors, and only just within the possibility of authorship. With this wisdom of life is the equal endowment of imaginative and of lyric power. He clothed the creatures of his legend with form and sentiments as if they were people who had lived under his roof; and few real men have left such distinct characters as these fictions. And they spoke in language as sweet as it was fit. Yet his talents never seduced him into an ostentation, nor did he harp on one string. An omnipresent humanity co-ordinates all his faculties. Give a man of talents a story to tell, and his partiality will presently appear. He has certain observations, opinions, topics, which have some accidental prominence, and which he disposes all to exhibit. He crams this part and starves that other part, consulting not the fitness of the thing, but his fitness and strength. But Shakspeare has no peculiarity, no importunate topic; but all is duly given; no veins, no curiosities; no cow painter, no bird-fancier, no mannerist is he: he has no discoverable egotism: the great he tells greatly; the small subordinately. He is wise without emphasis or assertion; he is strong, as nature is strong, who lifts the land into mountain slopes without effort and by the same rule as she floats a bubble in the air, and likes as well to do the one as the other. This makes that equality of power in farce, tragedy, narrative and love-songs; a merit so incessant that each reader is incredulous of the perception of other readers.

This power of expression, or of transferring the inmost truth of things into music and verse, makes him the type of the poet and has added a new problem to metaphysics. This is that which throws him into natural history, as a main production of the globe, and as announcing new eras and ameliorations. Things were mirrored in his poetry without loss or blur: he could paint the fine with precision, the great with compass, the tragic and the comic indifferently and without any distortion or favor. He carried his powerful execution into minute details, to a hair point; finishes an eyelash or a dimple as firmly as he draws a mountain; and yet these, like nature's, will bear the scrutiny of the solar microscope.

In short, he is the chief example to prove that more or less of production, more or fewer pictures, is a thing indifferent. He had the power to make one picture. Daguerre learned how to let one flower etch its image on his plate of iodine, and then proceeds at leisure to etch a million. There are always objects; but there was never representation. Here is perfect representation, at last; and now let the world of figures sit for their portraits. No recipe can be given for the making of a Shakspeare; but the possibility of the translation of things into song is demonstrated.

His lyric power lies in the genius of the piece. The sonnets, though their excellence is lost in the splendor of the dramas, are as inimitable as they; and it is not a merit of lines, but a total merit of the piece; like the tone of voice of some incomparable person, so is this a speech of poetic beings, and any clause as unproducible now as a whole poem.

Though the speeches in the plays, and single lines, have a beauty which tempts the ear to pause on them for their euphuism, yet the sentence is so loaded with meaning and so linked with its foregoers and followers, that the logician is satisfied. His means are as admirable as his ends; every subordinate invention, by which he helps himself to connect some irreconcilable opposites, is a poem too. He is not reduced to dismount and walk because his horses are running off with him in some distant direction: he always rides.

The finest poetry was first experience; but the thought has suffered a transformation since it was an experience. Cultivated men often attain a good degree of skill in writing verses; but it is easy to read, through their poems, their personal history: any one acquainted with the parties can name every figure; this is Andrew and that is Rachel. The sense thus remains prosaic. It is a caterpillar with wings, and not yet a butterfly. In the poet's mind the fact has gone quite over into the new element of thought, and has lost all that is exuvial. This generosity abides with Shakspeare. We say, from the truth and closeness of his pictures, that he knows the lesson by heart. Yet there is not a trace of egotism.

One more royal trait properly belongs to the poet. I mean his cheerfulness, without which no man can be a poet,—for beauty is his aim. He loves virtue, not for its obligation but for its grace: he delights in the world, in man, in woman, for the lovely light that sparkles from them. Beauty, the spirit of joy and hilarity, he sheds over the universe. Epicurus relates that poetry hath such charms that a lover might forsake his mistress to partake of them.* And the true bards have been noted for

---

*Emerson misattributes this statement to Epicurus. Plutarch in his *Morals* takes the idea from Xenophon. See the discussion in *The Collected Works*, vol. 4, p. 229.

their firm and cheerful temper. Homer lies in sunshine; Chaucer is glad and erect; and Saadi says, "It was rumored abroad that I was penitent; but what had I to do with repentance?"* Not less sovereign and cheerful,—much more sovereign and cheerful, is the tone of Shakspeare. His name suggests joy and emancipation to the heart of men. If he should appear in any company of human souls, who would not march in his troop? He touches nothing that does not borrow health and longevity from his festal style.

And now, how stands the account of man with this bard and benefactor, when, in solitude, shutting our ears to the reverberations of his fame, we seek to strike the balance? Solitude has austere lessons; it can teach us to spare both heroes and poets; and it weighs Shakspeare also, and finds him to share the halfness and imperfection of humanity.

Shakspeare, Homer, Dante, Chaucer, saw the splendor of meaning that plays over the visible world; knew that a tree had another use than for apples, and corn another than for meal, and the ball of the earth, than for tillage and roads: that these things bore a second and finer harvest to the mind; being emblems of its thoughts, and conveying in all their natural history a certain mute commentary on human life. Shakspeare employed them as colors to compose his picture. He rested in their beauty; and never took the step which seemed inevitable to such genius, namely to explore the virtue which resides in these symbols and imparts this power:—what is that which they themselves say? He converted the elements which waited on his command, into entertainments. He was master of the revels to mankind. Is it not as if one should have, through majestic powers of science, the comets given into his hand, or the planets and their moons, and should draw them from their orbits to glare with the municipal fireworks on a holiday night, and advertise in all towns, "Very superior pyrotechny this evening"? Are the agents of nature, and the power to understand them, worth no more than a street serenade, or the breath of a cigar? One remembers again the trumpet-text in the Koran,—"The heavens and the earth and all that is between them, think ye we have created them in jest?"† As long as the question is of talent and mental power, the world of men has not his equal to show. But when the question is, to life and its materials and its auxiliaries, how does he profit me? What does it signify? It is but a

*From *The Gulistan*, translated by James Ross (1823).
†From *Practical Philosophy of the Muhammadan People . . . the Akhlak-i-Jalay.*

Twelfth Night, or Midsummer-Night's Dream, or Winter Evening's Tale: what signifies another picture more or less? The Egyptian verdict of the Shakspeare Societies comes to mind; that he was a jovial actor and manager. I can not marry this fact to his verse. Other admirable men have led lives in some sort of keeping with their thought; but this man, in wide contrast. Had he been less, had he reached only the common measure of great authors, of Bacon, Milton, Tasso, Cervantes, we might leave the fact in the twilight of human fate: but that this man of men, he who gave to the science of mind a new and larger subject than had ever existed, and planted the standard of humanity some furlongs forward into Chaos,—that he should not be wise for himself;—it must even go into the world's history that the best poet led an obscure and profane life, using his genius for the public amusement.

Well, other men, priest and prophet, Israelite, German and Swede, beheld the same objects: they also saw through them that which was contained. And to what purpose? The beauty straightway vanished; they read commandments, all-excluding mountainous duty; an obligation, a sadness, as of piled mountains, fell on them, and life became ghastly, joyless, a pilgrim's progress, a probation, beleaguered round with doleful histories of Adam's fall and curse behind us; with doomsdays and purgatorial and penal fires before us; and the heart of the seer and the heart of the listener sank in them.

It must be conceded that these are half-views of half-men. The world still wants its poet-priest, a reconciler, who shall not trifle, with Shakspeare the player, nor shall grope in graves, with Swedenborg the mourner; but who shall see, speak, and act, with equal inspiration. For knowledge will brighten the sunshine; right is more beautiful than private affection; and love is compatible with universal wisdom.

Napoleon; or, the Man of the World[1]

AMONG THE EMINENT PERSONS of the nineteenth century, Bonaparte is far the best known and the most powerful; and owes his predominance to the fidelity with which he expresses the tone of thought and belief, the aims of the masses of active and cultivated men. It is Swedenborg's theory that every organ is made up of homogeneous particles; or as it is sometimes expressed, every whole is made of similars; that is, the lungs are composed of infinitely small lungs; the liver, of infinitely small livers; the kidney, of little kidneys, &c.* Following this analogy, if any man is found to carry with him the power and affections of vast numbers, if Napoleon is France, if Napoleon is Europe, it is because the people whom he sways are little Napoleons.

In our society there is a standing antagonism between the conservative and the democratic classes;[2] between those who have made their fortunes, and the young and the poor who have fortunes to make; between the interests of dead labor,—that is, the labor of hands long ago still in the grave, which labor is now entombed in money stocks, or in land and buildings owned by idle capitalists,—and the interests of living labor, which seeks to possess itself of land and buildings and money stocks. The first class is timid, selfish, illiberal, hating innovation, and continually losing numbers by death. The second class is selfish also, encroaching, bold, self-relying, always outnumbering the other and recruiting its numbers every hour by births. It desires to keep open every avenue to the competition of all, and to multiply avenues: the class of business men in America, in England, in France and throughout Europe; the class of industry and skill. Napoleon is its representative. The instinct of active, brave, able men, throughout the middle class every where, has pointed out Napoleon as the incarnate Democrat. He had their virtues and their vices; above all, he had their spirit or aim. That tendency is material, pointing at a sensual success and employing the richest and most various means to that end; conversant with mechanical powers, highly intellectual, widely and accurately learned and skil-

---

*Compare Emanuel Swedenborg's *The Animal Kingdom*, part 1, chapter 4, sect. 100–101.

ful, but subordinating all intellectual and spiritual forces into means to a material success. To be the rich man, is the end. "God has granted," says the Koran, "to every people a prophet in its own tongue."* Paris and London and New York, the spirit of commerce, of money and material power, were also to have their prophet; and Bonaparte was qualified and sent.

Every one of the million readers of anecdotes or memoirs or lives of Napoleon,[3] delights in the page, because he studies in it his own history. Napoleon is thoroughly modern, and, at the highest point of his fortunes, has the very spirit of the newspapers. He is no saint,—to use his own word, "no capuchin,"† and he is no hero, in the high sense. The man in the street finds in him the qualities and powers of other men in the street. He finds him, like himself, by birth a citizen, who, by very intelligible merits, arrived at such a commanding position that he could indulge all those tastes which the common man possesses but is obliged to conceal and deny: good society, good books, fast travelling, dress, dinners, servants without number, personal weight, the execution of his ideas, the standing in the attitude of a benefactor to all persons about him, the refined enjoyments of pictures, statues, music, palaces and conventional honors,—precisely what is agreeable to the heart of every man in the nineteenth century, this powerful man possessed.

It is true that a man of Napoleon's truth of adaptation to the mind of the masses around him, becomes not merely representative but actually a monopolizer and usurper of other minds. Thus Mirabeau plagiarized every good thought, every good word that was spoken in France. Dumont relates that he sat in the gallery of the Convention and heard Mirabeau make a speech. It struck Dumont that he could fit it with a peroration, which he wrote in pencil immediately, and showed it to Lord Elgin, who sat by him. Lord Elgin approved it, and Dumont, in the evening, showed it to Mirabeau. Mirabeau read it, pronounced it admirable, and declared he would incorporate it into his harangue tomorrow, to the Assembly. "It is impossible," said Dumont, "as, unfortunately, I have shown it to Lord Elgin." "If you have shown it to Lord Elgin and to fifty persons beside, I shall still speak it to-morrow:" and he did speak it, with much effect, at the next day's session. For Mirabeau, with his overpowering personality, felt that these things which his presence inspired were as much his own as if he had said

---

*See the Koran, sura X, verse 47.
†Friar of the order of St. Francis.

them, and that his adoption of them gave them their weight. Much more absolute and centralizing was the successor to Mirabeau's popularity and to much more than his predominance in France. Indeed, a man of Napoleon's stamp almost ceases to have a private speech and opinion. He is so largely receptive, and is so placed, that he comes to be a bureau for all the intelligence, wit and power of the age and country. He gains the battle; he makes the code; he makes the system of weights and measures; he levels the Alps; he builds the road. All distinguished engineers, savans, statists, report to him: so likewise do all good heads in every kind: he adopts the best measures, sets his stamp on them, and not these alone, but on every happy and memorable expression. Every sentence spoken by Napoleon and every line of his writing, deserves reading, as it is the sense of France.

Bonaparte was the idol of common men because he had in transcendent degree the qualities and powers of common men. There is a certain satisfaction in coming down to the lowest ground of politics, for we get rid of cant and hypocrisy. Bonaparte wrought, in common with that great class he represented, for power and wealth,—but Bonaparte, specially, without any scruple as to the means. All the sentiments which embarrass men's pursuit of these objects, he set aside. The sentiments were for women and children. Fontanes, in 1804, expressed Napoleon's own sense, when in behalf of the Senate he addressed him,—"Sire, the desire of perfection is the worst disease that ever afflicted the human mind." The advocates of liberty and of progress are "ideologists;"—a word of contempt often in his mouth;—"Necker is an ideologist:" "Lafayette is an ideologist."[4]

An Italian proverb, too well known, declares that "if you would succeed, you must not be too good." It is an advantage, within certain limits, to have renounced the dominion of the sentiments of piety, gratitude and generosity: since what was an impassable bar to us, and still is to others, becomes a convenient weapon for our purposes; just as the river which was a formidable barrier, winter transforms into the smoothest of roads.

Napoleon renounced, once for all, sentiments and affections, and would help himself with his hands and his head. With him is no miracle and no magic. He is a worker in brass, in iron, in wood, in earth, in roads, in buildings, in money and in troops, and a very consistent and wise master-workman. He is never weak and literary, but acts with the solidity and the precision of natural agents. He has not lost his native sense and sympathy with things. Men give way before such a man, as before natural events. To be sure there are men enough who are immersed in things, as farmers, smiths, sailors and mechanics generally; and we know how real and solid such men appear in the presence of scholars and grammarians: but these men ordinarily lack the power of arrangement, and are like hands without a head. But Bonaparte superadded to this mineral and animal force, insight and generalization so that men saw in him combined the natural and the intellectual power, as if the sea and land had taken flesh and begun to cipher. Therefore the land and sea seem to presuppose him. He came unto his own and they received him. This ciphering operative knows what he is working with and what is the product. He knew the properties of gold and iron, of wheels and ships, of troops and diplomatists, and required that each should do after its kind.

The art of war was the game in which he exerted his arithmetic. It consisted, according to him, in having always more forces than the enemy, on the point where the enemy is attacked, or where he attacks: and his whole talent is strained by endless manœuvre and evolution, to march always on the enemy at an angle, and destroy his forces in detail. It is obvious that a very small force, skilfully and rapidly manœuvring so as always to bring two men against one at the point of engagement, will be an overmatch for a much larger body of men.

The times, his constitution and his early circumstances combined to develop this pattern democrat. He had the virtues of his class and the conditions for their activity. That common-sense which no sooner respects any end than it finds the means to effect it; the delight in the use of means; in the choice, simplification and combining of means; the directness and thoroughness of his work; the prudence with which all was seen and the energy with which all was done, make him the natural organ and head of what I may almost call, from its extent, the *modern* party.

Nature must have far the greatest share in every success, and so in his. Such a man was wanted, and such a man was born; a man of stone and iron, capable of sitting on horseback sixteen or seventeen hours, of going many days together without rest or food except by snatches, and with the speed and spring of a tiger in action; a man not embarrassed by any scruples; compact, instant, selfish, prudent, and of a perception which did not suffer itself to be baulked or misled by any pretences of others, or any superstition or any heat or haste of his own. "My hand of iron," he said, "was not at the extremity of my arm, it was immediately connected with my head." He respected the power of nature and fortune, and ascribed to it his superiority, instead of valuing himself, like inferior men, on his opinionativeness, and waging war with nature. His favorite rhetoric lay in allusion to his star; and he pleased himself, as well as the people, when he styled himself the "Child of Destiny." "They charge me," he said, "with the commission of great crimes: men of my stamp do not commit crimes. Nothing has been more simple than my elevation, 't is in vain to ascribe it to intrigue or crime; it was owing to the peculiarity of the times and to my reputation of having fought well against the enemies of my country. I have always marched with the opinion of great masses and with events. Of what use then would crimes be to me?" Again he said, speaking of his son, "My son can not replace me; I could not replace myself. I am the creature of circumstances."

He had a directness of action never before combined with so much comprehension. He is a realist, terrific to all talkers and confused truth-obscuring persons. He sees where the matter hinges, throws himself on the precise point of resistance, and slights all other considerations. He is strong in the right manner, namely by insight. He never blundered into victory, but won his battles in his head before he won them on the field. His principal means are in himself. He asks counsel of no other. In 1796 he writes to the Directory: "I have conducted the campaign without consulting any one. I should have done no good if I had been under the necessity of conforming to the notions of another person. I have gained some advantages over superior forces and when totally destitute of every thing, because, in the persuasion that your confidence was reposed in me, my actions were as prompt as my thoughts."

History is full, down to this day, of the imbecility of kings and governors. They are a class of persons much to be pitied, for they know not what they should do. The weavers strike for bread, and the king and his ministers, knowing not what to do, meet them with bayonets. But Napoleon understood his business. Here was a man who in each moment and emergency knew what to do next. It is an immense comfort and refreshment to the spirits, not only of kings, but of citizens. Few men have any next; they live from hand to mouth, without plan, and are ever at the end of their line, and after each action wait for an impulse from abroad. Napoleon had been the first man of the world, if his ends had been purely public. As he is, he inspires confidence and vigor by the extraordinary unity of his action. He is firm, sure, self-denying, self-postponing, sacrificing every thing,—money, troops, generals, and his own safety also, to his aim; not misled, like common adventurers, by the splendor of his own means. "Incidents ought not to govern policy," he said, "but policy, incidents." "To be hurried away by every event is to have no political system at all." His victories were only so many doors, and he never for a moment lost sight of his way onward, in the dazzle and uproar of the present circumstance. He knew what to do, and he flew to his mark. He would shorten a straight line to come at his object. Horrible anecdotes may no doubt be collected from his history, of the price at which he bought his successes; but he must not therefore be set down as cruel, but only as one who knew no impediment to his will; not bloodthirsty, not cruel,—but woe to what thing or person stood in his way! Not bloodthirsty, but not sparing of blood,—and pitiless. He saw only the object: the obstacle must give way. "Sire, General Clarke can not combine with General Junot, for the dreadful fire of the Austrian battery."—"Let him carry the battery."—"Sire, every regiment that approaches the heavy artillery is sacrificed: Sire, what orders?"—"Forward, forward!" Seruzier, a colonel of artillery, gives, in his "Military Memoirs,"* the following sketch of a scene after the battle of Austerlitz.—"At the moment in which the Russian army was making its retreat, painfully, but in good order, on the ice of the lake, the Emperor Napoleon came riding at full speed toward the artillery. "You are losing time," he cried; "fire upon those masses; they must be engulfed: fire upon the ice!" The order remained unexecuted for ten minutes. In vain several officers and myself were placed on the slope of a hill to produce the effect: their balls and mine rolled upon the ice without breaking it up. Seeing that, I tried a simple method of elevating light howitzers. The almost perpendicular fall of the heavy projectiles produced the desired effect. My method was immediately followed by the adjoining batteries, and in less than no time we buried" some† "thousands of Russians and Austrians under the waters of the lake."

In the plenitude of his resources, every obstacle seemed to vanish. "There shall be no Alps," he said; and he built his perfect roads, climbing by graded galleries their steepest precipices, until Italy was as open to Paris as any town in France. He laid his bones to, and wrought for his crown. Having decided what was to be done, he did that with might and main. He put out all his strength. He risked every thing and spared

---

*Théodore Jean Joseph, baron Séruzier (1757–1821), *Mémoires militaries du B. Séruzier, colonel d'artillerie légère* (1823).

†As I quote at second hand, and cannot procure Seruzier, I dare not adopt the high figure I find (author's note). Emerson got his secondhand information on this "sketch" from Edward Bangs (*The Letters of Ralph Waldo Emerson*, vol. 4, pp. 168–170; see "For Further Reading"); the "high figure" he refused to adopt, 15,000, was an exaggeration.

nothing, neither ammunition, nor money, nor troops, nor generals, nor himself.

We like to see every thing do its office after its kind, whether it be a milch-cow or a rattle-snake; and if fighting be the best mode of adjusting national differences, (as large majorities of men seem to agree,) certainly Bonaparte was right in making it thorough. The grand principle of war, he said, was that an army ought always to be ready, by day and by night and at all hours, to make all the resistance it is capable of making. He never economized his ammunition, but, on a hostile position, rained a torrent of iron,—shells, balls, grape shot,—to annihilate all defence. On any point of resistance he concentrated squadron on squadron in overwhelming numbers until it was swept out of existence. To a regiment of horse-chasseurs at Lobenstein, two days before the battle of Jena, Napoleon said, "My lads, you must not fear death; when soldiers brave death, they drive him into the enemy's ranks." In the fury of assault, he no more spared himself. He went to the edge of his possibility. It is plain that in Italy he did what he could, and all that he could. He came, several times, within an inch of ruin; and his own person was all but lost. He was flung into the marsh at Arcola. The Austrians were between him and his troops, in the *mêlée*, and he was brought off with desperate efforts. At Lonato, and at other places, he was on the point of being taken prisoner. He fought sixty battles. He had never enough. Each victory was a new weapon. "My power would fall, were I not to support it by new achievements. Conquest has made me what I am, and conquest must maintain me." He felt, with every wise man, that as much life is needed for conservation as for creation. We are always in peril, always in a bad plight, just on the edge of destruction and only to be saved by invention and courage.

This vigor was guarded and tempered by the coldest prudence and punctuality. A thunderbolt in the attack, he was found invulnerable in his intrenchments. His very attack was never the inspiration of courage, but the result of calculation. His idea of the best defence consists in being still the attacking party. "My ambition," he says, "was great, but was of a cold nature." In one of his conversations with Las Casas, he remarked, "As to moral courage, I have rarely met with the two-o'clock-in-the-morning kind: I mean unprepared courage; that which is necessary on an unexpected occasion, and which, in spite of the most unforeseen events, leaves full freedom of judgment and decision:" and he did not hesitate to declare that he was himself eminently endowed with this "two-o'clock-in-the-morning courage, and that he had met with few persons equal to himself in this particular."

Every thing depended on the nicety of his combinations, and the stars were not more punctual than his arithmetic. His personal attention descended to the smallest particulars. "At Montebello, I ordered Kellermann to attack with eight hundred horse, and with these he separated the six thousand Hungarian grenadiers, before the very eyes of the Austrian cavalry. This cavalry was half a league off and required a quarter of an hour to arrive on the field of action, and I have observed that it is always these quarters of an hour that decide the fate of a battle." "Before he fought a battle, Bonaparte thought little about what he should do in case of success, but a great deal about what he should do in case of a reverse of fortune." The same prudence and good sense mark all his behavior. His instructions to his secretary at the Tuileries are worth remembering. "During the night, enter my chamber as seldom as possible. Do not awake me when you have any good news to communicate; with that there is no hurry. But when you bring bad news, rouse me instantly, for then there is not a moment to be lost." It was a whimsical economy of the same kind which dictated his practice, when general in Italy, in regard to his burdensome correspondence. He directed Bourrienne to leave all letters unopened for three weeks, and then observed with satisfaction how large a part of the correspondence had thus disposed of itself and no longer required an answer. His achievement of business was immense, and enlarges the known powers of man. There have been many working kings, from Ulysses to William of Orange, but none who accomplished a tithe of this man's performance.

To these gifts of nature, Napoleon added the advantage of having been born to a private and humble fortune. In his later days he had the weakness of wishing to add to his crowns and badges the prescription of aristocracy; but he knew his debt to his austere education, and made no secret of his contempt for the born kings, and for "the hereditary asses," as he coarsely styled the Bourbons. He said that "in their exile they had learned nothing, and forgot nothing." Bonaparte had passed through all the degrees of military service, but also was citizen before he was emperor, and so has the key to citizenship. His remarks and estimates discover the information and justness of measurement of the middle class. Those who had to deal with him found that he was not to be imposed upon, but could cipher as well as another man. This appears in all parts of his Memoirs, dictated at St. Helena. When the expenses of the empress, of his household, of his palaces, had accumulated great debts, Napoleon examined the bills of the creditors himself, detected overcharges and errors, and reduced the claims by considerable sums.

His grand weapon, namely the millions whom he directed, he owed to the representative character which clothed him. He interests us as he stands for France and for Europe; and he exists as captain and king only as far as the Revolution, or the interest of the industrious masses, found an organ and a leader in him. In the social interests, he knew the meaning and value of labor, and threw himself naturally on that side. I like an incident mentioned by one of his biographers at St. Helena. "When walking with Mrs. Balcombe, some servants, carrying heavy boxes, passed by on the road, and Mrs. Balcombe desired them, in rather an angry tone, to keep back. Napoleon interfered, saying 'Respect the burden, Madam.'" In the time of the empire he directed attention to the improvement and embellishment of the markets of the capital. "The market-place," he said, "is the Louvre* of the common people." The principal works that have survived him are his magnificent roads. He filled the troops with his spirit, and a sort of freedom and companionship grew up between him and them, which the forms of his court never permitted between the officers and himself. They performed, under his eye, that which no others could do. The best document of his relation to his troops is the order of the day on the morning of the battle of Austerlitz, in which Napoleon promises the troops that he will keep his person out of reach of fire. This declaration, which is the reverse of that ordinarily made by generals and sovereigns on the eve of a battle, sufficiently explains the devotion of the army to their leader.

But though there is in particulars this identity between Napoleon and the mass of the people, his real strength lay in their conviction that he was their representative in his genius and aims, not only when he courted, but when he controlled, and even when he decimated them by his conscriptions. He knew, as well as any Jacobin in France, how to philosophize on liberty and equality; and when allusion was made to the precious blood of centuries, which was spilled by the killing of the Duc d'Enghien, he suggested, "Neither is my blood ditch-water." The people felt that no longer the throne was occupied and the land sucked of its nourishment, by a small class of legitimates, secluded from all community with the children of the soil, and holding the ideas and superstitions of a long-forgotten state of society. Instead of that vampyre, a man of themselves held, in the Tuileries,† knowledge and ideas like their own, opening of course to them and their children all places of power

---

*Foremost museum of art in Paris.
†The royal palace in Paris.

and trust. The day of sleepy, selfish policy, ever narrowing the means and opportunities of young men, was ended, and a day of expansion and demand was come. A market for all the powers and productions of man was opened; brilliant prizes glittered in the eyes of youth and talent. The old, iron-bound, feudal France was changed into a young Ohio or New York; and those who smarted under the immediate rigors of the new monarch, pardoned them as the necessary severities of the military system which had driven out the oppressor. And even when the majority of the people had begun to ask whether they had really gained any thing under the exhausting levies of men and money of the new master, the whole talent of the country, in every rank and kindred, took his part and defended him as its natural patron. In 1814, when advised to rely on the higher classes, Napoleon said to those around him, "Gentlemen, in the situation in which I stand, my only nobility is the rabble of the Faubourgs."*

Napoleon met this natural expectation. The necessity of his position required a hospitality to every sort of talent, and its appointment to trusts; and his feeling went along with this policy. Like every superior person, he undoubtedly felt a desire for men and compeers, and a wish to measure his power with other masters, and an impatience of fools and underlings. In Italy, he sought for men and found none. "Good God!" he said, "how rare men are! There are eighteen millions in Italy, and I have with difficulty found two,—Dandolo and Melzi." In later years, with larger experience, his respect for mankind was not increased. In a moment of bitterness he said to one of his oldest friends, "Men deserve the contempt with which they inspire me. I have only to put some gold-lace on the coat of my virtuous republicans and they immediately become just what I wish them." This impatience at levity was, however, an oblique tribute of respect to those able persons who commanded his regard not only when he found them friends and coadjutors but also when they resisted his will. He could not confound Fox and Pitt, Carnot, Lafayette and Bernadotte, with the danglers of his court; and in spite of the detraction which his systematic egotism dictated toward the great captains who conquered with and for him, ample acknowledgments are made by him to Lannes, Duroc, Kleber, Dessaix, Massena, Murat, Ney and Augereau.[5] If he felt himself their patron and the founder of their fortunes, as when he said "I made my generals out of mud,"—he could not hide his satisfaction in receiving from them a sec-

---

*Working-class neighborhoods on the outskirts of Paris.

onding and support commensurate with the grandeur of his enterprise. In the Russian campaign he was so much impressed by the courage and resources of Marshal Ney, that he said, "I have two hundred millions in my coffers, and I would give them all for Ney."* The characters which he has drawn of several of his marshals are discriminating, and though they did not content the insatiable vanity of French officers, are no doubt substantially just. And in fact every species of merit was sought and advanced under his government. "I know" he said, "the depth and draught of water of every one of my generals." Natural power was sure to be well received at his court. Seventeen men in his time were raised from common soldiers to the rank of king, marshal, duke, or general; and the crosses of his Legion of Honor were given to personal valor, and not to family connexion. "When soldiers have been baptized in the fire of a battle-field, they have all one rank in my eyes."

When a natural king becomes a titular king, every body is pleased and satisfied. The Revolution entitled the strong populace of the Faubourg St. Antoine, and every horse-boy and powder-monkey in the army, to look on Napoleon as flesh of his flesh and the creature of *his* party: but there is something in the success of grand talent which enlists an universal sympathy. For in the prevalence of sense and spirit over stupidity and malversation,† all reasonable men have an interest; and as intellectual beings we feel the air purified by the electric shock, when material force is overthrown by intellectual energies. As soon as we are removed out of the reach of local and accidental partialities, Man feels that Napoleon fights for him; these are honest victories; this strong steam-engine does our work. Whatever appeals to the imagination, by transcending the ordinary limits of human ability, wonderfully encourages and liberates us. This capacious head, revolving and disposing sovereignly trains of affairs, and animating such multitudes of agents; this eye, which looked through Europe; this prompt invention; this inexhaustible resource:—what events! what romantic pictures! what strange situations!—when spying the Alps, by a sunset in the Sicilian sea; drawing up his army for battle in sight of the Pyramids, and saying to his troops, "From the tops of those pyramids, forty centuries look down on you;" fording the Red Sea; wading in the gulf of the Isthmus of Suez. On the shore of Ptolemais, gigantic projects agitated

---

*Napoleon was referring to Ney's brilliant defensive maneuvers while commanding the rear guard during the retreat from Moscow in 1812.

†Corrupt behavior by one in a position of trust.

him. "Had Acre* fallen, I should have changed the face of the world." His army, on the night of the battle of Austerlitz, which was the anniversary of his inauguration as Emperor, presented him with a bouquet of forty standards taken in the fight. Perhaps it is a little puerile, the pleasure he took in making these contrasts glaring; as when he pleased himself with making kings wait in his antechambers, at Tilsit, at Paris and at Erfurt.

We cannot, in the universal imbecility, indecision and indolence of men, sufficiently congratulate ourselves on this strong and ready actor, who took occasion by the beard, and showed us how much may be accomplished by the mere force of such virtues as all men possess in less degrees; namely, by punctuality, by personal attention, by courage and thoroughness. "The Austrians," he said, "do not know the value of time." I should cite him, in his earlier years, as a model of prudence. His power does not consist in any wild or extravagant force; in any enthusiasm like Mahomet's,[†] or singular power of persuasion; but in the exercise of common-sense on each emergency, instead of abiding by rules and customs. The lesson he teaches is that which vigor always teaches;—that there is always room for it. To what heaps of cowardly doubts is not that man's life an answer. When he appeared it was the belief of all military men that there could be nothing new in war; as it is the belief of men to-day that nothing new can be undertaken in politics, or in church, or in letters, or in trade, or in farming, or in our social manners and customs; and as it is at all times the belief of society that the world is used up. But Bonaparte knew better than society; and moreover knew that he knew better. I think all men know better than they do; know that the institutions we so volubly commend are go-carts and baubles; but they dare not trust their presentiments. Bonaparte relied on his own sense, and did not care a bean for other people's. The world treated his novelties just as it treats everybody's novelties,—made infinite objection, mustered all the impediments; but he snapped his finger at their objections. "What creates great difficulty," he remarks, "in the profession of the land-commander, is the necessity of feeding so many men and animals. If he allows himself to be guided by the commissaries he will never stir, and all his expeditions will fail." An example of his common-sense is what he says of the passage of the Alps in winter, which all writ-

---

*Napoleon failed to capture this city (formerly known as Ptolemais) on the coast of Palestine after a siege of ninety-one days.
†Alternate spelling for Muhammad.

ers, one repeating after the other, had described as impracticable. "The winter," says Napoleon, "is not the most unfavorable season for the passage of lofty mountains. The snow is then firm, the weather settled, and there is nothing to fear from avalanches, the real and only danger to be apprehended in the Alps. On those high mountains there are often very fine days in December, of a dry cold, with extreme calmness in the air." Read his account, too, of the way in which battles are gained. "In all battles a moment occurs when the bravest troops, after having made the greatest efforts, feel inclined to run. That terror proceeds from a want of confidence in their own courage, and it only requires a slight opportunity, a pretence, to restore confidence to them. The art is, to give rise to the opportunity and to invent the pretence. At Arcola I won the battle with twenty-five horsemen. I seized that moment of lassitude, gave every man a trumpet, and gained the day with this handful. You see that two armies are two bodies which meet and endeavor to frighten each other; a moment of panic occurs, and that moment must be turned to advantage. When a man has been present in many actions, he distinguishes that moment without difficulty: it is as easy as casting up an addition."

This deputy of the nineteenth century added to his gifts a capacity for speculation on general topics. He delighted in running through the range of practical, of literary and of abstract questions. His opinion is always original and to the purpose. On the voyage to Egypt he liked, after dinner, to fix on three or four persons to support a proposition, and as many to oppose it. He gave a subject, and the discussions turned on questions of religion, the different kinds of government and the art of war. One day he asked whether the planets were inhabited? On another, what was the age of the world? Then he proposed to consider the probability of the destruction of the globe, either by water or by fire: at another time, the truth or fallacy of presentiments, and the interpretation of dreams. He was very fond of talking of religion. In 1806 he conversed with Fournier, bishop of Montpellier, on matters of theology. There were two points on which they could not agree, viz. that of hell, and that of salvation out of the pale of the church. The Emperor told Josephine that he disputed like a devil on these two points, on which the bishop was inexorable. To the philosophers he readily yielded all that was proved against religion as the work of men and time, but he would not hear of materialism. One fine night, on deck, amid a clatter of materialism, Bonaparte pointed to the stars, and said, "You may talk as long as you please, gentlemen, but who made all that?" He delighted in the conversation of men of science, particularly of Monge and Berthollet;

but the men of letters he slighted; they were "manufacturers of phrases." Of medicine too he was fond of talking, and with those of its practitioners whom he most esteemed,—with Corvisart at Paris, and with Antommarchi at St. Helena. "Believe me," he said to the last, "we had better leave off all these remedies: life is a fortress which neither you nor I know anything about. Why throw obstacles in the way of its defence? Its own means are superior to all the apparatus of your laboratories. Corvisart candidly agreed with me that all your filthy mixtures are good for nothing. Medicine is a collection of uncertain prescriptions, the results of which, taken collectively, are more fatal than useful to mankind. Water, air and cleanliness are the chief articles in my pharmacopœia."

His memoirs, dictated to Count Montholon and General Gourgaud at St. Helena, have great value, after all the deduction that it seems is to be made from them on account of his known disingenuousness. He has the good-nature of strength and conscious superiority. I admire his simple, clear narrative of his battles;—good as Cæsar's; his good-natured and sufficiently respectful account of Marshal Wurmser and his other antagonists; and his own equality as a writer to his varying subject. The most agreeable portion is the Campaign in Egypt.[6]

He had hours of thought and wisdom. In intervals of leisure, either in the camp or the palace, Napoleon appears as a man of genius directing on abstract questions the native appetite for truth and the impatience of words he was wont to show in war. He could enjoy every play of invention, a romance, a *bon mot*,* as well as a stratagem in a campaign. He delighted to fascinate Josephine and her ladies, in a dim-lighted apartment, by the terrors of a fiction to which his voice and dramatic power lent every addition.

I call Napoleon the agent or attorney of the middle class of modern society; of the throng who fill the markets, shops, counting-houses, manufactories, ships, of the modern world, aiming to be rich. He was the agitator, the destroyer of prescription, the internal improver, the liberal, the radical, the inventor of means, the opener of doors and markets, the subverter of monopoly and abuse. Of course the rich and aristocratic did not like him. England, the centre of capital, and Rome and Austria, centres of tradition and genealogy, opposed him. The consternation of the dull and conservative classes, the terror of the foolish old men and old women of the Roman conclave, who in their despair took hold of any thing, and would cling to red-hot iron,—the vain at-

---

*Witty remark.

tempts of statists to amuse and deceive him, of the emperor of Austria
to bribe him; and the instinct of the young, ardent and active men every
where, which pointed him out as the giant of the middle class, make his
history bright and commanding. He had the virtues of the masses of his
constituents: he had also their vices. I am sorry that the brilliant picture
has its reverse. But that is the fatal quality which we discover in our pur-
suit of wealth, that it is treacherous, and is bought by the breaking or
weakening of the sentiments; and it is inevitable that we should find the
same fact in the history of this champion, who proposed to himself
simply a brilliant career, without any stipulation or scruple concerning
the means.

Bonaparte was singularly destitute of generous sentiments. The
highest-placed individual in the most cultivated age and population of
the world,—he has not the merit of common truth and honesty. He is
unjust to his generals; egotistic and monopolizing; meanly stealing the
credit of their great actions from Kellermann, from Bernadotte; in-
triguing to involve his faithful Junot in hopeless bankruptcy, in order to
drive him to a distance from Paris, because the familiarity of his man-
ners offends the new pride of his throne. He is a boundless liar. The of-
ficial paper, his "Moniteur," and all his bulletins, are proverbs for saying
what he wished to be believed; and worse,—he sat, in his premature old
age, in his lonely island, coldly falsifying facts and dates and characters,
and giving to history a theatrical *éclat*.* Like all Frenchmen he has a pas-
sion for stage effect. Every action that breathes of generosity is poisoned
by this calculation. His star, his love of glory, his doctrine of the im-
mortality of the soul, are all French. "I must dazzle and astonish. If I
were to give the liberty of the press, my power could not last three days."
To make a great noise is his favorite design. "A great reputation is a great
noise: the more there is made, the farther off it is heard. Laws, institu-
tions, monuments, nations, all fall; but the noise continues, and re-
sounds in after ages." His doctrine of immortality is simply fame. His
theory of influence is not flattering. "There are two levers for moving
men,—interest and fear. Love is a silly infatuation, depend upon it.
Friendship is but a name. I love nobody. I do not even love my broth-
ers: perhaps Joseph a little, from habit, and because he is my elder; and
Duroc, I love him too; but why?—because his character pleases me: he
is stern and resolute, and I believe the fellow never shed a tear. For my
part I know very well that I have no true friends. As long as I continue

---

*Brilliant performance.

to be what I am, I may have as many pretended friends as I please. Leave sensibility to women; but men should be firm in heart and purpose, or they should have nothing to do with war and government." He was thoroughly unscrupulous. He would steal, slander, assassinate, drown and poison, as his interest dictated. He had no generosity, but mere vulgar hatred; he was intensely selfish; he was perfidious; he cheated at cards; he was a prodigious gossip, and opened letters, and delighted in his infamous police, and rubbed his hands with joy when he had intercepted some morsel of intelligence concerning the men and women about him, boasting that "he knew every thing;" and interfered with the cutting the dresses of the women; and listened after the hurrahs and the compliments of the street, incognito. His manners were coarse. He treated women with low familiarity. He had the habit of pulling their ears and pinching their cheeks when he was in good humor, and of pulling the ears and whiskers of men, and of striking and horse-play with them, to his last days. It does not appear that he listened at key-holes, or at least that he was caught at it. In short, when you have penetrated through all the circles of power and splendor, you were not dealing with a gentleman, at last; but with an impostor and a rogue; and he fully deserves the epithet of *Jupiter Scapin*, or a sort of Scamp Jupiter.

In describing the two parties into which modern society divides itself,—the democrat and the conservative,—I said, Bonaparte represents the Democrat, or the party of men of business, against the stationary or conservative party. I omitted then to say, what is material to the statement, namely that these two parties differ only as young and old. The democrat is a young conservative; the conservative is an old democrat.[7] The aristocrat is the democrat ripe and gone to seed;—because both parties stand on the one ground of the supreme value of property, which one endeavors to get, and the other to keep. Bonaparte may be said to represent the whole history of this party, its youth and its age; yes, and with poetic justice its fate, in his own. The counter-revolution, the counter-party, still waits for its organ and representative, in a lover and a man of truly public and universal aims.

Here was an experiment, under the most favorable conditions, of the powers of intellect without conscience. Never was such a leader so endowed and so weaponed; never leader found such aids and followers. And what was the result of this vast talent and power, of these immense armies, burned cities, squandered treasures, immolated millions of men, of this demoralized Europe? It came to no result. All passed away like the smoke of his artillery, and left no trace. He left France smaller, poorer, feebler, than he found it; and the whole contest for freedom was to be begun again. The attempt was in principle suicidal. France served him with life and limb and estate, as long as it could identify its interest with him; but when men saw that after victory was another war; after the destruction of armies, new conscriptions; and they who had toiled so desperately were never nearer to the reward,—they could not spend what they had earned, nor repose on their down-beds, nor strut in their chateaux,—they deserted him. Men found that his absorbing egotism was deadly to all other men. It resembled the torpedo,* which inflicts a succession of shocks on any one who takes hold of it, producing spasms which contract the muscles of the hand, so that the man can not open his fingers; and the animal inflicts new and more violent shocks, until he paralyzes and kills his victim. So this exorbitant egotist narrowed, impoverished and absorbed the power and existence of those who served him; and the universal cry of France and of Europe in 1814 was, "Enough of him;" "*Assez de Bonaparte.*"

It was not Bonaparte's fault. He did all that in him lay, to live and thrive without moral principle. It was the nature of things, the eternal law of man and of the world which baulked and ruined him; and the result, in a million experiments, will be the same. Every experiment, by multitudes or by individuals, that has a sensual and selfish aim, will fail. The pacific Fourier† will be as inefficient as the pernicious Napoleon. As long as our civilization is essentially one of property, of fences, of exclusiveness, it will be mocked by delusions. Our riches will leave us sick; there will be bitterness in our laughter, and our wine will burn our mouth. Only that good profits which we can taste with all doors open, and which serves all men.

---

*Another name for the electric eel.

†Social reformer Charles Fourier proposed peaceful means to reform instead of revolution.

Address to the Citizens of Concord
(on the Fugitive Slave Law)[1]

FELLOW CITIZENS:

I accepted your invitation to speak to you on the great question of these days, with very little consideration of what I might have to offer; for there seems to be no option. The last year has forced us all into politics, and made it a paramount duty to seek what it is often a duty to shun.

We do not breathe well. There is infamy in the air. I have a new experience. I wake in the morning with a painful sensation, which I carry about all day, and which, when traced home, is the odious remembrance of that ignominy which has fallen on Massachusetts, which robs the landscape of beauty, and takes the sunshine out of every hour. I have lived all my life in this State, and never had any experience of personal inconvenience from the laws, until now. They never came near me to my discomfort before. I find the like sensibility in my neighbors. And in that class who take no interest in the ordinary questions of party politics. There are men who are as sure indexes of the equity of legislation and of the same state of public feeling, as the barometer is of the weight of the air, and it is a bad sign when these are discontented. For, though they snuff oppression and dishonor at a distance, it is because they are more impressionable: the whole population will in a short time be as painfully affected.

Every hour brings us from distant quarters of the Union the expression of mortification at the late events in Massachusetts, and at the behavior of Boston. The tameness was indeed shocking. Boston, of whose fame for spirit and character we have all been so proud; Boston, whose citizens, intelligent people in England told me, they could always distinguish by their culture among Americans; the Boston of the American Revolution, which figures so proudly in "John Adams's Diary,"* which the whole country has been reading; Boston, spoiled by prosperity, must bow its ancient honor in the dust, and make us irretrievably ashamed. In Boston, — we have said with such lofty confidence, — no

---

*The first volumes of the *Works of John Adams* (1850–1856), 10 vols., edited by Charles Francis Adams, had just been published (see p. 12).

fugitive slave can be arrested; — and now, we must transfer our vaunt to the country, and say, with a little less confidence, — no fugitive man can be arrested here; at least we can brag thus until tomorrow, when the farmers also may be corrupted.

The tameness is indeed complete. It appears the only haste in Boston, after the rescue of Shadrach[2] last February, was, who should first put his name on the list of volunteers in aid of the marshal. I met the smoothest of episcopal clergymen the other day, and allusion being made to Mr. Webster's treachery, he blandly replied, "Why, do you know I think *that* the great action of his life." It looked as if, in the city, and the suburbs, all were involved in one hot haste of terror,—presidents of colleges and professors, saints and brokers, insurers, lawyers, importers, manufacturers; — not an unpleasing sentiment, not a liberal recollection, not so much as a snatch of an old song for freedom, dares intrude on their passive obedience. The panic has paralyzed the journals, with the fewest exceptions, so that one cannot open a newspaper, without being disgusted by new records of shame. I cannot read longer even the local good news. When I look down the columns at the titles of paragraphs, "Education in Massachusetts," "Board of Trade," "Art Union," "Revival of Religion," what bitter mockeries! The very convenience of property, the house and land we occupy, have lost their best value, and a man looks gloomily on his children, and thinks, 'What have I done, that you should begin life in dishonor?' Every liberal study is discredited: Literature, and science appear effeminate and the hiding of the head. The college, the churches, the schools, the very shops and factories are discredited; real estate, every kind of wealth, every branch of industry, every avenue to power, suffers injury, and the value of life is reduced. Just now a friend came into my house and said, "If this law shall be repealed, I shall be glad that I have lived; if not, I shall be sorry that I was born." What kind of law is that which extorts language like this from the heart of a free and civilized people?

One intellectual benefit we owe to the late disgraces. The crisis had the illuminating power of a sheet of lightning at midnight. It showed truth. It ended a good deal of nonsense we had been wont to hear and to repeat, on the 19th April, the 17th June, the 4th July.* It showed the slightness and unreliableness of our social fabric, it showed what stuff

---

*April 19 commemorates the battles of Lexington and Concord, the first battles of the American Revolution. June 17 commemorates the Battle of Bunker Hill, another important battle of the Revolution fought in Boston. July 4 is Independence Day.

reputations are made of, what straws we dignify by office and title, and how competent we are to give counsel and help in a day of trial. It showed the shallowness of leaders; the divergence of parties from their alleged grounds; showed that men would not stick to what they had said: that the resolutions of public bodies, or the pledges never so often given and put on record of public men, will not bind them. The fact comes out more plainly, that you cannot rely on any man for the defence of truth, who is not constitutionally, or by blood and temperament, on that side. A man of a greedy and unscrupulous selfishness may maintain morals when they are in fashion: but he will not stick. However close Mr. Wolf's nails have been pared, however neatly he has been shaved, and tailored, and set up on end, and taught to say, "Virtue and Religion," he cannot be relied on at a pinch: he will say, morality means pricking a vein. The popular assumption that all men loved freedom, and believed in the Christian religion, was found hollow American brag. Only persons who were known and tried benefactors are found standing for freedom: the sentimentalists went downstream. I question the value of our civilization, when I see that the public mind had never less hold of the strongest of all truths. The sense of injustice is blunted,—a sure sign of the shallowness of our intellect. I cannot accept the railroad and telegraph in exchange for reason and charity. It is not skill in iron locomotives that marks so fine civility, as the jealousy of liberty. I cannot think the most judicious tubing* a compensation for metaphysical debility. What is the use of admirable law-forms and political forms, if a hurricane of party feeling and a combination of monied interests can beat them to the ground? What is the use of courts, if judges only quote authorities, and no judge exerts original jurisdiction, or recurs to first principles? What is the use of a Federal Bench, if its opinions are the political breath of the hour? And what is the use of constitutions, if all the guaranties provided by the jealousy of ages for the protection of liberty are made of no effect, when a bad act of Congress finds a willing commissioner?

The levity of the public mind has been shown in the past year by the most extravagant actions. Who could have believed it, if foretold, that a hundred guns would be fired in Boston on the passage of the Fugitive Slave Bill?† Nothing proves the want of all thought, the absence of stan-

---

*Iron tubes used to reinforce railway bridges or other structures.
†Supporters of the bill fired a one-hundred-gun salute on the Boston Common to celebrate its passage.

dard in men's minds more than the dominion of party. Here are humane people who have tears for misery, an open purse for want, who should have been the defenders of the poor man, are found his embittered enemies, rejoicing in his rendition,—merely from party ties. I thought none that was not ready to go on all fours, would back this law. And yet here are upright men, *compotes mentis*,* husbands, fathers, trustees, friends, open, generous, brave, who can see nothing in this claim for bare humanity, and the health and honor of their native state, but canting fanaticism, sedition and "one idea." Because of this preoccupied mind, the whole wealth and power of Boston—200,000 souls, and 180 millions of money,—are thrown into the scale of crime; and the poor black boy, whom the fame of Boston had reached in the recesses of a riceswamp, or in the alleys of Savannah, on arriving here, finds all this force employed to catch him. The famous town of Boston is his master's hound. The learning of the Universities, the culture of elegant society, the acumen of lawyers, the majesty of the Bench, the eloquence of the Christian pulpit, the stoutness of Democracy, the respectability of the Whig party are all combined to kidnap him.

The crisis is interesting as it shows the self-protecting nature of the world and of the Divine laws. It is the law of the world as much immorality as there is, so much misery. The greatest prosperity will in vain resist the greatest calamity. You borrow the succour of the devil and he must have his fee. He was never known to abate a penny of his rents. In every nation all the immorality that exists breeds plagues. Out of the corrupt society that exists we have never been able to combine any pure prosperity. There is always something in the very advantages of a condition which hurts it. Africa has its malformation; England has its Ireland; Germany its hatred of classes; France its love of gunpowder; Italy its Pope; and America, the most prosperous country in the Universe, has the greatest calamity in the Universe, negro slavery.

Let me remind you a little in detail how the natural retributions act in reference to the statute which Congress passed a year ago. For these few months have shown very conspicuously its nature and impractibility.

It is contravened,

1. By the sentiment of duty. An immoral law makes it a man's duty to break it, at every hazard. For virtue is the very self of every man. It is therefore a principle of law, that an immoral contract is void, and that an immoral statute is void, for, as laws do not make right, but are sim-

---

*Of sound mind (Latin); a legal term.

ply declaratory of a right which already existed, it is not to be presumed that they can so stultify themselves as to command injustice.

It is remarkable how rare in the history of tyrants is an immoral law. Some color, some indirection was always used. If you take up the volumes of the "Universal History," you will find it difficult searching. The precedents are few. It is not easy to parallel the wickedness of this American law. And that is the head and body of this discontent, that the law is immoral. Here is a statute which enacts the crime of kidnapping,—a crime on one footing with arson and murder. A man's right to liberty is as inalienable as his right to life.

Pains seem to have been taken to give us in this statute a wrong pure from any mixture of right. If our resistance to this law is not right, there is no right. This is not meddling with other people's affairs: this is hindering other people from meddling with us. This is not going crusading into Virginia and Georgia after slaves, who, it is alleged, are very comfortable where they are:—that amiable argument falls to the ground: but this is befriending in our own State, on our own farms, a man who has taken the risk of being shot, or burned alive, or cast into the sea, or starved to death, or suffocated in a wooden box, to get away from his driver: and this man who has run the gauntlet of a thousand miles for his freedom, the statute says, you men of Massachusetts shall hunt, and catch, and send back again to the dog-hutch he fled from.

It is contrary to the primal sentiment of duty, and therefore all men that are born are, in proportion to their power of thought and their moral sensibility, found to be the natural enemies of this law. The resistance of all moral beings is secured to it. I had thought, I confess, what must come at last would come at first, a banding of all men against the authority of this statute. I thought it a point on which all sane men were agreed, that the law must respect the public morality. I thought that all men of all conditions had been made sharers of a certain experience,[3] that in certain rare and retired moments they had been made to see how man is man, or what makes the essence of rational beings, namely, that whilst animals have to do with eating the fruits of the ground, men have to do with rectitude, with benefit, with truth, with something which *is*, independent of appearances: and that this tie makes the substantiality of life, this, and not their ploughing, or sailing, their trade or the breeding of families. I thought that every time a man goes back to his own thoughts, these angels receive him, talk with him, and that, in the best hours, he is uplifted in virtue of this essence, into a peace and into a power which the material world cannot give: that these moments counterbalance the years of drudgery, and that this owning of a law, be it called morals, religion, or godhead, or what you will, constituted the explanation of life, the excuse and indemnity for the errors and calamities which sadden it. In long years consumed in trifles, they remember these moments, and are consoled. I thought it was this fair mystery, whose foundations are hidden in eternity, which made the basis of human society, and of law; and that to pretend anything else, as that the acquisition of property was the end of living, was to confound all distinctions, to make the world a greasy hotel, and, instead of noble motives and inspirations, and a heaven of companions and angels around and before us, to leave us in a grimacing menagerie of monkeys and idiots. All arts, customs, societies, books, and laws, are good as they foster and concur with this spiritual element: all men are beloved as they raise us to it; all are hateful as they deny or resist it. The laws especially draw their obligation only from their concurrence with it.

I am surprised that lawyers can be so blind as to suffer the principles of Law to be discredited. A few months ago, in my dismay at hearing that the Higher Law was reckoned a good joke in the courts, I took pains to look into a few law-books. I had often heard that the Bible constituted a part of every technical law-library, and that it was a principle in law that immoral laws are void. I found, accordingly, that the great jurists, Cicero, Grotius, Coke, Blackstone, Burlamaqui, Montesquieu, Vattel, Burke, Mackintosh, Jefferson, do all affirm this.

I have no intention to recite these passages I had marked:—such citation indeed seems to be something cowardly, for no reasonable person needs a quotation from Blackstone to convince him that white cannot be legislated to be black, and shall content myself with reading a single passage.

Blackstone admits the sovereignty "antecedent to any positive precept of the law of Nature," among whose principles are, "that we should live honestly, should hurt nobody, and should render unto every one his due," etc. "*No human laws are of any validity, if contrary to this.*" "Nay, if any human law should allow or enjoin us to commit a crime" (his instance is murder) "we are bound to transgress that human law; or else we must offend both the natural and divine."

Lord Coke held, that where an Act of Parliament is against common right and reason, the common law shall control it, and adjudge it to be void. Chief Justice Hobart, Chief Justice Holt, and Chief Justice Mansfield held the same. Lord Mansfield, in the case of the slave Somerset, wherein the *dicta* of Lords Talbot and Hardwicke had been cited to the effect of carrying back the slave to the West Indies, said, "I care not for the supposed *dicta* of judges, however eminent, if they be contrary to all principle." Even the Canon Law says (in malis promissis non expedit servare fidem), "neither allegiance nor oath can bind to obey that which is wrong." Vatel is equally explicit. "No engagement (to a sovereign) can oblige or even authorize a man to violate the laws of Nature." All authors who have any conscience or modesty, agree that a person ought not to obey such commands as are evidently contrary to the laws of God. Those governors of places who bravely refused to execute the barbarous orders of Charles IX. to the famous St. Bartholomew's,[4] have been universally praised; and the court did not dare to punish them, at least openly. "Sire," said the brave Orte, governor of Bayonne, in his letter, "I have communicated your majesty's command to your faithful inhabitants and warriors in the garrison, and I have found there only good citizens, and brave soldiers; not one hangman: therefore, both they and I must humbly entreat your majesty, to be pleased to employ your arms and lives in things that are possible, however hazardous they may be, and we will exert ourselves to the last drop of our blood."

The practitioners should guard this dogma well, as the palladium* of the profession, as their anchor in the respect of mankind; against a principle like this, all the arguments of Mr. Webster are the spray of a child's squirt against a granite wall.

2. It is contravened by all the sentiments. How can a law be enforced that fines pity, and imprisons charity? As long as men have bowels, they will disobey. You know that the Act of Congress of September 18, 1850, is a law which every one of you will break on the earliest occasion. There is not a manly whig, or a manly democrat, of whom, if a slave were hidden in one of our houses from the hounds, we should not ask with confidence to lend his wagon in aid of his escape, and he would lend it. The man would be too strong for the partisan.

And here I may say that it is absurd, what I often hear, to accuse the friends of freedom in the north with being the occasion of the new stringency of the southern slave-laws. If you starve or beat the orphan, in my presence, and I accuse your cruelty, can I help it? In the words of Electra in the Greek tragedy,

"'T is you that say it, not I. You do the deeds, And your ungodly deeds find me the words."†

---

*Safeguard; after the legend of the statue of Pallas Athena in the city of Troy: So long as the statue was intact, the city would be safe.
†Sophocles' *Electra*, II, 626–627.

Will you blame the ball for rebounding from the floor; blame the air for rushing in where a vacuum is made or the boiler for exploding under pressure of steam? These facts are after the laws of the world, and so is it law, that, when justice is violated, anger begins. The very defence which the God of Nature has provided for the innocent against cruelty, is the sentiment of indignation and pity in the bosom of the beholder. Mr. Webster tells the President that "he has been in the North, and he has found no man, whose opinion is of any weight, who is opposed to the law." Ah!, Mr. President, trust not the information. The gravid old Universe goes spawning on; the womb conceives and the breasts give suck to thousands and millions of hairy babes formed not in the image of your statute, but in the image of the Universe; too many to be bought off; too many than that they can be rich, and therefore peaceable; and necessitated to express first or last every feeling of the heart. You can keep no secret, for whatever is true, some of them will unseasonably say. You can commit no crime, for they are created in their sentiments conscious of and hostile to it; and unless you can suppress the newspaper, pass a law against book-shops, gag the English tongue in America, all short of this is futile. This dreadful English speech is saturated with songs, proverbs and speeches that flatly contradict and defy every line of Mr. Mason's statute. Nay, unless you can draw a sponge over those seditious Ten Commandments which are the root of our European and American civilization; and over that eleventh commandment, "Do unto others as you would have others do to you," your labor is vain.

3. It is contravened by the written laws themselves, because the sentiments, of course, write the statutes. Laws are merely declaratory of the natural sentiments of mankind and the language of all permanent laws will be in contradiction to any immoral enactment. And thus it happens here: statute fights against statute. By the law of Congress March 2, 1807,* it is piracy and murder punishable with death, to enslave a man on the coast of Africa. By law of Congress September, 1850, it is a high crime and misdemeanor punishable with fine and imprisonment to resist the re-enslaving of a man on the coast of America. Off soundings, it is piracy and murder to enslave him. On soundings, it is fine and prison not to re-enslave. What kind of legislation is this? What kind of Constitution which covers it? And yet the crime which the second law ordains is greater than the crime which the first law forbids under

---

*Federal law that effectively ended the African slave trade by prohibiting the importation of slaves into the United States after January 1, 1808.

penalty of the gibbet. For it is a greater crime to reenslave a man who has shown himself fit for freedom, than to enslave him at first, when it might be pretended to be a mitigation of his lot as a captive in war.

4. It is contravened by the mischiefs it operates. A wicked law cannot be executed by good men, and must be by bad. Flagitious* men must be employed, and every act of theirs is a stab at the public peace. It cannot be executed at such a cost, and so it brings a bribe in its hand. This law comes with infamy in it, and out of it. It offers a bribe in its own clauses for the consummation of the crime. To serve it, low and mean people are found by the groping of the government. No government ever found it hard to pick up tools for base actions. If you cannot find them in the huts of the poor, you shall find them in the palaces of the rich. Vanity can buy some, ambition others, and money others. The first execution of the law, as was inevitable, was a little hesitating; the second was easier; and the glib officials became, in a few weeks, quite practiced and handy at stealing men.

But worse, not the officials alone are bribed, but the whole community is solicited. The scowl of the community is attempted to be averted by the mischievous whisper, "Tariff and southern market, if you will be quiet: no tariff and loss of southern market, if you dare to murmur." I wonder that our acute people who have learned that the cheapest police is dear schools, should not find out that an immoral law costs more than the loss of the custom of a southern city.

The humiliating scandal of great men warping right into wrong was followed up very fast by the cities. New York advertised in southern markets that it would go for slavery, and posted the names of merchants who would not. Boston, alarmed, entered into the same design. Philadelphia, more fortunate, had no conscience at all, and, in this auction of the rights of mankind, rescinded all its legislation against slavery. And the "Boston Advertiser," and the "Courier," in these weeks, urge the same course on the people of Massachusetts. Nothing remains in this race of roguery, but to coax Connecticut or Maine to outbid us all by adopting slavery into its constitution.

Great is the mischief of a legal crime. Every person who touches this business is contaminated. There has not been in our lifetime another moment when public men were personally lowered by their political action. But here are gentlemen whose believed probity was the confidence and fortification of multitudes, who, by fear of public opinion, or

---

*Wickedly shameful.

through the dangerous ascendency of southern manners, have been drawn into the support of this foul business. We poor men in the country who might once have thought it an honor to shake hands with them, or to dine at their boards, would now shrink from their touch, nor could they enter our humblest doors. You have a law which no man can obey, or abet the obeying, without loss of self-respect and forfeiture of the name of gentleman. What shall we say of the functionary by whom the recent rendition was made? If he has rightly defined his powers, and has no authority to try the case, but only to prove the prisoner's identity, and remand him, what office is this for a reputable citizen to hold? No man of honor can sit on that bench. It is the extension of the planter's whipping-post; and its incumbents must rank with a class from which the turnkey, the hangman, and the informer are taken, — necessary functionaries, it may be, in a state, but to whom the dislike and the ban of society universally attaches.

5. These resistances appear in the history of the statute, in the retributions which speak so loud in every part of this business, that I think a tragic poet will know how to make it a lesson for all ages.

Mr. Webster's measure was, he told us, final. It was a pacification, it was a suppression, a measure of conciliation and adjustment. These were his words at different times: "there was to be no parleying more;" it was "irrepealable." Does it look final now? His final settlement has dislocated the foundations. The state-house shakes likes a tent. His pacification has brought all the honesty in every house, all scrupulous and good-hearted men, all women, and all children, to accuse the law. It has brought United States swords into the streets, and chains round the court-house.

"A measure of pacification and union." What is its effect? To make one sole subject for conversation and painful thought throughout the continent, namely, slavery. There is not a man of thought or of feeling, but is concentrating his mind on it. There is not a clerk, but recites its statistics; not a politician, but is watching its incalculable energy in the elections; not a jurist, but is hunting up precedents; not a moralist, but is prying into its quality; not an economist, but is computing its profit and losses. Mr. Webster can judge whether this sort of solar microscope brought to bear on his law is likely to make opposition less.

The only benefit that has accrued from the law is its service to education. It has been like a university to the entire people. It has turned every dinner-table into a debating-club, and made every citizen a student of natural law. When a moral quality comes into politics, when a right is invaded, the discussion draws on deeper sources: general principles are laid bare, which cast light on the whole frame of society. And it is cheering to behold what champions the emergency called to this poor black boy; with what subtlety, what logic, what learning, what exposure of the mischief of the law, and, above all, with what earnestness and dignity the advocates of freedom were inspired. It was one of the best compensations of this calamity.

But the Nemesis works underneath again. It is a power that makes noonday dark, and draws us on to our undoing; and its dismal way is to pillory the offender in the moment of his triumph. The hands that put the chain on the slave are in that moment manacled. Who has seen anything like that which is now done?

The words of John Randolph, wiser than he knew, have been ringing ominously in all echoes for thirty years,—words spoken in the heat of the Missouri debate.* "We do not govern the people of the North by our black slaves, but by their own white slaves. We know what we are doing. We have conquered you once, and we can and will conquer you again. Aye, we will drive you to the wall, and when we have you there once more, we will keep you there and nail you down like base money." These words resounding ever since from California to Oregon, from Cape Florida to Cape Cod, come down now like the cry of Fate, in the moment when they are fulfilled. By white slaves, by a white slave, are we beaten. Who looked for such ghastly fulfilment, or to see what we see? Hills and Halletts, servile editors by the hundred, we could have spared. But him, our best and proudest, the first man of the North, in the very moment of mounting the throne, irresistibly taking the bit in his mouth and the collar on his neck, and harnessing himself to the chariot of the planters?

The fairest American fame ends in this filthy law. Mr. Webster cannot choose but to regret his loss. He must learn that those who make fame accuse him with one voice; that those who have no points to carry, that are not identical with public morals and generous civilization, that the obscure and private who have no voice and care for none, so long as things go well, but who feel the disgrace of the new legislation creeping like a miasma into their homes, and blotting the daylight,—those to whom his name was once dear and honored, as the manly statesman to whom the choicest gifts of nature had been accorded, disown him: that he who was their pride in the woods and mountains of New England, is

---

*Surrounding the passage of legislation that came to be known as the Missouri Compromise (1820–1821).

now their mortification,—they have torn down his picture from the wall, they have thrust his speeches into the chimney. No roars of New York mobs can drown this voice in Mr. Webster's ear. It will outwhisper all the salvos of the "Union Committees'" cannon. But I have said too much on this painful topic. I will not pursue that bitter history.

But passing from these ethical to the political view, I wish to place this statute, and we must use the introducer and substantial author of the bill as an illustration of the history.

I have as much charity for Mr. Webster, I think, as any one has. I need not say how much I have enjoyed his fame. Who has not helped to praise him? Simply, he was the one eminent American of our time, whom we could produce as a finished work of nature. We delighted in his form and face, in his voice, in his eloquence, in his power of labor, in his concentration, in his large understanding, in his daylight statement and simple force; the facts lay like strata of a cloud, or like the layers of the crust of the globe. He saw things as they were, and he stated them so. He has been by his clear perception and statement, in all these years, the best head in Congress, and the champion of the interests of the northern seaboard.

But as the activity and growth of slavery began to be offensively felt by his constituents, the senator became less sensitive to these evils. They were not for him to deal with: he was the commercial representative. He indulged occasionally in excellent expression of the known feeling of the New England people: but, when expected and when pledged, he omitted to speak, and he omitted to throw himself into the movement in those critical moments when his leadership would have turned the scale. At last, at a fatal hour, this sluggishness accumulated to downright counteraction, and, very unexpectedly to the whole Union, on the 7th March, 1850, in opposition to his education, association, and to all his own most explicit language for thirty years, he crossed the line, and became the head of the slavery party in this country.

Mr. Webster perhaps is only following the laws of his blood and constitution. I suppose his pledges were not quite natural to him. Mr. Webster is a man who lives by his memory, a man of the past, not a man of faith or of hope. He obeys his powerful animal nature;—and his finely developed understanding only works truly and with all its force, when it stands for animal good; that is, for property. He believes, in so many words, that government exists for the protection of property. He looks at the Union as an estate, a large farm, and is excellent in the completeness of his defence of it so far. He adheres to the letter. Happily he was born late,—after the independence had been declared, the Union agreed to, and the constitution settled. What he finds already written, he will defend. Lucky that so much had got well-written when he came. For he has no faith in the power of self-government; none whatever in extemporizing a government. Not the smallest municipal provision, if it were new, would receive his sanction. In Massachusetts, in 1776, he would, beyond all question, have been a refugee. He praises Adams and Jefferson, but it is a past Adams and Jefferson that his mind can entertain. A present Adams and Jefferson he would denounce.

So with the eulogies of liberty in his writings,—they are sentimentalism and youthful rhetoric. He can celebrate it, but it means as much from him as from Metternich or Talleyrand. This is all inevitable from his constitution. All the drops of his blood have eyes that look downward. It is neither praise nor blame to say that he has no moral perception, no moral sentiment, but in that region, to use the phrase of the phrenologists, a hole in the head. The scraps of morality to be gleaned from his speeches are reflections of the mind of others. He says what he hears said, but often makes signal blunders in their use to open the door of the sea and the fields of the earth, to extemporize government in Texas, in California, and in Oregon, and to make provisional law where statute law is not ready.

This liberalism appears in the power of invention, in the freedom of thinking, in the readiness for reforms; eagerness for novelty, even for all the follies of false science, in the antipathy to secret societies; in the predominance of the democratic party in the politics of the Union, and in the allowance of the public voice, even when irregular and vicious,—the voice of mobs, the voice of Lynch law, because it is thought to be on the whole the verdict, though badly spoken, of the greatest number. All this forwardness and self-reliance covers self-government; proceeds on the belief, that, as the people have made a government, they can make another; that their union and law are not in their memory, but in their blood and condition. If they unmake a law, they can easily make a new one. In Mr. Webster's imagination the American Union was a huge Prince Rupert's drop,* which, if so much as the smallest end be shivered off, the whole will snap into atoms. Now the fact is quite different from this. The people are loyal, law-loving, law-abiding. They prefer order, and have no taste for misrule and uproar. The destiny of this country is great and liberal, and is to be greatly administered. It is to be administered according to what is, and is to be, and not according to what is dead and gone. The Union of this people is a real thing, an alliance of

---

*Tear-drop-shaped glass ornament that can shatter easily.

men of one stock, one language, one religion, one system of manners and ideas. I hold it to be a real and not a statute Union. The people cleave to the Union, because they see their advantage in it, the added power of each.

I suppose the Union can be left to take care of itself. As much real Union as there is, the statutes will be sure to express; as much disunion as there is, no statute can long conceal. Under the Union I suppose the fact to be that there are really two nations, the north and the south. It is not slavery that severs them, it is climate and temperament. The south does not like the north, slavery or no slavery, and never did. The north likes the south well enough, for it knows its own advantages. I am willing to leave them to the facts. If they continue to have a binding interest, they will be pretty sure to find it out: if not, they will consult their peace in parting.

But one thing appears certain to me, that, as soon as the constitution ordains an immoral law, it ordains disunion. The law is suicidal, and cannot be obeyed. The Union is at an end as soon as an immoral law is enacted. And he who writes a crime into the statute-book, digs under the foundations of the Capitol to plant there a powder-magazine, and lays a train.

Nothing seems to me more hypocritical than the bluster about the Union. A year ago we were all lovers of the Union, and valued so dearly what seemed the immense destinies of this country, that we reckoned an impiety any act that compromised them. But in the new attitude in which we find ourselves the personal dishonor which now rests on every family in Massachusetts, the sentiment is changed. No man can look his neighbor in the face. We sneak about with the infamy of crime, and cowardly allowance of it on our parts, and frankly, once for all, the Union, such an Union, is intolerable. The flag is an insult to ourselves. The Union,—I give you the sentiment of every decent citizen—The Union! O yes, I prized that, other things being equal; but what is the Union to a man self-condemned, with all sense of self-respect and chance of fair fame cut off, with the names of conscience and religion become bitter ironies, and liberty the ghastly mockery which Mr. Webster means by that word. The worst mischiefs that could follow from secession and new combination of the smallest fragments of the wreck, were slight and medicable to the calamity your Union has brought us.

It did not at first appear, and it was incredible, that the passage of the law would so defeat its proposed objects: but from the day when it was attempted to be executed in Massachusetts, this result has become certain, that the Union is no longer desirable. Whose deed is that?

I pass to say a few words to the question, What shall we do?

1. What in our federal capacity is our relation to the nation?

2. And what as citizens of a state?

I am an Unionist as we all are, or nearly all, and I strongly share the hope of mankind in the power, and therefore, in the duties of the Union; and I conceive it demonstrated,—the necessity of common sense and justice entering into the laws.

What shall we do? First, abrogate this law; then, proceed to confine slavery to slave states, and help them effectually to make an end of it. Or shall we, as we are advised on all hands, lie by, and wait the progress of the census? But will Slavery lie by? I fear not. She is very industrious, gives herself no holidays. No proclamations will put her down. She got Texas, and now will have Cuba, and means to keep her majority. The experience of the past gives us no encouragement to lie by.

Shall we call a new convention, or will any expert statesman furnish us a plan for the summary or gradual winding up of slavery, so far as the Republic is its patron? Where is the South itself? Since it is agreed by all sane men of all parties—or was yesterday—that slavery is mischievous, why does the South itself never offer the smallest counsel of her own? I have never heard in twenty years any project except Mr. Clay's. Let us hear any project with candor and respect. It is impossible to speak of it with reason and good nature? It is really the project fit for this country to entertain and to accomplish.

Every thing invites emancipation. The grandeur of the design, the vast stake we hold; the national domain, the new importance of Liberia;* the manifest interest of the slave states; the religious effort of the free states; the public opinion of the world;—all join to demand it.

It is said, it will cost a thousand millions of dollars to buy the slaves,—which sounds like a fabulous price. But if a price were named in good faith,—with the other elements of a practicable treaty in readiness, and with the convictions of mankind on this mischief once well awake and conspiring, I do not think that any amount that figures could tell, founded on an estimate, would be quite unmanageable. Every man in the world might give a week's work to sweep this mountain of calamities out of the earth.

Nothing is impracticable to this nation, which it shall set itself to do.

---

*The African nation of Liberia was founded in 1821 with funds from the American Colonization Society; a number of reformers suggested black emigration to Liberia as a possible solution to conflicts over emancipation.

Were ever men so endowed, so placed, so weaponed? Their power of territory is seconded by a genius equal to every work. By new arts the earth is subdued, roaded, tunnelled, telegraphed, gas-lighted; vast amounts of old labor are disused; the sinews of man being relieved by sinews of steam. We are on the brink of more wonders. The sun paints; presently we shall organize the echo, as now we do the shadow. Chemistry is extorting new aids. The genius of this people, it is found, can do anything which can be done by men. These thirty nations are equal to any work, and are every moment stronger. In twenty-five years they will be fifty millions. Is it not time to do something besides ditching and draining, and making the earth mellow and friable? Let them confront this mountain of poison,—bore, blast, excavate, pulverize, and shovel it once for all, down into the bottomless Pit. A thousand millions were cheap.

But grant that the heart of financiers, accustomed to practical figures, shrinks within them at these colossal amounts, and the embarrassments which complicate the problem. Granting that these contingencies are too many to be spanned by any human geometry, and that these evils are to be relieved only by the wisdom of God working in ages,—and by what instruments,—whether Liberia, whether flax-cotton, whether the working out this race by Irish and Germans, none can tell, or by what scourges God has guarded his law; still the question recurs, What must we do?

One thing is plain, we cannot answer for the Union, but we must keep Massachusetts true. It is of unspeakable importance that she play her honest part. She must follow no vicious examples. Massachusetts is a little State. Countries have been great by ideas. Europe is little, compared with Asia and Africa. Yet Asia and Africa are its ox and its ass. Europe, the least of all the continents, has almost monopolized for twenty centuries the genius and power of them all. Greece was the least part of Europe. Attica* a little part of that,—one tenth of the size of Massachusetts. Yet that district still rules the intellect of men. Judæa† was a petty country. Yet these two, Greece and Judæa, furnish the mind and the heart by which the rest of the world is sustained; and Massachusetts is little, but, if true to itself, can be the brain which turns about the behemoth.

---

*Region in Greece that was ruled by the Athenians.

†Region surrounding Jerusalem where the Hebraic culture of the Old Testament developed.

I say Massachusetts, but I mean Massachusetts in all the quarters of her dispersion; Massachusetts, as she is the mother of all the New England states, and as she sees her progeny scattered over the face of the land, in the farthest South, and the uttermost West.

The immense power of rectitude is apt to be forgotten in politics. But they who have brought this great wrong on the country have not forgotten it. They avail themselves of the known probity and honor of Massachusetts, to endorse the statute. The ancient maxim still holds, that never was any injustice effected except by the help of justice. The great game of the government has been to win the sanction of Massachusetts to the crime. Hitherto they have succeeded only so far as to win Boston to a certain extent. The behavior of Boston was the reverse of what it should have been: it was supple and officious, and it put itself into the base attitude of pander to the crime. It should have placed obstruction at every step. Let the attitude of the state be firm. Let us respect the Union to all honest ends. But also respect an older and wider union, the law of nature and rectitude. Massachusetts is as strong as the Universe, when it does that. We will never intermeddle with your slavery,—but you can in no wise be suffered to bring it to Cape Cod and Berkshire.* This law must be made inoperative. It must be abrogated and wiped out of the statute-book; but whilst it stands there, it must be disobeyed.

We must make a small State great, by making every man in it true. It was the praise of Athens, "she could not lead countless armies into the field, but she knew how with a little band to defeat those who could." Every Roman reckoned himself at least a match for a province. Every Dorian did. Every Englishman in Australia, in South Africa, in India, or in whatever barbarous country their forts and factories have been set up,—represents London, represents the art, power and law of Europe. Every man educated at the northern schools carries the like advantages into the south. For it is confounding distinctions to speak of the geographic sections of this country as of equal civilization.

Every nation and every man bows, in spite of himself, to a higher mental and moral existence; and the sting of the late disgraces is that this royal position of Massachusetts was foully lost, that the well-known sentiment of her people was not expressed. Let us correct this error. In this one fastness, let truth be spoken, and right done. Here, let there be

---

*Cape Cod is a peninsula in eastern Massachusetts; the Berkshires are a mountain range in western Massachusetts.

no confusion in our ideas. Let us not lie, nor steal, nor help to steal, and let us not call stealing by any fine name, such as "union" or "patriotism." Let us know, that not by the public, but by ourselves, our safety must be bought. That is the secret of Southern power, that they rest not to meetings, but in private heats and courages. It is very certain from the perfect guaranties in the Constitution, and the high arguments of the defenders of liberty, which the occasion called out, that there is sufficient margin in the statute and the law for the spirit of the magistrate to show itself, and one, two, three occasions have just now occurred, and passed, in any of which, if one man had felt the spirit of Coke, or Mansfield, or Parsons, and read the law with the eye of freedom, the dishonor of Massachusetts had been prevented, and a limit set to these encroachments forever.

Fate[1]

Delicate omens traced in air
To the lone bard true witness bare;
Birds with auguries* on their wings
Chanted undeceiving things
Him to beckon, him to warn;
Well might then the poet scorn
To learn of scribe or courier
Hints writ in vaster character;
And on his mind, at dawn of day,
Soft shadows of the evening lay.
For the prevision is allied
Unto the thing so signified;
Or say, the foresight that awaits
Is the same Genius that creates.

IT CHANCED DURING ONE winter, a few years ago, that our cities were bent on discussing the theory of the Age. By an odd coincidence, four or five noted men were each reading a discourse to the citizens of Boston or New York, on the Spirit of the Times.[2] It so happened that the subject had the same prominence in some remarkable pamphlets and journals issued in London in the same season. To me, however, the question of the times resolves itself into a practical question of the conduct of life. How shall I live? We are incompetent to solve the times. Our geometry cannot span the huge orbits of the prevailing ideas, behold their return, and reconcile their opposition. We can only obey our own polarity. 'Tis fine for us to speculate and elect our course, if we must accept an irresistible dictation.

In our first steps to gain our wishes, we come upon immovable limitations. We are fired with the hope to reform men. After many experiments, we find that we must begin earlier,—at school. But the boys and

---

*Prophecies of future events.

girls are not docile; we can make nothing of them. We decide that they are not of good stock. We must begin our reform earlier still,—at generation: that is to say, there is Fate, or laws of the world.

But if there be irresistible dictation, this dictation understands itself. If we must accept Fate, we are not less compelled to affirm liberty, the significance of the individual, the grandeur of duty, the power of character. This is true, and that other is true. But our geometry cannot span these extreme points and reconcile them. What to do? By obeying each thought frankly, by harping, or, if you will, pounding on each string, we learn at last its power. By the same obedience to other thoughts, we learn theirs, and then comes some reasonable hope of harmonizing them. We are sure, that, though we know not how, necessity does comport with liberty, the individual with the world, my polarity with the spirit of the times. The riddle of the age has for each a private solution. If one would study his own time, it must be by this method of taking up in turn each of the leading topics which belong to our scheme of human life, and, by firmly stating all that is agreeable to experience on one, and doing the same justice to the opposing facts in the others, the true limitations will appear. Any excess of emphasis, on one part, would be corrected, and a just balance would be made.

But let us honestly state the facts. Our America has a bad name for superficialness. Great men, great nations, have not been boasters and buffoons, but perceivers of the terror of life, and have manned themselves to face it. The Spartan, embodying his religion in his country, dies before its majesty without a question. The Turk, who believes his doom is written on the iron leaf in the moment when he entered the world, rushes on the enemy's sabre with undivided will. The Turk, the Arab, the Persian, accepts the foreordained fate.

> "On two days, it steads not to run from thy grave,
>   The appointed, and the unappointed day;
>   On the first, neither balm nor physician can save,
>   Nor thee, on the second, the Universe slay."[*]

---

[*]Emerson's source is a German anthology of Persian poetry, *Geshichte der schönen Redekunste Persiens*. In his journals (*Journals and Miscellaneous Notebooks*, vol. 11, p. 103), he ascribes it to "Pindar of Rei in Cuhistan." The version given here is Emerson's translation from the German.

The Hindoo, under the wheel, is as firm. Our Calvinists, in the last generation, had something of the same dignity.* They felt that the weight of the Universe held them down to their place. What could *they* do? Wise men feel that there is something which cannot be talked or voted away,—a strap or belt which girds the world.

> "The Destiny, minister general,
>   That executeth in the world o'er all,
>   The purveyance which God hath seen beforne,
> So strong it is, that tho' the world had sworn
>   The contrary of a thing by yea or nay,
>   Yet sometime it shall fallen on a day
> That falleth not oft in a thousand year;
>   For, certainly, our appetites here,
>   Be it of war, or peace, or hate, or love,
> All this is ruled by the sight above."
>   Chaucer: *The Knight's Tale.*†

The Greek Tragedy expressed the same sense: "Whatever is fated, that will take place. The great immense mind of Jove is not to be transgressed."‡

Savages cling to a local god of one tribe or town. The broad ethics of Jesus were quickly narrowed to village theologies, which preach an election or favoritism. And now and then, an amiable parson, like Jung Stilling, or Robert Huntington,§ believes in a pistareen-Providence, which, whenever the good man wants a dinner, makes that somebody shall knock at his door, and leave a half-dollar. But Nature is no sentimentalist,—does not cosset or pamper us. We must see that the world is rough and surly, and will not mind drowning a man or a woman; but swallows your ship like a grain of dust. The cold, inconsiderate of persons, tingles your blood, benumbs your feet, freezes a man like an apple. The diseases, the elements, fortune, gravity, lightning, respect no persons. The way of Providence is a little rude. The habit of snake and spider, the

---

*Allusion to the Calvinistic belief in predestination which held that persons were either saved (the "elect") or damned (the "preterite") from birth.

†Lines 805–814.

‡From Aeschylus's *The Suppliants*, lines 1047–1049.

§Both believed that God would provide even the most basic needs for those who believed in his saving grace.

snap of the tiger and other leapers and bloody jumpers, the crackle of the bones of his prey in the coil of the anaconda,—these are in the system, and our habits are like theirs. You have just dined, and, however scrupulously the slaughter-house is concealed in the graceful distance of miles, there is complicity,—expensive races,—race living at the expense of race. The planet is liable to shocks from comets, perturbations from planets, rendings from earthquake and volcano, alterations of climate, precession of equinoxes. Rivers dry up by opening of the forest. The sea changes its bed. Towns and counties fall into it. At Lisbon, an earthquake killed men like flies. At Naples three years ago, ten thousand persons were crushed in a few minutes.* The scurvy at sea; the sword of the climate in the west of Africa, at Cayenne, at Panama, at New Orleans, cut off men like a massacre. Our western prairie shakes with fever and ague. The cholera, the small-pox, have proved as mortal to some tribes, as a frost to the crickets, which, having filled the summer with noise, are silenced by a fall of the temperature of one night. Without uncovering what does not concern us, or counting how many species of parasites hang on a bombyx;† or groping after intestinal parasites, or infusory biters, or the obscurities of alternate generation; —the forms of the sharks, the labrus,‡ the jaw of the sea-wolf paved with crushing teeth, the weapons of the grampus, and other warriors hidden in the sea,—are hints of ferocity in the interiors of nature. Let us not deny it up and down. Providence has a wild, rough, incalculable road to its end, and it is of no use to try to whitewash its huge mixed instrumentalities, or to dress up that terrific benefactor in a clean shirt and white neck-cloth of a student in divinity.

Will you say, the disasters which threaten mankind are exceptional, and one need not lay his account for cataclysms every day? Aye, but what happens once, may happen again, and so long as these strokes are not to be parried by us, they must be feared.

But these shocks and ruins are less destructive to us, than the stealthy power of other laws which act on us daily. An expense of ends to means is fate;—organization tyrannizing over character. The menagerie, or forms and powers of the spine, is a book of fate: the bill of the bird, the skull of the snake, determines tyrannically its limits. So is the scale of

---

*The Lisbon earthquake of 1755 was notorious for the devastation it caused. The earthquake at Naples occurred on December 17, 1857.

†Silkworm moth.

‡Killer whale.

races, of temperaments; so is sex; so is climate; so is the reaction of talents imprisoning the vital power in certain directions. Every spirit makes its house; but afterwards the house confines the spirit.

The gross lines are legible to the dull: the cabman is phrenologist so far: he looks in your face to see if his shilling is sure. A dome of brow denotes one thing; a pot-belly another; a squint, a pug-nose, mats of hair, the pigment of the epidermis, betray character. People seem sheathed in their tough organization. Ask Spurzheim, ask the doctor, ask Quetelet, if temperaments decide nothing? or if there be anything they do not decide? Read the description in medical books of the four temperaments,* and you will think you are reading your own thoughts which you had not yet told. Find the part which black eyes, and which blue eyes, play severally in the company. How shall a man escape from his ancestors, or draw off from his veins the black drop which he drew from his father's or his mother's life? It often appears in a family, as if all the qualities of the progenitors were potted in several jars,—some ruling quality in each son or daughter of the house,—and sometimes the unmixed temperament, the rank, unmitigated elixir, the family vice, is drawn off in a separate individual, and the others are proportionally relieved. We sometimes see a change of expression in our companion, and say, his father, or his mother, comes to the windows of his eyes, and sometimes a remote relative. In different hours a man represents each of several of his ancestors, as if there were seven or eight of us rolled up in each man's skin,—seven or eight ancestors at least,—and they constitute the variety of notes for that new piece of music which his life is. At the corner of the street, you read the possibility of each passenger, in the facial angle, in the complexion, in the depth of his eye. His parentage determines it. Men are what their mothers made them.

You may as well ask a loom which weaves huckaback,† why it does not make cashmere, as expect poetry from this engineer, or a chemical discovery from that jobber. Ask the digger in the ditch to explain Newton's laws: the fine organs of his brain have been pinched by overwork and squalid poverty from father to son, for a hundred years. When each comes forth from his mother's womb, the gate of gifts closes behind him. Let him value his hands and feet, he has but one pair. So he has but

---

*In ancient and medieval physiology, the body was said to contain four primary fluids, or humors—blood, phlegm, choler, and melancholy—that were thought to determine personality, or temperament.

†Coarse linen or cotton cloth used for toweling.

one future, and that is already predetermined in his lobes, and described in that little fatty face, pig-eyed, and squat form. All the privilege and all the legislation of the world cannot meddle or help to make a poet or a prince of him.

Jesus said, "When he looketh on her, he hath committed adultery."* But he is an adulterer before he has yet looked on the woman, by the superfluity of animal, and the defect of thought, in his constitution. Who meets him, or who meets her, in the street, sees that they are ripe to be each other's victim.

In certain men, digestion and sex absorb the vital force, and the stronger these are, the individual is so much weaker. The more of these drones perish, the better for the hive. If, later, they give birth to some superior individual, with force enough to add to this animal a new aim, and a complete apparatus to work it out, all the ancestors are gladly forgotten. Most men and most women are merely one couple more. Now and then, one has a new cell or camarilla† opened in his brain,—an architectural, a musical, or a philological knack, some stray taste or talent for flowers, or chemistry, or pigments, or story-telling, a good hand for drawing, a good foot for dancing, an athletic frame for wide journeying, etc.—which skill nowise alters rank in the scale of nature, but serves to pass the time, the life of sensation going on as before. At last, these hints and tendencies are fixed in one, or in a succession. Each absorbs so much food or force as to become itself a new centre. The new talent draws off so rapidly the vital force that not enough remains for the animal functions, hardly enough for health; so that, in the second generation, if the like genius appear, the health is visibly deteriorated, and the generative force impaired.

People are born with the moral or the material bias;—uterine brothers with this diverging destination: and I suppose, with high magnifiers, Mr. Frauenhofer or Dr. Carpenter might come to distinguish in the embryo at the fourth day, this is a Whig, and that a Free-soiler.3

It was a poetic attempt to lift this mountain of Fate, to reconcile this despotism of race with liberty, which led the Hindoos to say, "Fate is nothing but the deeds committed in a prior state of existence."‡ I find the coincidence of the extremes of eastern and western speculation in

---

*An allusion to the Bible, Matthew 5:28: ". . . whosoever looketh on a woman to lust after her hath committed adultery with her already in his heart" (KJV).

†Small room.

‡The source for this quotation about the Hindu concept of karma has not been identified.

the daring statement of Schelling, "there is in every man a certain feeling, that he has been what he is from all eternity, and by no means became such in time."* To say it less sublimely,—in the history of the individual is always an account of his condition, and he knows himself to be a party to his present estate.

A good deal of our politics is physiological. Now and then a man of wealth in the heyday of youth adopts the tenet of broadest freedom. In England, there is always some man of wealth and large connection planting himself, during all his years of health, on the side of progress, who, as soon as he begins to die, checks his forward play, calls in his troops, and becomes conservative. All conservatives are such from personal defects. They have been effeminated by position or nature, born halt and blind, through luxury of their parents, and can only, like invalids, act on the defensive. But strong natures, backwoodsmen, New Hampshire giants, Napoleons, Burkes, Broughams, Websters, Kossuths, are inevitable patriots, until their life ebbs, and their defects and gout, palsy and money, warp them.

The strongest idea incarnates itself in majorities and nations, in the healthiest and strongest. Probably, the election goes by *avoirdupois* weight, and, if you could weigh bodily the tonnage of any hundred of the Whig and the Democratic party in a town, on the Dearborn balance,† as they passed the hayscales, you could predict with certainty which party would carry it. On the whole, it would be rather the speediest way of deciding the vote, to put the selectmen or the mayor and aldermen at the hayscales.

In science, we have to consider two things: power and circumstance. All we know of the egg, from each successive discovery, is, *another vesicle;*‡ and if, after five hundred years, you get a better observer, or a better glass, he finds within the last observed another. In vegetable and animal tissue, it is just alike, and all that the primary power or spasm operates, is, still, vesicles, vesicles. Yes,—but the tyrannical Circumstance! A vesicle in new circumstances, a vesicle lodged in darkness, Oken thought, became animal; in light, a plant. Lodged in the parent animal, it suffers changes, which end in unsheathing miraculous capability in the unaltered vesicle, and it unlocks itself to fish, bird, or quadruped, head and foot, eye and claw. The Circumstance is Nature.

---

*Unidentified quotation.
†Type of scale invented by Henry Dearborn.
‡Small sac filled with fluid.

Nature is, what you may do. There is much you may not. We have two things,—the circumstance, and the life. Once we thought, positive power was all. Now we learn, that negative power, or circumstance, is half. Nature is the tyrannous circumstance, the thick skull, the sheathed snake, the ponderous, rock-like jaw; necessitated activity; violent direction; the conditions of a tool, like the locomotive, strong enough on its track, but which can do nothing but mischief off of it; or skates, which are wings on the ice, but fetters on the ground.

The book of Nature is the book of Fate. She turns the gigantic pages,—leaf after leaf,—never re-turning one. One leaf she lays down, a floor of granite; then a thousand ages, and a bed of slate; a thousand ages, and a measure of coal; a thousand ages, and a layer of marl and mud: vegetable forms appear; her first misshapen animals, zoophyte, trilobium, fish; then, saurians,—rude forms, in which she has only blocked her future statue, concealing under these unwieldy monsters the fine type of her coming king. The face of the planet cools and dries, the races meliorate, and man is born. But when a race has lived its term, it comes no more again.

The population of the world is a conditional population; not the best, but the best that could live now; and the scale of tribes, and the steadiness with which victory adheres to one tribe, and defeat to another, is as uniform as the superposition of strata. We know in history what weight belongs to race. We see the English, French, and Germans planting themselves on every shore and market of America and Australia, and monopolizing the commerce of these countries. We like the nervous and victorious habit of our own branch of the family. We follow the step of the Jew, of the Indian, of the Negro. We see how much will has been expended to extinguish the Jew, in vain. Look at the unpalatable conclusions of Knox, in his "Fragment of Races,"—a rash and unsatisfactory writer, but charged with pungent and unforgettable truths. "Nature respects race, and not hybrids." "Every race has its own *habitat.*" "Detach a colony from the race, and it deteriorates to the crab." See the shades of the picture. The German and Irish millions, like the Negro, have a great deal of guano* in their destiny. They are ferried over the Atlantic, and carted over America, to ditch and to drudge, to make corn cheap, and then to lie down prematurely to make a spot of green grass on the prairie.

One more fagot of these adamantine bandages, is, the new science of

---

*Dung of bats or seabirds, used for fertilizer.

Statistics. It is a rule, that the most casual and extraordinary events—if the basis of population is broad enough—become matter of fixed calculation. It would not be safe to say when a captain like Bonaparte, a singer like Jenny Lind, or a navigator like Bowditch, would be born in Boston: but, on a population of twenty or two hundred millions, something like accuracy may be had.*

'Tis frivolous to fix pedantically the date of particular inventions. They have all been invented over and over fifty times. Man is the arch machine, of which all these shifts drawn from himself are toy models. He helps himself on each emergency by copying or duplicating his own structure, just so far as the need is. 'Tis hard to find the right Homer, Zoroaster, or Menu; harder still to find the Tubal Cain, or Vulcan, or Cadmus, or Copernicus, or Fust, or Fulton, the indisputable inventor. There are scores and centuries of them. "The air is full of men." This kind of talent so abounds, this constructive tool-making efficiency, as if it adhered to the chemic atoms, as if the air he breathes were made of Vaucansons, Franklins, and Watts.

Doubtless, in every million there will be an astronomer, a mathematician, a comic poet, a mystic. No one can read the history of astronomy, without perceiving that Copernicus, Newton, Laplace, are not new men, or a new kind of men, but that Thales, Anaximenes, Hipparchus, Empedocles, Aristarchus, Pythagoras, Œnipodes, had anticipated them; each had the same tense geometrical brain, apt for the same vigorous computation and logic, a mind parallel to the movement of the world. The Roman mile probably rested on a measure of a degree of the meridian. Mahometan and Chinese know what we know of leap-year, of the Gregorian calendar,† and of the precession of the equinoxes. As, in every barrel of cowries, brought to New Bedford, there shall be one orangia,‡ so there will, in a dozen millions of Malays and Mahometans, be one or two astronomical skulls. In a large city, the most casual things, and things whose beauty lies in their casualty, are produced as punctually and to order as the baker's muffin for break-

---

*Everything which pertains to the human species, considered as a whole, belongs to the order of physical facts. The greater the number of individuals, the more does the influence of the individual disappear, leaving predominance to a series of general facts dependent on causes by which society exists, and is preserved.—Quetelet. (author's note).

†The modern calendar.

‡*Cowries:* common tropical marine mollusks; *orangia:* a tropical seashell of rare beauty.

fast. *Punch** makes exactly one capital joke a week; and the journals contrive to furnish one good piece of news every day.

And not less work the laws of repression, the penalties of violated functions. Famine, typhus, frost, war, suicide, and effete races, must be reckoned calculable parts of the system of the world.

These are pebbles from the mountain, hints of the terms by which our life is walled up, and which show a kind of mechanical exactness, as of a loom or mill, in what we call casual or fortuitous events.

The force with which we resist these torrents of tendency looks so ridiculously inadequate, that it amounts to little more than a criticism or a protest made by a minority of one, under compulsion of millions. I seemed, in the height of a tempest, to see men overboard struggling in the waves, and driven about here and there. They glanced intelligently at each other, but 'twas little they could do for one another; 'twas much if each could keep afloat alone. Well, they had a right to their eyebeams, and all the rest was Fate.

We cannot trifle with this reality, this cropping-out in our planted gardens of the core of the world. No picture of life can have any veracity that does not admit the odious facts. A man's power is hooped in by a necessity, which, by many experiments, he touches on every side, until he learns its arc.

The element running through entire nature, which we popularly call Fate, is known to us as limitation. Whatever limits us, we call Fate. If we are brute and barbarous, the fate takes a brute and dreadful shape. As we refine, our checks become finer. If we rise to spiritual culture, the antagonism takes a spiritual form. In the Hindoo fables, Vishnu follows Maya through all her ascending changes, from insect and crawfish up to elephant; whatever form she took, he took the male form of that kind, until she became at last woman and goddess, and he a man and a god. The limitations refine as the soul purifies, but the ring of necessity is always perched at the top.

When the gods in the Norse heaven were unable to bind the Fenris Wolf with steel or with weight of mountains,—the one he snapped and the other he spurned with his heel,—they put round his foot a limp band softer than silk or cobweb, and this held him: the more he spurned it, the stiffer it drew. So soft and so stanch is the ring of Fate. Neither brandy, nor nectar, nor sulphuric ether, nor hell-fire, nor ichor, nor po-

---

*English magazine known for its satirical cartoons.

etry, nor genius, can get rid of this limp band. For if we give it the high sense in which the poets use it, even thought itself is not above Fate: that too must act according to eternal laws, and all that is wilful and fantastic in it is in opposition to its fundamental essence.

And, last of all, high over thought, in the world of morals, Fate appears as vindicator, levelling the high, lifting the low, requiring justice in man, and always striking soon or late, when justice is not done. What is useful will last; what is hurtful will sink. "The doer must suffer," said the Greeks: "you would soothe a Deity not to be soothed." "God himself cannot procure good for the wicked," said the Welsh triad. "God may consent, but only for a time," said the bard of Spain.* The limitation is impassable by any insight of man. In its last and loftiest ascensions, insight itself, and the freedom of the will, is one of its obedient members. But we must not run into generalizations too large, but show the natural bounds or essential distinctions, and seek to do justice to the other elements as well.

Thus we trace Fate, in matter, mind, and morals,—in race, in retardations of strata, and in thought and character as well. It is everywhere bound or limitation. But Fate has its lord; limitation its limits; is different seen from above and from below; from within and from without. For, though Fate is immense, so is power, which is the other fact in the dual world, immense. If Fate follows and limits power, power attends and antagonizes Fate. We must respect Fate as natural history, but there is more than natural history. For who and what is this criticism that pries into the matter? Man is not order of nature, sack and sack, belly and members, link in a chain, nor any ignominious baggage, but a stupendous antagonism, a dragging together of the poles of the Universe. He betrays his relation to what is below him,—thick-skulled, small-brained, fishy, quadrumanous,†—quadruped ill-disguised, hardly escaped into a biped, and has paid for the new powers by loss of some of the old ones. But the lightning which explodes and fashions planets, maker of planets and suns, is in him. On one side, elemental order, sandstone and granite, rock-ledges, peat-bog, forest, sea and shore; and, on the other part, thought, the spirit which composes and decomposes nature,—here they are, side by side, god and devil, mind and matter, king

---

*These quotations from "the Greeks," "the Welsh triad," and "the bard of Spain" have not been identified.

†Having all four feet adapted as hands, as in nonhuman primates.

and conspirator, belt and spasm, riding peacefully together in the eye and brain of every man.

Nor can he blink the freewill. To hazard the contradiction,—freedom is necessary. If you please to plant yourself on the side of Fate, and say, Fate is all; then we say, a part of Fate is the freedom of man. Forever wells up the impulse of choosing and acting in the soul. Intellect annuls Fate. So far as a man thinks, he is free. And though nothing is more disgusting than the crowing about liberty by slaves, as most men are, and the flippant mistaking for freedom of some paper preamble like a "Declaration of Independence," or the statute right to vote, by those who have never dared to think or to act, yet it is wholesome to man to look not at Fate, but the other way: the practical view is the other. His sound relation to these facts is to use and command, not to cringe to them. "Look not on nature, for her name is fatal," said the oracle. The too much contemplation of these limits induces meanness. They who talk much of destiny, their birth-star, etc., are in a lower dangerous plane, and invite the evils they fear.

I cited the instinctive and heroic races as proud believers in Destiny. They conspire with it; a loving resignation is with the event. But the dogma makes a different impression, when it is held by the weak and lazy. 'Tis weak and vicious people who cast the blame on Fate. The right use of Fate is to bring up our conduct to the loftiness of nature. Rude and invincible except by themselves are the elements. So let man be. Let him empty his breast of his windy conceits, and show his lordship by manners and deeds on the scale of nature. Let him hold his purpose as with the tug of gravitation. No power, no persuasion, no bribe shall make him give up his point. A man ought to compare advantageously with a river, an oak, or a mountain. He shall have not less the flow, the expansion, and the resistance of these.

'Tis the best use of Fate to teach a fatal courage. Go face the fire at sea, or the cholera in your friend's house, or the burglar in your own, or what danger lies in the way of duty, knowing you are guarded by the cherubim of Destiny. If you believe in Fate to your harm, believe it, at least, for your good.

For, if Fate is so prevailing, man also is part of it, and can confront fate with fate. If the Universe have these savage accidents, our atoms are as savage in resistance. We should be crushed by the atmosphere, but for the reaction of the air within the body. A tube made of a film of glass can resist the shock of the ocean, if filled with the same water. If there be omnipotence in the stroke, there is omnipotence of recoil.

1. But Fate against Fate is only parrying and defence: there are, also,

the noble creative forces. The revelation of Thought takes man out of servitude into freedom. We rightly say of ourselves, we were born, and afterward we were born again, and many times. We have successive experiences so important, that the new forgets the old, and hence the mythology of the seven or the nine heavens. The day of days, the great day of the feast of life, is that in which the inward eye opens to the Unity in things, to the omnipresence of law;—sees that what is must be, and ought to be, or is the best. This beatitude dips from on high down on us, and we see. It is not in us so much as we are in it. If the air come to our lungs, we breathe and live; if not, we die. If the light come to our eyes, we see; else not. And if truth come to our mind, we suddenly expand to its dimensions, as if we grew to worlds. We are as lawgivers; we speak for Nature; we prophesy and divine.

This insight throws us on the party and interest of the Universe, against all and sundry; against ourselves, as much as others. A man speaking from insight affirms of himself what is true of the mind: seeing its immortality, he says, I am immortal; seeing its invincibility, he says, I am strong. It is not in us, but we are in it. It is of the maker, not of what is made. All things are touched and changed by it. This uses, and is not used. It distances those who share it, from those who share it not. Those who share it not are flocks and herds. It dates from itself;— not from former men or better men,—gospel, or constitution, or college, or custom. Where it shines, Nature is no longer intrusive, but all things make a musical or pictorial impression. The world of men show like a comedy without laughter:—populations, interests, government, history;—'tis all toy figures in a toy house. It does not overvalue particular truths. We hear eagerly every thought and word quoted from an intellectual man. But, in his presence, our own mind is roused to activity, and we forget very fast what he says, much more interested in the new play of our own thought, than in any thought of his. 'Tis the majesty into which we have suddenly mounted, the impersonality, the scorn of egotisms, the sphere of laws, that engage us. Once we were stepping a little this way, and a little that way; now, we are as men in a balloon, and do not think so much of the point we have left, or the point we would make, as of the liberty and glory of the way.

Just as much intellect as you add, so much organic power. He who sees through the design, presides over it, and must will that which must be. We sit and rule, and, though we sleep, our dream will come to pass. Our thought, though it were only an hour old, affirms an oldest necessity, not to be separated from thought, and not to be separated from will. They must always have coëxisted. It apprises us of its sovereignty and godhead, which refuse to be severed from it. It is not mine or thine, but the will of all mind. It is poured into the souls of all men, as the soul itself which constitutes them men. I know not whether there be, as is alleged, in the upper region of our atmosphere, a permanent westerly current, which carries with it all atoms which rise to that height, but I see, that when souls reach a certain clearness of perception, they accept a knowledge and motive above selfishness. A breath of will blows eternally through the universe of souls in the direction of the Right and Necessary. It is the air which all intellects inhale and exhale, and it is the wind which blows the worlds into order and orbit.

Thought dissolves the material universe, by carrying the mind up into a sphere where all is plastic. Of two men, each obeying his own thought, he whose thought is deepest will be the strongest character. Always one man more than another represents the will of Divine Providence to the period.

2. If thought makes free, so does the moral sentiment. The mixtures of spiritual chemistry refuse to be analyzed. Yet we can see that with the perception of truth is joined the desire that it shall prevail. That affection is essential to will. Moreover, when a strong will appears, it usually results from a certain unity of organization, as if the whole energy of body and mind flowed in one direction. All great force is real and elemental. There is no manufacturing a strong will. There must be a pound to balance a pound. Where power is shown in will, it must rest on the universal force. Alaric and Bonaparte must believe they rest on a truth, or their will can be bought or bent. There is a bribe possible for any finite will. But the pure sympathy with universal ends is an infinite force, and cannot be bribed or bent. Whoever has had experience of the moral sentiment cannot choose but believe in unlimited power. Each pulse from that heart is an oath from the Most High. I know not what the word *sublime* means, if it be not the intimations in this infant of a terrific force. A text of heroism, a name and anecdote of courage, are not arguments, but sallies of freedom. One of these is the verse of the Persian Hafiz, "'Tis written on the gate of Heaven, 'Woe unto him who suffers himself to be betrayed by Fate!'" Does the reading of history make us fatalists? What courage does not the opposite opinion show! A little whim of will to be free gallantly contending against the universe of chemistry.

But insight is not will, nor is affection will. Perception is cold, and goodness dies in wishes; as Voltaire said, 'tis the misfortune of worthy people that they are cowards; "un des plus grands malheurs des honnêtes gens c'est qu'ils sont des lâches." There must be a fusion of these two to generate the energy of will. There can be no driving force, except through the conversion of the man into his will, making him the will, and the will him. And one may say boldly, that no man has a right perception of any truth, who has not been reacted on by it, so as to be ready to be its martyr.

The one serious and formidable thing in nature is a will. Society is servile from want of will, and therefore the world wants saviours and religions. One way is right to go: the hero sees it, and moves on that aim, and has the world under him for root and support. He is to others as the world. His approbation is honor; his dissent, infamy. The glance of his eye has the force of sunbeams. A personal influence towers up in memory only worthy, and we gladly forget numbers, money, climate, gravitation, and the rest of Fate.

We can afford to allow the limitation, if we know it is the meter of the growing man. We stand against Fate, as children stand up against the wall in their father's house, and notch their height from year to year. But when the boy grows to man, and is master of the house, he pulls down that wall, and builds a new and bigger. 'Tis only a question of time. Every brave youth is in training to ride and rule this dragon. His science is to make weapons and wings of these passions and retarding forces. Now whether, seeing these two things, fate and power, we are permitted to believe in unity? The bulk of mankind believe in two gods. They are under one dominion here in the house, as friend and parent, in social circles, in letters, in art, in love, in religion: but in mechanics, in dealing with steam and climate, in trade, in politics, they think they come under another; and that it would be a practical blunder to transfer the method and way of working of one sphere, into the other. What good, honest, generous men at home, will be wolves and foxes on change! What pious men in the parlor will vote for what reprobates at the polls! To a certain point, they believe themselves the care of a Providence. But, in a steamboat, in an epidemic, in war, they believe a malignant energy rules.

But relation and connection are not somewhere and sometimes, but everywhere and always. The divine order does not stop where their sight stops. The friendly power works on the same rules, in the next farm, and the next planet. But, where they have not experience, they run against it, and hurt themselves. Fate, then, is a name for facts not yet passed under the fire of thought;—for causes which are unpenetrated.

But every jet of chaos which threatens to exterminate us, is convertible by intellect into wholesome force. Fate is unpenetrated causes. The water drowns ship and sailor, like a grain of dust. But learn to swim, trim your bark,* and the wave which drowned it, will be cloven by it, and carry it, like its own foam, a plume and a power. The cold is inconsiderate of persons, tingles your blood, freezes a man like a dew-drop. But learn to skate, and the ice will give you a graceful, sweet, and poetic motion. The cold will brace your limbs and brain to genius, and make you foremost men of time. Cold and sea will train an imperial Saxon race, which nature cannot bear to lose, and, after cooping it up for a thousand years in yonder England, gives a hundred Englands, a hundred Mexicos. All the bloods it shall absorb and domineer: and more than Mexicos,—the secrets of water and steam, the spasms of electricity, the ductility of metals, the chariot of the air, the ruddered balloon are awaiting you.

The annual slaughter from typhus far exceeds that of war; but right drainage destroys typhus. The plague in the sea-service from scurvy is healed by lemon juice and other diets portable or procurable: the depopulation by cholera and small-pox is ended by drainage and vaccination; and every other pest is not less in the chain of cause and effect, and may be fought off. And, whilst art draws out the venom, it commonly extorts some benefit from the vanquished enemy. The mischievous torrent is taught to drudge for man: the wild beasts he makes useful for food, or dress, or labor; the chemic explosions are controlled like his watch. These are now the steeds on which he rides. Man moves in all modes, by legs of horses, by wings of wind, by steam, by gas of balloon, by electricity, and stands on tiptoe threatening to hunt the eagle in his own element. There's nothing he will not make his carrier.

Steam was, till the other day, the devil which we dreaded. Every pot made by any human potter or brazier had a hole in its cover to let off the enemy, lest he should lift pot and roof, and carry the house away. But the Marquis of Worcester, Watt, and Fulton bethought themselves, that, where was power, was not devil, but was God; that it must be availed of, and not by any means let off and wasted. Could he lift pots and roofs and houses so handily? he was the workman they were in search of. He could be used to lift away, chain, and compel other devils, far more reluctant and dangerous, namely, cubic miles of earth, mountains, weight or resistance of water, machinery, and the labors of all men in the world; and time he shall lengthen, and shorten space.

It has not fared much otherwise with higher kinds of steam. The

---

*Boat.

opinion of the million was the terror of the world, and it was attempted, either to dissipate it, by amusing nations, or to pile it over with strata of society,—a layer of soldiers; over that, a layer of lords; and a king on the top; with clamps and hoops of castles, garrisons, and police. But, sometimes, the religious principle would get in, and burst the hoops, and rive every mountain laid on top of it. The Fultons and Watts of politics, believing in unity, saw that it was a power, and, by satisfying it, (as justice satisfies everybody,) through a different disposition of society,—grouping it on a level, instead of piling it into a mountain,—they have contrived to make of this terror the most harmless and energetic form of a State.

Very odious, I confess, are the lessons of Fate. Who likes to have a dapper phrenologist pronouncing on his fortunes? Who likes to believe that he has hidden in his skull, spine, and pelvis, all the vices of a Saxon or Celtic race, which will be sure to pull him down,—with what grandeur of hope and resolve is he fired,—into a selfish, huckstering, servile, dodging animal? A learned physician tells us, the fact is invariable with the Neapolitan, that, when mature, he assumes the forms of the unmistakable scoundrel. That is a little overstated,—but may pass.

But these are magazines* and arsenals. A man must thank his defects, and stand in some terror of his talents. A transcendent talent draws so largely on his forces, as to lame him; a defect pays him revenues on the other side. The sufferance, which is the badge of the Jew, has made him, in these days, the ruler of the rulers of the earth. If Fate is ore and quarry, if evil is good in the making, if limitation is power that shall be, if calamities, oppositions, and weights are wings and means,—we are reconciled.

Fate involves the melioration. No statement of the Universe can have any soundness, which does not admit its ascending effort. The direction of the whole, and of the parts, is toward benefit, and in proportion to the health. Behind every individual, closes organization: before him, opens liberty,—the Better, the Best. The first and worst races are dead. The second and imperfect races are dying out, or remain for the maturing of higher. In the latest races, in man, every generosity, every new perception, the love and praise he extorts from his fellows, are certificates of advance out of fate into freedom. Liberation of the will from the sheaths and clogs of organization which he has outgrown, is the end

---

*Storehouses for ammunition.

and aim of this world. Every calamity is a spur and a valuable hint; and where his endeavors do not fully avail, they tell as tendency.

The whole circle of animal life,—tooth against tooth,—devouring war, war for food, a yelp of pain and a grunt of triumph, until, at last, the whole menagerie, the whole chemical mass is mellowed and refined for higher use,—pleases at a sufficient perspective.

But to see how fate slides into freedom, and freedom into fate, observe how far the roots of every creature run, or find, if you can, a point where there is no thread of connection. Our line is consentaneous and far-related. This knot of nature is so well tied, that nobody was ever cunning enough to find the two ends. Nature is intricate, overlapped, interweaved, and endless. Christopher Wren said of the beautiful King's College chapel, "that, if anybody would tell him where to lay the first stone, he would build such another." But where shall we find the first atom in this house of man, which is all consent, inosculation,* and balance of parts?

The web of relation is shown in *habitat*, shown in hybernation. When hybernation was observed, it was found, that, whilst some animals became torpid in winter, others were torpid in summer. Hybernation then was a false name. The *long sleep* is not an effect of cold, but is regulated by the supply of food proper to the animal. It becomes torpid when the fruit or prey it lives on is not in season, and regains its activity when its food is ready.

Eyes are found in light; ears in auricular air; feet on land; fins in water; wings in air; and, each creature where it was meant to be, with a mutual fitness. Every zone has its own *Fauna*. There is adjustment between the animal and its food, its parasite, its enemy. Balances are kept. It is not allowed to diminish in numbers, nor to exceed. The like adjustments exist for man. His food is cooked, when he arrives; his coal in the pit; the house ventilated; the mud of the deluge dried; his companions arrive at the same hour, and awaiting him with love, concert, laughter, and tears. These are coarse adjustments, but the invisible are not less. There are more belongings to every creature than his air and his food. His instincts must be met, and he has predisposing power that bends and fits what is near him to his use. He is not possible until the invisible things are right for him, as well as the visible. Of what changes, then, in sky and earth, and in finer skies and earths, does the appearance of some Dante or Columbus apprise us?

---

*To join together by openings at the ends, as in veins and arteries.

How is this effected? Nature is no spendthrift, but takes the shortest way to her ends. As the general says to his soldiers, "if you want a fort, build a fort," so nature makes every creature do its own work and get its living,—is it planet, animal, or tree. The planet makes itself. The animal cell makes itself;—then, what it wants. Every creature,—wren or dragon,—shall make its own lair. As soon as there is life, there is self-direction, and absorbing and using of material. Life is freedom,—life in the direct ratio of its amount. You may be sure, the new-born man is not inert. Life works both voluntarily and supernaturally in its neighborhood. Do you suppose, he can be estimated by his weight in pounds, or, that he is contained in his skin,—this reaching, radiating, jaculating fellow? The smallest candle fills a mile with its rays, and the papillæ of a man run out to every star.

When there is something to be done, the world knows how to get it done. The vegetable eye makes leaf, pericarp, root, bark, or thorn, as the need is; the first cell converts itself into stomach, mouth, nose, or nail, according to the want: the world throws its life into a hero or a shepherd; and puts him where he is wanted. Dante and Columbus were Italians, in their time: they would be Russians or Americans to-day. Things ripen, new men come. The adaptation is not capricious.

The ulterior aim, the purpose beyond itself, the correlation by which planets subside and crystallize, then animate beasts and men, will not stop, but will work into finer particulars, and from finer to finest.

The secret of the world is, the tie between person and event. Person makes event, and event person. The "times," "the age," what is that, but a few profound persons and a few active persons who epitomize the times?—Goethe, Hegel, Metternich, Adams, Calhoun, Guizot, Peel, Cobden, Kossuth, Rothschild, Astor, Brunel, and the rest.

The same fitness must be presumed between a man and the time and event, as between the sexes, or between a race of animals and the food it eats, or the inferior races it uses. He thinks his fate alien, because the copula is hidden. But the soul contains the event that shall befall it, for the event is only the actualization of its thoughts; and what we pray to ourselves for is always granted. The event is the print of your form. It fits you like your skin. What each does is proper to him. Events are the children of his body and mind. We learn that the soul of Fate is the soul of us, as Hafiz sings:

> "Alas! till now I had not known,
> My guide and fortune's guide are one."

All the toys that infatuate men, and which they play for,—houses, land, money, luxury, power, fame, are the selfsame thing, with a new gauze or two of illusions overlaid. And of all the drums and rattles by which men are made willing to have their heads broke, and are led out solemnly every morning to parade,—the most admirable is this by which we are brought to believe that events are arbitrary, and independent of actions. At the conjuror's, we detect the hair by which he moves his puppet, but we have not eyes sharp enough to descry the thread that ties cause and effect.

Nature magically suits the man to his fortunes, by making these the fruit of his character. Ducks take to the water, eagles to the sky, waders to the sea margin, hunters to the forest, clerks to the counting-rooms, soldiers to the frontier. Thus events grow on the same stem with persons; are sub-persons. The pleasure of life is according to the man that lives it, and not according to the work of the place. Life is an ecstasy. We know what madness belongs to love,—what power to paint a vile object in hues of heaven. As insane persons are indifferent to their dress, diet, and other accommodations, and, as we do in dreams, with equanimity, the most absurd acts, so, a drop more of wine in our cup of life will reconcile us to strange company and work. Each creature puts forth from itself its own condition and sphere, as the slug sweats out its slimy house on the pear-leaf, and the woolly aphides on the apple perspire their own bed, and the fish its shell. In youth, we clothe ourselves with rainbows, and go as brave as the zodiac. In age, we put out another sort of perspiration,—gout, fever, rheumatism, caprice, doubt, fretting, and avarice.

A man's fortunes are the fruit of his character. A man's friends are his magnetisms. We go to Herodotus and Plutarch for examples of Fate; but we are examples. "*Quisque suos patimur manes.*"* The tendency of every man to enact all that is in his constitution is expressed in the old belief that the efforts which we make to escape from our destiny only serve to lead us into it: and I have noticed, a man likes better to be complimented on his position, as the proof of the last or total excellence, than on his merits.

A man will see his character emitted in the events that seem to meet, but which exude from and accompany him. Events expand with the character. As once he found himself among toys, so now he plays a part in colossal systems and his growth is declared in his ambition, his com-

---

*Each person undergoes his special penalty (Latin), from Virgil's *Aeneid* 6, 743.

panions, and his performance. He looks like a piece of luck, but is a piece of causation;—the mosaic, angulated and ground to fit into the gap he fills. Hence in each town there is some man who is, in his brain and performance, an explanation of the tillage, production, factories, banks, churches, ways of living, and society, of that town. If you do not chance to meet him, all that you see will leave you a little puzzled: if you see him, it will become plain. We know in Massachusetts who built New Bedford, who built Lynn, Lowell, Lawrence, Clinton, Fitchburg, Holyoke, Portland, and many another noisy mart. Each of these men, if they were transparent, would seem to you not so much men, as walking cities, and, wherever you put them, they would build one.

History is the action and reaction of these two,—Nature and Thought;—two boys pushing each other on the curb-stone of the pavement. Everything is pusher or pushed: and matter and mind are in perpetual tilt and balance so. Whilst the man is weak, the earth takes him up. He plants his brain and affections. By and by he will take up the earth, and have his gardens and vineyards in the beautiful order and productiveness of his thought. Every solid in the universe is ready to become fluid on the approach of the mind, and the power to flux it is the measure of the mind. If the wall remain adamant it accuses the want of thought. To a subtler force, it will stream into new forms, expressive of the character of the mind. What is the city in which we sit here, but an aggregate of incongruous materials, which have obeyed the will of some man? The granite was reluctant, but his hands were stronger, and it came. Iron was deep in the ground, and well combined with stone; but could not hide from his fires. Wood, lime, stuffs, fruits, gums, were dispersed over the earth and sea, in vain. Here they are, in reach of every man's day-labor,—what he wants of them. The whole world is the flux of matter over the wires of thought to the poles or points where it would build. The races of men rise out of the ground preoccupied with a thought which rules them, and divided into parties ready armed and angry to fight for this metaphysical abstraction. The quality of the thought differences the Egyptian and the Roman, the Austrian and the American. The men who come on the stage at one period are all found to be related to each other. Certain ideas are in the air. We are all impressionable, for we are made of them; all impressionable, but some more than others, and these first express them. This explains the curious contemporaneousness of invention and discoveries. The truth is in the air, and the most impressionable brain will announce it first, but all will announce it a few minutes later. So women, as most susceptible, are the best index of the coming hour. So the great man, that is, the man most imbued with the spirit of the time, is the impressionable man—of a fibre irritable and delicate, like iodine to light. He feels the infinitesimal attractions. His mind is righter than others because he yields to a current so feeble as can be felt only by a needle delicately poised.

The correlation is shown in defects. Möller, in his "Essay on Architecture," taught that the building which was fitted accurately to answer its end, would turn out to be beautiful, though beauty had not been intended. I find the like unity in human structures rather virulent and pervasive; that a crudity in the blood will appear in the argument; a hump in the shoulder will appear in the speech and handiwork. If his mind could be seen, the hump would be seen. If a man has a seesaw in his voice, it will run into his sentences, into his poem, into the structure of his fable, into his speculation, into his charity. And, as every man is hunted by his own dæmon, vexed by his own disease, this checks all his activity.

So each man, like each plant, has his parasites. A strong, astringent, bilious nature has more truculent enemies than the slugs and moths that fret my leaves. Such an one has curculios, borers, knife-worms: a swindler ate him first, then a client, then a quack, then smooth, plausible gentlemen, bitter and selfish as Moloch.

This correlation really existing can be divined. If the threads are there, thought can follow and show them. Especially when a soul is quick and docile; as Chaucer sings,

> "Or if the soul of proper kind
> Be so perfect as men find,
> That it wot what is to come,
> And that he warneth all and some
> Of every of their aventures,
> By previsions or figures;
> But that our flesh hath not might
> It to understand aright
> For it is warned too darkly."*

Some people are made up of rhyme, coincidence, omen, periodicity, and presage: they meet the person they seek; what their companion prepares to say to them, they first say to him; and a hundred signs apprise them of what is about to befall.

---

*"The House of Fame," lines 43–51.

Wonderful intricacy in the web, wonderful constancy in the design this vagabond life admits. We wonder how the fly finds its mate, and yet year after year we find two men, two women, without legal or carnal tie, spend a great part of their best time within a few feet of each other. And the moral is, that what we seek we shall find;* what we flee from flees from us; as Goethe said, "what we wish for in youth, comes in heaps on us in old age,"† too often cursed with the granting of our prayer: and hence the high caution, that, since we are sure of having what we wish, we beware to ask only for high things.

One key, one solution to the mysteries of human condition, one solution to the old knots of fate, freedom, and foreknowledge, exists, the propounding, namely, of the double consciousness. A man must ride alternately on the horses of his private and his public nature, as the equestrians in the circus throw themselves nimbly from horse to horse, or plant one foot on the back of one, and the other foot on the back of the other. So when a man is the victim of his fate, has sciatica in his loins, and cramp in his mind; a club-foot and a club in his wit; a sour face, and a selfish temper; a strut in his gait, and a conceit in his affection; or is ground to powder by the vice of his race; he is to rally on his relation to the Universe, which his ruin benefits. Leaving the dæmon who suffers, he is to take sides with the Deity who secures universal benefit by his pain.

To offset the drag of temperament and race, which pulls down, learn this lesson, namely, that by the cunning co-presence of two elements, which is throughout nature, whatever lames or paralyzes you, draws in with it the divinity, in some form, to repay. A good intention clothes itself with sudden power. When a god wishes to ride, any chip or pebble will bud and shoot out winged feet, and serve him for a horse.

Let us build altars to the Blessed Unity which holds nature and souls in perfect solution, and compels every atom to serve an universal end. I do not wonder at a snow-flake, a shell, a summer landscape, or the glory of the stars; but at the necessity of beauty under which the universe lies; that all is and must be pictorial; that the rainbow, and the curve of the horizon, and the arch of the blue vault are only results from the organism of the eye. There is no need for foolish amateurs to fetch me to admire a garden of flowers, or a sun-gilt cloud, or a waterfall, when I cannot look without seeing splendor and grace. How idle to choose a random sparkle here or there, when the indwelling necessity plants the

---

*Allusion to the Bible, Matthew 7:7: "Ask, and it shall be given you; seek, and ye shall find; knock, and it shall be opened unto you" (KJV).

†See the epigraph to the second part of Goethe's memoir *Poetry and Truth*.

rose of beauty on the brow of chaos, and discloses the central intention of Nature to be harmony and joy.

Let us build altars to the Beautiful Necessity. If we thought men were free in the sense, that, in a single exception one fantastical will could prevail over the law of things, it were all one as if a child's hand could pull down the sun. If, in the least particular, one could derange the order of nature,—who would accept the gift of life?

Let us build altars to the Beautiful Necessity, which secures all that is made of one piece; that plaintiff and defendant, friend and enemy, animal and planet, food and eater, are of one kind. In astronomy, is vast space, but no foreign system; in geology, vast time, but the same laws as to-day. Why should we be afraid of Nature, which is no other than "philosophy and theology embodied"? Why should we fear to be crushed by savage elements, we who are made up of the same elements? Let us build to the Beautiful Necessity, which makes man brave in believing that he cannot shun a danger that is appointed, nor incur one that is not; to the Necessity which rudely or softly educates him to the perception that there are no contingencies; that Law rules throughout existence, a law which is not intelligent but intelligence,—not personal nor impersonal,—it disdains words and passes understanding; it dissolves persons; it vivifies nature; yet solicits the pure in heart to draw on all its omnipotence.

Power[1]

> His tongue was framed to music,
> And his hand was armed with skill,
> His face was the mould of beauty,
> And his heart the throne of will.

THERE IS NOT YET any inventory of a man's faculties, and more than a bible of his opinions. Who shall set a limit to the influence of a human being? There are men, who, by their sympathetic attractions, carry nations with them, and lead the activity of the human race. And if there be such a tie, that, wherever the mind of man goes, nature will accompany him, perhaps there are men whose magnetisms are of that force to draw material and elemental powers, and where they appear, immense instrumentalities organize around them. Life is a search after power; and this is an element with which the earth is so saturated,—there is no chink or crevice in which it is not lodged,—that no honest seeking goes unrewarded. A man should prize events and possessions as the ore in which this fine mineral is found; and he can well afford to let events and possessions, and the breath of the body go, if their value has been added to him in the shape of power. If he have secured the elixir, he can spare the wide gardens from which it was distilled. A cultivated man, wise to know and bold to perform, is the end to which nature works, and the education of the will is the flowering and result of all this geology and astronomy. All successful men have agreed in one thing,—they were *causationists*. They believed that things went not by luck, but by law; that there was not a weak or a cracked link in the chain that joins the first and last of things. A belief in causality, or strict connection between every trifle and the principle of being, and, in consequence, belief in compensation, or, that nothing is got for nothing,—characterizes all valuable minds and must control every effort that is made by an industrious one. The most valiant men are the best believers in the tension of the laws. "All the great captains," said Bonaparte, "have performed vast achievements by conforming with the rules of the art,—by adjusting efforts to obstacles."

The key to the age may be this, or that, or the other, as the young orators describe;—the key to all ages is—Imbecility; imbecility in the vast majority of men, at all times, and, even in heroes, in all but certain eminent moments; victims of gravity, custom, and fear. This gives force to the strong,—that the multitude have no habit of self-reliance or original action.

We must reckon success a constitutional trait. Courage,—the old physicians taught, (and their meaning holds, if their physiology is a little mythical,)—courage, or the degree of life, is as the degree of circulation of blood in the arteries. "During passion, anger, fury, trials of strength, wrestling, fighting, a large amount of blood is collected in the arteries, the maintenance of bodily strength requiring it, and but little is sent into the veins. This condition is constant with intrepid persons."* Where the arteries hold their blood, is courage and adventure possible. Where they pour it unrestrained into the veins, the spirit is low and feeble. For performance of great mark, it needs extraordinary health. If Eric is in robust health, and has slept well, and is at the top of his condition, and thirty years old, at his departure from Greenland, he will steer west, and his ships will reach Newfoundland. But take out Eric, and put in a stronger and bolder man,—Biorn, or Thorfin,—and the ships will, with just as much ease, sail six hundred, one thousand, fifteen hundred miles further, and reach Labrador and New England. There is no chance in results. With adults, as with children, one class enter cordially into the game, and whirl with the whirling world; the others have cold hands, and remain bystanders; or are only dragged in by the humor and vivacity of those who can carry a dead weight. The first wealth is health. Sickness is poor-spirited, and cannot serve any one: it must husband its resources to live. But health or fulness answers its own ends, and has to spare, runs over, and inundates the neighborhoods and creeks of other men's necessities.

All power is of one kind, a sharing of the nature of the world. The mind that is parallel with the laws of nature will be in the current of events, and strong with their strength. One man is made of the same stuff of which events are made; is in sympathy with the course of things; can predict it. Whatever befalls, befalls him first; so that he is equal to whatever shall happen. A man who knows men, can talk well on poli-

---

*From Swedenborg's *The Animal Kingdom*, translated by James Garth Wilkinson, 2 vols. (Boston, 1843–1844).

tics, trade, law, war, religion. For, everywhere, men are led in the same manners.

The advantage of a strong pulse is not to be supplied by any labor, art, or concert. It is like the climate, which easily rears a crop, which no glass, or irrigation, or tillage, or manures, can elsewhere rival. It is like the opportunity of a city like New York, or Constantinople, which needs no diplomacy to force capital or genius or labor to it. They come of themselves, as the waters flow to it. So a broad, healthy, massive understanding seems to lie on the shore of unseen rivers, of unseen oceans, which are covered with barks, that, night and day, are drifted to this point. That is poured into its lap, which other men lie plotting for. It is in everybody's secret; anticipates everybody's discovery; and if it do not command every fact of the genius and the scholar, it is because it is large and sluggish, and does not think them worth the exertion which you do.

This affirmative force is in one, and is not in another, as one horse has the spring in him, and another in the whip. "On the neck of the young man," said Hafiz, "sparkles no gem so gracious as enterprise." Import into any stationary district, as into an old Dutch population in New York or Pennsylvania, or among the planters of Virginia, a colony of hardy Yankees, with seething brains, heads full of steam-hammer, pulley, crank, and toothed wheel,—and everything begins to shine with values. What enhancement to all the water and land in England, is the arrival of James Watt or Brunel! In every company, there is not only the active and passive sex, but, in both men and women, a deeper and more important *sex of mind*, namely the inventive or creative class of both men and women, and the uninventive or accepting class. Each *plus* man represents his set, and, if he have the accidental advantage of personal ascendency,—which implies neither more nor less of talent, but merely the temperamental or taming eye of a soldier or a schoolmaster, (which one has, and one has not, as one has a black moustache and one a blond,) then quite easily and without any envy or resistance all his coadjutors and feeders will admit his right to absorb them. The merchant works by bookkeeper and cashier; the lawyer's authorities are hunted up by clerks; the geologist reports the surveys of his subalterns; Commander Wilkes appropriates the results of all the naturalists attached to the Expedition; Thorwaldsen's statue is finished by stonecutters; Dumas has journeymen; and Shakspeare was theatre-manager, and used the labor of many young men, as well as the play-books.[2]

There is always room for a man of force, and he makes room for many. Society is a troop of thinkers, and the best heads among them take the best places. A feeble man can see the farms that are fenced and tilled, the houses that are built. The strong man sees the possible houses and farms. His eye makes estates, as fast as the sun breeds clouds.

When a new boy comes into school, when a man travels, and encounters strangers every day, or, when into any old club a new comer is domesticated, that happens which befalls, when a strange ox is driven into a pen or pasture where cattle are kept; there is at once a trial of strength between the best pair of horns and the new comer, and it is settled thenceforth which is the leader. So now, there is a measuring of strength, very courteous, but decisive, and an acquiescence thenceforward when these two meet. Each reads his fate in the other's eyes. The weaker party finds, that none of his information or wit quite fits the occasion. He thought he knew this or that: he finds that he omitted to learn the end of it. Nothing that he knows will quite hit the mark, whilst all the rival's arrows are good, and well thrown. But if he knew all the facts in the encyclopædia it would not help him: for this is an affair of presence of mind, of attitude, of aplomb: the opponent has the sun and wind, and, in every cast, the choice of weapon and mark; and, when he himself is matched with some other antagonist, his own shafts fly well and hit. 'Tis a question of stomach and constitution. The second man is as good as the first,—perhaps better; but has not stoutness or stomach, as the first has, and so his wit seems over-fine or under-fine.

Health is good,—power, life, that resists disease, poison, and all enemies, and is conservative, as well as creative. Here is question, every spring, whether to graft with wax, or whether with clay; whether to whitewash or to potash, or to prune; but the one point is the thrifty tree. A good tree, that agrees with the soil, will grow in spite of blight, or bug, or pruning, or neglect, by night and by day, in all weathers and all treatments. Vivacity, leadership, must be had, and we are not allowed to be nice in choosing. We must fetch the pump with dirty water, if clean cannot be had. If we will make bread, we must have contagion, yeast, emptyings, or what not, to induce fermentation into the dough: as the torpid artist seeks inspiration at any cost, by virtue or by vice, by friend or by fiend, by prayer or by wine. And we have a certain instinct, that where is great amount of life, though gross and peccant, it has its own checks and purifications, and will be bound at last in harmony with moral laws.

We watch in children with pathetic interest the degree in which they possess recuperative force. When they are hurt by us, or by each other, or go to the bottom of the class, or miss the annual prizes, or are beaten in the game,—if they lose heart, and remember the mischance in their chamber at home, they have a serious check. But if they have the buoyancy and resistance that preoccupies them with new interest in the new moment,—the wounds cicatrize,* and the fibre is the tougher for the hurt.

One comes to value this *plus* health, when he sees that all difficulties vanish before it. A timid man listening to the alarmists in Congress, and in the newspapers, and observing the profligacy of party,—sectional interests urged with a fury which shuts its eyes to consequences, with a mind made up to desperate extremities, ballot in one hand, and rifle in the other,— might easily believe that he and his country have seen their best days, and he hardens himself the best he can against the coming ruin. But, after this has been foretold with equal confidence fifty times, and government six per cents have not declined a quarter of a mill, he discovers that the enormous elements of strength which are here in play, make our politics unimportant. Personal power, freedom, and the resources of nature strain every faculty of every citizen. We prosper with such vigor, that, like thrifty trees, which grow in spite of ice, lice, mice, and borers, so we do not suffer from the profligate swarms that fatten on the national treasury. The huge animals nourish huge parasites, and the rancor of the disease attests the strength of the constitution. The same energy in the Greek *Demos*† drew the remark, that the evils of popular government appear greater than they are; there is compensation for them in the spirit and energy it awakens. The rough and ready style which belongs to a people of sailors, foresters, farmers, and mechanics, has its advantages. Power educates the potentate. As long as our people quote English standards they dwarf their own proportions. A Western lawyer‡ of eminence said to me he wished it were a penal offence to bring an English law-book into a court in this country, so pernicious had he found in his experience our deference to English precedent. The very word "commerce" has only an English meaning, and is pinched to the cramp exigencies of English experience. The commerce of rivers, the commerce of railroads, and who knows but the commerce of air-balloons, must add an American extension to the pond-hole of admiralty. As long as our people quote English standards, they will miss the sovereignty of power; but let these rough riders,—legislators in shirt-sleeves,—Hoosier, Sucker, Wolverine, Badger,§—or whatever hard head

---

*Scar over.

†Term used for the common people in ancient Greek city-states, such as Athens.

‡According to Edward W. Emerson, this "western lawyer" was Judge Halmer Hull Evans (1815–1877).

§Nicknames often used in political editorials for residents of Indiana, Illinois, Michigan, and Wisconsin, respectively.

Arkansas, Oregon, or Utah sends, half orator, half assassin, to represent its wrath and cupidity at Washington,—let these drive as they may; and the disposition of territories and public lands, the necessity of balancing and keeping at bay the snarling majorities of German, Irish and of native millions, will bestow promptness, address, and reason, at last, on our buffalo-hunter, and authority and majesty of manners. The instinct of the people is right. Men expect from good whigs, put into office by the respectability of the country, much less skill to deal with Mexico, Spain, Britain, or with our own malcontent members, than from some strong transgressor, like Jefferson, or Jackson, who first conquers his own government, and then uses the same genius to conquer the foreigner. The senators who dissented from Mr. Polk's Mexican war, were not those who knew better, but those who, from political position, could afford it; not Webster, but Benton and Calhoun.*

This power, to be sure, is not clothed in satin. 'Tis the power of Lynch law, of soldiers and pirates; and it bullies the peaceable and loyal. But it brings its own antidote; and here is my point,—that all kinds of power usually emerge at the same time; good energy, and bad; power of mind with physical health; the ecstasies of devotion, with the exasperations of debauchery. The same elements are always present, only sometimes these conspicuous, and sometimes those; what was yesterday foreground, being to-day background,—what was surface, playing now a not less effective part as basis. The longer the drought lasts, the more is the atmosphere surcharged with water. The faster the ball falls to the sun, the force to fly off is by so much augmented. And, in morals, wild liberty breeds iron conscience; natures with great impulses have great resources, and return from far. In politics, the sons of democrats will be whigs; whilst red republicanism, in the father, is a spasm of nature to engender an intolerable tyrant in the next age. On the other hand, conservatism, ever more timorous and narrow, disgusts the children, and drives them for a mouthful of fresh air into radicalism.

Those who have most of this coarse energy,—the "bruisers," who have run the gauntlet of caucus and tavern through the county or the state, have their own vices, but they have the good nature of strength and courage. Fierce and unscrupulous, they are usually frank and direct, and above falsehood. Our politics fall into bad hands, and church-

---

*Both Thomas Hart Benton and John C. Calhoun opposed President James K. Polk's war policy during the Mexican War (1846–1848), which led to the annexation of Texas, New Mexico, and California.

men and men of refinement, it seems agreed, are not fit persons to send to Congress. Politics is a deleterious profession, like some poisonous handicrafts. Men in power have no opinions, but may be had cheap for any opinion, for any purpose,—and if it be only a question between the most civil and the most forcible, I lean to the last. These Hoosiers and Suckers are really better than the snivelling opposition. Their wrath is at least of a bold and manly cast. They see, against the unanimous declarations of the people, how much crime the people will bear; they proceed from step to step, and they have calculated but too justly upon their Exellencies, the New England governors, and upon their Honors, the New England legislators. The messages of the governors and the resolutions of the legislatures, are a proverb for expressing a sham virtuous indignation, which, in the course of events, is sure to be belied.

In trade, also, this energy usually carries a trace of ferocity. Philanthropic and religious bodies do not commonly make their executive officers out of saints. The communities hitherto founded by Socialists,—the Jesuits, the Port-Royalists, the American communities at New Harmony, at Brook Farm, at Zoar,* are only possible, by installing Judas as steward. The rest of the offices may be filled by good burgesses. The pious and charitable proprietor has a foreman not quite so pious and charitable. The most amiable of country gentlemen has a certain pleasure in the teeth of the bull-dog which guards his orchard. Of the Shaker society, it was formerly a sort of proverb in the country, that they always sent the devil to market. And in representations of the Deity, painting, poetry, and popular religion have ever drawn the wrath from Hell. It is an esoteric doctrine of society, that a little wickedness is good to make muscle; as if conscience were not good for hands and legs, as if poor decayed formalists of law and order cannot run like wild goats, wolves, and conies;† that, as there is a use in medicine for poisons, so the world cannot move without rogues; that public spirit and the ready hand are as well found among the malignants. 'Tis not very rare, the coincidence of sharp private and political practice, with public spirit, and good neighborhood.

I knew a burly Boniface who for many years kept a public-house in

---

*New Harmony was a commune established on the Wabash River in Indiana. Brook Farm was a commune in West Roxbury, Massachusetts, founded by George Ripley and other transcendentalists. Zoar was another utopian community founded in Ohio by German separatists.
†Rabbits.

one of our rural capitals. He was a knave whom the town could ill spare. He was a social, vascular creature, grasping and selfish. There was no crime which he did not or could not commit. But he made good friends of the selectmen, served them with his best chop, when they supped at his house, and also with his honor the Judge, he was very cordial, grasping his hand. He introduced all the fiends, male and female, into the town, and united in his person the functions of bully, incendiary, swindler, barkeeper, and burglar. He girdled the trees, and cut off the horses' tails of the temperance people, in the night. He led the "rummies" and radicals in town-meeting with a speech. Meantime, he was civil, fat, and easy, in his house, and precisely the most public-spirited citizen. He was active in getting the roads repaired and planted with shade-trees; he subscribed for the fountains, the gas, and the telegraph; he introduced the new horse-rake, the new scraper, the baby-jumper, and what not, that Connecticut sends to the admiring citizens. He did this the easier, that the peddler stopped at his house, and paid his keeping, by setting up his new trap on the landlord's premises.

Whilst thus the energy for originating and executing work, deforms itself by excess, and so our axe chops off our own fingers,—this evil is not without remedy. All the elements whose aid man calls in, will sometimes become his masters, especially those of most subtle force. Shall he, then, renounce steam, fire, and electricity, or, shall he learn to deal with them? The rule for this whole class of agencies is,—all *plus* is good; only put it in the right place.

Men of this surcharge of arterial blood cannot live on nuts, herb-tea, and elegies; cannot read novels, and play whist; cannot satisfy all their wants at the Thursday Lecture, or the Boston Athenæum. They pine for adventure, and must go to Pike's Peak; had rather die by the hatchet of a Pawnee, than sit all day and every day at a counting-room desk. They are made for war, for the sea, for mining, hunting, and clearing; for hair-breadth adventures, huge risks, and the joy of eventful living. Some men cannot endure an hour of calm at sea. I remember a poor Malay cook, on board a Liverpool packet, who, when the wind blew a gale, could not contain his joy; "Blow!" he cried, "me do tell you, blow!" Their friends and governors must see that some vent for their explosive complexion is provided. The roisters who are destined for infamy at home, if sent to Mexico, will "cover you with glory," and come back heroes and generals. There are Oregons, Californias, and Exploring Expeditions enough appertaining to America, to find them in files to gnaw, and in crocodiles to eat. The young English are fine animals, full of blood, and when they have no wars to breathe their riotous valors in, they seek for travels as dangerous as war, diving into Maelstroms; swimming Hellesponts; wading up the snowy Himmaleh; hunting lion, rhinoceros, elephant, in South Africa; gypsying with Borrow in Spain and Algiers; riding alligators in South America with Waterton; utilizing Bedouin, Sheik, and Pacha, with Layard; yachting among the icebergs of Lancaster Sound; peeping into craters on the equator; or running on the creases of Malays in Borneo.[3]

The excess of virility has the same importance in general history, as in private and industrial life. Strong race or strong individual rests at last on natural forces, which are best in the savage, who, like the beasts around him, is still in reception of the milk from the teats of Nature. Cut off the connection between any of our works, and this aboriginal source, and the work is shallow. The people lean on this, and the mob is not quite so bad an argument as we sometimes say, for it has this good side. "March without the people," said a French deputy from the tribune, "and you march into night: their instincts are a finger-pointing of Providence, always turned toward real benefit. But when you espouse an Orleans party, or a Bourbon, or a Montalembert party,* or any other but an organic party, though you mean well, you have a personality instead of a principle, which will inevitably drag you into a corner."

The best anecdotes of this force are to be had from savage life, in explorers, soldiers, and buccaneers. But who cares for fallings-out of assassins and fights of bears, or grindings of icebergs? Physical force has no value, where there is nothing else. Snow in snow-banks, fire in volcanoes and solfataras† is cheap. The luxury of ice is in tropical countries, and midsummer days. The luxury of fire is, to have a little on our hearth: and of electricity, not volleys of the charged cloud, but the manageable stream on the battery-wires. So of spirit, or energy; the rests or remains of it in the civil and moral man, are worth all the cannibals in the Pacific.

In history, the great moment is, when the savage is just ceasing to be a savage with all his hairy Pelasgic strength directed on his opening sense of beauty:—and you have Pericles and Phidias,—not yet passed over into the Corinthian civility.‡ Everything good in nature and the world is in that moment of transition, when the swarthy juices still flow

---

*French political parties prominent during the Revolutionary and Napoleonic eras.
†Volcanic area or vent that appears in the late stages of volcanic activity.
‡The Pelasgians were an ancient people of Greece. Pericles commissioned the Greek sculptor Phidias (fifth century) to construct the Parthenon. The city of Corinth was famous for its elegance and luxury during the height of ancient Greek civilization.

plentifully from nature, but their astringency or acridity is got out by ethics and humanity.

The triumphs of peace have been in some proximity to war. Whilst the hand was still familiar with the sword-hilt, whilst the habits of the camp were still visible in the port and complexion of the gentleman, his intellectual power culminated: the compression and tension of these stern conditions is a training for the finest and softest arts, and can rarely be compensated in tranquil times, except by some analogous vigor drawn from occupations as hardy as war.

We say that success is constitutional; depends on a *plus* condition of mind and body, on power of work, on courage; that it is of main efficacy in carrying on the world, and, though rarely found in the right state for an article of commerce, but oftener in the supersaturate or excess, which makes it dangerous and destructive, yet it cannot be spared, and must be had in that form, and absorbents provided to take off its edge.

The affirmative class monopolize the homage of mankind. They originate and execute all the great feats. What a force was coiled up in the skull of Napoleon! Of the sixty thousand men making his army at Eylau, it seems some thirty thousand were thieves and burglars. The men whom, in peaceful communities, we hold if we can, with iron at their legs, in prisons, under the muskets of sentinels, this man dealt with, hand to hand, dragged them to their duty, and won his victories by their bayonets.

This aboriginal might gives a surprising pleasure when it appears under conditions of supreme refinement as in the proficients in high art. When Michel Angelo was forced to paint the Sistine Chapel in fresco, of which art he knew nothing, he went down into the Pope's gardens behind the Vatican, and with a shovel dug out ochres, red and yellow, mixed them with glue and water with his own hands, and having, after many trials, at last suited himself, climbed his ladders, and painted away, week after week, month after month, the sibyls and prophets. He surpassed his successors in rough vigor, as much as in purity of intellect and refinement. He was not crushed by his one picture left unfinished at last. Michel was wont to draw his figures first in skeleton, then to clothe them with flesh, and lastly to drape them.* "Ah!" said a brave painter to me, thinking on these things, "if a man has failed, you will

---

*Emerson knew of these anecdotes of Michelangelo from *Lives of the Most Eminent Painters and Sculptors*, by Giorgio Vasari (1511–1574).

find he has dreamed instead of working. There is no way to success in our art, but to take off your coat, grind paint, and work like a digger on the railroad, all day and every day."*

Success goes thus invariably with a certain *plus* or positive power: an ounce of power must balance an ounce of weight. And, though a man cannot return into his mother's womb, and be born with new amounts of vivacity, yet there are two economies, which are the best *succedanea*†—which the case admits. The first is, the stopping off decisively our miscellaneous activity, and concentrating our force on one or a few points; as the gardener, by severe pruning, forces the sap of the tree into one or two vigorous limbs, instead of suffering it to spindle into a sheaf of twigs.

"Enlarge not thy destiny," said the oracle: "endeavor not to do more than is given thee in charge."‡ The one prudence in life is concentration; the one evil is dissipation: and it makes no difference whether our dissipations are coarse or fine; property and its cares, friends, and a social habit, or politics, or music, or feasting. Everything is good which takes away one plaything and delusion more, and drives us home to add one stroke of faithful work. Friends, books, pictures, lower duties, talents, flatteries, hopes,—all are distractions which cause oscillations in our giddy balloon, and make a good poise and a straight course impossible. You must elect your work; you shall take what your brain can, and drop all the rest. Only so, can that amount of vital force accumulate, which can make the step from knowing to doing. No matter how much faculty of idle seeing a man has, the step from knowing to doing is rarely taken. 'Tis a step out of a chalk circle of imbecility into fruitfulness. Many an artist lacking this, lacks all: he sees the masculine Angelo or Cellini with despair. He, too, is up to Nature and the First Cause in his thought. But the spasm to collect and swing his whole being into one act, he has not. The poet Campbell said, that "a man accustomed to work was equal to any achievement he resolved on, and, that, for himself, necessity, not inspiration, was the prompter of his muse."

Concentration is the secret of strength in politics, in war, in trade, in short, in all management of human affairs. One of the high anecdotes of the world is the reply of Newton to the inquiry, "how he had been

---

*The painter is possibly Washington Allston; Emerson quotes his poem "The Paint King" in the essay "Nominalist and Realist" (see p. 275).

†Substitutes.

‡From Thomas Stanley's *History of the Chaldaick Philosophy* (1701).

able to achieve his discoveries?"—"By always intending my mind." Or if you will have a text from politics, take this from Plutarch: "There was, in the whole city, but one street in which Pericles was ever seen, the street which led to the market-place and the council house. He declined all invitations to banquets, and all gay assemblies and company. During the whole period of his administration, he never dined at the table of a friend."* Or if we seek an example from trade,—"I hope," said a good man to Rothschild, "your children are not too fond of money and business: I am sure you would not wish that."—"I am sure I should wish that: I wish them to give mind, soul, heart, and body to business,—that is the way to be happy. It requires a great deal of boldness and a great deal of caution, to make a great fortune, and when you have got it, it requires ten times as much wit to keep it. If I were to listen to all the projects proposed to me, I should ruin myself very soon. Stick to one business, young man. Stick to your brewery, (he said this to young Buxton,) and you will be the great brewer of London. Be brewer, and banker, and merchant, and manufacturer, and you will soon be in the Gazette."†

Many men are knowing, many are apprehensive and tenacious, but they do not rush to a decision. But in our flowing affairs a decision must be made,—the best, if you can; but any is better than none. There are twenty ways of going to a point, and one is the shortest; but set out at once on one. A man who has that presence of mind which can bring to him on the instant all he knows, is worth for action a dozen men who know as much, but can only bring it to light slowly. The good Speaker in the House is not the man who knows the theory of parliamentary tactics, but the man who decides off-hand. The good judge is not he who does hair-splitting justice to every allegation, but who, aiming at substantial justice, rules something intelligible for the guidance of suitors. The good lawyer is not the man who has an eye to every side and angle of contingency, and qualifies all his qualifications, but who throws himself on your part so heartily, that he can get you out of a scrape. Dr. Johnson said, in one of his flowing sentences, "Miserable beyond all names of wretchedness is that unhappy pair, who are doomed to reduce beforehand to the principles of abstract reason all the details of each

---

*Emerson took this anecdote from *Reflections on the Politics of Ancient Greece*, by German historian Arnold H. L. Heeren (1760–1842), translated by George Bancroft (1824).

†To be published as bankrupt.

domestic day. There are cases where little can be said, and much must be done."

The second substitute for temperament is drill, the power of use and routine. The hack is a better roadster than the Arab barb. In chemistry, the galvanic stream,* slow, but continuous, is equal in power to the electric spark, and is, in our arts, a better agent. So in human action, against the spasm of energy, we offset the continuity of drill. We spread the same amount of force over much time, instead of condensing it into a moment. 'Tis the same ounce of gold here in a ball, and there in a leaf. At West Point, Col. Buford, the chief engineer, pounded with a hammer on the trunnions of a cannon, until he broke them off. He fired a piece of ordnance some hundred times in swift succession, until it burst. Now which stroke broke the trunnion? Every stroke. Which blast burst the piece? Every blast. "*Diligence passe sens*," Henry VIII. was wont to say, or, great is drill. John Kemble said, that the worst provincial company of actors would go through a play better than the best amateur company. Basil Hall likes to show that the worst regular troops will beat the best volunteers. Practice is nine tenths. A course of mobs is good practice for orators. All the great speakers were bad speakers at first. Stumping it through England for seven years, made Cobden a consummate debater. Stumping it through New England for twice seven, trained Wendell Phillips. The way to learn German, is, to read the same dozen pages over and over again a hundred times, till you know every word and particle in them, and can pronounce and repeat them by heart. No genius can recite a ballad at first reading, so well as mediocrity can at the fifteenth or twentieth reading. The rule for hospitality and Irish "help," is to have the same dinner every day throughout the year. At last, Mrs. O'Shaughnessy learns to cook it to a nicety, the host learns to carve it, and the guests are well served. A humorous friend of mine thinks, that the reason why Nature is so perfect in her art, and gets up such inconceivably fine sunsets, is, that she has learned how, at last, by dint of doing the same thing so very often. Cannot one converse better on a topic on which he has experience, than on one which is new? Men whose opinion is valued on 'Change,† are only such as have a special experience, and off that ground their opinion is not valuable. "More are made good by exercitation, than by nature," said Democritus. The friction in nature is so enormous that we cannot spare any power. It is not question to ex-

---

*The direct electrical current generated by a battery.
†The stock exchange.

press our thought, to elect our way, but to overcome resistances of the medium and material in everything we do. Hence the use of drill, and the worthlessness of amateurs to cope with practitioners. Six hours every day at the piano, only to give facility of touch; six hours a day at painting, only to give command of the odious materials, oil, ochres, and brushes. The masters say, that they know a master in music, only by seeing the pose of the hands on the keys;—so difficult and vital an act is the command of the instrument. To have learned the use of tools, by thousands of manipulations; to have learned the arts of reckoning, by endless adding and dividing, is the power of the mechanic and the clerk.

I remarked in England, in confirmation of a frequent experience at home, that, in literary circles, the men of trust and consideration, bookmakers, editors, university deans and professors, bishops, too, were by no means men of the largest literary talents, but usually of a low and ordinary intellectuality, with a sort of mercantile activity and working talent. Indifferent hacks and mediocrities tower, by pushing their forces to a lucrative point, or by working power, over multitudes of superior men, in Old as in New England.

I have not forgotten that there are sublime considerations which limit the value of talent and superficial success. We can easily overpraise the vulgar hero. There are sources on which we have not drawn. I know what I abstain from. I adjourn what I have to say on this topic to the chapters on Culture and Worship.* But this force or spirit, being the means relied on by Nature for bringing the work of the day about,—as far as we attach importance to household life, and the prizes of the world, we must respect that. And I hold, that an economy may be applied to it; it is as much a subject of exact law and arithmetic as fluids and gases are; it may be husbanded, or wasted; every man is efficient only as he is a container or vessel of this force, and never was any signal act or achievement in history, but by this expenditure. This is not gold, but the gold-maker; not the fame, but the exploit.

If these forces and this husbandry are within reach of our will, and the laws of them can be read, we infer that all success, and all conceivable benefit for man, is also, first or last, within his reach, and has its own sublime economies by which it may be attained. The world is mathematical, and has no casualty, in all its vast and flowing curve. Success has no more eccentricity, than the gingham and muslin we weave

---

*"Culture" and "Worship" are the titles of essays that immediately follow "Power" in *The Conduct of Life*.

in our mills. I know no more affecting lesson to our busy, plotting New England brains, than to go into one of the factories with which we have lined all the watercourses in the States. A man hardly knows how much he is a machine, until he begins to make telegraph, loom, press, and locomotive, in his own image. But in these, he is forced to leave out his follies and hindrances, so that when we go to the mill, the machine is more moral than we. Let a man dare go to a loom, and see if he be equal to it. Let machine confront machine, and see how they come out. The world-mill is more complex than the calico-mill, and the architect stooped less. In the gingham-mill, a broken thread or a shred spoils the web through a piece of a hundred yards, and is traced back to the girl that wove it, and lessens her wages. The stock-holder, on being shown this, rubs his hands with delight. Are you so cunning, Mr. Profitloss, and do you expect to swindle your master and employer, in the web you weave? A day is a more magnificent cloth than any muslin, the mechanism that makes it is infinitely cunninger, and you shall not conceal the sleezy, fraudulent, rotten hours you have slipped into the piece, nor fear that any honest thread, or straighter steel, or more inflexible shaft, will not testify in the web.

Illusions[1]

Flow, flow the waves hated,
Accursed, adored,
The waves of mutation:
No anchorage is.
Sleep is not, death is not;
Who seem to die live.
House you were born in,
Friends of your spring-time,
Old man and young maid,
Day's toil and its guerdon,*
They are all vanishing,
Fleeing to fables,
Cannot be moored.
See the stars through them,
Through treacherous marbles.
Know, the stars yonder
The stars everlasting,
Are fugitive also,
And emulate, vaulted,
The lambent heat-lightning,
And fire-fly's light.
  When thou dost return
On the wave's circulation,
Beholding the shimmer,
The wild dissipation,
And, out of endeavor
To change and to flow,
The gas become solid,
And phantoms and nothings
Return to be things,
And endless imbroglio
Is law and the world,—

*Reward.

> Then first shalt thou know,
> That in the wild turmoil,
> Horsed on the Proteus,
> Thou ridest to power,
> And to endurance.

SOME YEARS AGO, IN company with an agreeable party, I spent a long summer day in exploring the Mammoth Cave in Kentucky.* We traversed, through spacious galleries affording a solid masonry foundation for the town and county overhead, the six or eight black miles from the mouth of the cavern to the innermost recess which tourists visit,—a niche or grotto made of one seamless stalacite, and called, I believe, Serena's Bower. I lost the light of one day. I saw high domes, and bottomless pits; heard the voice of unseen waterfalls; paddled three quarters of a mile in the deep Echo River, whose waters are peopled with the blind fish; crossed the streams "Lethe" and "Styx;"† plied with music and guns the echoes in these alarming galleries; saw every form of stalagmite and stalactite in the sculptured and fretted chambers,—icicle, orange-flower, acanthus, grapes, and snowballs. We shot Bengal lights‡ into the vaults and groins of the sparry cathedrals, and examined all the masterpieces which the four combined engineers, water, limestone, gravitation, and time, could make in the dark.

The mysteries and scenery of the cave had the same dignity that belongs to all natural objects, and which shames the fine things to which we foppishly compare them. I remarked, especially, the mimetic habit, with which Nature, on new instruments, hums her old tunes, making night to mimic day, and chemistry to ape vegetation. But I then took notice, and still chiefly remember, that the best thing which the cave had to offer was an illusion. On arriving at what is called the "Star-Chamber," our lamps were taken from us by the guide, and extinguished or put aside, and, on looking upwards, I saw or seemed to see, the night heaven thick with stars glimmering more or less brightly over our heads, and even what seemed a comet flashing among them. All the party were touched with astonishment and pleasure. Our musical

---

*In July 1850 Emerson visited Mammoth Cave in Kentucky while on a lecture tour.
†In Greek mythology, Lethe and Styx are rivers in the underworld of Hades.
‡A kind of firework.

friends sung with much feeling a pretty song, "The stars are in the quiet sky," etc., and I sat down on the rocky floor to enjoy the serene picture. Some crystal specks in the black ceiling high overhead, reflected the light of a half-hid lamp, yielding this magnificent effect.

I own I did not like the cave so well for eking out its sublimities with this theatrical trick. But I have had many experiences like it, before and since; and we must be content to be pleased without too curiously analyzing the occasions. Our conversation with Nature is not just what it seems. The cloud-rack, the sunrise and sunset glories, rainbows, and northern lights are not quite so spheral as our childhood thought them; and the part our organization plays in them is too large. The senses interfere everywhere, and mix their own structure with all they report of. Once, we fancied the earth a plane and stationary. In admiring the sunset, we do not yet deduct the rounding, coördinating, pictorial powers of the eye.

The same interference from our organization creates the most of our pleasure and pain. Our first mistake is the belief that the circumstance gives the joy which we give to the circumstance. Life is an ecstasy. Life is sweet as nitrous oxide; and the fisherman dripping all day over a cold pond, the switchman at the railway intersection, the farmer in the field, the negro in the rice-swamp, the fop in the street, the hunter in the woods, the barrister with the jury, the belle at the ball, all ascribe a certain pleasure to their employment, which they themselves give it. Health and appetite impart the sweetness to sugar, bread, and meat. We fancy that our civilization has got on far, but we still come back to our primers.

We live by our imaginations, by our admirations, by our sentiments. The child walks amid heaps of illusions, which he does not like to have disturbed. The boy, how sweet to him is his fancy! how dear the story of barons and battles! What a hero he is, whilst he feeds on his heroes! What a debt is his to imaginative books! He has no better friend or influence, than Scott, Shakspeare, Plutarch, and Homer. The man lives to other objects, but who dares affirm that they are more real? Even the prose of the streets is full of refractions. In the life of the dreariest alderman, fancy enters into all details, and colors them with rosy hue. He imitates the air and actions of people whom he admires, and is raised in his own eyes. He pays a debt quicker to a rich man than to a poor man. He wishes the bow and compliment of some leader in the state, or in society; weighs what he says; perhaps he never comes nearer to him for that, but dies at last better contented for this amusement of his eyes and his fancy.

The world rolls, the din of life is never hushed. In London, in Paris, in Boston, in San Francisco, the carnival, the masquerade is at its height. Nobody drops his domino. The unities, the fictions of the piece it would be an impertinence to break. The chapter of fascinations is very long. Great is paint; nay, God is the painter; and we rightly accuse the critic who destroys too many illusions. Society does not love its unmaskers. It was wittily, if somewhat bitterly, said by D'Alembert, "*qu'un état de vapeur était un état très fâcheux, parcequ'il nous faisait voir les choses comme elles sont.*"* I find men victims of illusion in all parts of life. Children, youths, adults, and old men, all are led by one bauble or another. Yoganidra, the goddess of illusion, Proteus, or Momus, or Gylfi's Mocking,—for the Power has many names,—is stronger than the Titans, stronger than Apollo. Few have overheard the gods, or surprised their secret. Life is a succession of lessons which must be lived to be understood. All is riddle, and the key to a riddle is another riddle. There are as many pillows of illusion as flakes in a snow-storm. We wake from one dream into another dream. The toys, to be sure, are various, and are graduated in refinement to the quality of the dupe. The intellectual man requires a fine bait; the sots are easily amused. But everybody is drugged with his own frenzy, and the pageant marches at all hours, with music and banner and badge.

Amid the joyous troop who give in to the charivari,† comes now and then a sad-eyed boy, whose eyes lack the requisite refractions to clothe the show in due glory, and who is afflicted with a tendency to trace home the glittering miscellany of fruits and flowers to one root. Science is a search after identity, and the scientific whim is lurking in all corners. At the State Fair, a friend of mine complained that all the varieties of fancy pears in our orchards seemed to have been selected by somebody who had a whim for a particular kind of pear, and only cultivated such as had that perfume; they were all alike. And I remember the quarrel of another youth with the confectioners, that, when he racked his wit to choose the best comfits in the shops, in all the endless varieties of sweet-meat he could only find three flavors, or two. What then? Pears and cakes are good for something; and because you, unluckily, have an eye or nose too keen, why need you spoil the comfort which the rest of us find in them? I knew a humorist, who, in a good deal of rattle, had a

---

*The hazy condition of things is upsetting because it makes us see things as they are (French).

†Serenade of raucous music performed in mockery.

grain or two of sense. He shocked the company by maintaining that the attributes of God were two,—power and risibility; and that it was the duty of every pious man to keep up the comedy. And I have known gentlemen of great stake in the community, but whose sympathies were cold,—presidents of colleges, and governors, and senators,—who held themselves bound to sign every temperance pledge, and act with Bible societies, and missions, and peace-makers, and cry *Hist-a-boy!* to every good dog. We must not carry comity too far, but we all have kind impulses in this direction. When the boys come into my yard for leave to gather horse-chestnuts, I own I enter into Nature's game, and affect to grant the permission reluctantly, fearing that any moment they will find out the imposture of that showy chaff. But this tenderness is quite unnecessary; the enchantments are laid on very thick. Their young life is thatched with them. Bare and grim to tears is the lot of the children in the hovel I saw yesterday; yet not the less they hung it round with frippery romance, like the children of the happiest fortune, and talked of "the dear cottage where so many joyful hours had flown." Well, this thatching of hovels is the custom of the country. Women, more than all, are the element and kingdom of illusion. Being fascinated, they fascinate. They see through Claude-Lorraines.* And how dare any one, if he could, pluck away the *coulisses*,† stage effects, and ceremonies, by which they live? Too pathetic, too pitiable, is the region of affection, and its atmosphere always liable to *mirage*.

We are not very much to blame for our bad marriages. We live amid hallucinations; and this especial trap is laid to trip up our feet with, and all are tripped up first or last. But the mighty Mother who had been so sly with us, as if she felt that she owed us some indemnity, insinuates into the Pandora-box^2 of marriage some deep and serious benefits, and some great joys. We find a delight in the beauty and happiness of children, that makes the heart too big for the body. In the worst-assorted connections there is ever some mixture of true marriage. Teague and his jade get some just relations of mutual respect, kindly observation, and fostering of each other, learn something, and would carry themselves wiselier, if they were now to begin.

'Tis fine for us to point at one or another fine madman, as if there were any exempts. The scholar in his library is none. I, who have all my life heard any number of orations and debates, read poems and miscel-

---

*Type of colored glass used by landscape painters to view a scene in subdued tones.
†Side-scenes or wings of a theatrical stage.

laneous books, conversed with many geniuses, am still the victim of any new page; and, if Marmaduke, or Hugh, or Moosehead, or any other, invent a new style or mythology, I fancy that the world will be all brave and right, if dressed in these colors, which I had not thought of. Then, at once, I will daub with this new paint; but it will not stick. 'Tis like the cement which the peddler sells at the door; he makes broken crockery hold with it, but you can never buy of him a bit of the cement which will make it hold when he is gone.

Men who make themselves felt in the world avail themselves of a certain fate in their constitution, which they know how to use. But they never deeply interest us, unless they lift a corner of the curtain, or betray never so slightly their penetration of what is behind it. 'Tis the charm of practical men, that outside of their practicality are a certain poetry and play, as if they led the good horse Power by the bridle, and preferred to walk, though they can ride so fiercely. Bonaparte is intellectual, as well as Cæsar; and the best soldiers, sea-captains, and railway men have a gentleness, when off duty; a good-natured admission that there are illusions, and who shall say that he is not their sport? We stigmatize the cast-iron fellows, who cannot so detach themselves, as "dragon-ridden," "thunder-stricken," and fools of fate, with whatever powers endowed.

Since our tuition is through emblems and indirections, 'tis well to know that there is method in it, a fixed scale, and rank above rank in the phantasms. We begin low with coarse masks, and rise to the most subtle and beautiful. The red men told Columbus, "they had an herb which took away fatigue;" but he found the illusion of "arriving from the east at the Indies" more composing to his lofty spirit than any tobacco. Is not our faith in the impenetrability of matter more sedative than narcotics? You play with jackstraws, balls, bowls, horse and gun, estates and politics; but there are finer games before you. Is not time a pretty toy? Life will show you masks that are worth all your carnivals. Yonder mountain must migrate into your mind. The fine star-dust and nebulous blur in Orion, "the portentous year of Mizar and Alcor,"* must come down and be dealt with in your household thought. What if you shall come to discern that the play and playground of all this pompous history are radiations from yourself, and that the sun borrows his beams? What terrible questions we are learning to ask! The former men believed in magic, by

---

*Allusion to astrology; Mizar and Alcor are two of the seven fixed stars in the constellation Ursa Major.

which temples, cities, and men were swallowed up, and all trace of them gone. We are coming on the secret of a magic which sweeps out of men's minds all vestige of theism and beliefs which they and their fathers held and were framed upon.

There are deceptions of the senses, deceptions of the passions, and the structural, beneficent illusions of sentiment and of the intellect. There is the illusion of love, which attributes to the beloved person all which that person shares with his or her family, sex, age, or condition, nay, with the human mind itself. 'Tis these which the lover loves, and Anna Matilda gets the credit of them. As if one shut up always in a tower, with one window, through which the face of heaven and earth could be seen, should fancy that all the marvels he beheld belonged to that window. There is the illusion of time, which is very deep; who has disposed of it? or come to the conviction that what seems the *succession* of thought is only the distribution of wholes into causal series? The intellect sees that every atom carries the whole of Nature; that the mind opens to omnipotence; that, in the endless striving and ascents, the metamorphosis is entire, so that the soul doth not know itself in its own act, when that act is perfected. There is illusion that shall deceive even the elect. There is illusion that shall deceive even the performer of the miracle. Though he make his body, he denies that he makes it. Though the world exist from thought, thought is daunted in presence of the world. One after the other we accept the mental laws, still resisting those which follow, which however must be accepted. But all our concessions only compel us to new profusion. And what avails it that science has come to treat space and time as simply forms of thought, and the material world as hypothetical, and withal our pretensions of *property* and even of self-hood are fading with the rest, if, at last, even our thoughts are not finalities; but the incessant flowing and ascension reach these also, and each thought which yesterday was a finality, to-day is yielding to a larger generalization?

With such volatile elements to work in, 'tis no wonder if our estimates are loose and floating. We must work and affirm, but we have no guess of the value of what we say or do. The cloud is now as big as your hand, and now it covers a county. That story of Thor, who was set to drain the drinking-horn in Asgard, and to wrestle with the old woman, and to run with the runner Lok, and presently found that he had been drinking up the sea, and wrestling with Time, and racing with Thought, describe us who are contending, amid these seeming trifles, with the supreme energies of Nature. We fancy we have fallen into bad company and squalid condition, low debts, shoe-bills, broken glass to pay for, pots to buy, butcher's meat, sugar, milk, and coal. "Set me some great task, ye gods! and I will show my spirit." "Not so," says the good Heaven; "plod and plow, vamp your old coats and hats, weave a shoestring; great affairs and the best wine by and by." Well, 'tis all phantasm; and if we weave a yard of tape in all humility, and as well as we can, long hereafter we shall see it was no cotton tape at all, but some galaxy which we braided, and that the threads were Time and Nature.

We cannot write the order of the variable winds. How can we penetrate the law of our shifting moods and susceptibility? Yet they differ as all and nothing. Instead of the firmament of yesterday, which our eyes require, it is to-day an eggshell which coops us in; we cannot even see what or where our stars of destiny are. From day to day, the capital facts of human life are hidden from our eyes. Suddenly the mist rolls up, and reveals them, and we think how much good time is gone that might have been saved, had any hint of these things been shown. A sudden rise in the road shows us the system of mountains, and all the summits, which have been just as near us all the year, but quite out of mind. But these alterations are not without their order, and we are parties to our various fortune. If life seem a succession of dreams, yet poetic justice is done in dreams also. The visions of good men are good; it is the undisciplined will that is whipped with bad thoughts and bad fortunes. When we break the laws, we lose our hold on the central reality. Like sick men in hospitals, we change only from bed to bed, from one folly to another; and it cannot signify much what becomes of such castaways,—wailing, stupid, comatose creatures,—lifted from bed to bed, from the nothing of life to the nothing of death.

In this kingdom of illusions we grope eagerly for stays and foundations. There is none but a strict and faithful dealing at home, and a severe barring out of all duplicity or illusion there. Whatever games are played with us, we must play no games with ourselves, but deal in our privacy with the last honesty and truth. I look upon the simple and childish virtues of veracity and honesty as the root of all that is sublime in character. Speak as you think, be what you are. Pay your debts of all kinds. I prefer to be owned as sound and solvent, and my word as good as my bond, and to be what cannot be skipped, or dissipated, or undermined, to all the *éclat* in the universe. This reality is the foundation of friendship, religion, poetry, and art. At the top or at the bottom of all illusions, I set the cheat which still leads us to work and live for appearances, in spite of our conviction, in all sane hours, that it is what we really are that avails with friends, with strangers, and with fate or fortune.

One would think from the talk of men, that riches and poverty were a great matter; and our civilization mainly respects it. But the Indians say, that they do not think the white man with his brow of care, always toiling, afraid of heat and cold, and keeping within doors, has any advantage over them. The permanent interest of every man is, never to be in a false position, but to have the weight of Nature to back him in all that he does. Riches and poverty are a thick or thin costume; and our life—the life of all of us—identical. For we transcend the circumstance continually, and taste the real quality of existence; as in our employments, which only differ in the manipulations, but express the same laws; or in our thoughts, which wear no silks, and taste no ice-creams. We see God face to face every hour, and know the savor of Nature.

The early Greek philosophers Heraclitus and Xenophanes measured their force on this problem of identity. Diogenes of Apollonia said, that unless the atoms were made of one stuff, they could never blend and act with one another. But the Hindoos, in their sacred writings, express the liveliest feeling, both of the essential identity, and of that illusion which they conceive variety to be. "The notions, '*I am*,' and '*This is mine*,' which influence mankind, are but delusions of the mother of the world. Dispel, O Lord of all creatures! the conceit of knowledge which proceeds from ignorance."* And the beatitude of man they hold to lie in being freed from fascination.

The intellect is stimulated by the statement of truth in a trope, and the will by clothing the laws of life in illusions. But the unities of Truth and of Right are not broken by the disguise. There need never be any confusion in these. In a crowded life of many parts and performers, on a stage of nations, or in the obscurest hamlet in Maine or California, the same elements offer the same choice to each new comer, and, according to his election, he fixes his fortune in absolute Nature. It would be hard to put more mental and moral philosophy than the Persians have thrown into a sentence:—

> "Fooled thou must be, though wisest of the wise:
> Then be the fool of virtue, not of vice."†

---

*From the *Vishnu Purana*, translated by H. H. Wilson (London, 1840), p. 585.
†From *Practical Philosophy of the Muhammudan People*, translated by W. F. Thompson (London, 1839), p. 95.

There is no chance, and no anarchy, in the universe. All is system and gradation. Every god is there sitting in his sphere. The young mortal enters the hall of the firmament: there is he alone with them alone, they pouring on him benedictions and gifts, and beckoning him up to their thrones. On the instant, and incessantly, fall snow-storms of illusions. He fancies himself in a vast crowd which sways this way and that, and whose movements and doings he must obey: he fancies himself poor, orphaned, insignificant. The mad crowd drives hither and thither, now furiously commanding this thing to be done, now that. What is he that he should resist their will, and think or act for himself? Every moment, new changes, and new showers of deceptions, to baffle and distract him. And when, by and by, for an instant, the air clears, and the cloud lifts a little, there are the gods still sitting around him on their thrones,—they alone with him alone.

Thoreau[1]

Henry David Thoreau was the last male descendant of a French ancestor who came to this country from the Isle of Guernsey.* His character exhibited occasional traits drawn from this blood, in singular combination with a very strong Saxon genius.

He was born in Concord, Massachusetts, on the 12th of July, 1817. He was graduated at Harvard College in 1837, but without any literary distinction. An iconoclast in literature, he seldom thanked colleges for their service to him, holding them in small esteem, whilst yet his debt to them was important. After leaving the University, he joined his brother in teaching a private school, which he soon renounced. His father was a manufacturer of lead-pencils, and Henry applied himself for a time to this craft, believing he could make a better pencil than was then in use. After completing his experiments, he exhibited his work to chemists and artists in Boston, and having obtained their certificates to its excellence and to its equality with the best London manufacture, he returned home contented. His friends congratulated him that he had now opened his way to fortune. But he replied, that he should never make another pencil. "Why should I? I would not do again what I have done once." He resumed his endless walks and miscellaneous studies, making every day some new acquaintance with Nature, though as yet never speaking of zoölogy or botany, since, though very studious of natural facts, he was incurious of technical and textual science.

At this time, a strong, healthy youth, fresh from college, whilst all his companions were choosing their profession, or eager to begin some lucrative employment, it was inevitable that his thoughts should be exercised on the same question, and it required rare decision to refuse all the accustomed paths and keep his solitary freedom at the cost of disappointing the natural expectations of his family and friends: all the more difficult that he had a perfect probity, was exact in securing his own independence, and in holding every man to the like duty. But Thoreau never faltered. He was a born protestant. He declined to give up his large ambition of knowledge and action for any narrow craft or profession,

---

*Island in the English Channel off the coast of Normandy.

415

aiming at a much more comprehensive calling, the art of living well. If he slighted and defied the opinions of others, it was only that he was more intent to reconcile his practice with his own belief. Never idle or self-indulgent, he preferred, when he wanted money, earning it by some piece of manual labor agreeable to him, as building a boat or a fence, planting, grafting, surveying, or other short work, to any long engagements. With his hardy habits and few wants, his skill in wood-craft, and his powerful arithmetic, he was very competent to live in any part of the world. It would cost him less time to supply his wants than another. He was therefore secure of his leisure.

A natural skill for mensuration, growing out of his mathematical knowledge and his habit of ascertaining the measures and distances of objects which interested him, the size of trees, the depth and extent of ponds and rivers, the height of mountains, and the air-line distance of his favorite summits,—this, and his intimate knowledge of the territory about Concord, made him drift into the profession of land-surveyor. It had the advantage for him that it led him continually into new and secluded grounds, and helped his studies of Nature. His accuracy and skill in this work were readily appreciated, and he found all the employment he wanted.

He could easily solve the problems of the surveyor, but he was daily beset with graver questions, which he manfully confronted. He interrogated every custom, and wished to settle all his practice on an ideal foundation. He was a protestant *à l'outrance,** and few lives contain so many renunciations. He was bred to no profession; he never married; he lived alone; he never went to church; he never voted; he refused to pay a tax to the State; he ate no flesh, he drank no wine, he never knew the use of tobacco; and, though a naturalist, he used neither trap nor gun. He chose, wisely no doubt for himself, to be the bachelor of thought and Nature. He had no talent for wealth, and knew how to be poor without the least hint of squalor or inelegance. Perhaps he fell into his way of living without forecasting it much, but approved it with later wisdom. "I am often reminded," he wrote in his journal, "that if I had bestowed on me the wealth of Crœsus, my aims must be still the same, and my means essentially the same."† He had no temptations to fight against,—no appetites, no passions, no taste for elegant trifles. A

---

*To the extreme (French).
†Compare H. D. Thoreau's "Conclusion" to *Walden*.

fine house, dress, the manners and talk of highly cultivated people were all thrown away on him. He much preferred a good Indian, and considered these refinements as impediments to conversation, wishing to meet his companion on the simplest terms. He declined invitations to dinner-parties, because there each was in every one's way, and he could not meet the individuals to any purpose. "They make their pride," he said, "in making their dinner cost much; I make my pride in making my dinner cost little." When asked at table what dish he preferred, he answered, "The nearest." He did not like the taste of wine, and never had a vice in his life. He said,—"I have a faint recollection of pleasure derived from smoking dried lily-stems, before I was a man. I had commonly a supply of these. I have never smoked anything more noxious."*

He chose to be rich by making his wants few, and supplying them himself. In his travels, he used the railroad only to get over so much country as was unimportant to the present purpose, walking hundreds of miles, avoiding taverns, buying a lodging in farmers' and fishermen's houses, as cheaper, and more agreeable to him, and because there he could better find the men and the information he wanted.

There was somewhat military in his nature, not to be subdued, always manly and able, but rarely tender, as if he did not feel himself except in opposition. He wanted a fallacy to expose, a blunder to pillory, I may say required a little sense of victory, a roll of the drum, to call his powers into full exercise. It cost him nothing to say No; indeed he found it much easier than to say Yes. It seemed as if his first instinct on hearing a proposition was to controvert it, so impatient was he of the limitations of our daily thought. This habit, of course, is a little chilling to the social affections; and though the companion would in the end acquit him of any malice or untruth, yet it mars conversation. Hence, no equal companion stood in affectionate relations with one so pure and guileless. "I love Henry," said one of his friends, "but I cannot like him; and as for taking his arm, I should as soon think of taking the arm of an elm-tree."†

Yet, hermit and stoic as he was, he was really fond of sympathy, and

---

*Emerson's source for these quotations has not been located; he may simply be reporting Thoreau's conversation.

†In his journals, Emerson records Elizabeth Hoar as saying, "I love Henry, but do not like him." Hoar (1814–1878), daughter of Concord lawyer Samuel Hoar, was engaged to marry Emerson's younger brother Charles, who died of tuberculosis before they could be wed; she remained a close friend of the Emerson family. The second quotation is Emerson's comment.

threw himself heartily and childlike into the company of young people whom he loved, and whom he delighted to entertain, as he only could, with the varied and endless anecdotes of his experiences by field and river: and he was always ready to lead a huckleberry-party or a search for chestnuts or grapes. Talking, one day, of a public discourse, Henry remarked, that whatever succeeded with the audience was bad. I said, "Who would not like to write something which all can read, like Robinson Crusoe? and who does not see with regret that his page is not solid with a right materialistic treatment, which delights everybody?" Henry objected, of course, and vaunted the better lectures which reached only a few persons. But, at supper, a young girl, understanding that he was to lecture at the Lyceum, sharply asked him, "Whether his lecture would be a nice, interesting story, such as she wished to hear, or whether it was one of those old philosophical things that she did not care about." Henry turned to her, and bethought himself, and, I saw, was trying to believe that he had matter that might fit her and her brother, who were to sit up and go to the lecture, if it was a good one for them.

He was a speaker and actor of the truth, born such, and was ever running into dramatic situations from this cause. In any circumstance it interested all bystanders to know what part Henry would take, and what he would say; and he did not disappoint expectation, but used an original judgment on each emergency. In 1845 he built himself a small framed house on the shores of Walden Pond, and lived there two years alone, a life of labor and study. This action was quite native and fit for him. No one who knew him would tax him with affectation. He was more unlike his neighbors in his thought than in his action. As soon as he had exhausted the advantages of that solitude, he abandoned it. In 1847,* not approving some uses to which the public expenditure was applied, he refused to pay his town tax, and was put in jail. A friend paid the tax for him, and he was released. The like annoyance was threatened the next year. But, as his friends paid the tax, notwithstanding his protest, I believe he ceased to resist. No opposition or ridicule had any weight with him. He coldly and fully stated his opinion without affecting to believe that it was the opinion of the company. It was of no consequence if every one present held the opposite opinion. On one occasion he went to the University Library to procure some books. The librarian refused to lend them. Mr. Thoreau repaired to the President, who stated to him the rules and usages, which permitted the loan of

---

*In fact, the year was 1846; the friend who paid the tax has been variously identified.

books to resident graduates, to clergymen who were alumni, and to some others resident within a circle of ten miles' radius from the College. Mr. Thoreau explained to the President that the railroad had destroyed the old scale of distances,—that the library was useless, yes, and President and College useless, on the terms of his rules,—that the one benefit he owed to the College was its library,—that, at this moment, not only his want of books was imperative but he wanted a large number of books, and assured him that he, Thoreau, and not the librarian, was the proper custodian of these. In short, the President found the petitioner so formidable, and the rules getting to look so ridiculous, that he ended by giving him a privilege which in his hands proved unlimited thereafter.

No truer American existed than Thoreau. His preference of his country and condition was genuine, and his aversation from English and European manners and tastes almost reached contempt. He listened impatiently to news or *bonmots* gleaned from London circles; and though he tried to be civil, these anecdotes fatigued him. The men were all imitating each other, and on a small mould. Why can they not live as far apart as possible, and each be a man by himself? What he sought was the most energetic nature; and he wished to go to Oregon, not to London. "In every part of Great Britain," he wrote in his diary, "are discovered traces of the Romans, their funereal urns, their camps, their roads, their dwellings. But New England, at least, is not based on any Roman ruins. We have not to lay the foundations of our houses on the ashes of a former civilization."

But, idealist as he was, standing for abolition of slavery, abolition of tariffs, almost for abolition of government, it is needless to say he found himself not only unrepresented in actual politics, but almost equally opposed to every class of reformers. Yet he paid the tribute of his uniform respect to the Anti-Slavery party. One man, whose personal acquaintance he had formed, he honored with exceptional regard. Before the first friendly word had been spoken for Captain John Brown,[2] he sent notices to most houses in Concord that he would speak in a public hall on the condition and character of John Brown, on Sunday evening, and invited all people to come. The Republican Committee, the Abolitionist Committee, sent him word that it was premature and not advisable. He replied,—"I did not send to you for advice, but to announce that I am to speak." The hall was filled at an early hour by people of all parties; and his earnest eulogy of the hero was heard by all respectfully, by many with a sympathy that surprised themselves.

It was said of Plotinus that he was ashamed of his body, and 't is very likely he had good reason for it,—that his body was a bad servant, and he had not skill in dealing with the material world, as happens often to men of abstract intellect. But Mr. Thoreau was equipped with a most adapted and serviceable body. He was of short stature, firmly built, of light complexion, with strong, serious blue eyes, and a grave aspect,—his face covered in the late years with a becoming beard. His senses were acute, his frame well-knit and hardy, his hands strong and skilful in the use of tools. And there was a wonderful fitness of body and mind. He could pace sixteen rods more accurately than another man could measure them with rod and chain. He could find his path in the woods at night, he said, better by his feet than his eyes. He could estimate the measure of a tree very well by his eye; he could estimate the weight of a calf or a pig, like a dealer. From a box containing a bushel or more of loose pencils, he could take up with his hands fast enough just a dozen pencils at every grasp. He was a good swimmer, runner, skater, boatman, and would probably outwalk most countrymen in a day's journey. And the relation of body to mind was still finer than we have indicated. He said he wanted every stride his legs made. The length of his walk uniformly made the length of his writing. If shut up in the house he did not write at all.

He had a strong common-sense, like that which Rose Flammock the weaver's daughter in Scott's romance commends in her father, as resembling a yardstick, which, whilst it measures dowlas and diaper, can equally well measure tapestry and cloth of gold. He had always a new resource. When I was planting forest trees, and had procured half a peck of acorns, he said that only a small portion of them would be sound, and proceeded to examine them and select the sound ones. But finding this took time, he said, "I think if you put them all into water the good ones will sink;" which experiment we tried with success. He could plan a garden or a house or a barn; would have been competent to lead a "Pacific Exploring Expedition;"* could give judicious counsel in the gravest private or public affairs.

He lived for the day, not cumbered and mortified by his memory. If he brought you yesterday a new proposition, he would bring you to-day another not less revolutionary. A very industrious man, and setting, like all highly organized men, a high value on his time, he seemed the only man of leisure in town, always ready for any excursion that promised well, or for conversation prolonged into late hours. His trenchant sense

---

*Most likely a reference to the expedition led by Charles Wilkes.

was never stopped by his rules of daily prudence, but was always up to the new occasion. He liked and used the simplest food, yet, when some one urged a vegetable diet, Thoreau thought all diets a very small matter, saying that "the man who shoots the buffalo lives better than the man who boards at the Graham House."* He said,—"You can sleep near the railroad, and never be disturbed: Nature knows very well what sounds are worth attending to, and has made up her mind not to hear the railroad-whistle. But things respect the devout mind, and a mental ecstacy was never interrupted." He noted what repeatedly befell him, that, after receiving from a distance a rare plant, he would presently find the same in his own haunts. And those pieces of luck which happen only to good players happened to him. One day, walking with a stranger, who inquired where Indian arrow-heads could be found, he replied, "Everywhere," and, stooping forward, picked one on the instant from the ground. At Mount Washington, in Tuckerman's Ravine, Thoreau had a bad fall, and sprained his foot. As he was in the act of getting up from his fall, he saw for the first time the leaves of the *Arnica mollis*.†

His robust common sense, armed with stout hands, keen perceptions and strong will, cannot yet account for the superiority which shone in his simple and hidden life. I must add the cardinal fact, that there was an excellent wisdom in him, proper to a rare class of men, which showed him the material world as a means and symbol. This discovery, which sometimes yields to poets a certain casual and interrupted light, serving for the ornament of their writing, was in him an unsleeping insight; and whatever faults or obstructions of temperament might cloud it, he was not disobedient to the heavenly vision. In his youth, he said, one day, "The other world is all my art; my pencils will draw no other; my jack-knife will cut nothing else; I do not use it as a means." This was the muse and genius that ruled his opinions, conversation, studies, work and course of life. This made him a searching judge of men. At first glance he measured his companion, and, though insensible to some fine traits of culture, could very well report his weight and calibre. And this made the impression of genius which his conversation sometimes gave.

He understood the matter in hand at a glance, and saw the limitations and poverty of those he talked with, so that nothing seemed concealed from such terrible eyes. I have repeatedly known young men of

---

*Boston boardinghouse run on the dietary system of Sylvester Graham.
†Medicinal plant used to treat sprains and bruises.

sensibility converted in a moment to the belief that this was the man they were in search of, the man of men, who could tell them all they should do. His own dealing with them was never affectionate, but superior, didactic, scorning their petty ways,—very slowly conceding, or not conceding at all, the promise of his society at their houses, or even at his own. "Would he not walk with them?" "He did not know. There was nothing so important to him as his walk; he had no walks to throw away on company." Visits were offered him from respectful parties, but he declined them. Admiring friends offered to carry him at their own cost to the Yellowstone River,—to the West Indies,—to South America. But though nothing could be more grave or considered than his refusals, they remind one, in quite new relations, of that fop Brummel's reply to the gentleman who offered him his carriage in a shower, "But where will *you* ride, then?"—and what accusing silences, and what searching and irresistible speeches, battering down all defenses, his companions can remember!

Mr. Thoreau dedicated his genius with such entire love to the fields, hills and waters of his native town, that he made them known and interesting to all reading Americans, and to people over the sea. The river on whose banks he was born and died he knew from its springs to its confluence with the Merrimack.* He had made summer and winter observations on it for many years, and at every hour of the day and night. The result of the recent survey of the Water Commissioners appointed by the State of Massachusetts he had reached by his private experiments, several years earlier. Every fact which occurs in the bed, on the banks, or in the air over it; the fishes, and their spawning and nests, their manners, their food; the shad-flies which fill the air on a certain evening once a year, and which are snapped at by the fishes so ravenously that many of these die of repletion; the conical heaps of small stones on the river-shallows, the huge nests of small fishes, one of which will sometimes overfill a cart; the birds which frequent the stream, heron, duck, sheldrake, loon, osprey; the snake, muskrat, otter, woodchuck and fox, on the banks; the turtle, frog, hyla and cricket, which make the banks vocal,—were all known to him, and, as it were, townsmen and fellow-creatures ; so that he felt an absurdity or violence in any narrative of one of these by itself apart, and still more of its dimensions on an inch-rule, or in the exhibition of its skeleton, or the specimen of

---

*Thoreau recorded his observations of the Concord River in his first book, *A Week on the Concord and Merrimack Rivers* (1849).

a squirrel or a bird in brandy. He liked to speak of the manners of the river, as itself a lawful creature, yet with exactness, and always to an observed fact. As he knew the river, so the ponds in this region.

One of the weapons he used, more important to him than microscope or alcohol-receiver to other investigators, was a whim which grew on him by indulgence, yet appeared in gravest statement, namely, of extolling his own town and neighborhood as the most favored centre for natural observation. He remarked that the Flora of Massachusetts embraced almost all the important plants of America,—most of the oaks, most of the willows, the best pines, the ash, the maple, the beech, the nuts. He returned Kane's "Arctic Voyage" to a friend of whom he had borrowed it, with the remark, that "Most of the phenomena noted might be observed in Concord." He seemed a little envious of the Pole, for the coincident sunrise and sunset, or five minutes' day after six months: a splendid fact, which Annursnuc* had never afforded him. He found red snow in one of his walks, and told me that he expected to find yet the *Victoria regia*† in Concord. He was the attorney of the indigenous plants, and owned to a preference of the weeds to the imported plants as of the Indian to the civilized man, and noticed, with pleasure, that the willow bean-poles of his neighbor had grown more than his beans. "See these weeds," he said, "which have been hoed at by a million farmers all spring and summer, and yet have prevailed, and just now come out triumphant over all lanes, pastures, fields and gardens, such is their vigor. We have insulted them with low names, too,—as Pigweed, Wormwood, Chickweed, Shad-blossom." He says, "They have brave names, too, — Ambrosia, Stellaria, Amelanchier, Amaranth, etc."

I think his fancy for referring everything to the meridian of Concord did not grow out of any ignorance or depreciation of other longitudes or latitudes, but was rather a playful expression of his conviction of the indifferency of all places, and that the best place for each is where he stands. He expressed it once in this wise:—"I think nothing is to be hoped from you, if this bit of mould under your feet is not sweeter to you to eat than any other in this world, or in any world."

The other weapon with which he conquered all obstacles in science was patience. He knew how to sit immovable, a part of the rock he rested on, until the bird, the reptile, the fish, which had retired from

---

*A hill in Concord.
†South American water-lily.

him, should come back and resume its habits, nay, moved by curiosity, should come to him and watch him.

It was a pleasure and a privilege to walk with him. He knew the country like a fox or a bird, and passed through it as freely by paths of his own. He knew every track in the snow or on the ground, and what creature had taken this path before him. One must submit abjectly to such a guide, and the reward was great. Under his arm he carried an old music-book to press plants; in his pocket, his diary and pencil, a spy-glass for birds, microscope, jack-knife, and twine. He wore a straw hat, stout shoes, strong gray trousers, to brave scrub-oaks and smilax, and to climb a tree for a hawk's or a squirrel's nest. He waded into the pool for the water-plants, and his strong legs were no insignificant part of his armor. On the day I speak of he looked for the Menyanthes,* detected it across the wide pool, and, on examination of the florets, decided that it had been in flower five days. He drew out of his breast-pocket his diary, and read the names of all the plants that should bloom on this day, whereof he kept account as a banker when his notes fall due. The Cypripedium† not due till to-morrow. He thought that, if waked up from a trance, in this swamp, he could tell by the plants what time of the year it was within two days. The redstart was flying about, and presently the fine grosbeaks, whose brilliant scarlet "makes the rash gazer wipe his eye,"‡ and whose fine clear note Thoreau compared to that of a tanager which has got rid of its hoarseness. Presently he heard a note which he called that of the night-warbler, a bird he had never identified, had been in search of twelve years, which always, when he saw it, was in the act of diving down into a tree or bush, and which it was vain to seek; the only bird which sings indifferently by night and by day. I told him he must beware of finding and booking it, lest life should have nothing more to show him. He said, "What you seek in vain for, half your life, one day you come full upon, all the family at dinner. You seek it like a dream, and as soon as you find it you become its prey."

His interest in the flower or the bird lay very deep in his mind, was connected with Nature,—and the meaning of Nature was never attempted to be defined by him. He would not offer a memoir of his observations to the Natural History Society. "Why should I? To detach the description from its connections in my mind would make it no longer

---

*Plant known as the bogbean or buckbean.
†Flower known as the lady's slipper.
‡Phrase from George Herbert's poem "Vertue," line 6.

true or valuable to me: and they do not wish what belongs to it." His power of observation seemed to indicate additional senses. He saw as with microscope, heard as with ear-trumpet, and his memory was a photographic register of all he saw and heard. And yet none knew better than he that it is not the fact that imports, but the impression or effect of the fact on your mind. Every fact lay in glory in his mind, a type of the order and beauty of the whole.

His determination on Natural History was organic. He confessed that he sometimes felt like a hound or a panther, and, if born among Indians, would have been a fell hunter. But, restrained by his Massachusetts culture, he played out the game in this mild form of botany and ichthyology. His intimacy with animals suggested what Thomas Fuller records of Butler the apiologist,* that "either he had told the bees things or the bees had told him." Snakes coiled round his leg; the fishes swam into his hand, and he took them out of the water; he pulled the woodchuck out of its hole by the tail and took the foxes under his protection from the hunters. Our naturalist had perfect magnanimity; he had no secrets: he would carry you to the heron's haunt, or even to his most prized botanical swamp,—possibly knowing that you could never find it again, yet willing to take his risks.

No college ever offered him a diploma, or a professor's chair; no academy made him its corresponding secretary, its discoverer, or even its member. Perhaps these learned bodies feared the satire of his presence. Yet so much knowledge of Nature's secret and genius few others possessed; none in a more large and religious synthesis. For not a particle of respect had he to the opinions of any man or body of men, but homage solely to the truth itself; and as he discovered everywhere among doctors some leaning of courtesy, it discredited them. He grew to be revered and admired by his townsmen, who had at first known him only as an oddity. The farmers who employed him as a surveyor soon discovered his rare accuracy and skill, his knowledge of their lands, of trees, of birds, of Indian remains and the like, which enabled him to tell every farmer more than he knew before of his own farm; so that he began to feel a little as if Mr. Thoreau had better rights in his land than he. They felt, too, the superiority of character which addressed all men with a native authority.

Indian relics abound in Concord,—arrow-heads, stone chisels, pestles, and fragments of pottery; and on the river-bank, large heaps of

---

*Keeper of bees.

clam-shells and ashes mark spots which the savages frequented. These, and every circumstance touching the Indian, were important in his eyes. His visits to Maine were chiefly for love of the Indian. He had the satisfaction of seeing the manufacture of the bark-canoe, as well as of trying his hand in its management on the rapids. He was inquisitive about the making of the stone arrow-head, and in his last days charged a youth setting out for the Rocky Mountains to find an Indian who could tell him that: "It was well worth a visit to California to learn it." Occasionally, a small party of Penobscot Indians would visit Concord, and pitch their tents for a few weeks in summer on the river-bank. He failed not to make acquaintance with the best of them; though he well knew that asking questions of Indians is like catechizing beavers and rabbits. In his last visit to Maine he had great satisfaction from Joseph Polis, an intelligent Indian of Oldtown, who was his guide for some weeks.

He was equally interested in every natural fact. The depth of his perception found likeness of law throughout Nature, and I know not any genius who so swiftly inferred universal law from the single fact. He was no pedant of a department. His eye was open to beauty, and his ear to music. He found these, not in rare conditions, but wheresoever he went. He thought the best of music was in single strains; and he found poetic suggestion in the humming of the telegraph-wire.

His poetry might be bad or good; he no doubt wanted a lyric facility and technical skill, but he had the source of poetry in his spiritual perception. He was a good reader and critic, and his judgment on poetry was to the ground of it. He could not be deceived as to the presence or absence of the poetic element in any composition, and his thirst for this made him negligent and perhaps scornful of superficial graces. He would pass by many delicate rhythms, but he would have detected every live stanza or line in a volume, and knew very well where to find an equal poetic charm in prose. He was so enamored of the spiritual beauty that he held all actual written poems in very light esteem in the comparison. He admired Æschylus and Pindar; but, when some one was commending them, he said that Æschylus and the Greeks, in describing Apollo and Orpheus, had given no song, or no good one. "They ought not to have moved trees, but to have chanted to the gods such a hymn as would have sung all their old ideas out of their heads, and new ones in." His own verses are often rude and defective. The gold does not yet run pure, is drossy and crude. The thyme and marjoram are not yet honey. But if he want lyric fineness and technical merits, if he have not the poetic temperament, he never lacks the causal thought, showing that his genius was better than his talent. He knew the worth of the Imagination for the uplifting and consolation of human life, and liked to throw every thought into a symbol. The fact you tell is of no value, but only the impression. For this reason his presence was poetic, always piqued the curiosity to know more deeply the secrets of his mind. He had many reserves, an unwillingness to exhibit to profane eyes what was still sacred in his own, and knew well how to throw a poetic veil over his experience. All readers of "Walden" will remember his mythical record of his disappointments:—

"I long ago lost a hound, a bay horse and a turtle-dove, and am still on their trail. Many are the travellers I have spoken concerning them, describing their tracks, and what calls they answered to. I have met one or two who have heard the hound, and the tramp of the horse, and even seen the dove disappear behind a cloud; and they seemed as anxious to recover them as if they had lost them themselves."*

His riddles were worth the reading, and I confide that if at any time I do not understand the expression, it is yet just. Such was the wealth of his truth that it was not worth his while to use words in vain. His poem entitled "Sympathy" reveals the tenderness under that triple steel of stoicism, and the intellectual subtility it could animate. His classic poem on "Smoke" suggests Simonides, but is better than any poem of Simonides. His biography is in his verses. His habitual thought makes all his poetry a hymn to the Cause of causes, the Spirit which vivifies and controls his own:—

> "I hearing get, who had but ears,
>   And sight, who had but eyes before;
> I moments live, who lived but years,
>   And truth discern, who knew but learning's lore."†

And still more in these religious lines:—

> "Now chiefly is my natal hour,
>   And only now my prime of life;
> I will not doubt the love untold,

---

*From the chapter "Economy" in *Walden*.
†This and the following quotation are from Thoreau's poem "Inspiration," but Emerson quotes the passages excerpted in the "Friday" and "Monday" chapters of *A Week on the Concord and Merrimack Rivers*.

Which not my worth nor want have bought,
Which wooed me young, and wooes me old,
And to this evening hath me brought."

Whilst he used in his writings a certain petulance of remark in reference to churches or churchmen, he was a person of a rare, tender and absolute religion, a person incapable of any profanation, by act or by thought. Of course, the same isolation which belonged to his original thinking and living detached him from the social religious forms. This is neither to be censured nor regretted. Aristotle long ago explained it, when he said, "One who surpasses his fellow-citizens in virtue is no longer a part of the city. Their law is not for him, since he is a law to himself."*

Thoreau was sincerity itself, and might fortify the convictions of prophets in the ethical laws by his holy living. It was an affirmative experience which refused to be set aside. A truth-speaker he, capable of the most deep and strict conversation; a physician to the wounds of any soul; a friend, knowing not only the secret of friendship, but almost worshipped by those few persons who resorted to him as their confessor and prophet, and knew the deep value of his mind and great heart. He thought that without religion or devotion of some kind nothing great was ever accomplished: and he thought that the bigoted sectarian had better bear this in mind.

His virtues, of course, sometimes ran into extremes. It was easy to trace to the inexorable demand on all for exact truth that austerity which made this willing hermit more solitary even than he wished. Himself of a perfect probity, he required not less of others. He had a disgust at crime, and no worldly success would cover it. He detected paltering as readily in dignified and prosperous persons as in beggars, and with equal scorn. Such dangerous frankness was in his dealing that his admirers called him "that terrible Thoreau," as if he spoke when silent, and was still present when he had departed. I think the severity of his ideal interfered to deprive him of a healthy sufficiency of human society.

The habit of a realist to find things the reverse of their appearance inclined him to put every statement in a paradox. A certain habit of antagonism defaced his earlier writings,—a trick of rhetoric not quite outgrown in his later, of substituting for the obvious word and thought its diametrical opposite. He praised wild mountains and winter forests for

---

*Emerson's source for this quotation has not been identified.

their domestic air, in snow and ice he would find sultriness, and commended the wilderness for resembling Rome and Paris. "It was so dry, that you might call it wet."

The tendency to magnify the moment, to read all the laws of Nature in the one object or one combination under your eye, is of course comic to those who do not share the philosopher's perception of identity. To him there was no such thing as size. The pond was a small ocean; the Atlantic, a large Walden Pond. He referred every minute fact to cosmical laws. Though he meant to be just, he seemed haunted by a certain chronic assumption that the science of the day pretended completeness, and he had just found out that the *savans** had neglected to discriminate a particular botanical variety, had failed to describe the seeds or count the sepals. "That is to say," we replied, "the blockheads were not born in Concord; but who said they were? It was their unspeakable misfortune to be born in London, or Paris, or Rome; but, poor fellows, they did what they could, considering that they never saw Bateman's Pond, or Nine-Acre Corner, or Becky Stow's Swamp; besides, what were you sent into the world for, but to add this observation?"

Had his genius been only contemplative, he had been fitted to his life, but with his energy and practical ability he seemed born for great enterprise and for command; and I so much regret the loss of his rare powers of action, that I cannot help counting it a fault in him that he had no ambition. Wanting this, instead of engineering for all America, he was the captain of a huckleberry-party. Pounding beans is good to the end of pounding empires one of these days; but if, at the end of years, it is still only beans!

But these foibles, real or apparent, were fast vanishing in the incessant growth of a spirit so robust and wise, and which effaced its defeats with new triumphs. His study of Nature was a perpetual ornament to him, and inspired his friends with curiosity to see the world through his eyes, and to hear his adventures. They possessed every kind of interest.

He had many elegancies of his own, whilst he scoffed at conventional elegance. Thus, he could not bear to hear the sound of his own steps, the grit of gravel; and therefore never willingly walked in the road, but in the grass, on mountains and in woods. His senses were acute, and he remarked that by night every dwelling-house gives out bad air, like a slaughter-house. He liked the pure fragrance of melilot.† He honored

---

*Learned, or scholarly ones (French).
†Sweet clover.

certain plants with special regard, and, over all, the pond-lily,—then, the gentian, and the *Mikania scandens*,* and "life-everlasting," and a bass-tree which he visited every year when it bloomed, in the middle of July. He thought the scent a more oracular inquisition than the sight,—more oracular and trustworthy. The scent, of course, reveals what is concealed from the other senses. By it he detected earthiness. He delighted in echoes, and said they were almost the only kind of kindred voices that he heard. He loved Nature so well, was so happy in her solitude, that he became very jealous of cities and the sad work which their refinements and artifices made with man and his dwelling. The axe was always destroying his forest. "Thank God," he said, "they cannot cut down the clouds!" "All kinds of figures are drawn on the blue ground with this fibrous white paint."

I subjoin a few sentences taken from his unpublished manuscripts, not only as records of his thought and feeling, but for their power of description and literary excellence:—

"Some circumstantial evidence is very strong, as when you find a trout in the milk."

"The chub is a soft fish, and tastes like boiled brown paper salted."

"The youth gets together his materials to build a bridge to the moon, or, perchance, a palace or temple on the earth, and, at length the middle-aged man concludes to build a wood-shed with them."

"The locust z-ing."

"Devil's-needles zigzagging along the Nut-Meadow brook."

"Sugar is not so sweet to the palate as sound to the healthy ear."

"I put on some hemlock-boughs, and the rich salt crackling of their leaves was like mustard to the ear, the crackling of uncountable regiments. Dead trees love the fire."

"The bluebird carries the sky on his back."

"The tanager flies through the green foliage as if it would ignite the leaves."

"If I wish for a horse-hair for my compass-sight I must go to the stable; but the hair-bird, with her sharp eyes, goes to the road."

"Immortal water, alive even to the superficies."

"Fire is the most tolerable third party."

"Nature made ferns for pure leaves, to show what she could do in that line."

"No tree has so fair a bole and so handsome an instep as the beech."

---

*Climbing vine known as climbing hempweed.

"How did these beautiful rainbow-tints get into the shell of the fresh-water clam, buried in the mud at the bottom of our dark river?"

"Hard are the times when the infant's shoes are second-foot."

"We are strictly confined to our men to whom we give liberty."

"Nothing is so much to be feared as fear. Atheism may comparatively be popular with God himself."

"Of what significance the things you can forget? A little thought is sexton to all the world."

"How can we expect a harvest of thought who have not had a seed-time of character?"

"Only he can be trusted with gifts who can present a face of bronze to expectations."

"I ask to be melted. You can only ask of the metals that they be tender to the fire that melts them. To nought else can they be tender."

There is a flower known to botanists, one of the same genus with our summer plant called "Life-Everlasting," a *Gnaphalium* like that, which grows on the most inaccessible cliffs of the Tyrolese mountains, where the chamois dare hardly venture, and which the hunter, tempted by its beauty, and by his love (for it is immensely valued by the Swiss maidens), climbs the cliffs to gather, and is sometimes found dead at the foot, with the flower in his hand. It is called by botanists the *Gnaphalium leontopodium*, but by the Swiss *Edelweisse*, which signifies *Noble Purity*. Thoreau seemed to me living in the hope to gather this plant, which belonged to him of right. The scale on which his studies proceeded was so large as to require longevity, and we were the less prepared for his sudden disappearance. The country knows not yet, or in the least part, how great a son it has lost. It seems an injury that he should leave in the midst his broken task which none else can finish, a kind of indignity to so noble a soul that he should depart out of Nature before yet he has been really shown to his peers for what he is. But he, at least, is content. His soul was made for the noblest society; he had in a short life exhausted the capabilities of this world; wherever there is knowledge, wherever there is virtue, wherever there is beauty, he will find a home.

POEMS

Each and All

Little thinks, in the field, yon red-cloaked clown*
Of thee from the hill-top looking down;
The heifer that lows in the upland farm,
Far-heard, lows not thine ear to charm;
The sexton, tolling his bell at noon,
Deems not that great Napoleon
Stops his horse, and lists with delight,
Whilst his files sweep round yon Alpine height;
Nor knowest thou what argument
Thy life to thy neighbor's creed has lent.
All are needed by each one;
Nothing is fair or good alone.
I thought the sparrow's note from heaven,
Singing at dawn on the alder bough;
I brought him home, in his nest, at even;†
He sings the song, but it cheers not now,
For I did not bring home the river and sky;—
He sang to my ear,—they sang to my eye.
The delicate shells lay on the shore;
The bubbles of the latest wave
Fresh pearls to their enamel gave,
And the bellowing of the savage sea
Greeted their safe escape to me.
I wiped away the weeds and foam,
I fetched my sea-born treasures home;
But the poor, unsightly, noisome things
Had left their beauty on the shore
With the sun and the sand and the wild uproar.
The lover watched his graceful maid,
As 'mid the virgin train she strayed,
Nor knew her beauty's best attire

---

*Farmer.
†Evening.

Was woven still by the snow-white choir.
At last she came to his hermitage,
Like the bird from the woodlands to the cage;—
The gay enchantment was undone,
A gentle wife, but fairy none.
Then I said, 'I covet truth;
Beauty is unripe childhood's cheat;
I leave it behind with the games of youth:'—
As I spoke, beneath my feet
The ground-pine curled its pretty wreath,
Running over the club-moss burrs;
I inhaled the violet's breath;
Around me stood the oaks and firs;
Pine-cones and acorns lay on the ground;
Over me soared the eternal sky,
Full of light and of deity;
Again I saw, again I heard,
The rolling river, the morning bird;—
Beauty through my senses stole;
I yielded myself to the perfect whole.

The Problem

I like a church; I like a cowl;
I love a prophet of the soul;
And on my heart monastic aisles
Fall like sweet strains, or pensive smiles;
Yet not for all his faith can see
Would I that cowlèd churchman be.

Why should the vest on him allure,
Which I could not on me endure?
Not from a vain or shallow thought
His awful Jove young Phidias brought;
Never from lips of cunning fell
The thrilling Delphic oracle;
Out from the heart of nature rolled
The burdens of the Bible old;
The litanies of nations came,
Like the volcano's tongue of flame,
Up from the burning core below,—
The canticles of love and woe:
The hand that rounded Peter's dome*
And groined the aisles of Christian Rome
Wrought in a sad sincerity;
Himself from God he could not free;
He builded better than he knew;—
The conscious stone to beauty grew.

Know'st thou what wove yon woodbird's nest
Of leaves, and feathers from her breast?
Or how the fish outbuilt her shell,
Painting with morn each annual cell?
Or how the sacred pine-tree adds
To her old leaves new myriads?

---

*The dome of Saint Peter's Cathedral in Rome was designed by Michelangelo.

Such and so grew these holy piles,
Whilst love and terror laid the tiles.
Earth proudly wears the Parthenon,*
As the best gem upon her zone,
And Morning opes with haste her lids
To gaze upon the Pyramids;
O'er England's abbeys bends the sky,
As on its friends, with kindred eye;
For out of Thought's interior sphere
These wonders rose to upper air;
And Nature gladly gave them place,
Adopted them into her race,
And granted them an equal date
With Andes and with Ararat.†

These temples grew as grows the grass;
Art might obey, but not surpass.
The passive Master lent his hand
To the vast soul that o'er him planned;
And the same power that reared the shrine
Bestrode the tribes that knelt within.
Ever the fiery Pentecost
Girds with one flame the countless host,
Trances the heart through chanting choirs,
And through the priest the mind inspires.
The word unto the prophet spoken
Was writ on tables yet unbroken;
The word by seers or sibyls told,
In groves of oak, or fanes of gold,
Still floats upon the morning wind,
Still whispers to the willing mind.
One accent of the Holy Ghost
The heedless world hath never lost.
I know what say the fathers wise,—
The Book itself before me lies,
Old *Chrysostom*, best Augustine,

---

*The temple of the goddess Athena built on the Acropolis at Athens was designed by Phidias.
†Mountains in western South America and eastern Turkey, respectively.

The Problem

And he who blent both in his line,
The younger *Golden Lips* or mines,
Taylor, the Shakspeare of divines.
His words are music in my ear,
I see his cowlèd portrait dear;
And yet, for all his faith could see,
I would not the good bishop be.

The Snow-storm

Announced by all the trumpets of the sky,
Arrives the snow, and, driving o'er the fields,
Seems nowhere to alight: the whited air
Hides hills and woods, the river, and the heaven,
And veils the farm-house at the garden's end.
The sled and traveller stopped, the courier's feet
Delayed, all friends shut out, the housemates sit
Around the radiant fireplace, enclosed
In a tumultuous privacy of storm.

    Come see the north wind's masonry.
Out of an unseen quarry evermore
Furnished with tile, the fierce artificer
Curves his white bastions with projected roof
Round every windward stake, or tree, or door.
Speeding, the myriad-handed, his wild work
So fanciful, so savage, nought cares he
For number or proportion. Mockingly,
On coop or kennel he hangs Parian* wreaths;
A swan-like form invests the hidden thorn;
Fills up the farmer's lane from wall to wall,
Maugre† the farmer's sighs; and at the gate
A tapering turret overtops the work.
And when his hours are numbered, and the world
Is all his own, retiring, as he were not,
Leaves, when the sun appears, astonished Art
To mimic in slow structures, stone by stone,
Built in an age, the mad wind's night-work,
The frolic architecture of the snow.

---

*White marble found on the island of Paros in the Aegean sea, and favored by ancient Greek sculptors.
†In spite of.

The Rhodora*

On Being Asked, Whence Is the Flower?

In May, when sea-winds pierced our solitudes,
I found the fresh Rhodora in the woods,
Spreading its leafless blooms in a damp nook,
To please the desert and the sluggish brook.
The purple petals, fallen in the pool,
Made the black water with their beauty gay;
Here might the red-bird come his plumes to cool,
And court the flower that cheapens his array.
Rhodora! if the sages ask thee why
This charm is wasted on the earth and sky,
Tell them, dear, that if eyes were made for seeing,
Then Beauty is its own excuse for being:
Why thou wert there, O rival of the rose!
I never thought to ask, I never knew:
But, in my simple ignorance, suppose
The self-same Power that brought me there brought
    you.

---

*Another name for the rhododendron, a flowering bush common to New England.

Uriel

It fell in the ancient periods
    Which the brooding soul surveys,
Or ever the wild Time coined itself
    Into calendar months and days.

This was the lapse of Uriel,
Which in Paradise befell.
Once, among the Pleiads* walking,
Seyd† overheard the young gods talking;
And the treason, too long pent,
To his ears was evident.
The young deities discussed
Laws of form, and metre just,
Orb, quintessence, and sunbeams,
What subsisteth, and what seems.
One, with low tones that decide,
And doubt and reverend use defied,
With a look that solved the sphere,
And stirred the devils everywhere,
Gave his sentiment divine
Against the being of a line.
'Line in nature is not found;
Unit and universe are round;
In vain produced, all rays return;
Evil will bless, and ice will burn.
As Uriel spoke with piercing eye,
A shudder ran around the sky;
The stern old war-gods shook their heads,
The seraphs frowned from myrtle-beds;
Seemed to the holy festival

---

*Cluster of stars in the constellation Taurus; in Greek mythology, they represent the six daughters of Atlas.
†The Persian poet Saadi.

The rash word boded ill to all;
The balance-beam of Fate was bent;
The bounds of good and ill were rent;
Strong Hades could not keep his own,
But all slid to confusion.

A sad self-knowledge, withering, fell
On the beauty of Uriel;
In heaven once eminent, the god
Withdrew, that hour, into his cloud;
Whether doomed to long gyration
In the sea of generation,
Or by knowledge grown too bright
To hit the nerve of feebler sight.
Straightway, a forgetting wind
Stole over the celestial kind,
And their lips the secret kept,
If in ashes the fire-seed slept.
But now and then, truth-speaking things
Shamed the angels' veiling wings;
And, shrilling from the solar course,
Or from fruit of chemic force,
Procession of a soul in matter,
Or the speeding change of water,
Or out of the good of evil born,
Came Uriel's voice of cherub scorn,
And a blush tinged the upper sky,
And the gods shook, they knew not why.

The Humble-bee

Burly, dozing humble-bee,
Where thou art is clime for me.
Let them sail for Porto Rique,*
Far-off heats through seas to seek;
I will follow thee alone,
Thou animated torrid-zone!
Zigzag steerer, desert cheerer,
Let me chase thy waving lines;
Keep me nearer, me thy hearer,
Singing over shrubs and vines.

Insect lover of the sun,
Joy of thy dominion!
Sailor of the atmosphere;
Swimmer through the waves of air;
Voyager of light and noon;
Epicurean of June;
Wait, I prithee, till I come
Within earshot of thy hum,—
All without is martyrdom.

When the south wind, in May days,
With a net of shining haze
Silvers the horizon wall,
And with softness touching all,
Tints the human countenance
With a color of romance,
And infusing subtle heats,
Turns the sod to violets,
Thou, in sunny solitudes,
Rover of the underwoods,

---

*The island of Puerto Rico in the Caribbean.

The Humble-bee

The green silence dost displace
With thy mellow, breezy bass.

Hot midsummer's petted crone,
Sweet to me thy drowsy tone
Tells of countless sunny hours,
Long days, and solid banks of flowers;
Of gulfs of sweetness without bound
In Indian wildernesses found;
Of Syrian peace, immortal leisure,
Firmest cheer, and bird-like pleasure.

Aught unsavory or unclean
Hath my insect never seen;
But violets and bilberry bells,
Maple-sap and daffodels,
Grass with green flag half-mast high,
Succory to match the sky,
Columbine with horn of honey,
Scented fern, and agrimony,
Clover, catchfly, adder's-tongue
And brier-roses, dwelt among;
All beside was unknown waste,
All was picture as he passed.

Wiser far than human seer,
Yellow-breeched philosopher!
Seeing only what is fair,
Sipping only what is sweet,
Thou dost mock at fate and care,
Leave the chaff, and take the wheat.
When the fierce northwestern blast
Cools sea and land so far and fast,
Thou already slumberest deep;
Woe and want thou canst outsleep;
Want and woe, which torture us,
Thy sleep makes ridiculous.

Hamatreya

Bulkeley, Hunt, Willard, Hosmer, Meriam, Flint,*
Possessed the land which rendered to their toil
Hay, corn, roots, hemp, flax, apples, wool and wood.
Each of these landlords walked amidst his farm,
Saying, ''Tis mine, my children's and my name's.
How sweet the west wind sounds in my own trees!
How graceful climb those shadows on my hill!
I fancy these pure waters and the flags
Know me, as does my dog: we sympathize;
And, I affirm, my actions smack of the soil.'

Where are these men? Asleep beneath their grounds:
And strangers, fond as they, their furrows plough.
Earth laughs in flowers, to see her boastful boys
Earth-proud, proud of the earth which is not theirs;
Who steer the plough, but cannot steer their feet
Clear of the grave.
They added ridge to valley, brook to pond,
And sighed for all that bounded their domain;
'This suits me for a pasture; that's my park;
We must have clay, lime, gravel, granite-ledge,
And misty lowland, where to go for peat.
The land is well,—lies fairly to the south.
'Tis good, when you have crossed the sea and back,
To find the sitfast acres where you left them.'
Ah! the hot owner sees not Death, who adds
Him to his land, a lump of mould the more.
Hear what the Earth says:—

---

*List of landowners who lived in Concord.

Earth-song

'Mine and yours;
Mine, not yours,
Earth endures;
Stars abide—
Shine down in the old sea;
Old are the shores;
But where are old men?
I who have seen much,
Such have I never seen.

'The lawyer's deed
Ran sure,
In tail,
To them, and to their heirs
Who shall succeed,
Without fail,
Forevermore.

'Here is the land,
Shaggy with wood,
With its old valley,
Mound and flood.
But the heritors?—
Fled like the flood's foam.
The lawyer, and the laws,
And the kingdom,
Clean swept herefrom.

'They called me theirs,
Who so controlled me;
Yet every one
Wished to stay, and is gone,
How am I theirs,
If they cannot hold me,
But I hold them?'

When I heard the Earth-song,
I was no longer brave;
My avarice cooled
Like lust in the chill of the grave.

Give All to Love

Give all to love;
Obey thy heart;
Friends, kindred, days,
Estate, good-fame,
Plans, credit and the Muse,—
Nothing refuse.

'T is a brave master;
Let it have scope:
Follow it utterly,
Hope beyond hope:
High and more high
It dives into noon,
With wing unspent,
Untold intent;
But it is a god,
Knows its own path
And the outlets of the sky.

It was never for the mean;
It requireth courage stout.
Souls above doubt,
Valor unbending,
It will reward,—
They shall return
More than they were,
And ever ascending.

Leave all for love;
Yet, hear me, yet,
One word more thy heart behoved,
One pulse more of firm endeavor,—
Keep thee to-day,
To-morrow, forever,

Free as an Arab
Of thy beloved.

Cling with life to the maid;
But when the surprise,
First vague shadow of surmise
Flits across her bosom young,
Of a joy apart from thee,
Free be she, fancy-free;
Nor thou detain her vesture's hem,
Nor the palest rose she flung
From her summer diadem.

Though thou loved her as thyself,
As a self of purer clay,
Though her parting dims the day,
Stealing grace from all alive;
Heartily know,
When half-gods go,
The gods arrive.

Merlin*

I

Thy trivial harp will never please
Or fill my craving ear;
Its chords should ring as blows the breeze,
Free, peremptory, clear.
No jingling serenader's art,
Nor tinkle of piano strings,
Can make the wild blood start
In its mystic springs.
The kingly bard
Must smite the chords rudely and hard,
As with hammer or with mace;
That they may render back
Artful thunder, which conveys
Secrets of the solar track,
Sparks of the supersolar blaze.
Merlin's blows are strokes of fate,
Chiming with the forest tone,
When boughs buffet boughs in the wood;
Chiming with the gasp and moan
Of the ice-imprisoned hood;
With the pulse of manly hearts;
With the voice of orators;
With the din of city arts;
With the cannonade of wars;
With the marches of the brave;
And prayers of might from martyrs' cave.

---

*The sixth-century Welsh poet Myrddin, rather than the magician of Arthurian legend.

Great is the art,
Great be the manners, of the bard.
He shall not his brain encumber
With the coil of rhythm and number;
But, leaving rule and pale forethought,
He shall aye climb
For his rhyme.
"Pass in, pass in," the angels say,
"In to the upper doors,
Nor count compartments of the floors,
But mount to paradise
By the stairway of surprise."
Blameless master of the games,
King of sport that never shames,
He shall daily joy dispense
Hid in song's sweet influence.
Forms more cheerly live and go,
What time the subtle mind
Sings aloud the tune whereto
Their pulses beat,
And march their feet,
And their members are combined.

By Sybarites beguiled,
He shall no task decline;
Merlin's mighty line
Extremes of nature reconciled,
Bereaved a tyrant of his will,
And made the lion mild.
Songs can the tempest still,
Scattered on the stormy air,
Mold the year to fair increase,
And bring in poetic peace.
He shall nor seek to weave,
In weak, unhappy times,
Efficacious rhymes;
Wait his returning strength.
Bird that from the nadir's floor
To the zenith's top can soar,
The roaring orbit of the muse exceeds that journey's
    length.

Nor profane affect to hit
Or compass that, by meddling wit,
Which only the propitious mind
Publishes when 'tis inclined.
There are open hours
When the God's will sallies free,
And the dull idiot might see
The flowing fortunes of a thousand years;
Sudden, at unawares,
Self-moved, fly-to the doors,
Nor sword of angels could reveal
What they conceal.

II

The rhyme of the poet
Modulates the king's affairs;
Balance-loving Nature
Made all things in pairs.
To every foot its antipode;
Each color with its counter glowed:
To every tone beat answering tones,
Higher or graver;
Flavor gladly blends with flavor;
Leaf answers leaf upon the bough;
And match the paired cotyledons.*
Hands to hands, and feet to feet,
In one body grooms and brides;
Eldest rite, two married sides
In every mortal meet.
Light's far furnace shines,
Smelting balls and bars,
Forging double stars,
Glittering twins and trines.
The animals are sick with love,
Lovesick with rhyme;
Each with all propitious Time
Into chorus wove.

---

*First pair of leaves produced by a flowering plant.

Like the dancers' ordered band,
Thoughts come also hand in hand;
In equal couples mated,
Or else alternated;
Adding by their mutual gage,
One to other, health and age.
Solitary fancies go
Short-lived wandering to and ire,
Most like to bachelors,
Or an ungiven maid,
Nor ancestors,
With no posterity to make the lie afraid,
Or keep truth undecayed.
Perfect-paired as eagle's wings,
Justice is the rhyme of things;
Trade and counting use
The self-same tuneful muse;
And Nemesis;
Who with even matches odd,
Who athwart space redresses
The partial wrong,
Fills the just period,
And finishes the song.
Subtle rhymes, with ruin rife
Murmur in the hour of life,
Sung by the Sisters as they spin;
In perfect time and measure they
Build and unbuild our echoing clay.
As the two twilights of the day
Fold us music-drunken in.

Xenophanes

By fate, not option, frugal Nature gave
One scent to hyson and to wall-flower,
One sound to pine-groves and to waterfalls,
One aspect to the desert and the lake.
It was her stern necessity: all things
Are of one pattern made; bird, beast and flower,
Song, picture, form, space, thought and character
Deceive us, seeming to be many things,
And are but one. Beheld far off, they part
As God and devil; bring them to the mind,
They dull its edge with their monotony.
To know one element, explore another,
And in the second reappears the first.
The specious panorama of a year
But multiplies the image of a day,—
A belt of mirrors round a taper's flame;
And universal Nature, through her vast
And crowded whole, an infinite paroquet,*
Repeats one note.

---

*Parrot.

Concord Hymn[1]

Sung at the Completion of the
Battle Monument, July 4, 1837

By the rude bridge that arched the flood,
    Their flag to April's breeze unfurled,
Here once the embattled farmers stood
    And fired the shot heard round the world.

The foe long since in silence slept;
    Alike the conqueror silent sleeps;
And Time the ruined bridge has swept
    Down the dark stream which seaward creeps.

On this green bank, by this soft stream,
    We set to-day a votive stone;
That memory may their deed redeem,
    When, like our sires, our sons are gone.

Spirit, that made those heroes dare
    To die, and leave their children free,
Bid Time and Nature gently spare
    The shaft we raise to them and thee.

Voluntaries[2]

Low and mournful be the strain,
Haughty thought be far from me;
Tones of penitence and pain,
Moanings of the tropic sea;
Low and tender in the cell
Where a captive sits in chains,
Crooning ditties treasured well
From his Afric's torrid plains.
Sole estate his sire bequeathed,—
Hapless sire to hapless son,—
Was the wailing song he breathed,
And his chain when life was done.

What his fault, or what his crime?
Or what ill planet crossed his prime?
Heart too soft and will too weak
To front the fate that crouches near,—
Dove beneath the vulture's beak;—
Will song dissuade the thirsty spear?
Dragged from his mother's arms and breast,
Displaced, disfurnished here,
His wistful toil to do his best
Chilled by a ribald jeer.

Great men in the Senate sate,
Sage and hero, side by side,
Building for their sons the State,
Which they shall rule with pride.
They forbore to break the chain
Which bound the dusky tribe,
Checked by the owners' fierce disdain,
Lured by 'Union' as the bribe.
Destiny sat by, and said,

457

'Pang for pang your seed shall pay,
Hide in false peace your coward head,
I bring round the harvest day.'

II

Freedom all winged expands,
Nor perches in a narrow place;
Her broad van seeks unplanted lands;
She loves a poor and virtuous race.
Clinging to a colder zone
Whose dark sky sheds the snowflake down,
The snowflake is her banner's star,
Her stripes the boreal streamers are.
Long she loved the Northman well;
Now the iron age is done,
She will not refuse to dwell
With the offspring of the Sun;
Foundling of the desert far,
Where palms plume, siroccos blaze,
He roves unhurt the burning ways
In climates of the summer star.
He has avenues to God
Hid from men of Northern brain,
Far beholding, without cloud,
What these with slowest steps attain.
If once the generous chief arrive
To lead him willing to be led,
For freedom he will strike and strive,
And drain his heart till he be dead.

III

In an age of fops and toys,
Wanting wisdom, void of right,
Who shall nerve heroic boys
To hazard all in Freedom's fight,—
Break sharply off their jolly games,
Forsake their comrades gay
And quit proud homes and youthful dames
For famine, toil and fray?

Yet on the nimble air benign
Speed nimbler messages,
That waft the breath of grace divine
To hearts in sloth and ease.
So nigh is grandeur to our dust,
So near is God to man,
When Duty whispers low, *Thou must*,
The youth replies, *I can.*

IV

O, well for the fortunate soul
Which Music's wings infold,
Stealing away the memory
Of sorrows new and old!
Yet happier he whose inward sight,
Stayed on his subtile thought,
Shuts his sense on toys of time,
To vacant bosoms brought.
But best befriended of the God
He who, in evil times,
Warned by an inward voice,
Heeds not the darkness and the dread,
Biding by his rule and choice,
Feeling only the fiery thread
Leading over heroic ground,
Walled with mortal terror round,
To the aim which him allures,
And the sweet heaven his deed secures.
Peril around, all else appalling,
Cannon in front and leaden rain
Him duty through the clarion calling
To the van called not in vain.

Stainless soldier on the walls,
Knowing this,—and knows no more,—
Whoever fights, whoever falls,
Justice conquers evermore,
Justice after as before,—
And he who battles on her side,
God, though he were ten times slain,

Crowns him victor glorified,
Victor over death and pain.

V

Blooms the laurel which belongs
To the valiant chief who fights;
I see the wreath, I hear the songs
Lauding the Eternal Rights,
Victors over daily wrongs:
Awful victors, they misguide
Whom they will destroy,
And their coming triumph hide
In our downfall, or our joy:
They reach no term, they never sleep,
In equal strength through space abide;
Though, feigning dwarfs, they crouch and creep,
The strong they slay, the swift outstride:
Fate's grass grows rank in valley clods,
And rankly on the castled steep,—
Speak it firmly, these are gods,
All are ghosts beside.

Days

Daughters of Time, the hypocritic Days,
Muffled and dumb like barefoot dervishes,
And marching single in an endless file,
Bring diadems and fagots in their hands.
To each they offer gifts after his will,
Bread, kingdoms, stars, and sky that holds them all.
I, in my pleached* garden, watched the pomp,
Forgot my morning wishes, hastily
Took a few herbs and apples, and the Day
Turned and departed silent. I, too late,
Under her solemn fillet† saw the scorn.

---

*Woven or plaited.
†Narrow headband.

The Chartist's Complaint[3]

Day! Hast thou two faces,
Making one place two places?
One, by humble farmer seen,
Chill and wet, unlighted, mean,
Useful only, triste and damp,
Serving for a laborer's lamp?
Have the same mists another side,
To be the appanage* of pride,
Gracing the rich man's wood and lake,
His park where amber mornings break,
And treacherously bright to show
His planted isle where roses glow?
O Day! and is your mightiness
A sycophant† to smug success?
Will the sweet sky and ocean broad
Be fine accomplices to fraud?
O Sun! I curse thy cruel ray:
Back, back to chaos, harlot Day!

---

*Extra profit or gain enjoyed as a perquisite.
†Person who seeks favor by flattery.

Terminus

It is time to be old,
To take in sail:
The god of bounds,
Who sets to seas a shore,
Came to me in his fatal rounds,
And said: "No more!
No farther shoot
Thy broad ambitious branches, and thy root.
Fancy departs: no more invent;
Contract thy firmament
To compass of a tent.
There's not enough for this and that,
Make thy option which of two;
Economize the failing river,
Not the less revere the Giver,
Leave the many and hold the few.
Timely wise accept the terms,
Soften the fall with wary foot;
A little while
Still plan and smile,
And—fault of novel germs—
Mature the unfallen fruit.
Curse, if thou wilt, thy sires,
Bad husbands of their fires,
Who, when they gave thee breath,
Failed to bequeath
The needful sinew stark as once,
The Baresark marrow to thy bones,
But left a legacy of ebbing veins,
Inconstant heat and nerveless reins,—
Amid the Muses, left thee deaf and dumb,
Amid the gladiators, halt and numb."
  As the bird trims her to the gale,
I trim myself to the storm of time,
I man the rudder, reef the sail,

Obey the voice at eve obeyed at prime:
"Lowly faithful, banish fear,
Right onward drive unharmed;
The port, well worth the cruise, is near,
And every wave is charmed."

Glossary of Names

Achilles. In Greek and Roman mythology, central protagonist in Homer's *Iliad;* according to legend, his father, Thetis, dipped him in the river Styx to make him immortal.

Adams, John (1735–1826). Second president of the United States and an influential figure in the drafting and ratification of the Declaration of Independence and the United States Constitution.

Adams, John Quincy (1767–1848). Son of John Adams; sixth president of the United States and a longtime member of the House of Representatives; known as Old Man Eloquence.

Aeschylus (525–456 B.C.). Greek lyric poet and dramatist.

Aesop (6th century B.C.). Greek writer of fables.

Africanus, Scipio (237–183 B.C.). Conqueror of Carthage.

Agamemnon. Leader of the Greek forces in the Trojan War, the basis for Homer's epic poem the *Iliad.*

Agrippa, Cornelius (1486–1535). German physician.

Alaric (c.370–410). King of the Visigoths and conqueror of Rome in 410.

Alembert, Jean Le Rond d' (1717–1783). French mathematician and philosopher.

Alfred (849–899). King of Wessex; united the Saxons against the Danes.

Ali (c.602–661). Fourth caliph of Mecca; cousin and son-in-law of the prophet Muhammad.

Aligheri, Dante (1265–1321). Italian poet; author of the *Divine Comedy*, an epic poem that recounts the author's journey through Hell (the Inferno), Purgatory, and Paradise.

Alphonso X (1221–1284). Spanish king and patronage of science and the arts; also known as Alphonso the Wise.

Allston, Washington (1779–1843). American artist and author.

Ames, Fisher (1758–1808). Federalist congressman and lawyer.

Anaxagoras (c.500–428 B.C.). Greek philosopher.

Anaximenes (c.600–500 B.C.). Greek philosopher.

Angelo. See Michelangelo.

Antommarchi, Francesco (1780–1838). Corsican anatomist who attended Napoleon as physician at Saint Helena.

Antonio. Character from Shakespeare's *The Merchant of Venice.*

Apollo. In Greek mythology, god of prophecy, medicine, poetry, and music; said to be the leader of the nine Muses, patron goddesses of the arts, the daughters of Zeus and Mnemosyne.

Ariosto, Ludovico (1474–1533). Italian epic and lyric poet.

Aristarchus of Samos (c.300–200 B.C.). Greek astronomer who anticipated Copernicus in proposing a sun-centered model of the solar system.

Aristotle (384–322 B.C.). Greek philosopher; student of Plato.

Arminius, Jacobus (1560–1609). Dutch theologian of the Reformed Church who modified Calvin's strict definition of predestination.

Arnim, Elizabeth von (1785–1859). German romantic writer who published what she claimed to be her correspondence with Goethe; also known as Bettine.

Arrian (95–180). Greek stoic philosopher and historian.

Astor, John Jacob (1763–1848). German-born American fur trader; made a fortune in real estate by purchasing much of the undeveloped land on Manhattan island, New York.

Ate Dea. Goddess of infatuation or moral recklessness.

Aubrey, John (1626–1697). English antiquary and author of *Lives of Eminent Men.*

Augereau, Pierre-François-Charles (1757–1816). Marshal of France and duke of Castiglione.

Augustine (Saint; 354–430). Bishop of Hippo; influential Christian theologian.

Aurora. In Greek and Roman mythology, goddess of dawn; begged Zeus to make her lover, Tithonus, immortal but forgot to ask for eternal youth and so Tithonus grew older and older; also known as Eos.

Bacon, Francis (1561–1626). English philosopher who championed the inductive method of modern science and insisted that all scientific theories be based on observable data.

Baresark. See Berserkir.

Beaumont, Francis (c.1584–1616). Often wrote in collaboration with John Fletcher; their best-known plays are *Philaster, The Maid's Tragedy,* and *A King and No King.*

Beaumont, Jean-Baptiste-Armand-Louis-Léonce Élie de (1798–1874). French geologist.

Behmen, Jacob (1575–1624). German mystic and theologian who claimed divine revelation; also known as Jakob Boehme.

Bellarmine, Robert (1542–1621). Italian Jesuit theologian; prominent figure in the Catholic Reformation.

Bentham, Jeremy (1748–1832). English philosopher, jurist, and political theorist; founder of utilitarianism, which argued that the greatest good for the greatest number should be the principle used to judge the effectiveness of social institutions.

Benton, Thomas Hart (1782–1858). Senator from North Carolina (1821–1851).

Bering, Vitus Jonassen (1680–1741). Danish navigator who explored the northern Pacific.

Berkeley, George (1685–1753). Irish-born English bishop and philosopher.

Bernadotte, Jean-Baptiste (1763–1844). Soldier and diplomat; a rival to Napoleon on the battlefield and in the political arena.

Berserkirs. Norse warriors who overwhelmed opponents by fighting in a frenzy of rage.

Berthollet, Claude-Louis (1748–1822). French chemist.

Berzelius, Jöns Jakob (1779–1848). Swedish chemist.

Betterton, Thomas (c.1635–1710). Well-known Shakespearean actor.

Bettine. See Arnim, Elizabeth von.

Beza, Theodore (1519–1605). French theologian; associate of John Calvin.

Bivar, Rodrigo Díaz de (c.1040–1099). Legendary Spanish hero; also known as El Cid and El Campeador.

Blackmore, Sir Richard (c.1650–1729). English physician and poet.

Blackstone, William (1723–1780). English lawyer and author of *Commentaries on the Laws of England* (1765–1769).

Boethius (c.475–525). Roman Neoplatonist philosopher and statesman; author of *De consolatione philosophiae* (*The Consolation of Philosophy*).

Bonaparte, Napoleon (1769–1821). French military leader who conquered most of Europe and had himself proclaimed emperor of France.

Boniface. Gregarious innkeeper in George Farquhar's play *The Beaux's Stratagem* (1707).

Borrow, George Henry (1803–1881). English author and adventurer; published *The Zincali, or . . . the Gypsies in Spain* (1841) and other works based on his travels as a translator and agent for the British and Foreign Bible Society.

Boscovitch, Ruggiero Giuseppe (1711–1787). Italian physicist who proposed an early atomic theory of matter.

Boswell, James (1740–1795). Scottish biographer who was said to have spent his career following great men rather than being one himself.

Bourbon-Condé, Louis-Antoine-Henri de (1772–1804). Executed by Napoleon for conspiracy; also known as Duc d'Enghien.

Bowditch, Nathaniel (1773–1838). American mathematician and astronomer; author of *The New American Practical Navigator* (1802).

Brahmins. Priestly class of the Hindu religion; charged with interpreting the Vedas, the sacred texts of Hinduism.

Brant, Joseph (1742–1807). Chief of the Mohawk; fought under Sir William Johnston in the French and Indian War and on the side of the British in the American Revolution.

Brougham, Henry Peter (1778–1868). English statesman; supporter of the Reform Act of 1832.

Brown, John (1800–1859). American abolitionist who led the attack on Harper's Ferry, Virginia (now West Virginia), on October 16, 1859, for which he was tried and executed.

Bruce, Thomas (1766–1841). Seventh earl of Elgin and a British diplomat.

Brummel, George (1778–1840). Famous as a British dandy; also known as Beau Brummel.

Brunel, Isambard (1806–1859). Designer of the first Atlantic steamer, the *Great Western*.

Bruno, Giordano (1548–1600). Italian philosopher.

Buch, Christian Leopold von (1774–1853). German geologist; student of Abraham Gottlob Werner.

Buffon, Georges-Louis Leclerc de (1707–1788). French naturalist; keeper of the Jardin des Plantes, the botanical gardens in Paris, which Emerson visited in 1833.

Buford, Napoleon Bonaparte (1807–1883). American soldier and engineer who taught natural philosophy at West Point in 1834 and 1835.

Burke, Edmund (1729–1797). British statesman and philosopher; opposed the French revolution and Napoleon's rise to power.

Burlamaqui, Jean-Jacques (1694–1748). Swiss jurist.

Byron, George Gordon; called Lord Byron (1788–1824). English poet.

Cadmus. Phoenician prince and mythical founder of Thebes; said to have invented the Phoenician alphabet and to have conjured an army with the teeth of a dragon he slew.

Caesar, Julius (c.100–44 B.C.). The most famous of the Roman Caesars.

Cain, Tubal. Biblical metalworker (see Genesis 4:22).

Calhoun, John C. (1782–1850). American politician; vice president under John Quincy Adams and Andrew Jackson.

Calvin, John (1509–1564). Protestant reformer.

Campbell, Thomas (1777–1884). Scottish poet.

Cardano, Girolamo (1501–1576). Italian mathematician and naturalist.

Carnot, Lazarre-Nicholas-Marguerite (1753–1823). French general; served as war minister under the Consulate but opposed Napoleon's elevation to emperor.

Carpenter, William B. (1813–1885). English biologist; published findings on the uses of the microscope.

Cary, Lucius (c.1610–1643). English Parliamentary leader.

Cato the Younger (95–46 B.C.). Roman statesman who, because of his devotion to the principles of the early republic, opposed Caesar; when defeated in Africa, he committed suicide and urged his people to make peace with Caesar.

Causabon, Isaac (1559–1614). Geneva-born theologian and classical scholar.

Cecil, Sir Robert (1563–1612). English statesman and first earl of Salisbury.

Cellini, Benvenuto (1500–1571). Italian sculptor and engineer.

Cervantes, Miguel de (1547–1616). Spanish writer; author of *Don Quixote*.

Chalmers, Alexander (1759–1834). Editor of *The Works of the English Poets, from Chaucer to Cowper* (1810).

Chapman, George (c.1559–1634). Translator of Homer's *Iliad* and *Odyssey*.

Charles II (1630–1685). King of England following the Restoration.

Charles V (1500–1558). King of Spain and Holy Roman Emperor.

Charles XII (1682–1718). King of Sweden.

Chatham, Lord. See Pitt, William.

Chaucer, Geoffrey (c.1343–1400). English poet, author of *The Canterbury Tales*.

Chiffinch, William (1602–1688). Page to English king Charles II; notorious as a spy and informer to the king.

Christina (1626–1689). Queen of Sweden.

Chrysostom, John (Saint; c.345–407). Archbishop of Constantinople; known for his eloquent denunciations of the rich.

Cicero, Marcus Tullius (106–43 B.C.). Roman statesman and poet.

Cid. See Bivar, Rodrigo Diaz de.

Circe. In Homer's *Odyssey*, the enchantress who transformed Odysseus's crew into swine.

Clarendon. See Hyde, Edward.

Clarke, Henri-Jacques-Guillaume (1765–1818). French soldier and duke of Feltre; Napoleon's war minister.

Clarkeson, Thomas (1760–1846). English abolitionist who helped end the British slave trade.

Clay, Henry (1777–1852). Kentucky politician; served as secretary of state; influential in drafting compromise legislation that included the Fugitive Slave Law.

Cobden, Richard (1804–1865). British economist and politician.

Coke, Edward (1552–1634). English jurist.

Coleridge, Samuel Taylor (1772–1834). English Romantic poet and critic.

Collier, John Payne (1789–1883). Controversial Shakespeare scholar and editor.

Columbus, Christopher (1451–1506). Credited with European discovery of North and South America.

Condillac, Etienne Bonnot de (1715–1780). French philosopher who claimed that because all knowledge comes from the senses, there are no innate ideas.

Copernicus, Nicholas (1473–1543). Polish astronomer who posited the sun-centered model of the universe that replaced the Ptolemaic system, in which the sun was thought to revolve around Earth.

Coriolanus, Gnaeus Marcius (6th–5th century B.C.). Roman general.

Corvisart, Jean-Nicholas (1755–1821). French physician and anatomist; Napoleon and Josephine's doctor in Paris.

Cotton, Charles (1630–1687). English writer and poet whose translation of Montaigne's *Essais* was widely read.

Cowley, Abraham (1618–1667). English metaphysical poet.

Crichton, James (1560–1582). Scottish adventurer and scholar; called "the Admirable Crichton" because of his athleticism and intellectual abilities.

Croesus (6th century B.C.). King of Lydia in Asia Minor; said to have been the richest man in the world.

Cromwell, Oliver (1599–1658). Lord Protector of England following the English Civil War.

Cudworth, Ralph (1617–1688). English philosopher; one of the Cambridge Platonists.

Cupid. Roman god of love.

Cuvier, Georges (1769–1832). French anatomist and paleontologist.

Daguerre, Louis-Jacques-Mandé (1789–1851). French physicist; developed an early technique of making photographs, called "daguerreotypes."

Dalton, John (1766–1844). English chemist and physicist who proposed a modern version of atomic theory.

Dandolo, Vincenzo (1758–1819). Italian chemist and patriot; joined Napoleon to help liberate Italy from the Austrians.

David (10th century B.C.). King of Israel; author of the biblical Book of Psalms.

Davy, Sir Humphrey (1778–1829). English chemist and physicist.

Dekker, Thomas (c.1570–1632). English dramatist best known for his comedy *The Shoemaker's Holiday.*

Democritus (5th century B.C.). Greek philosopher who proposed an early atomic theory of matter.

Descartes, René (1596–1650). French philosopher, scientist, and mathematician.

Dessaix, Joseph-Marie (1764–1834). French count; served Napoleon throughout his career.

Devereux, Robert (1567–1601). Second earl of Essex; English soldier and courtier.

Diogenes (c.412–323 B.C.). Greek philosopher.

Donne, John (1572–1631). English poet and minister; considered the greatest of the metaphysical poets.

Dorians. One of the four main peoples of ancient Greece.

Druids. Ancient Celtic sect.

Dryden, John (1631–1700). English poet, dramatist, and critic.

Due d'Enghien. See Bourbon-Condé, Louis-Antoine-Henri de.

Dumas, Alexandre (1802–1870). French novelist and playwright; worked with numerous collaborators; known as Dumas père.

Dumont, Pierre-Etienne-Louis (1759–1829). Reports the anecdote on pages 332–333 in his *Recollections of Mirabeau, and of the Two First Legislative Assemblies of France* (1833), pp. 63–67.

Duroc, Geraud-Christophe-Michel (1772–1813). Duke of Friouli; Napoleon's aide de camp in the Italian campaign.

Dyce, Alexander (1798–1869). Scottish clergyman and scholar; edited a nine-volume edition of Shakespeare, as well as the works of a number of other Elizabethan and Jacobean dramatists.

Earl of Essex. See Devereux, Robert.

Eldin, Lord. See Scott, John.

Elgin, Lord. See Bruce, Thomas.

Emmerich, Leopold Franz (1794–1849). Prince of Hohenlohe; reputedly a miracle-healer.

Empedocles (c.495–435 B.C.). Greek philosopher who held that the universe was composed of four elements: earth, fire, water, and air.

Epaminondas (c.410–362 B.C.). Theban general who defeated the Spartans at Leuctra (371 B.C.).

Erasmus, Desiderius (c.1466–1536). Dutch humanist and editor; author of *The Praise of Folly*.

Eric the Red (10th century). Norse chieftain and navigator who discovered and colonized Greenland.

Eril, Francesco Melzi d' (1753–1816). Italian politician; joined Napoleon to help liberate Italy from the Austrians.

Essenes. Obscure Jewish religious sect around the time of Jesus.

Euclid (3rd century B.C.). Greek mathematician whose *Elements* formed the basis of geometry.

Eulenstein, Charles (1802–1890). Popular musician who played the jew's harp, a small lyre-shaped instrument held in the teeth and strummed with a finger.

Euler, Leonhard (1707–1783). Swiss mathematician and physicist.

Fichte, Johann Gottlieb (1762–1814). German post-Kantian romantic philosopher whose work was a precursor to Hegel.

Ficino, Marsilio (1433–1499). Italian philosopher and translator of the Neoplatonists who had a profound influence on Renaissance humanism.

Flammock, Rose. Character in Sir Walter Scott's novel *The Betrothed* (1825).

Flamsteed, John (1646–1719). English astronomer who published the first of the Greenwich star catalogues.

Flaxman, John (1755–1826). English illustrator.

Fletcher, John (1579–1625). Often wrote in collaboration with Francis Beaumont; their best-known plays are *Philaster, The Maid's Tragedy*, and *A King and No King*. Some scholars believe that Fletcher collaborated with Shakespeare on *Henry VIII* and *The Two Noble Kinsmen*.

Fontanes, Louis (1757–1821). French marquis, poet, and politician; strong supporter of Napoleon when he had himself declared emperor of France.

Ford, John (c.1586–1640). Best known for his revenge tragedy *'Tis Pity She's a Whore*.

Fourier, Charles (1772–1837). Theorist of socialism whose ideas greatly influenced the Brook Farm experiment and the associationist movement in general.

Fournier, Marie-Nicholas (1760–1834). Chaplain and almoner to Napoleon; made bishop of Montpellier in 1806.

Fox, Charles James (1749–1806). British orator and statesmen; played a significant role in the third coalition against Napoleon.

Fox, George (1624–1691). English religious reformer and founder of the Religious Society of Friends (Quakers).

Franklin, Benjamin (1706–1790). American writer, scientist, and statesman.

Franklin, Sir John (1786–1847). Arctic explorer and governor of Tasmania; credited with discovering the Northwest Passage.

Frauenhofer, Joseph von (1787–1826). German optician who made improvements to the telescope.

Fries, Elias Magnus (1794–1878). Swedish botanist who proposed the modern classification of fungi and lichens.

Fuller, Thomas (1608–1661). English clergyman and author.

Fulton, Robert (1765–1815). American inventor of steamboats.

Furies. In Greek mythology, avatars of justice.

Fust, Johann (c.1400–1466). German printer associated with Johann Gutenburg, the inventor of movable type.

Galileo. See Galilei, Galileo.

Galilei, Galileo (1564–1642). Italian astronomer, mathematician, and physicist whose work confirmed the Copernican theory of the solar system.

Garrick, David (1717–1779). Renowned Shakespearean actor.

Gautama, Siddhartha (c.536–483 B.C.). The Buddha; founder of the religion and philosophy of Buddhism.

Gentili, Alberico (1552–1608). Italian-born legal scholar whose work laid the foundation for international law.

Gentoo. Variant of "Hindu."

Gibbon, Edward (1737–1794). English historian; author of *The History of the Decline and Fall of the Roman Empire* (1776–1788).

Gilbert, William (1544–1603). English physician who contributed to the study of magnetism.

Gnostics. Early Christian sect that promised salvation through an occult knowledge that was revealed to them alone.

Goethe, Johann Wolfgang von (1749–1832). German poet and dramatist.

Gorgias of Leontini (5th century B.C.). Rhetorician and sophist whose ideas were refuted in several of the dialogues of Plato.

Gracchus, Tiberius Sempronius (163–133 B.C.), and his brother Caius Sempronius Gracchus (154–121 B.C.). Known as the Gracchi. Roman statesman and social reformers.

Graham, Sylvester (1794–1851). Proponent of vegetarianism.

Grand Turk. Emerson's reference on page 198 is possibly to Suleiman the Magnificent (1494–1566), sultan of the Ottoman Empire.

Gray, Thomas (1716–1771). English poet.

Greene, Robert (c.1558–1592). English prose writer and dramatist; his *Pandosto* may have served as the basis for Shakespeare's *The Winter's Tale.*

Grotius, Hugo (1583–1645). Dutch jurist who wrote on the rights and duties of states (see p. 374).

Guizot, François (1787–1874). French historian and statesman.

Gustavus II Adolphus (1594–1632). King of Sweden; played a decisive role in the Thirty Years War.

Gylphi. In Norse mythology, king of Sweden known for his deception.

Hades. In Greek mythology, god of the underworld.

Hafiz (c.1319–1389). Persian lyric poet whose original name was Muhammad Shams al-Din Hafiz.

Hales, John (1584–1656). English scholar and clergyman.

Hall, Basil (1788–1844). British naval commander and author of travel narratives.

Hallet, Benjamin Franklin (1797–1862). Editor of the *Boston Post*; supported the proslavery candidate Franklin Pierce in the presidential election of 1852. Appointed district attorney of Boston under the spoils system; as such, was responsible for prosecuting those who violated the Fugitive Slave Law.

Hamatreya. Variation on Maitreya, a Hindu god in the *Vishnu Purana* who loses all worldly ambition when the earth sings a song to him.

Hampden, John (1594–1643). English Parliamentary leader.

Handel, George Frideric (1685–1759). German-born British composer.

Hardwicke, Philip Yorke, first earl of (1690–1764). English jurist who set precedent on laws of equity.

Haydn, Franz Joseph (1732–1809). Austrian composer.

Hegel, Georg Wilhelm Friedrich (1770–1831). German philosopher.

Helen of Argos. In Homer's *Iliad*, beautiful woman who marries Paris, which leads to the outbreak of the Trojan War.

Heraclitus (c.535–475 B.C.). Greek philosopher who held that the only constant was change.

Herbert, Edward (1583–1648). English philosopher, poet, and diplomat; brother of George Herbert; one of the "two Herberts" Emerson mentions on page 321.

Herbert, George (1593–1633). English metaphysical poet, brother of Edward Herbert; one of the "two Herberts" Emerson mentions on page 323.

Hercules. In Greek mythology, hero known for his strength.

Hermes. Greek god of invention.

Herodotus (c.484–425 B.C.). Greek historian who created a memorable account of the Persian Wars in his *Histories*.

Herschel, Sir William (1738–1822). German-born English astronomer; updated John Flamsteed's Greenwich star catalogues.

Heywood, Thomas (c.1574–1641). English playwright best known for his tragedy *A Woman Killed with Kindness*.

Hill, Isaac (1789–1851). New Hampshire editor and politician who opposed the abolitionists.

Hipparchus (2nd century B.C.). Greek astronomer.

Hippias of Elis (5th century B.C.). Rhetorician and sophist whose ideas were refuted in several of the dialogues of Plato.

Hobart, Henry (1563–1625). One of three English chief justices who wrote the opinion in the case of Somerset, which led to the abolition of slavery in the British colony of the West Indies.

Hohenlohe. See Emmerieh, Leopold Franz.

Holt, John (1642–1710). One of three English chiefjustices who wrote the opinion in the case of Somerset, which led to the abolition of slavery in the British colony of the West Indies.

Home, Sir Everard (1756–1832). Scottish surgeon.

Homer (9th-8th century B.C.). Greek author of the *Iliad* and the *Odyssey*.

Huber, François (1750–1831). Swiss naturalist who studied the life cycle of the honeybee.

Hudson, Henry (c.1570–l611). Explored much of the North Atlantic in search of a northern passage to the Pacific.

Huntington, William (1745–1813). English minister of working-class origins.

Hutton, James (1726–1797). Scottish geologist whose work was influential in the geological dating of Earth.

Hyde, Edward (1609–1674). First earl of Clarendon; wrote *History of the Rebellion and Civil Wars in England* (1702–1704).

Iachimo. Villainous character in Shakespeare's *Cymbeline*.

Iamblichus (4th century). Syrian philosopher of the Neoplatonist school; student of Porphyry.

Ignatius of Loyola (1491–1556). Roman Catholic saint who founded the Society of Jesus, members of which are called "Jesuits."

Isocrates (436–338 B.C.). Pupil of Socrates; teacher of Athenian orators.

Jacobi, Friedrich Heinrich (1743–1819). German romantic philosopher.

Jacobins. Political party that supported the Reign of Terror and other extreme measures following the French Revolution.

James I (1566–1625). King of Great Britain who authorized the King James Version of the Bible (1611).

Jefferson, Thomas (1743–1826). Third president of the United States and principle author of the Declaration of Independence.

Jeremiah. Old Testament prophet, central figure of the Book of Jeremiah.

John. Disciple of Jesus; author of epistles and one of the gospels of the New Testament of the Bible.

Johnson, Samuel (1709–1784). English author; leading literary scholar and critic of his day.

Jonson, Ben (1572–1637). English playwright and poet best known for his comedies *Volpone*, *Epicene*, and *The Alchemist*.

Josephine (1763–1814). Napoleon's wife, born Marie-Josèphe-Rose Tascher de La Pagerie.

Jove. In Roman mythology, god of the heavens.

Judas. Disciple who betrayed Jesus.

Julian (Saint). Patron saint of travelers and hospitality.

Jung-Stilling, Johann Heinrich (1740–1817). German physician and mystic who called himself Heinrich Stilling.

Junot, Andoche (1771–1813). French soldier and duke of Abrantès; fought with distinction in Napoleon's campaigns in Italy and Egypt; was appointed governor general of Portugal.

Jupiter. The supreme god in Roman mythology.

Kane, Elisha Kent (1820–1857). American naval officer and explorer who attempted to establish a route to the North Pole.

Kant, Immanuel (1724–1804). German philosopher who countered the empiricism of John Locke and others by arguing that our knowledge of objective reality is conditioned by the structures of the knowing mind.

Kean, Edmund (1787–1833). Famous Shakespearean actor. His son Charles John Kean (1811–1868) was also an actor, principally in melodramas.

Kellermann, François-Etienne de (1770–1835). Duke of Valmy; one of Napoleon's most able cavalry generals.

Kemble, John Philip (1757–1823). Prominent Shakespearean actor.

Kepler, Johannes (1571–1630). German astronomer who discovered that the planets move in elliptical orbits around the sun.

Kléber, Jean-Baptiste (1753–1800). French soldier; served in Napoleon's Egyptian campaign.

Knox, John (c.1514–1572). Scottish religious reformer; founder of Scottish Presbyterianism.

Knox, Robert (1791–1862). Scottish anatomist and ethnologist; in *The Races of Men, a Fragment* (1850), proposed a theory of race that was used to justify racial prejudice.

Kossuth, Lajos (1802–1894). Hungarian patriot who helped establish independence of Hungary in the revolution of 1848; Emerson officially welcomed him to Concord in May 1852, during Kossuth's tour of the United States.

Kotzebue, August Friedrich Ferdinand von (1761–1819). German dramatist.

Krishna. Eighth incarnation of Vishnu, the supreme deity of Hinduism.

Kyd, Thomas (1558–1594). English dramatist best known for *The Spanish Tragedy.*

Lafayette, Marie-Joseph-Paul-Yves-Roch-Gilbert du Motier, marquis de (1757–1834). French general and politician who led the French forces against the British in the American Revolution; stood in political opposition to Napoleon even as he continued to serve in governmental positions under him.

Lamartine, Alphonse-Marie-Louis de (1790–1869). French romantic poet, novelist, and statesman.

Landor, Walter Savage (1775–1864). English writer.

Landseer, Sir Edwin Henry (1802–1873). English painter famous for his sentimental renditions of animals.

Lannes, Jean (1769–1809). Duke of Montebello and marshal of France; fought with distinction in Napoleon's Italian and Egyptian campaigns.

Laplace, Pierre-Simon de (1749–1827). French marquis, mathematician, and philosopher.

Las Casas. See Las Cases, Emmanuel-Augustin-Dieudonné de.

Las Cases, Emmanuel-Augustin-Dieudonné de (1766–1842). French count and historian; Napoleon's companion and informal secretary during his first year of exile at Saint Helena; also known as Las Casas.

Lavoisier, Antoine (1743–1794). French chemist and physicist; a founder of modern chemistry.

Layard, Sir Austen Henry (1817–1894). English archaeologist and politician; author of *Nineveh and Its Remains* (1849).

Leibnitz, Gottfried Wilhelm (1646–1716). German philosopher and mathematician who proposed a "consistent rationalism," which maintained that the universe forms one context in which each occurrence can be seen in relation to every other; his theory of "correspondences" relates the external world to the internal world of human consciousness.

Leonidas (5th century B.C.). King of Sparta who was killed in 480 B.C. defending the pass at Thermopylae against the Persian army led by Xerxes.

Lessing, Gotthold Ephraim (1729–1781). Philosopher, critic, and dramatist.

Lind, Jenny (1820–1887). Swedish-born British soprano.

Linnaeus, Carolus (1707–1 778). Swedish botanist and taxonomist who originated the modern scientific system for the classification of plants and animals.

Locke, John (1632–1704). English philosopher and political thinker.

Lucan (39–65). Roman poet.

Luther, Martin (1483–1546). German religious reformer whose writings inspired the Protestant Reformation.

Lyncaeus. In the Greek myth of Jason and the Argonauts, Lyncaeus served as lookout because of his keen eyesight.

Mackintosh, Sir James (1765–1832). Scottish writer, philosopher, and lawyer.

Macready, William Charles (1793–1873). Well-known Shakespearean actor.

Malone, Edmund (1741–1812). Irish scholar who proposed that the second and third parts of *Henry VI* were source plays rewritten by Shakespeare.

Malthus, Thomas Robert (1766–1834). English economist.

Mani or Manes (c.216–276). Founder of Manicheanism, a religion based on a dualistic conception of existence in which the world is equally divided between forces of good and evil, and between spirit and matter, matter being understood as a corrupting influence.

Marlowe, Christopher (1564–1593). Playwright best known for *Dr. Faustus*, *The Jew of Malta*, and *Edward II*.

Marvell, Andrew (1621–1678). English metaphysical poet.

Mason, James Murray (1798–1871). Senator from Virginia; drafted the Fugitive Slave Law.

Masséna, André (1758–1817). Duke of Rivoli and prince of Essling; marshal of the empire under Napoleon.

Massinger, Phillip (1583–1640). English playwright best known for his comedies *A New Way to Pay Old Debts* and *The City Madam*.

Maya. Hindu goddess of illusions.

Mencius (4th century B.C.). Confucian philosopher; also known as Meng-tsu or Meng-tzu.

Meno (5th century B.C.). Disciple of Gorgias (see Plato's dialogue *Meno*, 80 A–B).

Menu. That is, Manu; reputed author of the Hindu sacred text *Laws of Manu*. As is the case with Homer, some scholars think that Manu is a historical person; others believe the name became attached to a narrative passed down through oral tradition.

Merlin. Magician and counselor to the king in the legend of King Arthur.

Metternich, Klemens (1773–1859). Foreign minister and chancellor of the Austrian empire.

Michelangelo (1475–1564). Full name: Michelangelo di Lodovico Buonarroti Simoni; Emerson refers to him as Angelo. Italian painter, sculptor, architect, and poet.

Middleton, Thomas (1570?–1627). English dramatist best known for his tragedy *The Changeling*.

Millenialists. Group that believes in the advent of a thousand-year period of blessedness on Earth (see the Bible, Revelations 20).

Milton, John (1608–1674). English poet; author of *Paradise Lost* and *Paradise Regained*.

Minerva. Roman goddess of wisdom.

Mirabeau. See Riqueti, Honoré-Gabriel.

Möeller, Georg (1784–1852). German architect who wrote *Essay on the Origin and Progress of Gothic Architecture* (1825).

Moloch. Phoenician god to whom children were burned in sacrifice.

Momus. Greek god of laughter or mockery.

Monge, Gaspard (1746–1818). French mathematician and principle founder of l'Ecole Polytechnique.

Mons, Jean Baptiste van (1765–1842). Belgian horticulturalist who improved varieties of fruit trees through hybridization.

Montaigne, Michel de (1533–1592). French essayist.

Montesquieu, Charles-Louis de Secondat (1689–1755). Philosopher and jurist; his *The Spirit of Laws* (1748) was a major contribution to political theory in eighteenth-century Europe.

Moravians. Protestant sect of the seventeenth and eighteenth centuries.

More, Henry (1614–1687). English philosopher; one of the Cambridge Platonists.

More, Sir Thomas (Saint; 1478–1535). English statesman; author of *Utopia*.

Moses. Old Testament prophet who led the exodus from Egypt.

Mozart, Wolfgang Amadeus (1756–1791). Austrian composer; first achieved fame as a child prodigy.

Muhammad (c.570–632). Prophet of Islam and author of the Koran.

Murat, Joachim (1767–1815). Marshal of France, and from 1808, king of Naples.

Murray, William (1705–1793). One of three English chief justices who wrote the opinion in the case of Somerset, which led to the abolition of slavery in the British colony of the West Indies.

Necker, Amne-Louise-Germaine. (1766–1817). Baroness of Staël-Holstein; also known as Madame de Staël. Writer.

Necker, Jacques (1732–1804). French financier and statesman; father of Madame de Staël (Anne-Louise-Germaine Necker).

Nemesis. Greek goddess of retribution and fate.

Neptune. In Roman mythology, god of the sea.

Newton, Sir Isaac (1642–1727). English physicist and mathematician who discovered the laws of motion and the calculus, once called the method of fluxions.

Ney, Michel (1769–1815). Marshal of France, duke of Elchingen, and prince of Moskowa.

Noah. Builder of the Ark (see the Bible, Genesis 6–9).

Oberlin, Johann Frederic (1740–1826). Lutheran clergyman, educator, and social reformer.

Œnopides of Chiops (5th century B.C.). Greek mathematician who disputed with Pythagoras over who discovered the obliquity of the ecliptic.

Oegger, Guillaume (1790?–1853?). French Catholic priest and follower of *Emanuel Swedenborg*; his works stress the possibility of linking the natural and spiritual worlds.

Oersted, Hans Christian (1777–1851). Danish physicist and chemist who made early discoveries in the science of electromagnetism.

Oken, Lorenz (1779–1851). German naturalist, founder of modern celluar theory in biology.

Omar (c.586–644). Second caliph of the Muslims; also known as 'Umar I.

Paganini, Niccolò (1782–1840). Italian composer and violinist.

Paine, Thomas (1737–1809). American political theorist and writer.

Paley, Willam (1743–1805). English theologian and utilitarian philosopher.

Pan. Greek god of fertility.

Paracelsus, Philippus Aureolus Theophrastus Bombastus von Hohenheim (1493–1541). Swiss physician and alchemist.

Parmenides (5th century B.C.). Greek philosopher whose ideas are central to Plato's *Parmenides*.

Parry, Sir William Edward (1790–1855). British explorer of the North Pole.

Parsons, William (c.1570–1650). Lord justice of Ireland.

Paul (Saint). Disciple of Jesus and author of epistles of the New Testament; his three missionary journeys are described in Acts of the Apostles, a book of the New Testament of the Bible.

Peel, Sir Robert (1788–1850). English statesman and prime minister.

Peele, George (1556–1596). English dramatist and poet; best known for the play *The Old Wives' Tale*.

Pericles (c.495–429 B.C.) Athenian statesman who established peace with Sparta.

Pestalozzi, Johann Heinrich (1746–1827). Swiss educational reformer whose ideas influenced Emerson's friends Bronson Alcott and Elizabeth Peabody.

Petrarch, Francesco (1304–1374). Italian lyric poet whose sonnets helped define the form.

Phidias (c.490–432 B.C.). Greek sculptor who designed the Parthenon.

Phillips, Wendell (1811–1884). American abolitionist known for his oratorical skills.

Philolaus (5th century B.C.). Greek Pythogorean philosopher.

Phocion (c.402–318 B.C.). Athenian general and statesman.

Phosphorus. Greek god known as the light-bringer; a personification of the morning star.

Pico della Mirandola, Giovanni (1463–1494). Italian philosopher and translator of the Neoplatonists; he had a profound influence on Renaissance humanism.

Picus Mirandola. See Pico della Mirandola, Giovanni.

Pilpay (6th century B.C.). Indian philosopher; reputed author of a collection of animal fables and proverbs; also known as Bidpai.

Pindar (c.520–438 B.C.) Greek lyric poet.

Pisistratus (c.605–527 B.C.); also Peisistratus. Greek statesman; tyrant of Athens.

Pitt, William (1708–1778). First earl of Chatham. English statesman and great orator; called the Elder Pitt and the Great Commoner.

Pitt, William (1759–1806). Second son of William Pitt, first earl of Chatham. English statesman who had great influence during the years of the French Revolution and the Napoleonic wars; led the first and second coalitions against France; called the Younger Pitt.

Plato (c.427–347 B.C.). Greek philosopher (see Emerson's lecture on Plato, pp. 296–315).

Plotinus (c.205–270). Roman Neoplatonic philosopher who practiced a form of asceticism in the belief that the soul could become closer to God by removing it as much as possible from the senses.

Plutarch (c.46–120). Greek biographer famous for his *Parallel Lives.*

Pluto. In Roman mythology, god of the underworld.

Pollock, Robert (1798–1827). Scottish minister and poet.

Polycrates (6th century B.C.). Tyrant king of Samos.

Pope, Alexander (1688–1744). English poet of the Enlightenment period who published a translation of Homer's *Odyssey* in 1725.

Porphyry (c.234–c.305). Neoplatonic philosopher; student of Plotinus; wrote of his vision of union with God.

Port-Royalists. Members of the Port-Royal abbey and school in France, founded by the Jansenists and known for the brilliance of its intellectuals, including Racine and Pascal.

Poussin, Nicolas (1594–1665). French painter of the Classical school.

Proclus (c.410–485). Greek Neoplatonic philosopher.

Ptolemy (2nd century). Greco-Egyptian mathematician and astronomer who proposed a model of the solar system that placed Earth at the center.

Pylades. In Greek mythology, Orestes' closest friend. When the Furies were pursuing Orestes for the murder of his mother, Clytemnestra, Pylades tried to deceive them by masquerading as Orestes.

Pym, John (c.1583–1643). Puritan Parliamentary leader.

Pyrrho (c.360–270 B.C.). Skeptical Greek philosopher who maintained that nothing could be known with certainty.

Pythagoras (c.582–507 B.C.). Pre-Socratic philosopher who thought that all reality could be expressed in numbers; also taught a theory of the transmigration of souls.

Quakers. Common name for the Religious Society of Friends, founded by George Fox (1624–1691).

Quetelet, Lambert (1796–1874). Belgian mathematician who helped establish the science of statistics.

Quietists. Protestant sect of the seventeenth and eighteenth centuries.

Rabelais, Francois (c. 1494–1533). French humanist and physician; author of *Gargantua and Pantagruel.*

Raleigh, Sir Walter (1554–1618). English explorer, courtier, and poet who organized expeditions to colonize the North American continent.

Randolf, John (1773–1833). United States senator and congressman from Virginia.

Ricardo, David (1772–1823). English economist.

Richard I (1157–1199). King of England; known as Richard the Lion-Hearted.

Riqueti, Honoré Gabriel (1749–1791). Comte de Mirabeau. French revolutionary and political leader, known for his rousing speeches in the States-General and the Constituent Assembly.

Rosa, Salvator (1615–1673). Italian landscape painter.

Rothschild, Mayer Amschel (1744–1812). German-Jewish banker.

Rousseau, Jean-Jacques (1712–1778). French philosopher, writer, and political theorist.

Rowe, Nicholas (1674–1718). English dramatist who edited the first substantial edition of Shakespeare's plays and wrote the first biography of Shakespeare.

Russell, Lord William (1639–1683). English Whig politician executed after being implicated in the Rye House Plot to execute Charles II and his brother James.

Saadi (c.1213–1291). Eminent Persian poet; author of *Gulistan* (*The Rose Garden*); also known as Sa'di and Seyd.

Sallust (c.86–34 B.C.). Roman historian.

Santi, Raphael (1483–1520). Italian Renaissance painter; often referred to as simply Raphael; surname sometimes given as Sanzio.

Saracens. Term commonly used in the Middle Ages to designate the Arabs and, by extension, Muslim peoples in general.

Sarpi, Paolo (1552–1623). Venetian statesman and theologian.

Scanderbeg (c.1404–1468). National hero of Albania whose real name was George Kastrioti.

Scapin. The devious valet in Molière's comedy *Les Fourberies de Scapin* (*The Rogueries of Scapin*).

Schelling, Friedrich Wilhelm Joseph von (1775–1854). German philosopher.

Schlegel, August Wilhelm von (1767–1845). German poet, literary historian, and translator.

Schlegel, Friedrich von (1772–1829). German romantic literary historian and philosopher.

Schuyler, Philip John (1733–1804). American Revolutionary general, member of the Continental Congress, and U.S. senator.

Scott, John (1751–1838). First earl of Eldon. British statesman and lawyer; staunch opponent of reform.

Scott, Sir Walter (1771–1832). Scottish novelist and poet.

Shakers. Radical sect of Quakers so called because members would shake in spiritual ecstasy during religious services.

Sidney, Sir Philip (1554–1586). English author, soldier, and courtier.

Siegfried. German folk-hero whose story is told in the *Nibelungenlied*, an epic poem of the thirteenth century.

Siegmund, Dagobert (1724–1797). Count von Wurmser. One of the Austrian generals Napoleon defeated in the Italian campaigns of 1796 and 1797.

Simonides (5th century B.C.). Greek lyric poet.

Smith, John (1618–1652). English philosopher; one of the Cambridge Platonists.

Socrates (c.470–399 B.C.). Greek philosopher; central figure of Plato's dialogues.

Solon (c.630–c.560 B.C.). Athenian statesman and reformer; established set of laws that were the basis of classical Athenian democracy.

Somerset, Edward (1601–1667). Marquis of Worcester; amateur mechanical engineer who proposed an early model for the steam engine.

Sophocles (c.496–406 B.C.). Greek tragic dramatist; his *Antigone* tells the story of the daughter of Oedipus, who disobeyed Creon, king of Thebes, in order to give proper burial to her brother Polynices, who had been killed while leading a rebellion against the state.

Sophron (5th century B.C.). Greek writer from Syracuse known for his dialogues.

Spartans. People of the ancient Greek city-state of Sparta, famous for their military prowess, strength, and perseverance.

Spenser, Edmund (c.1552–1599). English poet best known as author of *The Faerie Queene.*

Spinoza, Benedict (1632–1677). Dutch rationalist philosopher who claimed that God is nature in its fullness.

Spurzheim, Johann (1776–1832). German physician who proposed the pseudoscience of phrenology, which evaluated personality traits through a "reading" of the bumps on the skull.

Staël, Madame de. See Necker, Anne-Louise-Germaine.

Stewart, Dugald (1753–1828). Scottish philosopher of the common-sense school.

Swedenborg, Emanuel (1688–1772). Swedish theologian and mystic who developed a doctrine of correspondence between the inner and outer worlds.

Sybarites. People of ancient Sybaris, a city known for its luxury and hedonism.

Sydenham, Floyer (1710–1787). Translator of Plato, Plotinus, Proclus, and other Neoplatonists.

Sydney. See Sidney, Sir Philip.

Talbot, Charles (1685–1737). Jurist in the slave case of 1729 that was overturned in the Somerset case.

Talleyrand-Périgord, Charles-Maurice de (1754–1838). French diplomat.

Talma, François-Joseph (1763–1826). French actor admired by Napoleon, who sought out his friendship.

Tasso, Torquato (1544–1595). Italian poet best known for his epic *Jerusalem Delivered*.

Taylor, Jeremy (1613–1667). Anglican bishop and theologian.

Taylor, Thomas (1758–1835). Translator of Plato, Plotinus, Proclus, and other Neoplatonists.

Terminus. Roman god of boundaries.

Thales (7th-6th century B.C.). Greek philosopher.

Theosophist. One who seeks to understand divine principles through contemplation.

Thersites. One of the Greek soldiers in Homer's *Iliad*, known for his ugliness, bad temper, and lack of respect for those of higher rank.

Thor. Norse god of thunder.

Thorfinn Karlsefni (11th century). Scandinavian navigator and explorer.

Thorwaldsen, Bertel (1770–1844). Danish sculptor; the sculpture referred to on page 392 is his *Lion of Lucerne*, a large-scale memorial to the Swiss guard, carved from the native rock at Lucerne, that was designed by Thorwaldsen but completed by his assistants.

Timaeus (flourished c.400 B.C.). Greek astronomer whose name is attached to one of Plato's dialogues, which embodies a theory of the universe.

Timoleon (4th century B.C.). Greek statesman and general known as the scourge of tyrants.

Timon. Character from Shakespeare's *Timon of Athens*.

Tiraboschi, Girolamo (1731–1794). Historian of Italian literature.

Titans. In Greek mythology, the original gods, a race of giants who were overthrown by the Olympians.

Troubadors. Medieval lyric poets who flourished in southern France from the eleventh to the thirteenth centuries.

Turgot, Anne-Robert-Jacques (1727–81). French economist and political reformer.

Ulysses. King of Ithaca; hero of Homer's *Odyssey*.

Uriel. One of the archangels; in Milton's *Paradise Lost*, introduced as the archangel of the sun.

Vane, Sir Henry (c.1613–1662). Puritan who served briefly as colonial governor of Massachusetts (1636–1637) before returning to England, where he was eventually executed for treason by the Restoration government.

Vattel, Emmerich de (1714–1767). Swiss jurist and author of *The Law of Nations* (1758).

Vaucanson, Jacques de (1709–1782). French mathematician and inventor of automata.

Viasa. Legendary author of the Vedas, the sacred literature of Hinduism.

Vieta, François (1540–1603). French mathematician, founder of algebra; also known as Francois Viète.

Virgil (70–19 B.C.). Roman poet; author of the *Aeneid* and other works.

Vishnu. In the Hindu trinity, the savior of humanity.

Vitruvius (lst century B.C.). Roman architect and engineer.

Vittorio, Count Alfieri (1749–1803). Italian poet and patriot.

Voltaire. Assumed name of François-Marie Arouet (1694–1778). French philosopher and writer; a deist who rejected the idea that Jesus was divine.

Vulcan. Roman god of fire and metalworking.

Walpole, Horace (1717–1797). English man of letters.

Walton, Izaak (1593–1683). English writer and biographer.

Warburton, Bishop William (1698–1779). English bishop and scholar; with Alexander Pope, edited an eight-volume edition of Shakespeare.

Warton, Thomas (1728–1790). Historian of British literature.

Warwick. Character from Shakespeare's *Henry VI* plays.

Washington, George (1732–1799). First president of the United States and commander in chief of the Continental army during the American Revolution.

Waterton, Charles (1782–1865). British naturalist; author of *Wanderings in South America* (1825).

Watt, James (1736–1819). Scottish engineer who invented the modern steam engine.

Webster, Daniel (1782–1852). American statesman, lawyer, and orator.

Webster, John (c.1580–c.1634). English dramatist best known for his revenge tragedy *The Duchess of Malfi*.

Wellesley, Arthur (1769–1852). First duke of Wellington. English general who defeated Napoleon at Waterloo.

Wellington. See Wellesley, Arthur.

Werner, Abraham Gottlob (1750–1817). German mineralogist and geologist.

Wesley, John (1703–1791). English evangelical preacher, founder of Methodism.

Wieland, Christoph Martin (1733–1813). German poet, novelist, critic, and translator.

Wilkes, Charles (1798–1877). American naval officer and explorer; published *Narrative of the United States Exploring Expedition* (1844), an account of his explorations of Antarctica and the Pacific.

William of Orange (1533–1584). William I, prince of Orange; won independence for Netherlands from Spain; this is most likely who Emerson refers to on page 338.

Winkelried, Arnold (14th century). Swiss hero credited with the defeat of the Austrians at the Battle of Sempach in 1386.

Witt, Jan de (1625–1672). Dutch statesman influential in the peace treaties that put an end to the Anglo-Dutch Wars.

Woden. Norse god of war.

Wonder. In Greek mythology, mother of Iris; a messenger of the gods; associated with the rainbow; also known as Thaumas or Miracle.

Wotton, Sir Henry (1568–1639). English poet and diplomat.

Wren, Christopher (1632–1732). English architect.

Wurmser. See Siegmund, Dagobert.

Xenophanes (c.560–c.478 B.C.). Pre-Socratic Greek philosopher who taught the unity of all existence.

Xerxes (c.519–459 B.C.). King of ancient Persia opposed by Leonidas and his 300 Spartans at Thermopylae.

Yoganidra. Goddess of illusion in Hindu mythology.

Zeno (4th century B.C.). Greek philosopher and founder of Stoicism.

Zoroaster (c.628–551 B.C.). Religious prophet of ancient Persia.

Endnotes

Grateful acknowledgment is due to the editors of *The Collected Works of Ralph Waldo Emerson* (5 vols. to date, edited by Alfred R. Ferguson, Joseph Slater, and Douglas Emory Wilson, Harvard University Press, 1971–); Emerson's *Journals and Miscellaneous Notebooks* (16 vols., edited by William H. Gilman, Ralph H. Orth, et al., Harvard University Press, 1960–1982); and *The Later Lectures of Ralph Waldo Emerson, 1843–1871* (2 vols., edited by Ronald A. Bosco and Joel Myerson, University of Georgia Press, 2001).

Readers who have further questions about Emerson's sources or other textual matters should refer to the notes and textual apparatus of *The Collected Works*. A bibliography of other resources is also included in this edition; see "For Further Reading."

Nature

1. (p. 7) *Nature:* Originally published in 1836, *Nature* was Emerson's first book and remains perhaps the most systematic statement of the idealist philosophy he would develop and moderate in *Essays* (1841) and *Essays: Second Series* (1844). Emerson republished *Nature* in 1849 as the introductory piece to *Nature, Addresses and Lectures.* "The American Scholar" address, "An Address to the Senior Class in Divinity College, Cambridge" (which appears in this volume as "An Address" on p. 67), "Man the Reformer," and "The Transcendentalist" were all included in that volume. Each in its way comprises the ideas expressed in *Nature* adapted for a specific audience—college undergraduates, future ministers, the entrepreneurs of the emerging middle class, and Boston's wealthy elite.

2. (p. 7) *A subtle chain of countless rings . . . Mounts through all the spires of form:* In the 1836 edition of *Nature*, Emerson used as his epigraph the following quotation from the Neoplatonist philosopher Plotinus (c. 205–270 A.D.). "Nature is but an image or imitation of wisdom, the last thing of the soul; nature being a thing which doth only do, but not know." In the 1849 edition, he replaced it with verses of his own, following a pattern he had begun in *Essays: Second Series* (1844).

3. (p. 9) *It builds the sepulchres of the fathers:* An allusion to the Bible, Luke 11:47–48, "Woe unto you! for ye build the sepulchers of the prophets, and your fathers killed them. Truly ye bear witness that ye allow the deeds of your fa-

thers: for they indeed killed them, and ye build their sepulchers" (King James Version). Emerson is calling his readers to be the prophets of today, to be future oriented in their thinking, instead of simply memorializing the great thinkers of the past.

4. (p. 9) *Every man's condition is a solution in hieroglyphic to those inquiries he would put:* This reference to the pictographic writing of ancient Egypt, first deciphered in 1821 by Jean-François Champollion, announces a major theme that Emerson will develop in subsequent chapters of *Nature*, especially chapter IV, "Language," where he will claim, "Every natural fact is a symbol of some spiritual fact" (p. 21).

5. (p. 10) *all which Philosophy distinguishes as the* NOT ME: Emerson borrows the phrase "Not Me" from Thomas Carlyle's *Sartor Resartus* (1833–1834). He arranged for the publication of the American edition (1836) and wrote its introduction.

6. (p. 12) *I become a transparent eyeball:* Emerson's description of becoming "a transparent eyeball" is perhaps the most famous passage in *Nature*. Much commented on and often parodied, it nonetheless remains a powerful statement of transcendence—a metaphor for how perceiving the divinity of the natural world and of one's self can cause one to leave behind the conventional attitudes and beliefs of society.

7. (p. 14) *They all admit of being thrown into one of the following classes; Commodity; Beauty; Language; and Discipline:* These "classes" outline the progression Emerson will follow in the next four chapters as he traces the uses of Nature from its practical, material use to its symbolic use as a sign of ethical laws.

8. (p. 15) *he realizes the fable of Æolus's bag:* In Homer's *Odyssey* (book 10), Aeolus, the god of winds, gives Odysseus a bag of favorable winds to be used in the event that his ship is becalmed. However, in order to reach home sooner, his crew releases them all at once, unleashing a storm that drives them off course. In this paragraph, Emerson is referring to the fact that modern science and technology have accomplished what past civilizations could not—the progress that has occurred from "the era of Noah to that of Napoleon."

9. (p. 17) *The dawn is my Assyria . . . the night shall be my Germany of mystic philosophy and dreams:* Emerson is drawing a contrast between the empiricist tradition of Scottish common sense philosophy (Bacon, Locke, Hume) and the idealist tradition of post-Kantian German romantic philosophy (Schelling, Fichte, Hegel). Assyria was an ancient city empire in western Asia known for its wealth and the luxury of court life; Paphos was an ancient city in Cyprus and an important seaport during the Hellenistic period.

10. (p. 18) *when Leonidas and his three hundred martyrs consume one day in dying:* Leonidas—king of Sparta killed in 480 B.C. defending the pass at Thermopylae against the Persian army led by Xerxes—is the first in a series of examples of heroes and heroic actions.

11. (p. 21) *Every natural fact is a symbol of some spiritual fact:* Emerson's sense of

the symbolic correspondence between natural objects and spiritual concepts is derived largely from his reading of Emanuel Swedenborg, whose doctrine of correspondence between inner and outer worlds struck Emerson, at this early stage in his career, as a way to overcome the dualism inherent in human experience. For examples of Emerson's efforts to address the dualistic nature of human experience, see "Compensation" (p. 138), "Nominalist and Realist" (p. 277), and "Fate" (pp. 386, 388).

12. (p. 23) *The same symbols are found to make the original elements of all languages:* The theory of the origins of language that Emerson gives in this and subsequent paragraphs was common during the romantic period. Emerson will use it to claim that poets possess a revolutionary power insofar as they can use language to reshape the values of society (p. 24), a claim similar to that made by Percy Bysshe Shelley in his "A Defense of Poetry" (1821): "Poets are the unacknowledged legislators of the world." Compare this with Emerson's essay "The Poet" (p. 228).

13. (p. 25) *It is the standing problem which has exercised the wonder and the study of every fine genius since the world began; . . . of Leibnitz, of Swedenborg:* Each of the "fine geniuses" in this list sought to explain "the relation between mind and matter."

14. (p. 25) *There sits the Sphinx:* "The riddle of the sphinx" refers to the mystery of human existence. It is taken from the story of Oedipus in Greek mythology. The sphinx was a monster with a lion's body, an eagle's wings, and the head and breasts of a woman. It guarded the road to Thebes and challenged all travelers with a riddle; if they failed to answer correctly it would kill and eat them. When Oedipus solved the riddle, the sphinx killed itself. The riddle: "What walks on four legs at dawn, two legs at noon, and three legs in the evening." Oedipus's answer: "Man," because dawn, noon, and evening refer to the stages of human life: in childhood we crawl, in adulthood we walk, in old age we use a cane.

15. (p. 27) *Discipline:* Emerson's title for this chapter refers to the self-discipline individuals must exercise in order to intuit properly the symbolic meaning of natural phenomena. His claim that "every natural process is a version of a moral sentence" obliges us to "read" the ethical significance of the natural world and of human actions.

16. (p. 30) *The fable of Proteus has a cordial truth:* In Greek mythology, Proteus was the sea god who tended the seals of Poseidon; he could change shape to evade capture, but if caught and held he would foretell the future. Compare this with Emerson's reference to Proteus in the poem that serves as the headnote to "Illusions" (pp. 405–406).

17. (p. 33) *The frivolous make themselves merry with the Ideal theory:* The "Ideal" theory that Emerson summarizes in the previous paragraph is drawn from the philosopher George Berkeley. See his *Three Dialogues between Hylas and Philonous* (1713) for a clear synopsis of his argument that ideas are known only in the mind and thus there is no existence of matter independent of perception:

esse est percipi (roughly, "being is perception"; more accurately, "what is is what is perceived to be").

18. (p. 42) *we learn that man has access to the entire mind of the Creator, is himself the creator in the finite:* Compare this passage with Emerson's description of becoming a "transparent eyeball" in chapter 1, "Nature": "I am part or particle of God" (p. 12). This faith in the divinity of the individual is the foundation on which Emerson builds his philosophy of self-reliance. Compare also with "Self-Reliance": "We lie in the lap of immense intelligence . . ." (p. 123).

19. (p. 46) *we learn to prefer imperfect theories, and sentences, which contain glimpses of truth, to digested systems which have no one valuable suggestion:* Emerson apparently is renouncing the systematic approach to knowledge that he practiced in the earlier chapters of *Nature*, where he traced the uses of nature from their use as commodities to their use as signs of ethical laws. This sets the stage for the prophetic pronouncements in the paragraphs that follow, which Emerson claims were sung to him by a "certain poet." The "poet" is Emerson himself. He will repeat this gesture in his essay "The Poet" (see p. 223).

20. (p. 47) *Thus my Orphic poet sang:* "Orphic" is an allusion to Orpheus. a musician in Greek mythology who charmed Hades with his song so that he could bring his wife, Eurydice, back from the underworld. Emerson's close friend and fellow transcendentalist Bronson Alcott would later contribute to the *Dial* a series of aphorisms under the title "Orphic Sayings."

The American Scholar

1. (p. 50) *The American Scholar:* In his address to the Phi Beta Kappa society at Harvard, Emerson applied the idealist philosophy he had worked out in *Nature* to the institution of higher education. "Why should we not have a poetry and philosophy of insight and not of tradition, and a religion by revelation to us, and not the history of theirs?" he had asked in his introduction to *Nature* (p. 9). Now he urged his audience to take that question to heart in their studies, to be "Man Thinking" rather than "the parrot of other men's thinking" (p. 51).

2. (p. 55) *There is then creative reading as well as creative writing:* Compare this passage with "The Poet": "An imaginative book renders us much more service at first, by stimulating us through its tropes, than afterward, when we arrive at the precise sense of the author" (pp. 227–228). Emerson's criticism of the rote learning practiced in the university, where students memorize the work of famous poets, philosophers, and scientists instead of writing poetry, philosophy, and science of their own, shares much in common with his criticism of social conformity in "Self-Reliance."

3. (p. 56) *The preamble of thought, the transition through which it passes from the unconscious to the conscious, is action:* Compare this passage with Emerson's discussion of virtuous actions in chapter III, "Beauty," of *Nature*: "We are

taught by great actions that the universe is the property of every individual in it" (p. 18). In "The American Scholar," Emerson is following a similar progression from perception to action to thought.

4. (p. 58) *Authors we have, in numbers, who . . . ramble round Algiers, to replenish their merchantable stock:* Emerson refers here to a common practice among writers of his day, many of whom would travel to Europe, the Middle East, or the frontier and then publish narratives based on their experiences. He may have had in mind, particularly, Washington Irving, whose *The Conquest of Granada* (1829) and *Legends of the Alhambra* (1832) are based on his experiences in the Mediterranean during his stint as ambassador to Spain, and James Fenimore Cooper, whose novel *The Prairie* (1827), the third of his famous Leatherstocking Tales, transplanted his hero from the wilderness of upstate New York to the western frontier.

5. (p. 59) *I hear therefore with joy whatever is beginning to be said of the dignity and necessity of labor to every citizen:* Emerson is referring to the "associationist" movement, inspired by socialist and utopian thinkers who believed that all should share equally in the labor needed to support a community. A number of Emerson's close friends and colleagues founded Brook Farm, a utopian community in West Roxbury, Massachusetts, based on associationist principles. Although Emerson was supportive of the enterprise, he refused to join.

6. (p. 65) *This idea has inspired the genius of Goldsmith. . . . of Gibbon, looks cold and pedantic:* In this paragraph, Emerson contrasts the Enlightenment tradition represented by Alexander Pope, Samuel Johnson, and Edward Gibbon with pre-Romantic (Oliver Goldsmith, Robert Burns, and William Cowper) and Romantic writers (Goethe, William Wordsworth, and Thomas Carlyle). The Romantic emphasis on the common experiences of everyday people makes the objective, rational style of the Enlightenment seem "cold and pedantic."

An Address

1. (p. 67) *An Address:* In his address to the graduating class of the Divinity School at Harvard, Emerson applied his transcendental philosophy to the institution of the ministry, telling his audience that, in order to be a spiritual force in the lives of their parishioners, they would need to liberate themselves from "the dogmas of our church," which are "wholly insulated from anything now extant in the life and business of the people" (p. 76). While his call for a radical break from traditions that are dead was well received when addressed to the Phi Beta Kappa Society, in the halls of the Divinity School it was more controversial. Many faculty members were outraged. The following year Professor Andrews Norton, in his own address to the school, publicly condemned Emerson as an atheist, and Emerson was not invited back to speak at Harvard for more than three decades.

2. (p. 72) *In this point of view we become very sensible of the first defect of historical*

Christianity: "Historical Christianity" refers to what came to be known as "the higher criticism," an approach to Christian texts that emerged in Germany and that applied to the interpretation of scripture the scientific methods used by historians and archaeologists.

3. (p. 72) *All who hear me . . . as the Orientals or the Greeks would describe Osiris or Apollo:* Developing his argument that Christianity has become a "Mythus," Emerson claims that Christ is to Europe what Osiris (the goddess of fertility) was to Egypt and Apollo (god of music, poetry, and prophecy) was to Greece. The region we now call the Middle East (including Egypt) was commonly referred to as "the Orient" in the eighteenth and nineteenth centuries.

4. (p. 79) *The imitator dooms himself to hopeless mediocrity:* Compare this passage with the second paragraph of "Self-Reliance": "There is a time in every man's education when he arrives at the conviction that envy is ignorance; that imitation is suicide" (p. 114).

5. (p. 81) *All attempts to contrive a system . . . ending to-morrow in madness and murder:* A reference to the fact that, during the French Revolution, efforts to reorganize society along strictly rational codes of conduct ultimately led to the Reign of Terror, in which thousands of people were executed.

Man the Reformer

1. (p. 83) *Man the Reformer:* In this lecture, Emerson responds to the associationist movement, under whose banner many of his fellow transcendentalists embarked on experiments in communal living at Brook Farm and Fruitlands. Although sympathetic to intentions behind these projects, Emerson insisted that society could not be reformed unless individuals first reformed themselves. Emerson's criticism of the materialism of American society and of conformity with those values, which leads individuals away from "the lesson of self-help," anticipates Henry David Thoreau's criticisms of "Economy" in the first chapter of *Walden* (1854).

2. (p. 97) *the time will come when we too shall hold nothing back, but shall eagerly convert more than we now possess into means and powers:* Compare this passage with the concluding sentence of "Experience": ". . . the true romance which the world exists to realize will be the transformation of genius into practical power" (p. 254).

The Transcendentalist

1. (p. 98) *The Transcendentalist:* This essay is by no means a self-portrait. Instead, it should be read as a counterbalance to the more pragmatic views expressed in "Man the Reformer." Emerson takes the point of view of an outside observer "describing a class of young persons whom I have seen" (as he wrote in a letter to his aunt Mary Moody). His intention was to encourage his Boston audience

to see the value of allowing some members of society to pursue their own path, regardless of how impractical it may seem to them. "When every voice is raised for a new road or another statute, or a subscription of stock . . . will you not tolerate one or two solitary voices in the land, speaking for thoughts and principles not marketable or perishable?" (p. 112). Henry David Thoreau would make the same point in the concluding paragraph of "Resistance to Civil Government" (1849): "I please myself with imaging a State at last which can afford to be just to all men, . . . which even would not think it inconsistent with its own repose, if a few were to live aloof from it, not meddling with it, nor embraced by it, who fulfilled all the duties of neighbors and fellow-men."

2. (p. 103) *It is well known to most of my audience, that the Idealism of the present day acquired the name of Transcendental, from the use of that term by Immanuel Kant:* Emerson's knowledge of Kant's philosophy is mainly derived from Coleridge and Carlyle, and his understanding of the term "transcendental" as referring to "whatever belongs to the class of intuitive thought" is much broader than Kant's definition of the term.

3. (pp. 109–110) *The worst feature of this double consciousness is . . . the two discover no greater disposition to reconcile themselves:* In "Fate" Emerson will again address the problem of our "double consciousness" but in more positive terms: "One key, one solution to the mysteries of human condition, one solution to the old knots of fate, freedom, and foreknowledge, exists, the propounding, namely, of the double consciousness. A man must ride alternately on the horses of his private and public nature" (p. 388).

4. (p. 110) *Patience, then, is for us, is it not? Patience, and still patience:* Compare this passage with the concluding paragraph of the "The American Scholar": "Patience,—patience;—with the shades of all the good and great for company; and for solace, the perspective of your own infinite life; and for work, the study and the communication of principles, the making those instincts prevalent, the conversion of the world" (p. 66).

5. (p. 110) *In the eternal trinity of Truth, Goodness, and Beauty:* Emerson is adapting the fundamental doctrine of the Trinity in Christianity, in which God is said to exist in three persons who were held to be separate and equal, yet one: God the Father, God the Son (who became incarnate as Jesus), and the Holy Spirit proceeding from Father and Son. Interestingly, the Unitarian branch of Congregationalism, to which Emerson belonged when a minister, denied the Trinity. Compare this passage with a paragraph from "The Poet" that begins "For the Universe has three children . . ." (p. 215).

6. (p. 111) *Antony:* In this hypothetical exchange, Emerson names his transcendentalist after Saint Anthony (251?–c.350), the father of Christian monasticism. According to tradition, Saint Anthony endured every temptation the devil could devise while living as a hermit. The temptations of Saint Anthony became a popular theme in Western art and literature.

Self-Reliance

1. (p. 113) *Self-Reliance:* Perhaps the most famous of Emerson's essays, "Self-Reliance" contains some of his strongest statements of individualism. However, when Emerson makes such bold claims as "the only right is what is after my constitution, the only wrong what is against it" (p. 116), it is important to see that his conviction is grounded in a belief that all genuine actions proceed from divinity. "We lie in the lap of immense intelligence, which makes us organs of its activity and receivers of its truth. When we discern justice, when we discern truth, we do nothing of ourselves, but allow a passage to its beams" (p. 123).

2. (p. 117) *I would write on the lintels of the door-post,* Whim: Compare to the Bible, Exodus 12. The last of the plagues Moses called down upon Egypt was God's promise to strike down the firstborn of every household in the land. He had Moses instruct the Israelites to paint their doorposts with the blood of a sacrificed lamb and promised to "pass over" those households thus marked. By implication, Emerson wants the obligations of social conformity to "pass over" him.

3. (p. 120) *Pythagoras was misunderstood . . . and Newton:* In this list Emerson names individuals who had a revolutionary effect on western culture.

4. (p. 133) *Hudson and Behring accomplished so much in their fishing-boats as to astonish Parry and Franklin:* In this sentence Emerson contrasts the accomplishments of four explorers: Vitus Jonassen Bering and Henry Hudson accomplished more than the later Arctic explorers William Parry and John Franklin, who were better equipped. Emerson's larger point is that the power of the human will, not technology, accomplishes great endeavors.

Compensation

1. (p. 136) *Compensation:* This essay can be seen as a bridge between "Self-Reliance" and "Spiritual Laws." While acknowledging that there are limits to the human will, Emerson nevertheless insists that our failures, and even the tragedies we suffer, contribute to our growth and development. "When he is pushed, tormented, defeated, he has a chance to learn something; he has been put on his wits, on his manhood; he has gained facts; learns his ignorance; is cured of the insanity of conceit; has got moderation and real skill" (p. 149). Emerson will return to this theme in "Experience" and "Fate," essays that also consider those forces that limit our self-reliance.

2. (p. 146) *the emerald of Polycrates:* Polycrates, concerned about his consistent good fortune, threw his most prized possession, an emerald ring, into the sea to placate the gods. The next day he found the ring in the belly of a fish that was served to him, an omen of his subsequent overthrow and death.

3. (p. 152) *The voice of the Almighty saith, 'Up and onward for evermore!':* Compare this passage with the conclusion of "Experience": "Never mind the

ridicule, never mind the defeat; up again, old heart! it seems to say, there is victory yet for all justice" (p. 254).

Spiritual Laws

1. (p. 154) *Spiritual Laws:* In this essay, Emerson catalogues the fundamental truths revealed by self-reliant action. While acknowledging the unique and subjective quality of each individual mind, Emerson insists that the legitimacy of our thoughts and actions depends on how well we communicate them to others. Despite his criticisms of social conformity in "Self-Reliance," in "Spiritual Laws" he affirms that society is the ultimate safeguard of truth. "A man passes for that he is worth. What he is, engraves itself on his face, on his form, on his fortunes, in letters of light which all men may read but himself. Concealment avails him nothing, boasting nothing" (p. 168).

2. (p. 154) *In these hours the mind seems so great that nothing can be taken from us that seems much:* Compare this passage with Emerson's account of the death of his son, Waldo, in "Experience" (p. 236).

3. (p. 155) *What we do not call education is more precious than that which we call so:* Compare this passage with Emerson's criticisms of "the book-learned class" in "The American Scholar" (p. 54).

4. (p. 156) *the Transcendental club:* Emerson was one of the founding members of the Saturday Club, which later became known as the Transcendental Club, a group of intellectuals who met periodically to discuss current philosophical and scientific ideas. Among the best-known members were Henry David Thoreau, George Ripley, Bronson Alcott, Margaret Fuller, Francis Henry Hedge, and Theodore Parker. The *Dial*, edited by Fuller and Emerson, published the writings of many of its members.

5. (p. 160) *What a man does, that he has. . . . his infinite productiveness:* In this and subsequent paragraphs, the first sentence gives a "spiritual law" that Emerson then elaborates in the sentences that follow.

6. (p. 163) *"My children . . . you will never see anything worse than yourselves":* In his journals, Emerson attributes this comment to "my Grandfather" (*Journals and Miscellaneous Notebooks*, vol. 4, p. 212).

7. (p. 166) *Our philosophy is affirmative, and readily accepts the testimony of negative facts, as every shadow points to the sun:* Compare this passage with "Experience": "Skepticisms are not gratuitous or lawless, but are limitations of the affirmative statement, and the new philosophy must take them in and make affirmations outside of them, just as much as it must include the oldest beliefs" (p. 249).

8. (p. 171) *The poet uses the name of Cæsar, of Tamerlane, of Bonduca, of Belisarius:* Emerson likely has in mind Shakespeare's *Tragedy of Julius Caesar;* Philip Marlowe's *Tamburlaine,* which recounts the Mongolian ruler's conquests; John Fletcher's *Bonduca,* about the British queen who led a rebellion against the Ro-

mans; and Jean François Marmontel's *Bélisaire*, a novel about the Roman general under Justinian.

Friendship

1. (p. 172) *Friendship:* Emerson had long been aware that the transcendence of social conformity, the aspiration to be self-reliant, could lead to alienation. In *Nature,* he acknowledged that, in moments of transcendence, "the name of the nearest friend sounds then foreign and accidental: to be brothers, to be acquaintances,—master or servant, is then a trifle and a disturbance" (p. 12), and in "Self-Reliance" he urged his readers to place their obligation to the truth above their obligations to family and friends (p. 127). In "Friendship," he examines more closely what is necessary "to stand in true relations with men in a false age" (p. 178).

2. (p. 175) *And I must hazard the production of the bald fact amid these pleasing reveries, though it should prove an Egyptian skull at our banquet:* Emerson refers to an ancient Egyptian custom in which a skeleton was placed on the banquet table during celebrations to remind diners that, since death is inevitable, they should enjoy themselves to the fullest.

3. (p. 178) *Every man alone is sincere. At the entrance of a second person, hypocrisy begins:* Compare this passage with "Self-Reliance": "It is easy in the world to live after the world's opinion; it is easy in solitude to live after our own; but the great man is he who in the midst of the crowd keeps with perfect sweetness the independence of solitude" (p. 118).

The Over-Soul

1. (p. 186) *The Over-Soul:* Emerson often uses the term "Over-Soul" to refer to divinity. He sometimes uses it interchangeably with the philosophic concept "Being" and the theological concept "Universal Spirit." Compare this passage with his discussion of "Intuition" in "Self-Reliance" (p. 123).

2. (p. 191) *That third party or common nature is not social; it is impersonal; is God:* Henry David Thoreau makes a similar observation in the "Solitude" chapter of *Walden:* "However intense my experience, I am conscious of the presence and criticism of a part of me, which, as it were, is not a part of me, but spectator, sharing no experience, but taking note of it; and that is no more I than it is you."

3. (p. 193) *The trances of Socrates; . . . the illumination of Swedenborg; are of this kind:* In this sentence Emerson lists a series of revelatory experiences. The apostle Paul's conversion on the road to Damascus is described in the Bible, Acts 9:1–19.

4. (p. 196) *The great distinction between teachers, sacred or literary; between poets like Herbert, . . . Mackintosh and Stewart:* In this series of poets and philoso-

phers, Emerson contrasts those who write from their own experience of the transcendent or divine with those who make objective, rational arguments about the possibility of divinity.

5. (p. 196) *All men stand continually in the expectation of the appearance of such a teacher:* Compare this passage with the conclusion of "An Address" (to the Divinity School at Harvard): "I look for the new Teacher . . ." (p. 82), and Emerson's earlier exhortation to his audience: "Be to [your parishioners] a divine man; be to them thought and virtue" (p. 79).

6. (pp. 197–198) *But the soul that ascendeth to worship the great God, is plain and true; . . . the earnest experience of the common day:* Compare this passage with Emerson's emphasis on "the near, the low, the common" in "The American Scholar," (p. 64).

Circles

1. (p. 202) *Circles:* In this essay, Emerson's idealist philosophy takes its most progressive turn. Having affirmed the universal nature of truth in "Spiritual Laws" and "The Over-Soul," Emerson now insists that all social institutions and all human knowledge are continually subject to new revolutions of thought. His role as an intellectual and an artist is not to propose a new set of ideas to reform society but to unsettle the ideas currently in place to make way for the emergence of better ones. "I unsettle all things," he writes. "No facts are to me sacred; none are profane; I simply experiment, an endless seeker, with no Past at my back" (p. 210).

2. (p. 202) *St. Augustine described the nature of God as a circle whose center was everywhere, and its circumference nowhere:* According to the editors of *The Collected Works* (pp. 253–254), Emerson's source for this idea is not the writings of Saint Augustine himself, but John Norris's *An Essay Towards the Theory of the Ideal or Intelligible World* (2 vols., London, 1701–1704); however, the idea appears in numerous other works read by Emerson, including Sir Thomas Browne's *Religio Medici* (1643) and Samuel Taylor Coleridge's *Aids to Reflection* (1825).

3. (p. 203) *You admire his tower of granite. . . . the effect of a finer cause:* In this example of a tower of granite, Emerson illustrates his idealist philosophy: that material objects are symbols of thought, and that therefore new ideas can transform the world. Compare this passage with chapter VI of *Nature*, "Idealism": "Seen in the light of thought, the world always is phenomenal" (p. 40).

4. (p. 204) *Resist it not; it goes to refine and raise thy theory of matter just as much:* Compare this passage with "Experience": "The new statement will comprise the skepticisms as well as the faiths of a society, and out of unbeliefs a creed shall be formed" (p. 249).

5. (p. 210) *No facts are to me sacred; none are profane; I simply experiment, an endless seeker, with no Past at my back:* Compare this passage with chapter VII of

Nature, "Prospects": "A wise writer will feel that the ends of study and composition are best answered by announcing undiscovered regions of thought, and so communicating, through hope, new activity to the torpid spirit" (p. 46).

The Poet

1. (p. 213) *The Poet:* In this essay, Emerson develops an idea central to the "Language" section of *Nature* (see note 12). He describes poets as "liberating gods" because their use of metaphor can free readers from conventional ways of thinking (p. 227). Scholars recognize this essay as inaugurating a distinctively American poetic tradition. Emerson's observation "We have yet had no genius in America, with tyrannous eye, which knew the value of our incomparable materials, and saw, in the barbarism and materialism of the times, another carnival of the same gods whose picture he so much admires in Homer" (p. 230) is often said to anticipate Walt Whitman's *Leaves of Grass.*

2. (p. 215) *For the Universe has three children . . . the Knower, the Doer, and the Sayer:* Compare this passage with Emerson's discussion of "the eternal trinity of Truth, Goodness, and Beauty" in "The Transcendentalist" (p. 110).

3. (p. 220) *The inwardness, and mystery. . . . they are all poets and mystics:* Compare this paragraph on political symbolism with *Nature* (p. 24). "The great ball" is an allusion to a promotional stunt used by the Whig party in the presidential campaign of 1840 that involved large, wooden-framed balls covered with leather and decorated with slogans such as "Keep the ball rolling." Emerson goes on to list a variety of political symbols current in the 1840s. In political parades, manufacturing towns such as Lowell, Lynn, and Salem would be represented by floats shaped like the goods they produced. W. H. Harrison used "the log cabin" and "the cider barrel" in his 1840 campaign for presidency to remind voters of his frontier origins. The "hickory stick" was the symbol of Andrew Jackson, seventh president of the United States, whose nickname was "Old Hickory." "The palmetto tree" was associated with Senator John Calhoun of South Carolina, a staunch defender of the interests of the southern plantation aristocracy.

4. (p. 223) *I remember that a certain poet described it to me thus:* As in the concluding chapter of *Nature,* Emerson creates a persona to communicate his ideal philosophy; see note 19.

5. (p. 228) *I think nothing is of any value in books excepting the transcendental and extraordinary:* Compare this passage with "The American Scholar": "There is then creative reading as well as creative writing" (p. 55).

Experience

1. (p. 234) *Experience:* One of Emerson's most deeply personal essays, "Experience" may have been motivated in part by the death of his first-born son,

Waldo, at the age of five. This tragedy may also have reawakened memories of the death of his first wife, Ellen Tucker, and of his brothers Edward and Charles. While in "Circles" Emerson had found the endless succession of knowledge and events to be an inspiration to new thoughts and endeavors, "Experience" offers a darker view on the impermanence of reality. "I take this evanescence and lubricity of all objects, which lets them slip through our fingers then when we clutch hardest, to be the most unhandsome part of our condition" (p. 237). Yet despite these limitations, Emerson still makes the affirmative statement: "Onward and onward. In liberated moments we know that a new picture of life and duty is already possible" (pp. 248–249).

2. (p. 235) *like those that Hermes won with dice of the Moon, that Osiris might be born:* In ancient Egyptian mythology, the Sun god placed a curse on his wife, Rhea, for her infidelity, which prevented her from giving birth on any day of the year. Hermes won an additional five days from the Moon, and Osiris was born on the first of these.

3. (p. 239) Pero si muove: The Italian phrase translates as "still it moves," words allegedly murmured by Galileo immediately after he was forced by Roman Catholic authorities to deny publicly his discovery that Earth moves around the sun.

4. (p. 243) *the Vatican, the Uffizii, or the Louvre:* These museums are in Rome, Florence, and Paris, respectively. Three paintings are mentioned just above: *The Transfiguration,* by Raphael; *The Last Judgment,* by Michelangelo; and *The Communion of Saint Jerome,* by Il Domenichino.

5. (p. 252) *In Flaxman's drawing of the Eumenides . . . the Furies sleep on the threshold:* In Aeschylus's tragedy *Eumenides,* Orestes was ordered by Apollo to avenge the murder of his father, who was killed by his wife, Clytemnestra, and her lover, Aegisthus. Orestes does so but nonetheless is pursued by the Furies for matricide. He flees to Athens, where he eventually is put on trial and acquitted.

Politics

1. (p. 255) *Politics:* While the painful lesson that "all things fade" was traumatic for Emerson in "Experience," in "Politics" he again makes the impermanence of things a motive for revolutionary thinking. In the first sentence, he reminds his readers that each law and each institution of the State was "the act of a single man" meant to address "a particular case" and that, therefore, all are subject to change: "they are all imitable, all alterable; we may make as good; we may make better" (pp. 255–256). This pragmatic belief that laws are subject to individuals, and not the reverse, was a powerful incentive for Emerson's resistance to the Fugitive Slave Law and his public support of abolition in the decade leading up to the Civil War. See his "Address to the Citizens of Concord" on the Fugitive Slave Law, included in this edition.

2. (p. 255) *Phœbus stablish must:* In Greek mythology, the sons of Amphion (or Antiope) erected around Thebes a wall made of stones that would move when Amphion played her lyre. Phoebus Apollo was the god of light, music, and poetry. Emerson seems to mean that Phoebus must establish or stabilize the city-state erected by Amphion's sons. This will be accomplished by the "meeting" of the Muses and the Virtues in the next two lines.

3. (p. 396) *We must trust infinitely to the beneficent necessity which shines through all laws:* Compare this passage with the conclusion of "Fate": "Let us build altars to the Beautiful Necessity" (p. 389).

Nominalist and Realist

1. (p. 267) *Nominalist and Realist:* This essay is in many ways a summation of the various themes developed in *Essays: Second Series.* Emerson proposes a dualistic antagonism in human nature to account for the apparent contradiction between his belief in self-reliance and his experience that we are all subject to external forces that shape and mold our sense of ourselves. "All the universe over, there is but one thing, this old Two-Face, creator-creature, mind-matter, right-wrong, of which any proposition may be affirmed or denied" (p. 277). Emerson will return to this dualistic conception of human nature in "Fate."

2. (p. 269) *Webster cannot do the work of Webster:* Emerson's opinion of Webster changed dramatically after Webster supported the legislation that came to be known as the Compromise of 1850, which included the Fugitive Slave Law.

3. (p. 271) *The eye must not lose sight for a moment of the purpose. . . . they respect the argument:* Compare this passage with "The Poet": "For it is not meters, but a meter-making argument, that makes a poem" (p. 217).

4. (p. 273) *Alphonso of Castille fancied he could have given useful advice:* When the Ptolemaic system of astronomy was explained to Alphonso X, he is alleged to have said that if God had consulted him the universe would have had a better and simpler design.

5. (p. 278) *If we could have any security against moods!:* Compare this passage with "Experience": "Life is a train of moods like a string of beads, and as we pass through them, they prove to be many-colored lenses which paint the world their own hue" (p. 237).

Uses of Great Men

1. (p. 280) *Uses of Great Men:* This is the introductory lecture to the series Emerson published as *Representative Men* in 1850. The series as a whole bears some similarity to Thomas Carlyle's *Heroes, Hero Worship and the Heroic in History,* but unlike Carlyle, Emerson does not present his biographical subjects as models to imitate. Instead, each represents a characteristic approach to human experience, as the subtitles of each lecture suggest: Plato's life is exemplary of "the

Philosopher's" approach; Shakespeare's, of that of "the Poet." Each of these different representative types is meant to check and balance the others and so help Emerson's audience realize their own approach to life. "Other men are lenses through which we read our own minds," he writes. "Each man seeks those of different quality from his own, and such as are good of their kind; that is, he seeks other men, and the *otherest.* The stronger the nature, the more it is reactive" (p. 281).

2. (p. 287) *The dominion of Aristotle, the Ptolemaic astronomy, the credit of Luther, of Bacon, of Locke:* In this series, Emerson lists intellectuals whose philosophical, scientific, or theological systems were greatly influential, but eventually overturned by subsequent thinkers.

Plato; or The Philosopher

1. (p. 296) *Platonists! . . . Picus Mirandola:* The city of Alexandria, famous for its library, was a center for Neoplatonist thought. Many of the Neoplatonist philosophers Emerson admired studied there, including Plotinus and Proclus. "The Elizabethans" refers broadly to English philosophers, scientists, and writers of the Renaissance that flourished in Great Britain under the reign of Queen Elizabeth.

2. (p. 298) *He was born 427 . . . and died . . . in the act of writing, at eighty-one years:* The editors of *The Collected Works* surmise that Emerson drew this biographical information from Thomas Stanley's *The History of Philosophy* (1701).

3. (p. 299) *Before Pericles came the Seven Wise Masters . . . or from mind:* Under the peace established during Pericles' reign (see p. 17), Athens flourished. "The seven wise masters" refers to a series of ancient Greek political leaders and philosophers, including Thales (seventh century), who is said to have introduced geometry to the Greeks. By "partialists" Emerson seems to mean materialist as opposed to idealist philosophers.

4. (p. 300) *"In the midst of the sun is the light . . . the imperishable being":* The Vedas are the sacred literature of Hinduism. This specific quotation is probably drawn from Henry Thomas Colbrooke's "On the Religious Ceremonies of the Hindus, and the Brahmens Especially" in *Miscellaneous Essays* (1837). See the discussion in *Collected Works,* vol. 3, p. 180.

5. (p. 303) *whether a swarm of bees settled on his lips:* Emerson is referring to the legend that when Plato was an infant, bees made a honeycomb in his mouth, signifying his later talent as an orator and rhetorician—that is, he was "honey-tongued."

6. (p. 311) *Socrates again, in his traits and genius. . . . he was what our country-people call an old one:* See the conclusion of Plato's *Symposium.* As with the biographical information for Plato, Emerson takes most of the anecdotes of Socrates given in this and the following paragraphs from Thomas Stanley's *The History of Philosophy* (1701).

Shakespeare; or The Poet

1. (pp. 317–318) *Here is the tale of Troy . . . which all the London 'prentices know:* Emerson alludes to a number of narratives that may or may not have served as the basis for some of Shakespeare's plays. Shakespeare is known to have drawn heavily from sources, such as the chronicles of Raphael Holinshed and Edward Hall, which gave the history of "the royal Henries" from Henry I (1068–1135) to Henry VIII (1491–1547).

2. (p. 319) *In Henry VIII. I think I see plainly the cropping out . . . vicious ear:* Emerson's contention that *Henry VIII* is not entirely the work of Shakespeare has been maintained by modern scholarship, which generally treats the play as a collaborative work by Shakespeare and John Fletcher.

3. (p. 320) *But Chaucer is a huge borrower:* Emerson took most of his information on Chaucer's sources from Thomas Warton's *History of English Poetry* (1824). Modern scholarship has proven much of it to be inaccurate; yet Emerson's larger point—that Chaucer, like Shakespeare, worked from a literary tradition—is sound.

4. (p. 321) *Vedas, Æsop's Fables . . . are not the work of single men:* In this series, Emerson names a number of works that are thought to be the product of hundreds of years of oral tradition rather than the work of a single author.

5. (p. 322) *the Shakspeare Society . . . Gammar Gurton's Needle:* Founded in 1840, the Shakespeare Society of London published a multivolume edition of pre-Shakespearean drama edited by John Payne Collier, James Orchard Halliwell, and others, some volumes of which Emerson borrowed from Longfellow. "Ferrex and Porrex" is an alternate title for the early British tragedy *Gorboduc* (1561), by Thomas Sackville and Thomas Norton. *Gammar Gurton's Needle* is one of the earliest British comedies (written sometime between 1552 and 1563) by "Mr. S., Master of Art," probably William Stevenson.

6. (p. 323) *it was with the introduction of Shakspeare into German, by Lessing, and the translation of his works by Wieland and Schlegel:* Lessing, Wieland, and von Schlegel were influential in presenting Shakespeare as an exemplary writer to their romantic contemporaries. Similarly, Goethe and Coleridge repeatedly cite Shakespeare as an exemplary artist in their critical writings.

Napoleon; or, The Man of the World

1. (p. 331) *Napoleon; or, The Man of the World:* Emerson included Napoleon in *Representative Men* because he saw him as exemplary of the mindset of the middle class, which in the nineteenth century became the dominant political class in Europe and America for the first time in western history. "The instinct of active, brave, able men, throughout the middle class every where, has pointed out Napoleon as the incarnate Democrat" (p. 331). Although he placed great value on Napoleon's ability to accomplish what he set his mind to do, at

the end of the essay Emerson judges Napoleon a failure because he lacked moral conscience. "Here was an experiment, under the most favorable conditions, of the powers of intellect without conscience. . . . It came to no result. All passed away like the smoke of his artillery, and left no trace" (p. 346).

2. (p. 331) *In our society there is a standing antagonism between the conservative and the democratic classes:* Compare this passage with Emerson's discussion of "the two great parties which, at this hour, almost share the nation between them" in "Politics" (p. 260).

3. (p. 332) *anecdotes or memoirs or lives of Napoleon:* In this lecture, Emerson takes quotations and anecdotes from numerous memoirs and historical accounts of Napoleon's life, including Napoleon's own *Memoirs of the History of France during the Reign of Napoleon, Dictated by the Emperor at Saint Helena to the Generals Who Shared His Captivity; and Published from the Original Manuscripts Corrected by Himself* (1823–1824), Comte Emmanuel Augustin Dieudonné de Las Cases's *Mémorial de Sainte Hélène. Journal of the Private Life and Conversations of the Emperor Napoleon at Saint Helena* (1823), Louise Antoine Fauvelet de Bourrienne's *Private Memoirs of Napoleon Bonaparte, During the Periods of the Directory, the Consulate, and the Empire* (1830), Barry Edward O'Meara's *Napoleon in Exile; or, A Voice from St. Helena* (1822), Augustin Louis Caulaincourt's *Recollections of Caulaincourt, Duke of Vicenza* (1838), and Franceso Antommarchi's *The Last Days of the Emperor Napoleon* (1825). Emerson's quotation and borrowing from these and other works will not be identified in this edition. Readers interested in Emerson's sources for this lecture should consult volume 4 of *The Collected Works.*

4. (p. 333) *Lafayette is an ideologist:* Along with his role in the American Revolution, Lafayette was an important figure in the French Revolution and its aftermath. Napoleon often used the term *idéologue* in a derogatory sense to dismiss his political opponents as idealistic dreamers who were out of touch with reality.

5. (p. 340) *He could not confound Fox and Pitt . . . Ney and Augereau:* In the first list, Emerson names some of Napoleon's political opponents; in the second, a number of Napoleon's trusted generals and political supporters, many of whom were awarded imperial titles for their service.

6. (p. 344) *His memoirs, dictated to Count Montholon. . . . The most agreeable portion is the Campaign in Egypt:* Emerson refers in this paragraph to *Memoirs of the History of France during the Reign of Napoleon* (see note 3 above), which Napoleon I dictated to Baron Gaspard Gourgaud (1783–1852) and Count Charles-Tristran de Montholon (1783–1853), both of whom were generals under Napoleon and accompanied him to Saint Helena when he was exiled. Julius Caesar wrote commentaries on the Gallic and Civil Wars.

7. (p. 346) *I omitted then to say. . . . the conservative is an old democrat:* Compare this passage with "Nominalist and Realist": "The rabid democrat, as soon as he is senator and rich man, has ripened beyond possibility of sincere radicalism,

and unless he can resist the sun, he must be conservative the remainder of his days" (p. 277).

Address to the Citizens of Concord (on the Fugitive Slave Law)

1. (p. 348) *Address to the Citizens of Concord:* On May 3, 1851, Emerson delivered this address at the request of his fellow citizens of Concord, thirty-six of whom signed a petition asking him to state publicly his "opinion upon the Fugitive Slave Law and upon the aspect of the times." In it, he strongly condemned the law for its violation of the moral principles "which made the basis of human society, and of law" (p. 353). After speaking in Concord, he went on to deliver the address in several Massachusetts towns to support Free-Soil candidate John G. Palfrey in his political campaign for Congress. Emerson's commitment to abolition is obvious. He advocates civil disobedience in no uncertain terms: "This law must be . . . abrogated and wiped out of the statute-book; but whilst it stands there, it must be disobeyed" (p. 364).

2. (p. 349) *after the rescue of Shadrach:* Frederick "Shadrach" Minkins (also known as Jenkins) was the first person to be arrested under the Fugitive Slave Law in Boston. On the day of his arrest (February 15, 1851) members of the Boston Vigilance Committee, an abolitionist organization, rescued Minkins from the courthouse and arranged for his passage to Canada via the Underground Railroad. A month and half later, on April 3, 1851, Thomas Sims was arrested under the law, and great lengths were taken by public authorities to prevent a similar rescue attempt, including the enlistment of volunteers to help defend the courthouse. Heavy iron chains were placed across the courthouse doors, and when Judge Lemuel Shaw arrived to try the case he had to duck under the chains to enter.

3. (p. 352) *I thought that all men of all conditions had been made sharers of a certain experience:* The "certain experience" Emerson refers to is similar to the moments of transcendence he describes in *Nature*, "Self-Reliance," "The Over-Soul," and elsewhere. Compare, for example, with his description in "Self-Reliance" of "the sense of being which in calm hours rises" (p. 123).

4. (p. 354) *Those governors of places who bravely refused to execute the barbarous orders of Charles IX. to the famous St. Bartholomew's:* Emerson's source for this anecdote about the Viscount d' Orthe's response to the orders of Charles IX of France following the St. Bartholomew's Day massacres is Emmerich von Vattel's *The Law of Nations; or, Principles of the Law of Nature* (Northampton, Massachusetts, 1820).

Fate

1. (p. 366) *Fate:* The introductory essay to *The Conduct of Life* (1860), "Fate" is perhaps the best of Emerson's later essays. In it Emerson returns to the problem raised in "Compensation" and "Experience": To what extent is the human will subject to circumstance? Nature no longer figures as a beneficial resource for human development, as it did in *Nature;* instead, it is antagonism, all the forces that rend and tear. "The way of Providence is a little rude. The habit of snake and spider, the snap of the tiger . . . these are in the system, and our habits are like theirs" (pp. 368–369). Yet this antagonism, Emerson argues, is also what incites the human will to action. "For, though Fate is immense, so is power, which is the other fact in the dual world, immense" (p. 376). And that power ultimately is the power of thought. "Forever wells up the impulse of choosing and acting in the soul. Intellect annuls Fate. So far as a man thinks, he is free" (p. 377).

2. (p. 366) *four or five noted men were each reading a discourse to the citizens of Boston or New York, on the Spirit of the Times:* Emerson delivered a lecture entitled "The Spirit of the Times" in New York City on January 29, 1851. After Thomas Carlyle's essay "Signs of the Times" was published in 1829, a number of English writers had published on the theme, including William Hazlitt (*The Spirit of the Age,* 1825) and John Stuart Mill (*The Spirit of the Age,* 1831).

3. (p. 371) *this is a Whig, and that a Free-soiler:* That is, a conservative, or a liberal—the Whigs were the political party that opposed the Democrats. The Free-soilers were a political party that opposed the expansion of slavery into the territories. When Emerson first lectured on fate in 1851, the Whigs supported the Fugitive Slave Law, while the Free-soilers opposed it. See Emerson's discussion of "the two great parties which, at this hour, almost share the nation between them," in the essay "Politics," (p. 260).

Power

1. (p. 390) *Power:* In *The Conduct of Life* (1860), "Power" is the essay that immediately follows "Fate." It bears some similarities with "Self-Reliance" but perhaps more with "Napoleon; or, The Man of the World." In the first paragraph Emerson affirms that "Life is a search after power," and he even holds off from discussing the moral and intellectual checks that must be placed on power until the subsequent essays in *The Conduct of Life,* "Culture" and "Worship," because "this force or spirit [is] the means relied on by Nature for bringing the work of the day about." Emerson had stressed the value of practical success in earlier works such as "Man the Reformer," but never had he bracketed off power from spiritual growth as a pragmatic necessity.

2. (p. 392) *Shakspeare was theatre-manager, and used the labor of many young men,*

as well as the playbooks: See Emerson's lecture "Shakspeare; or The Poet," for his discussion of Shakespeare's use of sources (pp. 317–322).

3. (p. 398) *running on the creases of Malays:* This is a reference to the practice of running barefoot across a row of swords (creases) planted blade up in the ground as a demonstration of courage and strength.

Illusions

1. (p. 405) *Illusions:* The concluding essay of *The Conduct of Life* (1860), "Illusions" tempers the strains of Emerson's paean "Power" earlier in the volume, by reminding us of the impermanence of reality: "Science has come to treat space and time as simply forms of thought, and the material world as hypothetical, and withal our pretensions of *property* and even of self-hood are fading with the rest." Amidst this relativity, "we must work and affirm, but we have no guess of the value of what we say or do" (p. 411). As in "Circles" and "Experience," the succession of thought, the ongoing revolution of new ideas and new civilizations in each era throughout history, testifies to the vanity of human endeavor. Like the stoic philosophers he admired, Emerson's conclusion is that we must cling to truth: "Whatever games are played with us, we must play no games with ourselves, but deal in our privacy with the last honesty and truth.... Speak as you think, be what you are. Pay your debts of all kinds" (p. 412).

2. (p. 409) *Pandora-box:* In Greek mythology, Pandora was sent by Zeus to punish mankind and its benefactor Prometheus, who had given to humans the gift of knowledge. Pandora was given in marriage to Epimethus, Prometheus's simple brother, and she bore with her a box she was told not to open. Her curiosity prevailed, and she opened the box, releasing all the evils that afflict humanity. Only hope remained within the box.

Thoreau

1. (p. 415) *Thoreau:* Emerson delivered part of this biographical sketch as the eulogy at Thoreau's funeral in May 1862. A year later, a revised version was printed in the *Atlantic Monthly*. Rich in personal memories of Thoreau, it captures as few other essays do the character and personality of the man who has been called Emerson's "anti-disciple."

2. (p. 419) *Before the first friendly word had been spoken for Captain John Brown:* Emerson is referring to Thoreau's "A Plea for John Brown," which Thoreau delivered while Brown was being held for trial. Emerson had heard Brown speak in Boston in 1857 and spoke to raise funds for the relief of Brown's family after his execution.

Poetry

1. (p. 456) *Concord Hymn:* This poem was first published as a pamphlet that was distributed at the dedication ceremony for the monument commemorating the battles of Lexington and Concord (April 19, 1775), the first battles in the American Revolutionary war.

2. (p. 457) *Voluntaries:* Emerson wrote this poem to commemorate Colonel Robert Gould Shaw and the men of the Massachusetts 54th Regiment who were killed in the assault on Fort Wagner, South Carolina, on July 18, 1863. The 54th Regiment was the first Union regiment to enlist African Americans.

3. (p. 462) *The Chartist's Complaint:* This poem was written as a companion piece to "Days." The Chartists were political and social reformers in England who campaigned for workers' rights and other reform measures. In his 1847–1848 lecture tour in England and Scotland, Emerson followed the Chartist movement closely and with sympathy, writing in his journal, "I fancied, when I heard that the times were anxious and political, that there is to be a Chartist revolution on Monday next, . . . that the right scholar would feel,—now was the hour to test his genius" (*Journals and Miscellaneous Notebooks*, vol. 10, p. 310).

Inspired by Ralph Waldo Emerson

> I celebrate myself,
> And what I assume you shall assume,
> For every atom belonging to me as good belongs to you.
> —Walt Whitman

More than a poet, more than an essayist, and more than a philosopher, Emerson was an American presence. During his prolific career as a writer and lecturer, he achieved an almost guru-like status among the literati and youth of nineteenth-century America. His transcendental exhortations for cultural and national rebirth predate Ezra Pound's famous creed "Make it new."

The most preeminent of Emerson's disciples was Walt Whitman, who has been called the quintessential American poet and the "father of free verse." When his *Leaves of Grass*—a slim, self-published tract of twelve untitled poems—first appeared in 1855, Whitman was an unknown, yet he believed his was precisely the type of voice Emerson hoped America would produce, as described in his essay "The Poet" (1844):

> We have yet had no genius in America, with tyrannous eye, which knew the value of our incomparable materials, and saw, in the barbarism and materialism of the times, another carnival of the same gods whose picture he so much admires in Homer. . . . Our log-rolling, our stumps and their politics, our fisheries, our negroes and Indians, our boats and our repudiations, the wrath of rogues, and the pusillanimity of honest men, the northern trade, the southern planting, the western clearing, Oregon, and Texas, are yet unsung (p. 230).

Whitman, with characteristic self-assurance, believed he was exactly the poet Emerson was looking for. Hoping for a favorable response, Whitman sent Emerson a copy of the first edition of *Leaves of Grass*. In return he got what is probably the most famous letter in American literary history:

CONCORD, MASSACHUSETTS, 21 JULY, 1855

DEAR SIR—

I am not blind to the worth of the wonderful gift of "Leaves of Grass." I find it the most extraordinary piece of wit and wisdom that America has yet contributed. I am very happy in reading it, as great power makes us happy. It meets the demand I am always making of what seemed the sterile and stingy Nature, as if too much handiwork, or too much lymph in the temperament, were making our western wits fat and mean.

I give you joy of your free and brave thought. I have great joy in it. I find incomparable things said incomparably well, as they must be. I find the courage of treatment which so delights us, and which large perception only can inspire.

I greet you at the beginning of a great career, which yet must have had a long foreground somewhere, for such a start. I rubbed my eyes a little, to see if this sunbeam were no illusion; but the solid sense of the book is a solid certainty. It has the best merits, namely, of fortifying and encouraging.

I did not know until I, last night, saw the book advertised in a newspaper, that I could trust the name as real and available for a post-office. I wish to see my benefactor, and have felt much like striking my tasks, and visiting New York to pay you my respects.

R. W. EMERSON

What Whitman did next drew sharp criticism from some of Emerson's acquaintances and from future scholars. Without Emerson's permission, he used the letter to promote *Leaves of Grass*. In October 1855, he gave it to Charles A. Dana, who printed it in the *New York Tribune* as an endorsement of the book by one of the nation's leading literary figures. In the second, expanded edition of *Leaves of Grass* (1856), Whitman had the phrase "I greet you at the beginning of a great career. R.W. Emerson" printed on the book's cover, and he included Emerson's letter in the introduction as the premise for his own reply, in which, under the guise of thanking Emerson, he described his ambition to be the poetic voice of the nation.

Master, I am a man who has perfect faith. Master, we have not come through centuries, caste, heroisms, fables, to halt in this land today. Or I think it is to collect a ten-fold impetus that any halt is made. As nature, inexorable, onward, resistless, impassive amid the threats and screams of disputants, so America. Let all defer. Let all attend respectfully the leisure of These States, their politics, poems, literature, manners, and their free-handed modes of training their own off-spring. Their own comes, just matured, certain, numerous and capa-ble enough, with egotistical tongues, with sinewed wrists, seizing openly what belongs to them. They resume Personality, too long left out of mind. Their shadows are projected in employments, in books, in the cities, in trade; their feet are on the flights of the steps of the Capitol; they dilate, a larger, brawnier, more candid, more demo-cratic, lawless, positive native to The States, sweet-bodied, completer, dauntless, flowing, masterful, beard-faced, new race of men.

Emerson was more annoyed than angered by Whitman's eager self-promotion. He is reported to have said that he would have qualified his praise if he had known it was to be published, and he tried to persuade Whitman to edit out some of the more sexually explicit passages from later editions of *Leaves of Grass*. Nonetheless, he stood by his initial recognition of Whitman's genius, and supported Whitman throughout his career, writing him letters of recommendation and sending contri-butions when Whitman's family and friends sought assistance for the controversial poet. Emerson's letter to Whitman marked the beginning of a long and complex friendship between the two men.

Many who have disapproved of Whitman's lack of decorum have praised his disregard for poetic convention, and indeed Whitman was a major innovator in both the style and the content of his poetry. His poems stray from rhyme and traditional meter, and instead embrace the line—no matter how long or short—as a musical unit. He employs the cadence of simple, even idiomatic speech to "sing" national identity and destiny, philosophy and spiritualism, and frank autobiography. Whit-man's work—especially his celebration of himself as a rough working man, and his openness about sexuality and homosexuality—has influ-enced many American poets. Among his successors are Hart Crane, Henry Miller, William Carlos Williams, and the Beat poets, including Allen Ginsberg.

Whitman revised *Leaves of Grass* throughout his life. The ninth, so-called death-bed edition (1892) encompasses his entire career and in-cludes the poems "I Sing the Body Electric," "When I Heard the Learn'd Astronomer," the elegy for Abraham Lincoln "When Lilacs Last in the Dooryard Bloom'd," and a final version of "Song of Myself" totaling more than 1,300 lines.

Comments & Questions

In this section, we aim to provide the reader with an array of perspectives on the text, as well as questions that challenge those perspectives. The commentary has been culled from sources as diverse as reviews contemporaneous with the works, letters written by the author, literary criticism of later generations, and appreciations written throughout the works' history. Following the commentary, a series of questions seeks to filter Essays and Poems *by Ralph Waldo Emerson through a variety of points of view and bring about a richer understanding of these enduring works.*

Comments

WALT WHITMAN

Emerson, in my opinion, is not most eminent as poet or artist or teacher, though valuable in all those. He is best as critic, or diagnoser. Not passion or imagination or warp or weakness, or any pronounced cause or specialty, dominates him. Cold and bloodless intellectuality dominates him. (I know the fires, emotions, love, egotisms, glow deep, perennial, as in all New Englanders—but the facade hides them well— they give no sign.) He does not see or take one side, one presentation only or mainly, (as all the poets, or most of the fine writers anyhow)— he sees all sides. His final influence is to make his students cease to worship anything—almost cease to believe in anything, outside of themselves. . . .

The best part of Emersonianism is, it breeds the giant that destroys itself. Who wants to be any man's mere follower? lurks behind every page. No teacher ever taught, that has so provided for his pupil's setting up independently—no truer evolutionist.

—*Specimen Days & Collect* (1882–1883)

MATTHEW ARNOLD

We have not in Emerson a great poet, a great writer, a great philosophy-maker. His relation to us is not that of one of those personages; yet it is a relation of, I think, even superior importance. His relation to us is more like that of the Roman Emperor Marcus Aurelius. Marcus Aurelius is not a great writer, a great philosophy-maker; he is the friend and

515

aider of those who would live in the spirit. Emerson is the same. He is the friend and aider of those who would live in the spirit.

—*Discourses in America* (1885)

W. L. COURTNEY

That quality in Emerson which communicates impulse and inspiration is equally due to the ancestry of preachers and the habits of a lecturer. There is a freshness, a vitality, a breezy force of life and spirits, which not only animate the writer's style, but add wings to the reader's thoughts. Socrates, long ago, found that the best way of getting hold of men was to talk with them. The living intercourse between men's minds was thus promoted by "the lively and animated word," which went from one to the other, and got better as it went. Emerson, who was in some respects a true disciple of Socrates, himself knew the secret of "sowing and planting knowledge" by oral communication. No one has better single thoughts or phrases. No one can, in a word or two, draw a better or fresher picture of nature, not as though it were a mere matter of canvas and oil-paints, but as a living and working agency, carrying on its thousand offices through a thousand different lines of activity. "The world is new, untried. Do not believe the past. I give you the universe a virgin to-day." "Truth is such a fly-away, such a sly-boots, so untransportable and unbarrelable a commodity, that it is as bad to catch as light." "Men have come to speak of the Divine revelation as something long ago given and done, as if God were dead." "It is God in us which checks the language of petition by a grander thought." "A good reader can nestle into Plato's brain and think from thence; but not into Shakespeare's. We are still out of doors." The words seem alive, as though they were not so much the cold abstract results of thought as themselves furnished with hands, and feet, and wings. They are all fresh coined in the mint of nature; in Emerson's beautiful phrase, "one with the blowing clover and the falling rain."

—*Fortnightly Review* (August 1, 1885)

EDWIN PERCY WHIPPLE

The noblest passages in [Emerson's] writings are those in which he celebrates this august and gracious communion of the Spirit of God with the soul of man; and they are the most serious, solemn, and uplifting passages which can perhaps be found in our literature. Here was a man who had earned the right to utter these noble truths by patient meditation and clear insight. Carlyle exclaimed, in a preface to an English edition of one of Emerson's volumes: "Here comes our brave Emerson, with *news* from the empyrean!" That phrase exactly hits Emerson as a transcendentalist thinker. His insights were, in some sense, revelations; he could "gossip on the eternal politics"; and just at the time when science, relieved from the pressure of theology, announced materialistic hypotheses with more than the confidence with which the bigots of theological creeds had heretofore announced their dogmas, this serene American thinker had won his way into all the centres of European intelligence, and delivered his quiet protest against every hypothesis which put in peril the spiritual interests of humanity. It is curious to witness the process by which this heresiarch has ended in giving his experience, that God is not the Unknowable of Herbert Spencer, but that, however infinitely distant He may be from the human understanding, He is still intimately near to the human soul.

—*American Literature and Other Papers* (1887)

OLIVER WENDELL HOLMES, SR.

One of Mr. Emerson's biographers has claimed that his Phi Beta Kappa Oration was our Declaration of Literary Independence. But Mr. Emerson did not cut himself loose from all the traditions of Old World scholarship. He spelled his words correctly, he constructed his sentences grammatically. He adhered to the slavish rules of propriety, and observed the reticences which a traditional delicacy has considered inviolable in decent society, European and Oriental alike. When he wrote poetry, he commonly selected subjects which seemed adapted to poetical treatment,—apparently thinking that all things were not equally calculated to inspire the true poet's genius. Once, indeed, he ventured to refer to "the meal in the firkin, the milk in the pan," but he chiefly restricted himself to subjects such as a fastidious conventionalism would approve as having a certain fitness for poetical treatment. He was not always so careful as he might have been in the rhythm and rhyme of his verse, but in the main he recognized the old established laws which have been accepted as regulating both. In short, with all his originality, he worked in Old World harness, and cannot be considered as the creator of a truly American, self-governed, self-centred, absolutely independent style of thinking and writing, knowing no law but its own sovereign will and pleasure.

—*Over the Teacups* (1891)

GEORGE SANTAYANA

The source of [Emerson's] power lay not in his doctrine, but in his temperament, and the rare quality of his wisdom was due less to his reason than to his imagination. Reality eluded him; he had neither diligence nor constancy enough to master and possess it; but his mind was open to all philosophic influences, from whatever quarter they might blow; the lessons of science and the hints of poetry worked themselves out in him to a free and personal religion. He differed from the plodding many, not in knowing things better, but in having more ways of knowing them. His grasp was not particularly firm, he was far from being, like a Plato or an Aristotle, past master in the art and the science of life. But his mind was endowed with unusual plasticity, with unusual spontaneity and liberty of movement—it was a fairyland of thoughts and fancies. He was like a young god making experiments in creation: he botched the work, and always began again on a new and better plan. Every day he said, "Let there be light," every day the light was new. His sun, like that of Heraclitus, was different every morning.

—*Interpretations of Poetry and Religion* (1900)

LESLIE STEPHEN

One charm of Emerson is due to affable reception of all opinions. On his first appearance in a pulpit he is described as "the most gracious of mortals, with a face all benignity," and preached with an indefinite air of simplicity and wisdom. His lectures radiate benignity and simplicity. He had no dogmas to proclaim or heretics to denounce. He is simply uttering an inspiration which has come to him. He is not a mystagogue, affecting superinducal wisdom and in possession of the only clue to the secret. If you sympathize, well and good; if you cannot, you may translate his truth into your own. The ascent into this serene region, above all the noise of controversy, has its disadvantages. Carlyle complains gently that his friend is in danger of parting from fact and soaring into perilous altitudes. He is "soliloquizing on the mountain tops." It is easy to "screw oneself up into high and ever higher altitudes of transcendentalism," to see nothing beneath one but "the everlasting snows of the Himalaya, the earth shrinking to a planet, and the indigo firmament sowing itself with stars." Come back to the earth, he exclaims; and readers of Emerson must occasionally echo the exhortation. And yet, in his own way, Emerson was closer to the everyday world than Carlyle himself; and it is the curious union of the two generally inconsistent qualities which gives a peculiar flavour to Emersonian teaching.

—*National Review* (February 1901)

Questions

1. Emerson is often thought of as the man who created "a truly American, self-governed, self-centered, absolutely independent style, . . . knowing no law but its own sovereign will and pleasure," in the words of Oliver Wendell Holmes, Sr. Certainly Holmes saw a discrepancy between the way Emerson actually lived his life and this perceived ideal, but is this near-legendary Emersonian style still an important part of the American national character?

2. "To believe your own thought, to believe that what is true for you in your private heart, is true for all men—that is genius." So Emerson wrote, probably aware that others defined that kind of belief as madness. What do you think? Is Emerson's genius crazy?

3. A contemporary of Emerson's, James Margh, wrote that his lectures "contain with scarcely a decent disguise nothing less than an Epicurean Atheism dressed up in a style seducing and to many perhaps deceptive." Margh is referring to the stoic philosophy of Epicurus, who believed that events are the product of chance, and that the greatest good, therefore, is to be found in the avoidance of pain and suffering, or in their acceptance as inevitable facts of existence. Is there any evidence in the *Essays* of this Epicurean Atheism?

4. The historian Louis Manand wrote of Emerson that "his thought plays continually with the limits of thought, and his greatest essays are efforts to get at the way life is held up, in the end, by nothing." This characterization of Emerson's writing makes him seem very modern, a kind of Samuel Beckett. Is Menand going too far, or can you pinpoint evidence of the void behind Emerson's apparent optimism and idealism?

For Further Reading

Biographical Resources

Allen, Gay Wilson. *Waldo Emerson: A Biography.* New York: Viking, 1981.

Cole, Phyllis. *Mary Moody Emerson and the Origins of Transcendentalism: A Family History.* New York: Oxford University Press, 1998.

Emerson, Ralph Waldo. *Emerson in his Journals.* Selected and edited by Joel Porte. Cambridge, MA: Belknap Press of Harvard University Press, 1982.

————. *The Selected Letters of Ralph Waldo Emerson.* Edited by Joel Myerson. New York: Columbia University Press, 1997.

Richardson, Robert D., Jr. *Emerson: The Mind on Fire.* Berkeley: University of California Press, 1995.

Rusk, Ralph L. *The Life of Ralph Waldo Emerson.* New York: Scribner's, 1949.

Von Frank, Albert J. *An Emerson Chronology.* New York: G. K. Hall, 1994.

Collections of Essays

Buell, Lawrence, ed. *Ralph Waldo Emerson: A Collection of Critical Essays.* Englewood Cliffs, NJ: Prentice Hall, 1993.

Mott, Wesley T., and Robert E. Burkholder, eds. *Emersonian Circles: Essays in Honor of Joel Myerson.* Rochester, NY: University of Rochester Press, 1997.

Myerson, Joel, ed. *A Historical Guide to Ralph Waldo Emerson.* New York: Oxford University Press, 2000.

Porte, Joel, and Saundra Morris, eds. *The Cambridge Companion to Ralph Waldo Emerson.* Cambridge and New York: Cambridge University Press, 1999.

Selected Critical Studies

Gougeon, Len. *Virtue's Hero: Emerson, Antislavery, and Reform.* Athens: University of Georgia Press, 1990.

Robinson, David M. *Apostle of Culture: Emerson as Preacher and Lecturer.* Philadelphia: University of Pennsylvania Press, 1982.

Sealts, Merton M., Jr. *Emerson on the Scholar.* Columbia: University of Missouri Press, 1992.

Whicher, Stephen E. *Freedom and Fate: An Inner Life of Ralph Waldo Emerson.* Philadelphia: University of Pennsylvania Press, 1953.

Zwarg, Christina. *Feminist Conversations: Fuller, Emerson, and the Play of Reading.* Ithaca, NY: Cornell University Press, 1995.

Historical Background

Capper, Charles, and Conrad Edick Wright. *Transient and Permanent: The Transcendental Movement and Its Contexts.* Boston: Massachusetts Historical Society; distributed by Northeastern University Press, 1999.

Miller, Perry, ed. *The Transcendentalists: An Anthology.* Cambridge, MA: Harvard University Press, 1950.

Packer, Barbara. "The Transcendentalists." In *The Cambridge History of American Literature*, edited by Sacvan Bercovitch, vol. 2, *Prose Writing, 1820–1865*, pp. 329–604. Cambridge: Cambridge University Press, 1995.

Reynolds, Larry J. *European Revolutions and the American Literary Renaissance.* New Haven, CT: Yale University Press, 1988.

Von Frank, Albert J. *The Trials of Anthony Burns: Freedom and Slavery in Emerson's Boston.* Cambridge, MA: Harvard University Press, 1998.

Other Works Cited in the Introduction

Emerson, Ralph Waldo. *Journals and Miscellaneous Notebooks.* 16 vols. Edited by William H. Gilman, Ralph H. Orth, et al. Cambridge, MA: Harvard University Press, 1960–1982.

———. *The Letters of Ralph Waldo Emerson.* Edited by Ralph L. Rusk and Eleanor M. Tilton. 9 vols. New York: Columbia University Press, 1939–1995.

(continued)

Jude the Obscure	Thomas Hardy	1-59308-035-2	$6.95
The Jungle	Upton Sinclair	1-59308-118-9	$7.95
The Last of the Mohicans	James Fenimore Cooper	1-59308-137-5	$7.95
Les Liaisons Dangereuses	Pierre Choderlos de Laclos	1-59308-240-1	$8.95
Little Women	Louisa May Alcott	1-59308-108-1	$6.95
Lost Illusions	Honoré de Balzac	1-59308-315-7	$9.95
Main Street	Sinclair Lewis	1-59308-386-6	$9.95
Mansfield Park	Jane Austen	1-59308-154-5	$5.95
The Metamorphosis and Other Stories	Franz Kafka	1-59308-029-8	$6.95
Moby-Dick	Herman Melville	1-59308-018-2	$9.95
My Ántonia	Willa Cather	1-59308-202-9	$5.95
Narrative of Sojourner Truth		1-59308-293-2	$6.95
The Odyssey	Homer	1-59308-009-3	$5.95
Oliver Twist	Charles Dickens	1-59308-206-1	$6.95
The Origin of Species	Charles Darwin	1-59308-077-8	$7.95
Paradise Lost	John Milton	1-59308-095-6	$8.95
Persuasion	Jane Austen	1-59308-130-8	$5.95
The Picture of Dorian Gray	Oscar Wilde	1-59308-025-5	$5.95
A Portrait of the Artist as a Young Man and Dubliners	James Joyce	1-59308-031-X	$7.95
Pride and Prejudice	Jane Austen	1-59308-201-0	$6.95
The Prince and Other Writings	Niccolò Machiavelli	1-59308-060-3	$5.95
The Red Badge of Courage and Selected Short Fiction	Stephen Crane	1-59308-119-7	$4.95
Republic	Plato	1-59308-097-2	$7.95
Robinson Crusoe	Daniel Defoe	1-59308-360-2	$5.95
The Scarlet Letter	Nathaniel Hawthorne	1-59308-207-X	$5.95
The Secret Agent	Joseph Conrad	1-59308-305-X	$8.95
Selected Stories of O. Henry		1-59308-042-5	$5.95
Sense and Sensibility	Jane Austen	1-59308-125-1	$5.95
Siddhartha	Hermann Hesse	1-59308-379-3	$6.95
The Souls of Black Folk	W. E. B. Du Bois	1-59308-014-X	$5.95
The Strange Case of Dr. Jekyll and Mr. Hyde and Other Stories	Robert Louis Stevenson	1-59308-131-6	$5.95
A Tale of Two Cities	Charles Dickens	1-59308-138-3	$5.95
Three Theban Plays	Sophocles	1-59308-235-5	$7.95
Thus Spoke Zarathustra	Friedrich Nietzsche	1-59308-278-9	$7.95
The Time Machine and The Invisible Man	H. G. Wells	1-59308-388-2	$6.95
Treasure Island	Robert Louis Stevenson	1-59308-247-9	$4.95
The Turn of the Screw, The Aspern Papers and Two Stories	Henry James	1-59308-043-3	$5.95
Uncle Tom's Cabin	Harriet Beecher Stowe	1-59308-121-9	$7.95
Vanity Fair	William Makepeace Thackeray	1-59308-071-9	$7.95
Walden and Civil Disobedience	Henry David Thoreau	1-59308-208-8	$6.95
The War of the Worlds	H. G. Wells	1-59308-362-9	$5.95
Ward No. 6 and Other Stories	Anton Chekhov	1-59308-003-4	$7.95
Wuthering Heights	Emily Brontë	1-59308-128-6	$5.95